DETECTIVE MAIER MYSTERIES COLLECTION

THE COMPLETE SERIES

TOM VATER

Copyright (C) 2023 Tom Vater

Layout design and Copyright (C) 2023 by Next Chapter

Published 2023 by Next Chapter

Cover art by CoverMint

This book is a work of fiction. Names, characters, places, and incidents are the product of the author's imagination or are used fictitiously. Any resemblance to actual events, locales, or persons, living or dead, is purely coincidental.

All rights reserved. No part of this book may be reproduced or transmitted in any form or by any means, electronic or mechanical, including photocopying, recording, or by any information storage and retrieval system, without the author's permission.

THE CAMBODIAN BOOK OF THE DEAD

DETECTIVE MAIER MYSTERIES BOOK 1

To the ones of the first hour...Janey, Lo, Flintman, Rockoff and Pesey (RIP)

Cambodia: Where the Appalling is Commonplace

— JERRY REDFERN

IN THE SHADOW OF ENLIGHTENMENT

IN RETROSPECT, Maier could see that the catastrophe in Cambodia had been the turning point. But in retrospect, everything always looked different.

War was never simple. As soon as the first shot was fired, carefully made plans changed beyond recognition. As soon as the blood flowed, everything was unpredictable, and no one got away scot-free.

Most men were simply blown away by the willful mayhem, like dry leaves in a fast wind.

Others found themselves in the horror of the moment and got stuck there, making the world die, over and over. A few went by another route, on and on, into themselves, until they experienced a kind of epiphany, a moment of arrival.

War correspondent Maier was about to arrive.

Maier and Hort sat on a crumbling wall near to what was left of the railway station in Battambang, or what was left of this once-picturesque and industrious town in north-western Cambodia. Perhaps a school had stood here forty years earlier. A few metres of tired red brick work was all that␣was had survived the recent vagaries of history. At midday, the wall offered no shade. It was just a structure to sit next to. Better than being exposed, in a world of dust, misery and possible aggravation. A group of men cowered next to the two journalists on low stools. They drank rice wine as if their lives depended on it. Perhaps it did.

Garbage and dust-devils blew across the shabby, run-down space between the wall and the railway tracks – scraps of paper, plastic bags, and diapers. Who had money for diapers around here? Where could you even buy nappies in Cambodia?

A young woman with a pinched face served the rancid drink from an old oil canister. There was only one glass, which went around in a circle. People in Cambodia drank quietly and with great concentration. Everyone was waiting. The railway station was a good place to wait. The trains were less reliable than the next glass, as the Khmer Rouge, Pol Pot's feared communist army, frequently mined the tracks between the capital Phnom Penh and Battambang. The Khmer Rouge was the main reason why people were waiting. Despite UN sponsored elections, boycotted by the communists, the war just would not die. Most Cambodians wanted peace, and peace meant waiting.

Hort passed Maier a joint. "The war will be over in a few weeks, Maier. 1997 is our year. At least that what they say in Phnom Penh. Around here, people not so sure."

Hort laughed, as the Khmer sometimes do when they don't feel like laughing.

Maier wiped the sweat from his eyes, rearranged his matted beard and shrugged his shoulders. "Your country is sick of war, Hort. And you are getting married next week, when we are through and you have earned yourself a sack full of money."

The young Khmer was working as Maier's fixer and had been accompanying him for the past four years, every time the German journalist had been on assignment in Cambodia. Four years and six visits to this cursed country. And yet Maier had fallen into uneasy love with this sunny and wicked paradise.

Hort had saved his life on at least two occasions. In a few days, Maier would be the best man at his young friend's wedding, hopefully without making a drunken pass at Hort's attractive sister.

What would Carissa, beautiful and twisted Carissa, say if she found him in the sack with a young Khmer woman? What would be left, when the war really ended, when the international media left this tired land to its own devices? Maier had come with the war. Would he not also disappear with the war? Move on to the next war? Lack of choice wasn't the issue. War was always in vogue.

Hort interrupted him in his thoughts.

"As long as Pol Pot is alive, we not find peace. Why don't UN arrest and kill him?" Hort answered the question himself, "My people no longer have expectation that anyone come and help."

An old woman, her lined forehead almost hidden beneath a faded krama, the traditional chequered scarf many Khmer wore, her eyes black and numb like the tropical small hours, passed the two men slowly and silently spat on the hot dusty ground in front of Maier.

Hort's contorted stare followed her.

"I think I could do with a glass of rice wine myself."

Maier and his fixer were waiting for an officer serving with a regiment of government troops. Their contact was involved in peace negotiations with the last remnants of the Khmer Rouge fighters. The civil war, which had prevented recovery since the demise of the communists' agrarian utopia in 1979, some eighteen years before, was drawing to a close. The government in Phnom Penh had some control over most of the country, or at least over what was left of Cambodia after a half century of catastrophic politics, war and genocide. Every time he made eye contact with a Khmer, Maier could see that that wasn't much.

The Khmer Rouge had retreated to the west, to the provinces bordering Thailand. Several conflagrations had taken place in Battambang in recent weeks. Nasty, dark stuff.

Maier knew there wasn't much time left. One of the great nightmares of the twentieth century was drawing to a close and Cambodia was moving towards an uncertain but less violent future. He'd come back to find out what that future might look like from the country's last battlefield. Finding out anything in Cambodia usually involved waiting. Maier had been waiting for three days. Today, Hort had assured him, the interview would materialise. Hort had been equally optimistic the previous day and the day before that.

A group of young men in torn work clothes, their dusty, hard feet in plastic flip-flops, walked past the wall, smoking cigarettes and talking quietly amongst themselves. Maier had picked up enough Khmer to understand that the conversation revolved around him. Was the tall foreigner a soldier? Was he looking for a girl? One look from Hort made them shut up.

"What gift do you give my future wife on her wedding day, Maier?"

The young Khmer could hardly wait to return to Phnom Penh. Two extended families were waiting on the groom and his tall, white employer – his protector. They had already put up the marquee.

"If you keep bugging me, Hort, I will buy her a sack of cold, fried frogs." Maier grinned at the young man – for his friend's assurance – as the Khmer did not always understand his sarcasm. How many miles had he already travelled with Hort, how many cruelties had he documented, while his fixer had stood next to him, his face expressionless? How many drunk and trigger-happy soldiers had they passed together at road blocks? Perhaps he really was the young Khmer's lucky charm.

Maier got distracted by a young woman in a bright purple sarong. He noticed the boy as well, but you noticed so many things. You had to choose, and Maier chose the woman. Hort, too, held his breath for a second. The woman passed the wall without looking at the men and crossed the railway tracks. Maier could not see her face, but he was sure that she was beautiful. He followed the languid sway of her hips and let his thoughts meander. The war was practically finished and he felt happier than he had in a long time. His plan to stop working in the conflict news business had become more appealing in recent months, but since his return to Cambodia, he had enjoyed his work, and after all, a plan was only a plan.

Later, as he sat on the back of a pick-up slowly rumbling towards Phnom Penh, he would suddenly recall the most important moment: the short cropped hair and the fixed stare, the dusty brown baseball cap, which the boy had pulled deep into his face and which had not suited the young Khmer Rouge at all. But you saw people with fixed stares everywhere, especially in this mad and lost part of the world.

The boy had appeared on the potholed road. He wore ripped T-shirt and black trousers and he was barefoot. Why had Maier not looked at him more closely?

The youth dropped his bag next to the woman who was serving the rice wine. She had her back turned to Maier and he barely noticed the brief exchange between the two. It looked like an everyday conversation. It was an everyday conversation. A few seconds later, the boy was on his way and Maier had forgotten him. He stared across the tracks, but the girl in the bright sarong had also dropped out of sight. Maier briefly turned towards the woman serving the moonshine. She had started a heated argument with her customers. He didn't understand a word the woman said. She had a strong accent, and whatever she was saying, quickly fell victim to the mean, silent aggression of the day. He didn't really want to hear another petty argument between people who'd had everything but their souls disenfranchised. And perhaps those as well. The smell of the tropics, saturated with reincarnation and ruin, this hypnotising combination of extremes, of promise and danger, of temptation and failure, had convinced him once more that it was all worth it; he'd chosen the best job in the world. In a few hours, when the interview would finally be in the can, he would drink with Hort. He still had a small bottle of vodka in his bag, and they were bound to be able to organise a few oranges in Battambang. No rice wine for Maier. And in a few days, after the wedding, he'd be flying back to Hamburg. That was the plan.

"I'm really looking forward to your wedding, Hort. It will be a special day for me as well."

"The day you ask for my sister's hand?"

The years with Maier had changed the Khmer as well. Occasionally he tried his luck with irony, in a gentle Cambodian way.

Maier replied drily, "Carissa will cut my balls off. Or I'll have to flee and will never be able to return to Cambodia."

"That a shame, Maier. Maybe it better you keep your hands off my sister and follow your western lifestyle."

Suddenly, the three drinkers next to Maier wrested the sack off the wine-seller and jumped up. Hort jerked to his feet and gave Maier a hard push. The explosion extinguished his friend's warning. The bomb blew most of the wall straight past Maier. The woman who'd been selling the wine was torn to pieces. Screams and smoke. Maier lay flat on the ground for a few long seconds, not daring to move. Even the sky was on fire. Turning his head, he could see twisted bodies through the clouds of black fumes, shapes covered in blood and dust, frozen in black burns. A couple of lean-tos that had been built against the wall were ablaze. Maier shook his legs and arms; everything was still there. One of the young men who'd been sitting behind him was alive. Caked in blood, he cried softly, as he tried to pull a friend from under the rubble. It was too late. A wooden beam had completely severed his companion's legs from his torso.

Hort had disappeared. Perhaps he had fallen before the explosion had gone off. But Maier knew that his friend had been sitting between himself and the woman selling the wine and had jumped up to warn him. The sudden realisation that his friend and fixer was dead came as a physical blow, as if some unchallengeable force had risen from the earth below him and was suddenly ripping the skin off his back, fear and sorrow racing up his neck made of needles and knives, into his head where everything contracted in panicked spasms. He sat in debris, trying to breathe, waiting for something to come back, for time to go on. In the silence following the attack, a couple of dogs barked in the distance and the whine of a motorbike grew louder. Women cried, somewhere to his right. Otherwise, all he could hear was a high-pitched ringing tone in his ears. Maier forced himself up and climbed through the smoke across the strewn-around brickwork. He had to be sure.

The bomb had taken Hort straight through a big hole in the wall of a building that had been destroyed decades ago. A quick look was enough. Hort was dead.

Without a doubt, the bomb had been meant for Maier. The Khmer Rouge hated westerners, especially journalists. And the Cambodian army had known that Maier would be waiting by the station. Virtually anyone with a modicum of energy could get hold of explosives in this country.

Maier moved away from the carnage and disappeared as best as he could into the crowd that was beginning to gather by the railway tracks. He had to get away before the police and the military showed. He ran to one of the nearest shacks, dived into a small shop, pulled his cell phone from his pocket and called Carissa. Then he tied a krama around his head and jumped a passing pick-up truck bound for the capital.

He'd call his editor once he'd returned to Hamburg and hand in his notice. Maier was no longer a war correspondent.

PART I

THE GOLDEN PEACOCK

1

THE WIDOW

Dani Stricker crossed the Paradeplatz and walked down the Planken, towards Mannheim's historic water tower. It was an old tradition. With Harald, she'd walked down the city's shopping mile every Saturday afternoon, no matter what the weather had been like. For twenty years.

The Cambodian woman frequently remembered her arrival in Mannheim in 1981. The shops had dazzled her and she'd thought that the fountain in front of the Kaufhof, the biggest mall in town, sprayed liquid gold instead of water into the air. She'd been sure of it. The people, the Germans, they were huge. And rich. Today she could see the differences in incomes and lifestyles, but in those early months, she'd almost believed that money grew on trees in Germany. Of course, money didn't grow on trees anywhere, unless you owned the tree. She knew that now.

Everything had been strange. Dani had never seen a tram, never mind an escalator. Such things did not exist in Cambodia. In the supermarket, she'd been overwhelmed by the enormous variety of cats and dogs available in tins, which crowded the shelves of an entire aisle. The first pretzel that Harald had bought her had tasted disgusting. She'd felt she was going to suffocate on the heavy, salty dough. But she'd forced herself to eat it anyway, for Harald.

As scary and foreign as her new home had been then, she had not wanted to return to Cambodia. There, death lived in the rice fields and would be able to find her people in their flimsy huts even a hundred years from now, to drag them from their homes into the darkness and make them vanish forever. Dani had been homesick, but she'd understood even then that the country she called home no longer existed. No one returned from the long night that had covered Cambodia like a suffocating blanket for decades. Only ghosts flourished in the rice paddies. Harald had saved her life. Harald was Dani's hero. Everything she had seen and learned in the past twenty years had come from Harald. And now, Harald was dead.

Sometimes, they'd taken the tram from the city centre to Harald's house in Käfertal. Sometimes she'd taken the tram into town all by herself, as Harald hadn't been keen on public transport. She'd never learned to drive. Now she really needed the tram, was dependent on it for the first time in her life. Now she was alone. She would sell the BMW straight away.

Dani boarded a Number 4 in front of the water tower. An inspector silently took her ticket, looked at it with deliberate, antagonistic care and handed it back, having switched his expression to trained boredom. A couple of rows behind Dani, two youths with coloured hair and buttons in their ears raised their voices against the police state. After the funeral, she'd put the car in the local newspaper and hope for a buyer.

The tram slowly passed the city cemetery. Harald had died on October 11th, just a week ago. The poplar leaves blew around the pavement like shiny, copper-coloured bank notes. That looked pretty disorderly by Mannheim's standards, but a municipal employee would soon come with a machine and hoover the leaves out of this world and into another.

One day, Dani's coffin would be laid to rest here as well, thousands of miles from home. She'd promised Harald. Nevertheless, the idea of a burial remained unsettling. How would she fare in the next life if she was not cremated? But promises had to be kept. She'd learnt that as a young girl, working alongside her mother on the family's farm. Without keeping promises, life wasn't worth a thing. It wasn't worth much anyway.

Her parents and her sister hadn't been cremated either. She dreamed that if she returned to Cambodia, she would be able to locate the mass grave in which they'd been dumped. Her contact had suggested starting some investigations, but Dani had turned his offer down. Too many old bones belonging to too many people lay in those graves and she would never really be certain.

Her mobile rang. The foreign number. The call Dani had been waiting for. She'd been waiting for more than twenty years. It was time to let her past bleed into her present life. The past, the present and the future coexisted next to each other. Every child in Cambodia knew that. But here, in Germany, in the West, one's life cycle was split into distinct parts. Dani wasn't interested in the parts alone. She knew them too well. Now she would finally take steps to take control, to bring closure to reunite past, present and future. Revenge could do that. Anonymous and ruthless revenge.

Dani took a deep breath and answered the call.

"Hello?"

"Everything is ready. Tomorrow I will be in Bangkok to catch a flight to Phnom Penh."

Dani was surprised. The man spoke Khmer, albeit with a strong accent. A *barang*. Dani was shocked at her own reaction. After all, Harald had also been a *barang*, a white man. As a child she'd never asked herself whether the term the Khmer used for Westerners had positive or negative connotations. During the Khmer Rouge years, *barang* had meant as much as devil or enemy. She forced herself back into the present.

"Find him and get in touch when you have learned what has happened to my sister. Force him to talk. When you have proof of what happened to her, kill him."

The man at the other end of the conversation said nothing. He had been recommended by a fellow Cambodian whom she had met on the long journey from a refugee camp on the Thai-Cambodian border to Germany, some twenty years earlier. The *barang* had apparently done jobs like this in Cambodia before.

"If that doesn't work, please kill him immediately."

The miserable ticket inspector passed her again. He was in another world. A world she had learned to love. A world in which you were not pulled out of your house in the middle of the night, to be butchered, because you allegedly worked for the CIA. She was back in the rice paddy behind her farm. The feeling of displacement was so intense, she was sure she was able to count the clouds above her family home if she only looked up. She could almost taste *prahok*, the pungent, fermented fish paste, which her mother prepared every day, the best *prahok* in the village. One day, the Khmer Rouge, the Red Khmer, had come and killed everyone who had worked for the CIA. It was only after Dani had lived in Germany for some years, that she'd learned what the CIA was.

She was flustered and tried to find the right word to continue the conversation.

"I mean, that's what I hired you for."

"Yes, you did," he answered.

She had no idea what else to tell a contract killer, an assassin. There was nothing to say.

"Be sure to get the right man."

"I have received your money and the information. I will only call you one more time. Please do not worry."

The man had a gentle, almost feminine voice. She knew that was meaningless of course. In the past week she had transferred some fifty thousand Euro, a large part of her inheritance, to the various accounts of this man. Harald would have understood. Or would he? He would have accepted it. But Dani had never dared to tell her husband about her plan. And now it was too late.

The man hung up. She stood motionless and stared at the silent phone, unable to disconnect from what she'd just said and heard. Six thousand miles east of a small town in southern Germany, death would stalk through the rice paddies once again, in search of the red devil that had destroyed Dani Stricker's life. She almost forgot to get off in Käfertal.

"Last stop, all change," the miserable inspector shouted. She smiled at the man. He wouldn't beat her to death.

2

MAIER

MAIER, private detective, forty-five years old, 190 cm tall, perfectly trilingual, single, handlebar moustache, greying locks, currently cut almost short, leaned back in his economy seat, as much as he could, and smiled at the Thai stewardess who was coming his way. Maier had broad shoulders and green eyes and he looked a little lived in. Light boots, black cotton pants, a white shirt with too many pockets and one of those sleeveless vests with yet more pockets – he'd never quite managed to shake the fashion crimes of the war correspondent. At least he'd knocked the cigarettes on the head.

His father had turned up in Germany, from somewhere further east, sometime in the early Forties, despite the Nazis. He'd had green eyes and blond hair, and he'd been an attractive man, so attractive that the German girls, who had lost their husbands at the front, fell in love with him. Even in Hitler's Germany, the Other seemed to have its attraction. At least as long as the Other called itself Maier and travelled with correct, possibly fake papers.

He had survived the war in the arms of young women and had fled to England in the closing months before returning to post-war Germany. In the mid-Fifties he had washed up on Ruth Maier's doorstep in Leipzig, told her just that and hung around. But not for long. After eleven months, he'd disappeared and had never been heard of again.

Sometimes Maier asked himself how many siblings he might have. He wondered whether his father was still alive. And whether he might have worked for the Soviet secret service during the war? And whether he had worked for the Stasi later? Maier had never met his father. His love of women, his restlessness and his looks were the sole assets he had inherited from his old man. That's what Ruth Maier had said.

His mother had been right of course. Maier didn't enjoy staying put very much. After he'd finished his studies in Dresden, he had worked as an international correspondent in Poland, Czechoslovakia, Bulgaria and Yugoslavia. How he got the job without too much maneuvering, he never found out. Perhaps his father had had something to do with it.

When East Germany had begun to collapse, Maier had fled across Hungary to West Germany and had eventually ended up in Hamburg. After the Berlin Wall had fallen, Maier had expected to see life with different eyes. Finally, he'd be able to write what he wanted. He had been yearning for a new joy, an entirely new existence and he had almost found it. In the new Germany he had, after many years of working abroad, the right connections in the media and was soon hired by the news agency dpa.

Maier rarely woke up in his small, impersonal apartment in Altona. He was on the road for the most part, on assignment – German holidaymakers from Mallorca to Vegas, German investors in Shanghai, German footballers in Yaoundé. There was always something to report some place. And Maier didn't feel at home anywhere. He'd fallen in love a few times, but somehow, he'd never hung around.

The power of money in the new Germany first disorientated him; later it became an irritation. He still felt as if he'd been catapulted from the fantastical dereliction of the old system into the depressing realities of the new one. Maier became ambivalent, despite the fact that, for the first time in his life, in the new Germany, he had the freedom to work. But life was too short to wash cars, watch TV or rent a video from the shop down the road. Maier chose the quickest, most radical way out of the German workaday life he could think of: he became a war correspondent.

After eight years down the front of the nasty little wars of the late twentieth century – from the Israeli occupation of the Palestinian Territories to the civil wars in the former Yugoslavia and the high-altitude conflict in Nepal – he'd filed his last story four years earlier in Cambodia, had flown home and, after some soul-searching and a little retraining, had joined the renowned Hamburg detective agency Sundermann. Since then, Maier had been entrusted with cases all over Asia. He'd tracked down the killers of an Australian climber who'd apparently had a fatal accident in one of India's most remote valleys; negotiated the release from Bang Kwang Prison, Thailand's most notorious jail, of a man who'd fallen foul of the country's draconian lèse-majesté law; and uncovered a pedophile ring amongst Singapore's judiciary, though this most disturbing case had been stopped in its tracks by higher powers before the detective could wrap up his mission. He thought of himself as a fish, passing in silence through a big sea, catching prey here and there, occasionally unable to take a bite out of it for fear of being swallowed whole by more powerful predators. He didn't miss the near-death adrenaline rush he had been addicted to in his last life.

And yet, Maier took his new job seriously. The years as a correspondent had left him with contacts in every major city in South and Southeast Asia. He always went down to the wire to get his case solved. His work as a crisis journalist had left him hardened, and determined as the hounds of hell. Maier could walk over corpses to get to the heart of a case. The truth, even if neither palatable nor publishable, was everything to him. Sundermann hadn't been disappointed by his new detective.

When he was off work, Maier was a directionless romantic with desert sand in his shoes and a modicum of vanity in his eyes. That's how he imagined his father had been.

"Vodka Orange, please."

The stewardess's hand touched his arm as she placed the plastic glass on the collapsible table in front of him. The slight, barely noticeable gesture made him smile.

She was young, beautiful and, for a few bucks, she risked her life day in and day out. Cambodian Air Travel, the only airline that currently flew from Bangkok into Phnom Penh, ran overworked and ancient Russian propeller planes, dying air-wrecks long past retirement that barely managed to clear the Cardamom Mountains. The pilots were Russian, vets from Afghanistan, who'd once flown attack helicopters against armed resistance fighters. In Cambodia air space, the

Russians' worst enemy was alcohol. Planes that crashed over the remote and heavily mined forests of Cambodia were rarely found.

A cursory glance at his fellow passengers suggested that the almost forgotten kingdom he was heading for had changed since Maier's last visit. Young, self-confident backpackers in search of post-war adventures, a French tour group in search of temples, and a few old men in search of women, or children, or anything else that would be available in hell for a few dollars, had replaced the soldiers, gangsters and correspondents who had dared to fly into Phnom Penh a few years earlier.

In those days, he'd travelled by helicopter into a darker place, where men had routinely barbecued the livers of their enemies on open fires, sitting on the edges of paddy fields in the shadows of solitary palm trees. They, men that Maier knew well, had travelled and lived with, had wolfed down the organs in the belief that they were ingesting their enemies' souls, as their victims had watched, holding their eviscerated stomachs, slowly bleeding to death. Just one of many reasons why the dead could never rest and the country was beset by ghosts and demons, some of them his very own.

"Do you live in Phnom Penh, sir?" the young stewardess asked him, as she, placed a small carton, in which Maier could see an old-looking biscuit and an overripe banana, next to his empty plastic glass. She did this with her best bit of barely trained elegance, which was breathtaking.

"No, I am on holiday."

"Another drink perhaps?"

Maier hesitated for a second, and then opened his eyes wide enough to let the girl look inside his inside.

"Vodka orange?"

The stewardess's gaze dropped to the floor of the aisle before she rushed off.

Maier's thoughts returned to the task at hand. A strange case. A case without a crime.

The detective let the one and only conversation he'd had with his client run though his head once more.

"I want you to visit my son and find out what he's up to. You have to understand that Rolf is the black sheep of the Müller-Overbeck family," the woman had said without greeting or introduction. Her voice had been dead flat.

Mrs. Müller-Overbeck, whose husband had made his fortune with the first post-war coffee empire in the Bundesrepublik, had shot him a nervous, imperious glance. Ice cold and in her mid-sixties. Just like her gigantic villa in Blankenese, built by some Nazi before the war. With a haircut that could have dried out an igloo, silver, stiff and expensive, the woman had simply looked ridiculously affluent. What the rich thought of as low key. The skirt, fashionable and a touch too tight, and the blouse, uniquely ruffled, and finally the many thin gold bracelets dangling from her pale wrists like trophies, hadn't helped. But there'd been something unscripted in her performance, which Maier had supposed to be the reason for his presence in the Müller-Overbeck universe. She'd been agitated. It was hard to be ice-cold and agitated at the same time. How did the Americans say? It was lonely at the top. Life was a lottery. Maier had instinctively understood that this woman's expectations of service were in the rapacious to unreasonable bracket.

"You know the country?"

"I am the expert for Asia at Sundermann's. And I worked in Cambodia as a war correspondent for dpa."

Mrs. Müller-Overbeck had winced, "There is war over there? Rolf is caught up in a war? I thought he ran some kind of business for tourists there?"

"The war finished in 1998. The country is currently being rebuilt."

Listening hadn't been one of the strengths of Hamburg's coffee queen. Another reason for Maier to say as little as possible.

"I don't understand why he wanted to go there. To a country at war. I can remember the post-war years in Germany all too well. I don't understand why he'd want to go and look at the suffering of others. But Rolf has always been difficult. An A in English and an F in Maths, everything had to be extreme… Of course, the family is hoping that he'll come back and take over the reins. He's such a clever boy."

She hadn't offered Maier a drink. Not even a promotional gift, a politically correct cup from Nicaragua perhaps. He'd pondered whether she ever drank coffee. She'd seemed a woman who'd never done anything that involved any acceleration of the inevitable ageing process.

"You will find him and watch him. I am paying your usual rate for two weeks. Then you will call me. And I will, on the basis of your meticulously detailed and inclusive report, which you will have sent to me by email, prior to our call of course, decide whether you will be recalled to Germany or whether I will make further payments so that you may make additional enquiries."

Mrs. Müller-Overbeck had smelled of money and avarice, but not of coffee. It looked as if Maier would become the babysitter to Hamburg's rich heirs. There had been moments when he had wished the Wall back. In his thoughts, he'd cursed Sundermann, his boss.

"Mr. Maier, my expectations are very high and if I get the impression that you are unable or unwilling to fulfil them, then I will mention your agency to my friend, Dr. Roth, who sits on the city council."

His eyes tuned to truthful and trustworthy, Maier had nodded in agreement, and had let Mrs. Müller-Overbeck work on him, her scrawny, pale and lonely hands fragile as thin glass, held together by gold, coming up and down in front of him to emphasise the message.

"If my son is involved in any illegal or dangerous business over there, then please have his business uncovered in such a way that he is immediately deported back to Germany."

"Mrs. Müller-Overbeck, that kind of action can be very dangerous in Cambodia."

The coffee queen had reacted with irritation. "That's why I am not sending a relative. That's why you are going. I expect results, solutions, not doubts. I want to see my son where he belongs."

"I can't force your son to come back home."

"Tell him he is disinherited if he won't budge. No, do not tell him anything. Just report to me. And please be discreet. Rolf is my only son. You never know, in these countries, so far away…"

Maier had only then realised that Mrs. Müller-Overbeck was crying. The tears would surely turn to ice in seconds. She'd patted her sunken cheeks with a silk handkerchief.

"Preliminary investigations have told us that your son is a business partner in a small dive shop in a beach resort. He appears to be reasonably successful at what he is doing."

Mrs. Müller-Overbeck had abandoned all efforts to save her face and blurted in despair and with considerable impatience, "I could have told you that myself. I want to know with what kind of people he is doing business, whether he has a woman, what kind of friends he has. I want to know everything about his life over there. I want to know why he is there and not here. And then I want him back."

"You don't need a private detective to find that out. Why don't you just fly over there and visit him?"

"Don't be impertinent. You are being well paid, so ask your questions in Asia, not here. Goodbye, Maier. Please remember every now and then that your agency's licenses are granted by the city of Hamburg. And I am a significant part of our great city. That will keep you up to speed."

"This is co-pilot Andropov speaking. Please return your seats to upright position. We're about to land at Phnom Penh International Airport. The temperature in Phnom Penh is thirty-three degrees, local time is 6.30. We hope you enjoyed flying Cambodian Air Travel. Look forward to welcoming you on our flights again soon. On behalf of captain and the crew, have a pleasant stay in Cambodia. Hope to see you 'gain soon."

The stewardess passed Maier's seat, wearing her most professional smile. There was no way to get through now. Maier sighed inwardly and turned to the window.

Cambodia was down there, a small, insignificant country, in which the history of the twentieth century had played out as if trapped in the laboratory of a demented professor.

French colony, independence in 1953, a few years of happily corrupt growth and peace under King Sihanouk, followed by five years of war with CIA coups, Kissinger realpolitik, US bombs, a few hundred thousand dead and millions of refugees – the most intense bombing campaign in the history of modern warfare was the opening act for the communist revolution of Pol Pot and the Khmer Rouge, who killed a quarter of the country's population in less than four short years. The genocide was choked off by the Vietnamese, unwelcome liberators, and almost two decades of civil war followed. Finally, UNTAC, the United Nations Transitional Authority of Cambodia, had shown up, organised elections of sorts and had then fled the burnt out, tired country as quickly as possible. The last Khmer Rouge fighters had thrown in their blood-soaked towels in 1997 and joined the county's government troops. Maier had stood right next to them. It had been a painful process.

Since then, Cambodia had known peace – of sorts.

The women were beautiful. It had always been like that, if you were to believe the silent stone reliefs of countless apsaras, the heavenly dancers of the Angkor Empire that graced thousand-year-old temple walls in the west of the country. The highly paid UN soldiers had noticed the sensuousness of the women too and had promptly introduced HIV, which now provided the only international headlines of this otherwise forgotten Buddhist kingdom – a kingdom that had ruled over much of Southeast Asia eight hundred years ago. Past, present and future, it was all the same, every child in Cambodia knew that. Maier was looking forward to it. All of it.

The plane made a wide curve and barely straightened for its landing approach, descending with the coordination of a happy drunk towards the runway. The sky was gun-metal grey. Dark, heavy clouds hung low to the east of the city over the Tonlé Sap Lake. The country below looked dusty and abandoned. Here and there Maier spotted a swamp in this semi-arid desert, a rubbish-filled fish pond or a clogged-up irrigation canal. Dots of sick colour spilled on a blank, diseased landscape.

The aircraft abruptly lost altitude. Glittering temple roofs amidst the grey metal sheds of the poor that spread like tumors around the airport, shot past. Beyond the partially collapsed perimeter fence, children dressed in rags raced across unpaved roads or dug their way through gigantic piles of refuse. The Wild East.

The Cambodian Air Travel flight began to shake like a dying bird and Maier couldn't help but overhear one of the passengers in the seats behind him, a dour but voluptuous Austrian woman.

"Gerhard, are we crashing? Will we die, Gerhard?"

Maier spotted a few skinny cows grazing peacefully on the edge of the runway. Then they were down.

Welcome to Cambodia.

3

THE PEARL OF ASIA

"Vodka orange, please."

The Foreign Correspondents Club, the FCC, was Maier's first port of call in Phnom Penh. As the sun set, Maier sat on the front terrace on the first floor of the handsome French colonial-era corner building and watched the action along Sisowath Quay, the wide road that ran along the banks of the Tonlé Sap River. Since his last visit three years earlier, things had changed. Some of the roads in town had been resurfaced and, in the daytime, the city was safe. Amnesties and disarmament programs run by the government and international aid organizations had wrestled the guns from the hands of the kids.

Sisowath Quay woke up in the late afternoon and made a half-hearted attempt to resurrect the flair of the Fifties, when the Cambodian capital had been known as the Pearl of the East. Half the establishments along the river road were called something like L'Indochine. Pastis was served on the sidewalks and the cute young waitresses in their figure-hugging uniforms had learned to say bonjour. The bistros, bars and restaurants did brisk business with the tourists who had, looking for temples, somehow got lost and ended up in the city. A few galleries had opened, offering huge and garish oil paintings of Angkor Wat. Too loud for the waiting room at Mrs. Müller-Overbeck's dentist back in Blankenese, but just right for the current batch of visitors.

And the anarchy of the recent past remained visible. Small groups of cripples, most of them men, victims of a few of the millions of landmines that had been buried across the country, were gathering on the footpaths. Those with crutches limped up and down the broken pavement, carrying hawkers' trays filled with photocopied books about genocide, torture and the terrible human cost of land mines.

"Only two dollar," was the call that followed tourists brave enough to walk as night fell. Most of the unfortunates merely followed the wealthy visitors with their dead eyes, tried to sell drugs or simply begged for something, anything to get them through the night. To survive in this country could be called fortunate – or not. Those who no longer had eyes were guided in mad circles by orphaned children as they played sad, lamenting songs on the srang, a small, fiddle whose body was tied off with the skin of a cobra. Emaciated, dried up cyclodrivers moved their pedal-powered rickshaws along the quay in slow motion as if in funeral processions, while the motorised transport rolled like a dirty wave around them. Thousands of small mopeds, driven by motodops, provided the only public transport. Huge four-wheel-drives that had, for the most part, originated with the many NGOs in town and were now driven by heavily armed young thugs, the children of the corrupt upper classes, of government cronies and the upper echelons of the military. The Toyotas smuggled in from Thailand, with the steering wheel on the wrong side – you drove on the right in Cambodia, on the left in neighbouring Thailand and any which way you preferred on Sisowath Quay after dark – rarely displayed number plates. Some of the drivers were too young to look above the steering wheel. The countless bars on the side streets branching off from the river were filled with young women in tight clothes. For a few dollars you could take any one of them back to your hotel.

Directly above the steep banks of the river, the municipal authorities had built a wide promenade where the inhabitants of Cambodia's capital could enjoy the fresh breeze while the tourists could get excited about photographing the resident elephant. The US dollar was still the main currency in circulation, if the price list on the FCC's was anything to go by. The riel, the country's currency, wasn't worth much. Only the poor used it.

Maier found himself getting depressed. Here on Sisowath Quay, as the sun sunk into the slow moving, broad river, dotted with small fishing barges, a shoot-out before dinner was wholly imaginable, just as it had been four years earlier. Some change.

"Hey Maier, long time no see, mate. You're missing the boom."

Carissa Stevenson had once been the best and most attractive foreign journalist in Phnom Penh. After UNTAC had packed up its tanks, the media had left and the country had slipped from the international front pages, Carissa had stayed on. She'd stayed after Hort had died and Maier had said goodbye to his old life. Now, as he got up and put his arms around his former colleague and sometime partner, he noticed that the four years in the sun of a country the world had forgotten had given her a positively golden bloom. Carissa radiated life force.

"Hey Carissa, you look great, better than anyone I've seen lately. The heroin must be getting better in these parts."

"Well, it's getting cheaper all the time, Maier."

The woman from Nelson, New Zealand broke into a slightly lopsided and gorgeous smile. Rings around her fingers and hammocks under her dark eyes, lined with kohl. Dressed all in red. The skirt was tight and short. The long, frizzled hair was white.

White!

Maier remembered Carissa as ash blond.

"I don't suppose you've come to Phnom Penh for a holiday? And you're not here for me either. And there's no big story to be scooped. Apart from the daily rapes and murders, the governing kleptocracy, rampaging elephants and the occasional drug overdose by some third-tier member of the European aristocracy, it's pretty quiet. The good old and wild times, when Cambodia could shock the world are long gone. So, what's left? Angelina Jolie is shooting a film here soon. Have you become a reporter for the stars, mate?"

"I haven't worked as a journo for years, Carissa. I'm a private detective now. And I'm here on business."

Carissa laughed drily and, with a languid, studied gesture, waved for service. The waiter, at the far end of the teak top bar, nodded. It was as it had always been. Everyone knew what Carissa wanted. Maier remembered the exciting weeks in Phnom Penh – nights on the terrace of her colonial-era villa, crushed by sex, amphetamines, alcohol and marihuana, as gunfire rattled through the darkness around them. Life had been uncomplicated then. One just had to react to whatever had been going on.

The trips up-country were just as vivid in his memory. He'd often travelled with soldiers loyal to Hun Sen, the country's new leader, a young and ruthless ex-Khmer Rouge who had gone over to the Vietnamese. The soldiers had gone out to hunt Khmer Rouge. Looking danger in the eye had become habitual, like smoking, and had given Maier the illusion of eternal life. Somehow, he'd lost that later. On the day the bomb with his name on it had killed Hort, it had disappeared altogether. Now, as he looked at his old partner, he could clearly see his past in her familiar, so-familiar face.

"I don't fucking believe it. A private detective? I'll call you Holmes from now on."

"There are better private detectives."

He gave her his card.

"Marlowe is probably more appropriate."

Carissa expelled a short, mocking laugh. She hadn't lost her charm, or her cynicism. She smelled good too. She leant dangerously close to Maier and for a second he turned his eyes away from the street and fell into hers, like a fever.

"And how can I be of assistance to solve the great gumshoe's case?" she whispered with the broadest Kiwi accent he'd heard in years.

"I am not sure I can let you in on the confidential aspects of this case," he replied just as softly.

Carissa pulled a face and began to search through her handbag, until she'd found a half-smoked joint.

"You won't convince me with that. Is Cambodia the only country left in the world where smoking weed is still legal?"

"No longer, at least not on paper. The Americans put the heat on and parliament has passed the relevant laws. But what does that mean here? There are three restaurants in town that have happy pizza on their menu. One slice is enough to take you straight back to the good old UNTAC days. You can even choose, appropriately for the consumer age – happy, very happy and extremely happy. I've just covered it for High Times."

"Shame, that's not why I came back. But it's great to see you."

Carissa looked at him impatiently and passed the joint.

"So, tell me why you came back to Phnom Penh. I'll promise not to publish a word without your permission."

"I am looking for a young man who runs a scuba diving business in Kep. You know, the beach place near the Vietnamese border."

"Yeah, I fucking know the place. We had sex in an old ruined church there once, remember? A pigeon shat on your arse."

Maier did remember.

"There's only one dive place. It can only be Rolf or Pete. Rolf's German, Pete's a Brit. The outfit's called Pirate Divers, something original like that. Pete's in town. Those two aren't hard to find."

Maier took a quick drag and passed the joint back to the journalist.

"Well, if Pete is here already, I would like to meet him. Where does he go at night?"

"The English guy? But your case surely has to be about the German? Has he done anything wrong? I hope he's not a child molester, but I suppose he wouldn't have slept with an old lady like me if he went for the young ones."

"As far as I know, he is nothing of the sort. But I don't know much and that's why I am here."

"Is there a warrant out for him in Germany?"

"No. How long have you known Rolf Müller-Overbeck?"

Carissa grinned with only a modicum of embarrassment.

"Don't sound so formal, Maier. I picked Rolf up in the Heart of Darkness bar. On his first night in town. That was six months ago, in April, around New Year. You know, when everyone throws water and talc at each other and everyone gets wet. Rolf's the kind of guy who's straight in there, no hesitation. He poured a bucket of ice water over my head and I took my revenge."

"How did he seem to you?"

Carissa laughed, "Quite flexible for a bloke, especially for a German. Spontaneous, friendly and naïve – as far as Asia's concerned. He hadn't caught yellow fever yet. I was down in Kep in May to celebrate my birthday. I saw Rolf again that night and he still hadn't been infected. But that has, as far as I know, changed now. What do you want from him?"

"Confidential. But as far as I know, he has not committed a crime. Yellow fever?"

"Oh, you know, the unhealthy fixation on Cambodian women

many male foreigners arrive with or acquire here. They think that Cambodian girls are the most beautiful females in the world, which has a lot to do with the fact that they don't talk back. As long as the money keeps rolling in. Once the boys become infected, I'm out of the race, completely. Naturally. I talk back."

"And the English guy?"

"…is kind of a smooth operator, a wide-boy as they'd say where he comes from. But the dive business seems to be going good since Rolf got in as a partner. He invested and manages to get German customers via their website. The dive industry's in its infancy here. Those two are real pioneers. They won't get rich but I'm sure they get by."

Maier was suddenly exhausted. The long flight and the short joint, the unfamiliar heat and the city air, saturated with petrol fumes, the anarchy on the street, and on top, his old lover – it was simply great to be back in Cambodia and float in clouds of nostalgia. This case would be more fun than Mrs. Müller-Overbeck had had in her entire life.

Carissa raised her glass, "Mr. Private Detective, if you don't come home with me tonight, I'll do everything in my power to make your case more complicated."

4

INTO THE HEART OF DARKNESS

BY 9 O'CLOCK, the city burnt out. For a few short hours, the daily struggle for survival of almost all the city's inhabitants' ground to a halt. As soon the sun disappeared into the Tonlé Sap River, the shops closed and the pedestrians got off the river promenade. The opposite side of the slow-moving water had already fallen into silent, mosquito-sodden darkness. Perhaps the river was not to be trusted: after all it changed direction twice a year. Yes, Cambodia was a special place.

The one-legged entrepreneurs faded from the sidewalks and soon only hardened motodops, pushing ketamine, brown sugar and girls, all at the same time if desired, cruised up and down Sisowath Quay. Homeless families, just in from the countryside to look for jobs in the construction industry, were camped in front of closing restaurants. These people had to share the concrete floor with cockroaches and rats for as long as it took to find employment and a roof over their heads.

Maier sat on the back of Carissa's 250cc Yamaha dirt bike. The Kiwi journalist drove like the devil down Street 154 and didn't hesitate to take a cop's right of way on Norodom Boulevard.

"If you drive too slowly at night, you get harassed by kids with guns."

Phnom Penh remained a wonderful, frightening backwater. If the Cambodian capital had been safer, investors would have built a sea of chrome-and-glass monstrosities. But there were enough buildings from the French colonial days and the optimistic post-independence era of the Fifties left standing to get a feeling for the city's history, even at sixty miles an hour.

The Khmer Rouge had laid siege to and finally taken Phnom Penh in April 1975. In the following weeks, the victorious revolutionaries emptied the city of its people. The entire population was driven into the countryside onto collectives to work as rice farmers. Overnight, schools, post offices, banks and telephone exchanges were made obsolete. Money no longer existed. The Pearl of Asia became a ghost town.

The forced exodus of the Seventies and the lack of investment in subsequent decades saved the city's character from demolition. As neighbouring Bangkok grew into a Bladerunner-like cityscape, Phnom Penh remained provincial. Much of Cambodia's urban population had been butchered in the communists' Killing Fields and many of the capital's current inhabitants were landless farmers who'd drifted into town since the end of the war in search of work.

After dark, dogs, cats and rats, all about the same size, ruled the garbage dumps, which spread across almost every street corner. Here and there, fairy lights glimmered in the darkness, beacons of hope and all its opposites to guide the night people towards massage brothels which could be found in the small alleys off the main strips. The red light was Phnom Penh's only vital sign at night. The best party going was at the Heart, as the motodops called the city's most popular bar without a great deal of affection.

"How d'you want me to introduce you to Pete?"

"As your victim. And as a potential business victim. You can tell him that I am on the way to Kep and that I am planning to invest there."

On Rue Pasteur, close to the nightclub, a small traffic jam clogged the road. Rich kids, the sons of the families who plundered the country, were trying to park their king-sized SUVs with horns blaring, while mouthing off to their compatriots. It appeared to be a fairly well-established and reasonably safe ritual – the children of the privileged were all surrounded by their personal teams of bodyguards. The street was in a permanent state of détente, and just a few small steps short of apocalypse. With these people around, there would be occasional fuck-ups.

A food stall was mobbed by prostitutes – taxi girls. The young

Khmer seemed to eat all day long – perhaps a reaction to periodic famines, which had many villages in its grip, even today. Ever since the Khmer Rouge had taken over the government and beaten educated Cambodians to death, there'd not been enough food to go around. Some Khmer hadn't had enough to eat for twenty-five years.

The music in the Heart of Darkness was loud. The bar was packed three-deep. A small laser swished like a searchlight across the crowded dance floor to the sounds of Kylie Minogue's 'Can't get you out of my head' – the vaguely futuristic dazzle caused a slight culture shock. The Heart was a different world. Backpackers, worn out, sleazy ex-pats and young, rich local thugs gyrated in front of the massive bass bins. Everyone danced in his or her own personal hedonistic movie. Taxi girls threw yaba pills, cheap methamphetamines from Thailand, into each others' mouths. Bowls of marihuana graced the long bar. The smoke of a hundred joints hung above the cashiers like a storm cloud.

The Heart was a Cambodian institution, a collection point for all those who couldn't sleep at night and had money to burn.

Carissa made her way towards the bar. Maier followed her through the dense throng, her white head guiding him. The pool table was run by shredders, young and beautiful taxi girls who played the tourists for their wallets. On the wall above the table, a faded photograph of Tony Poe, a CIA operative who'd made his name collecting the heads and ears of his communist enemies during the Secret War in Laos in the Sixties, faced onto the dance floor. Maier had heard the stories from UN soldiers. Poe had been so awful, he'd eventually become the template for Marlon Brando's Colonel Kurtz in Apocalypse Now. Maier smiled to himself. That was how small and post-modern the world had become. The Heart of Darkness was probably the best-known watering hole in Southeast Asia.

But you had to take care in here. The squat Khmer bouncer who was in charge of bets at the pool table wasn't the only man who carried his gun more or less openly in his belt. Maier was keen to avoid trouble. After all, he'd only landed a few hours ago.

"Shit, it is loud in here."

"You're getting old," Carissa laughed over her shoulder and passed him an ice cold can of Angkor Beer.

Maier didn't like beer. Nor did he like yaba and disco music. Yaba meant mad medicine. Just the right kind of drug for Phnom Penh.

'Holidays in Cambodia' by the Dead Kennedys blasted from the speakers. Maier could at least remember this one. Good sounds to kick back to and watch the dance on the volcano. And what a dance it was. Jello Biafra screamed "Pol Pot, Pol Pot, Pol Pot," and the girls, who'd perhaps never heard of the man who'd killed their mothers and fathers, uncles and aunts, gobbled more pills as the sweat of three hundred drunks dripped from the ceiling onto the dance floor.

By the pool table, a life-size sandstone bust of Jayavarman VII, the greatest of the ancient Angkor kings, stood, softly lit, in an alcove. The thousand-year-old god-king sucked up the chaotic scene in the room with empty eyes. Maier sympathised. In the Heart, he felt as old as a god-king. An even older white man, his shirt open to his belt buckle, had climbed the bar with two girls and waved at the crowd, a bottle of red wine spilling from his right hand. The hair on his head and chest stood in all directions and he looked like an electrified dancing bear. Perhaps he'd once been a butcher or owned a tanning studio in the burbs of Europe. And one day that had suddenly felt like no longer enough.

Maier felt the man, but he had no desire to swap places. In the clouds of marihuana smoke behind the pool table, one of the young shredders began to open the trouser belt of a helpless, drunken and equally young tourist. Maier had just read in the Phnom Penh Post that the staff of the US Embassy was banned – by the US government – from entering the Heart. Had this decision been made for security reasons or out of prudish concern for America's brightest?

"The English guy's already here, at a table behind the bar. And he's with bad company."

"With some of these nouveau riche thugs?"

Carissa leaned heavily into Maier and tried to make herself understood above the din of the music. "No, with real gangsters. People who don't belong in here."

Maier shrugged and pulled a face, "So, what are we waiting for? Introduce me."

"Hey Pete."

"Wow, Carissa, babe, you look stunning, as always. May I introduce to you, gentlemen, Phnom Penh's classiest import from New Zealand."

Maier saw straight away that all the chairs were occupied by problems. The skinny Brit with the bright red hair and the sunken cheeks, a tough little pirate, had jumped up and embraced Carissa. Maier guessed him in his mid-thirties. The silver chain around his wrist was heavy enough to sink a water buffalo. He wore a Manchester United shirt, with the collar up, and moved in a cloud of cheapish deodorant. He counteracted this with a strong-smelling Ara, the cigarette of choice for taxi girls and motodops, stuck in his nicotine-stained fingers. Two full packs and three mobile phones lay on the table in front of him. So, this was the business partner of Rolf Müller-Overbeck: the wide-boy from the mean streets of Britain. Not completely unlikeable, but definitely not trustworthy.

The other two men at the table, both Khmer, were of a different ilk – one was young, the other old, though they came from the same dark place. They were smoking Marlboros and looked at Carissa as if she were a piece of meat. These days, Maier didn't encounter men like these very often. There weren't that many. Both of them had been defined and molded by war. They were men who'd killed and thought nothing of it.

Maier's presence had been registered. He could almost physically feel being observed and judged. Was he a potential danger or an opportunity to further their interests? What was the English guy doing with guys like this in a cosmopolitan filling station on a Saturday night?

The older man was in his mid-sixties. He had glued his short hair to his square, box-shaped head with gel. His neck was non-existent. He wore a black polo shirt and looked too casual in a grey pair of polyester slacks. Like a toad on a golf course. This man had worn a uniform for most of his life.

The youngster next to him was his son, mid-twenties, wide hip-hop jeans, a Scorpions T-shirt, and a baseball cap, worn back to front on his equally square head, his thick, hairless arms defaced by backstreet tattoos. The boy had been born and had grown up during the civil war, a stark but no less assuring contrast to his formerly revolutionary father.

Luckily, all the chairs were taken. It was better to stand around people like this.

Carissa exchanged kisses with Pete. "My old friend Maier is on the way to Kep, guys. He wants to poke around down there, see if there's anything worth investing in."

Pete's handshake was hard and dry. His dark eyes sparkled frivolously in his sunken face, which seemed deathly pale, despite a deep suntan. Pete looked like a guy who had nothing to lose and loved playing for huge stakes. Maier thought him largely pain-free.

"Maier, mate. Come and visit. An old friend of Carissa's is always welcome. And my partner is a kraut too. At least you look like a kraut."

Pete winked at him as if they were secret co-conspirators and whispered in a hoarse tone, "Kep was made for people like us. Nice beach town, built by the French, who're long gone, thank fuck. It's a bit shambolic down there, but things are getting better. Haven't you heard? Cambodia's booming. Now's a great time to get your investments in, mate."

The old man had got up. Pete threw him a few clunky chunks of Khmer. The son had also stood up, showing off the pistol in the belt of his low-slung ghetto pants. The older man bowed slightly.

"My name is Tep. I am number one in Kep. My friends call me Tep."

Maier couldn't imagine that this man had friends. The handshake was soft and moist, like creeping death.

Maier extrapolated a little – the man had Khmer Rouge and genocide written all over his face. Had some of the old comrades of the politburo, those who had survived the vagaries of history, become investors? Was that the price of peace?

The younger man with the gun didn't introduce himself, but that was OK.

Tep smiled silently at Maier. The sonic sins of a Britney Spears song hung suspended between the two men, creating a strange, cheap, disposable mood. What was a man like that doing in a place like this? Tep should have died in the jungle a long time ago.

"I run a few businesses in Kep. I can help you if you need anything in Kep. Come to visit on my island. And bring your girlfriend."

The old man's English was simple and barely understandable. Carissa pulled at Maier's sleeve, as the detective tried to look as uninformed as possible.

"Beer?"

Pete had already ordered five cans of Angkor Beer and banged them on the table. Tep sat back down, a shadow of irritation shooting across his face, and turned to Carissa. The antipodean journalist was waiting for him.

"Aren't you a former Khmer Rouge general? Aren't you the guy who blew up the Hotel International in Sihanoukville? Perhaps you remember, a tourist from New Zealand died in that attack, General Tep?"

For a split second, the old man's eyes burst into flames.

Pete laughed nervously, "Wow, Carissa, babe, Carissa, we aren't here to reheat old rumours, are we? It's great to see you, babe."

Pete, Maier decided, was capable of balancing a tray full of landmines, which was just as well in this place, at this moment.

Tep didn't get a chance to answer. A young Khmer with a shaved head, dressed in an immaculate white silk suit, dead drunk and sporting a slight similarity to the bust of the god-king, had pulled his gun at the next table. A flat-footed tourist had just stepped on his brand-new, imported Nikes. Enraged the young Khmer had spilt his beer onto a row of green pills he'd lined up in front of him, which he now tried to rescue from the ash-sodden slop on his table directly into his mouth. The hapless tourist had already disappeared into the throng.

There'll be trouble in a minute, was the only thought that came to Maier's mind.

The bald playboy swallowed his last pills and got up to scan the crowd for a likely scapegoat who was going to pay, one way or another, for someone else's clumsiness. Someone would have to pay. With a theatrical gesture he whipped his gun from his belt and waved it around the room.

Sometimes things happened quickly. The skinhead climbed onto his chair and began to scream hysterically. Tep nodded to his son and turned to Maier, "Don't make any problems in Kep. Investors are welcome, snoops and stupid people are not. You see."

The first shot, the one to drive up the courage, went straight into the ceiling. The Heart stopped in its tracks. The DJ cut the music. The house-lights flashed on, illuminating a hundred twisted, strung-out faces in mid-flight. Carissa grabbed for Maier's shoulder and pulled him to the sticky ground. Pete had already vanished. Punters rushed for the exit. The old general made no effort to move. His son got up and slunk behind the rebel in the white suit who stood on his chair, turning around and around, levelling his gun towards the surrounding tables.

Pop, pop, pop

The tourists screamed in panic. The playboy skinhead was dead by the time he hit the table in front of Maier, which collapsed in a hail of bottles, cans and cigarette butts.

Tep's son had shot him in the back.

That's how easy it was to die in Cambodia.

The boy helped his father get up and made a path for the old man to get behind the bar.

"Follow them." Maier grabbed Carissa, "There must be another exit."

The muggy night air felt good after the two beers Maier shouldn't have drunk and a murder he hadn't wanted to witness. But outside there was only Cambodia. Shots rang down the street. Car windows smashed. A small gang of motodops raced down Rue Pasteur, into the darkness. Girls screamed. Saturday night in Phnom Penh.

"So, this is the most popular nightclub in the country," he said, more to himself than anyone around him.

The windows of the police station that stood hidden behind a high wall directly opposite the Heart, remained dark, despite the gunfire. No policeman who earned twenty dollars a month would get involved in this weekend orgy of adolescent violence unless there was extra money to be made. The situation would eventually bleed itself to death.

The general pulled his polo shirt straight and stared down the road, an expression of faint amusement on his flat features. The old man didn't seem overly concerned about his son's state of mind, after the youngster had just killed a man in cold blood in front of several hundred witnesses.

"Thanks, Mr. Tep, your son saved our lives."

The general looked at Maier, his eyes fixed and devoid of message.

"Kep is a quiet town. You can relax. Come and visit on my island. Ask local fishermen how to get to my villa on Koh Tonsay. Germans always welcome. And forget what happen here tonight."

His car pulled up.

Carissa had freed her 250 from the chaos of parked bikes in front of the Heart and Maier lost no time jumping on the back. A few seconds later, they crossed Norodom Boulevard.

"Fucking hell, Maier, as soon as you turn up, the bullets start flying. The article I'm going to write about this tomorrow will be sensational. Son of former KR general shoots son of oil executive in Cambodia's most cosmo nightclub. That'll make waves. You'll have to drink beer without me tomorrow."

"I don't like beer."

5

CHRISTMAS BAUBLES

Carissa's heavy breasts floated above Maier's heavy head, as seductive as the baubles that his mother had fastened to the Christmas tree forty years ago. In his drunken state, a few heartbeats short of sunrise, this absurd association made passing sense. Gram Parson's "Hickory Wind" was playing on Carissa's laptop. The song, which she'd always liked, took Maier back to his early assignments in Cambodia. Another job, another life. Dangerous thoughts percolated in his mind.

"The nights were never long enough with you."

"What nights, Carissa? Mostly we did it on the roof of your villa in the mornings, because we were working at night or because we were too wasted."

"Nothing much's changed with ten years having passed then."

"Probably not."

"Then I still turn you on?"

"Yes, you do."

"Everything's all right then."

Carissa rolled out from under the mosquito net and stretched in front of the open window of her apartment.

Life wasn't easy in the tropics, but a sunrise that you could never witness in Europe was about to point its first light fingers across the horizon, and get caught up in a decadent play of glittering sparks on the golden roof of a neighbouring temple before beginning to dance around Carissa's neck and shoulders. Maier groaned.

"Why didn't you stay?"

"For the same reason I will go to Kep alone."

Carissa turned towards Maier in the faint light. Now she looked like the Hindu goddess Kali, irresistible and merciless.

"Why?"

"Because I do not like to watch my best friends die. And this country finishes off even the best. Especially the best."

"So, you expect problems on the coast?"

"I do not expect anything. I don't even really know why I am here yet. But I am sure that the son of my client is up to his neck in shit."

"I survived quite well without you for the past ten years, Maier. You're just commitment-shy."

"That I am. But that has nothing to do with me going to Kep alone."

"Then you love me a little bit and want to save me from the evil in this world?"

Maier sensed the sarcasm in her voice and replied as calmly as he could. "That I do and that is what I want to do."

"All men are the fucking same," she hissed, lifted the net and fell towards him.

Maier was alone in his dream, crossing the country on foot. Everything was on fire. The air was filled with the stench of burned flesh. The smell was so bad that he was permanently retching. The corpses of lynched monks, policemen who had been skinned alive, dismembered teachers, postal workers, rotten and hollowed out by maggots, of engineers who'd been half eaten by stray dogs, artists who'd been shot, judges who'd been beaten to death and decapitated students whose heads grinned from thousands of poles that had been rammed into the rice fields, piled up by the roadside and slowly slid into shallow graves that they themselves had dug earlier. Except for a few farmers with closed faces, virtually all the adults had been killed. General Tep and his horde of undernourished, angry humans, clad in black pajamas and armed with blood-soaked machetes and sticks, marched with torches across the dying land and burnt one village after another to the ground.

Maier reached one of the villages, a typically dysfunctional cooperative on the verge of starvation, destined to fail because no one had any tools and all the tool makers had been killed.

Tep had caught a woman who'd been grilling a field rat over a smoldering, badly smelling fire. Angkar, the mysterious and powerful organization that fronted and obscured the communist party of Cambodia, had forbidden the private preparation and consumption of food. What Angkar said was law. And all those who opposed the laws or broke them, were taken away for re-education or training and were never seen again. Angkar could not be opposed.

There was good reason for this. Those who ate more than others were hardly exemplary communists and were not completely dedicated to help Kampuchea rise from the ashes of its conflicts. Those who ate in secret had other things to hide. With traitors in its midst, Kampuchea had no chance to fight the imperialist dogs. The enemy was without as well as within. And the CIA was everywhere.

Tep had no choice. He beat the woman to death with a club, split her head right open. As the woman's skull cracked, a small noise escaped, "Pfft," and the world lay in pieces.

The woman had two daughters. The girl in the rice field had watched her mother's murder and was running towards her father who was working under a hot sun with his second, younger daughter.

Tep, soaked in blood, the liver of the woman in his fist, followed the girl. He listened as the father shouted to his daughters to flee. When he finally reached the man, he tried to kill him with a hammer, the last hammer in the village. Tep hit the man in the face, again and again, but he would not die. Tep began to sweat. Maier stood next to Tep. He was sweating as much. He was witness. He couldn't stop a thing. The younger daughter stood a little to the side. She wore her hair short and like the rest of her insignificant family, wore black pajamas. She was a product of Angkar and had grown up in a children's commune. She barely knew her father. She was a child of Angkar.

"What is your name?" Tep smiled gently at the girl.

"My name is Kaley."

"Your father is an enemy of Angkar, Kaley. He works for the CIA."

The girl smiled and looked down at the broken man, who lay beside her, breathing in hard spasms. Tep handed the hammer to the girl. She might have been twelve years old.

After she'd done as ordered, he shouted for his men to cut the man open and devour his liver.

The older girl had run and reached the edge of the forest beyond the paddy fields. Maier was also running. He looked back across his shoulder.

Tep's men were queuing up to rob the little sister of her innocence, life and liver. Some had leathery wings and hovered above their victim like attack helicopters. *Flap-flap-flap-flap.*

A white spider, as tall as a house, appeared on the edge of the village. The men shrank back and made a tight circle around the girl and her dying father. The white spider moved slowly towards the circle. It didn't hesitate; it just took its time. Maier ran on, his mind locked in terror. He no longer dared to turn. The fire rolled across the family, the village and the land. Maier's tears were not sufficient to put out the flames.

"Maier, are you crying in your sleep? Have you missed me that much or did you go soft back home in Deutschland?"

The morning breeze ran coolly across his sweat-soaked back and he crept deeper into the arms of the girl who'd become a woman. Carissa lifted her head, her white hair alive like the tufts of the Medusa.

6

SELF-DEFENSE

PETE'S HAIR looked more fiercely red in bright, merciless daylight than it had in the damp flickers of the Cambodian night. It didn't look natural. The Englishman was just devouring his very English breakfast at the Pink Turtle, a pavement restaurant on Sisowath Quay – scrambled eggs, bacon, sausage, baked beans, toast and grilled tomatoes, all of it swimming in a half centimetre of fat.

Despite the previous evening's shooting and a royal hangover, the dive shop owner was in a good mood. A can of Angkor Beer sat sweating next to his delectable culinary choice.

"So, this French guy walks into a bank the other day. The newest bank in town. Just opened. Air-con and all. And he walks up to the cashier and pulls out a shooter. There are three security guys in this bank, armed with pump actions. But they don't know what to do, they're so fucking surprised. A *barang* robbing a bank? How mad is that? But then the French geezer makes a mistake. As the cashier hands him a bag full of dollars, he puts his gun down on the counter. He just lost it for a sec. That's when they jump him. It's just too easy. Fucking prick's in jail, looking at twenty. Had gambling debts and they threatened to cut his girl's throat, only she was in on it. Great Scambodian fairy tale, so fucking typical."

Carissa ordered two coffees. Pete was on a roll.

"The dive business is going good, mate, it really is. We have great dive sites a half hour away by long-tail boat. Our customers get to see turtles and reef sharks, and there's plenty of titan trigger fish and large barracuda out there. As long as they don't overdo the dynamite. But I'm an optimist. We're searching for new dive spots all the time. There are hundreds of wrecks. And every year, more and more tourists come here. The first real beach resort just opened. That's Tep's of course."

"And what else does Tep do?" Maier asked, his eyes recovering behind a pair of mirror shades.

Pete shrugged his narrow shoulders, "Yeah, I agree, mate, that didn't look too cool last night. It was well ugly. But luckily, this kind of thing doesn't happen too often. Almost never."

The Englishman must have noticed a shadow of doubt cross Maier's face, "It was virtually self-defense."

Maier smiled, "Virtually."

Carissa laughed throatily, "The boy shot the bald guy in the back, Pete. Only in Cambodia is this called self-defense, and only if you know the right people and have sacks full of cash."

"You were always very principled, babe. You know exactly how things stand and fall here. In a small dump like Kep everyone knows and respects the boss. Otherwise you can't run a business or do anything. In Cambodia, you need good connections and a strong will to live."

Carissa, resigned boredom painted across her face, shrugged lazily.

"Always the same excuses. And you screw the taxi girls because you are really humane employers who believe in equal opportunities and don't want to see them exploited by Gap in the garment factories."

Pete stopped concentrating on his beans and winked at Maier, "Some get bitter as they get older. Others realise what they've missed. Life's a short and meaningless trip crammed with suffering and emptiness. I knew that when I was five years old. You don't need the Buddha to realise that. I think it's best to fish for as much money and pussy as possible. Come on, babe, Carissa, you're not so different."

The journalist rolled her eyes in silence and lit a crinkled joint she had fished out of her handbag. How quickly you got used to the small rituals of friends, Maier thought.

"Does Tep have enough connections upstairs in the government to suppress the incident in the Heart?"

"Yeah, he does. He's got old mates in government. The bald

playboy in the Armani suit went mad on drugs and shot himself. There are witnesses who swear he took a bunch of pills before he pulled his gun, put it to his chest and pulled the trigger. Over and over, apparently. That ketamine is strong."

"Then I don't have a real story. Just a suicide on drugs won't do." Carissa complained.

The Englishman grinned at her.

"No, you don't, unless you want a shed load of trouble."

"So, what else does your influential friend do?"

"Tep's a businessman. He knows he can't be too greedy. He needs us foreigners as much as we need him. And unfortunately, the country also needs can-do guys like Tep. Together we create employment opportunities. And not just for taxi girls, as Carissa likes to think."

"This doesn't really answer my question."

"You're a pretty curious type, Maier. Normally the krauts are a bit more reticent."

Maier let the remark pass, almost.

"Before I invest anything here, I want to know how much disappears in the quicksand. And that did not look too good last night. I have read good things about Kep, but I have also heard good things about Koh Samui."

Pete relaxed, pushed his plate away, lit an Ara and laughed drily. "Maier. Don't be so German, so pessimistic. Come down to the coast and meet my partner, Rolf. He's just as much a true human being as you two, and still, he's happy. And anyway, people shoot each other on Samui all the time. Every month, people go AWOL and are found later, half-eaten and drifting in the Gulf. I know, cause most of them are countrymen of mine. That's how it is in these parts. That's why we're here and not at home."

Pete beamed at his breakfast companions.

"But in contrast to the overcrowded, unfriendly beaches in Thailand, Kep is stunningly beautiful and quiet, just totally fucking idyllic. We have a few hours of electricity a day, no traffic, no disco, no Internet. And on top of that, Kep has plenty of traces of this country's sad history, something you Germans usually go for, no?"

Maier had gotten tired of the Englishman's jokes and had withdrawn into himself. "Two world wars and one world cup" appeared to define Pete's idea of Germans. He was hardly unique. Southeast Asia was a favourite destination for the UK's piratical and lawless white trash underclass.

But the little red-haired, wrinkled man hadn't finished, "Just one thing, mate, a friendly piece of advice. People who get too curious about how things work in Cambodia, people who ask too many questions, are in danger of giving the impression that they might not be around for the reasons they say they are. If Tep gets this impression, it can have really heavy consequences. It's better to let life roll along at its natural pace down there and to roll with it. That way, most questions will be answered anyway. I'm sure you understand me."

"I must be lucky then that I let life roll at its natural pace last night." Maier laughed.

Pete reached across the table and slapped Maier's shoulder like an old friend. "You're a fun guy to be around, Maier. That's why my advice comes flowing your way. Our community down there in Kep is so small that every newcomer is looked at, like under a magnifying glass. It's just a local reflex. We don't mean anything by it. And anyway, you come with the best of references."

Maier looked across at Carissa. Was this skinny little Englishman threatening him or was it all just talk? Maier didn't want to fall in love with his old colleague again, but now he was worried and that was never a good sign. The detective rarely worried. Worries made life, this short and meaningless journey of suffering and emptiness, more complicated. The Buddha had been right about most things.

But Maier had no time to philosophise. The young waitress of the Pink Turtle appeared with a tray, loaded with three whiskeys, on the rocks.

Just like the freebooter he was, Pete had remembered the most important thing of all.

"I know, Maier, you don't like drinking beer. It makes you very likeable somehow. Let's drink Jack Daniels to the man who doesn't like beer! Cheers."

Maier didn't like whiskey much either but he lifted his glass. He was on duty.

7

ON THE BEACH

Maier was the day's first punter in the Last Filling Station. The ramshackle bar stood on the edge of a beach in a palm orchard, a few hundred metres west of what was left of Kep-sur-Mer. More than a hundred villas slowly crumbled into the brush along the coast towards the Vietnamese border. Kep was a ghost town about to be reconquered by the jungle. Even the Angkor Hotel, near the crab market, was in a pitiful condition, its pockmarked walls protected by downwardly mobile shards of sheet metal. Maier had taken a room right under the roof. During the night, the rain had roared all around him, loud enough to drown out the noise of the television, which, powered by a car battery, had run at top volume in what passed as a lobby until dawn. Just as well that all good roads in the world led to a bar. And the Last Filling Station was special. It was the only bar in Kep, and in the mornings, it served the desperate.

"This town has seen better days."

"It has. But the impression of total collapse is misleading, buddy. Kep has had a demanding history and it ain't done yet."

The old man behind the counter gave a friendly nod and lit a joint. The moist and pungent smoke rolled through the heavy air towards Maier. The bar's proprietor was a small, fat man with hairy, tattooed arms that stuck out of an old, sleeveless Bruce Springsteen T-shirt. Born in the USA, no doubt about it. His lumpy face, in which two beady eyes threatened to drown, descended to several ridges of double chins. His voice had crawled out of a Louisiana backwater and forgotten to dry off. The thumb on his right hand was missing. He was a character.

In the Last Filling Station, the Vietnam War was celebrated like a nostalgic road trip. Behind the counter, the shelf crammed with mostly empty liquor bottles had been welded together from machine gun parts. A torn cloth of the Rolling Stones' tongue hung like a pirate flag from a wooden pole that had been lodged, with the help of a couple of CBU bomb cases, into the ground in the centre of the small square room. The fan squawked like a tired seagull and barely managed to turn the air. Spent mortar shells and hand grenades hung suspended from the ceiling around the fan. Willie Peter canisters, once the receptacles for white phosphorus, which burned through skin like napalm, served as ashtrays.

It was too early to smoke and drink. Maier had only just started working.

"First time in Kep?"

"Yes."

"But not the first trip to Cambodia, right?"

The American had a good eye for people.

"No, I was here a few times between '93 and '97, came as a journalist."

The American's tiny eyes lit up.

"Is there anything to report from Kep that the world might be interested in?"

"No idea. I no longer work in the media business."

The man behind the counter shrugged.

"That's probably for the best. Folks who ask too many questions around here end up floating in the soup pretty damn soon."

"You've already asked me three questions, be careful," Maier laughed and offered the American his hand. The bar owner's thumbless paw was huge and badly scarred.

"Maier."

"Les. Les Snakearm Leroux."

"Really?"

"Really! My momma called me Lesley Leroux. And they called me Snakearm in Vietnam."

"Snakearm?"

"Because I could squeeze the life out of a python with one hand."

"No shit?"

"No shit. Made a heap of money in some dark places in Saigon, right up to the day we abandoned ship and honour. That was three questions, buddy. One more and I'll shoot you dead."

"Vodka orange?"

"Bang."

The war vet was an instantly likeable guy. And the Last Filling Station was the perfect place to drink your troubles away on a lonely near-equatorial morning. Not that Maier had anything to be mournful about. Not yet. He was only just getting started.

"So, what happened here? Was the town destroyed in the war?"

The American shook his head.

"Kep was the Saint Tropez of Cambodia. The French showed up in the late nineteenth century and started it off with a few hotels, churches and brothels between the jungle and the sea. In the Fifties, Kep became popular with Khmer high society who came down from Phnom Penh and built weekend villas. They had it all just the way they wanted it – waterskiing and cocktail parties, barbecues and Rock'n'Roll bands on the beach. But the good life ended with Sihanouk's departure. Rich folks boarded up their houses and stopped coming. The KR were here from '71 to '77 and they did kill quite a few locals, but there wasn't much fighting here. Then in '79, when the 'Nam invaded, the harvest didn't happen. People broke into the houses and stripped them, even chiseled the steel out of the walls. Whatever they got, they exchanged with the Vietnamese for rice. Hard times."

Les coughed thick clouds of smoke across the dark, scratched wood of the bar.

"But that was all a long time ago. Now we got three hotels in Kep and the first scuba diving outfit opened some while ago. At weekends it gets really crowded with locals who come for the crabs. The crabs are fucking delicious, you should try them. About a dollar a kilo. Otherwise, backpackers, weekenders from Phnom Penh, adventurers and lunatics. Which crowd d'you run with, Maier?"

A young Vietnamese woman with a closed face and short black hair that was trying to grow in several directions at once appeared silently in the door between the bar and kitchen and handed Maier his Vodka orange. Les had his hands full with his joint.

"That's the fashion in Vietnam these days. The girls want to look like the guys in the boy bands."

Van Morrison's "Brown-Eyed Girl" poured from the speakers that hung amongst the ordnance from the ceiling. The wall facing the sea had been almost completely destroyed and replaced by thin wooden slats. The other walls, in which various calibers had left their marks, were covered with framed photographs of the American wars in Vietnam, Laos and Cambodia.

Les pointed to a faded image of a young man in jeans, sporting a huge moustache, posing in front of a helicopter, "I was a pilot. First, I flew Hueys out of Danang for the Navy. Later I worked for Air America in Laos. Black Ops. Top Secret. This shot was taken in Vientiane. We flew weapons, troops and drugs for the CIA. Then, from '73 on, I was here, until the KR took over."

"You must have been on one of those last buses full of foreigners to leave Phnom Penh, which the Khmer Rouge accompanied to the Thai border?"

"No, wasn't there. Just prior to that, I evacuated employees from our embassy. I flew an overloaded Huey to one of our ships. After the last flight, we tipped the bird off the ship and into the sea, just like my colleagues did off Saigon. You can't imagine how that felt."

"So why did you come back?"

Les Snakearm Leroux looked around his bar as if he'd just entered it for the very first time.

"I ain't a historian or anything. But I saw a lot in the war. I saw a lot of war. Not all of us were junkies, at least not all of the time. I knew even then that politics was behind the rise of the KR. We ran an awesome air campaign against suspected Vietnamese positions inside Laos and Cambodia. We killed thousands of civilians and carpet-bombed their fields. How is a Khmer farmer supposed to understand that a plane drops from the sky and burns his village to the fucking ground? Just think, one payload dropped from a B-52 bomber destroys everything over a three square kilometre area. Everything. Nothing's left after that. We atomised people. We vaporised them. Hundreds of thousands died. And that was before the KR ever took over."

Les lit the next joint. Maier was sure that the pilot shared his story, his trauma, his life, with anyone who came through his door with open ears.

It was a good story.

"Anyway, buddy, the war years were my best. We lived from day to day, hour to hour. We drank through the nights and learned Vietnamese, Lao, Thai and Khmer from the taxi girls. Many of us also consumed industrial quantities of opium, heroin, LSD, amphetamines and marihuana, uppers and downers. And in the morning, we were back up in the mountains to pick something up or drop something off, to set fire to some village, to carry on killing. As I said, my best years."

A bout of coughing interrupted his nostalgia.

"When it was all over, I had no desire to go back home. The New Orleans that I'd left more than ten years earlier no longer existed. That's how it goes in war, I guess. It changes the perspective, and stands everything that you learn about life on its damn head. Back home everything was too much and too little at the same time. And every fucking hippy I passed in the street shouted abuse at me. I had to ask myself, was I a war criminal or not. How much of our responsibility can we shift to others? I had changed into something else in the East. I was burnt out from being burnt out. I couldn't face queuing up in a supermarket. Never again."

Maier nodded and lifted his glass.

"I would like another Vodka orange."

Les seemed to be adrift in reminiscences, and stood nervously fumbling with the napkins on his bar. Was there a signal or did the Vietnamese have the ears of a bat? Maier was not sure, but seconds later, he had a second glass in his hand and the young woman was already disappearing back into the kitchen.

"You know the rest. We never forgave the Vietnamese and that's why we supported the KR in the Eighties – embargo, famine, civil conflict – that's the American way of war. Until UNTAC turned up, with guys like you in the luggage."

The American laughed without malice.

Maier'd had enough history lessons and changed the subject.

"And how long have you been in Kep?"

Les looked into his eyes for a second and lowered his voice.

"Black op, buddy, you catch my drift. I may be an alcoholic, but I ain't stupid. You're no tourist and in a second you're gonna tell me that you've come here to buy land. And then you carry on asking questions."

Maier did not think too long about his answer. It was too early to make enemies in Kep.

"I am looking for a piece of land. I have heard that Kep will soon participate in the national economic boom."

"Soon." The old vet laughed. "Maier, if I stumble across a piece in the dark, I'll keep it warm for you. Ha-ha. You're all right, aren't you?"

"I am alright. And an old friend of Carissa Stevenson."

Les passed Maier the joint.

"If you'd told me that earlier… Carissa celebrated her last birthday in this shack, back in May. Carissa's my soul sister. As long as my joint is open, she's got credit."

A *barang* entered. Within a split second, the light in Les' eyes faded.

"Howdy, Maupai."

The new arrival pulled a sour face. He looked like a man who'd recently retired to a life of leisure and hadn't yet worked out what to do with the free time at his disposal. He was about the same age as Les, in his mid-sixties, but he was a different type altogether. A man who'd probably spent his entire life in the same job and the same marriage. If such people could live here – the man wasn't a tourist, he was wearing a worn but reasonably clean linen suit, a white shirt, the three top buttons undone – then Cambodia was on its way. But where to?

Maupai had thick grey hair that fell across his forehead in a lock that was too heavy for its own good. A gold chain hung around his neck. A French bank director perhaps, used to the good life, who had aspirations to be a mid-career Belmondo or late-career Cassel. More like Belmondo with a season ticket for the opera.

"My wife's not well. And the doctors talk about the sea breeze."

"Your wife's not well, cause you're always in a foul mood and because you screw the local girls."

"A beer."

Les shrugged. The Vietnamese woman handed the man a can of Angkor. *My Country, My Beer*, it said on the can. He looked across at Maier, lit an Alain Delon, Cambodia's fanciest cigarette, and raised his can.

"Be careful if you're considering buying land in Kep, monsieur. Many of the documents of the old properties which you will be shown are fakes."

Maier tried his most respectable smile.

"Is real estate the only subject people talk about?"

The man nervously brushed his hair from his eyes and laughed defensively, "The only subject that is safe to speak with strangers about. Everything else our little community talks about is so evil, you won't want to know."

He put special emphasis into the evil, like a real estate salesman or a priest talking up an unspeakable product to keep consumers tied to their wares.

"Maier."

The hand shake was slack. His English was perfect, but for the pronunciation. His voice was full of pride he took in his own importance.

"Henri Maupai, from Paris. I was regional director of Credit Nationale, but I got out of the rat-race early. Life is too short for working only, n'est-ce pas?"

Maier grinned at the Frenchman. That's exactly what he looked like. Like a man who wanted to get something out of life, but had somehow missed the boat. Really a good-looking guy, but way too boxed in. Here, he could let go. Maier tried to imagine Madame Maupai.

"Well, you don't look like much of a backpacker, Monsieur Maupai."

"Ha," the man laughed drily. "This Lonely Planet, the Guide de Routard, they should be banned. The people who travel with a book like that, they leave their brains at home. The little bastards come and destroy everything. They fuck on the beach and upset the locals. They drive their bikes too fast and sleep in the old villas, so they are not paying anyone anything. They hardly bring any money into the country anyhow and they bargain for every riel, and if the room price in the guidebook is lower than offered, they have a fit. This generation is a weird one, incomprehensible. And just think, we put them into the world. We gave them life, everything."

His second swig finished the can and he waved at Les. The Vietnamese girl silently put another can on the bar. She smiled, but not at her customer. Maier didn't like the man much. One couldn't fall in love with every-one.

"I have retired here with my wife. I grew up in a France that no longer exists. My children left home. In my time, one might have bought a little holiday house or apartment in Provence, but these days, too many Arabs and Africans live there. They steal your car while you are sitting in it. The concept of the Grande Nation is dead, completely dead. There's a McDonalds, Burger King or kebab on every street corner. If the Arabs don't burn our cars, the Americans force their fast food down our throats."

The second can was empty.

"Ca m'enerve. Compared to that, the Khmer are just great. Here the communists killed everyone who could think, but at least the Cambodians have respect, and they smile when I ask them something."

Maier silently played with the bar mat and tried to look neutral.

"Maupai is our village racist. He doesn't enjoy life," Les offered.

"You just enjoy life because you fuck your little Vietnamese and take drugs all day."

"You hit it on the head there, buddy," Les chuckled, not trying very hard to diffuse the Frenchman's aggression.

"Have another beer, Maupai, and enjoy the unique ambience of the Last Filling Station. Soon you're gonna die from misery."

"Enjoy, enjoy, you're just running away from something. One day Kep will be returned to its former glory and guys like you will be thrown out. Kep will bloom, I tell you. Just like it did fifty years ago. A little island of civilization in this tired country. Imagine if we had kept l'Indochine. There would be hospitals, schools, roads, electricity and good coffee."

Les sighed and turned to Maier, "People travel around half the world because they don't like their own country and then they complain about how things are done in their adopted home."

Maier was content everywhere. Maier never spent enough time anywhere to get bored. But the Frenchman was drunk and wouldn't let go.

"That's all just talk. You know as well as I do, how mad and murderous the Khmer really are. How can one be happy in a country like Cambodge, a land with so much sorrow? Look at what happened to Monsieur Rolf. A pleasant countryman of yours by the way, Monsieur Maier. A young man from a good family, that much was immediately clear. He came with great ideas and ideals. He wanted to help. And look what happened. And then take a good long look in the mirror."

"One day I'll bar you from the premises, Maupai, because you have a big mouth. You can go sit on the beach, converse with the dogs and get eaten by crabs."

The retired bank director laughed loudly, his bitterness gurgling in his throat like long suppressed bile, "By then there will be a bistro and a wine bar here and only the rats will visit you. Until that time, you need my money. See you tomorrow. Salut."

Maupai slammed a handful of dollar notes onto the bar and walked out into the sun. Les shrugged while the Vietnamese gathered up the money. ZZ Top played from the speakers overhead.

"Don't ask me about the young German straight away, otherwise I might really think you're a snoop, buddy."

Maier also paid. There was no sense in putting a man like Les under pressure during a first meeting. The conversation would continue another time.

"Nice to meet you, Les Leroux. I will be in the area for a while, so I will drop by again. Great bar."

"You alright, Maier, ain't you?"

"I am, yes."

"Then take care. And don't believe everything you hear. Kep is a small place. Everyone knows everyone else and everyone thinks they know everything there is to know about everyone else. Almost everything. It's wonderful, really."

8

KALEY

A SANDY POTHOLED track led from the Last Filling Station to the crab market. To the north of what passed for town, the densely forested Elephant Mountains rose into a gun-metal grey sky that had conspired with the jungle to fall down and bury everything. You always had to fear the worst in Cambodia. And usually it wasn't too far off the mark if you did.

Kep was no exception. The villas of the rich and gone stood on overgrown plots of land, demarcated by crumbling concrete fences and grandiose entrance gates. The side streets that branched off from the coast road had been claimed by tall grasses, and, following the rains, the former streets had turned into ponds and small streams, in which millions of black tadpoles flicked about, hoping to grow four legs before the water evaporated. Kep was an untapped archaeological dig of the very recent past, waiting to be rediscovered by twenty-first century history students. Cows grazed in the middle of traffic crossings. Twenty-year-old palm trees had replaced the street lamps and grew from the foundations of the old buildings. If nature had its way, all traces of human activities would disappear within a few years. No buildings, no streets, not even thoughts.

Maier walked from property to property, aimlessly at first, in order to think, and to get the vodka and the joint out of his system. He hadn't smoked for a long time. In Germany it no longer suited his lifestyle. But here… he laughed at himself; anything was possible in Cambodia.

Maier took a closer look at some of the abandoned properties. Some of the buildings were occupied by penniless Khmer – most of these casual tenants had no belongings and simply strung a piece of tarpaulin between walls that remained standing, to find refuge from the rain. Feral-looking children grew up beneath the improvised plastic roofs. But for the squeal of an infant or the squawk of a chicken, the silence amongst the buildings was complete. Lizards slid silently across hot stones. If not for these occasional signs of life, Maier thought, Kep might have been the perfect town to encounter a ghost. For the Khmer, ghosts were as real and commonplace as the monsoonal rains. And down here in the blinding humidity of an inebriated morning, it was easy to empathise with their superstitions.

The crab market, a long row of wooden sheds, which lingered under palm trees in front of a ruined colonial rest house, appeared abandoned. Young salesgirls dozed in their hammocks, dogs scratched themselves on the broken tarmac and the surf slashed hesitantly across the narrow, dirty beach. A few hysterical seagulls circled above heaps of rubbish. Maier bought a bottle of water and sat in the shadow of a tall coconut palm. His mind replayed the Frenchman's drunken speech. What had happened to Müller-Overbeck?

The woman appeared silently, like a cat. Maier's eyes had fallen shut for just a second. Now they were open and the detective held his breath.

The famous, impenetrable smile of the Cambodians, the sourir Khmer, a phrase the French had coined a hundred years earlier, was shining down on him like a floodlight at the Millerntor-Stadion. She was the most beautiful woman Maier had ever seen. Not quite perfect, in fact, not perfect at all. But breathtakingly, stunningly beautiful.

"Hello, Maier."

The detective was lost for words. That didn't happen very often. The woman was well informed.

"My name is Kaley."

She stood in front of him, stock-still, tall for a Khmer, wearing a colourful sarong with flower patterns and a black blouse. Her hair fell straight down to her hips, like a waterfall of black pearly drops cascading in the midday sunshine that just touched her face, fragmented by palm leaves overhead. She studied him.

Maier recalled old Cambodian ghost stories. Perhaps Kaley was a vision. Had someone slipped something into his vodka? The detective swore never to drink or smoke in the mornings again.

Kaley was barefoot. Silver rings curled around her toes; the nails painted in a garish red. Her hips were broad, perhaps she was a mother. The black blouse was buttoned up, her prominent breasts vibrated slightly underneath the worn cloth. Her neck was delicate and thin, fragile even. Maier guessed she was between thirty and forty. But he found it hard to guess. Perhaps she was two thousand years old. Maier pulled himself up and looked into her face with care. Through the pitch-black eyes of this woman, you could see all the way into the heart of the world. Or at least into the heart of this unhappy country. A risky business.

She put her hands together in the traditional greeting and slowly, ever so slowly, and with the utmost elegance, sat down, two metres away under the next palm tree, and stared at him. Directly, openly, vulnerable, invincible. Maier felt his balls contract. Some men would kill for a woman like this one.

"I am looking for my sister, Maier. Can you help me?"

Her English was pretty good. But Maier could hardly focus on what she said. He was completely captivated by what she looked like. A long red scar crossed her right cheek, which gave her a crude and mystical aura. A broad white tuft of hair cut across her forehead and across her face like a knife, parallel to the mark on her skin. Her extraordinary physical uniqueness reinforced his first impression: he was facing a formidable, exceptional being.

Maier had been around long enough to evolve from atheist to agnostic. The Khmer lived in a different world to the *barang*, a world in which ghosts were as real as a cup of tea. This enabled curious visitors to open doors in their heads through which they could peer into this other world, which was subject to different laws. Maier enjoyed looking. Borderline situations were always crowded with ghosts. Kaley was different from any other woman he'd ever met. For the first time in his life, Maier felt fear in the presence of an unarmed, friendly woman. A strange, foreign feeling and one he relished. Mostly it was her black, so very black eyes. The expression in her eyes made him want to offer her some commitment, a promise, a finger, anything, even if it would bind them to the bitter end.

Her end, not his.

Maier felt callous for a second. Then he remembered to breathe slowly and enjoy life.

"How do you know my name, Kaley?"

"Les told me. Les my friend."

"Was your sister just here a moment ago?"

"No."

"When did you last see your sister?"

Her expression remained impassive. She just kept looking at him. He had the feeling that she was very close to him now and that she could sense something in him that he had no conscious knowledge of.

"When I am little girl. In our rice field. But now she is coming back to come and get me. I think that maybe you see her?"

Maier shook his head.

"What gave you that idea?"

"Les told me that you are good man with good heart."

"I am a man."

"I know."

Maier began to sweat, sitting in the shade.

"I have to go."

"Where do you have to go, Kaley? Stay another moment."

As soon as the words passed his lips, Maier knew he shouldn't have asked.

"Les said you are good man," she said stubbornly. But she stayed. And smiled at him. He'd be responsible for what was to come. He'd asked her to stay.

Maier knew she'd go with him. He only had to ask. And then she would never be able to sit in front of him as she did now. He remained silent. Her first question had been her last. You were only asked this question once in a lifetime, or at all. It was like a Grail. He offered her his water. She took a swig and handed him the bottle back. A few drops ran down her chin and fell onto her black cotton blouse where they turned to steam.

"I tell you a story. An old Khmer story that people tell in the village at night."

Maier nodded to her with encouragement.

"A long time ago, a rich woman live in Kep. Her name Kangaok Meas. She very cruel woman and treat her husband and her slaves very bad. Kangaok Meas have slave called Kaley. Kangaok Meas beat and curse Kaley every day. Even Kaley work in the field all day, she hardly have enough to eat. When Kangaok Meas find out Kaley is pregnant, she send her husband away to the harvest and make her work harder. On the day Kaley get her pains, Kangaok Meas beat the girl with a yoke and shout, 'Because you love your husband, you forget that you are my slave. I will kill you and your child.'

"The husband of Kangaok Meas felt sorry for Kaley, but he scared of his wife. When she angry, she bite him, scratch his face and kick into his balls, so he almost fall sick. Soon Kangaok Meas died and was reborn as the child. The people in the village hated the child. Not even Kaley like the child. Ten years pass and one day, Kaley tell her daughter to work. Now Kaley daughter work in the sugarcane field from morning to night time. Then she marry the man who is no good, always drunk. When the girl get pregnant, the husband beat her and she die with her child."

Somehow, Kaley took something like a bow in front of him as she rose and for a split-second Maier could see into her blouse. Her breasts shifted with the rhythm of her sparse, elegant movements. Kaley moved so slowly that he could enjoy the eternal second. These were forbidden fruits. You did not look at the cleavage of a ghost, a goddess or a cursed being.

"Thank you, Maier."

Kaley departed as silently as she'd come. He was alone. More alone than he'd ever been in his entire life. In a sudden flash, helped along by her outlandish tale, the monotonous, lazy rush of the surf and the shrill squawking of the seagulls, he was acutely aware of the terrible transience of life's most wonderful moments. He sat in the shadow of the palm tree, as if paralysed, desperate to stop time.

A long while later, Maier shook his head. He'd made a promise to a vision, he knew that much. He smiled. Now he was in the story, in the case and on the case. Now, he was sure, he had the case of a lifetime to work on.

And who had named her Kaley?

9

DOG LOVER

THE POLICEMAN WAS in his mid-fifties. Maier was standing on the first floor of a dilapidated villa when he saw him approach on a small motorcycle. He was fat and every time he drove through a pothole, the rusty vehicle beneath him bounced him around like a balloon. An old German Shepherd ran behind in his wake.

The ruined villa stood on oddly angled concrete pillars, had round windows and a spiral staircase with aspirations that extended beyond the first floor. The building, which lingered in the centre of a long-abandoned palm orchard, looked like an unlikely prop from a war movie.

The policeman, now stationary and sweating heavily, waved up to Maier. He took his cap off to wipe his broad forehead and, and, with these few gestures, he managed to convey the impression of an officer who'd not worked this hard in a long time. Maier jumped down the broken stairs and met the man halfway.

The handshake was almost wet, like his eyes. The man sweated so hard that he seemed to cry permanently. He also chewed betel – periodically, he spat huge blood-red gobs of juice onto the floor. A well-oiled side-arm hung from his belt. Otherwise, this cop looked scruffy.

The dog had caught up and sniffed his way around Maier. Maier liked dogs and the policeman's companion quickly lost interest.

"Police dog. Very good dog."

The policeman patted the head of the exhausted animal. People in Cambodia rarely showed this much affection to their domestic animals.

"Soksabai."

"Do you want to buy this house?"

His English was not bad, nor was it very clear.

"I am just looking around."

"This property for sale. But you go quick. Prices go up every year. Fifty percent."

The officer of the law swayed back and forth in front of Maier and for a second it looked as if he was about to embrace the German detective. The two men stood, silently facing each other. The cop looked at Maier with crying eyes.

"Where you from?" he managed after a while.

"From Germany."

"Germany is rich country."

It sounded like "I want to fuck you".

Maier let the statement stand.

"My name Inspector Viengsra."

"My name is Maier."

Inspector Viengsra pulled a small red pill from his breast pocket and pushed it into his mouth. His teeth were almost completely black, perhaps that's why he didn't smile much.

"Yaba?" Maier asked innocently.

The policeman nodded gently and grinned, without showing teeth.

"You're friend of Mr. Rolf?"

"No."

The inspector pulled a face and then pulled Maier onto a broken stone bench in the shadow of an old mango tree.

"If you want to buy land in Kep, you need friend. No friend, no land. Very difficult. Many people not honest, many document not right."

Maier shook his head in shock.

The public servant nodded solemnly and, wincing and with some difficulty, pulled a document from his hip pocket.

"Here you see. This is real. For this beautiful house."

Maier turned around. The ruin which he had just wandered through was about to collapse. The armed real estate man next to him was going the same way.

"Just fifty thousand dollars. Good price. The *barang* buy. We build Kampuchea again. Every year more."

"I will think about it."

The policeman leaned over a little too far towards Maier. "And be careful if you see the beautiful woman with the cut on her face."

Maier nodded respectfully.

"I fight many years. I fight Khmer Rouge. I fight many battle and massacre."

Maier sat, waiting for more.

"Death is a lady, monsieur, I tell you. Every time I fight the enemy, I see the woman. Death is a lady. Every time she come, we all know, someone die. But you never know who goes with the lady. Sometime the enemy, sometime my friend. Maybe me next time."

The policeman yawned and scratched his balls.

"Why is the woman with the scar so dangerous? The war is over now."

Maier was not going to get an answer. Despite his intake of amphetamines, Cambodia's finest had fallen asleep on the broken bench.

Maier left quietly. The dog didn't budge.

Police dog.

Nice dog.

10

THE REEF PIRATES

Reef Pirate Divers was an appropriate name for Kep's only scuba-diving outfit. Tourism in Cambodia was limited to the temples of Angkor. Beyond the magnificent ruins, the country was still waiting for wealthy foreigners. You could tell in this shop.

The office of the dive business was located in a small traditional family home that rested on high stilts on Kep's main beach. A few hundred metres to the east, a long stone pier stretched into the shallow water of the Gulf of Thailand. A large sculpture of a nude woman, recently painted in glistening white, rested regally at the end of the pier.

The compressors were located in a concrete shed. The bottles, wet suits, BCDs, regulators, masks, fins, snorkels and weights hung in a long wooden pavilion, underneath a grass roof that didn't look like it would survive a rainy season. Reef Pirate Divers was a modest enterprise.

A few tourists, geared up to dive, were just clambering onto a long-tail fishing boat. A young Khmer was loading the bottles.

Kaley stood on the beach, talking to Pete, who was shouting into two phones simultaneously until he recognised Maier.

"Our German hero and investor! Hello Maier. Hey Rolf, the other kraut I told you about has turned up."

With his Porsche shades, his torn T-shirt and a pair of faded shorts that sported stark prints of white skulls on black cloth, Pete looked like a man intent on spending the rest of his life on a beach. Rolf looked the stereotypical involuntary heir to an industrial fortune. Maier couldn't imagine this instantly likeable, good-looking young man sitting in an office to count coffee beans. But he was no pirate either.

Rolf was more than ten years younger than Maier, and he looked like he'd enjoyed a healthier life. He had a deep golden tan from working outdoors. A couple of well tattooed sharks circled one another between his shoulder blades. His dark straight hair fell just over his broad shoulders. Around his waist, he'd wrapped a red karma, like a belt. He was half a head taller than his English partner. A tiny earring sparkled on his left lobe, but that didn't make him any less acceptable for a visit to grandmother. Rolf Müller-Overbeck was one of those who'd always been lucky in life. Until the day he had decided to visit Cambodia.

"Hello Maier. Pete already told me about the mayhem at the Heart. You're an old friend of Carissa's? I'm Pete's partner, Rolf."

Strong handshake, chiseled features, open smile, steel-blue eyes. He looked more like Till Schweiger than his mother. With long hair. Maier's gaze drifted to Kaley, whom Pete hadn't introduced. Maier detected a moment of insecurity in the eyes of the young German who continued, "My girlfriend, Kaley. She's helping us with our business."

Seeing the girl for the second time, Maier was still mesmerised.

Kaley had changed her sarong and now wore cool silvery green. She had put up her hair with a couple of wooden chopsticks. She looked like a mermaid, so beautiful that men might construct a pier in her honour. Kaley nodded politely and offered a cool hand. How could she have such cool hands in this heat?

"Nice to meet you, Maier. I hope Cambodia is beautiful for you," she said in broken English. She smiled as you smiled when meeting strangers. Maier smiled back, hesitantly. He was finding it hard to get used to the young woman's hypnotic eyes.

"Hey, Maier, we have a spare space on the boat, why don't you hop on? Know how to dive?"

"I have not dived for a couple of years. But yes, of course, that could be fun."

For some reason, the Englishman was upset and lit a cigarette before throwing it into the surf a few seconds later. Rolf on the other hand was relaxed, almost glacial. The very definition of the successful German. Perhaps he was trying to make a good impression on his clients, three girls and a boy from Frankfurt, barely out of their teens and heavily tattooed on legs and shoulders.

"You can dive with me; I don't have a dive buddy. We go out beyond Koh Tonsay, there are some good rock formations and swim-throughs."

Ten minutes later, Maier sat, zipped into a wetsuit, next to Samnang, the captain, in the stern of the open boat which slowly slid out into the Gulf of Thailand. He tried to remember how to operate his equipment. Koh Tonsay was the largest island off the coast of Kep, partially forested and almost uninhabited. King Norodom Sihanouk had called it L'Île des Ambassadeurs – the Island of Ambassadors – and thrown extraordinarily decadent, private parties on its beaches. Countless criminals had later been imprisoned on this speck of paradise and were then called upon to defend the coast from pirates. Today, a few families, the former inmates' offspring, lived in a modest fishing community on the main beach. The island's royal residence had long been swallowed up by the jungle.

The locals called Koh Tonsay Rabbit Island. Apparently, seen from the air, it looked like a rabbit. How the fishermen knew this was a mystery, but Maier had a harder case to crack.

"Where do you come from in Germany?" Maier asked Rolf, who sat on a wooden plank in front of him and was playing with his dive computer.

"I was born in Hamburg where I grew up and where I started and terminated my university education. Prior to coming here, I'd never really been anywhere by myself."

That sounded like almost like a crime, but the young German grinned across the water, barely a worry on his face.

"And how long have you been in Cambodia?"

"Well, about six months or so. It's hard to believe, but I was at the dentist a while back, sitting in the waiting room and reading these articles about Germans who emigrated. One story was about a man from

Bottrop who settled in Kampot, a small town thirty kilometres up the coast towards Sihanoukville. That read a lot better than my studies and the constant hassle from my mother to take over the family business. It's not easy growing up in one of the typically traditional Hamburg trading families. I mean, they, we, are just very conservative," Rolf explained. "I had some money and I basically dropped everything – my girlfriend, my studies, my apartment, and my mother…especially my mother. And now I'm the owner of a dive shop in Kep."

"The dream of the German emigrant has come true?"

Rolf turned again and looked past Maier, across the water back to the receding shore.

"Well, not quite."

Maier saw conflicting emotions cross the prominent features of the young coffee heir from Hamburg. But Rolf said nothing more and began to tap away at his dive computer again.

Maier tried to defuse the sudden tension between them, "I live in Hamburg as well. I rent a flat in Altona. But I am hardly ever there. I have come down to Kep to talk to the local expats about the economic climate. I might even buy something. Plenty of nice properties around."

The young man was himself again and turned around to look the detective square in the eye.

"To be really honest, I wouldn't bother. Kep is a little brothel town, a seedy hole on the beach," Rolf laughed, his voice filled with bile, "A ghost town turned into a whorehouse. The dead rise to get in on the boom. Can you understand that? I thought about selling my shares in Reef Pirates, but what would happen to Kaley if I closed shop and disappeared?"

"Ah, women, always complicated."

The younger German turned towards Maier, his face twisted with worry, his eyes drilling into the detective like dark blue, dying stars. "I can't leave her. Impossible. That would be the end of her. And morally speaking, me as well."

That sounded almost like a confession or some long-learned, melancholy statement. Maier decided to provoke the younger man, "Well, you don't have to take it so seriously, I am sure. She would not be the first Cambodian girl a white man has left behind. Women get over this kind of thing. And the way she looks, she would find a new friend soon, no?"

Rolf replied angrily, "You want to fuck my girlfriend, Maier? You another sleaze ball washing up in Cambodia? Kaley is not a taxi girl; she no longer works in that business."

Maier raised his hands in defense, "Hey, Rolf, sorry, I misunderstood completely. You have a serious relationship here and you can't just leave her."

Maier felt a little cheap. But only a little.

A pod of dolphins played in the dark blue ahead of the boat. The tourists from Frankfurt craned their necks in excitement and Samnang revved his engine in order to keep up. The dolphins were game and dived under the boat, jumped clear of the placid water and did pirouettes ahead of the divers. They had no problems outrunning the longtail.

Koh Tonsay lay just a few kilometres off the Cambodian coast. A little further east a much larger island loomed from the sea – Phu Quoc. Rolf pointed to the fog-laden ridges of the huge landmass.

"The Khmer say it's theirs. The Vietnamese say the same thing. But the Vietnamese have the upper hand, as usual."

The colour of the water was changing as the boat got closer to Rabbit Island. And Maier, who was looking over the side of the boat, could see the sandy sea floor broken up by small rock formations. Rolf got busy checking his customers' equipment. A few hundred metres ahead, a small fishing boat had just pulled anchor and was leaving.

Rolf shook his head in frustration, "No one is allowed to fish around here. Even the governor is keen to save the coral and I will report these idiots later."

Samnang slowed down and let the boat slide on under its own momentum. The dolphins had followed them into the shallow water and were now circling the spot the fishing boat had just abandoned. What was there to see for a dolphin?

Rolf was asking himself the same question.

"Friends, we have reached the first dive site, but before we all jump into the water, I'll check with my friend Maier what the dolphins are so curious about. They must be attracted by something. Otherwise they wouldn't be circling over this spot. So, make yourselves comfortable for a few minutes. Our captain, Samnang, will put up an umbrella. Drinks in the cool box. On the house."

The young coffee heir had already checked his gear and opened Maier's bottle.

"Everything OK? Ready for the jump into the unknown? No fear?"

Maier shook his head, "No problem, scuba diving is like cycling... Once you have learned it..."

"Let's go."

11

BLUE, RED AND DEAD

Samnang had dropped a small anchor. The boat bobbed about in the clear water as Maier wrestled into his BCD, pulled his fins over his feet, donned his mask, checked the regulator and dropped backwards into the Gulf of Thailand.

The sea floor loomed barely ten metres below them. The water was warm and crystal clear. Maier could see about twenty metres. The water crackled in his ears as he descended and equalised. The dolphins had disappeared. Rolf hovered below Maier and waved to him to follow.

Maier had learned to dive in Cuba in the Eighties with a bunch of crazy KGB guys and after his last big case in Thailand he'd travelled on a liveaboard to the Burma Banks to dive with hammerhead sharks. But he'd never been on duty, on the job, so to speak, underwater.

Dark rocky pinnacles rose like stalagmites from the gently descending sea bed. Maier was swimming through a park of miniature cathedrals. As soon as he reached Rolf, a solitary great barracuda came to check the visitors out and lay perfectly still next to them in the water. The predator looked like an expensive sports car. Maier got so close, he could count the razor-sharp teeth in its open jaws.

Rolf lost no time and, checking his compass, swam off, a few metres above the sea floor. Maier followed suit. While no coral grew here, the variety of fish was surprising. Lobsters waved their long white feelers from the nooks and crannies of the rocks, a moray eel and countless small colourful reef fish vied for his attention. A shoal of squid suddenly appeared in front of them, lined up in formation like a squadron of fighter jets. Seconds later, they shot away into the deep blue, in one single, coordinated movement. Maier paddled hard behind the young man from Hamburg and tried to concentrate on his breathing. They weren't deep, but he was going to have to do the second dive with the same bottle. He slowly inhaled, slowly exhaled, until he found his rhythm.

The sea floor began to fall away steeply below the two divers. They were about to slide into a cauldron-shaped depression, littered with rocks as large as minibuses. Rolf stopped at the edge of this abyss and moved closer towards one of the rock formations.

Suddenly, two dark shadows appeared out of the blue – and moved lightning-fast directly towards the two divers. That had to be the dolphins. But there was something wrong. The two animals seemed to be bumping into one another as they got closer. Rolf pulled Maier's wetsuit and pressed him against the rock.

The reef shark, its head swinging wildly back and forth, shot a few centimetres past the detective's arm. A young dolphin had pushed the predator off its course. Amidst an explosion of bubbles Maier briefly caught Rolf's eye. The young German was alert but remained relaxed. He moved further into the rock and pointed in the direction from where the shark had attacked.

Maier had dived with reef sharks many times, but he'd never seen one race towards a diver so aggressively. Reef sharks hunted more modest prey. There had to be blood in the water, a lot of blood. Perhaps another, injured, shark, hooked on a line, was driving his predatory brothers and sisters mad. Maier looked around, but the shark had not returned, not yet. The detective pointed to the surface, but Rolf shook his head and began to search the pockets of his BCD. Seconds later, he pulled out a red plastic hose, unrolled it and filled it with air from his regulator. The two-metre-long safety buoy shot to the surface like a rocket.

Rolf grabbed Maier's arm and they descended further into the cauldron. Maier checked his air; his bottle was half full and they were at twenty-four metres. No problem, yet.

Rolf urged him on, as close as possible to the large rocks that made the area look like an abandoned scrap yard. After twenty metres, the younger German stopped, slid, as best he could, into a narrow cave and pointed ahead.

They were very close. The centre of the cauldron was a hellish place. Maier felt cold. Fear spread through his wetsuit like ice water.

Twenty to thirty reef sharks had gathered and were nervously cruising around their find. Ten metres ahead of the two divers, a man floated, his feet chained to a stone, dressed in a torn shirt and jeans, upright in the water. One of the sharks had already ripped away his right arm and part of the shoulder. Blood swelled in small clouds around his injury.

The man was dead.

Maier was ready to retreat, but Rolf shook his head again and pulled Maier deeper into the cave he'd found.

He looked up, but the reef sharks had gone. The scene in front of the two divers was ghostly. The man hung in the blue water, all alone, as if waiting for something. Maier couldn't see whether the corpse was Khmer or foreign.

A huge, dark shadow appeared at the opposite rim of the cauldron and descended, like a malignant avalanche, down the slope towards the dead man. Maier wasn't sure what they were facing – a blue shark, a tiger shark? He had no idea. Whatever it was, it was monster size. Definitely not friendly. Definitely wound up by the blood.

The shark was bigger than many of the rocks in its way and seemed in no hurry to reach its prey. But its slack movements were deceiving. Within seconds, the huge creature had passed the dead man and was gliding straight towards the two divers. Maier could feel the blood pumping in his temples. The shark had reached the cave. Black, dead eyes. Mouth, jaws, teeth. Maier had heard that some sharks closed their eyes seconds prior to taking a bite while dislocating their jaws. But this shark kept its eyes open. It must have been close to four metres long, as large and as heavy as the hammerhead sharks in the Burma Banks. And a lot meaner.

As the shark reached the narrow cave, Rolf pressed the buttons of both his regulators and the water filled with clouds of bubbles. The shark, irritated, changed course and disappeared behind them. Maier thought he could hear the boat engine above them, but Rolf grabbed hold of his jacket and shook his head. Maier understood, they could no longer ascend safely. They'd been too deep for too long to go to the surface without safety stops. Rolf checked Maier's bottle and shook his head again. Maier no longer had enough air.

Maier tried to bend his head back. The fissure into which they had squeezed led deeper into the rock and widened above them. Rolf had the same idea. They pumped up their BCDs and slowly ascended while pushing deeper into the rock. Rolf had found Maier's alarm buoy, filled it with air and let it rise to the surface.

At eight metres, they had reached the upper lip of the rock. Maier could see the boat clearly above them but he did not dare raise his head above the rock. He turned slowly.

The large shark had forgotten about the two divers and was slowly circling the man below them. A few reef sharks had returned but they kept cautiously to the rim of the cauldron. A metal clunk distracted Maier. Samnang had lowered a full bottle, tied to a weight-belt onto the rock. Rolf carefully pulled the precious air into their crevice. Maier's bottle was almost empty and he changed regulator. Rolf had enough air and calmly watched the drama below them. Maier sucked on his new bottle greedily.

The shark swam in a wide curve and coiled, like a tightened spring. As the huge fish came face to face with its victim, it sped up. Then it was upon the dead man. In the last moment before impact, the shark turned on its side and shot forward like a rocket. Maier had no idea whether the fish shut its eyes or dislocated its jaw. The water filled with blood.

Rolf pulled him up then, his computer had indicated a safe ascent. The reef sharks were back and fought over the legs of the man.

Maier had never climbed into a boat as fast. Samnang pulled him out of the water. The young tattooed tourist from Frankfurt asked, "So, are we going in now, or what?"

12

ONE HOT, ONE COLD

"You still want to invest here, Maier?"

Rolf Müller-Overbeck leaned drunkenly into the bar of the Last Filling Station. His long hair dripped with sweat. The young German's question didn't sound sarcastic. Maier was counting his dollar bills for the next round of drinks. There'd been many rounds already.

The Last Filling Station was packed. Even Les Snakearm Leroux served beer tonight. It looked like the entire foreign community was present. Maier looked around – a pretty strange life you led here, isolated from the locals, but, he knew, that was the norm all over Asia. Unbridgeable culture gaps and huge income disparity precluded integration. The Khmer sat on the floors of their huts and drank illegal rice wine that had been distilled in the jungle. The foreigners sat on plastic chairs and drank cheap beer. To make things worse, Kep's expatriates sat in segregated clusters, divided by nationalities, at several metal tables.

Still, the entire room had murder on its mind. Murder talk in at least four languages. And with every translation, the details became increasingly sketchy, the truth more remote, the shark ever larger.

The French, including Monsieur and Madame Maupai, sat in the centre of the action. A second table was occupied by a noisy group of Scandinavians tourists. They'd heard about the killing from the

German kids and kept away from the local *barang*. As if murder was contagious. Perhaps in Cambodia it was.

"What kind of shark was it?" was Maier's first contribution in a while, a change in subject without changing the subject.

He'd decided by now that he'd have to keep his true intentions in Kep secret. He had a feeling the murder in the Gulf was in some way connected to his new young friend, the coffee heir from Hamburg. Luckily, nothing brought men closer together than the shared survival of dangerous adventure. Hanging out with the man he was hired to shadow now came naturally.

"It was a tiger shark. I've done more than four hundred dives off the coast of Kep, but I've never seen a monster like that. Tigers don't usually show up in shallow water, but perhaps El Niño has something to do with it," Rolf swallowed hard, "A friend told me that he saw a big shark off the west coast of Thailand a few months ago, while snorkeling! I didn't believe it then. Maier, we were fucking lucky. A tiger shark! Luckily, I didn't see how it finally mauled Sambat, poor bastard. But I'm still in shock."

"The fact that such a big fish came into shallow water must have had something to do with the victim and all that blood. Sharks can smell blood for miles. Who was the victim?"

"Guy called Sambat. Worked with his sister for an NGO in Kampot, a few miles down the coast. The NGO looks after orphans. The two of them were orphans themselves – and one of their parents was a *barang*. They were born shortly after the Vietnamese invasion in '79. It's a kind of miracle they survived at all. I didn't know Sambat well, but he was a nice guy."

"A great guy," Les added, "He often came on his half-dead Yamaha from Kampot for a beer. He was really a serious man, reflective and pragmatic, really amazing for his age. Just like his twin sister. In fact, he dropped in yesterday and talked about abductions of children to Bokor."

"Bokor?"

"The old hill station, stuck up on a plateau in the Elephant Mountains, buddy. Maier, if there's a building in this world that's haunted, the Bokor Casino is it. Built by the French as a pleasure palace in the Twenties and full of ghosts, just crammed with'em, like no Hollywood haunted house ever could be. The area around it's a national park."

Maupai suddenly stood next to Maier, "And today it is all fucked. *Ça m'enerve.* Bokor was a French institution and one of the most exclusive hotels in l'Indochine. Guests came from all over the world to lose their money in Le Bokor Palace."

He leaned past his wife towards Maier, "If Kep-sur-Mer was once the Côte d'Azur of Asia, then Bokor was the Monte Carlo of Indochina."

The Frenchman's eyes had glazed over, he was badly drunk.

"Believe me, Monsieur Maier. Bokor is a monument to our greatest days. And perhaps to Cambodia's greatest days too."

"Chérie, please sit down with Hervé and Celine, otherwise they will think that we don't want them here. They came all the way from Paris."

Madame Maupai did look poorly. She was about ten years younger than her husband and might once have been a great beauty. Now she was in her mid-fifties and she'd probably bought her skin-tight dress in a children's clothes store in Paris. The high heels didn't help, as she had the legs of a stork. Her face was deeply lined, the march of time barely disguised by a thick coat of make-up underneath which she sweated. Her eyes lay deep in dark caverns beneath darker brows and she wore her hair short. Her illness had progressed so far that the attempts to hide it were pathetic. Despite all this, she exuded more dignity than her husband.

Maupai gestured impatiently.

"Let me drink my beer in peace, Joséphine. You hassle like a bloody Arab."

Madame was obviously used to the tone and, without another word, she returned to the table of their friends.

"Everything is broken. C'est comme ça." Maupai groaned, without turning around.

The silent Vietnamese girl pushed two cans of beer across the counter at him. Maier waved briefly to the young woman. A few seconds later he had a Vodka orange in his hand.

Rolf didn't look as if he wanted to talk to the Frenchman and turned his back on him.

"Maier. Let's drive up to Bokor tomorrow. Great place. Change of scene. My customers from Frankfurt have left for Kampot. After our experience yesterday, they aren't going to dive in Cambodia. I could do with a break from the business, working is hard work. And I have to go visit Mikhail."

"Mikhail?"

"Mikhail. Mikhail is a true original, an exceptional guy and a free spirit. A Russian who's been doing guided tours through Bokor Casino for the past weeks. Nothing official, but I'd like to offer his service to my clients, as long as there's no development up there. That man's an enigma. Never answers a question directly. Knows more about Kep than all of us put together, even though he's only been here once, and very briefly. But he tells a good story. He's an interesting guy. Sits in the clouds and drinks with the park rangers. And no one knows whether he's a real Russian. He does seem Russian though. He drinks like a Russian."

Maier drifted away, wondering about what abductions of children might have to do with his case. He was missing too many pieces to form any assumptions. And Maupai didn't like being ignored.

"You probably want a break from your luxury slut? Isn't that a bit of an extreme swing, from Kaley to the homo Russian on the hill?"

Rolf suddenly looked stone cold sober.

'Waiting for the Man' by the Velvet Underground came to an end and for a second one could have heard a pin drop in the Last Filling Station.

"Maupai, you're a drunken asshole, a real pig. My 'luxury slut' told me that a guy like you would never get near her, not even for a thousand dollars. So shut up, my friend, before you really offend someone."

The Frenchman had gone pale and looked ready to counter with more hate speech, but Hervé, Céline and Madame Maupai pulled him back to their table. Dylan's "Subterranean Homesick Blues" started up and the Scandinavians paid and left.

Maier felt like relaxing after his dive, but he hesitated taking his glass to the beach and letting them fight it out. He'd find out more if he stayed around until the community began to throw punches at itself.

Pete had chosen the right moment to arrive. The wiry Englishman stood in the door of the Last Filling Station, flanked by two young women.

"Yes, friends, my old lady couldn't make it tonight, so I brought my secretaries, Mee and Ow. I will be giving some language lessons tonight."

Pete propelled the two girls, both Vietnamese, towards the bar.

"Only joking of course. They already know more than enough English. What would you like to drink, dears? Beer, whiskey, Coke, juice or maybe a glass of soya milk?"

The silent waitress pushed two glasses of Coke across the counter at the two girls. She had nothing to say, not even to her compatriots.

Les leaned across to Maier, "My girlfriend hasn't said a word since she was five years-old. She saw the ghost of her mother in her father's bed. The next morning the father was dead. Since then, she's been stumm."

"How do you communicate?"

"Ah, well, you know, buddy. She's been working for me for the past three years and she sleeps in my bed. I provide a roof over her head. She doesn't have anyone else. I think we communicate OK. If it's something important, she can write some English. And I do remember some Vietnamese."

The two young girls began to dance to the sounds of The Doors. For an instant Maier felt transported into a bad American war movie. So, this was what the Wall had fallen for.

"Pete, where did you find these two fine ladies? Did you drive all the way to Kampot to get them?"

"Maier, mate, you haven't had much of a look-see, have ya? Seen the two huts above the Angkor Hotel? That's our very own village brothel, poorly disguised as a barber's shop. One large, one small. You must have seen the handmade signs. The large hut is home to my two friends and a few of their compatriots. In the small hut, we had Kangaok Meas, our very own peacock girl. But she's not around now."

"Kangaok Meas?"

"Yes, Maier, the golden peacock. Never heard the story? You are usually pretty quick, aren't ya?"

Somewhere in the back of his head, new wheels began to spin, but Maier wasn't sure whether they were turning in the right direction. The redhead hadn't finished, "Probably the same Kangaok Meas that caused poor Sambat to drown. The police in Kep have decided to ignore the incident as there's no corpse, no crime scene. No need to make statements. And the dive business is saved. Long live Cambodia."

Rolf stared angrily at Pete. Maier gently held the young man's arm and said quietly, and in German, "Obvious that would happen. Whoever wanted to get rid of the young man had already cleared it with the local authorities. They dropped him right on a dive site. Don't start an argument with your business partner over this."

Marvin Gaye came on and Pete became distracted by the bored gyrations of his companions. With the girls in his arms he looked ten years older. One of the girls wore a jacket.

"Are you cold or do you have a machine gun under there? A machine gun?" he inquired rudely.

The girl didn't understand a word.

"One hot, the other one cold, not bad, eh?"

Before Rolf could open his mouth, Pete stepped forward and embraced his partner, "Come on, Rolf, it's Friday night. The night's warm, the girls are willing and if you screw one of these two, it won't rain."

He winked at Maier. "The entire village goes there. The fishermen can only afford short time on a wooden bunk under a leaky roof. Our good friend Maupai, on the other hand, could enjoy a Friday night sandwich, just like me, if he only understood that his covert afternoon excursions aren't particularly discreet."

Maupai had been listening to the Englishman and now stood up, dropping his Alain Delon.

"Here, Maupai, one hot and one cold," Pete taunted.

Before the furious Frenchman could lash out, Les stepped around the bar and grabbed Maupai from behind. The old American looked ready to crush the Frenchman. Maier almost burst out laughing – old men impatient as young pups, doing a hundred eighty miles towards their own demise. The return of Snakearm Leroux, gambler of a thousand Saigon nights. The bank director itching for a fist fight. You only got that here.

Les squeezed until Maupai had gone red like an overripe peach. Maier looked across at the French table, but there would be no help for the village racist from his own quarter.

Les finally let go, disgusted, "No fights in the Last Filling Station. And you're much too old for this."

He turned to Pete, "Take your guests away with you. No one likes you today."

"Why, are you going to shoot me with your M-16 if I don't?"

The American laughed, "Of course, buddy. I've been looking for a good reason ever since you first came into my bar. Now I got one."

13

THE CASINO

Maier rode ahead. There wasn't enough road left to be able to admire the landscape. He concentrated on the potholes and sandy ridges that had carved the old mountain road into a rutted graveyard trail.

The first thirty kilometres led through dense jungle. Maier didn't see a soul by the roadside.

He tried to circle each pothole, some of them half-metre craters, in order to get through the mud, gravel and sand as quickly as possible. Every now and then, he could hear Rolf rev his bike behind him. Both sides of the road were hedged in by giant ferns and tall grasses. Small streams ran through the brush and underneath old, partly-collapsed bridges. The canopy threw long and deep shadows. Tigers were said to survive here. The birds, unseen, managed to create enough song to occasionally filter through the roar of his machine.

On steep curves, the road had washed away altogether. During the rainy season, the lateritic soil turned into an ocean of rust-coloured mud. Maier gripped the handlebars hard to avoid losing control of his machine and continued to slither up the mountain. Sweat ran down his back, despite the shade.

An hour into the drive, it got noticeably cooler. The wet, impenetrable forest loosened up. Light that looked like dirty milk poured through the trees. Quite suddenly, on a sharp corner in the road, the blackened ruin of a large house loomed into a grey sky. The sun had vanished behind thick wisps of cloud.

Maier stopped in front of the once handsome building and cut his engine.

The Bokor Plateau lay right ahead, a highland area of shrubs and low, gnarled trees, dotted with twisted rock formations. A cold wind made his vest stick to his sweaty T-shirt and blew black clouds across the sickly horizon. An old water tower and a copper-coloured chateau-style building rose from a barren cliff a few kilometres away. Beyond the two buildings, there was nothing. That had to be the end of the road. As Rolf pulled up next to him and killed his bike, Maier felt as if he'd lost his hearing: the silence, but for a whisper of wind, had a finality, like death.

"This ruin here's the Black Villa. The building used to be one of Sihanouk's residences, when he visited Bokor in the Fifties."

The royal villa stood empty and windowless. The floor tiles had been smashed, and the walls were covered in obscene graffiti. The squat servants' quarters had already been swallowed by the jungle. Nature was going about its business to reclaim all it could. Nobody lived here.

"Quite a trip up, no? A vibe away from the beach."

Rolf, psyched by the drive through the jungle, looked like a man without a worry in the world, as he used his krama to push his long, wet hair from his face.

"The casino hotel over there was opened in the Twenties. Only the super-rich could afford to come up here."

Maier was taken by the landscape. The plateau, with its eerie remnants of long-faded privilege, looked like a post-apocalyptic archaeological dig. The rolling monochromatic grassland lay dotted with concrete ruins as far as he could see. It did have a vibe. A malign current ran straight through this place. Maier wasn't a religious man, but the word godforsaken crossed his mind for the second time since getting off his bike. Bokor was perfect to burn a witch or two.

"You are the history expert, Rolf. Did the Khmer Rouge reside here as well?"

The coffee heir shook his head.

"The communists came in 75' but never stayed for long. In the Eighties, the Cambodian military occasionally had shoot-outs with the

KR up here. The rebels would walk up through the jungle, kill a few soldiers, drop a few mines and disappear the way they'd come."

Heavier, grey clouds crawled up the mountain behind them. Seconds later the view across the highland had been swallowed up by dirty white fog. The milky nothing brought the ghosts of war. Maier felt like he could almost hear them march. The ghosts of the French, the Khmer Rouge, the Vietnamese, the ghosts of victims and perpetrators. It was time to move.

Maier got back on his bike. Suddenly, he heard steps behind him. A young, broad-shouldered man in uniform, a machine gun casually slung across his shoulder, peeled out of the fog. Rolf approached him.

"Soksabai, Vichat. How are you?"

The park ranger answered something in Khmer. The closer he got, the smaller and less dangerous he looked.

"This park full of poachers and ghosts," the Khmer laughed, when he saw Maier looking at the gun.

Vichat wasn't long past twenty. His uniform was frayed and he wore cheap plastic sandals. His weapon was in working order though.

"The poachers shoot deer, boar, sometimes the elephant. Or they come with chainsaw and steal the tree. But ghosts very bad. Last week one ranger disappear. Before, he tell me he talk to three young girl, all dress in black."

The young ranger whispered, "Like Khmer Rouge."

Vichat pointed to Rolf's bike and into the fog.

"My bike break down. Take me to ranger station. Not safe out here alone."

A few hundred metres along the road, they came across the ranger's motorcycle, marooned in a ditch with a flat tire.

The fog got denser the further they rolled across the plateau. Maier opened his throttle and slithered across moist rocks and broken tarmac. The clouds lifted around them and Maier spotted a church tower ahead. A few hundred metres on and the road split again. The fog had already swallowed Rolf. Maier could no longer hear the young German's engine and took the right turn. He passed several overgrown plots of land, fronted by opulent gates that lead nowhere.

Bokor must have once been one of the most exclusive and beautiful holiday destinations in the world. More than a thousand metres above sea level, the colonial rulers of Indochina had forced their subjects to build a magnificent, almost paradise-like resort, a French Shangri-La, surrounded by tropical forests teeming with tigers and elephants.

There wasn't much left of that glory now.

The road ended abruptly and a huge, dark shadow loomed out of the fog. He got off the bike, pushed it to the side of the road and walked the last fifty metres to the Bokor Palace. As he got closer, the casino peeled out of the mist like a Victorian ghost ship. He slowed and stopped. This was some building. It had personality. The black, cavernous windows of the erstwhile luxury hotel stared at Maier like the dead eyes of long-fallen soldiers. The roof was topped by four crumbling towers. A wide moss-covered stairway led up to the main entrance. The grey, bullet-riddled walls were overgrown by a red, luminous fungus, which looked like a torn and bloody carpet that had been hung out to air a hundred years ago and forgotten about. Spent gun cartridges, evidence of past wars, crunched underneath his feet as he stood at the foot of the stairway.

Maier hadn't planned to go in, but just as he was about to kick his bike back into life, he heard someone walking inside the building. He looked around. There was no one within his limited field of vision. A few crows circled above Maier, the first animals he'd noticed since emerging from the jungle. A dog barked behind the building.

Maier began to ascend the stairs. He felt exhausted. It was hard to take each step, as if walking uphill against a strong wind. This building was tired of visitors. At the same time, the yawning entrance door at the top of the stairs appeared to try to suck him inside.

A half century ago, people had lost their money and perhaps their lives in Bokor Palace. During the war, hundreds if not thousands had certainly lost their lives here. He reached the top of the stairway and passed the threshold.

The lobby was smaller than the detective had expected. The reception lay behind a kicked-in dark window, a tiny and barren office. Lamps and fittings, light switches and furniture had been removed. From both sides of the lobby, long corridors stretched away into darkness. The yellowing, damp walls were covered with the traces and thoughts of earlier visitors. A few obscene drawings could still be made out. Maier stepped into a ballroom. Some joker had carved the sentence "Everyone will die" into the moist plaster above the door frame. The heavy, cast iron fireplace lay smashed by the door. Otherwise, the room was empty. Fog hemorrhaged through the large broken windows on the opposite side of the cavernous hall No one had danced on the tiled floor for decades.

The wind picked up and began to whistle through the old building. He could hear a girl call. On the first floor. A loud bang shook him into action.

Bang, bang, bang, bang.

The noise came from above. It didn't sound like gunshots. Maier walked back to the entrance door and looked up the stairs. The narrow, worn steps were deserted. The afternoon light was fading. Soon it would be dark.

Bang, bang, bang, bang.

He scrambled up the stairs as quickly as possible, trying to avoid garbage and lose tiles. Empty rooms, dirty and dead. The tubs and washbasins had all been smashed. The tapestry had peeled off the walls. Traces of war lingered everywhere – many rooms were connected by holes, large enough for a man to step through. Rusty cartridges and shotgun parts lay amongst other debris. Dark water stood in muddy puddles everywhere.

The noise came from the west wing of the sprawling building. As Maier stopped in one of the rooms, catching his breath, he heard a noise, very close, behind him and spun around. Out of the corner of his eye, he sensed, more than he saw, a shiny purple sarong rush past. He stepped into the corridor. Maybe it had been a child. He couldn't see anyone. But something was wrong. He walked towards the noise, towards a large dark room next to the stairway, towards its door and the black beyond. Now it sounded like a machine, though not regular enough.

Bang, bang, bang, bang.

Maier stepped through the door.

The room was empty. Large holes had been hewn into the floor.

Maier could see down to the ballroom below. A weak light flickered nervously though the holes. At the far end of the empty room a second door opened into a second darkness. The noise which had turned the empty room into an echo chamber originated in the next room.

Maier crossed the broken floor carefully and looked into darkness. A cold night wind blew in his face.

The last room was empty.

A plastic bag had been caught up in the tiny bare place and blew jerkily from wall to wall.

Bang, bang, bang, bang.

Maier let the plastic bag continue its madness-inducing racket and returned to the first room. He lay down by the largest hole and tried to peer down into the ballroom. He could still see the flickering light and began to crawl forward in order to push his head further through the unlikely window to the scene below.

A light flashed and suddenly he could see clearly, but there wasn't time to take in what he saw. Someone yanked him from his lookout with huge force. He tried to turn and kick, but it was too late. He felt his ear rip open as he passed the rim of the hole, a second later the proverbial blunt object connected with the back of his head.

Loud voices woke Maier. He couldn't have been unconscious for long. It was pitch dark and the wind had calmed, but the detective could hear heavy raindrops hitting the roof of the casino. He still lay in the room in which he'd been attacked. He slowly turned on his back and touched his head. Nothing broken. His ear was still there as well. Voices poured up from the ballroom. Maier looked around. He was alone. Whoever had clubbed him over the head was an amateur assassin or no friend of the people in the ballroom. They certainly wouldn't have left him alive if they'd caught him spying. What he'd seen for just an instant was hard to digest. Life-changing. And not for the better.

Maier, riding his stubborn streak, crawled up to the hole a second time while trying to keep an eye on the door behind him.

The ceremony, if that's what it had been, had ended. Kaley and Tep's son stood together, talking. The woman had washed the blood off her chest and now wore a white T-shirt. He couldn't see anyone else. Maier had a headache. The plastic bag behind him began to do the rounds once more.

Bang, bang, bang, bang.

Kaley looked up to the ceiling, towards Maier, before quickly dropping her gaze again. She'd seen him. He snuck out of the room as quietly as possible and felt his way along the corridor to one of the stairways in a far wing of the casino.

The stairs he found had partially collapsed, but he didn't have a choice of escape routes. He had to get out but escaping via the main stairway he had come up on was too risky. Maier climbed as carefully as possible into the gloom below him. Metal bars reached like petrified snakes out of the torn walls, ready to impale careless passers-by. On the ground floor, Maier saw another shadow rush from the corridor into a room as he emerged but by the time he'd come to a halt and held his laboured breath, he couldn't hear a thing. He turned and carried on until he reached the basement. The water stood up to his ankles. Something stank, but he wasn't sure what it was. A few metres ahead, Maier could see another set of stairs that led out into the open. He waded slowly towards the weak light, trying not to stumble in the cold, dead water. Several times he bumped into large soft objects. He didn't stop.

Maier climbed the slippery stairs as quietly as possible. As he emerged from the basement, he spotted Inspector Viengsra, the policeman he'd met in Kep, on the balustrade that encircled the casino property, sitting in the rain, next to a four-wheel drive. He had his back turned. The dog sat between the policeman's legs.

As Maier passed, the cur raised its head and looked briefly in his direction. But Maier was every dog's friend.

He found his bike, snapped it into neutral and pushed it as quickly as possible back to the last crossing. The fog was slowly drifting away and he could see the roof of the ranger station, barely a kilometre below. Lights twinkled down there. Maier let the bike roll.

14

MOTHER RUSSIA

THE GIANT STOOD on the wide steps of the station and toasted Maier with his bottle and a wide, mischievous grin across his face.

"Tourists get lost around here regularly and it's a miracle that no one has fallen off the cliff down into the jungle. Some, I've been told, are thrown off by the ghosts of the casino. You were too heavy for the ghosts?"

Maier hadn't expected a welcoming committee, much less a camp, quite possibly drunk Russian with a poetic bent. For a second he was tempted to throw the few phrases of Russian he remembered from school at the man, but then he decided to say nothing.

Mikhail had charisma. His command of English was perfect, even playful, his accent that of a Hollywood bad guy.

"Well, young man, have you been rendered speechless? Let's start at the beginning, dear. What's your name, and what dark power propelled you to enrich this godforsaken part of the world with your delightful presence?"

The Russian wore shorts and a big shirt that flopped open over his huge, smooth belly. His long grey hair framed an unshaven, beetroot-red face. He looked like someone who tried to give an impression of sloth and laziness. The eyes of this freewheeler were sharp and alive though, sober in the extreme, and reminded Maier of his own – eyes you could switch on and off. The Russian was a few centimetres taller than Maier. Next to the park rangers, he was humongous.

Maier sensed that the Russian was a man with a mission, just like himself. Cambodia was merely a stopover for a man like Mikhail. This old Soviet hippy was, despite his extrovert drunkenness, nowhere near the end of his line yet. Maier liked him instantly.

"Leave it be, Mikhail. I just came off my bike."

Rolf and the young ranger had appeared behind the Russian.

"What, my name travels ahead of me? You heard of me in Kep and defied the dangers of the jungle just to come and see me? Perhaps you heard of me as far away as Kampot or Sihanoukville? Or did someone whisper my name to you in the capital? I mean, young man, there's not much to see up here except for me."

Rolf and the young ranger looked carefully into his blood-encrusted ear.

"What happened?"

Maier realised only now that the right shoulder of his vest was soaked in blood.

"I fell off the bike at the last crossing. I had taken my helmet off, started driving, puddle ahead, deep pothole, and bang, I fell flat on my face and must have passed out. The rain woke me up. But the bike would not start again."

The Russian translated into Khmer.

The ranger seemed to understand at least part of what Mikhail said and shook his head in disbelief.

"Vichat thinks that you were up in the casino, fighting with ghosts."

"Is he serious?"

"Serious, young man. He also suggests that we sow your ear back to your head. Vichat is the man here who knows about first aid. He told me he even amputated a leg once."

The Khmer looked at Maier questioningly and pulled a small mirror from his pocket. In the weak light of a single bulb, the detective did not need a thorough self-examination to decide that something had to be done.

"Is there any vodka?"

"Tonight, you will have to make do with whiskey, Maier. Otherwise there's the always reliable local rice wine, a drink that makes good people bad."

"Is there any ice?"

Rolf handed him a full bottle.

"Be a man, Maier."

Maier took a swig. Vichat began to clean the wound with alcohol.

The four men sat outside the ranger station. Vichat spoke quietly on his radio set to a girl in Kampot, far below them on the coast.

"You want to offer guided night safaris though the casino?"

The Russian looked across at Maier and nodded, his voice dripping with sarcasm.

"I've been doing this for a while, with people who come up here by themselves. But I don't know what to do if something happens to a tourist. Some people fall off their bikes before they've even seen the casino."

Rolf shrugged in frustration.

"It was just an idea Pete, Mikhail and I had. Mikhail does a great tour through the hotel, it's a total ghost ride. I almost shat myself."

The Russian grinned with mock malice and showed yellow teeth.

"While Pete wanted to bed a couple of girls in the casino the first night he was up here. How is our happy-go-lucky British pirate? Does he still dream of infinite power and undeserved wealth?"

Rolf didn't answer.

"Come on, Rolf, you're not stupid. You know how to run a business. You're good-looking. You still have a nice character. Be careful that you don't get stuck in the wrong country with the wrong people. Cambodia really sticks to some."

"Are you going to tell me Kaley is a slut as well?"

Mikhail laughed and poured himself another glass.

"Deep inside, you know what she is, Rolf. Just be careful that you don't end up in the rain one day. You never know. But the local slut she's not – that's me! That's my privilege."

Rolf didn't answer.

Maier coughed into the silence. "Well, are you going to let me in on something?"

"Only if you sleep with me tonight, young man."

Mikhail laughed himself into a coughing fit.

"Here comes a well-preserved German of young middle-age with an alleged sack of gold and tells anyone who will listen that he wants to invest, though he hasn't looked at a single piece of land. And he wants to be let in on something? Into our dark secrets?"

"Why would I invest in a country like Cambodia if I didn't know who pulls the strings, at least locally? Especially in a small place like Kep."

"You're right, Maier. Don't be so touchy. You don't need to justify yourself. You know how it is in Cambodia. People react to people who ask questions. Hardly anyone does, so it's noticeable. In time, you will make best friends here. Kep is full of nice people."

Rolf interrupted the monologue.

"So, nothing's going to come of it?"

"Of what, dear? Of us? Nothing, I think. You are too romantic. And you like the ladies too much. And the sad thing is, Rolf, that most of the women around here are so skinny that they almost look like men. Isn't that depressing? The poor suckers come from Moscow, Berlin and London, frustrated and fragmented by their luscious, voluptuous devotschkas and fall in love with these passive shrimps. Not with me, but with these skinny nothings, who have no tits and no asses. No opinions either. It's all about power. None of these girls are any good in bed. You need brains, imagination to be any good in bed. You have to be a bit of an artist. Like me. The tough guys from the West, they only come here to load one of these little mice on the back of their rented chopper cycles and drive around like apparatchiks."

Maier was definitely amused. Mikhail was a freak, a prophet of the damned. A man not to be interrupted.

"But power is something very temporary, very transient. The moment these men look away from their shrimps, they are getting ripped off. It was just the same for the French. Look around. This place was once a dream destination. And what happened? After fifteen years, it was all finished. The casino closed and the power evaporated. Even the Khmer, Sihanouk and Cambodia's elite couldn't save the dream. That's why I love it up here. Man defines himself here. The French played around with the country, the Americans flattened it, and the communists had graves dug for the entire population, socialist mass graves. Those exist in my part of the world too. What about yours, Maier?"

The Russian burped quietly and stumbled on without waiting for an answer, "And now the business types turn up. People like you. Do you really think you can help this country? Wouldn't it be better to throw all the foreigners out for five years, so that the brothels close and golf courses aren't built in national parks?"

"Is anyone building a golf course up here?"

Vichat increased the volume on his two-way radio. The girl on the coast started to sing. The Russian fell silent. They listened to the young Khmer woman's love song. The moon had risen above the casino, clearly visible above them. The church and several other buildings rose out of the darkness like tombstones. North of the casino, the old water tower appeared to walk, like a UFO from a Fifties sci-fi movie, across the darkened highland. The girl's voice sounded eerily metallic through the tiny speakers, but it dripped with genuine emotion. Words of love amidst war of the worlds.

The song brought movement into the tall grasses beyond the station. Maier remembered good times in the old communist Germany, long walks with young women who'd also had beautiful voices. Even his headache was subsiding. Vichat smiled himself into a quiet daze. The song ended and the girl on the coast, a thousand metres below the plateau on which the four men sat, whispered good night and signed off.

"So, what about the golf course?"

"Maier, you're a Prussian hunting dog. The tears haven't dried yet and you're already asking again. Was it not full of love, young man?"

"I can imagine how we could spoil a place so remote and lovely, and a national park to boot, but I would like to know firsthand of course."

The huge Russian slapped his back

"Haven't you noticed yet, that we can spoil anything? Not just here, but in our backyards too. Why bother with Cambodia? Our backyards are legendary. Or is this just your roundabout way of asking more questions about what you're really after but don't want to tell us about?"

Mikhail had dispensed with his glass. He lifted the bottle to his mouth and took a long swig before he continued. "You'll find strange bedfellows in Kep if you're looking to invest. Some people think the town is a gold mine. Others think the casino is a symbol for past glories. As I said, there are a million ways to spoil the world. And in Cambodia, they have all been tried. All of them."

Maier turned to Rolf. "A golf course, up here? Who will pay for it? They would have to rebuild the road first, that would take years."

The younger German didn't answer.

Mikhail changed the subject.

"Rolf, I would love to do the tours, but in a few months, or perhaps weeks, the fun and games up here will be finished. You know it. And I'm not worth any kind of investment. I am broke and happy, that's why I sit up here and drink."

Rolf had nothing to say and stared into the void, his face distorted by something stronger than annoyance.

"If you think Cambodia's so corrupt, why don't you go back to Russia?"

The giant laughed bitterly.

"To Russia? You'll make me cry, if you force me to think about my country. Our rivers are poisoned and dried up, inflation is as high as the Kremlin walls, and life on the street is as brutal as a weekend in a Siberian gulag. We're being ruled by evil bratschnicks, who want to take away our freedom, our culture and our right to drink excessively. We're being watched around the clock, blackmailed and threatened and we're at war everywhere. Just like it's always been. Mother Russia. The newscasters lie that the world will end soon. The president lies that it won't end. I like being here. For the Khmer, the end of the world won't come as a surprise. One golf course more or less won't make a difference."

Rolf interrupted the Russian, "There's a Cambodian investor in Kep who wants to construct a golf course up here. Perhaps he has the necessary contacts in the government to get permission to build in a national park."

"And that would be Tep?"

"Ah, Maier, so well informed. Then you must know that the resident foreigners in Kep are being asked to come in on the project. In some instances that request looks like an order."

Rolf nodded. "Yes, Pete's on board."

The Russian laughed. "Children, children. Everyone wants to have a go. The French, the Scandinavians. Last week, three Japanese showed up here, industrial spies, came from Saigon in a four-wheel drive and had a look at the area. Sweat shop on the beach, resort on the mountain. Everyone thinks you can put a golden cow onto this cliff. But the French already tried that."

"And who exactly is Tep? Or rather, what is he? I met him a few days ago in the Heart of Darkness."

Mikhail grinned, "Well, then you know everything there is to know. You don't look stupid, Maier, even if you fall off your bike without reason."

It was getting cold. Vichat carried his radio transceiver into the ranger building. But the young man stopped for a second and looked at Maier, "Tep no good. Tep Khmer Rouge. Tep, he fight here, he live here. Maybe he think Bokor belong to him."

The ranger disappeared into his room. Mikhail stared after him, his eyes full of longing.

"He's got a great behind, that Vichat. But he prefers to listen to the warble of his girl, instead of throwing himself into my open arms."

Mikhail leaned back like a fat diva and looked into the night sky, theatrical, self-important and mocking, "The world's not fair. Not even in Cambodia."

"And Inspector Viengsra works for Tep?"

Rolf and Mikhail laughed.

Mikhail had found his glass and filled it, then drained it in one long swig.

"The dog lover? Has he shown you any property papers which he happened to have with him, when he passed you on his bike? There's only one thing to say. The relationship between Viengsra and Tep is the same as between the inspector and his dog – symbiotically bestial."

"And how dangerous is the policeman?"

The Russian laughed dryly, "It always depends who's swinging the hammer. It's all connected to gravity. And our dog lover is affected by it as much as anyone. Most of the time, he sleeps. Sometimes he does evil things for his boss. Kill the dog and he's finished."

Maier felt sick. But only a little.

"And what does Tep have to do with the execution of that young man, Sambat?"

"You'll find out Maier, of that I have no doubt."

15

MOSQUITO

Maier was getting drunk. That seemed to be the best strategy in Kep. He needed a break. The case needed air. The Russian on the mountain had made him suspicious. Something didn't fit the program. Maier wasn't even sure whether the man was really Russian or gay. It could all be an elaborate act. Despite his doubts, or perhaps because of them, he liked Mikhail.

Back on the beach, his fifth Vodka orange done with, he'd asked Les to show him to a hammock. Now he hung in an alcohol bubble between two posts under a straw shade on the flat roof of the Last Filling Station and listened to the surf. The crab boats slowly moved up and down the coast. He could hear them putter back and forth, but he was too lazy to lift his head and look out across the sea. The surf made him sleepy. Soon the mosquitoes would come and eat him.

Rolf, the good-looking and self-confident coffee heir, a man who had everything going for him in life, was trapped in a web of trouble that Maier couldn't decode. Not yet. The detective was sure that his young compatriot wanted to get out. As soon as Maier could make a more informed judgment on Rolf's entanglement, he would provoke a situation, which would present Müller-Overbeck with an opportunity to slip away. If the younger man didn't take him up on his offer, he'd report to his mother, the Hamburg ice queen. He wasn't here to solve local mafia crimes. Still, the girl Kaley wouldn't leave his increasingly cloudy thoughts. In his drink-addled mind, Maier laid out every shred of information he had – her story, her smell, her weightlessness, her hips, the promise he'd made and the moment in the ballroom of the casino. Then he left those shards of facts right there, laid out, and dozed off, dark thoughts on his mind.

"Yeah, yeah, mate, you have no choice. But the apple isn't nearly as sour as you make it out to be."

The scratchy voice of Pete the Englishman woke Maier.

"I didn't come here to invest in some crazy esoteric scheme with the entire expatriate community. Our business is doing well, better than it did when you ran it by yourself. Without me, you'd still be saving for the next set of equipment."

The two owners of Reef Pirate Divers sat directly beneath the entrance to the Last Filling Station, and therefore directly beneath Maier. The sunset melted in epic brushstrokes across the evening sky and the mosquitoes were getting ready to attack. Maier didn't dare to move for fear of being discovered. Defenseless, he let the insects descend.

"Let's pull in your countryman first. He looks like he's got money. But he's not stupid. We just have to find his weak point."

"It's bad enough I'm involved in all this shit," Rolf countered weakly.

The Brit laughed venomously, "It says in our contract that I have the right to sell Reef Pirate Divers. But I've no intention of pulling you across the table. We sell the shop, invest in the casino or the golf course, or the dinosaur park, if you like. You know, there are at least two guys in Phnom Penh who want to buy the dive shop; two guys who have the necessary cash."

"I don't want any more deals with Tep. He's dangerous. He probably killed Sambat."

The two men fell silent. Only the buzzing of thousands of insects was audible.

Pete began to talk at Rolf once again.

"You can't prove that. And anyway, we're in Cambodia. This isn't our country. We're guests here. All we can do is adapt to local circumstances, invest our money wisely and hope that the locals will also profit. Not just Tep, but hundreds, perhaps thousands of workers he'll have to hire."

"You know that more people will die. Sambat was just the beginning. I don't understand why Tep would get rid of a guy who has nothing to do with Bokor in such a cruel and crazy way. Sambat worked with orphans."

Pete didn't answer.

"I've had enough. I want to get out and I'll take Kaley with me."

The Englishman hissed back angrily, "Then you lose all your dough, mate. And you know that you can't take her out of here. Kaley belongs to Kep. You're not the only one she's connected to. It's ridiculous that she's living with you, mate. Kaley belongs to all of us. I told you that the day after the accident. If you're sleeping with her, you know the score," Pete coughed and lit a cigarette, "So, here's some advice. It fucking rained."

"You're a bastard."

"Rolf, there's so much money in all this. The entire business community of Kep will participate in the rebuilding of the casino. And everyone here knows about Kaley. Even Kaley believes that she's the reincarnation of the Kangaok Meas. That's the reason you could hush up the accident. Otherwise you'd be in jail or on the run. And I don't think she'd even go with you. Most importantly, Tep is also convinced she's the Kangaok Meas, otherwise he would've killed her a long time ago."

Maier had an overwhelming urge to scratch himself.

Rolf had got to his feet below him.

"Faith is just something we hang on to, despite the fact that we know it's an illusion. I believe in the Kangaok Meas. Kaley is like a golden peacock. But there has to be a way to free a person from this ridiculous superstition, this darkness of tradition. And from Tep. The old man's not a ghost, but an ex-general who has lost his moral compass. He dreams of the times when he could go around bashing people's heads in with a hammer."

"Well, wish me a quick death, Rolf, if you believe in all this esoteric mumbo-jumbo."

16

RAIN

"I NEED something against insect bites. Vodka orange, please."

The Vietnamese girl silently served Maier his drink.

Les rolled the next joint, quickly and with four fingers.

"I'm surprised you lasted as long up there."

"I fell asleep. I started drinking too early today."

"That happens."

"Normally it happens to other people."

The American laughed, "I fell asleep on the roof last year, buddy. Just like you. I got dengue fever. It shook me three weeks straight. Without my girl, I wouldn't have made it. Besides the girl, there's no cure for it. That's why the Brits call it break-bone fever."

'Black Dog' blasted from the speakers. Maier didn't really like rock music, but the sounds suited the Last Filling Station. Anything was better than disco. And Les was a nice guy. It was time to get answers and nice people were always the first toehold in the answer game.

"Did it rain after you slept with Kaley, Les?"

The American didn't say anything at all. Maier began to worry that he'd overstretched his direct approach. Les probably had a gun or a club under his counter.

"Yes," the owner of the Last Filling Station said, looking anything but happy after spilling his confession.

"Tell me the story, Les."

"It's a long story and you don't want to hear it, Maier. Not if you plan to invest around here."

"I'm not going to invest in Kep, Les."

The old war vet growled.

"So, what the hell are you doing here?"

"I am a private detective. I am trying to solve a case involving a German client. In order to get closer to solving it, I need to know about the accident and I need to know the story of the rain. You are the only person in Kep I can ask. You are involved in all this here, just like everyone else, and you are also the one who has the least to lose if the community ever goes pop. And that is very likely, and very soon too."

"Might be your head that goes pop, Maier."

"Les, the first time I came into your bar, you could see I was not just another hapless westerner about to drop a million into a hole in Southeast Asia. And you asked me whether I was OK. I mean, what a question to ask."

"Maier, I got nothing against you, buddy. But you got no idea what kind of a swamp you're sliding into here. The people in Kep are cursed – the Khmer, the Vietnamese and the *barang*. All of them. It don't matter what you are looking for here, all you'll find is Cambodian curse."

"And you don't find that scary, Les?"

The American brushed his thumb-less hand across the faded tattoos on his left arm.

"I have seen whole valleys go up in flames, turned to steam by the payloads of B-52s. For my country, I poured napalm over children and I pushed men out of helicopters. In Khe Shan, we were attacked by Vietcong who had loaded syringes taped to their arms, syringes filled with heroin. Every time I walked out of the compound after a battle and found a dead soldier, I had myself a shot. It was always Grade A quality. I saw ghosts. Before death stalks the paddies, a young woman appears. Everyone, every child, who's served at the front will tell you this. I see the same ghosts and accept the same laws of nature that people here have faith in. Kep's my final destination – as the name of my modest establishment should tell to you."

Maier looked Les straight in the eyes. "Then you lose nothing if you tell me what is going on here."

Les looked uncertain and began to roll another joint.

"What kind of music do you listen to, Maier?"

The detective shrugged in his vest.

"You have found my weak point, Les."

"People who don't like music are strange, Maier. What did you do in your last life?"

"As I told you, I was a journalist, first in East Germany, then, after the fall of the Wall, in West Germany."

The American's eyes widened with surprise. "You're a commie?"

Maier laughed and tried to steer the conversation into more profitable waters.

"I was a journalist for six years in communist Germany. I was born there and grew up there. I was a war correspondent working for an agency in the reunited Germany for eight years. I've seen a few ghosts too, in my time."

The American digested the news and changed the subject. "Kaley was married to Tep's oldest son. He was a real piece of work, worse than the second son, whom you know from the Heart. This guy, Hen, he was a cop in Kep. He stole from tourists and set a small bungalow operation on fire that wouldn't pay him his bribes. He also had something to do with the bomb at the hotel in Sihanoukville which killed a foreigner. He opened a small brothel behind the Angkor Hotel and brought some girls in from Saigon. Kaley had Hen's child eight years ago, a daughter. A beautiful girl called Poch. Hen used to beat Kaley. At that time there weren't that many foreigners in town. But we all knew what was going on. Kaley was the most beautiful woman in Kep. She still is today. Back then, she looked totally irresistible. It hurt to watch her being mistreated. But no one did a thing. Perhaps we were all sadistic swine, because we couldn't have her for ourselves. Of course, the entire expatriate community was scared of Hen and his father. Two years ago, Poch borrowed a hammer from the neighbours and beat her father to death in his sleep. Shortly after, Kaley and the kid stood in front of my door. What could I do? I took them both in. I slept with her and it rained. A few days later, she went back to Tep."

Les sighed. His eyes had glazed over with sadness and loss.

"Tep took his revenge. He installed Kaley in the brothel and invited the men from the plantations. It always rained afterwards and local people believe that anyone who sleeps with Kaley is cursed and will die a violent death."

"What do you think?" Maier asked and lifted his empty glass.

Moments later, an ice-cold Vodka orange stood in front of him. Drinking was part of the job – Maier repeated this troubling thought like a mantra and held on to the bar.

"I don't think I got much time left. That's why I didn't throw you out."

"And what happened to the daughter?"

Les held up his hands in defense, "You'll have to ask Rolf that. And now go home, I've had enough of you."

Maier left some dollar bills on the counter and drifted into the night. He'd not been this smashed in a long time.

17

ENLIGHTENMENT

Though Maier had spent years in Southeast Asia, he'd stayed away from the taxi girls. He wasn't averse to the looks of Asian women, and he'd communed with a few. But for Maier, sex had to be an explosive exchange, a kind of celebration of body and soul. If the woman wasn't hot for it, then neither was Maier.

Taxi girls weren't hot for it.

And when the occasional hotel receptionist or flight attendant had sought to slip between Maier's sheets, usually she'd done so in the hope of being able to hang on to him. Sex was weapon and tool in Asia, especially as long as so many women couldn't emancipate themselves. How often had he looked at a Cambodian woman's behind and then taken the young lady from Bremen or Santa Barbara who'd been drinking at the next table home with him? As a war correspondent, he'd never had to worry about finding partners for the long nights on the road. A lonely NGO worker or reporter could be found even in the world's darkest recesses. For a private eye, having a love life was more complicated. Maier rarely told people what he did. But at the age of forty-five, his remarkable eyes had never let him down yet. Eyes like magical flashbulbs.

Lying in Maier's hotel room, Carissa slowly turned in bed so he could admire her in his own time. Her hips gleamed with sweat and

Maier watched a large drop of moisture slide down a smooth thigh, before it was trapped in the hollow of her knee.

"You should meet Raksmei, Sambat's sister. She's no shrimp. Half *barang* and half Khmer, a ravishing-looking woman. If you ever look into her eyes properly, you'll never share a bed with me again. That said, she's too young for you."

Sex and death stuck close to one another. The little death and the big death. Carissa had heard of the underwater execution and travelled down from the capital in search of the story.

"The NGO is called Hope-Child and Raksmei founded the orphanage and pulled in the foreign donors. Her brother Sambat used to help her, but for the past year, he has been hunting down pedophiles and kidnapping their victims right from under their noses. You know, some of these sex tourists that come here – as well as well-connected locals – are after kids. Sambat had very good connections in the media. Even had a couple of Swiss guys busted, with the help of journalists. They had this mutually beneficial relationship and as he was half-*barang*, he thought he'd be reasonably safe. Raksmei thinks that his murder has something to do with Bokor."

Maier slowly slid his hand down Carissa's spine. Despite the conversation, he found it hard to keep his fingers off her. He liked this woman more than he remembered liking her back then.

"Why are these two young Khmer so active? You definitely need protection if you're going to kidnap trafficked children from their captors. This sounds so incredible."

"Raksmei and Sambat are orphans. No one knows anything about their parents. That means that the most beautiful woman in Cambodia is alone right now, drowning in sorrow, vulnerable. Why don't you go and see her? She might help you with your case. As you won't let me help you…"

"You can help me any which way you want, Carissa. I am powerless. And I like older women."

The Kiwi journalist pushed a few stray white hairs from her face and laughed.

"When I first met Raksmei, she thought I was an old woman. In Cambodia, only old women have white hair. In her eyes I must have looked sixty."

"You'd pass for fifty any time."

The kick in the ribs hurt.

"Maier, you're a low-down chauvinist."

"Let's celebrate that."

"Help me with my story. You know much more than I do about what's going on here. What's happening up there at the casino?"

Maier held his aching side and contemplated into which cheek of her delectable arse he would sink his fingers and twist. Then he shrugged and feigned innocence.

"I have no idea what is going on at the casino. I was in Bokor but not in the casino. I fell off my bike and broke my head open, as you can see."

Carissa carefully pulled a lock of hair away from his ear.

"I can see a man who got whacked over the head with a blunt object and won't admit it. Maier, you're a right bastard. You pump me all the time and give nothing back."

"I like pumping you, Carissa."

"Until your case is solved, then you run off and work some other exotic locale where you'll also pump a journalist or an NGO secretary who is so lonely that she'll go to bed with a down-at-heel private eye and think it's romantic."

Maier had nothing to say. She was right, he also knew women in Kathmandu, Bangkok and Singapore. Women with whom he'd almost stayed. And now, in his room at the Angkor Hotel, with his old flame in his arms, he could imagine staying with her. It was all pretty romantic.

"Can you imagine me moving back to Phnom Penh? What would I do? Prove that half the older men in town have committed crimes against humanity?"

Carissa sighed, "No, of course not. We're both used to our freedoms. And after forty, people rarely change. But I have another seven years to go before I am forty, Maier. You're too old for me. Your life has already run its course. Mine's almost still ahead of me."

Maier had only recently started thinking about his age. He had got as far as deciding to avoid wars for the rest of his life. He'd decided that he wanted to grow old. But a relationship, or a family, the concept of permanent cohabitation in compromise lay a long way off. Still, he felt hurt by Carissa's sarcasm.

"Don't be macho now and don't start feeling sorry for yourself.

You're great in bed and I have to be careful, otherwise I'll fall in love with you a second time. You're a strange man. Just looking into those eyes of yours, which never rest until they see something pleasant or foul, makes me dizzy. But then they move off somewhere else. You're an obsessive. You're like a child in a toy shop, blown away by all that's on display and you go all the way to get it. Life just offers too much to a man like you. And that's why you're so lonely, Maier."

She crawled into his arms. He didn't have to look at her to know she smiled sadly.

"There's a Chinese curse…"

"Yeah, Maier, with which you tried to impress me years ago. 'May we live in interesting times.' You're cursed, lover. All those years ago, it was just your way to pull me in, now it's the truth."

A few minutes later, they'd reached another place, free from the obligations of verbal communication.

18

DAWN

He woke up alone. The bed was still warm. The night and the hangover from the day before stuck deep in his bones. What a woman.

She couldn't have gone far. For the second time since his return to Cambodia, Maier was suddenly scared for his old girlfriend. He got up, put on a pair of shorts and went downstairs. It was just getting light. The guard lay snoring in his hammock. The sun would remain hidden behind the Elephant Mountains for a while yet and it was refreshingly cool. The early morning looked innocent; a few birds rushed over his head along the almost deserted shore road, an old woman stood by the roadside and, still half asleep, wrapped her krama around her head before she set off for the crab market, laden down with plastic buckets. Even at a considerable distance, he could make out the red hair of the Englishman. Carissa sat on the beach with Pete.

Not that Kep had a real beach, but he could see the two clearly on the sandy strip below the road. Pete gesticulated wildly, but at this distance Maier couldn't make out what he was saying. He stepped out into the day.

"Good morning, Maier. I'm just trying to explain to your old lover here, that her investigations could kill her, if she insists on digging around down here."

For once, the detective shared the same opinion as the wrecked-looking dive operator.

"You look like you had a wild night, Pete."

"I always have wild nights, mate. At least since I've lived in Cambodia."

He lit a red Ara and blew smoke-rings into the perfect morning air.

"I don't understand you people. The country is beautiful. The people are polite and a bit retarded. The women are hot and always within reach. Genocide has its good sides too. Come on, Maier. Germany is wealthy today because we flattened you in World War Two. And we flattened you because you killed too many people. It's the same here. In twenty years, Cambodia will be back on its legs. And if we make the right decisions now, we'll be able to contribute to the rebuilding of a nation. We'll be the new colonial masters, independent of state power or ideology. We take what we can, wherever we can. That's called globalisation. The published truth about a few not totally legal investments won't stop or even slow the development of this country."

By now, Maier had made up his mind that he didn't care for the Englishman.

Pete sighed. "You're idealists. The world is bad. We have to make the best of it."

Maier laughed. "Your world is bad, Pete. Our world is OK."

He knew this was all just posturing, his old girlfriend wouldn't be put off by the Englishman. She would follow her story to its bitter end. Any journalist in her situation would want to know why Sambat had been killed.

Pete got up and wiped the sand off his pants. He looked stressed.

"Maier, mate, don't come back to me later and tell me that I didn't warn you. I'm assuming that your investor story is bullshit and that you're some kind of journo as well."

Maier looked across to Carissa but her face was turned and hidden under her white hair. All of a sudden, he was angry. Angry at Carissa, who'd risk her life for a story about a few old murders. Angry at Pete who'd risk anyone's life for a few dollars. The probable result was the same and went with the locality: killing and burying were still acceptable solutions to all sorts of problems in this broken land. And many foreigners took to the local traditions like fish took to water. Maier no longer felt like holding back.

"I am not a journalist, Pete. But I might become your worst nightmare yet. If anything happens to Carissa, I will personally order the tiger shark back and make sure he gets fed."

The English pirate jerked his head in surprise and met Maier's stare with expressionless eyes. Not a good sign. Most people were scared of Maier when he threatened, as he threatened rarely. There was no hope for this man.

"Yeah, Maier, mate, now I'm almost impressed by you. Wow. So, I'll say it again. The future of Kep won't be defined by you two ageing angels. Even yours truly here will have just a tiny hand in what's going to happen."

Without another word, the red-haired pirate got up and walked along the shore towards the market. Carissa hadn't moved. Now she turned to Maier. She had tears in her eyes.

"Who the fuck do you think you are, Maier? No one hears a thing from you for four years and then suddenly you show up and throw everything into disorder. You fuck your old girlfriend for a few nights and pull every scrap of information she has from her, only to solve your enormously important case. You're here for a few hours and people start dying like flies. But you give nothing yourself and make grand speeches how you will take your revenge on that little wanker, if he burns a hole into your mattress. Mate, wake up."

Maier waited until she'd calmed down.

"Ok, Carissa, I will tell you everything I know, but you have to promise me not to go to see Mikhail in Bokor. I was wrong. I think it is a trap."

"Maier, I'm not going to promise you anything. I know Mikhail, he's eccentric, but he's not a murderer. And he knows more about the people here than you do."

The sun had risen above the Elephant Mountains. It was starting to get hot. Carissa looked beautiful. But Maier couldn't bring himself to apologise for his emotional agnosticism.

"Ok, wait one more day and we'll go together. I have been invited for dinner by Tep."

"On the island?"

"On his island. Pete will take me across later."

Carissa looked at Maier for a long time. She looked like a white goddess in the bright morning sunlight, a divine entity who'd just appeared on earth to find a prince. It was probably already too late for Maier. He wasn't prince material.

"Maier, you might not come back from there. Pete is close to Tep, very close. And if he assumes that you're some kind of snoop or investigative journalist and passes that impression on to Tep, then that nasty old general will get rid of you."

"A few days ago, I deposited a large chunk of money in a bank to which Tep has connections. Enough money for a house down here. I am sure he knows about it and will try to convince me to come in with him on his schemes. The true reason why I am here is to get Rolf out of Cambodia. But he will not leave without his girl. I am trying to find out what is forcing him to stay and what Kaley has to do with Tep. And the only way to find that out is to accept the invitation."

Carissa thought for a while.

"What happens when the case is done? You'll just disappear again?"

Maier swallowed hard. Maier had no idea what Maier wanted.

"I don't know what will happen. I won't stay in Phnom Penh."

He didn't say anything.

"Perhaps you might tag along to Hamburg?"

The goddess from New Zealand said nothing and stared across the placid water. Maier rearranged his beard and tried to rearrange his thoughts.

"Perhaps," she said, finally.

Maier felt queasy. He'd reached a place he was not familiar with. He smiled. Finally, a real challenge, something totally new.

"Don't get happy yet, old man. First, we have to solve the case," she mumbled and fell into his arms. A few hundred metres away, he watched Pete turn around and stare back at them.

19

DOWN BELOW

Rolf Müller-Overbeck lay in the hammock he'd probably slept in. He looked wasted. His long hair was greasy and some food had got caught in his days-old stubble. In fact, he looked almost dead.

The dive shop was deserted. Neither Pete nor Samnang, nor any of the other employees could be seen.

"Holidays?"

Rolf barely moved, and waved him away with tired arms.

"There's a story doing the rounds in Phnom Penh that someone got eaten by a shark down here. I suppose my customers from Frankfurt told everyone in their guest house horror stories. We have only cancellations for the next few weeks. I've sent our workers home."

Maier sat on the wooden stairs to the office of Reef Pirates.

"And where is Kaley?"

"Kaley's gone."

Maier looked past the dive-shop owner out to sea. Koh Tonsay was almost completely obscured by fog. The sky had turned dark grey again. It was incredibly humid. A singular morning had given way to a depressing day.

"I've had enough, I can tell you that, Maier. If I could see a way out of Kep, I'd jump into a taxi right now and go directly to the airport in Phnom Penh."

"So, what's stopping you?"

"I can't sell my share in the business. And I can't leave without offering Kaley an opportunity to leave as well."

"Has she stopped turning up for work?"

"No, she's just gone. Back to her barber shop behind the hotel. Since then it has rained twice. I can't bring myself to go up there. But I'm far enough in my thinking now that I no longer care about the money. I have to leave. I'm getting sucked into this morass here so deeply that I'm drowning."

The young German looked at Maier with large paranoid eyes, partially visible under his matted hair.

"I still have a life ahead of me, I think. But if I stay here… I really thought that we could do something for people. But anything we try to set up here comes down to exploiting those who need protecting most. I almost agree with Mikhail now. Maybe all the foreigners should leave, so the country can make up its own mind where it wants to go."

Maier had a question on the tip of his tongue, but he couldn't formulate it. The young German was completely overwhelmed by his present circumstances. Without the help of others, he'd never make it out alive.

"I am not sure that would help. I think the Cambodians are perfectly capable of screwing themselves up, even without the help of foreigners."

Maier had the feeling that all the locals he'd spoken to, whether Khmer or foreign, suffered from a common psychosis that was connected to Kaley. Something was afoot that had nothing to do with real estate.

"What happened to Kaley's daughter, by the way?" Maier remembered.

A strange, strangulated noise emanated from Rolf's mouth. After a while he said with a cold, tired voice, "It's like this in Kep, Maier: if you buy land and become part of the community, you're privy to information which outsiders don't have access to. Cambodia has many secrets. The first foreigners who came here all speak Khmer and they know the area, the people and even the ghosts. You understand?"

"I will most likely buy one of the ruins in Kep, Rolf. I have just been waiting for my money."

"You're buying from Tep?"

"I am answering a dinner invitation on his island tonight."

Rolf turned back and forth in his hammock to make sure no one else was in hearing distance.

"I wouldn't do that, Maier. That could be a really dangerous trip. I'm not sure you understand, but it's your soul that becomes corrupted here. You're forced to make realisations that don't exist in Hamburg, at least not in the Hamburg I grew up in. Here you cross a threshold. In this sense, Kep is probably the most exclusive beach resort in the world. Where else would you be able to witness an underwater execution? I warned you."

"Not to go to the island or not to buy land?"

"I told you a few days ago that Kep is changing from ghost town to pimp town. I wasn't entirely right. I think the ghosts still have the upper hand. The Khmer say that people who were killed but not cremated never come to rest. Every Khmer has seen ghosts. Some people even believe that some people are not people at all, but are really ghosts. And that they can bring great sorrow and suffering to others."

Rolf really got going now.

"It's amazing that we abandon part of our rational western thinking, our Eurocentric view of the world, after a few months in this country, amazing how quickly that happens. It's a process that erodes the space between reality and illusion. Opinions are just like clothes."

Maier laughed drily. But he was not sure what was going on. Too many pieces of the puzzle were missing. The scene in the ballroom flashed through his head, again.

"Ghosts, you might be right, Rolf. I saw some when I was here in '93."

The young German turned away.

"If you buy land, let's talk about ghosts again. And if you want to buy the dive shop, let me know. Until then, take care of yourself."

20

L'AMOUR

Maier had an hour to kill until Tep's boat would pick him up. Enough time to get a haircut. He passed the Angkor Hotel and walked up the hill to the two small huts.

Mee and Ow sat in the shade of a mango tree and were doing their make-up. Both of them wore gloves that reached all the way up to their elbows, to keep the tropical sun off their skins. They looked at Maier with the curiosity reserved for a passing dog. It was too early for professional enthusiasm.

The huts stood a hundred metres above the Angkor Hotel on a lightly forested hillside. They looked ready to be torn down. The bamboo walls had fist-sized holes and the sheet metal roofs had rusted through in places. General Tep hadn't invested much in the less than salubrious village whorehouse.

Maier passed the women, nodded and entered the second hut. Two barber chairs, torn red leather, stood in front of a dirty mirror beneath a long counter. The counter and the mirror stood on the forest floor. The walls were covered with faded posters of Cambodian boy bands and starlets. No sign of a barber.

At the far end of the hut he could see a beaded curtain. Maier heard voices. As he was about to cross the threshold into the hut, he could hear Mee and Ow curse behind him. It sounded like curses.

The detective hesitated. He didn't carry a weapon and he had no business here. But he separated the bead strings and carefully stuck his head into the small, dark room beyond.

As he parted the curtain, the light that fell through flickered across her skin. Kaley lay naked on a wide wooden bunk. Four unadorned walls and a small, rickety side table scarred with cigarette burns, the only other piece of furniture in the room, made up the picture. A bunch of hundred-dollar bills lay crumpled on the table. A spent syringe and a packet of blue tablets lay next to the money. He could smell expensive aftershave, cheap alcohol, sweat and death – a disconcerting combination of odours. Maier felt a little dizzy. There were moments in life when he wanted to throw up without being drunk or sick.

This was what they called "all the way down".

Maupai had heard the Vietnamese girls outside and was just buttoning up his trousers. His gold chain shone on his hairless chest. His white shirt was soaked with sweat, the grey hair hung off his head like a long-used dishcloth.

A phone rang.

"Monsieur Maier, in Cambodia, thank God, there are fewer rules to observe than in France, but in a brothel, everyone must queue. As a newcomer you might not be aware of this. That's why I'm not put out enough, after you've brought my enjoyable Saturday afternoon to an abrupt end, to have you killed."

The phone continued to ring. It had started to rain. Kaley moved slowly on the bed and looked up at Maier.

Maupai pulled a mobile, a rare luxury in Cambodia, from his pocket. Maier noticed that blood had soaked through the right sleeve of Maupai's shirt. The Frenchman had been shooting up.

"Allo?"

Kaley made no effort to cover up with the torn blanket that lay on the bunk next to her. She smiled at Maier sensuously. At least that's how it looked. But he wasn't quite sure what he was facing on the bunk. The tension in the small windowless room was unbearable. The rain started hammering onto the roof with greater force.

Maupai was still on the phone as he fell onto the bunk next to the girl. Despite the twilight in the room, Maier could see that the Frenchman had lost it. He no longer looked like a retired film star.

"Bad news, Maupai?"

The Frenchman dropped his phone.

" Ma femme...elle est morte. Joséphine is dead. She died at Calmette Hospital in Phnom Penh this afternoon."

Maupai began to scratch himself nervously. He couldn't look into Maier's face.

"The doctors always talked about fresh air. They just wanted to get rid of us," he whispered.

Maier shook his head. He found it hard to have pity for the Frenchman.

"While you are in here, having sex with your neighbour's friend, your wife dies? Maupai, you have problems."

The former bank director hadn't heard him. He was miles away, his eyes drifting towards something beyond the beaded curtain.

Outside, the Vietnamese girls were giggling. One hot, one cold. Where could you go in such a situation? What did it mean, to have arrived in this hut, at this juncture in your life? Weighty stuff zapped through Maier's head. His eyes wandered to the most beautiful woman he'd ever seen, who seemed to wrap herself around her own golden-brown body. Now she lay curled like a python. He could hear her sigh. Somewhere, water dripped into the room.

After an embarrassing eternity, the Frenchman got up. He stood like an automaton and did up the buttons of his shirt, slowly, pedantically, one by one, looking straight ahead into the big nothing.

"Maier, do you have a gun?"

"No, I do not. And you do not need one, Maupai. Can you not hear it is raining? Is that not your rain, your own personal rain of death? Save yourself the gun and enjoy the few remaining days you have, before the curse catches up with you."

"And I will die a terrible, violent death. Oh, Joséphine, I will not be able to tell you of my adventures. I only did it to save our marriage. Now there's just the wait, for the end."

"Maupai, get lost."

The Frenchman turned and looked at the woman on the bunk, as if he'd just stepped into the room.

Kaley answered his gaze with a dark smile. As the Frenchman began to return the smile, his face twisted into a grotesque mask – perhaps trying to process the terror that was waiting for him outside.

"I will leave you alone now. See you on the other side. You'll have to make your sacrifice as well, Monsieur Maier. Just like young Rolf.

Just like all of us. The Kangaok Meas demands that we destroy ourselves, before we are reborn as gods," he whispered as his voice grew hoarser.

Maier smiled along with them. Now all three of them were smiling and the world was fine.

Kaley stretched slowly and looked at the two men as if she had nothing to do with the room or its male visitors, as if the two intruders were alien, incomprehensible phenomena, propelled into her life by some dark, malignant force.

Maupai left without another word.

Maier turned and sat next to Kaley on the bunk. He had nothing to say and no reason to stay. Kaley wouldn't answer his questions.

And still he asked, "Why did you not stay with Rolf?"

"I need money."

"Rolf has money."

"I work for my papa. He is an important man, a powerful man."

"I know, I will have dinner with him tonight."

"I know."

"I have not found your sister yet."

Kaley leaned forward and pulled Maier's shoulder. Her smile was open, perfect, warm. Her breasts shook ever so slightly. Sweat ran off her golden-brown shoulders. She looked like an angel in reverse.

"I know. And you find her. I am sure. Do you want me help you, Maier?"

"I don't think this will help finding your sister."

Kaley sighed. "Maybe the Kangaok Meas is just story."

"Perhaps. But I am no longer sure who you are."

"I am Kampuchea," she hissed and wrapped herself around him.

He wanted to tell her that he'd seen her in the casino. He wanted to tell her what he'd seen. He remembered her look to the ceiling. She had to know that he'd been there. But there was no point in saying anything. He couldn't tell someone who lived where she lived and tried to hang on, someone about whom he knew next to nothing – he could not tell someone like that about good and evil, about what it might mean to be human. He only had the right to do that if he looked into the abyss at the end of the world himself. Maier wasn't sure whether he was qualified for spiritual insights. He almost felt like he was back in school. In a school where students studied darkness and its habitués.

"Maier, drink. Les says you are friend."

Maier grabbed the whiskey bottle which she had pulled from underneath the bunk and took a long swig. Red Label. He almost wretched it back up; the cheap booze was so bad. He quickly took another swig.

"Les my friend. He like the others, but he my friend."

"And Rolf?"

She said nothing for a while. The rain had almost stopped. The drumming on the roof had turned to an irregular tapping. It sounded like the bag in the casino. He had to get out.

"Rolf so far away. He scared of Kaley."

She looked at him sadly.

"He is probably not the only one," Maier said drily, but she didn't understand him.

"He not understand."

Maier leaned back into a moist bamboo wall and buttoned up his shirt. He could feel the cheap booze stick in his beard, like glue. He took another swig. He wanted to get out. He needed to get out. He wanted to stay. Everything began to turn. He wanted this woman, but he had to solve the case.

Maier didn't fight, he merely dropped. His hands began to shake. Cold sweat ran across his face. He sank into himself. Kaley would catch him and carry him across the fire into a new life and a new Cambodia.

The woman began to sing.

Pete shook him awake.

"Maier, welcome to Club Kep. Wake up, mate, we're already late. You're expected for dinner."

Maier had a furious headache. He was alone in the shed with Pete. Kaley had disappeared. Maier stood up and stumbled about uncertainly. He looked down his front. Had he slept with her? What kind of drink had that been? He tried to focus in silence and pulled his clothes straight.

The English pirate laughed hoarsely, "She just lies there like she's dead, no? Just like I told you."

Maier rolled his eyes and asked, "Can you not imagine that such an experience is different for everyone?"

"No, Maier, I can't."

The world looked better outside. Maupai was nowhere to be seen. The two Vietnamese girls had disappeared as well. Maier stumbled after the Englishman, down the hill to the beach. The sun had just set above Koh Tonsay and Samnang was waiting, motor running.

21

L'ÎLE DES AMBASSADEURS

MAIER ENJOYED THE TRIP. No rain clouds and no dolphins. No tourists from Frankfurt. Samnang passed the eastern shore of the island in a wide arc. Coconut palms lined the picture-postcard beach.

The young Khmer captain stared across the water without expression. Maier didn't find this reassuring, but the sunset hung like a Turner painting and lent the day plenty of painful *Endzeitstimmung*. He was sailing into the beginning of the end of something.

The redhead from England was also quiet and smoked one Ara after another.

As a journalist, Maier had always known why he worked in dangerous situations. He had a mission, a job, to go to hell, to visit places where no one would go voluntarily, to collect information and impressions and to carry them back into the world to remind the people back home how easy their lives were. It had also been a way to get to know the new reunited Germany, by working with other Germans who were on the road. Maier had loved the friendships and the cut-throat competition of war reporting. He'd met the same remarkable people over and over – in Rwanda, in Bosnia, in Cambodia, in Afghanistan. Everyone spinning the wheel, until they'd used up their survival points. After some years a sad routine became apparent. One friend after another died. A few got out of the game because their partners couldn't take it any longer. Maier had stayed on. Until Battambang.

But nothing had really changed. Maier was back in Cambodia, back in the country of his dead friend, Hort. He was sitting on a boat transporting him into a tropical Heart of Darkness, surrounded by people who didn't know why he was here, but who wanted to kill him anyhow.

His client circle back home had shrunk and become more exclusive and he no longer needed to look as closely at political conditions as in his last life. He no longer needed to work as transparently as a journalist either, and this was one aspect of his new profession that Maier liked. As a journalist one was often tied to a truth, usually not one's own. All that mattered for a detective was to close one's case successfully. This didn't have to have anything to do with truth, not one's own and not that of others either.

But detectives and journalists followed common threads – snooping around, unearthing information and asking questions, the search for informants, and, in conflict countries, the ever-present danger of being killed for asking one question too many.

Maier would have to be very careful tonight. He could only hope that the former Khmer Rouge general had made the effort to check his financial background.

They had already turned to the south side of Koh Tonsay. Samnang slowed the engine and lifted the propeller out of the shallow water. A white, solitary bungalow stood two hundred metres ahead, a little set back from the beach amidst a coconut plantation. Tep liked things private.

"This is it. The Villa Ambassade."

Three girls ran along a narrow wooden pier. A speedboat was moored to the rickety structure and bounced gently up and down in the waves. Pete had climbed to the front of the boat and dropped the small anchor into the water. The boy, Tep's son, whom Maier had already seen in action in the Heart, appeared behind the three girls.

As he stood up, Maier could hardly believe his eyes. The girls were around twelve or thirteen and wore identical black pajama suits, complimented by crude flipflops cut from spent car tires – the uniform of the Khmer Rouge. Their hair was cut short, they wore red krama around their necks and carried Kalashnikovs. What a show of force.

Welcome to my genocide. Samnang stayed in the boat and Maier could feel that Pete had tensed up. But it was too late for second thoughts. They'd arrived at the place he'd wanted to visit all along. He ignored the pier and jumped into the shallow water. The Englishman followed and lit an Ara.

The youngest and meanest girl got off the pier, stepped right to the water's edge and pointed the gun at Pete's chest.

"No smoking," she barked.

There was no arguing with the weapon or the girl, but Pete wasn't sure how to get rid of the cigarette. The girl looked like she would shoot him if he dropped it into the water.

"That's how you give up smoking," he mumbled and gave his Ara to Samnang.

"In a minute she'll tell us that smoking is decadent."

Maier didn't feel much like joking. He already had the feeling that he was a prisoner. He followed the boy to the villa. The girls marched slowly after them. Not a word of greeting.

"Be really careful what you say here. Tep is very eccentric. Especially when he's at home. Just keep focused on the business."

"Is he trying to bring back the Seventies? Does he have many of these killer girls?"

"Many."

Maier shook his head.

The Khmer Rouge had long stopped functioning as a guerrilla force. No one in Cambodia dressed and walked like these girls any more. Once again, his thoughts drifted back to what he had seen through the hole in the floor of the casino.

Their host was waiting for them on the wooden veranda of his villa. The veranda faced the jungle. The man obviously didn't think much of sunsets. Today the old Khmer was in uniform. His short hair had been cropped shorter and stood in stubbles on his square head. Tep wore the uniform of a Khmer Rouge general.

The old soldier nodded without a word and waved Maier to a rattan chair. He didn't offer his hand. There were only two chairs on the veranda. The boy and the three girls in black lined up behind Tep. Pete had disappeared.

A large tattered flag graced the wall of the bungalow. Maier was pretty sure that the three yellow Angkor towers set against the red background had once served as the colours of Democratic Kampuchea, the short-lived Cambodia of the Red Khmer.

Kaley stepped out onto the veranda, with two glasses of wine balanced on a plastic tray. She too was dressed in black. She had put her hair up under a black Mao cap and didn't know him. She handed him one of the glasses without a word. The flag and the outfits, all this iconography of failure, reminded Maier of skinhead gatherings in Germany, but these people looked more serious and spookier.

Tep was watching him attentively. Maier watched back. He had the feeling that he wasn't being appraised by the old man alone. You could easily get paranoid in the presence of Khmer Rouge, but he felt he was being observed by someone else. The door which led into the villa was covered by a curtain. Maier thought he could make out someone breathing behind the cloth. It wasn't Pete, of that he was sure. No, this sounded like a much older man.

Maier's brain suddenly did somersaults. Perhaps Pol Pot, Brother Number One, was still alive. Perhaps he hadn't been poisoned by the Thais, but had retired to the idyll of Koh Tonsay. Crazy idea.

"Mr. Maier, you are our guest for almost two weeks now and you not come to visit me in my home. And you meet everyone else in Kep. Maybe you like to find friend because you have no friend?"

Maier cleared his throat. "I have been trying to understand the investment."

Tep smiled like a gentle, slightly senile pensioner.

"And how is investment climate in Kep?"

"It seems that all roads, and boats, lead to your doorstep."

Maier wasn't sure how to address the man. Comrade didn't seem a good choice. And he wasn't going to call him General.

"Yes, they do," the general confirmed. "All roads lead to Tep. But you visit the very small one-way streets in Kep. I hear that you go to Bokor Casino to look."

The eyes of the old man didn't go well with his friendly-grandpa style interrogation technique. They drilled right through Maier. He'd have to choose his next words very carefully.

"True, I was in Bokor a few days ago. I only saw the casino from the outside. An amazing building."

Tep nodded.

"It so run down. I will change it. Bokor is very special place in

Cambodia. I will make resort there, maybe even golf course. What do you think, Mr. Maier?"

"I don't understand why you are so keen on tourism, as well as the past?"

Maier realised immediately that he'd made a mistake.

"Which past, Mr. Maier?"

There was no turning back. Maier had pushed ahead too far and too quickly.

"Your past, Tep. You are surrounded by children in black uniforms. That's a tradition from a time when foreigners were not welcome here."

The Khmer laughed and shook his head.

"You wrong, Mr. Maier. Cambodia always welcome the foreigner, even in Angkor time. Only foreigner who want to make problem, who want to know our business, who maybe want to stop Cambodia become great country again, like Vietnamese, or American, we don't like to see."

Maier didn't say anything. He started wondering whether the three machine guns that were loosely pointing in his direction were slowly homing in. But he didn't look directly at the girls. He had his hands full with Tep.

"You see, Mr. Maier, all foreigner who come to Kep and stay more than holiday, I meet. And you understand, in Cambodia today, the government very weak. So, in the province, the local man has to do the best to rebuild the country. We need to rebuild the country, Mr. Maier. We have little money. America bomb everything and when we beat the foreign enemy, the Vietnamese, our real enemy, invade. Stay ten years, no problem. Big problem for Khmer. Vietnam make problem for Cambodia long time, take our land, destroy our country. We cannot do business with Vietnamese or American. So, I ask, I meet clever man like you and I think, you work for this side or that side? Maybe you here to make problem for Cambodia, take our land or take our woman and child?"

Maier shrugged and answered, "You know all about the activities of the *barang* in Kep and hence you should know that I am here to help Cambodia. Cambodia needs contact with the rest of the world. You cannot do it alone. The world is too small a place for that today."

The old Khmer suddenly leaned forward and grabbed for Maier's right wrist.

"The whole world want to help Cambodia. The UN, the CIA, the newspapers and many people think they can fuck the women and kidnap the children, put people in factories, where they make clothes for *barang* for a few riel. All this just to make economy in your country strong. And then you come and tell us we are murderers. Are you this people, Mr. Maier?"

Maier sat motionless and took his time to answer. Tep continued to hold on to his wrist. The breath of the old man was stale and used up.

"I came to you tonight to discuss business. If you want to accuse me of other things, get your information right. A man with your connections should be able to find out whether I am just talking or whether I really have the money to buy a villa or two and restore them."

The general laughed sourly. "That right, Mr. Maier. I am honest with you. I cannot find out why you come here. I spend my life in Kep. I come from Kampot Province, where I grow up in a village. But I cannot decide if you want to make problem for my country and steal from Cambodian people, or if you are useful to rebuild Cambodia."

Tep rose and grabbed Maier's left hand as well. The detective wondered whether he'd be asked to dance next.

"Mr. Maier, I tell you a story about Cambodian village. You know, local people in Cambodia are very superstitious. One day a group of monk come to my village. The monk is telling the villagers that they can kill all bad spirits in the village, if the villagers give them money and the animals. The villagers happy for help fighting many bad spirits, give the monk their animals and the money, and the monk leave the village. In the evening, a young boy is walking home from his rice field, when meet the group of monk. The monk drinking and eating. They kill all the animals already. They very drunk. The boy run home and tell his mother about the monk. The mother not believe her son and take him to the monk. The monk tell the mother, her son have the bad sprit inside and not his fault what he say. The monk tell the mother to leave the boy. They promising to help the boy. The mother agree and the monk take the boy and torture him for a week. After, the monk leave the boy almost dead near the village and disappear. Is the boy clever or stupid?"

Maier was certain now that a third person was a silent participant in their conversation. In the silence between the general's words, he felt a shadow leaning over him.

"I am poor farmer son when French are here. My uncle die, building the road to Bokor. Like many other Cambodian, he die for the French. Later my brother work as guard in big villa. One day, the son of owner drive his car into a tree and tell his father my brother the driver. The father was friend of King Sihanouk. They arrest my brother and take him to the jail in Kampot. We never see him again. You see, no matter who rule Cambodia, the people without power never can do anything."

"Tep, we face the same situation in Germany. We have a lot in common. I grow up under a socialist government as well."

"You are from East Germany? Why you tell people in Kep you are from Hamburg?"

The old Khmer knew too much. Maier felt dizzy again. No ordinary Khmer Rouge, general or not, would know where Hamburg was. He made a last effort to worm himself out of being a suspect, which likely meant being convicted and executed in Tep's world.

"I live in Hamburg. Until 1989, I worked in East Berlin, as well as in Hungary, Poland, Czechoslovakia and Romania."

The Khmer loosened his iron grip somewhat.

"Did you work for the Staatssicherheitsdienst? Do you know HVA?"

Maier didn't expect this question. The HVA, the Hauptverwaltung Aufklärung, had been East Germany's secret service, its CIA. Maier had bumped into its agents in Eastern Europe, had even tried to seduce one of them in Breslau once. He shook his head. He hardly felt the needle penetrate his skin. The old Khmer smiled. Maier began to sink.

A voice, a German voice, ancient and thin, like cold clear soup, hissed behind him, "He never worked for the Stasi. A man like him would've been noticed in the Runde Ecke right away. But we can never be one hundred percent sure."

Tep let go of Maier's hands. The detective tried to turn but it was too late. He felt the thin white hand on his shoulder more than he saw it. For a few seconds, Kaley's smile crossed his inner eye, then everything went dark.

PART II
THE WHITE SPIDER

22

THIRIT'S WISDOM

You could rely on the Germans, even when it came to death.

They'd phoned Dani Stricker immediately after Thirit, her turtle, had died. Dani wasn't surprised. Her time in Germany was coming to an end. Without Harald, she felt more like a stranger every day, more than she'd felt for the past twenty years.

She hurried through the rainy park to the Mannheim botanical house.

Harald had brought her here when she'd first arrived in Germany. The heavy, humid air reminded Dani of the rainy season back home. She got homesick every time she entered the huge building, but she'd never told Harald. And they'd come back, as often as Harald had found the time, to admire the crocodiles in the entrance hall, and the Mongolian gerbils racing about in their enclosure, or they walked through the butterfly garden, before they drifted across to the reptiles who lived in several rows of glass tanks. Only the large turtles lived outside.

Citizens could support one of these slow creatures and for her twentieth birthday, Harald had registered Dani as the godmother of Thirit, a tortoise from Southeast Asia.

In the years that followed, Thirit had become the closest connection Dani had to home. Once she had mastered some German, she'd taken the tram to the park every month and had told Thirit about her childhood. Thirit had known all of Dani's secrets, had listened to the young Cambodian woman for hours, as she had told her of her unfortunate sister Kaley. Thirit had had to listen to terrible stories, of murdered monks Dani had seen lying on the road in her village, of communes where people only worked and never ate, of friends' parents who had been picked up for 'training' by Angkar one night and had never been seen again. Thirit had never commented or thrown in a critical remark. A real friend never did that.

The guard of the botanical house, a young man in a muscle shirt, welcomed Dani. He was utterly taken by her, she noticed. Some western men were fascinated by Asian women and the park employee probably had no idea that she was ten years older than him. She felt something like longing, but the feeling was quickly swept away by thoughts of the coming weeks.

"Very sorry, Frau Stricker, but Thirit died last night. These animals have a life expectancy of ten to fifteen years. Yours was almost twenty years old."

Dani wasn't sure how she was to react. The Germans expressed their commiserations like other people, but surely no one expected tears for a turtle.

Dani didn't have any.

"Can I see Thirit one more time?"

The young man shrugged his shoulders in embarrassment and looked at the floor.

"Unfortunately, one of my colleagues already disposed of the animal. We had hoped that you might want to sponsor another turtle…"

Dani shook her head sadly.

"I'm leaving Mannheim in a few days. Thanks for informing me."

She left the man standing there, admiring her, and walked through the doors of the botanical house.

Her life in Mannheim was over.

But where next?

Her phone rang. She ran to a nearby closed café and stood under the awnings.

"You asked me to call once more. I have found your sister. And the man you're looking for. Everything is going as planned. Do you have any further instructions?"

Dani's heart beat all the way into her skull.

"My sister is alive? You have no doubt?"

"Absolutely sure. There's no doubt. She lives in Kep, on the coast."

Desperate thoughts raced through her mind. She had sworn not to return to her country. She'd tried to become a German for twenty years. But it only took a few seconds to change her mind.

"I'm coming to Cambodia."

For several seconds, there was no answer.

Finally, the man answered calmly, "Don't come here. The situation is complicated and dangerous."

"I want my sister. Where is she?"

"Perhaps you should wait a week or two. But I would really advise you not come."

Dani resented the man's advice. She had to see her sister.

"I am Khmer. I know my country is dangerous. You work for me and I will come to pick up my sister."

The man chuckled, "Ok, don't say I didn't warn you. Send your flight details to this number. Be patient. You hired me to get rid of the man. Has that changed?"

"No."

Dani shook the ice-cold rain from her hair. The man had hung up.

23

SHADOW PLAY

MAIER LAY on a bunk covered with a straw mat. He couldn't move anything but his eyes. It was almost dark. The room in which he lay smelled of old stone, of moss, of wild animals. A suite in a luxury hotel it wasn't.

Outside, from somewhere unimaginably far away, he could hear birdsong, perhaps a few insects. No people, no engine noises. Maier felt incredible and assumed his mental well-being to be the result of the drug they'd given him. Or perhaps his euphoria had something to do with the fact that he was still alive. Wherever he was now, his life couldn't be worth much to anyone but himself.

Shadows moved around him. He tried to turn his head – to no avail. He was paralysed.

"You see, Maier, it's my mission to find out who you are. I will not let you go. You can no longer walk anyway. The general told me that you might want to invest in us, but I am convinced it's too late for that. Things have gone too far. Our relationship is not transparent and unnecessarily complicated. For this reason, I will take you back to 1976, metaphorically speaking, and I will interrogate you before you are disposed of. I'm sure you understand. Tried and trusted methods."

Maier could almost see the man, not directly see him, but feel his presence. He spoke German.

Maier wasn't scared. It was too late for that. It was probably too late for Müller-Overbeck and Kaley as well.

He was alone again. Shadows brushed through space for long seconds. Time had slithered into a black hole. The back of Maier's head hoped that they had given him Flunitrazepam, Ruppies, R2s, Ropys, Flunies or something similar. He couldn't remember a thing but his head was clear.

Had he been permanently damaged? He wasn't worth much if he remained paralysed. He tried to laugh. After a while, the mosquitoes attacked. Maier groaned; he was the perfect meal.

Children's voices. Serious children's voices. No laughing. Light. Shadow. Orders. Maier managed to turn his head. His eyes were swollen, but he could see that he lay under an old mosquito net. Caught in the net of a huge spider. The room in which he lay was bathed in soft late afternoon sunlight, which flooded through an open, stone-framed window, like the blood of a freshly slaughtered buffalo. The walls were constructed from huge carved blocks of stone. He'd been taken to an old temple ruin of the Angkor Empire.

Someone removed the net. Three young girls, their hair cut short, all of them dressed in black uniforms, looked down at him. Their oblique expressions, perfectly synchronised, made him feel like a victim.

"Maier, were you born in Leipzig?"

The voice was old and tired, yet sharp and focused at the same time. Full of cold, bureaucratic routine. The man spoke a peculiar German. Maier thought he could detect a faint Eastern European accent. Whoever was outside his field of vision, in the process of deciding what would happen to him, had conducted thousands of interviews like this.

"Yes."

"Maier, are you working for an intelligence service?"

"No."

The girl nearest to him drove her fist into his face.

Maier cursed.

"Maier, did you study political sciences in Berlin and Leipzig between 1976 and 1982?"

"Yes."

"You worked as a foreign correspondent in the GDR? You travelled abroad?"

"Yes."

"That means you were trusted not to defect, trusted at the highest level?"

"That's true."

"I don't see any reason why the relevant offices would have had so much trust in you."

Maier didn't know what to say. The second girl hit him hard on his right thigh. The child was good at her job, with immovable face and trauma rings around her eyes. The pain was terrible, a good sign as far as Maier was concerned. A little more beating and he would be able to walk again. He didn't say anything for a while.

"I was a good journalist."

"Did you work in Cambodia at the time?"

"No."

"You absconded to the West before the Wall came down?"

"I had an offer from dpa to work as a foreign correspondent in Eastern Europe and South Asia."

"Your ideological turn-about presented no problems for you?"

"There was no ideological turn. I was a journalist in the GDR, then in the reunited Germany. And then I stopped."

"Yes, yes, Battambang, '97. A bomb that killed a Cambodian colleague. A man called Hort, through whom you met your girlfriend Carissa Stevenson."

"I don't have a girlfriend. The man was my fixer, my employee. Ms. Stevenson is an old colleague."

The third girl stepped up and hit him in the face. Maier's brain had started to crank up properly and he could make a pretty good guess at the next questions. As well as at the attached trap. He saw no way out.

"Carissa Stevenson is not your girlfriend?"

"No."

"Then you have no real interest in whether she's dead or alive?"

"Of course, I have an interest, professional as well as motivated by friendship. We have known each other since the UNTAC years. Hort introduced her to me, as you said."

"Didn't you just tell me that you no longer work as a journalist? How can your interest be professional? Are you lying to me, Maier?"

"No."

The first of the three girls had stepped very close to Maier, holding a long acupuncture needle. She gently lifted his right arm and pushed the needle through the palm of his hand.

Maier passed out.

"Maier, were you born in Leipzig?"

"Yes."

"Maier, are you working for an intelligence service?"

"No."

The second girl hit him in the face.

"Are you Christian?"

Maier tried to shake his head.

"That's a shame, Maier. I'd always give a German Christian a second chance. You have another ten days of interrogations ahead of you. Choose your answers carefully and the young ladies will keep the needles away from your testicles."

Slow, scuffled steps receded. Maier hadn't seen his interrogator. The three girls continued to watch him; their faces twisted by nameless resentment. Maier tried to breathe slowly and evenly to get his heartbeat back under control. Borderline experiences in Cambodia. He coughed with exhaustion and closed his eyes. Perhaps it was better to be tortured with eyes closed. The detective was on the verge of burnout. Short and sharp panic attacks shot like black pinballs from one corner of his drug-addled brain to another. He heard a cockerel crow outside. He felt like screaming himself, but he wasn't that far gone yet. Or perhaps he'd already passed the screaming stage. He let himself slide downwards.

Maier lay on the wide stone terrace of a temple ruin. He knew he was badly injured. Dense jungle reached to the horizon ahead. Dark green, light green and a thousand shades in between for which there were no words. Not a soul down there. He couldn't move. He could only stare at the green hell beneath him, above him, all around him. He managed to lift his right hand. The breeze almost pulled it away. As he looked past his dismembered thumb, he could see the blue evening sky.

. . .

Maier noticed that the walls of the room he lay in were covered in bas-reliefs. A gigantic battle unfolded around him. He gazed at the scene for some time without understanding. Then he slowly remembered what the thousand-year-old carvings represented.

Gods and demons pulled at opposite ends of a naga, a mythical snake, which had curled around the sacred Mount Mandhara. Through the labour of gods and demons, the ocean of cosmic milk which surrounded the sacred mountain grew more and more stormy and eventually gave up amrita, the nectar of immortality.

Heavenly apsaras – sacred celestial nymphs with perfect breasts and swaying hips – floated above the scene and gazed down at him with serene expressions.

This old Hindu myth could also be found on the walls of Angkor Wat. But Maier had never seen this version of the masterpiece he now marveled at, despite feeling rotten and depressed. There was nothing left to do but look.

Carissa had gone ahead and rounded a curve in the forest road. He'd just heard her voice, then she'd been swallowed by the jungle. Unarmed and curious. Greedy for the new. Maier ran up the mountain as fast as he could. Animals that no white man had seen lived in the huge trees along the roadside. But Maier couldn't see animals. He didn't want to see or hear them.

Where was she? His woman?

Carissa lay on the road, sleeping peacefully.

Maier took in every detail of the crime scene. An army of ants had constructed a highway across her naked belly. Her white hair obscured most of her face. He could not read her last scream.

The bullet had entered the skull from behind and emerged below the lower jaw. Carissa would never say another word. Everything, almost everything was blown away. The ants began to consume her eyes. The tiny soldiers danced around her dark unreachable pupils like kohl.

A girl with short frizzy hair washed him. She was older than his earlier tormentors, around twenty perhaps. She was different. She didn't smile nor did she look as numb as the black creatures with the needles. She kept her pale blue almond-shaped eyes low. Maier recognised that in another life she'd be beautiful. But one couldn't choose. Perhaps in the next life.

"My name is Raksmei. Eat something, Maier."

Maier expected another beating when he didn't answer. He didn't want to eat. Not even a Vodka orange would have helped right now. He could smell shit and old leather. He could hear something hovering, flapping its wings, outside, beyond his reach.

Kaley sat next to him and held his injured hand.

"My name is Raksmei. Eat something."

"I haven't found your sister yet."

"That does not matter. You have done your best."

Had his best been all that good?

"Have you come to Cambodia to arrest the German?"

"No."

"The old man is sure you here because of him."

"Who is he?"

"He is very old. He comes and goes. For more than twenty years."

He felt himself drift in shallow water. The current was slow. He could stretch out and drift away, like a message in a bottle. He was embedded in silence, as if submerged in cotton wool, or fresh snow. In the absence of peace of mind, this was pretty good. There was no fresh snow in Cambodia. The water was tropically warm. Something moved in front of him. A white spider, as big as a car, sat on the water's surface. Long white legs bopped up and down, gnarled like ancient tree trunks.

The spider turned towards Maier.

"Maier, do you work for a security service?"

"No."

"Are you Christian?"

"No."

"What do you know about Project Kangaok Meas?"

His legs began to get caught up in the spider's net. He felt himself sink. People could drown in just thirty centimetres of water. He needed answers.

He was a detective, a journalist, an adventurer, a ladies' man, a lone wolf. All just shells.

Maier screamed into the room, "You smell like a Stasi spook. Why haven't you cut my nose off yet? Why haven't you bugged my cell? Why haven't you asked me whether I work for the CIA? Or the KGB? Or the IRA, the PLO or al-Qaeda? I don't need to look at you to identify you. You smell of old files and the sweat of the dead you have on your conscience."

Exhausted, Maier fell back onto his bunk.

Kaley and Raksmei had disappeared.

The spider sat in the corner of the room and laughed blood.

"What, what, what?"

"If I told you that I knew something about the sun and the moon, I would be lying."

"The sun and the moon? You're working for the sun and the moon? Maier, we're not on the same team."

Grey spittle dropped from the creature's lower jaw and spread across the stone floor like something indescribable, searching out Maier's cold flesh.

"The only thing I know is what I will do with you."

Maier started singing to himself. The smell was unbearable, like rotten, atrophied flesh. The three girls, dressed in black bikinis, floated into the room on a long black surfboard made from old car tires, wrapped in barbed wire. The scarred, bent back of the spider burst open and thousands of tiny black spiders wearing black rubber shoes flooded the cell. In seconds, floor, walls and ceiling were covered in cold, black energy.

Then they began to crawl up his legs. Maier was caught. Maier was composed. This is what the end looked like, felt like.

"Sometimes the same's different, but mostly it's the same."

The Khmer Rouge had forbidden everything. Shopping, music, gossip, prayer, love and even laughing and crying had been punishable by death or worse. But in the moment of dying, prohibitions didn't apply. Maier didn't feel like praying, so he laughed. That seemed perfectly reasonable. It was part of being human. Insanity was the solution.

Maier got up and pushed the three girls aside.

What was his small suffering in comparison to the decades-long chaos Cambodia had experienced?

He stepped to the window, and, without turning, without searching for the eye of his tormentor, without bothering with the small spiders that were eating the world, he let go and rose into the clear blue evening sky.

24

BIG SISTER

DANI STRICKER COULD HARDLY BELIEVE it. She didn't recognise a thing. The country looked utterly foreign to her.

The new airport was different to what she had expected. What had she expected? The buildings were practically shining and the arrival hall was as neat and clean as the departure lounge in Frankfurt. Everything smelled new. The immigration officer wore a real uniform, hardly looked at her and, once she'd paid the twenty US dollars for a tourist visa, he stamped her German passport without pulling a face or asking for a bribe.

Her arrival card read, "Welcome to Cambodia".

Fear and pleasure, a strange euphoria shot through her. The war, which she carried in the back of her head like the memory of an absent child, was nowhere to be seen. Outside, the taxi drivers hustled around her and carried her bags to a waiting car. She felt like she knew all Khmer people. After all, they were her people. Then she flushed, acutely aware that she'd been away for twenty years. And that almost all the people she had once known were dead. Only her sister, Kaley, remained alive. And that man.

It was hotter and more humid than the botanical house back in Mannheim. The air smelled sweet and heavy, saturated by the smell of blooming flowers and cheap talcum powder, the way Danny remembered from her childhood. The scene in front of her flickered from foreign to home, from alien to familiar, back and forth, rapidly.

She looked around, perhaps expecting her hired assassin to emerge from the crowd to hand her the head of the man whose death she'd wished for all these years. But of course, she didn't know the man and she couldn't see anyone who might have fitted the bill.

A family of Scandinavians, with five blonde children, tried to lift several heavy suitcases from their cab. The children screamed excitedly; the parents looked stressed. A tour group, Japanese, living up to the cliché, their necks bent forward, straining against the weight of their huge cameras, filed past her into the sun. A huge and pale *barang* in a loud Hawaiian shirt stood near the taxi rank and gesticulated into his telephone. The man had an impossibly red face and briefly looked distractedly in her direction. Who were these people? Who came here voluntarily? And why? Dani had bought a travel guide, but she was still surprised to see tourists. Her last impressions of her homeland, her overland escape, on foot, through a ruined and vicious country, were hard to connect with the reality of this new Cambodia.

In early 1979, she'd fled her commune, had walked along the heavily mined road leading west towards Thailand, had forced herself not to drink from ponds filled with the corpses, sometimes entire families, who'd been butchered or poisoned. Again, and again, she had lain hidden in the brush for hours to avoid patrolling Khmer Rouge units. Most of these soldiers had been undisciplined children with murder in their eyes. Again, and again, she'd thought about her sister whom she had left behind. Her life was worth nothing. Once she'd eaten a dog, a piece of dog that she had found, half cooked by the heat, on the broken tarmac. A man had appeared and tried to kill her with a stone until she gave up the carcass and ran. The man had had a leg missing. He'd not been able to follow her. She'd passed pagodas that had been turned into pigsties. In Sysophon, she'd seen five shorn heads lined up on poles. The Buddha statues, those that hadn't been smashed to pieces, had cried in their temples.

The land she had walked across was silent. Throughout her entire month-long journey, she hadn't heard or seen a single motorised vehicle. She had heard the footsteps of ghosts preceding and following her, all the way to the border.

Countless times, she had passed dead soldiers and civilians. The victims had been young and old, male and female, Buddhist and Muslim, Cambodians and Vietnamese. Cambodia had become a country where cannibalism had become commonplace. She'd noticed that the killers had often cut the livers from their victims and grilled and eaten the organs right next to the corpses. Intestines, swollen by fat black maggots, had burst from slit stomachs. Others had lain in the brush, tied together and beaten to death. Yet others, many more, had lain in open ditches, half buried and half left to the elements. The wild animals had long abandoned this cursed land and migrated into Thailand or Laos. The dead had rotted in their pits, untouched. Dani had walked on, even though she had hardly a will to live left. She'd kept thinking about her little sister whom she had abandoned to the Khmer Rouge. What was the point of survival if everything one experienced was the suffering and death of others? There had been no future. The future had been forbidden by Angkar, along with everything else.

She looked her driver in the eyes. He was about her age. He wouldn't meet her curious gaze and turned his head. A shock ran through Dani Stricker. No question, the horror was still here. People remembered in silence. It was embarrassing. It was still there, beneath the glittering surface of the new Cambodia. It didn't fit in with this new life, but it served as a foundation for everything she was trying to absorb right now. She wished she had Harald with her, but he'd died with her old life. She was alone.

Dani took a deep breath and got into the old beaten-up Toyota. How many lives could a person experience in the few short years one lived consciously? She shook her head. That was truly a *barang* question. No wonder her home had become an alien place. She'd become so German.

As a young woman, she'd once visited Phnom Penh. She remembered a sleepy, clean town with wide boulevards. Not much of that city had made the jump into the twenty-first century. All hell had come out to play on the airport road into town. Cambodia was waking up. After the dark years, the process looked a phenomenal challenge.

The traffic was hair-raising. Hundreds of mopeds, many loaded with families or impossibly large piles of goods, drove on both sides of the road in all directions. Mothers clutched two or three children, riding side-saddle behind their husbands. No one wore a helmet. New temples, new apartment blocks and new businesses sprouted from every street corner. The taxi passed the university. The buildings looked overgrown and run down, but the young students, dressed in pressed white shirts and blue trousers or skirts, were streaming through the entrance gates into the road, laughing and kidding each other like students in other countries. Cambodia screamed new. Huge billboards promoting the country's three political parties lined the roadside. Policemen stood in small clusters at busy crossings, machine guns casually slung across their shoulders, and dared each other to stop a vehicle and rob the driver for the coming weekend's drinking money. Some things hadn't changed.

"You want me to take you to a good hotel? I can find a very cheap room for you."

Dani, tired, shook her head.

"I have a reservation at Hotel Renakse. Please take me there. You know, the hotel in front of the Royal Palace."

The driver gazed at her in the rearview mirror with empty eyes. She hadn't forgotten her mother tongue but the man could tell that she didn't belong here.

Dani's mobile phone rang and she dug it out of her handbag.

"Rent a car, a four-wheel drive if possible, and come up to Siem Reap. Take a room and wait for my call. My last call."

"Your last call?"

"Yes, in a few days it'll all be done. When you have found your sister, leave the country immediately. No one will follow you beyond Cambodia's borders."

"So far you haven't done anything for the money I paid you."

The man laughed drily and said in English, "That's how it is in this business. The clients want unmentionable things done and at the same time they demand information."

He hung up. Dani Stricker wound down the window, leaned back and stared into the traffic, lost in her thoughts.

25

THE NEEDLE

HE LAY on the same bunk when he woke the next morning. The hallucinations of the previous day had receded. He could hear birdsong in the jungle. Maier still existed. He lay in a thousand-year-old temple in the dark heart of Cambodia, alive and mentally intact. But he was no longer in the mood for it. Today would be his last day. A knife, a bullet, an injection, he didn't care which. It just had to be quick.

"Do we know each other?"

The White Spider. Maier recognised the man immediately, despite the fact that he'd never seen him before.

Today he'd reverted to his human shape. The man was at least seventy, as tall as Maier, but twenty kilos or so lighter. He wore khaki jeans, a thin white cotton shirt and a tie. He stood, slightly bent, over the detective. The Omega on his wrist was likely accurate to the second. He probably had leather wings under his shirt. His face hung back in the shadows; Maier couldn't make him out clearly.

"Who am I?"

"I have never seen you before. And now that I have seen you, I never want to see you again."

The White Spider smiled thinly. He combed through his thin silver hair. His hands were huge, his fingers long and thin like hairless bones.

He stared down at his prisoner with narrow blue eyes that sparkled in a thin face. He looked like someone who enjoyed a good bottle of wine, who read the right books and who never sat in the sun. Culture had never saved anyone from themselves.

"I can have you killed straight away, without further discussion. Wouldn't you like to cling to the hope that you can talk yourself out of this for a little while longer? Don't you have a will to live, Maier? Are you even a real German?"

His voice was as thin as the fingers on his pale hand. A voice that came to Maier from far away. A voice that knew no resistance and no doubt.

"Why were you sent to Cambodia?"

Maier looked past the man now into the clear sky, towards freedom. Then he pulled back into the cell. Where he belonged. Outside, everything would be different.

The world he had left no longer existed. In his absence, everything had continued turning, without his input, his hopes and his fears. He embraced the darkness now. Here he'd make his deal with the devil that stood in front of him now.

"I can see neither life nor hope in your eyes. I don't really know why I am here. You are German. Me too. Still, someone should dig a ditch in a rice field and throw you in it, along with your friends. That's where you belong. I belong to the world. Not just Germany, but the world."

The man was silent.

"I assume my kidnapping and imprisonment is down to the paranoia of a few crazy holdovers of long-gone wars. You must think I have stumbled upon some dark secret from your past."

Maier gasped for air. A voice in his head was trying to make him panic and chanted "Shitty cards, shitty cards", over and over.

Maier lay, the man stood. He seemed to contemplate something. Maier tried to relax. Just a little. He couldn't ask this man to continue torturing him. His capacity to absorb pain was exhausted. Freedom or death, one was as urgent as the other. Sometimes, the same was different, but mostly, it was just the same. Maier had thought to the end. Losing was better than hesitating.

The White Spider turned towards the window. For him too, there was no way out. The deal was on the table. Perpetrator and victim had united into an organism called brute. The interrogation had ended. All that was left was the clean-up.

Raksmei appeared next to the White Spider. Maier had the feeling he'd met the girl somewhere before. But her eyes were the same as on the previous day. Pale blue and far away. A Khmer with blue eyes?

He couldn't reach her. She held a syringe in her right hand.

"Tell me why you're here and I may let you live."

Maier could detect a faint expression of hope in the old man's face.

"You know why I am here. You have always known."

The next tome he raised his head, was alone with Raksmei. He couldn't move. The sun fell through the window the same way it had done the previous day.

A day without Maier.

It had all gone so quickly, this life.

The young woman knelt next to him, tied him off, found a vein and stuck the needle into his arm. Maier smiled and opened his eyes wide enough to let her look inside.

The world was full of shit and gasoline, baby.

2 6

HOMECOMING

Dani Stricker had tears in her eyes. She couldn't help it after sitting in a crab shack in Kep all afternoon. She'd discarded her hired assassin's advice. Siem Reap could wait. Once, a long time ago, in another life, she'd come here, with her sister. They'd run away from the paddy fields for a day to see the ocean. Their parents had never allowed them to go so far from the village. Dani's sister had been very young then. With the few riel Dani had taken from the family purse, she'd bought steamed crab for her sister.

Her cell phone rang.

"Where are you?" the voice with the strong *barang* accent enquired without a word of greeting.

"At home. I've come home. I'm in Kep."

She hoped that she didn't sound tearful. She could still taste the lemon sauce which came with the crab on her lips. The man said nothing a while.

"You are an idiot," he hissed finally, "I told you not to come back to Cambodia. I told you I found your sister. Now you're in Kep and in danger and so is she. The man you want dead isn't dead yet."

She didn't like the tone of the man's voice. She was paying him well. Before she could protest, he carried on, "If you have transport, leave immediately. Go back to Phnom Penh and wait for me to get in touch. And I mean immediately. I'll call you back when it is safe for you to have a beach holiday. You're jeopardising your sister's life."

The line went dead. Dani was furious. Who did he think he was? Cambodia was her country. No one could be of any danger to her here. No one was even likely to recognise her. She ordered a pot of green tea. She could still return to the capital tomorrow. The man was clearly paranoid. She so missed her sister.

Dani watched the mellow surf lapping against the rocks below the shack. She heard steps approaching and looked up expecting the waitress and her tea. Instead, a girl with short hair, dressed in black pajamas approached quickly and grabbed her roughly by the hair. She jerked back in surprise, but it was too late. The girl plunged a needle into Dani Stricker's throat and pushed the plunger.

27

BILGE WATER AND MEKONG WHISKEY

THE WATER SLAPPED against the side of the wooden boat. The smell of rotten fish was overwhelming. Had Maier had more room to maneuver, he would have stuffed bits of cloth or pieces of wood into his nostrils, but he lay less than twenty centimetres below the boat's deck in bilge water. He was trapped.

He'd managed to vomit twice without suffocating or being discovered. Did he want to be discovered?

He could see across the lake through a small hole in the side of the boat. Phnom Krom, the mountain at the western end of the Tonlé Sap, bopped up and down a few kilometres away. Grasses and plastic rubbish floated close by.

The boat was being loaded. Heavy boxes packed with fish crashed onto the deck, which pressed down onto Maier. The wooden boards above his head were bending closer and closer. He wanted to scream, but most of all, he wanted to know more.

Why was he still alive? Had the young woman helped him escape? What was he doing under the deck of a fishing boat? How long had he been unconscious?

A loud, authoritarian voice barked an order. The men who were loading the boat stopped toiling.

Maier could detect uniforms in the shallow water outside, moving towards the boat. Now he saw one of the men who'd been loading the fish, a Khmer fisherman, skinny and brawny, his back, bent from years of hard labour, burnt almost black by the sun. A policeman grabbed the man by the throat and screamed at him. Everywhere Maier could see now, uniforms were closing in. If Cambodian policemen stalked around in dirty water, up to their hips in the sauce, holding their Kalashnikovs above their heads, their uniforms muddy, they had to be under great pressure to produce results. Or they'd been promised a fat reward. They were looking for him.

But who knew that he lay under the planks of a boat on the Tonlé Sap? He barely knew himself. Someone had taken him from the temple to the lake shore and loaded him onto the boat. As much as he tried to stretch, he could not see or hear the young woman who had executed him with her syringe.

The commanding officer now stood directly in front of Maier's spyhole and scratched his balls. Two of the officer's minions crashed about above Maier and began to bang on the wooden deck. Through the narrow gaps between the planks he could see that the men were trying to figure out how solid the deck was. Sweat and frustration dripped down on him.

A few minutes later they gave up and began to wade towards the next boat. The policeman in front of Maier growled, spat into the dirty water and disappeared.

The boat's engine coughed into life. The screw hit the water and the vessel began to move. Maier could see Cambodia pass through the tiny hole by the side of his head. Unnoticed, he slid through the floating village of Chong Neas, beneath Phnom Krom. An hour later, the boat passed the flooded forests of Kompong Phluk, whose fishermen lived in huts constructed on high poles. The boat didn't stop. Maier could hear the sound of a transistor radio from afar, a girl singing a mournful tune across the water, before sinking back into the rhythm of the engine and the rush of the water.

In the afternoon, the mosquitoes devoured Maier. He let himself go. What else could he do? He was sure the men on the boat didn't know of their stowaway. He was a ghost and he tried to live the moment. After the days in the temple cell, he felt slightly euphoric, despite the insects, the vomit, the water, and his present imprisonment.

As evening came, they reached the mouth of the Stung Sangkar River. Every now and then he saw faint lights on the shore, lined by poor fishing communities. Then the night swallowed the land and only the gurgling water reminded Maier that he was still alive.

He woke up with a start. He was cold. The boat had stopped at a pier, probably in the early hours of the morning. A few weak bulbs flickered above an embankment. He could hear drunken voices.

The boat must have reached Battambang, the largest town on the Stung Sangkar. He began to shake. The sun would soon be up. Battambang had hotels and telephones. He would ring Carissa. His lover was the only person he could trust. But first he had to get out of his water taxi.

The detective lifted his bite-covered arms and pushed hard against the wooden planks above him. The wood bent a little, but there was no moving it. They had laid him below deck and then nailed everything shut. He would freeze to death before sunrise. He hadn't drunk or eaten anything for at least sixteen hours.

After an eternity, he heard steps on the pier above him.

"Maier?"

A woman's voice, quiet and self confident. Khmer.

Maier groaned, "Yes?"

"I will get you out, but it will take some time. I don't want to make a noise. Everybody think you dead."

"I do too," he answered weakly.

28

BATTAMBANG

A COUPLE OF DAYS LATER, Maier was back on his feet. But he couldn't run from himself. He slept under a net in a neat, small room located in an unremarkable family home on the edge of town, a bottle of water under his arm.

Every few hours, he woke, bathed in sweat, listening to the panic recede, and cursed the world. He hadn't seen Raksmei since his rescue. Twice a day, the family with whom he stayed invited him to eat. Rice and *prahok*. Maier didn't eat much. The boys who lived in the house tried to animate him to play football, but he wouldn't leave the safety of the net.

She suddenly stood in his room, a pile of newspapers under her arm. Jeans, white cotton shirt, leather sandals. She'd parted the short hair with a garish plastic hair clip. He noticed small golden rings in her ears. She hadn't worn those in the temple.

"I have only bad news for you, Maier."

Maier looked at her silently.

Raksmei appeared to be two people at the same time, changing and shifting from one moment to another. The blue eyes were confusing. There couldn't be many children her age who were half-Khmer and half-*barang*. Carissa had been right; the girl was special. She reminded Maier of someone. He hoped that his brain was only temporarily muddled by the drugs they'd given him. The drugs she'd given him.

"Maybe you read article in Phnom Penh Post first."

She left a phone and a bottle of Mekong Whiskey and disappeared. Maier didn't feel like bad news.

CAMBODIAN WITH GERMAN PASSPORT KILLED IN KAMPOT

Daniela Stricker, a Cambodian carrying a German passport, was found dead in her hotel room in Kampot. A 42-year old Canadian was arrested near the Green Apsara Guest House while trying to flee on a motorcycle and has made a full confession. The murder weapon, a golf club, was found at the crime scene.

The police in Kampot are looking for a 45-year old German real estate speculator. Police investigations suggest the man left Kampot a day before the crime took place. It is not clear whether the man is a suspect. A week ago, Sambat Chuon, an employee of Hope-Child, a Kampot based NGO, was registered as missing. The local police dismissed any possibility that the disappearance and the murder of the German national could be connected. According to a German Embassy spokesman speaking on condition of anonymity, Mrs. Stricker was from the town of Mannheim and had been recently widowed. Suicide has been ruled out.

A passport photo accompanied the brief article. The woman's face was familiar. After staring at the image for a while, he knew. This had to be Kaley's sister. Shit. And the German speculator? Maier didn't have to speculate all that much – he was being set up. He still held the paper in his hand when the young woman returned two hours later.

"Do you see my brother die?"

"No."

"But you are diving near where my brother die, right?"

"Your brother was sunk with stones around his feet. When my dive partner and I reached him, he was already dead and there was nothing we could do for him. The water was full of sharks. I am sorry."

"I sure it all the same story."

Maier swallowed, "Me too."

"You are journalist?"

"No."

She'd saved his life. He had to tell her the truth. There was no one else in Cambodia who'd listen to him.

"I am a private detective. I am here to look out for a young German man in Kep. I was hired by his mother. It's Rolf, the owner of Reef Pirate Divers."

Raksmei watched him for a while.

"He disappear. I hear he have problem with partner and go to Phnom Penh to sell business."

She hesitated.

"You not here to find out what happen in Kep and Bokor and why somebody kill my brother and this lady?"

"No, I did not come for this reason. But we both think all this is connected and I am sure my client is up to his neck in trouble."

Raksmei nodded sadly.

"Raksmei, why did you save my life? And what were you doing in that temple with those people?"

"I look for murder of my brother. I want to know what happen to all the children who disappear from Kampot in last two years."

"And?"

"The people who stay in old Khmer temple near Siem Reap, they trade with property on the coast. From Koh Kong to Sihanoukville and to Kep. But I think this is front for something different. Do you know Kangaok Meas Project?"

"The old man in the temple asked me the same question. A woman in Kep told me a story about Kangaok Meas, an old Cambodian story."

"The story of golden peacock and Kaley?"

"Yes."

"Kaley is Khmer Rouge. She with Tep, old Khmer Rouge General, who use her to get *barang* business partner. Maybe she mad. I not know her much."

"She asked me to find her sister. I think the German woman killed is her sister. I am pretty sure."

Raksmei looked at Maier doubtfully.

"I think Tep kill her family long time ago. He call her Kaley. She Tep slave, I think."

"That is possible, but it is too simple, Raksmei. All the men who slept with her in Kep allegedly fall under a curse. They say if it rains after a man has spent a night with Kaley, he will die a violent, agonising death. All the locals and westerners in Kep believe this."

"Old story from old Cambodia. Do you believe in ghosts, Maier?"

Maier hesitated to answer. In this country one lost touch with reality even quicker than one's life.

"Since I lay on that bunk in the temple, I believe in anything. Perhaps the horrors of the past left something here in Cambodia. So many unimaginable crimes have been committed in this country. It's hard to see how things could be as they were before. Some of the horror sticks."

"I never see ghost, Maier. But the Khmer, they live with ghost every day. But my brother and this lady not kill by ghost."

"No."

Maier read the article once more.

"I will go and visit the man who is in jail in Kampot. The man accused of Dani Stricker's murder."

"Maier, the Cambodian government say you missing. Everybody looking for you. Tep know many police. He not stop until he find you, dead or alive."

"And you too."

"Yes, me too. You want to know why I save you? Alone I can do nothing. I save you because I think you crazy to come to Cambodia to solve crime. Maybe you so crazy you help me. I want to know what happen with my brother and what happen in the temple with the young girls."

Raksmei sat down on the cool tiled floor and appeared to be ordering her thoughts.

"I run orphanage in Kampot. A few month ago, my brother find out that some of the girl we report missing are on Bokor mountain. He go up there one time but he not tell me what he see. Tep want to find the money to buy casino and make all new. I think this connected to Kangaok Meas Project."

"Could I make an international phone call?"

"Good to hear from you, Maier," Sundermann said. "We were getting a bit worried. Two days ago, Frau Müller-Overbeck paid us a visit. She was very upset when she told us that her son had disappeared. I assume you're on his trail?"

"Her son is in Phnom Penh. He is trying to sell his business. That's all I can say right now."

"She'll pay a fat bonus if you bring him back to Hamburg."

"Dead or alive?"

"It's that serious, Maier?"

"People who are close to this young man are dying. He is deeply involved in a crooked real estate deal with occult overtones."

"That sounds like Cambodia, Maier."

"And the police are looking for me at this point. No one knows why I am here, though, or who I really am, so there's no need to worry. I need another week to solve the case and get the young man out of here."

"Don't put your life on the line out there, Maier. You're one of the best. If it gets hairy, then slink across the border into Thailand and we'll send Altwasser as a replacement. I will pass your news on to Frau Müller-Overbeck. Don't bother with the report. It's all under control this end."

"It is already very hairy. I will be in touch."

"Alive, please, Maier. If he dies, there will be a lot of trouble and no bonus."

Sundermann wasn't a bad boss. Maier had all the freedom he wanted to do his work. He was expected to work independently and discreetly. And he was expected to produce results.

"I have one week left, then I need to take the young man back to Germany," Maier said.

"You go to Phnom Penh and find this man."

"He refuses to leave Cambodia without his girl."

"Girl?"

"Kaley, the girl in the story of the Kangaok Meas."

Raksmei slowly shook her head.

"Not possible. I think she belong to General Tep. No one can help. My NGO cannot help. She too old."

Kaley's desperate request to find her sister had sounded genuine.

But Maier was beginning to think that the mysterious beauty was either mad or did indeed work for the general.

"Somehow Kaley is at the centre of all this though. I saw her in the temple."

Raksmei shook her head.

"Not possible, Maier. Kaley is in Kep."

"She sat next to me on my bunk and asked me where her sister was."

"I think you dream, Maier."

"And the White Spider? The old German?"

Raksmei took her time to answer.

"A *barang* who speak Khmer and Vietnamese. Speak very well. A friend of General Tep. He here long time. He live and speak like Asian man. No like Khmer Rouge man. But maybe he here in Khmer Rouge time. I don't know."

"Are you scared of this man?"

"I don't know. He always friendly to me. But everyone scare the White Spider. Everyone shaking when he come into the room. He not like people speak bad with him, disagree with him. He never shout. Always speak very quiet."

"Do you think Tep is scared of the man?"

Raksmei shook her head.

"Tep is old friend. They like brother and brother. I never see Khmer and *barang* good friend like this. But all the girl in the temple very fear from him."

"How many girls live in the temple? Do you know?"

"Maybe twenty. They come and go in big black car. They all look and talk same same."

Raksmei stared into empty space, lost in thought.

'Did the Khmer Rouge not manipulate children to get them to brand their own parents as traitors or anti-communists?"

"I know, Maier. They do that before, long time before. Young Khmer people like me not know much about Khmer Rouge time. We not want to remember and the parents not want to talk about these times. But I know, the soldiers who come to Phnom Penh in 1975, many of the children, young boys and girls."

"Do you know who your parents are?"

Again, Raksmei took her time to answer.

"No. Somebody tell me my father is *barang*. My brother, he say same same. Papa is *barang*. But maybe mama is *barang*. I don't know. I think I'm born in 1980."

"At that time, there were not many *barang* in Cambodia?"

Raksmei nodded.

"No *barang*. The Khmer Rouge throw out all the foreigner or kill them. But maybe there is some exception."

Maier realised he was hurting the girl with his questions and changed the subject.

"How did you get into the temple?"

"I know General Tep long time, since I am little girl. He help me and my brother. We grow up with old lady in Kampot. I call her aunty, but she not aunty. She die eight years before. After that I live with my brother in her old house. Tep, he give money and food. I remember him long time."

"I hadn't imagined Tep to be a generous man."

Raksmei laughed, but Maier could sense that the girl was angry.

"One time he try to chat me up. When I start Hope-Child, he give some money. After my brother gone, I give up NGO and offer to Tep I can work for him. He accept."

"And why does he tell you about his dark secrets?"

"In Cambodia, people like this, man like this. They not think that a woman they know long time can make problem for them."

Maier laughed drily.

"That's not a Cambodia phenomenon. It's like that everywhere."

But Maier still had doubts. A large piece of the puzzle was still missing.

"I have to go to Kampot."

Raksmei brushed her short hair across her forehead and smiled. She pulled a small wad of dollar bills and his passport from her pocket.

"I find in your room in the temple. Tonight, I take you to Phnom Penh. From there you go alone."

After she'd left, Maier opened the bottle of whiskey.

29

FREEZER

Maier pressed ten dollars into the hand of the man on duty. The lucky recipient pulled a stretcher from the ice box and disappeared. The mortuary in Calmette, Phnom Penh's barely functioning government hospital, was silent, dirty and cold. The hospital was a place to die in. A last way-station. The doctors bargained hard for every dollar. The medical equipment, such as it was, did not work and cockroaches ruled the grey building with impunity, day and night. During the UNTAC days, the hospital had gained the moniker "Calamity". Patients and their families lay on mats in the corridors. In the yard, the sick slept under mosquito nets on the bare ground. Nurses demanded hard cash for every shot of morphine. No one who was admitted was expected to recover, but Calmette was the best hospital in the country. Maier hesitated for a second before he pulled the cloth back.

The journey from Battambang to the capital had been wonderful. He travelled through Raksmei's country, a country whose stories he'd absorbed for many years, and had written about in his articles. He felt alive. Raksmei had warned him that the roads and trains between Battambang and Phnom Penh would be watched. Maier preferred to remain dead for now. This had called for a journey on the Funny Train.

The French had brought the railroads to Cambodia, but since the end of the war, only one train a day commuted between the capital and Battambang and, after decades of neglect, the tracks were in pitiful condition. The three-hundred-kilometre journey took around twenty hours. Usually the train was so packed that every available bit of roof space of the gutted and rusty carriages was occupied.

Maier had suffered through the trip in the Nineties. In those days, the journey had been free for passengers prepared to ride in the first two carriages. This hadn't been a charitable gesture by the railway authorities. The front of the train had been regularly blown up by landmines that Khmer Rouge units had dropped onto the tracks during the night.

As the roads around Battambang were unnavigable during the rainy season and virtually useless the rest of the year, local people constructed their own trains – from old tractor axles, water pumps and a home-made wooden platform – the Funny Trains.

These unlikely and unsafe vehicles transported up to ten passengers at a time and moved down the tracks significantly faster than the regular train. When two Funny Trains met, one could be quickly dismantled, deposited next to the rails, until the tracks were free once more.

The young man who operated the unusual vehicle didn't say a word, which was fine with Maier. The detective spent the day in silence, a water bottle in his hand, dressed in a torn shirt and the pants of a Cambodian farmer, a krama around his head. He tried to process the events of the previous days. He didn't do too well. His thoughts turned back to his mission again and again. He knew Kaley's sister had been killed but he had no idea why. This German Khmer had not seen her sister for years, decades even. He had to see for himself. He thought of Hort. Right now, the necessity of knowing felt like a yoke around his neck.

Village children ran along with them, waving and screaming at the top of their lungs, then Maier was left to his thoughts again. The driver stopped in Pursat and bought a bag of fried frogs. All that was left of the French-era train station was a single wall, against which the male passengers of passing trains urinated. Just like Battambang.

Maier ate nothing.

The Funny Train reached Phnom Penh Airport after dark. Maier jumped off, paid the driver and took a taxi into town. Every bone in his body seemed to have moved during the bumpy ride. He rented a cheap room in a guest house at Boeung Kok where he'd left money and a couple of phones. Then he waited for dawn.

Maier had seen, photographed and examined many corpses. Death made the human body unfamiliar. Whatever had made the person who'd left the body behind was no longer there.

There's wasn't much left of her head. Whoever had swung the golf club had wanted not just to kill. Daniela Stricker's face was totally disfigured. The lower jaw was missing. The back of her skull had also been bashed in. As if the murderer had wanted to obscure the identity of his victim.

After a while, he forced himself to search her torn clothes.

Her hands and arms were punctured by small round holes, which had become infected. She had been tortured, most likely by the three little girls. He turned the woman around. He could see livor mortis on her hip and along her back. The discolouring of her skin suggested she'd been moved a few hours after her death. He took another close look at her head. No doubt about it, Ms Stricker had been tortured, shot, moved from the scene of the crime, and then been beaten with a golf club. The police had covered up the true murder.

Maier would have to travel to Kampot to talk to the man in jail there. He heard voices approaching the door of the mortuary. The detective pushed the dead woman back into her cooling slot.

The employee burst in and gesticulated wildly. Maier didn't lose a second, pressed another twenty dollars in the man's hand and followed him through the only door, up a set of stairs and into a small office. Seconds later he saw the boy, Tep's son, his baseball cap turned backwards as usual, pass the door, followed by three young girls. The girls wore jeans and T-shirts today. They wore their hair short and their expressions left no doubt that they'd come from the temple Maier had been held at. The boy carried a revolver.

The hospital employee behind Maier shook like a leaf and started mumbling to himself. The small room they were in had one window. Maier told the man to close the window behind him, and escaped into the bright morning sun.

Who'd known that he'd be at Calmette Hospital today? Was the appearance of the boy and his three angels a coincidence or had he been betrayed?

The detective tied his krama around his head and marched, his head bowed, through the entrance gate of the hospital and disappeared in the crowds on Monivong Boulevard.

30

ROLF

Rolf Müller-Overbeck's handsome looks had all but faded. Maier almost didn't recognise the young coffee heir, who lay sprawled in an armchair in the back of Restaurant Edelweiß. The young German didn't react as Maier threw himself onto a sofa opposite and pulled off his krama.

"Hello, Rolf."

"Hello, Maier. Thought you'd been fed to the fish in front of Koh Tonsay. Almost feel like I'm meeting an old friend. Time flies."

The young German dropped the filter of a burnt-out cigarette into an overflowing ashtray and stared blankly at Maier. His clothes were dirty. His shirt was ripped across his right shoulder. He looked almost as desperate as the legless beggars who moved up and down Sisowath Quay.

"You don't seem to be particularly happy about my survival."

Rolf shrugged.

"It's all over, Maier. My business has been stolen and my woman has disappeared, probably kidnapped, probably not to be saved. Your appearance doesn't make much different in the larger scheme of things."

"Perhaps I can help you."

The younger man laughed bitterly, "Help me? Everybody wants to help me. Help me to buy land, help me to start a business, help to cheat the locals, to pull them across the table and to rape them. I don't know why you turned up in Kep, but since you did, things have been going downhill. And now you want to help me?"

"What happened?"

Rolf pulled another cigarette from his crumpled shirt and began fiddling with a cheap plastic lighter.

"Why should I tell you anything? You make it all worse."

"After what you have just told me, it cannot get much worse. I can assure you that I have nothing to do with the problems in Kep."

Maier knew that he didn't sound convincing. Rolf said nothing.

A smiling waitress arrived with two cans of beer.

"Vodka orange," Maier ordered and handed one of the cans back to the young woman.

"Last week we found out that the land documents most of the *barang* in Kep hold are fakes. Tep cheated us and then offered generously to transfer our investments to the casino. Otherwise it would all be gone and we could leave Kep. And if that wasn't acceptable, the general's little killer girls would chase us away. As expected, my partner Pete signed the new contract with Tep. Without asking me."

"And where is Kaley?"

"Disappeared. Inspector Viengsra came and took her. After I refused to invest in the casino, I received a letter. I found it under my door at the dive shop office."

The younger German pulled a piece of paper from his breast pocket.

Maier scanned the page, which had been torn from a child's exercise book. If Rolf wanted to see Kaley again, it read in broken English, he'd have to pay fifty thousand US dollars. The deadline for the drop had already passed.

"I don't have fifty thousand US dollars. Anyway, this doesn't mean anything. Who knows what would have happened if I'd paid?

Maier looked into Rolf's eyes. The coffee heir was all the way down. The moment had come to push forward, directly into his heart.

"What happened to Kaley's daughter?"

Rolf brushed the long hair from his gaunt face and looked at Maier with a hostile expression.

"You're telling me that you have nothing to do with what's going on in Kep and you ask me so personal a question?"

"Why is the question personal?"

"Because I killed Poch, Kaley's daughter."

Maier went for a mild smile. He knew he'd driven Rolf into a corner, exactly where he wanted him. The pressure to confess, to communicate, to share his suffering had to be overwhelming.

"You don't look like someone who kills small children. What happened?"

"Yes, I'm a child killer and everyone in Kep knew that and knows that and they keep their mouths shut because Tep makes them. I'm the child killer of Kep. That's the secret of our little community."

Maier said nothing. He was waiting for more.

"I was driving our jeep between Kampot and Kep. Pete sat next to me. Suddenly, a black shadow ran across the road and it went bang."

The young German finished his beer and waved the can in the direction of the waitress.

"We stopped. A small girl was lying in front of the car in the middle of the road. She was alive for a few more minutes, but she didn't say anything. Just this little bundle of suffering and death. Her name was Poch. She was Kaley's daughter."

"She wore black pajamas?"

Rolf nodded distractedly.

"She had short hair?"

"Yes, just like her girlfriends who stood by the side of the road a few minutes later. I can remember exactly what they looked like. They were angry, angry as I've never seen anyone. They had murder in their eyes. I almost had the feeling that it wasn't directed at me, but at their little friend. As if Poch had been running away from them. But that didn't make sense. And then her mother came."

Rolf swallowed hard.

"You see, Maier, I can't leave Kaley behind. And now it looks like I can't take her with me. As I said, everything is broken. Just read the paper."

"Are you sure that Kaley would leave the country with you?"

Rolf wouldn't make eye contact with Maier. He stared silently across Sisowath Quay.

"I'm not sure."

The younger man was about to break into tears. Instead he lit his cigarette and hid behind a cloud of smoke. He pushed the current edition of the Cambodia Daily across the table at Maier and stabbed his finger angrily at the main feature.

"Kaley is only the tip of the iceberg that's drifting around Kep. She never asked me to take her with me. But who, in her situation, would say no?"

Maier understood that the young man had no clear idea of the priorities of his girlfriend. If she still had priorities.

"You remember what Vichat, the park ranger in Bokor, told us about his colleague who'd disappeared, and the girls he'd seen in the ruins?"

31

ACTIVIST FOUND DEAD AT HOME

Preah Sim, well-known human rights activist and director of the Cambodian Human Rights Society, was found yesterday in his room on Street 278. Sim was 28 years old. Neighbours confirmed to a correspondent from the Cambodian Daily that three young women had visited the activist in the afternoon.
The homicide department of the Phnom Penh police force initially insisted on suicide, but a demonstration by hundreds of workers of the garment industry in front of the Rue Pasteur police station and pressure from the opposition Sam Rainsy Party forced the authorities to reconsider the case. Prime Minister Hun Sen, at a CPP party function in Stung Treng, regretted the death and promised a swift resolution to the case.

"IF YOU HAVE money you can do anything here. It goes all the way to the top. You can cover up murder and accidents as if they'd never happened. But someone somewhere always gets caught up in this. Do you understand what's happening here? And why you can't help me?"

Maier read the article again.

"You have money in Germany. Ask your family. Your mother would send you the money straight away."

Rolf rose angrily, "What do you know about my mother, about my life, Maier?"

"I am a private detective from Hamburg. Your mother hired me–"

"To spy on my life, because she thinks I can't do it alone. Or because she can't bring herself to sell the family business to a stranger. Unbelievable. You're a bastard, Maier."

The younger German had gone pale with anger. He was on a roll, his voice heavy with sarcasm and malice

"So, Detective Maier already knows that a German woman has been killed near Bokor, and that he's one of the suspects. All your own fault, Maier. Or my mother's, who won't let go of her son."

"But you won't manage to get out of here by yourself. I can help you to find Kaley."

Rolf laughed.

"You're wanted for the murder of a German tourist and now you want to save my girlfriend. Maier, don't cross my path again."

The young man threw a few bills on the table and disappeared in the throng on Sisowath Quay. Rolf was well informed. But not well enough to know who the dead German tourist was. Maier stayed behind, alone, enveloped in dark thoughts.

32

CAMBODIA DAILY

THE YOUNG JOURNALIST watched Maier nervously across a table of the Boat Noodle Restaurant. A few of the surrounding tables were occupied by employees – Khmer and *barang* – of the NGOs who had their offices in the adjacent buildings.

He could see that the young man wasn't comfortable, though he'd chosen the restaurant. Maier was in a hurry and journalists were badly paid in Cambodia. The detective pushed a hundred-dollar bill across the table at Sorthea Sam. The young writer stared at the money and asked in French, "What do you expect for this money? That's more than I earn in a month. I don't think that I have information that is worth one hundred dollar to you."

Maier guessed that the man was very frightened. Otherwise he would have taken the money straight away.

"I have a few questions in relation to the article on the death of the human rights activist. The story you wrote."

"A crazy, dangerous story that will never be resolved," the journalist answered in a shaky voice, and finally, without looking at Maier, slipped the money in his breast pocket.

"Who were the three girls who visited the victim on the day of the murder? Why were the children even mentioned?"

Sorthea Sam looked across his shoulder.

"You say you are a detective from Germany? Not a journalist?"

"No."

"And you are here to watch a German who might be involved in this?"

Maier ordered a coffee and nodded. The young Khmer ordered tea and a glass of water. Sorthea Sam lit a red Ara and sat quite still, smoking in silence. Finally, the young man began to talk.

"Eyewitness accounts. Preah Sim lived in an apartment block not far from the palace. We spoke to the neighbours. The police didn't. Four families in the same building confirmed that they saw the three girls arrive and go into Preah Sim's room. They came out shortly afterwards, moments before Preah Sim emerged, bleeding heavily. A black SUV, tinted windows, no plates, dropped the kids off and collected them again. The police published a photograph of a young man who allegedly stabbed Preah Sim. The suspect is in prison and the case is closed."

"And the girls?"

The young journalist mulled over his answer.

"I only mentioned the girls because I had a strange visitor a few weeks ago. A young man came to see me. He was half Khmer and half *barang*. His name was Sambat and he was working for an NGO in Kampot that was looking after orphaned children. I had heard of Sambat before he visited me, from a colleague with whom he had followed and exposed a Swiss pedophile. Otherwise I would never have believed the story he told me."

Maier stirred his coffee and tried to look as unconcerned as possible.

"Sambat told me that he had seen these girls do military training at Bokor. I thought, this guy is mad, but Sambat was a serious man. I snooped around a bit after that and found out that a former Khmer Rouge general is trying to buy the casino. I even sent someone to Bokor, but there was no trace of the girls. My informant only met a drunken Russian. But then one of the park rangers told him about the girls. The story is so bizarre that I checked back with a few contacts I have in government here. When I mentioned the name of this general a couple of times, I was told to let the matter drop. At the same time, I found out that the son of this general had shot some nouveau riche kid in the Heart of Darkness bar in front of a hundred witnesses. That killing was suppressed as well."

The Khmer laughed bitterly.

"I never wrote the story. I never heard from Sambat again, except for the news that he'd disappeared. When Preah Sim was killed and the neighbours talked about the girls, I remembered Sambat. Do you know what happened to him?

"He is dead."

Sorthea Sam looked at Maier in disbelief.

"Dead?"

"He was killed in Kep two weeks ago. The corpse was fed to the sharks, so that they could declare him missing. No body, no murder."

The journalist looked scared.

"How do you know?"

"I was there."

"Where?"

"At the crime scene. I was scuba-diving off the Kep coast and watched how sharks ripped the young man apart. He'd been sunk alive, with stones around his feet."

The Khmer nervously shrugged his shoulders and lit a cigarette.

"Another reason not to follow this story any further. That could become very unhealthy for me. And for you too."

Maier sank back into his chair and relaxed. He also felt like a cigarette but he repressed the urge. He'd hated himself as a smoker too much to start smoking again.

"So, what is your theory? Is there anything in it?"

"My theory is absurd, monsieur."

"I would like to hear it any way."

"Money. It's all about money. Everything in Cambodia is about money. There's never enough and the Cambodian government is doing everything it can to shovel international aid into its own pockets, to sell the land to foreign investors and deny our people any opportunity to live a decent life. There are more than enough orphaned girls in Cambodia. It's a brilliant idea. If I had not stumbled across it, I would not have connected Sambat with Preah Sim. But like this…"

Maier smiled softly. He was on the right track.

"Will you pick up the murders again now, with what I have told you?"

The young Khmer shook his head.

"No body, no story. I believe you, but I assume I can't quote you.

And the case of Preah Sim is still hot and it is unlikely that they will let the young man who is sitting for it go. He has a good alibi, but his family was forced to stand as witness against him. The man was betrayed by his own father. What does that take? You can imagine what kind of pressure my newspaper will be under if I continue my investigations."

Maier finished his coffee and waited. He had the feeling that the journalist had something more for him.

"I have a small consolation for you – there was another murder three months ago and three girls were seen near the scene of the crime. That one had nothing to do with politics. The wife of a minister had her husband's second wife disfigured with acid. The girl died of shock in hospital. A young man was arrested and sentenced shortly after. They never touched the wife of the minister. I reported the case and interviewed a few of the witnesses. One mentioned the girls. It didn't mean anything at the time. Now we are talking about at least four dead."

Maier thanked the writer and thought of the fifth victim – Daniela Stricker, Kaley's sister.

33

KAMPOT

AN HOUR LATER, Maier raced a Kawasaki dirt bike through the suburbs of the capital, on his way to Kampot. The road south had improved since the UNTAC days, but the traffic was still life-threatening. He needed to reach Daniela's alleged killer alive, but he knew that time was running short.

Cambodia knew no driving licenses, nor was there a minimum age for drivers, and most private vehicles had no number plates. No one was insured. Every few kilometres, Maier passed an accident. Every time, a small crowd gathered and people stood staring at a mangled motorbike or its dead or dying driver. No one tried to help. No one called an ambulance. Ambulances and doctors were for the rich, who, in the event of an emergency, would have themselves taken to Phnom Penh Airport and medivacced to Bangkok. If there was enough time. Less fortunate members of the population died, in the event of a serious accident, right by the roadside. Just like today. Just like every day. Despite the traffic, Maier reached the small river town before sundown and drove directly to the prison.

Kampot was a sleepy community, held together by a few blocks of French colonial and Chinese buildings from the early twentieth century, which spread around a large Art Deco-style market hall. Many of the old buildings were in need of restoration. Especially the old jail.

The prison was in the centre of town, on the banks of a stagnant, dirty pond. Coconut palm trees and high grasses grew around the compound. The prison wall was topped with rusty barbed wire that had once been electrified, decorated by torn pieces of prison clothing. An old watchtower leaned away from the wall across the street as if trying to escape its responsibility.

Maier parked his bike in front of a café on the other side of the pond and walked through the open prison gate. A group of soldiers sat around a rickety plastic table and played cards. They didn't notice him pass.

The main building looked like a French small-town apartment block from the Fifties – four stories, rectangular and drab, thought up by bureaucrats. The two other buildings that served as accommodation for the guards had survived from the colonial era and were about to collapse.

Maier walked through the main entrance into the cool semi-darkness of the almost empty reception hall. A naked bulb flickered uncertainly in the ceiling. A soldier sat in a dirty green shirt and faded shorts at an empty table and played with his mobile phone. The building was deadly quiet. There couldn't be many inmates.

"Soksabai."

The guard raised his eyes, an expression of well-worn boredom on his blank face.

Maier offered his hand and looked the man directly in the eyes, smiling broadly. The guard put his phone down carefully and accepted the handshake and the enclosed ten dollars with a gentle, impenetrable smile.

As in any proper prison, a large keyring hung from a rusty nail on the wall behind the desk. The guard slipped the money into his pocket, grabbed the keys and waved for Maier to follow. He wore no shoes and Maier followed the patter of his bare feet along a pitch-dark corridor. The cells on the ground floor were all empty. The guard stopped and felt along the wall for a switch. In the light of a solitary bulb, Maier followed him up a naked stairway to the first floor. The layout was the same. Maier followed the soldier along a corridor until they reached the third cell. The guard switched the cell light on and unlocked the heavy steel door.

An unimpressive man in his forties sat, obviously confused, on the edge of a bunk.

Maier nodded to the man and turned to the guard, but the soldier had already disappeared. He'd left the door open.

The man didn't move and stared into empty space, like a deer that had been caught in a car's headlights. He was unshaven and had black rings under his eyes. He didn't look dangerous. Another victim.

The damp cell had no windows. The bunk was the only piece of furniture. The half-finished plate of rice and *prahok* on the floor had been taken over by cockroaches. The room stank, as it does when misery gains the upper hand. The man must have sat in darkness all day.

"Good afternoon, my name is Ernst. I am a representative of the International Red Cross. I have been sent to see how you are being treated."

The man looked at him in disbelief.

"What time is it?"

"Two o'clock in the afternoon," Maier lied. "I am here to ask you how you are being treated. Do you understand my question?"

"Is this a joke?"

Maier shook his head with a serious expression in his eyes and showed the man an ID card of the Red Cross.

"Your name is Renfield? Wayne Renfield?"

The prisoner was still watching him doubtfully. Maier felt his fear. This man was scared of being killed. He nodded carefully.

"Are you the only prisoner here?"

The man shook.

"I think so. There was an old man on this floor a while back, but he died. Every now and then they put some motorcycle thieves in here, so they don't get lynched by irate villagers."

"How long have you been here?"

Renfield suddenly fell to his knees and looked up at Maier.

"Can you get me out of here? I'm sitting here waiting for someone to come and kill me. I'm innocent. It couldn't have been me. I was already sitting here before the woman got murdered. I've never killed anyone. I was only here for the kids. They gave me one year…"

Maier didn't care much for the men who came to Cambodia to abuse children. It brought out his vigilante side. He tried to push evil thoughts aside. But not altogether. The children who'd tortured him in the temple cell had been on his mind all day.

"I can help you, Mr. Renfield. But you have to trust me. You have to tell me why you are here. I am sure this is a local misunderstanding, and that we can resolve it, if you did not commit the murder of which you are accused."

Maier sat down on the bunk next to the man and offered him his hand. The handshake of the Canadian was coated in fear.

"What was your name again?"

"Ernst, Robert Ernst. The Red Cross in Phnom Penh sent me, after we read an article about you in the Phnom Penh Post."

Renfield was skinny and tall and had a chin like Kirk Douglas. His cheeks were grey and his white fingers shook nervously. He had chewed his nails down to the tips of his fingers. He wore torn, stinking socks, baggy and stained khaki pants and a stone-washed denim shirt. He wiped his hand continuously through his greasy hair that dropped across his shoulders. Not a pretty picture.

But Maier wasn't here to hand out Christmas presents. So, they would come to kill this man.

"You told me you were already incarcerated here before the murder?"

"That's what I tried to explain to the cops in Phnom Penh. This English guy with bright red hair, who said his name was Pete, came to see me a week ago and told me I was free to go. He told me Tep had bailed me out and that I owed him a favour. No problem, I thought. Either I fuck off out of the country right away or I pay my debts. The English guy left the keys to a motorbike and disappeared. He left the cell door open; it was unbelievable. I simply walked out. I got on the bike and drove off towards Kep to go and thank Tep. No one tried to stop me."

Maier looked into the eyes of the prisoner and tried to smile with a neutral, officious expression.

"And what happened next?"

The Canadian jerked around. "You don't believe me either, do you? This is just another trap. You'll tell me I'm free to go and then I get shot in the back on the way out."

With a calming gesture, Maier tried to wave the man's paranoia away.

"I am not in a position to free you, Mr. Renfield. I merely want a statement from you so that we can help you from Phnom Penh. Now that I have your statement, I am sure you will be released soon," Maier laughed politely, "Of course, I cannot just take you with me."

"I understand, I understand," the prisoner mumbled eagerly and tried to relax.

"So, you never saw the woman you allegedly murdered?"

"Never saw her. Never met her. Have no idea who she might be."

Renfield swallowed. Perhaps he realised that the truth wasn't doing him any favours.

"You understand? You must understand. I didn't knock her off. I was right here in jail and after the English guy had given me the bike keys I left. That sounds mad, but that's how it was. And the soldiers who guard this dump said nothing to their colleagues; otherwise they would have lost face."

There was nothing more to find out.

"Mr. Ernst, how does it look? Will I ever see the prairies of Alberta again? Will I get out of here alive, or am I sitting in a trap, waiting to be sacrificed for something I didn't do?"

Maier looked at the man. The truth was secondary today. It was time to go.

"Mr. Renfield, I will tell your embassy and the police in Phnom Penh that I am of the opinion that you are not the killer of Mrs. Stricker. The Red Cross has no sympathy for you in regards to your actual crimes, the abuse of children, and we will pass this on to the Cambodian authorities. I assume you will be able to serve the rest of your sentence in Phnom Penh, while the murder of the woman is likely to be resolved later this week. Have a nice day."

Maier got up and shook the Canadian's hand once more. Still moist and full of dread. Renfield knew how quick the end could come in Cambodia. That's why he'd told the truth. This pedophile had not killed nor disfigured Daniela Stricker.

Maier left the man in his cell and felt his way back to the stairway.

Downstairs, the guard had returned his attention to his mobile phone. He nodded to Maier and smiled gently. The detective escaped into the humid afternoon.

34

THE LAST FILLING STATION

MAIER SPENT the night in a small guest house in Kampot. The next day he stayed in his room, had his food delivered to his door, slept and dreamt empty dreams.

When it got dark, he got on the bike and drove to Kep.

"I need a gun. It cannot be difficult to buy a gun in Cambodia, surely?"

Maier had waited until just after midnight before he'd dropped into the Last Filling Station. Les had shown no surprise as the detective had entered his bar.

"The red snoop is back," was all he'd said.

The old American nodded at the Vietnamese girl and seconds later a .22 caliber revolver and a box of cartridges lay on the bar counter in front of Maier.

"This little thing is not registered, buddy. And it's small, so you won't go through the wall behind you when you pull the trigger. I don't want to see it again. Get rid of it when you're done. You owe me a hundred and fifty US dollars."

Maier loaded the weapon.

"Turn up the music for a minute, Les."

The detective stepped outside and walked down to the beach. A loud rock song blasted from the bar and shattered the humid silence. *I am the world's forgotten boy, the one who searches and destroys.*

Maier stepped up to a palm tree, kept five metres distance and pulled the trigger. The bullet burst the tree bark. He waited until the song had finished.

"You don't trust anybody?"

"Kaley's sister was not killed by the Canadian who is sitting in jail in Kampot. At the time of the murder, that man was already in a cell. Pete helped him get out and he was picked up again immediately. The woman was tortured and shot in Bokor. The work with the golf club was meant to hide this."

The American nervously brushed his hand across a tattooed arm as if trying to cure an itch. The old war veteran looked as if he was going to despair. Maier was sure he could trust this man. Les called for the Vietnamese girl. The silent woman appeared from the kitchen, carrying two more guns. Les spoke a few words of Vietnamese to her and gave her a keyring. The girl gesticulated angrily. But the American shook his head gently and took the weapons from her hands.

Maier realised only now that Raksmei had been sitting at one of the darkened tables at the back of the bar since he'd arrived.

"I wait for you long time, Maier."

She looked incredible in a pair of old and very tight jeans and a pink, buttoned-up shirt. Her blue eyes were lined with black kohl. Her short frizzy hair stood in all directions and had been dyed a soft red. She looked ready for a wild Saturday night in Phnom Penh, but it was Wednesday and she sat in the only bar in Kep.

"The whole world wants a piece of Maier. Tep's people were waiting for me in Phnom Penh."

Maier had planned to ask Les whether the old soldier could take him to Bokor without being noticed, but it would have to wait.

"What you do with the gun, Maier? Shoot the ghost?"

Maier laughed, "I would not dare pay a second visit to Tep's without a gun."

"You go back island?"

"Yes, tomorrow morning. Alone."

Raksmei nodded seriously.

"No problem, Maier. I not come with you. If Tep catch me, I am dead. I not think he like that I help you run away."

Maier nodded thankfully.

Raksmei finished a glass of water and stood up.

"You take me to Kampot? You not stay in Kep tonight? Pete is at the dive shop and son of Tep come here today looking for us. And he ask for you in Kampot."

The American nodded in agreement.

"Yeah, the English guy dropped by with a lawyer from Phnom Penh and showed me copies of my land ownership papers. He told me that all the papers I had were fake. He's been doing the rounds for days, with all the *barang* who bought land in Kep. Usually the same story. Either we invest the money in the casino and pay rent for the properties we bought or we can get out. The Scandinavians already left. A few of the French have too. Maupai is still here. He came in yesterday, drunk, and told me that the casino would be saved through the cooperation of the local expatriate community. If you believe that, he will rule Bokor like the Sun King one day and Indochina will make a comeback. He's basically gone insane since the death of his wife."

"What happened to Kaley?"

"Inspector Viengsra charged her with prostitution and took her away. Shortly after, Tep's son chased Rolf out of Kep. As far as I know, our young German hero is in Phnom Penh."

Les laughed without joy.

"That was a few days ago. Since then no one's seen Kaley in Kep. But Tep's still here. Sometimes he's over at his island, sometimes up at the brothel and sometimes at his beach resort."

Maier gave the American his best smile and said goodbye.

"I will be in touch."

"If you need anything else, buddy, let me know." He paused, then added, "You are alright, Maier, aren't you?"

"I am alright. Please organise me a boat that I can take to the island tomorrow."

Two minutes later, Maier raced without lights along the coast road to Kampot, his revolver in a pocket of his vest. Raksmei sat behind him, her arms slung around his waist, her right hand on his weapon.

Maier had made all his decisions in the hospital in Phnom Penh.

"If you ever look into her eyes properly, you'll never share a bed with me again."

When he stopped at the offices of Hope-Child, the girl behind him had fallen asleep. He switched off his engine and shook her awake.

"Maier, come in, your hotel might no longer be safe."

"It is almost certainly safe. I checked in under a false name."

In the light of a pale half moon, Raksmei stepped towards him and threw her arms around the detective. Maier looked at her eyes. What a terrible and beautiful place this country was. He looked past her, tried to feel Carissa in the darkness of the tropical night, but she wasn't there.

Raksmei climbed back on his bike and they drove to his guest house.

Carissa's words followed him like a warning.

"Don't get happy yet, old man. First we have to solve the case."

He finally took Raksmei where he could see her and opened his eyes for a second time, wide enough to let her look in. She stared back, from a place Maier could only guess at. Her skin was like the surface of a placid ocean, from a world in which placid oceans existed. When he slid his hand down her back, from her shoulders to the bottom of her spine, she shuddered slightly. She showed no fear, nor obvious joy, but enough silent lust to pull him down into the water.

They lay next to each other in his room, silent and sweating.

Hours later, after her breathing had calmed, he stood next to her, revolver in hand and stared down at the beautiful sleeping shape of the girl. Her face had a very serious expression. So familiar.

It was time to go.

Maier got dressed quietly, reloaded the gun, and collected Raksmei's clothes. No one would follow him this time. As he stood outside the door in the dark corridor he waited and typed a message into his mobile phone. The reception along the coast was not great and Maier hoped that his brief instructions made it to Kep.

He locked the room and threw Raksmei's clothes behind the reception.

It had started to rain.

Maier pushed his motorbike to the old bridge, the only one which led across Prek Kampong Bay, before he started the engine and slowly drove towards Bokor. When he reached the edge of the jungle, he ditched the bike and started walking. He never saw nor heard the three youthful black shadows peeling out of the fog behind him and closing in.

35

HELL IS EASY

MAIER FELT great and assumed his mental well-being to be the result of the drug he had been given. Everything in his head repeated itself over and over, at unfathomable speeds. He knew that he'd been lying on his bunk for ten thousand years. He could feel himself lying there ten minutes ago. Or perhaps his euphoria could have something to do with the fact that he was still alive. Wherever he was now, his life couldn't be worth much to anyone but himself.

Outside, somewhere unimaginably far away, he could hear birdsong, perhaps a few insects. No people, no engine noises. Familiar, but he couldn't put his finger on it.

After some time, he managed to move his head.

The White Spider sat in front of him. He was alone. The man was so old, a single kick would end it all. But Maier couldn't even move his little toe. He couldn't even see far enough along his body to check whether he still had his toes.

"I assume that you feel reality has become more flexible. In a few days you'll be able to find your way around the inside of your head again. You will then be able to sort your visions from your life."

Maier watched the man in silence. He didn't want to try to speak yet.

"You're in a monastery near Bokor. You've been with us for a week, and you've been doing well. Some other guests would have gone insane by now, or expired. But we haven't amputated anything yet. No one knows that you're here and no one's out there looking for you. You've been reported missing to the authorities. People go missing in Cambodia all the time. And you're wanted in connection with the death of a German tourist, I have heard. The police found a gun with your prints on it that has been counter-checked with the German authorities."

Maier tried to focus on the man's wristwatch. There were walls in his head and they kept moving about, which made it impossible to form judgments. He needed to make judgments on what the man had just told him. But he couldn't.

"What do you want with me?"

Maier was surprised, the question had simply slipped out of him.

The old man heard him and leant forward.

"I like precise answers, it comes with my background. You, on the other hand, ask precise questions. I'm not used to that."

He seemed to be searching for words.

"I've not been asked anything for a very long time."

"What's your background?" Maier ventured, light-headed.

"My background is in vermin removal. I realised as young man that this was my calling and I never got away from it again. I've had different experiences in life and have done different jobs, but I always felt most comfortable in my first job. I'm sure you understand. Through the vagaries and coincidences of life, I've become a mirror of the twentieth century. A mirror for the blind. Look closely, without blinking. Concentrate."

Maier's head was clear now. He could see the man in front of him, but he had not caught up with himself yet. Some large chunk of his life, his personality, appeared like a dream which, following his return to consciousness, threatened to disappear down a black hole. That might've had its good sides, but he couldn't put his finger on anything positive. He wasn't even sure whether he was still truly Maier, whether he'd ever been truly Maier, or whether he might be Maier again at some point in the future. He'd lost his desire to make judgments. He was happy.

"I will tell you my story very slowly, Maier. I am a Catholic. I believe in hell. I'm familiar with it. My hell can only be days away. That's how it is when you grow old. After a long and productive life, one can't help becoming a little cynical. You used to be a journalist, now you're a detective. You grew up in a totalitarian country, but now you live in apparent freedom. You've seen a lot during your travels. That's why you can and will write down my story. That's why you're here now. That's why you're breathing."

The White Spider nodded at him, a celebratory expression in his pale blue eyes.

"Yes, I am appointing you as my biographer. I will pay you for your services, every day. With your life. Your work will enable you to continue living. You'll be my Scheherazade. I'll show you things only a few people have seen. And if you manage to bring my story to paper, you'll earn the right to live, until our next session."

Maier tried to nod, but his head wouldn't move.

"And if you do a good job, you'll soon understand again who you are and how to read the truth."

Maier inhaled, exhaled, tried not to shit himself with fear. Succeeded.

"But you must choose, Maier, between life and death. And if you choose life, it'll be my life. My story."

The old man got up and staggered towards Maier. A young, beautiful woman with short frizzy hair and inscrutable blue almond-shaped eyes had appeared next to him. A European? Maier couldn't be sure.

He had seen her somewhere before. Maier thought about her so hard that his head almost exploded, but he couldn't recall the name of the woman or where he might have met her. Her name had disappeared into the black hole.

She wore black pajamas and stood in bare feet. She held two syringes in her hands. The left syringe was filled with blue liquid. The right one was clear. She didn't smile and looked right through him.

"You're my biographer, Maier, and I will make you the witness of my life's work. What do you think, helping an old friend, a countryman, far away from home, to take leave of the world? What do you think of your assignment? Isn't my offer irresistible?"

The White Spider bent over Maier and watched him attentively. Maier knew that the most important moment in his life lay in his own green eyes right now. In his eyes, which he'd used all his life to seduce women and to pull the truth from people. Perhaps his life had all been one long preparation for this moment. For a few seconds, he opened his eyes to let the old man look in.

The White Spider nodded sympathetically and the girl put the syringe with the clear liquid aside. Seconds later he felt the needle in his arm and fell into the sky.

"Don't worry. Everything is simple and straightforward in hell. You don't need a translator and there are no questions to ask. Just make sure you don't blink, Maier."

36

THE TWENTIETH CENTURY

MAIER WOKE IN THE MORNING, wheelchair-bound. He sat on a wide stone platform, just above a towering cliff from which the coastline was visible. He heard voices somewhere, but he couldn't see anyone. He breathed in and out deeply. It seemed the best way to find out whether he was still hallucinating or whether he had returned to some reality.

Shit, he'd been caught a second time.

The forest had crept across the stones for centuries and had spread so much that one had to step right up to the temple wall to get an idea of the building's dimensions.

Maier could move his arms and turned the wheelchair around. Lizards and squirrels chased along the hot stones and invisible birds sang from the trees. It didn't look like hell. But Maier had never been sure whether he'd recognise hell if he happened to end up in it. He remembered the old German's offer. How long had he been here? Suddenly, the mental floodgates broke, and a thousand questions rushed like an avalanche through Maier's head. What had happened? How much of what he took for reality was hallucination? He needed answers.

He remembered the girl who had given him the injection. Then it was all gone again and he sat in a wheelchair and admired the view and the jungle.

Maier heard voices behind him and turned his wheelchair once more.

"Ah, good morning, Maier."

The White Spider spoke English today, out of respect for his companion – a tiny Japanese man who looked like a butterfly collector. The man was in his mid-fifties and wore a green saggy cotton hat, short khaki jeans and a shirt with a thousand pockets. He wore three cameras around his neck. Only the large net and the jar full of chloroform were missing.

A girl, dressed in black, followed the man, carrying a heavy camera tripod.

The Japanese nodded amiably at Maier.

"Are you also a guest of the Khmer Rouge? Everyone always says how unpredictable and dangerous these people are, but this is my second trip."

Maier must have had questions written on his face, because the little man continued.

"I'm here to stock up on my collection of objects from the Angkor period. And the White Spider is a reliable supplier."

Maier wasn't surprised. He knew that smugglers, bandits and former Khmer Rouge soldiers had long sold the finest carvings and statues to private collectors from around the world. The Khmer Rouge had advanced from murderers to co-conspirators and suppliers of the bourgeoisie.

The Japanese man lit a red Ara and theatrically blew smoke through his nostrils.

"We have a saying in Japan, 'Kiken nashi niha, yorokobi mo nai'. It means as much as 'Without danger, there is no happiness'."

Maier was not sure whether he really agreed with anything the art collector said. The pleasure of being close to the White Spider was a dubious one and didn't stand in any kind of relation to the risk one took. But the Japanese hadn't understood that yet.

The White Spider smiled at Maier and said, "Your assignment starts today, Maier. My assistants will provide you with a laptop. You should start taking notes immediately. The quality of your documentation will dictate the quality of your life."

The Japanese visitor had walked along the platform to the edge of the cliff and began to take pictures. Every so often he turned and snapped the small group around Maier.

"You see, Maier, in our business, discretion is everything. This man is not discreet. He's a good customer, but this time he brought cash. And as you can see, he's clearly a security risk. What do you think, Maier?"

"Why don't you take his camera? You are the boss around here."

"That's right," the old German laughed and waved for the collector's assistant. The girl waited until the art collector looked at the world through his view finder, before she smashed the tripod into the back of his head. The Japanese man dropped to the ground like a sack of flour. Two more girls, dressed identically, emerged from the temple, took the man's cameras and threw them into the forest below. The collector could no longer move and cried softly. The three girls dragged him away like roadkill.

"It's essential to kill with enthusiasm. I learned that in the Balkans a long time ago. If you don't have enthusiasm for your line of work, then change job. Killing's not an occupation for dispassionate people."

He added, with an almost cheeky gleam in his pale eyes, "Neither is living."

The girl who'd given Maier the last injection put a laptop computer onto his lap and pushed his wheelchair after the White Spider.

"I'm Raksmei, Maier. You can't remember me but you will. I have given you drugs. I will help you," she whispered behind him. Maier didn't react. He suspected that this girl was the sister of Sambat, the boy who'd been executed in Kep. But he didn't trust his judgement. When had he last seen her? How had she managed to get inside?

A second girl helped lift Maier over the threshold of the temple.

The Japanese lay on a rusty hospital stretcher in an almost dark, damp hall. A few candles, stuck to the base of a pillar on which a statue of Buddha or Ganesh might have once stood, threw an eerie, unpredictable light into the room. Maier could smell blood and garbage.

"We prepare our girls for all eventualities. Everyone has to be ready for combat at any time. Ready without hesitation, without thinking, without having to look into the eyes of their commander, without sentimentality, they will be able to successfully go through with the job at hand, so to speak. The readiness to overcome incredible odds and challenges is an old Khmer Rouge tradition, especially when it comes to health care. And our art collector will make the perfect cadaver to bring our students closer to becoming accomplished surgeons."

The White Spider snapped his fingers and the girls tied the Japanese to the stretcher. Raksmei had a syringe ready, but the old man shook his head.

"Unfortunately, we cannot afford to waste medication indiscriminately. We have to do without during training."

The old German nodded to the youngest girl, who rolled a small steel table to the stretcher. The Japanese had woken up and, with a confused expression, looked around the dark hall. When the girl approached him, he screamed so loud that Maier thought his head might burst. Without hesitation, the girl grabbed a bone saw off the steel table and began to amputate the art collector's right leg. Screaming still, the Japanese shat himself and passed out. Urine and blood mixed below the stretcher.

In an instant Maier understood where he was, what he was and what would be expected of him.

"Yes, Maier, everything is becoming clear now. Now you're ready to accompany me on my last journey. Now you're my biographer."

37

THE BIOGRAPHER

MAIER WAS EMPTY AND TIRED. The continuous hallucinations had worn him down. The murder he'd witnessed had numbed him. He'd written the first entry in his biography.

The White Spider oversees two girls attempting to amputate a man's leg in a temple hall near Bokor Palace. There are no qualified medical personnel present. In order to simulate war-like conditions, no medication is administered to the patient during the operation. The patient, a Japanese national, dies during the procedure, presumably from blood loss and shock.

It was hard to write more than a few lines about the butchering in the temple hall. It was hard to write anything.

Now he sat, still in a wheelchair, in the shadow of the old casino and watched twenty girls, still in their teens, as they were being drilled in close combat by Tep and his son. He remembered nothing of the journey from the temple to the hill station.

It was agreeably cool on the plateau and the pale morning sun barely managed to pierce the clouds of fog which hung between the crumbling buildings of the French hill station. The training was as brutal as the operation had been on the previous day, and Maier was sure that some the girls would not survive their apprenticeship. Again, and again, Tep, dressed in a tracksuit like a football coach, made the girls attack each other with bamboo sticks, while his son pulled one or another girl out of the mêlée and let her smoke yaba on the casino steps. The cheap amphetamine had its desired effect. After three or four pills, the girls were so highly motivated that they picked up a machete without hesitation.

Inspector Viengsra sat on the balustrade surrounding the property. He smoked one Ara after another and watched the drama. The policeman wasn't in any condition to participate in physical training.

The White Spider appeared next to Maier and looked down at him, smiling broadly. The old German wore a freshly-pressed, spotless white shirt, and a large black floppy hat, under which his pale blue eyes roamed like fog lights.

"I see you are taking notes. That's great. Everything should be noted, even our mistakes. No one's perfect."

Maier wasn't sure whether the old man referred to the death of the Japanese man or the training of the girls. If he continued writing for his captor he'd be as guilty of the crimes he documented as the actual killers. Every sentence he put to paper was part report, part confession. That of the White Spider, as well as his own. The moment had come to make a fundamental decision. As if the White Spider had read Maier's thoughts, the old man turned and snapped his fingers.

Raksmei pushed a second wheelchair next to Maier.

"Oh, no."

Carissa sat next to him and smiled unhappily. Her face was as white as her hair. In the pale morning light, she looked so very beautiful and broken. He looked at her in silence.

"You were right, Maier, I shouldn't have followed you. You don't bring any luck to girls. But it's good to see you."

"I'm not exactly having the time of my life. For now, think yourself lucky you've still got legs. I begged you, told you this was one investigation you should have left your fingers off."

The White Spider stepped between the two.

"In order to motivate you properly, I have invited your girlfriend to join us for a while. Unfortunately, Ms Stevenson seems to have similar problems with her legs as you did and cannot walk at present. Whether we will operate on the lady in the next few days depends on your literary abilities. You understand me, Maier?"

Maier nodded numbly and began to write.

Extreme hand-to-hand combat. The apprentices are fighting with sticks and machetes in front of the Bokor casino. Amphetamines are used deliberately and excessively to motivate the fighters. The results are remarkable. At least one of the girl fighters is unable to continue and tries to cut her throat with her own knife.

A girl had brought a chair and the old German sat down next to Maier.

"What is your name?"

The White Spider didn't answer for some time. Finally, he cleared his throat and looked at the detective with something akin to fatherly pride.

"I keep forgetting that you're my biographer. Your detective career is over. I have to get used to that. Keep writing, keep writing."

Maier managed to smile at the man with forced benevolence.

"My name is Lorenz, Hilmar Lorenz. I was probably born in Düsseldorf in 1925. I grew up in an orphanage. I joined the Deutsches Jungvolk when I was ten. At thirteen I was in the Hitlerjugend, and at seventeen, the SS," the old man smiled with distant pride.

In 1943, I worked in Croatia, Bosnia and Herzegovina. That's where I found my calling. I worked as a point man between the SS and the Ustashe. I worked in the camps. Tens of thousands, Maier, tens of thousands of people marched past me to their deaths. I was part of a gigantic machine. When we began to take heavy casualties on the Eastern front, I knew that the German dream had failed. A year later, in September 1944, Tito urged some Croatian and Bosnian troops to change sides and join the Partisans. I still remember that morning clearly. I acted immediately. Out of necessity and conviction, I might add. I like to be on the winning side. As I had a lot of intelligence information, the Partisans didn't kill me. In order to prove my worthiness, I was ordered to lead the communists, disguised in Ustashe uniforms, into my own Ustashe camp. I became a Trojan Horse. The Partisans and I killed everyone. We killed my friends and colleagues, fellow fighters, even the prisoners. Everyone. That's what saved me. I was accepted, I was on Tito's side. I performed an ideological U-turn. Ideology is secondary. It's not about the 'Why', it's all about the 'How'."

Maier took notes and tried to remember what he could of southern Europe during World War II. The Ustashe had been the most feared fascist militia in the Balkans and had been every bit as brutal as the Khmer Rouge. Lorenz wasn't too far off the mark – it hardly mattered whether totalitarian systems were left- or right wing. The Germans and Dachau, the Khmer Rouge and the Killing Fields, the Americans and Vietnam. Death knew no ideology. One could become a war criminal in any culture.

Maier continued to write.

Lorenz proved to be flexible, ruthless and cunning enough to integrate himself into the communist power clique. In 1945, Hilmar Lorenz, under the assumed name of Yvan Nazor, organised a series of massacres along the Austria-Slovenian border. Thousands of Ustashe units as well as countless Wehrmacht soldiers perished in these efforts. Following the foundation of Yugoslavia, he became a member of the internal security services.

"I only got to meet Tito after the war ended. I wasn't the only SS-Standardjunker who made a career in a communist country. In Vietnam, scores of my old SS colleagues fought for the communists against the French. That didn't surprise me. I was a child of totalitarianism. That's why I was sent to Cambodia as a Yugoslavian diplomat in 1973. Tito knew that he had the right man in the right place. For me it was like a third spring."

The girls had completed their training for the day, and Tep, followed by his son, approached Maier. The general looked at Maier as if he were inspecting a flat tire on his SUV and grinned, "Not long now, Maier."

When the Khmer Rouge marched victoriously into Phnom Penh on April 17th 1975 and took power, Hilmar Lorenz was Yugoslavia's diplomatic representative to Cambodia. In the following months, Lorenz took part in a number of secret meetings of the Cambodian communist party's central committee. Often, he was the only

European present. In 1976, Yugoslavia donated nine million dollars towards rebuilding the shattered nation. Lorenz stayed in Cambodia until 1979, aside from a few short trips to Belgrade, and would only be recalled after the Vietnamese invasion.

"I don't understand what you are doing here today. Surely there are other, more vicious regimes, which would go to great lengths to utilise your services and expertise?"

The White Spider appeared to play through all possible answers to Maier's question. Finally, he bent forward and began to admonish his prisoner.

"Please do try and keep the irony out of the voice of the biographer. Otherwise I'll have it removed with a knife. A man like you wouldn't be able to survive such a loss. It's very simple, Maier. I've grown old. My experience and services were very much in demand in 1975. I was probably as old then as you are now. In the new Cambodia, I'm not needed, officially. But I came back for nostalgic reasons and the country can use any kind of help with its reconstruction. I'm a consultant. I think that's the going term nowadays."

Following the disintegration of Yugoslavia, Lorenz visited the German embassy in Belgrade. With the help of partly forged documents, he managed to prove that he had a right to German citizenship. Neither his past in the Waffen-SS, nor his work as a Yugoslav intelligence agent was uncovered during the application process, and since 1991, Lorenz has been a German citizen again.

"I was a pensioner, a damn pensioner, like millions of others. Germany has grown old and careful. But I was in no mood to die in a small apartment in Darmstadt. I returned to Cambodia with UNTAC, just like you, though not as a journalist, but as an investor. I used the money I got from the sale of my apartment and bought land in Phnom Penh. And one day, during a visit to Kep, I bumped into Tep, my old friend Tep, with whom I had crisscrossed his country thirty years before to take stock of the revolution. He was almost destitute and I bought him a piece of land on the coast. A thanks and a token of remembrance, for the good times. We both made a fortune when land prices shot into the sky a few years later. Enough money to get mad ideas."

The old German's mobile phone rang. He said nothing on answering the call. After a while he slowly got up and walked towards the black SUV that stood waiting next to the casino. Raksmei, the young woman whom Maier had thought to be European, the little sister with the needles, helped the White Spider into his vehicle.

Before the German got into the car, he called for Viengsra, the policeman who'd fallen asleep next to his dog. Lorenz shook his head in resignation, carefully climbed onto the backseat, closed the door and lowered the window. He grinned at Maier, as if he'd just had a brilliant idea, and shouted, "When tourists come to visit the casino, we retreat to the pagoda. We have had some problems with a Russian who lives up here. But you're welcome to stay. Your legs should almost be usable again. Tep's son will keep you company and will assist you in getting rid of this useless policeman. I am relying on you, Maier."

The old man slammed the door of his car shut. The moment of no return had come as quickly as Maier had expected. While he didn't like the policeman, he didn't want to kill him. He didn't want to kill anyone. He wanted to go through life without taking a life. This was the final journey Lorenz had mentioned. A journey into the human off-side.

The old German lowered his window and laughed, "And don't wait too long. A man awake and in fear of his life is more dangerous than a man who's asleep. Until tomorrow."

The White Spider retreated into the darkness of the car and the dark window slid up silently. As the SUV pulled off, the window lowered once more.

"That was just a joke, Maier. We still need the policeman. I wish you an enjoyable evening. Keep writing. I want a story, not a notebook. Write with style and flair if you want to save your girlfriend's legs."

38

THE HANGMAN'S BOUDOIR

"Were you ever married?"

Lorenz smiled happily. The young fighting girls had cleared some of the overgrown garden behind the casino. Carissa, Maier and the White Spider sat in wheelchairs in the morning sun. The view across the Gulf of Thailand was gorgeous, the ridges of islands in the distance half submerged in clouds, the water placid and calm.

"Now, Maier, we're getting closer to each other. Your critical, well-structured thinking is coming into play. Perhaps this is your true calling. Perhaps you lived your entire life in preparation for this moment. Now you're asking the questions that a good biographer would think of. You're beginning to dig for the morsels of information that lie buried between the lines of the official version – exactly the things that make a man what he is. You're writing my testament."

Maier had turned his notes into prose during the night. He was no poet, but he weighed every word. The fear that the little shrimps would amputate Carissa's legs if he didn't produce sat deep in his bones. To avoid this scenario, he needed to write like a Nobel winner.

Maier's most difficult assignment had only just started.

"I was married twice. I met my first wife in Croatia in 1942. She worked in a women's camp, in which I was employed as representative of the Reich. I was very young, almost a teenager. Her father was a German, her mother from Croatia. I could never have married her back in Germany. She was ten years older than me. We were married by the camp commander. As I said, I was young. And I had no urge, like many of my colleagues, to rape the female inmates. They were too sick, and anyway, that kind of thing stood everything on its head. My mission and my ideological convictions stood in the way. We were trying to get rid of these people. A few months into the marriage, I was told that my wife was protecting one of the inmates."

The old man took a deep, rattling breath and continued, "She'd married me in order to save her friend, perhaps her lover, perhaps a dissident. My wife even told me in which part of the camp her friend was housed. She never really thought about what kind of a man she'd married. Isn't that strange? I didn't bother finding out who her friend was."

The White Spider sat facing Maier, eyes glazed over, drifting through the memories of his youth. Maier said nothing. He had opened a dark door in the White Spider's head. He hoped he wouldn't drown in the flood of memories that was pouring out.

He was the biographer of death.

"Though she was older than me, she had a much lower rank. The next day I went to visit the camp commander. I told him the truth. At the same time, I informed the SS in Zagreb. The commander wouldn't have agreed to my suggestions without pressure from the outside. As I said, I was still young."

Maier took notes, in direct speech. He would rewrite the text later. Somehow.

The White Spider leaned forward and brushed his old thin hand through Carissa's white hair. The journalist recoiled from the pale, skinny fingers and looked past him, her gaze fixed.

"Yes, Maier, women. I learned early. If you really want to achieve something in life you'll have to do without some things, some circumstances and even relationships, which we take for granted, which we feel we have a right to, simply because we're alive. But it's not like that. Man has no right. He takes it. Think of what will happen to the world if we let everybody reproduce, on and on and on. The lack of natural resources, our environmental vandalism, climate change, the little wars in the developing world: all results of our irrational attitude towards reproduction. One day this will bring us down. I won't be around to see it. But think about it. In China, the government tries to control population growth by passing laws. It doesn't work, because the system is so corrupt, but in principle, the Chinese are on the mark."

"What was your first wife's name?"

The White Spider looked at Maier directly. The question had brought him back from his philosophical meanderings.

"Take notes, Maier, this was one of the key events in my life. I remember exactly how I stepped into my office that morning, after talking to the commander. The day is so clear in my memory, as if it had all happened yesterday. It was a bloody cold day. Sixty inmates had frozen to death the previous night. My wife was a guard in a place called Stara Gradiška, the women's camp of Jasenovac. Her brother worked with her. He was really a nice man. But he had no ideology. He was an opportunist. A typical Croatian. I ordered two other Croatian guards into the office, very reliable men. Then I had her brother called. His name was Miroslav. I told him that my wife had been cheating me. Of course, he tried to defend his sister. He knew exactly what it was all about. My two helpers garroted him right in front of my desk. My secretary passed out."

The old German had got so excited he was out of breath and now coughed quietly into a white handkerchief.

"Take notes, Maier," he repeated. "I'm in the mood to have the odd toe removed from your girlfriend's foot. My girls never get enough practice. The visit of the Japanese collector was a rare opportunity to simulate the conditions of a field hospital in a combat situation."

Maier began to write in silence. He didn't dare to look across at Carissa. Lorenz looked at the detective, his eyes filled with expectation. Maier swallowed.

"You didn't tell me your first wife's name."

"That's correct, Maier. That's how it goes when you tell stories. I am getting there. Just a little bit more."

Maier nodded and briefly glanced past the old German, at life. It was a long way away and he didn't belong there. He had taken his place, close to the cold flame of the old white devil.

"I filled in an execution order for the entire block my wife had mentioned. About three hundred women and children. I had the camp commander sign it. The document contained very precise instructions as to how the inmates were to be killed. My wife was ordered to get them to dig their own graves. It was her job to kill them, with a shovel to the back of the head, one by one. After the thirty-eighth execution, Nada shot herself in the head."

Maier and the White Spider sat, united. Maier looked at his captor and fell through black eyes into the depths of a bottomless ocean. Lorenz grabbed his wrist and smiled gently, "I killed my second wife myself, Maier."

39

ALL'S FAIR IN LOVE AND WAR

MAIER AND CARISSA had spent a second night on the roof of the casino. The boy had cradled his AK like a baby and had fallen asleep on the stairs in front of them. Four of the girls took turns guarding them during the night. They hadn't spoken or slept much. Just before dawn, Carissa had moved in his arms.

"Maier, we need to get out of here. I feel sick all the time."

"I'm not exactly doing great either. Just be glad you still have your legs. Today we can walk again. Lorenz knows that everything here is going down the drain. He talks about dying all the time. Perhaps he has enough and wants to provoke an end, even if, or precisely because this would destroy his plans in Cambodia."

Carissa got up and fished a crumpled joint from her trouser pocket.

"By the way, Rolf went crazy in Kep the other day. He had a fight with Pete at the crab market and then broke into Tep's resort. I don't know if he stole anything. After that he disappeared. Kaley was taken away by the policeman. I actually expected to see her up here in Bokor."

Maier had caught up.

"They pumped me full of drugs and took me from the island to a temple north of Angkor, deep in the jungle. The stuff they gave me really crushed my mind. I didn't know what was happening, or where I was. I even thought you'd been killed on the road to Bokor. But I escaped, found out that Kaley's sister, a German, had come to Cambodia, presumably searching for her sister, and got killed by Tep. I just missed him at Calmette where I went to make sure it really was Kaley's sister. I got caught again."

Maier's memory was back – he could remember that Raksmei had guided him through his toxic dreams, but he wasn't sure what had happened in his mind and what hadn't. He didn't have the energy to look closely at the past days, to separate hallucination from fact. He had caught up and found his centre once more, but the recent past appeared as several narratives that were coagulating into a new reality, its only objective survival.

"Did they interrogate you?" She wouldn't make eye contact with Maier.

"Yes," she mumbled.

A gust of wind brushed across the casino roof and Carissa took a deep drag on her joint. Maier shook his head. Carissa brushed her hand through his short hair.

"I think that Mikhail's involved in all this. But when I came to visit, he wouldn't tell me a thing. On the way back to Kampot, Tep stopped me on the forest road and took me to the pagoda on the plateau. I spent last week in a hole there. They didn't kill me, because the old German thinks that you'll cooperate better if I'm alive."

The fog lifted as the sun rose. Below them, the Gulf of Thailand stretched towards Malaysia. Phu Quoc, Koh Tonsay and a few smaller islands were clearly visible. Fishing boats moved up and down in front of Rabbit Island.

The boy had gone downstairs. Maier couldn't see anyone around the casino. The old buildings of the hill station, the post office, the church, the mayor's office, the old water tower, surrounded by rough rock formations and tall grasses – the entire community looked like a place from which man had been banished a long time ago.

During Sihanouk's reign in the Sixties, the roads had been surfaced and lit by gas lights. The staff had worn pressed white uniforms and had spoken enough French to supply the guests with the illusion of savoir vivre at the end of the world. The cocktails had flowed night after night and the king had seduced countless women.

There'd even been a toy train up here. The rich could be absurd anywhere.

There wasn't much left of the good times. As Vichat had said, Bokor was ruled by ghosts.

"Today, we get down to business. I am sure that Kaley is here. I am ready for anything. I will not let them torture us again."

Maier turned to Carissa.

"By the way, do you know what role Raksmei plays in all this?"

Carissa shook her head and squashed her joint on the red fungus which covered the rooftop.

"I don't know. It looks like she's the old man's assistant. But she hasn't been up here long. I have no idea what her game is. I thought I knew that girl. And I think many of the girls that are being trained here come from the orphanage she ran in Kampot. A terrible thought. But I don't understand what they're doing here. What are they being trained for? Are Tep and the old man planning a second revolution?"

Carissa looked burnt out. Her white hair stood in all directions and the black rings under her eyes lent her a ghostlike quality, hardly softened by the morning light.

"I have an idea. Have a look at the papers when we are back in Phnom Penh, for unsolved political or otherwise remarkable murders. I mean professional assassinations. I would be surprised if witnesses did not see young girls near the scene of the crime."

Carissa nodded in silence.

"I have the feeling that we got involved in something that's a little too heavy for us. What do you think, Maier?"

Maier returned her gaze and said, with all the optimism he could muster, "Today we find Kaley and disappear."

Raksmei stepped onto the casino's rooftop, two syringes in her hands. The boy stood behind her; gun pointed at Maier. Behind the boy, two girls in black, remote-controlled eyes fixed on their prisoners, stood on the stairway.

Raksmei closed in on Maier and said in halting English, "A car is waiting for you downstairs. Be quick and you will get there before this shot takes effect and your legs give out."

He had no choice. The boy would shoot him if he tried to run and the shrimps would skin him before he'd reached the stairs. Raksmei's expression didn't change as she pushed the needle into Maier's arm. He felt dirty.

The old police station lay a kilometre below the ranger station. The boy raced the SUV as quickly as possible along the potholed road.

There was no sign of Mikhail, but Maier could see Vichat standing on the terrace of the ranger station. Ten minutes later, the boy hit the brakes in front of the overgrown building. A sign on the wall next to the broken door read Police Municipale. Like the other buildings scattered across the plateau, the former station was a ruin.

The White Spider was waiting in the shade of a mango tree, carrying his oversized hat in his thin nervous hands. Lorenz wore a worn, snow-white linen suit.

Two wheelchairs stood at the ready. The boy and Inspector Viengsra lifted Maier and Carissa into their chairs. The boy placed the computer on his lap and pushed him into the building. The White Spider followed him slowly.

"You're doing well, Maier. You're finding your feet. But you keep things a little short. Please do unfold your talents a little more, put a little more oomph in it, a little flair. And do ask me whatever you like, if there's something you don't understand."

Les Snakearm Leroux sat in a chair in the office of the former station. The cells and toilets that Maier could see were empty and smashed up. Just like Les. The American pilot wasn't sitting. He had been tied to the chair.

Lorenz waved for the boy.

"Leave us alone today. These two here can't move and for me, it's a lot more exciting to be surrounded by three people who'd like to kill me. Raksmei will help if there's a problem."

The boy and the inspector looked at the old man in disbelief, but he waved a tired hand and his henchmen disappeared. Seconds later, the car started outside. Lorenz waited theatrically, until the engine noise had faded.

"As you know, Lesley Leroux is the owner of a bar in Kep. Having been told that we caught you here, he came up on the plateau and walked into the arms of our girls. Unfortunately, it turned out that Les had done a spell as a prisoner of war some years back and we weren't able to find out who'd informed the old man. Now, he's no able longer to tell us."

Maier couldn't look away. The American had some serious head-wounds and they had sawed off his left thumb. He had been bandaged but he was still bleeding like a recently butchered animal. He was alive.

"Did Leroux work for you, Maier?"

The biographer shook his head.

The White Spider sat down heavily on a rickety stool; the only option other than the chair Les had been tied to. The weak sunlight fell through the window onto his gaunt face, which appeared to dissolve into thousands of tiny wrinkles.

Maier stared into empty space, fascinated. He barely noticed he was chewing his tongue. This time Raksmei's shot had been anything but paralysing. Amphetamines massaged his brain and urged him to jump up. He was wide awake, and sitting opposite his adversary, irrationally happy. He didn't dare look at Carissa for fear of giving himself away too early.

All's fair in love and war.

He would choke the old bastard to death.

"You're alright, Maier, aren't you?"

The American had raised his battered head. Maier looked Les in the eye and nodded.

"It's over, Les."

"That's good. I've had enough. This countryman of yours is worse than the Vietcong,"

"You are OK now, Les."

Lorenz had gotten up and stepped impatiently in front of the American.

"Maier, you are here to write my story, not to help this decadent drunk die."

Maier really saw him as a spider, a tough old tarantula, working her last net.

"Tell me the end of your story. What are you doing here?"

The old man looked at Maier with pity in his pale eyes, as if he were an about-to-be crushed cockroach or a poisoned rat – something that was dying.

"You're right, of course. I appear like a dinosaur to you. Irony is rising up inside you. But you're wrong about me. I am not that old-fashioned, Maier. It's all about the money today. Dollars, euros, yen. Ideologies, racial theories, national pride, honour itself, these are all outmoded concepts that belong to the time of my youth. Those were simple years when people in Europe knew less. Today, they know everything, everything but values. They know too much. The West swims in an ocean of useless information – gossip, rumours, lies. I've made peace with all that. I won't die in Germany or for Germany. But I will tell you why I returned to Cambodia. Please take notes."

Maier contemplated killing the man with his laptop. Instead he opened his file.

"I am all ears, Herr Lorenz."

The old man grinned.

"In contrast to our American friend here, who has eaten his."

Now he laughed like a small boy.

Carissa hissed impatiently in her wheelchair next to Maier.

"For the past two years, we've been offering an exclusive service. All in line with the priorities of the new century. For a substantial amount of money, you can hire us to get rid of your political enemy, your competitor, your lover, your lover's lover or husband's lover or members of your family. Anyone. You can read about it in the papers. I'm surprised, Ms. Stevenson, that no one from your professional circle has cottoned on to us yet. We've shut down a few local journalists already. Our ladies work in Vietnam, Thailand, Laos and of course Cambodia for clients with the right money. As soon as we find the right teachers to train our staff in language skills, we'll go global."

"You will teach these girls English with a stick?"

The old man, full of pride, ignored the detective's sarcasm.

"You see, Maier, Cambodia has an oversupply of young girls. There are no jobs. Even prostitution doesn't offer every pretty girl an opportunity. The war killed too many men and yet women don't get any opportunities. Tep, my old friend, wants to buy Bokor. That's looking good, we just need a bit more money. Thanks to his efforts in Kep, not a great deal more. Then we can throw out the rangers and train more girls. We'll soon have to leave our temple hideaway. The tourists are coming. That's why we'll be restoring the casino. We'll build a swimming pool, a golf course and a heliport, all the stuff Bokor needs in the twenty-first century. As an alibi for the real business at hand. Don't you agree it's a solid plan?"

"And where do the girls come from?"

Lorenz sat heavily.

"From orphanages, from mothers who can't feed their children. Cambodia is a country of unlimited possibilities."

Hilmar Lorenz returned from Germany to Cambodia in the early Nineties and, with the help of former Khmer Rouge officers, started setting up an assassination service with global ambitions – the Kangaok Meas Project.

Lorenz's guardians are educated according to the inhuman and extreme values of the Khmer Rouge. Members of his organization have allegedly committed more than fifty murders in Phnom Penh, Siem Reap and Sihanoukville in the past two years. The organization is also active in neighbouring countries.

Raksmei held two syringes in her hands and stood behind the White Spider.

Maier closed the laptop.

The girl pushed the first needle into the old man's back.

Lorenz turned and tried to grab the girl but the sedative worked quickly and he slumped forward on his chair.

Raksmei walked around the tall bent-over figure and pushed him upright. Lorenz looked up at her in surprise.

"Raksmei?"

Maier and Carissa had both stood up. Raksmei grabbed hold of the old German's arm, pulled the sleeve of his white shirt up and gave him a second shot, without bothering to tie him off first.

"For Sambat, my brother."

She gently smiled at the old man and brushed his silver hair straight.

"Raksmei, you know who I am?" Lorenz asked with an uncertain tone in his voice. It didn't suit him.

She didn't answer.

"How long has he got?"

"He can talk thirty minutes. Then one hour quiet. Then dead."

Carissa untied Les from his chair.

"Is it over, Maier?"

"It is all over. We will say goodbye to Bokor now."

Without turning around, Carissa and Raksmei grabbed Les and led him outside, into the sun.

Lorenz's eyes followed his daughter in silence.

"I was a good man. A friend of the people. When the Vietnamese invaded in '79, I could have hidden in my embassy. I would have been safe there. But I fled with Tep. I knew that my career in Yugoslavia was finished. I couldn't let Tep down. He was a good soldier and he took our mission seriously. He was my friend."

Maier sat back into his wheelchair. Slowly, ever so slowly, he was beginning to relax. For the first time in a week, he wasn't in mortal danger and he knew what was going on. The White Spider was drooling. Paralysis was slowly setting in. Maier was watching a man die.

"After Phnom Penh had fallen, we came down here and slept in a cooperative. In the morning we planned to head west to the Cardamom Mountains, as good a place as any to disappear for a while. Just before we left, Tep caught a woman roasting some animal over an open fire. Angkar had forbidden any such act. Tep was as loyal to Angkar as I am to him. That's how it is in war, Maier. Even while we were being chased by the enemy, he took a hammer and killed the woman. Her husband worked in a field nearby with his daughter. Tep walked up to the man. I stood on the edge of the field and saw exactly what he did. He said something about Angkar to the little girl and hit her father. The man fell to the ground. He gave the little girl the hammer. These are the moments, Maier, on the edge of everything, when we get close to the gods. I had moments like that in Croatia."

The voice of the old man was getting weaker. His eyes had glazed over. Outside, in front of the police station, Maier could hear the flapping of leathery wings.

"I'm almost gone, Maier. Not even my daughter wants to watch me die. No one will bury me. Tep won't let you get away, but even that no longer matters now. The Kangaok Meas Project is running. My last engagement. You see, the girl who killed her father in the rice-field, her name was Kaley. Tep took her with us. He gave her to me as a present and thus saved her life. I took her the same afternoon. She couldn't have been much older than thirteen. Raksmei and Sambat are my children. My children with Kaley. She was the reason why I came back to this small, primitive, insignificant country. Her sister also came back from Germany to find Kaley. Tep got rid of her."

The White Spider gasped for air. Then he calmed and let the toxin work its way to his core.

"And as you may know, Maier, Tep married Kaley off to his oldest son, who was killed by Kaley's youngest daughter, Poch. With a hammer, I might add. When Tep tried to train the girl as one of our assassins, she ran in front of the jeep of that young German guy. The little girl lived like Kaley, following only her own laws. Just like Raksmei, who just killed her father. Everything repeats itself again and again, like in the old story about the Kangaok Meas, which these uneducated half-people keep alive with their superstitions."

"Does Raksmei know who her parents are?"

The old man coughed up some blood and shook his head.

"No. Tep insisted that Raksmei and Sambat should grow up as orphans. The Khmer Rouge often separated children from their parents. Later, when Raksmei had grown up a bit, shortly after I came back to Cambodia, he tried to seduce her. She must have been the same age as Kaley, when she gave birth to my children. It almost broke our friendship. Now I wonder why I was so cross."

The White Spider laughed.

"But she's not stupid, this daughter of mine. She was never scared of me. When she was brought to the temple a few weeks ago, I was sorely tempted to tell her the truth. But I would've had to tell her everything, including the fact that I was responsible for the death of her brother. Tep was sure she'd be reliable and she knew something about drugs. So she became your poisoner."

The voice of the old man seemed to drift away from him. His lips barely moved.

"But in her heart, she always knew. Do you really think a woman like Raksmei can kill her own father without recognising him? I'm proud of my daughter."

"Does Kaley know that she is Raksmei's mother?

The old German laughed, just.

"She knows nothing. After the birth, Tep took the kids away from her and had them sent back to Kampot with the Khmer Rouge. She thinks her children are dead. Do you understand why I returned to Cambodia as soon as possible? I wanted to make sure my children had a chance."

"And then you killed your son? What chance did he have?"

"A misunderstanding. War is never simple. As soon as the first shot is fired… Sambat was here and watched the Kangaok Meas ceremony."

"What ceremony?"

"Maier, Tep found out that my son was here and Viengsra killed him and threw him in the sea."

Maier looked at the dying man without pity.

"He didn't kill him. He drowned your son alive. He tied stones to his feet and drowned him."

For the first time, Maier could detect particles of pain in the eyes of the old man. He didn't have much time left.

"And where is Kaley now?"

"Maier, you didn't understand me. The Kangaok Meas is a concept of the Immaterial, a manifestation of the sensuous, a golden peacock, reborn in each generation. And in this life, Kaley belongs to Kep, to Bokor. She's the whore of Cambodia and all who sleep with her will experience a violent end. That's what the locals believe. More importantly, that's what Kaley believes."

What had Rolf said? There had to be a way to free people from the darkness of tradition, even from superstition.

Maier was less idealistic. People, whether highly educated or illiterate, always stayed the same. The killing technique changed, but the thought was the same.

The White Spider coughed blood and slid deeper into his chair.

"When I slept with Kaley, she was still a child. You must understand. We were at war. There was nothing to eat. And Tep and I saved her. At that time, we couldn't see that she was the Kangaok Meas. We only realised that later."

Lorenz fought for breath.

"Lift me up, Maier. Don't let me die like a rat. Please do me one last favour and call my daughter back in."

Maier shook his head.

The White Spider stared up at him, his gaunt long face wracked by pain and anger.

"How many people have you poisoned, Hilmar Lorenz?"

Maier wanted to kick him, but one didn't kick dead people.

The White Spider's phone rang. Without turning, Maier left the former police station.

40

DEATH IN THE TEA PLANTATION

"The butchers will be here in a few minutes and they will be looking for us."

Les sat against the wall, almost passed out, "I know a trail, past the old jail and into the jungle. It's difficult to follow us there."

"Will he be able to make it?"

Raksmei looked at Maier. She nodded.

Les groaned. The young woman had a syringe in her hand. The White Spider's daughter looked breathtaking and deadly. Suddenly Maier felt like a human being again. A human being pumped to the gills with amphetamine.

"That's my last one. He will make it with this shot."

Raksmei tied off the American's arm. A dog started barking. Carissa and Raksmei helped the battered war veteran to his feet.

The trail led downhill. After a few minutes they crossed two narrow streams and Les managed to walk without help. The path got steeper. Les walked silently and, despite his injuries, overtook the other three.

After an hour they reached the bottom of a valley. An overgrown, barely visible building lay off to the left of the trail.

"The old prison."

Raksmei made no effort to stop and followed Les along the narrow trail that led between tall grasses.

"The trail will divide a bit further. The left path leads back to the Black Villa, the right trail drops down into the jungle. We go right. The road is bound to be guarded."

Carissa and Raksmei crashed into Maier, thrown to the floor by the power of the explosion, and pressed them into the soil. Just ahead, a round hole had been ripped from the trail. Raksmei had blood on her face but she started to get up. Someone was screaming behind them. The hunters were on their way.

Maier knew that they had only seconds. They had to leave.

"Carissa, take Raksmei into the jungle. I will see you in Kampot. Rent a car to go to the border. I will distract the dogs and meet you tomorrow."

Carissa was unhurt. She grabbed the young Khmer woman's arm.

"If there are more mines on this trail, we're fucked."

But there was no time to ponder. Tep's men were barely a hundred metres behind them.

"Let's go."

The two women ran down the hill. There was no sign of Les. The bushes were dripping with blood. The American could not have survived. Before Maier could take a step, the boy and Viengsra stood behind him.

The inspector smiled like a toothless child and spoke first. "Monsieur Maier, my dog found you."

The boy had his finger on the trigger and grinned.

The two men led Maier across to the overgrown prison.

"We mine the trail this morning. Otherwise you escape. Someone wait for the girl at Black Villa already. General Tep very angry. You kill his friend."

Maier stumbled ahead of the two men. Suddenly the boy grabbed him by the shoulder and pushed him into dense undergrowth, past the abandoned building. A trail opened and they stood in front of the main entrance of the old French jail. Maier fell up the slippery stairs.

"We wait for Tep. He want to see you die. He want to take you life, Monsieur Maier."

The boy pushed Maier inside the building. The roof had partly fallen in but a few of the cells beyond the entrance hall looked intact.

The first thing Maier saw was a red head which jumped up and down behind a barred window.

"Maier, you're still alive? I never would 've thought."

The boy opened the only functioning cell door and pushed Maier inside.

Pete was pale and looked bewildered. He was unshaven and his gaunt cheeks had become hollower. His voice was so hoarse that Maier had problems understanding him.

"Yeah, Maier, I haven't eaten for days. These fuckers simply forgot about me. Maier, do you have anything to eat?"

The steel door slammed shut behind Maier.

"My liver?"

The English man didn't smile.

"Maier, I've seen it before. You can't eat anything for days after, if you see something like that."

"They'll take your liver too, Pete."

The cell was empty. Small trees sprouted from the broken moss-covered walls. In a few years the roots would crack the wall open and the building would collapse. Not soon enough.

Pete staggered around in circles, shaking with panic. Maier looked around. The roof had holes, but it was more than four metres up. There was no getting up there.

"Have you got a fag?"

"I don't smoke."

Pete looked at him with unfathomable anger, before he began circling the cell again. The round smooth face of the policeman appeared at the cell window. Inspector Viengsra was chewing betel. He lost a thread of red spit and smiled.

"The White Spider show Tep and his son how to skin people."

The man was so simple, one had to be scared. But Maier didn't want to give up. One hour.

"I hope I not watch. Sometime they go too far, too far, Monsieur Maier."

"Watch?" Maier asked, not expecting an answer, and stepped up to the window to laugh in the inspector's face.

"They will roast you and your dog as well, Inspector. The White Spider is dead and we got away. You have failed. It will all be your fault when we are dead. You will see how Cambodia gets rid of people who fail."

Genuine worry spread across the moon-shaped face of the policeman as he looked down at the prisoners. Then he laughed carelessly.

"I help him grill. He need my help. Tep not eat three liver, for sure."

Suddenly the boy called out in front of the prison.

"Viengsra?"

Someone fired a shot.

The policeman's crying eyes blinked in panic and he pulled his weapon. Pete ran to the cell window and tried to look past the inspector. Viengsra started to shoot, wildly. After a few seconds only the click of the empty gun was audible.

"Shit, the boy is dead."

Pete stepped away from the window.

"Tep wouldn't kill his own son, would he?"

Two more shots rang through the entrance hall of the prison.

The power of the bullets threw Inspector Viengsra to the cell window.

The cell door opened and the next bullet caught Pete in the forehead.

Maier remained standing in the middle of the room.

"Yes, young man, wrong time, wrong place."

Mikhail stepped into the cell, bowed theatrically and raised his weapons.

"I thought all the while you were involved in something up here. Should I shoot you straight away?"

Maier had put up his hands.

"What are you doing here, you damn gopnik? Correct answer please, your life hangs by the proverbial thread, a thread so delicate even the king of Cambodia has never seen it."

"I am a private detective. From Hamburg. I work for a family in Hamburg, to bring their son back to Germany. Rolf is the son."

Mikhail laughed, pushed his grey locks out of his face and carefully lowered his weapons.

"Good answer, Maier. I know all this already. And good thing too you got rid of the old Nazi. But things like that, they make waves. And I don't like waves. That's why I live up here."

Maier knew it was pointless to ask the Russian what he was doing in Bokor. One could not ask a man like that questions.

"I am looking for the Kangaok Meas," Maier said.

"Usually everyone runs away when that name is mentioned. Rolf will never get the girl. But he will try. People are like that. They believe in things they know not to exist. As a Russian, I sympathise. But you, you man, you have the East in your eyes. That's why you'll manage to solve your case, detective."

The dog of the policeman had pushed into the cell and sniffed at Maier's legs.

"It's better we disappear. This place will be swarming with black shrimps soon."

"The road is blocked. The trail through the forest might be mined."

"I know that, Maier. I found Les outside. Poor man. Survived three wars and then died up here in the great nothing."

Mikhail shot the dog.

41

THE ROOF OF THE WORLD

THE ROOF of the casino was the last place where Tep would search for Maier. Mikhail had led him back to the old hotel on a different trail, through tall grasses past the old water tower. By afternoon, the Bokor Palace had become a hive of activity. SUVs, all of them black and without number plates, arrived one after another and dropped off groups of girls. Lexus was the preferred brand for the killers. Mikhail and Maier had entered through the basement and climbed one of the broken stairways to the top of the building. Now they were watching the scene below from one of the crumbling towers at the front side of the building.

The Russian stared down grimly at the preparations for the great summit of the Kangaok Meas Project. Maier knew that Mikhail had almost shot him. He was in the way.

Shortly after dark, Tep arrived with his son, the White Spider and Viengsra. Some of the girls lined the three corpses up on straw mats in front of the casino.

For a while the old general stood in front of the remains of the people closest to him, lost in thought. It wasn't his best day. Maier counted twelve girls who stood to attention behind Tep. After an hour, he turned away and walked into the building. The girls carried the corpses around the casino building to the edge of the Bokor plateau and doused them in kerosene. The loud hiss of the flames reached all the way to the rooftop. Two of the girls heaped wood onto the corpses, while a third used a stick to push hands and feet that stuck out of the fire back into the flames. After an hour, nothing remained but three dark spots and a few bones on the ground. One of the girls began to shovel the ash and bones over the side of the cliff. Maier almost smiled. That was how war criminals ended – some of them. But the death of the White Spider was hardly a victory. Men like Lorenz would never become extinct.

A huge, rusty water tank stood in the centre of the roof. The round steel container offered the only protection from the evening's cold wind. Mikhail spread a dirty krama on the shadow side of the tank and pulled a tin of corned beef, two baguettes, mangos and a bottle of vodka from his bag.

As far as Maier could remember, he had consumed nothing but rice and *prahok* during his incarceration. He had already noticed that his trousers weren't as tight as they had been. Nothing got rid of excess fat quicker than torture. He grabbed one of the mangos and devoured it like a starved animal, squeezing the yellow flesh from the skin into his mouth.

The Russian was in good spirits.

"The story of the Kangaok Meas is centuries old. The reincarnation in the story, the continuation of evil, from one generation to the next, originates with the brand of Hinduism that some of the kings of Angkor followed. Brahmin priests were very influential at the Khmer court and they spread the belief in the continuation of the soul. On top of that, you have the archaic animist belief system of the Khmer and the cruel history of the last decades. We're in Cambodia, dear, not in Vladivostok or Germany. This place is haunted. I know this country."

Maier shook his head. He was a detective, not an exorcist. Mikhail slapped his shoulder and grinned with yellow teeth.

"Maier, everyone will believe what they want. I've had so many extreme experiences in my life, that I have no options left but to remain open to everything. I'm a collector. That's a respectable profession. I collect situations."

The Russian took a swig of vodka from the bottle and handed it to Maier. The alcohol woke him up. He was beginning to feel in tune with himself once more.

"Why did you not shoot me?"

"Maier, young man, I'm not a mass murderer. Three thugs were enough for me. And I need your help tonight. Vichat and the other rangers will not come near the casino at night. They're very scared of the shrimps."

"I love vodka. Did you know that?"

"Yes, dear, I remember talking about drinking at length after you'd fallen off your motorbike."

"Was that you?"

Mikhail brushed a huge hand through his greasy grey hair and appeared to evaluate what the detective had said.

"My dear Maier, you ask as many questions as one would expect from a detective."

"That's what the White Spider said as well."

The Russian laughed until his face had gone the way of a tomato.

"Then you know that you have to be careful in Cambodia if you look over another man's shoulders."

He winked at Maier and coughed.

"So be careful."

Maier had dozed off when the Russian shook him by the shoulder.

"Maier, the shrimps are searching the casino. They will be up here in a minute."

The fat Russian had already packed the baguette and vodka and was in the process of climbing into the water tank. Maier jumped up and followed him.

A few seconds later, they could hear voices in the stairway.

The shrimps weren't alone. Tep had stepped onto the roof and spoke French.

"Tonight, we have the last initiation of the Kangaok Meas in the casino. A little earlier than planned, but this damn detective from Germany make many problem for us. Many big problem. Today he kill my son."

"I am sorry to hear that. Have you caught Monsieur Maier?"

Maier recognised the voice of the other man immediately. He sat next to Mikhail in knee-deep rancid water and tried to hold his breath. The two men stood directly in front of the water tank now, while the shrimps searched the roof. The Russian had pulled a gun and pointed it directly at the thin rusty wall of the tank.

"I get him. Tomorrow we have money to buy casino. Tonight, we blow it up. I catch the German OK. I watch all roads to Phnom Penh. Nothing to stop us now. In two years, we open resort and golf course. No problem."

The Frenchman had walked a few steps away.

"Can't you lend me one of your girls, Tep?"

The general hissed angrily, "You never have enough, Maupai. You are strong man. We are same age and you want girl more than me. More than Khmer Rouge general. This kill you one day. I tell you, keep fingers away from Kangaok Meas and my staff."

The voices receded, but Mikhail waved to Maier to remain seated. For a while they heard nothing. Suddenly someone began to scratch the underside of the tank they were in. After endless seconds, one of the girls shouted an order and everyone trooped back down the stairway.

Mikhail and Maier rose from the cold, dirty water and climbed back onto the roof terrace.

"What did they say?"

Maier translated the conversation between Tep and the Frenchman.

The Russian took a long swig of vodka and grinned. "You see, young man, I'm not the only one warning about Kaley."

The girls had used duct tape to fasten a packet of explosives and a timer to the underside of the water tank. Mikhail ripped the packet off and examined it.

"Maier, this little packet is going to do much damage to the building. They must have installed something similar in the basement. That's where I have to go."

The collector of situations had taken the package apart and stuffed half the explosive into his pocket. Then he reattached the rest exactly as the girls had left it.

He got up, his face beetroot, and checked his revolver.

"It's best you stay here. This bomb here has been defused. But they won't notice if they come back and check. I come and get you when the

Kangaok Meas appears. Tonight, I'll show you why Rolf must up give this woman."

Maier didn't think he'd have another chance to ask the Russian anything.

"What are you doing here, Mikhail?"

"Maier, they'll never build a golf course here. I'm sure. I'm the king of Bokor. This is my home. No need to know more about me."

"I would like to know in whose interest you are working."

The Russian hesitated, then he pulled a torch from his pocket and handed it to Maier.

"You'll need it tonight, dear. And here's some good advice from a man who's been everywhere: If you find yourself in a minefield, as sometimes happens in Cambodia, then follow the sticks in the ground, otherwise you will end up like Les. Don't forget that. Follow the sticks."

The giant disappeared down the stairs without another word.

Maier was alone. Almost alone.

"Oh, Maier."

Maier turned around, but the voice had not come from the stairway. Kaley stood in front of him. She wore a green sarong and the black shirt she'd worn when he'd first met her. She had put up her hair with the help of two chopsticks, which emphasised her beautiful face, interrupted in its perfection only by her bright shining scar. A timeless, unreal beauty. She smiled uncertainly and held up the palms of her hands. Maier remembered the words of the inspector. Death was a woman.

"Hello, Kaley."

There was only one way onto the roof of the casino. Kaley had not come that way. The woman smiled past Maier.

"You look beautiful, Kaley."

She pulled her sarong straight. The expression of modesty that crossed her face was so remote that Maier could barely breathe. She was fearsome. Suddenly she took a step forward and embraced Maier, clawing at his back with her hands.

"Oh, Maier."

Maier took her in his arms, though he had no desire to be near her. She smelled of the red fungus that had grown all over the casino walls.

Kaley didn't want to let go.

"Kaley, tell me what happened."

When she finally disentangled herself, she climbed on to the balustrade of casino roof, sat down and let her feet dangle towards the ground.

"You catch me if I fall, Maier?"

"Of course."

Without another word, she slipped forward, but Maier had already grabbed her under the arms. He almost expected her to dissolve into thin air, but she fell back into his arms. She was light, but not as light as one would expect a ghost to be.

"Maier, the people not leave me alone."

"What kind of people?"

"The people who take me from the rice-field. They do terrible thing. I see many time. The Kangaok Meas in Bokor is no good."

She lay in his arms like a drunk.

"Do you know what you are, Kaley?"

The young woman laughed unhappily.

"I am dead, you alive."

"So, you know who I am?"

She looked into his eyes for the first time.

"You are Maier."

She lowered her gaze.

"How long has the Kangaok Meas been coming here, Kaley?"

Kaley shook her head.

"Long time. Many years."

"Is the Kangaok Meas scared?"

"I am reborn. I am dead, you alive."

"Can I help you somehow, Kaley?"

The Khmer began to cry.

"You promise you find my sister, Maier."

He didn't answer her. He couldn't. Not now. Not after all the death that had manifested around this woman. Kaley began to dance across the roof.

"Can you dance, Maier?"

"Not well."

"Good for me."

She touched him lightly on the shoulders and led him to the centre of the rooftop. Grey clouds rushed across the edge of the plateau. The old water tower looked like it was ready to march away, in the face of all the horror. Maier thought he could hear an orchestra play faintly, somewhere far away, as the fog slowly slid across the casino like creeping death and Kaley waltzed him effortlessly across the roof of the world. Had the vodka been drugged?

A few seconds later it was pitch dark.

42

FAITES VOS JEUX

"Gentlemen, we gather tonight to celebrate the last Kangaok Meas ceremony in Bokor Palace. Before we proceed, I like to tell you, everyone who know about our project is one hundred percent with us. You have doubt in our business, now is time to go."

Tep's voice echoed through the casino's ballroom, as a dozen or so investors sat down in a row of rattan chairs. The general was in uniform tonight. A revolver hung from his belt. Even in mourning, the old communist looked ready for battle. A few of the men carried briefcases. The room was lit by fat yellow candles usually used in temples. Maier recognised most of the men in the warm twilight – all of them foreigners who had bought property in Kep.

Two girls, dressed in black, stood behind a small bar and mixed cocktails. A straw mat lay in the centre of the otherwise empty hall. Music emanated from an unseen source. Maier knew the song, a mournful tune usually played during Cambodian cremations. Kaley had led Maier into the room in which he'd been beaten unconscious on his first visit. Now they lay next to each other beside two holes in the floor and stared down into the ballroom.

"Do you know that I have been here before, Kaley?" Maier whispered.

Kaley nodded.

"Do you know who attacked me when I was lying on the floor?"

Kaley shook her head.

"I not remember. It not important. Today you not worry. I hide you if someone coming."

The ballroom had settled into silence. Now and then the ice cubes in the guests' glasses tinkled through the great nothing.

Something began to move in the semi-darkness at the end of the ballroom. Tep clapped his hands together.

"With your payments, we buy the casino, stop the rangers and build most exclusive resort in Southeast Asia. We pay a high price to do this. Enemy force kill my son and Inspector Viengsra today. For this reason, very difficult for me to celebrate. But finances for project now sure. Our agency, Kangaok Meas Project, now working. My staff travel all the region for mission. Every day, we more rich."

The general's speech was followed by polite applause.

Kaley stepped into the light, followed by twenty girls with short cropped hair, dressed in black pajamas and rubber sandals. The Kangaok Meas looked unbelievably beautiful and cruel. Kaley wore a dress made from fine gold chains over a black thong. She wore her hair down, almost reaching her broad hips. Her body had a golden sheen. The scene below Maier looked both ridiculous and terrible, like a sequence in a Hollywood movie with a huge budget badly spent.

Maier pulled his head out of his observation hole and wouldn't have been surprised if she'd still been lying next to him, but she was gone. Rather, she'd appeared below. But how had she managed to change so fast?

The investors held their breath as the Kangaok Meas swayed past them. She shot a quick glance to the ceiling before she stood next to Tep. Tonight, the long scar, accentuated by the white strand of hair, gave her a demonic aura, and split her face in two in the twilight of the ballroom.

Maier made no efforts to hide. The Kangaok Meas locked her glassy eyes with his again, then she turned wordlessly towards the general.

The girls had lined up in two rows, silently facing each other.

The old general barely looked at Kaley and continued, his voice heavy with emotion. "Tonight, I dedicate for my son. Also, my very good old friend, Herr Lorenz, is killed today. I will catch killer. For me difficult to lose old friend. More difficult to lose two, son and one good friend. This is story of Cambodia."

Tep clapped his hands again and Kaley began to walk up and down the rows of girls. Her face was shiny and cold.

She was grinding her jaws. She must have taken something for this performance. Passing the girls three times, she pointed at two of the identically-dressed, prospective assassins.

The two girls stepped forward, while the rest of the group spread across the ballroom.

Maupai talked excitedly with another Frenchman next to him, but Maier couldn't follow the conversation.

Kaley started to walk from one guest to the next to collect their briefcases. Tep took each case and lined them up in a long row on the bar.

Kaley waved to the two girls who immediately started to approach each other. A low round of applause rose from the investors. The two girls circled, their eyes full of murder. One of the girls lashed out. The second girl took the hit to the face without trying to dodge her opponent. Instead she went with the blow and slid towards her attacker like mercury. The first girl looked up but it was already too late. A small piece of metal flashed in the hand of the attacker. A split second later, she pushed the nail into her adversary's eye socket. The loser fell to the floor screaming. Kaley stepped between the two fighters.

But for the screams of the injured girl, the ballroom was absolutely silent. Tep waved for two other girls who pulled the loser onto the straw mat in the centre of the room and began to kick her.

Kaley stood on the edge of the mat and slowly pulled off her slip. Like a dark angel, she stepped closer to the injured girl and bent downwards, her back turned to the investors.

Two of the men had jumped up and were dropping their trousers as quickly as possible. Maier began to understand what would happen now. He could hear the beating of leathery wings outside the building. He didn't want to watch any longer and he had no idea how to stop what he was seeing.

This was war.

Kaley grabbed hold of the head of the injured girl and slowly, theatrically, pulled the nail from her eye. The girl screamed. Blood spurted across Kaley's breasts, but the Kangaok Meas hardly noticed.

She was now crouched on all fours above her victim. The first investor had almost reached and was about to make a grab for her legs. At the last moment, he was pushed aside by a second man.

"I have earned this. I'm the most important investor, n'est-ce pas?"

Maupai grabbed the Kangaok Meas by the hips and tried to climb the undead woman.

Kaley held the bloody nail in her hand and turned briefly to the Frenchman, smiling broadly, before she plunged the metal into her victim's remaining eye.

The Frenchman's head exploded a second later. He fell on top of her like an old sack.

Rolf stepped out of the shadows, two revolvers in his hands and stared wild-eyed at Kaley.

Tep waved for his girls who began to close in on the young German from all directions, but Kaley ordered them to retreat. She rose slowly and approached Rolf, smiling faintly. Her breasts and belly were smeared with blood. Without a word, she knelt down in front of him and began to open the belt of his trousers. Rolf began to shake and raised the two guns. The tension in the room was unbearable.

Maier jumped up, ready to run downstairs and storm the show, but what would be the point. He'd be totally outgunned down there.

"Not yet," he said to himself and lay back down.

Rolf stared down at Kaley, crying, his two revolvers centimetres from her head.

The ballroom exploded.

Maier was thrown against the wall of the room he lay in. In seconds the space filled with dust which wafted up from the ballroom. Maier fought his way back to the hole but there was nothing to see. It was pitch dark below him.

Somewhere a smaller explosion went off and a wall collapsed. More dust. He crawled down the main stairs to the entrance, half-blind, and made it outside. It was pouring with rain. The casino's basement was on fire and thick cement dust poured out of the building's windows. The floor of the ballroom had collapsed and had swallowed all those who'd been present. The detective sunk helplessly into the wet grass in front of the building.

A car started behind Maier. One of the SUVs shot forward. Maier could see Tep in the weak light of the driver's cabin. The old general held on to the wheel, bleeding heavily and stared blindly into the darkness. Kaley emerged from the burning building and marched down the stairs. She looked untouched. In her hands, she carried the briefcases full of money. She stopped in the light of the car's headlights in front of Maier and looked at him, in apparent confusion.

"You find my sister, Maier."

Seconds later she was gone. The general revved the engine and the car slithered away into the darkness. Maier sat alone, in front of the burning casino, knowing he'd never be able to fulfil his promise.

After a long while, Maier mounted the steps to the hotel. The ballroom was a smoking bomb crater. He stared into the darkness, but he couldn't see a thing. His torch didn't reach to the bottom. He would have to go down there.

He left the casino and circled the building until he found the back entrance to the basement. The same entrance through which he'd escaped on his first visit. Maier climbed downwards.

The water was still knee deep but the basement floor was littered with large chunks of the ceiling. Someone moaned ahead of Maier and the detective stopped and tried to listen into the darkness.

"Rolf, Rolf, are you down here?"

Shadows moved around him. Someone coughed a few metres ahead. Maier walked on, deeper into the bowels of the building. Then he saw Rolf in the light of his weak flickering torch. The young German lay on a piece of beautifully tiled ballroom floor with which he'd fallen. But he wasn't alone. The girls lay around him in the stinking water as if waiting for something. Of course, they were dead, but that didn't mean much in Cambodia.

He grabbed hold of the young coffee heir and pulled him in the direction of the stairs. The girls made no efforts to stop him, but they followed Maier with their eyes through the dark water towards the exit. Death was a lady. Rolf was conscious. Maier couldn't see any gratuitous injuries on the young man. The rain had stopped.

The detective stumbled from car to car until he found one with the keys in the ignition. He loaded Rolf onto the back seat and raced off without looking back, towards the coast, away from the cursed Bokor Palace, away from the dead shrimps, away from this damn case.

43

ENDGAME

"What happened, Maier?"

The detective shook his head in exhaustion and pointed at the car. Carissa had pounced on him as soon as he'd reached the guest house in Kampot.

She looked indescribable, all in red. Before he could say anything, she handed him a Vodka orange and a half-smoked joint. Maier couldn't have imagined a better breakfast.

In a few rushed sentences he told his old flame what had happened during the night. Carissa looked on with concern.

"Raksmei wants to stay here, wants to take over the orphanage again. Do you think Tep will come back to take his revenge? After all she played a double game to avenge her brother."

Maier shrugged his shoulders.

"I don't think that she is in danger. Tep escaped, but he is badly injured. I doubt he will seek revenge. He has known Raksmei too long. She is his best friend's daughter and he may not know that she crossed her father."

Carissa looked at Maier in disbelief.

"The White Spider was in Cambodia in the Seventies. He worked as a Yugoslavian diplomat while the revolution was in full swing here. He fled with Tep when the Vietnamese invaded. On the way to Thailand, they killed a family near Kep and abducted and raped the youngest daughter, Kaley. After the war, Kaley had two children with the old German. Tep took the children and hid them in Kampot. More recently, the White Spider returned to Cambodia to be closer to these children. But when he got here, he had this idea of starting an assassination service. He made Kaley a kind of chairperson of the whole project."

"And what happened after the casino blew up?"

Maier shrugged. "Even before the casino went up, things were very strange. I think I had a flashback from the drugs that Raksmei had given me in the temple. After Mikhail had disappeared, I spent the early evening with Kaley on the rooftop. She was like a ghost."

Carissa shot Maier a look full of pity before turning her head.

"I am serious. A few minutes after the casino went up, Kaley emerged from the burning building, not a scratch on her, got into a car with Tep and bags full of money and drove off. Everyone else in there, except for Rolf, died. I cannot explain it."

Maier noticed that Carissa looked embarrassed by his lack of a credible story and dropped the subject.

"I am sure that Tep has returned to his temple hideaway. Maybe he still has a few slaves there who will look after him. I still don't know who Mikhail really is, what he was doing up on the plateau and what his connection to us and to Tep is. But I think this strange Russian means to confuse. He has not played his last card yet. I think it is best we cross into Thailand as quickly as possible, to be safe. Then we will see what we can do."

Carissa embraced him, "Yes, Maier, let's check into a hotel in Bangkok and not leave the room for a week."

"Do you have a passport?"

She shook her head.

"Rolf doesn't have one either. But I think we can cross at Koh Kong."

The muddy road to the border led through the Cardamom Mountains. The small group was forced to cross four rivers, swollen by the rains, their vehicle loaded onto improvised bamboo platforms operated by skinny men dressed in rags. At nightfall, they reached the border town of Koh Kong.

Maier drove the car directly to the pier. The small town was – but for a handful of casinos where rich, gambling-addicted Thais lost their fortunes – a collection of wooden huts built on high stilts. The settlement appeared to slide slowly into the tepid dirty coastal waters of the Gulf of Thailand. Children and pigs played amongst the crumbling houses. Policemen sat on shaded balconies, drank beer and played with their guns. As soon as Maier had got out of the car, tough teenagers tried to sell him marihuana, opium, heroin and other teenagers. Maier grabbed the boy who spoke the best English, pulled him back to the car and pressed twenty dollars into his hand.

"What's your name?"

"Somchai," the boy lied.

"I need a speedboat to Thailand. My two passengers don't have passports. We have to avoid the Thai border post."

Somchai, hardly older than fourteen and already thoroughly disillusioned with life, grinned brazenly at Maier.

"Tausend dollar, mister... Kein problem."

Maier laughed. "If you can get me a boat in ten minutes, I will give you forty thousand dollars. What do you think?"

Somchai laughed back. "I think you cheat me, *barang*. If you have forty thousand dollar in your car, you not need me."

Maier opened the door, pulled the keys from the ignition and dangled them in front of the boy's nose.

"Get me a boat to Thailand and the car is yours. It is not registered. It does not have plates and it is brand new. There is even some petrol in the tank."

The boy didn't hesitate. He skipped around the car and jumped into the passenger seat.

"No problem, mister, you drive."

Minutes later, they stopped in front of a small guest house. An old, toothless Khmer lay in a hammock next to the door.

Somchai beamed. "This my grandfather. He has boat. Small boat, but very fast."

The boy woke the old man and implored him in Khmer. The alleged grandfather stared at Maier and the car and finally asked in French. "You are being followed? By the police? By bad elements?"

Maier shook his head.

"We were attacked and robbed in Sihanoukville. My friend is injured and needs a doctor."

The old Khmer took a long hard look at Rolf, almost as long as at the car. Maier knew that the man didn't believe a word of his story. But that hardly mattered. This was business.

"OK, tonight I take you across the border to Trat. Take a room in my guest house and buy new clothes in the market. If you arrive in Thailand the way you look now, you'll be arrested."

Maier looked down his shirt front. The man was right. And sensible. He looked used up. His vest was torn and frayed, his trousers black with dirt and dried blood. He wouldn't make it to Bangkok like this. Appearance was everything in Thailand.

He dragged Rolf to a small room. Carissa left to buy clothes, while Maier took a shower. Then he showered his client and gulped down a plate of loc lac, fried beef topped by a fried egg. After the long journey Maier felt like he was eating an exotic delicacy. Even Rolf swallowed a few bites in silence. The young coffee heir was still in shock.

Late at night, Somchai and his grandfather came to pick up the small group. Rolf and Maier had changed into loud beachwear. Maier had sacrificed his moustache. Carissa had dyed her hair black and Rolf had hidden his blank eyes behind mirrored sunglasses.

This time, Somchai insisted on driving. The boy could hardly see above the steering wheel, but he handled the heavy SUV like a champion driver. A few minutes' drive took them to a dilapidated wooden pier, which jutted out between two abandoned stilt houses into the Stung Koh Poi River. Maier grabbed the keys from the ignition, his only bargaining chip, and walked out onto the pier.

"Your boat."

Maier looked down at a plastic bowl, a tiny fiber-glass dingy with an ancient outboard engine. The contraption bopped precariously around in the filthy water. Maier turned to the old man with a doubtful expression.

The Khmer smiled widely at his client.

"No problem, Monsieur. I have done this trip many times. I drop you at a pier from where you can get a taxi to Bangkok. Avoid the buses, they are often stopped by the military close to the border. A taxi with three *barang* inside is no problem."

Somchai helped Rolf into the small vessel, which was tied off between the two houses. When the boy had jumped back up to the pier, he held his hand out to Maier. The detective gave him the keys for the car.

Maier didn't turn around as they slowly oozed through the black water out into the Gulf of Thailand. The boat was a bit too small, but the old man was a good captain. As soon as they'd left Koh Kong behind, he opened up the engine and they sped across the open sea towards freedom. An hour later, the small vessel was far from the Cambodian coast in international waters. As Koh Kong faded into the darkness behind them, Maier relaxed. Cambodia was done. The case had bled itself to death. It was almost time to lick the wounds and celebrate being alive.

Around midnight, the boat changed direction and raced towards the bright lights of the Thai coastline. Rolf had passed out next to him, but Carissa sat in front of the boat, wide awake, her eyes scanning the empty night.

44

THE CITY OF ANGELS

THE TV SPAT silent images of crises in other places. The air-con was going full blast and sounded like a coven of witches, out of sight, flying circles, riding their brooms, exhaling arctic breath, somewhere above his head. Carissa had fallen asleep, fully clothed, on the bed next to him. It was breakfast time. Or 2am in Hamburg. Sundermann answered on the second ring.

"Maier, you hit the big city?"

"Yes, I just dropped Rolf Müller-Overbeck in hospital. He is almost safe and sound and will come out of this with a couple of scratches, both mental and physical."

Maier squinted into the morning. He was exhausted and not in the mood for a debriefing. He looked across at Carissa who managed to look beautiful even as she slept with her mouth open and her face drawn.

3000 miles to the west, his boss started congratulating him.

"Maier, we spoke to the family while you were en route. Frau Müller-Overbeck is as close to happy as she'll ever get."

He knew that Sundermann's compliments sometimes came with a catch.

"You've done great work, but we aren't done."

Maier felt irritation rising in his throat. He was so completely done.

"The case is not closed? We've done everything the ice queen hired us for, haven't we?"

Sundermann took his time and chose his words carefully, "As I said, Frau Müller-Overbeck is virtually ecstatic that her son is back in what she calls the 'real world' and that he's well cared for. But you know these wealthy clients. Enough is never enough, Maier. Easy is never easy. I know you're fed up and exhausted, but this morning she paid a fat bonus, and asked that you visit Rolf in hospital when he is himself again. And the young heir will ask you to return to Cambodia, to find the woman and to get her out. The family pays, because Rolf has promised that he will return to Hamburg if Kaley is safe. We gather that she's back at that temple where they kept you prisoner. What do you think?"

Maier was sick to his stomach. He felt like a babysitter for Hamburg's rich again. Unnecessary. And not in the mood to return to the hell he'd just escaped from. Maier had seen enough of the jungle temple.

"I don't want to appear negative, but I think it's almost impossible to free Kaley from the twists and turns of her past. The distance between the two, it is enormous – cultures, mentalities, education, expectations. Rolf ignores the fact that she is so deeply traumatised by the war that she has an obligation to her past."

The sour hiss of the static between Hamburg and the Thai capital bled into Maier's dull, tired head. Some case. But Sundermann wasn't going to let his detective's sober assessment sway him. Maier could already hear the wheels crunching.

"Maier, none of this matters. We took the case and you've resolved everything this far. But now the family Müller-Overbeck is throwing more money at us in order to help their son close this chapter of his life. That's why you'll visit him in hospital tomorrow."

"Were you threatened with the city council?"

"I was," the agency director admitted. "I have to be politician as much as I have to be businessman. Let's give the gods of Blankenese the feeling that they can rely on us. It's good for me and good for you. And for the German coffee industry."

Without a great deal of conviction, Maier consented.

"You know that I won't achieve what Rolf expects. He wants me to ease his guilt, because he killed the woman's daughter."

"Maier, do your thing. I know you can. Work your magic one last time. Go and see Rolf, check the water temperature and do as our client suggests. She's threatening to break my left hand while piling money in the right one."

Maier hung up and looked across at Carissa. So much for her suggestion to spend a week in bed together. He guessed she would go back to Phnom Penh. He almost envied her for feeling at home there, for having somewhere to go.

Rolf Müller-Overbeck lay in a private suite in Crescent Hospital, a few minutes off Sukhumvit Road in downtown Bangkok. The hospital was one of the most expensive in Southeast Asia and served as a collection point for countless tourists and wealthy Thais, as well as ailing family members of dictators from neighbouring countries.

As Maier entered the room, four giggling nurses were making the bed. Rolf sat in a wheelchair and conducted the girls' efforts. Maier felt a quick flashback go through him – to the young girls, dressed all in black, who'd lined up by his bunk, needles in hand.

"Hello, Maier, good to see you. Sorry I lost it with you in Phnom Penh. You saved my life."

The young German had regained some of the colour in his face and almost looked like a hero. His hair had been cut short, his earring had disappeared and Maier noticed that the coffee heir was starting to cultivate a moustache, a little like his own.

"Rolf, you are looking good. I am glad we got you out. It would have been a shame to throw your life away in Cambodia."

Maier thought he could detect a more thoughtful expression on his client's face.

"Maier, I simply didn't know what to do after I'd killed that little girl. Pete took charge of the situation so quickly, there was no choice. I was...not assertive enough. I made mistakes. Now it's so long ago that it's become unreal in my memory."

The nurses lifted Rolf off the wheelchair onto his bed and waved goodbye, giggling on the way out.

"Do they help you go to the toilet as well?"

Rolf laughed. "Probably, if I asked them to."

Then he became serious again.

Maier sat down on the sofa that stood next to the patient's bed.

"Did Kaley ever tell you anything about her sister?"

The young man from Hamburg shook his head in surprise, "She told me almost nothing of her past. I only know that she was married to Tep's son."

"And you want me to go back there and find Kaley for you?"

"Maier, I want to know who she really is and why she took part in this terrible ceremony in the casino. I want to know whether anything can be done to change her situation. I didn't manage that but I owe her. I killed her child."

Rolf had tears in his eyes. Maier decided to tell Rolf no more about Kaley and the men and children in her life. Or about Daniela, her dead German sister. These stories were best kept in the files. Maier left. Outside in the leaden Bangkok heat, he stopped to catch his breath. As futile as so many things he had done since working on this case. He wasn't going to get around his last pilgrimage to Cambodia. Maier flagged a taxi and headed straight for the airport.

45

HER EYES SAID GOODBYE

SIEM REAP, formerly a provincial French town, was on its way to becoming Cambodia's second capital. The world had rediscovered the spectacular ruins of the Angkor Empire, and the land-mines around the temples had been cleared. The tourists were back. Since the international airport had opened, investors, who circled like vultures above the UNESCO world heritage site, could not get hotels, restaurants, shopping centres, massage parlours, casinos and bars off the ground quick enough.

In the brand new Siem Reap International Airport, the immigration officer had photographed Maier, who was travelling under a false name on a clean French passport. Bangkok made such things possible.

Maier rented a motorbike and drove out to the temples. The town's first traffic light had just been installed and was guarded by three policemen with loudspeakers, who were giving twelve-hour-long lessons in basic traffic rules to passing motorists. Ten minutes later, he circled the broad moat that stretched around Angkor Wat.

The world's largest temple lay in the morning sun like a sleeping colossus, but the detective didn't stop. Instead, he opened the throttle and shot through the southern gate into Angkor Thom, the old Khmer capital, past the Bayon temple and its two hundred or so gigantic faces that smiled down stoically at Maier, challenging him to drive further into the jungle. It was too early for the tour groups and buses and

Maier had the roads all to himself. Many of the ruins were surrounded by dense forest and Maier had to brake hard now and then to avoid mowing down one of the many monkeys who enjoyed sitting on the tarmac before it got hot.

Maier left Angkor Thom via the Victory Gate and ran past the eastern Baray, a huge reservoir built by the Angkor kings to help run the thousand-year-old empire's powerhouse economy. Village children jumped into the street as Maier passed, waving postcards and cans of Coke, hoping to make a few riels off this early traveler.

Beyond Banteay Srey, the Citadel of Women, the road turned into a red lateritic track. Maier pushed on as fast as possible. He'd planned to return to Siem Reap the same day and catch a night flight back to Bangkok.

Small settlements stretched along the dusty road, huts on stilts, without electricity or water. Until recently, there'd been jungle behind the huts, but the poor who lived here had logged and burnt it for rich landowners – the land looked like a wasted moonscape.

Beng Melea had been built in the twelfth century, following the same basic design as Angkor Wat.

Maier stopped in front of the overgrown temple. A CMAC crew, known to its international donors as the Cambodian Mine Action Center, was working close to the temple. Twenty young men in blue uniforms roped off a small piece of land next to the ruin and began to search the dry ground, metre by metre. It would take years, if not decades, to remove all the mines and explosives buried in Cambodia.

Maier drove along a narrow path into the forest, which forked several times. He followed fresh tire tracks deep into the jungle of northwest Cambodia. An hour into his journey, the track broadened. Maier slowed as a crumbling stone tower emerged from the foliage ahead. He had reached his destination and pushed the bike off the track into the forest. Small green parrots chased through the canopy above and Maier could see a few flying foxes sleeping in the trees. The world was fine. For a while Maier sat at the bottom of a tree, letting the silence settle. This time he wasn't going to be overrun by murderous teenage girls.

The temple was smaller than Beng Melea and completely subsumed by the forest. Maier didn't see anyone, but he approached the ruin slowly and with care. He circled the building. The structure had only one tower. Two others had collapsed and pulled down part of the roof with them. An SUV stood parked behind the temple. The engine was still warm. The car was unlocked and Maier found a gun in the glove compartment. He stared at it, then left it where he'd found it. Partially-burnt suitcases crammed with cash filled the boot and the back seat.

Suddenly he heard voices from the temple interior and hunkered down behind the sandstone wall which surrounded the building. Something stank. Terribly. Slowly, ever so slowly, he raised his head above the wall.

Pete and Inspector Viengsra were barely recognisable. The two men grinned yellow teeth at Maier. The detective dropped back down behind the wall. Tep had brought their heads from Bokor, driven them onto wooden stakes and set them up at the entrance to the temple. Flies cruised in thick, shape-shifting clouds around what was left of the two men. Pete's formerly red hair had turned rust brown and the eyes of the policeman were missing. Even on Maier's side of the wall, the smell was unbearable. He retreated to his bike, vomited into the bushes and sat in the shade until the sun dropped into the trees.

A couple of hours later, he picked a different entrance for his second attempt to enter the temple. This time he got lucky. He could hear the general's voice reverberate around the temple ruin. The old soldier spoke English.

"Cambodia no longer need you. Your men and your children are dead. All dead. Your power used up. The curse of the Kangaok Meas coming to an end."

Maier slid into an alcove that might once have housed an apsara. Inside, he could barely make out Tep in the semi-darkness. The general wore a bandage around his neck and had his hands up. Kaley pointed a gun at Tep's chest. A couple of torches lodged in the temple walls lit the scene.

Would she shoot, if Tep attacked her?

Tep smiled and Maier knew that the old general didn't feel threatened. He continued in Khmer.

"Please come. I will take you back to the car. There's no need for the gun. We're both Khmer."

Maier couldn't work out why the old general had spoken English to Kaley. Did he know the detective had arrived?

Tep and Kaley had turned off into a narrow corridor. Maier

followed slowly. He was still spooked by the young murder girls and desperately hoped he wouldn't meet one in the dark. But the temple was abandoned. Tep and Kaley were the only survivors of the Kangaok Meas Project. The general and Kaley pressed on, with Maier following at what he considered a safe distance. He cursed himself for having left the gun in Tep's car. He'd have to jump the old man at the next corner. But the detective hung back too far behind the strange couple.

When Maier finally stepped from the narrow corridor into the open, it was too late. Tep didn't make deals. The old man had led Kaley into a logged clearing and disarmed her. Kaley stood stock still, forlorn and confused. The general was already fifty metres away, limping back towards his car.

Suddenly he spun around, saw Maier and shouted, "We give life to Kangaok Meas, my friend Lorenz and me. And when we need to, we take it as well. Today I finish our dream."

Kaley stared at her tormentor without comprehension. Maier stopped on the lowest step of the temple stairway and called to her.

"Hello, Kaley."

She didn't turn. He called to her again. More than ever he now thought of her as a ghost. What had he been thinking, trying to save this shattered woman?

"Kaley."

Tep raised his gun and fired a couple of shots at the detective. Maier dropped to the ground, looking for something to hide behind, but the old general was too far away and the bullets hit the temple walls a few metres away. Tep didn't come back for Maier, an easy target on the bottom step of the temple stairway. Mercy was hardly in the former Khmer Rouge soldier's repertoire of sentiments. So why didn't the Cambodian come and finish him off?

The clearing in front of the Khmer ruin had gone dead silent. The general had stopped walking, his gun empty. As if waiting for something. For the end.

Maier waved at the woman and slowly started walking towards her, watching the general as well as the ground ahead. He didn't have to go far to understand how Tep had trapped Kaley and was using her as bait. But it was too late to turn back. A few metres to his right, a handful of warning signs for landmines had been thrown to the forest floor. Tep must have had them removed. The old general obviously knew how to cross the clearing without losing a limb. But Maier didn't. The detective suddenly had the feeling that the last unresolved questions of his case were about to be answered. Everything was falling into place. What had the Russian told him, before he'd left the roof of the casino?

"Don't forget, follow the sticks."

It had sounded like nonsense. But the Russian wasn't stupid and had never said anything unnecessary. Mikhail's remark suddenly burnt like a flame through Maier's mind and he took another look at the clearing.

Mikhail was a step ahead. He had known even then, on the roof of the casino, that Maier would end up in a minefield. And not just in any minefield. In this minefield.

At a distance of about two metres, small sticks rose from the dry forest floor. Some had been broken and kicked away. Perhaps Tep had tried to obscure the safe way out of the clearing, but after studying the ground for some time, Maier could see a clear route all the way to the petrified woman. One just had to know. Without worrying too much, Maier stepped onto the dusty ground and slowly walked towards Kaley, who looked at him in shock.

After a few metres, something like dizziness overcame him. He stopped, only to notice that his sweat-soaked shirt was sticking to his back. Fear. It was all in the mind, he told himself. The Russian hadn't killed him in Bokor. There had to be a reason. Mikhail did nothing without reason. Mikhail had foreseen this situation.

Tep still stood on the edge of the clearing and watched Maier. He was too far away to shoot them. But he didn't want to walk back out into the minefield. Which didn't stop him cursing Maier.

"Maier, so good to see you so close to death. You will go a traditional way, I promise you. I tell you our first meeting, we not like snoops in Cambodia. Have nice day with lady. Today is last one for you."

The old soldier turned in disgust and got into his car.

Kaley shook her head, a few metres ahead of him. For the first time, Maier saw her, the Kangaok Meas, as a human being, fragile and vulnerable, without the aura, just like anyone else.

"And how do we get out of here?"

"Just the same way we came in. As a man in Bokor told me, follow the sticks."

Maier looked at the ground in front of him. On the way out of the clearing, Tep had torn away many of the sticks. The way they'd come, back to the temple looked more promising.

"Look at the small sticks in the ground. We have to follow their path. Here and there some have collapsed but we should be able to see my footsteps."

They began to walk back slowly.

Maier went first. Now and then he turned and looked back at Tep, who sat in his car, waiting for him or the woman to die. Thirty metres more.

Suddenly they reached open ground. Maier couldn't see any of the sticks. They were so close to the temple now. So close, fifteen steps, no more. Fifteen steps of death. Maier stood looking desperately for his footprints when Kaley passed him. She made directly for the temple. She almost had a spring in her step. Maier followed carefully and turned once more.

The general had been waiting for Maier's turn and waved from the car's driving seat before he bent forward to put the key in the ignition.

The explosion threw the heavy SUV into the air. The heat of the flames was incredible. One of the axles came off and flew, tires burning, across the temple wall. A second explosion ripped the car apart, perhaps the petrol tank had caught fire.

"Let's go, back into the temple."

Maier squeezed past Kaley and took up the trail through the minefield. The last few steps towards safety were clearly visible. A few seconds later he stood with Kaley on the broad stairs of the temple. Maier wiped the sweat from his forehead and sat down in the shadow of the narrow corridor that led into the temple interior. Kaley had a dreamy expression on her face. An expression that Maier hadn't seen before.

She stepped towards the detective and embraced him.

"Thank you, Maier, you are good man. Les is right."

The scene he'd watched through the hole in the floor of the casino flashed through Maier's head. He never did have a chance to fulfil his promise. He'd been deluding himself and the woman too. As she stepped away from him, he held out his hand, but he knew instinctively that she wouldn't take it. Kaley was done with taking and had long given everything she had ever had. Just like Cambodia. All she expected him to do now was to witness her last pathetic, heroic act. She turned away from him and, no longer choosing her steps carefully, left the safety of the temple and walked into the night. Maier did not try to stop her or follow her. But neither did he leave. He owed her that much, perhaps more, much more.

There were times when Maier liked to remember the gentle attempts by his friend Hort to make him laugh, especially when there was absolutely nothing to laugh about. Those were the moments when he thought he could understand his dead friend Hort.

Then the exploding landmine ripped away all his thoughts. The ground shook briefly. A cloud of dust rose from the tired earth. It was all over.

Maier, stunned, remained on the temple steps. Absentmindedly, he put his hands into the pockets of his vest and pulled out a strange object. After staring at his find mindlessly for a short eternity, he recognised it as one of Carissa's half-smoked, crumpled joints. The detective lit up and watched parrots at play in the canopy on the edge of the clearing. Rolf Müller-Overbeck was going to be distraught. As Maier followed the exuberant dive-bombing of the small green birds that squawked above his head, his mind drifted away from the carnage and he experienced a sudden moment of almost absolute certainty. It was time to go and see his woman.

46

A MIRROR FOR THE BLIND

Sundermann had sunk deep into his wicker chair and watched Maier and Carissa fight over the best parts of the dinner they were sharing. Eclectic world music dripped from invisible speakers through the Foreign Correspondents Club. A faint breeze from the river cut through the heat.

Maier was pleased. His mission was ending back where it had begun. Down in the street, the hustlers, the limbless and the hopeless congregated just as they had for days, weeks, months and years. Tourists stumbled along, avoiding the drug dealers and taxi girls who tried to separate the visitors from their cash. A little circus of cross-cultural absurdities.

But things were looking up. Cambodia was coming out of its self-prescribed dark age, blinking, insecure, proud and with so little care for her past that her very immediate future would likely be a happy one. Beyond the next ten minutes though, everything was speculation. The culture of impunity was the only ticket in town.

Other guests kept looking back at Maier and his partner. Some men walked past them several times. Carissa looked stunning. Her hair had turned white once again and her shiny green dress, tailored from Thai silk, perfectly complemented the large red ruby, suspended from a thin gold chain around her neck, which wanted to get lost in her cleavage.

Maier detested paperwork and had debriefed himself over an excellent sea food salad, several enormous wood-fired pizzas and many tall glasses of Vodka orange. The orange juice was freshly squeezed and the detective was happy. Sundermann and Carissa were on their third bottle of Beaujolais, when Maier finally ended with his account of his moment in the mine field. Sundermann appeared to be as sober as at the start of the evening.

Maier had respect for his boss, who was ten years older, drank like a world champion and looked after the handful of detectives he employed like a kind uncle. And Sundermann had a discreet, if noisy style – suits by Armani, close shave, an expensive pair of rimless glasses, a tie for every occasion, a likeable open smile and a compliment or calming word for every client. Maier liked working with the best. He had learned, a long time ago, in his life as a war correspondent, that working with amateurs led to calamities. It was no different for detectives. He could trust Sundermann. Sundermann had come all the way to Phnom Penh to personally sign off on Maier's Cambodian adventure. And Sundermann always asked the right questions.

Just like Carissa. The journalist excused herself and Sundermann switched to German.

"Who's this Mikhail? A colleague?"

"First, I thought he was just a cynic, a former mercenary, who wanted to take things in his own hands up there. But I guess he was a man with a plan."

"An investigator?"

Maier shook his head in doubt.

"That man's an assassin, not a detective. He didn't hesitate for a second to kill Pete in that jail and he almost shot me dead. He also didn't defuse the explosives on the hotel roof, he just moved the clock of the timer forward."

"So why didn't he shoot you?"

Maier hesitated, tried to process his thoughts from assumptions into usable information.

"It was a calculated risk. I am sure of that. This crazy Russian decided in that split second, with his finger on the trigger, that I could be useful to him. But how, I have no idea. Not exactly. I have my theories."

Sundermann nodded.

"No, Mikhail was no Russian Rambo. I think he was a sleeper who had been waiting for something near that casino. I'm sure he has a military background."

Maier knew that the chances of ever tracking down the Russian were minute.

"Our research here in Cambodia didn't turn up a thing. Disappeared into thin air. Same at the borders, no sign of him. But that doesn't really mean anything, aside from the fact that he's a pro."

"Maier, I have heard, from a source in southern Germany, that someone else was after the woman. Perhaps an associate of the White Spider. Or our friend Mikhail. Perhaps you were used to provoke the events in the casino. The question is, was there another case, some kind of mission going, in connection with Kaley, while you were in Cambodia? And does it have anything to do with Lorenz?"

"We know some of the answers to this already. Kaley's sister, one Daniela Stricker, who was killed by Tep or his son, had lived in southern Germany for twenty years. She had a German passport, and then turned up after all these years on Cambodia's coast and promptly got killed."

"That we know. But we don't know why she came back or whether she was connected to someone else in this story."

Maier shrugged. "Perhaps she hired the Russian to find her sister. I am sure he wired the car at the temple. He planted the sticks in the minefield. In a way I finished his job for him. And mine. Quite brilliant."

Sundermann didn't have to say anything. Maier knew his boss agreed.

"I have a feeling I will meet Mikhail again," said Maier. "But I doubt we will find out exactly what is role was in all this. He is a slippery customer."

Sundermann nodded thoughtfully and let it go. As he passed a sealed manila envelope to his detective, Carissa floated back onto the Foreign Correspondents Club's terrace.

"The notes for Laos," Sundermann said. "Your next case. I trust it will be a walk in the park compared to your Cambodian mission. When you are done here, fly to Hamburg and meet your next client. I rely on you, Maier. Travel safely"

Maier made a grab for the case files and an almost full bottle of wine and pulled Carissa away from the table and through the club. The world turned around them and Maier knew that everything was OK, would be OK. He would beat his traumas. He would start right away. Carissa would help him.

"Let's go to bed and celebrate."

Carissa laughed, her eyes full of challenge. "Yes, Maier, let's party like there's no tomorrow."

Maier was too happy and too drunk to think about her words or to notice the dark look simmering beneath her smile as they descended the broad stairs into the rubbish strewn street.

They jumped a tuk-tuk to the Hotel Renakse, a charming former royal guest house opposite the palace, a few hundred meters from their dinner party, and for Maier the most romantic place in the city. They propped each other up as they slowly walked through the hotel garden up the pebbled drive and through the colonial-era building's sparsely furnished corridors. The night was dark and cool. The floor tiles danced under their feet. A bird called from the river, answered by the cry of a lone drunk. Everything was good and Maier wallowed in his illusions, throwing furtive glances at the journalist, who responded with the happy-sad looks of someone hopelessly in love. This was the closest he might ever get to it. To something essential. Once in the room, they fell into a fever. Even youth was somehow with them and the last thing Carissa said to Maier as he drifted into sleep, burnt itself into his mind like a rust-colored tropical sunset after the rains, "All through our dinner, I was on the verge of having an orgasm, Maier. You were the most handsome man in Phnom Penh tonight, no doubt about it. It's uncanny you came back here. And it's been good knowing you all these years. And so much more."

When Maier woke in the morning, she was gone. Her smell still clung to the sheets, but he knew that Carissa had said goodbye. His life was empty and without worry, just as he wished it to be. It hurt. He got up and went to the bathroom to examine his psyche.

With bright red lipstick, she had written one of his favourite quotes on the mirror.

"We live as we dream."

ACKNOWLEDGMENTS

Thanks to my family, especially my wife Aroon Thaewchatturat and my brother Marc Eberle – both played instrumental roles in getting me to finish The Cambodian Book of the Dead.

Thanks to my friend Hans Kemp for embarking on an adventure called Crime Wave Press and helping to get Detective Maier on the road. Lucy Ridout did a great early edit.

In 1995, I crossed from Thailand into Cambodia at Hat Lek, racing in a speed boat up the jungle-fringed Koh Kong River, with troops dug in on both sides. The other passengers besides my travel companion and me were a man who had a suitcase chained to his wrist and a sex worker on her way home from Pattaya. The sky was gun metal grey. I was hooked.

Cambodia is a land of stories, both beautiful and beautifully poignant – an obvious location for the first job for German detective Maier, a former war correspondent who investigates crimes around Asia. Throughout my many subsequent trips, I was touched by the friendliness of the Cambodians and shocked by what they have to put up with.

Those who provided insights: Youk Chang (at DCCAM), David Chandler, Soparoath Yi, Poch Kim, Luke Duggleby, Gerhard Joren, Roland Neveu, Kraig Lieb, Barbara Lettner, Jane Elizabeth, Jochen Spieker, Joe Heffernan, Chanthy Kak, Julien Poulson, Kosal Khiev, Chris Kelly, Tassilo Brinzer and Marie Phoue. Thanks also to my agent Philip Patterson at Marjacq in London.

The amazing Emlyn Rees put the shine to the text.

Maier will be back in *The Man with the Golden Mind*.

THE MAN WITH THE GOLDEN MIND

DETECTIVE MAIER MYSTERIES BOOK 2

1

THE HONEY TRAP

LAO PEOPLE'S DEMOCRATIC REPUBLIC, OCTOBER 1976

THE TWO MEN crossed the river road as the sun set on the other side of the Mekong, over Thailand. Hammers and sickles set against blood-red backgrounds fluttered from a row of sorry-looking poles by the water. This was the Laotian way to remind the Thais who'd won the war.

It was early November. The rains had stopped, but the river remained swollen and muddy. The revolution, a long time in coming, had come. And gone. Vientiane looked less like a national capital than a run-down suburb of Dresden with better weather. The sun, a misty, dull red fireball, sunk into the turgid current in slow motion.

Once the American infrastructure – a few office blocks and residential areas, the CIA compound at Kilometer 14, a handful of churches, bars, brothels, clinics and aid agencies – had been removed, closed down or reassigned, there was nothing left to do but to enjoy socialism. The locals lingered in hammocks or went about their business in culturally prescribed lethargy as they'd done for centuries.

Once it got dark, Laotians disenchanted with the revolution would take to modest paddle boats to flee across the water to the free world. The authorities, glad to be rid of these vaguely troublesome citizens, turned a blind eye or two. Laos was that kind of place. Not even the politburo took anything too serious. And if it did, no one ever heard about it. No one worried about the consequences of this or that so long as it didn't make any waves in the here and now. Some workers' utopia.

The two men walked at a healthy but innocuous pace. The German Democratic Republic's newly appointed cultural attaché to Laos, Manfred Rendel, strode purposefully ahead, a harried expression on his face. He was the younger though hardly the fitter of the two, and sweated profusely in his polyester suit. No one would have called him handsome, not even from across the river and the free world. Rendel needed to lose weight both in body and mind. For now, it was the mind that was in the process of unburdening itself.

"I tell you, it's serious. Thought it better we meet on the street than in my office, where half the world's likely to listen in. Especially our friends, the Viets."

The second man, broad-shouldered and in his early fifties, his blond hair cropped short, cautiously brought up the rear. He had just arrived in town and wore an innocuous, short-sleeved white shirt with gray slacks, black shoes, no tie. He kept his eyes locked to the ground and took care not to look directly at passers-by. He walked the way a predator might move through dense jungle, purposefully, quietly and acutely aware of everything around him. Elegant in a way it was hard to put a finger on. A casual onlooker might have assumed him to be a rather superfluous character, a slightly ruffled subordinate of the more dynamic man up front. A very careful observer would have noted that this man achieved near invisibility without a great deal of effort.

"She asked for me, specifically?"

Rendel nodded. "Asked for your codename. She said Weltmeister. Loud and clear. Was a bit of a shock. I mean, no one knows that name. Mentioned Long Cheng as well. And gold. American gold. Lots of American gold."

Rendel's eyes flashed greedily.

The older man ignored the attaché's predilection for vice and profiteering and carefully scanned both sides of the potholed river road ahead of them. Everything looked as it always did. The courtyard of the Lane Xang, the riverside's best hotel, lay deserted but for the usual half dozen party limos that parked there for the weekend, their drivers lounging under a rickety wooden stand to the left of the building, plucking hair from their chins with steel tweezers, and playing cards.

It was Saturday evening and the country's decision makers were most likely lying half dead in their suites, nursing their foreign liqueur hangovers, fawned over by taxi girls, exhausted from celebrating the revolution the night before or getting ready to do it all over again. Unlimited supplies of Russian vodka, local sex slaves and an entrenched feudal mindset that was immune to both the benefits and strictures of communism could do terrible things to a government, even one that had partaken in beating the world's mightiest superpower.

Prior to the revolution, the same drivers had sat in the same spot, waiting for their American employers to emerge from the same kind of weekend carnage.

The traffic was light. A group of female students, dressed in white blouses and dark sarongs, cycled past and threatened to distract the attaché from the clandestine nature of his walk. But the passing girls didn't manage to stop Manfred Rendel grinning with all the severity of a man who'd spent his entire life steadfastly refusing to develop a sense of humor, "Must have practiced pronouncing it. It rolled right off her tongue. Wouldn't tell me anything else. Good-looking little number, too. Pale skin, Chinese features. Nice tits. Bad teeth. Savage basically. She calls herself Mona. And she said the magic word. Weltmeister."

The older man shook his head and hung back, as if trying to distance himself from his old friend who reveled in the loss of his moral compass. But it was just a reaction on his side to hearing his code name spoken by someone else. For the first time in decades.

"A Hmong girl perhaps. But hardly anyone knows my codename. A few Viets, maybe. And they'd never blab. Even at our embassy here, no one knows. The past is the past."

His cover had been blown. Someone was on to him. Somebody knew he'd been to Long Cheng. Someone was on to the fact that he had been to the secret American base not just as a Vietnamese agent, but that he'd lived and worked there for the CIA. And whoever had made him, they were organized and they were close. But it never occurred to Weltmeister to tell his old friend the truth. The truth hadn't propelled him to the top of his profession.

Right now, he needed more information. If the cat was out of the spook sack, he was finished. As were all those others, who had sponged off his genius years ago. If the U48 surfaced, people would be soiling their government-issue suits from Washington to Moscow, from Hanoi to Bangkok. Retirees across several continents would scramble to hide ill-gotten gains and fear for the retraction of past honors, or worse. No one would be happy. Heads would roll in the White House and the Kremlin. A small but vital aspect of twentieth-century history would have to be rewritten. The man codenamed Weltmeister shrugged. Who cared about Realpolitik? His life was on the line. The trenches he'd dug, the palisades he had carefully erected around himself were about to be overrun. He'd have to check out of the program, batten down the hatches, close the loopholes and sink into the dust of history, never to reemerge. His war was coming to an end. He'd have fun ending it on his terms.

"No one knows except you, Manfred."

Rendel stopped in his tracks on the crumbling pavement and turned back to his friend, his face flushed with anger and, deeper down, beneath the layers of fat, slothdom and greed, a little fear.

"Well, I didn't shop you. And I resent that remark. How long have we known each other? Didn't I help you get laid at college in Leipzig all those years ago? When you acted like an introvert spy who'd come in from the cold? Semester after semester, I talked you up with the girls without ever hinting at what a truly twisted individual you really were. Didn't I help facilitate your current position? You have changed sides more often than the oldest whore in Vientiane, and the first thing I do when your name comes up is call you. Isn't that what trust is made of?"

The older man smiled sardonically, "You know how it is in our line of work. Take no prisoners."

But Weltmeister chuckled disarmingly as he spoke, and Rendel let the threat pass. The cultural attaché was a sentimental man.

As daylight faded, the Mekong receded into the almost-silent tropical night, filled with mosquitoes and military patrols who would have the streets cleared in a couple of hours. Only the cicadas would be singing in Vientiane tonight. Across the river in Si Chiang Mai, the nearest town on the far shore, primitive rock music throbbed from unseen speakers. This was the Thai way to remind the Laotians that the forces of evil had been beaten but not vanquished, and that the river served as one of the most important Cold War fault lines in the world.

The clandestine meeting was coming to an end.

"I mean it, Manfred. Let's play the old game. A little subterfuge. You meet her. Tell her you're Weltmeister. See what she's got for us."

It was the younger man's turn to laugh.

"First, I'll see what she's got for me. This girl is a honey trap if ever I've seen one. I might as well taste the honey before I pry the trap open."

Weltmeister shrugged. "Just get the intel. Find out what she wants. Don't scare her with your cock. Just be me. And if she's Hmong, remind her that the war is over and that the good guys won. The Americans won't be back."

2

THE MOST SECRET PLACE ON EARTH

Two nights and a day later, Rendel and Weltmeister hid Mona under a tarpaulin in the back of the attaché's jeep and left town. The Hmong girl was desperate to get into the mountains and reunite with her brother, the man who knew where the gold was stashed. The man who'd given his sister one of the most secret codes of the American war in Asia. The man who'd sent her to the city. She'd spent the night with Rendel, only to intone the same mantra over and over again.

"We meet brother Léon. Léon meets Weltmeister. Very good."

And that was all he could lure out of her.

Outside the capital, the roads were muddy tracks lined by impenetrable walls of bamboo forest interspersed with tiny settlements and their adjacent fields. Children dressed in rags waved at them from the roadside. Neither man waved back.

The Laotian military stopped them at several roadblocks: Rendel's embassy credentials and a few cartons of American cigarettes provided smooth transitions. They spent the first night in a paddy field hut just north of Ban Houay Pamon. Rendel kept pestering the girl about the gold she'd shown him in Vientiane.

"Are you sure there is more of this gold up there?"

"You see, I tell the truth. Long Cheng, big American airport, many boxes gold. My brother, Léon, he show you. We meet in Long Cheng. You help me and Léon go America. We all rich. I help you."

Thousands of these hill tribe people had been caught up in the almost twenty-year-long war. Some had fled to refugee camps in Thailand, from where they had moved on to France and the US, while others lingered in the Laotian jungles, their futures blighted by their erstwhile alliance with the Americans. Weltmeister didn't have any interest in gold, nor did he care about the escape plans of a few CIA-trained Hmong rebels.

Mona was probably leading them into a trap. But he felt reasonably safe as long as Rendel kept up the charade of pretending to be his alter ego, the elusive superspy. The three travelers all had their private agendas. Loyalty, greed and the need for anonymity would be battling it out soon enough. Weltmeister relished the fact. He didn't like loose ends.

They entered Xaisomboun District. Beyond the small town of the same name, a trader's outpost mired in mud and the deprived locals' long faces, traffic petered out. Wild animals, so little known they'd never been on television, occasionally ran, scuttled, slithered or jumped across the road in front of the vehicle. The district, until recently the heart of the US Secret War in Laos, was off limits to everyone except Laotian military and local farmers. Even comrades, be they Soviet or German, weren't welcome. It was a different story for the Vietnamese. They went everywhere and de facto ruled parts of the country. Victors' justice.

The road snaked deeper into the hills, wearing down the jeep's suspension and the travelers' patience with every pond-sized hole in their path. Halfway through the second day of automotive torture, Mona told them to stop.

"Many army post before we reach Long Cheng. We walk from here."

They pushed the jeep into thick brush. As Rendel pulled the key from the ignition, only the faint tick of the hot engine was audible.

Weltmeister inhaled the forest. He loved the silence. Silence, he'd long decided, was his hobby.

Rendel unloaded several backpacks and a couple of shovels and pulled a gun from under the passenger seat.

"Manfred, how much gear did you bring? Are you planning to tunnel through to Vietnam?"

The attaché grinned. "Need something to carry at least some of that gold away with us. Once we figure the situation down there, we take what we can and try and work out a way to come back with a larger vehicle. Was thinking of burying some of it."

Weltmeister held out his hand. "Give me the gun then. I'm a better shot than you."

"In your dreams. This is my Dienstpistole from back home, the gun I was issued at the Ministry of State Security, on my very first day at work."

Weltmeister stood waiting, his hand out, an easy smile on his face, waiting for his friend to hand over his duty pistol. Rendel snorted and laughed. The older man didn't move. Rendel stood in doubt for a long moment, then his sentimental side got the better of him.

"Well, you're my old friend. Look after it."

He handed the Makarov and two boxes of cartridges to his partner.

They dropped away from the track into the jungle. Mona walked ahead, barefoot, resolute and sensuous. If she was concerned about the gun, she didn't show it.

"Stay on the path. Maybe land mine around."

Rendel was right behind her, hypnotized by the swing of her narrow hips while Weltmeister cautiously made up the rear. The narrow trail led upwards. The tree cover started to thin. An hour later, they reached Skyline Ridge, the Americans' last defense. The view was breathtaking.

The gigantic former US air base of Long Cheng, codename Lima Site 20A, lay in a wide, verdant valley beneath them. A couple of years earlier, this unlikely location had been the world's busiest airport. And no one had ever heard of it.

Weltmeister pulled a pair of binoculars out of his pack.

The runway, long enough to take large transport planes, was intact and stretched towards high karst stone formations. The American field agents who'd lived here for almost two decades had likened them to a pair of pointed breasts. Dense jungle punctuated by bomb craters spread across the hills beyond the valley.

Everything looked familiar to him. He knew this valley as intimately as any place on Earth.

A ramshackle collection of wooden shacks spread on both sides of the runway, augmented here and there by small clusters of more ambitious concrete structures, the former CIA offices. Long Cheng had been the nerve center of the agency's clandestine war in Laos, a covert slice of a larger conflict fought to contain communism in Indochina. A conflict that had cost more than four million lives and had taken some twenty years to grind itself and the region into dust.

A US-financed secret army, a mercenary force of hill tribe soldiers and their families, some fifty thousand people, had lived in Long Cheng for more than a decade. Most of the fighters had died. Even their children, sent into battle by the CIA, had been lost to the final years of the war.

Weltmeister could see a couple of Laotian patrols on the cracked tarmac. A cow, a long rope dragging behind the animal, meandered towards the mountains, following a faded white line. There were no other signs of life.

The communists had overrun the base a year or so earlier, and since then the secret city, the second largest in the country, had simply died. Weltmeister, in the service of the Vietnamese at the time, had helped oversee the end of the airfield.

Now the jungle, spurred on by the recent rains and the almost complete absence of human activity, was on the move, determined to wrestle Long Cheng back under its control.

Weltmeister laughed inwardly at the sacrosanct absurdities his various paymasters engaged in and the lengths they were prepared to go to, to see their demented visions through. Only the jungle really knew what it was doing.

The thrill of having returned to the scene of his crimes was weighed down by bitterness and misgivings. The devil always ruled both sides.

But Weltmeister wasn't a religious man. And he wasn't driven by ideology either. Rather, he was motivated by a lifelong desire for anonymity. His existence as a nobody kept him focused and interested. He'd never felt a need for family or friends. For security reasons, he had almost completely denied himself the affections of others and avoided confessions. Almost.

His lack of preference for a particular life had made him an excellent spy in Nazi Germany, and after the war, in East Germany, in the US and finally in Southeast Asia. And now, despite being the best in the business, one of his former selves had been found out. The great cloak-and-dagger game, which until a year or so ago he had thought to be the true love of his life, hung in the balance.

It was time for a purge.

3

FINGERPRINT FILE

"So, the gold is down there, near the runway?"

Mona nodded distractedly and pulled a small mirror from her shirt.

"What time now?" she asked, her voice a monotone of defiance.

"Three o'clock."

"We wait one hour. Before sun goes down, I send signal, my brother. Then we go meet."

Rendel grinned at her, watching a thin rivulet of sweat run from her neck into her cheap polyester shirt.

"No," she said, a flash of anger in her eyes that Weltmeister hadn't seen before.

He liked her righteous indignation. After all, she'd slept with creepy Rendel to get them here. Now that they were here, there was no more need for pretense. The honey trap had withdrawn its sticky content. They were close. The trap was about to snap shut.

They descended towards the base just before sunset. Mona, dead sure her brother had seen her signal, walked with a renewed spring in her step. They quickly dropped down from their vantage point, carefully keeping low brush between themselves and the lazily patrolling troops on the runway. Fifteen minutes later, they'd reached the first shacks. Whatever trap had been set; they were about to walk right into it.

The formerly bustling city was in a state of rapid decline. The roads and trails between the shacks were rutted. The detritus of war lay scattered everywhere – sheet metal, rusting tins of American foodstuff, shreds of clothing, torn and frayed Stars and Stripes, shell casings of every imaginable caliber. The girl led the two men into the heart of the decaying jumble of buildings, towards the concrete structures they'd seen from the ridge.

Weltmeister remembered the way perfectly well. He'd walked along the narrow alleys hundreds of times. But there was no need to let his companions know how deep his connection with Long Cheng was.

The girl stopped in her tracks quite suddenly and tried to orient herself.

"Guten Abend."

They stood surrounded by armed men. The Hmong militia fighters, some of them teenagers, dressed in rags and carrying heavy weapons, had popped up like ghosts. The youngest couldn't be more than twelve years old. Mona fell into the arms of a handsome boy and whispered rapidly. No one else spoke. Everyone stared at the white men.

As the girl recounted their journey in her own language, the boy, no more than sixteen, watched the two Germans like a hawk. He was tall and pale, with thick black hair and a wispy goatee, and, to Weltmeister, very familiar. Léon Sangster had grown from child to man in three short years. The war had sped things up. His bloodshot eyes burned like black pools of burning coal and he smelt of lao khao, the local rice wine. Growing up as an American in this wilderness had freed the young man from some of the constraints of one culture and trapped him within those of another.

Weltmeister had recognized him immediately. There'd always been something feral about Léon. And, he noticed, the girl had it as well. But unlike her half-caste brother, Mona was all Asian.

The other men looked battle-scarred and resigned to the routine boredom and brutality of war. Weltmeister would have to play this very carefully. Whatever she was telling her brother, who'd failed to recognize him so far, didn't enamor them to the young man. Léon was more Sturm und Drang than Weltmeister liked. A sensitive boy, driven by righteous and rightful anger.

Léon looked at him more closely then. "You look familiar. I've seen you somewhere before," he spat in fluent American English.

Weltmeister smiled affably and shook his head in mock confusion.

"That seems unlikely, young man."

The young Hmong waved the thought away, led them to a two-story house and entered. His fighters spread around the building and melted away into the shadows to keep an eye out for passing Laotian patrols. The siblings sat down on wooden bed frames without mattresses, the only pieces of furniture in the dilapidated room, facing their visitors. Shovels and sledgehammers leant in an untidy row in the far corner. Otherwise, the room was empty.

Weltmeister noticed that they sat on the old frames in deliberate poses, stiff and tense. One of Léon's soldiers stayed in the room, casually leaning against the back wall, a Kalashnikov strapped across his shoulder. The gold had to be close.

The two Germans remained standing.

"You speak my language?" Rendel barked across the room.

The boy shook his head, and got straight down to business, "You'll help us move the gold. We give you twenty percent when we reach Vientiane. Then you help us cross the Mekong into Thailand."

Rendel nodded, keeping up with the English, wearing his best expression of integrity.

"You are Weltmeister?"

"Yes," Rendel lied.

The boy smiled for the first time. It wasn't a friendly smile. There was too much doubt in it.

"I was here when Long Cheng fell last year. My father was one of the last remaining CIA case officers, Jimmy Sangster. My mother was a Hmong princess. Mona is my half-sister. This isn't about politics. It's about us. We want out."

Léon fell silent. Outside, darkness came quickly, the subtropical night descending on the spy city, which was without electricity. Mona stared at her brother in the fading half light, her eyes full of admiration.

Weltmeister felt a little sick. This was war, or its immediate aftermath, he told himself. Things were messy. He'd seen all this before. Humanity. Hope. Suffering. Disappointment. And this time, Long Cheng wasn't safe. The beautiful teenage girl, the daughter of legendary CIA case officer Jimmy Sangster who'd given his life for the country, had led them into a heart of darkness he felt no desire to linger in. Familiar and highly dangerous. He was taking a huge risk. To find out what this boy knew about him. What he remembered.

"The Americans left thousands of us on the runway. Women and children. Old people. We didn't know anything about when the last plane flew out. Our leader, General Vang Pao, escaped in a CIA helicopter and went to America. When the communists closed in on the runway, we fled into the jungle. We thought the Americans would come back to save us. We'd given them everything."

Léon looked emotional, the desperate last days of the American war at the forefront of his mind.

"Surely you could have been on a plane? You had great connections," Rendel wondered with his usual lack of tact.

"Our parents loved both their children and their countries.", Léon continued slowly, his voice filled with resentment, "Mona is all I have in this world. And now she has brought me Weltmeister."

"Why me? How do you know this name?"

"The file, it's in the file."

"What file?" Rendel demanded.

"The file my father was responsible for. The file you put together for the Vietnamese. The U48. The file that killed my father. The file you came looking for."

Rendel stared at the young man with his best neutral expression.

The man with the codename Weltmeister knew he was coming to the end of his journey and silently got ready to enter the next phase of his life. He discreetly clicked the safety off his friend's gun.

4

THE END

"The U48?" Rendel asked.

"Come on, Weltmeister. The secret Vietnamese file? All the names of all the double agents the Viet Cong ran in Vietnam, Laos, Cambodia and Thailand? Even yours. Weltmeister? Can you imagine what we will get if we sell you to the Americans? Or the Vietnamese?"

"Have you read the file?" the real Weltmeister asked, careful to weigh his question with as little urgency as possible.

Léon shook his head, but kept his eyes on Rendel. "No, only glanced at it, at some names, at your name, but we knew you would come back to Laos for it."

"Where is the file?" Rendel kept pushing.

The boy broke into his troubling smile again.

"With my father and my mother."

"You said they were killed?" the attaché, exasperated by the young man's monosyllabic answers, asked.

"I buried them. You see, they never planned to escape without the file and my mother refused to leave her family. The agency left us stranded. Perhaps they'd planned to sacrifice us."

Weltmeister got up, walked to the only window in the room and stared out into the night.

Rendel did his best to sound unconvinced, "If the file is still here, the Vietnamese will also be looking for it."

The boy answered, "The Vietnamese dogs shot my mother and father. I buried them with the gold, our last batch of heroin, and the file. My father couldn't leave. He was too attached to this place, this situation. When the Vietnamese and the Pathet Lao attacked, I ran away. I thought the war would continue. That we'd get our revenge. Our justice. But our fight is finished. We're finished. Now I'm back to take the file and some of the gold with me to a new life in the West. With Mona."

The attaché did his best not to look out of his depth. "So how did you guess I was Weltmeister and why did you send your sister?"

"My father told me there was a superspy on the list, a German who worked for the US. A lone wolf and a double agent. The man who betrayed Long Cheng. He told me that this man would come because the cover for his identity depended on getting the list. Some of our supporters in Vientiane have been watching the German embassy. And then you arrived and took up your post. I knew it was my only shot to find closure. And to get the gold out."

"Where is the file?" Weltmeister repeated with more urgency.

The young Hmong looked at him with renewed interest. Weltmeister looked away, nothing more than a casual move of the head. For a split second, a thought seemed to pass through Léon's mind, then it was gone.

Mona got up and pushed the bed frames aside as her brother handed the two men a shovel and a hammer.

"Right here," he said, pointing at the floor, "Start digging."

"Scheisse," Rendel screamed and fell through the floor as it collapsed around him. Their breakthrough shattered the near silence of their work. They'd found their treasure. The trap had opened and closed.

Dust swirled around the room and Weltmeister edged his way to the door. He could hear feet rushing around the building. Probably Léon's men. He carefully opened the door and slipped outside. Far off, from somewhere on the runway, he could hear shouting. The Laotian military was up and running. Time was up. They'd been made. He slunk back inside and shone his torch into the hole in the center of the room.

Rendel was making a lot of noise.

"Get me out of here. I've broken my bloody leg."

Weltmeister shivered uncomfortably. He hadn't felt this nervous since escaping the Gestapo in Berlin more than thirty years earlier. Timing was everything now.

Léon suddenly loomed in front of him, "Now I know you. I saw you in Long Cheng. A long time ago, when I was a kid. Now I remember your eyes."

The Hmong sucked in his breath as more unpleasant realizations appeared to flood his mind. He shook his head in disbelief.

"You're the devil who…"

The man codenamed Weltmeister shot the boy. Léon fell beside Rendel into his parents' grave. His next shot killed the Hmong soldier before he had time to move his weapon. Mona screamed and made for her brother, but the third bullet caught her in the neck. Weltmeister stood still, listening into the night. None of the other Hmong rebels around the building seemed to have heard the shots. Rendel's Dienstpistole, with a silencer, was a reliable tool.

"I'll get you out, Manfred; don't worry."

He climbed down into the chamber below the building's floor. His torch flicked across Rendel who had suffered an open break in his left leg and looked like he was about to pass out. This place wasn't made for cultural attachés with shattered femurs.

To his right, the low-ceilinged chamber was filled with boxes and metal ammunition cases, rusty but intact. The first one he pried open contained gold bars. The second one was packed with sealed bags of Double Uoglobe heroin. He took one of each and stashed them in his pack. But the file was nowhere to be seen.

Léon was still alive.

"Where is my sister?"

"She went outside to get help," Weltmeister answered in a kind tone.

"You save my sister; I tell you about the file. Promise?"

He made eye contact with the young man and nodded solemnly. Léon hadn't seen his sister die.

The Hmong pointed to the far side of the chamber.

"In the bag under my father's head. Promise."

The young man passed out, a pool of blood spreading under his prone figure. He'd be dead soon enough.

The remains of Léon's parents lay in a crumpled embrace in the far corner of the chamber. Weltmeister assumed that Léon had dragged them there after they'd been killed. He found the bag and pried it from under the decomposed head of Jimmy Sangster, his former colleague.

Inside he found his grail.

The man who'd sat at tables with beggars and kings, who'd deceived the Gestapo, the CIA, the TC2 and the Stasi, allowed himself a vague smile as he peeled a bundle of papers from an oilcloth bag. His handwriting was still legible. A neat list of names, codenames, ages, birthplaces, and photographs, including, most importantly, his own, covered page after page. Memos and reports followed.

The U48. The file that had eluded him the last time he'd been in Long Cheng.

The trail to Weltmeister ended here. For a second, he contemplated burning the document. This was the only copy, the only clear evidence of who he was. Of what he'd done. But he knew he wouldn't do it. The U48 was too valuable. And he knew he was too vain. He'd created this file as much as he had created his persona. The file, he knew, was one of the great masterpieces of the western world. You could hold it up to a Picasso or a Gauguin. It had to live on in some shape or form. Who'd be mad enough to burn the Mona Lisa, even if she were to harbor uncomfortable truths?

Rendel regained consciousness and moaned, "We must leave. The Laotians will be here any minute. I can walk if you hold me. Don't leave an old friend behind."

"Sorry, Manfred, you know how it is in our line of work. Take no prisoners. Silence is everything."

Weltmeister turned to his old friend, raised the other man's Dienstpistole and pulled the trigger.

Without losing another second, he wiped the Makarov clean and pressed it into Rendel's limp right hand, climbed out of the chamber and pushed Mona down into what was becoming a mass grave. Then he moved the bed frames over the hole. Pushed together they covered the collapsed floor. There was nothing to be done about the terrible stink that would soon lead anyone within a mile to the gold and heroin. Outside, gunshots began to sound across the valley. The Laotians had noticed the activity and were on their feet. It was time to leave the most secret place on Earth. His eyes drifted across the room one last time. All this money. All this bad karma. He sighed. The list was all that mattered.

A few minutes later, he'd cleared the huts and was climbing out of the valley. The Laotian troops guarding the airstrip would finish off the rest of the Hmong.

PART I

MAIER

1

A HELL OF A CLIENT

HAMBURG, GERMANY, NOVEMBER 2001

"In 1976, for a few short months, my father was the German Democratic Republic's cultural attaché in Laos. He was an old Asia hand. He knew the region. But he was killed shortly after he arrived and his body was never repatriated. In fact, we know almost nothing about his death. I want you to find out why and how it happened. Who killed him? And I'd like you to find him, if possible. Retrieve his body, in fact."

Julia Rendel didn't waste time. The assignment was on the table before she'd given herself a chance to sip her coffee – black, very strong, no sugar. Nor did Maier's elegant client appear to be perturbed by the fact that half the customers and all the staff in the rather bourgeois but frighteningly trendy Herr Max were twisting their heads to get a better look at her. The detective guessed her to be in her mid-thirties. She had the gift and the money.

Her dark hair was piled high in an unruly and, at least to Maier, pleasing creation. Unruly hair didn't come cheap in Germany. Her chunky jade earrings, probably from Burma, accentuated her long, pale neck. Her face was narrow, with high cheekbones and full lips. The stuff of movies and broken hearts. Her eyes shone with this knowledge like black stars. Her pale skin and slim nose somehow accentuated the fact that she was half-Asian. Her wardrobe said dressed-to-kill detectives in the most subtle way. Julia Rendel's silk blouse was low-key but made no attempt to close over her alluring cleavage. The jeans she wore looked like they'd been molded around her.

Maier could see why Ms. Rendel might have sought his services. She spoke German with a slight Saxony accent and, like himself, had probably grown up in the East. Her father must have been one of the top dogs at what Maier assumed had been a reasonably important embassy in Vientiane. Following the defeat of US forces across Southeast Asia in the mid-Seventies, the GDR, along with other Soviet-aligned countries, had quickly built up a strong presence in Laos.

"I know this is an unusual case, Maier. My father was killed a long time ago in what was then still a war zone. In fact, I made my peace with his murder when I was a teenager. I was ten when he died and I barely remember him. My mother is half-Cambodian, half-French. My parents met in Phnom Penh in the early Sixties, but my father never married her. He left her and took me to Laos. After he was killed, the GDR authorities told me next to nothing, took me back to Germany and placed me in a foster home."

She took a sip of coffee and continued. "You see, without a bit of family background, this story isn't going to make any sense. When the Khmer Rouge took over in Cambodia in 1975, my mother disappeared. For a long time, I thought she'd been killed but she eventually showed up in a refugee camp on the Thai border in the Eighties. I managed to get her back to Germany in '89. I hadn't seen her for almost fifteen years."

She stopped short of another revelation and shot Maier a searching glance. He could feel she was surprised when he made eye contact. Most people didn't notice his piercing green eyes until he wanted them to.

"My father wasn't a good man. Not much of a family man. Until very recently, I'd pretty much stopped thinking about my family's history. One grows out of trying to come to terms with these things."

Maier had ordered a mineral water and was toying with the metal lid of the three-Euro bottle, keeping his counsel. In Europe, it was near impossible to uncover the motives for a man's murder twenty five years after the fact. Finding the actual killer was even more unlikely. In Southeast Asia, no one kept records. People were conditioned to forget, not to remember. Especially in a war zone. But all this was immaterial. The woman intrigued Maier more than the case of her deceased father.

Julia Rendel was the most attractive client he'd been hired by. He liked her instantly, though he was careful not to show it. In fact, she was so likeable that Maier, for a fleeting moment, thought her a Trojan horse, a honey trap of some kind. But he quickly dismissed his hunch. Ms. Rendel was paying top rate to Maier's agency.

Julia Rendel casually waved for the waiter. She had an easy way with people, authoritative without being demanding, ever so slightly manipulative while projecting quite the opposite. In the overcrowded afternoon rush hour in Herr Max, everything appeared to revolve around her. Maier enjoyed the show. One of the café's pumped-up and stressed-out employees rushed to their table and almost stood to attention. With practiced nonchalance, Ms Rendel ordered another coffee strong enough to make a dead man laugh and waited until they were alone again before she continued speaking, "I had an identity crisis a few years back. But let me take you there in a roundabout way that is pertinent to your job. I finished high school in the GDR, late because I'd been in Asia. In the early Nineties, a friend of my father's adopted me. I was already grown up, of course, but I had no money or prospects. He was a painter and another terrible egomaniac, though a more successful one than my father. He paid for my education. Only the best. We moved to London. I read political science at Oxford, then went to the States and did a PhD in Asian studies and international relations at Princeton, and finally a stint as an intern at the Bundestag in Berlin so that I'd get reacquainted with the machinations of the fatherland. You know, champagne debates and cocaine in the parliamentary toilets. My step-daddy had also been a GDR diplomat in the old days and had even served in Southeast Asia during the Seventies. If he hadn't come into my life, I'd have become a kindergarten teacher or a clerk. So, you see, I'm set for great things. In fact, I felt like my stepfather had me groomed for great things. I still do."

Something unhealthy crossed her face then, but it was so subtle and potentially scary that Maier refused to acknowledge it.

"Great things being, Ms Rendel?"

She looked at him sharply, perhaps trying to figure out whether to take offence from his interruption. She decided not to.

"Well, this is the odd thing. Despite my father and my stepfather having been part of the old communist regime, I was told that all doors were open for me in the new, reunited Germany. Politics, foreign affairs, lobby groups, think tanks, you name it. Once I finished my studies, all these different bodies were virtually battling each other to pull me in. OK, I'd been to Oxford and Princeton, but I wasn't sure I deserved all that attention. I'd done nothing to prove myself in any way."

Maier experienced a strange feeling of déjà vu. Hadn't his own career, albeit years earlier and in a different political system, started in a similar vein? He'd been one of the best journalism graduates in his class. But his meteoric rise to foreign correspondent, both an honor and a calculated risk usually bestowed only on the most reliable party members, had come off without a hitch, at a time when East Germany wasn't keen to deal with the loss of face that defectors incurred.

Whatever doubts she was mulling over, Julia Rendel shrugged them off and continued, "I decided to push my luck and change track completely. I joined an NGO called TreeLine. Heard of it?"

Maier was familiar with the organization. TreeLine monitored forest cover in developing nations and released reports on illegal logging and government corruption, most notably in Asia. Its critics, including a plethora of corrupt politicians in said parts of the world, claimed that TreeLine was a Eurocentric outfit, a political tool to push European environmental agendas with little understanding of or sympathy for the situation on the ground in poor countries. Whatever their sins, the more moderate of these unlikely commentators had a point. NGOs rarely prioritized circumstances on the ground. It was a game of donors and budgets.

He kept his thoughts to himself and said nothing.

"Ah, you're a careful man, Maier. I like it. We'll get on."

"Get on, Ms. Rendel?"

"Oh, yes, I'll be in Laos when you start your investigation. And please call me Julia."

"Please call me Maier."

He shot her a quick glance, encouraging his client to continue.

"I am TreeLine's senior analyst for Southeast Asia. I'm based in Bangkok, but we're most active in Laos and Cambodia."

This time, Maier couldn't help himself and quipped, "Because trees don't need saving in Thailand?"

Julia laughed, "No, Maier, because the people who finance TreeLine view Laos and Cambodia at best as uncooperative countries. And, if we did report on Thailand, we wouldn't be able to run our office there. Did I tell you my job was sleazy? But it puts me where I want to be right now, and I can still strive for a more worthy existence later. Everything a person does is preparation for something else, right?"

Maier laughed politely.

She snapped, "And don't patronize me, Mr. Detective. You appear to see the world in equally jaded terms as I do; you are an expert on Asia and a charming if slightly detached man, which I'd say is almost interesting, though unhealthy, given that I've hired you. I'm impressed. Our mutually complementary abilities of deduction will make our professional relationship that much easier; I'm sure. As long as you remember that I'm your employer."

Maier shrugged and tried to guide his client back to the case.

"So, what about these new developments?"

She shot him a look that made his stomach flutter. For a split second, he could detect a razor-sharp mind, as well as an unhealthy degree of admiration he felt he hardly deserved, but was happy to entertain anyhow.

"As I said, interesting. I have a suite at the Atlantic. After a couple of months of shitting in the woods, I feel I deserve a few days of unbridled luxury."

Maier grinned, "Bumped into the Atlantic's resident rock star yet?"

"The really very gracious Udo Lindenberg and I had a long evening of absolutely divine champagne together last week. He's an absolute sweetie. He sat down at his piano and sang 'Sonderzug nach Pankow' for me, and I've had red roses from him every day since. But don't get jealous, Maier; he wasn't interested in me. He's seen too much in this life. More than you, perhaps."

"What was that about keeping it professional?"

"Oh yes, Maier, we will. Don't worry. Anyway, you're hired and I expect you to put your heart as well as your very sharp mind into the job at hand. I'll send out a couple of emails this afternoon, warning Laos of our imminent arrival. I trust you'll also be available to dine with me in my suite at 8pm sharp. You and I being good Germans, no matter how wayward, I'm sure we'll both manage to be on time. I'll fill you in on the rest of the case then. Room 172. See you."

Her piece said, Julia Rendel was gone in an instant, leaving Maier with a barely touched second cup of coffee and an inappropriately large banknote to pay the bill. Maier pocketed some of the change, thinking of it as a modest advance on his expenses.

2

I'LL BE YOUR SISTER

DETECTIVE MAIER LOITERED naked in front of the full-sized mirror. At 190 cm, his reflection barely fitted into the solid teak frame, courtesy of Hamburg's prestigious Hotel Atlantic Kempinski, that he drunkenly leant against. He studied his lived-in face, the deepening lines that spread around his eyes and along his cheeks. One day, it would all be gone to hell. But his shoulders were broad and he was in good shape at forty-five, all things considered. He still had hair on his head. He didn't need glasses. He enjoyed his vanity and made no bones about it. Old age held off for another day.

He looked deeper into the mirror and could just make out the vague outline of Julia, who lay asleep across the huge bed in the shadows behind him.

His boss, Sundermann, had told him to go on holiday, take it easy, to digest and reflect on the horrors he'd encountered on his last case. His recent trip to Cambodia had been a hard slog, physically and emotionally demanding.

Since returning to Hamburg, he'd been making the effort. He got rid of his moustache – a woman who'd left him, one he'd really liked, had ridiculed him for it. And now that she had gone, he'd followed her advice and shaved it off. That kind of action – too little, too late – appeared to be symptomatic for the way he failed in his relationships. He ran near his apartment in Altona. On days he felt particularly energetic, he went and exercised amongst the flower displays at Planten un Blomen, a mile or so east of his apartment. He refrained from drink, drugs, sex and even Bratkartoffeln - roast potatoes - a German staple food he was partial to.

He saw a psychiatrist who did his best to detect symptoms of post-traumatic stress disorder. He watched television. He bought clothes. He polished up his French while forgetting whatever Russian he'd learned in school. He tried to be ordinary. He tried to live down his last job. He tried to accept that the women who fell into his arms fled them just as quickly when they took a closer look.

Maier loved his current job, just as he'd been a hundred percent committed when he'd been a war correspondent. Being a relatively successful detective was one hell of a journey.

Born in Leipzig in 1954, to his sweet mother Ruth and a father he'd never met, Maier had done exceedingly well. Following his studies in Dresden and Berlin he worked as a journalist for the East German state organ, Neues Deutschland, and covered foreign affairs in Poland, the Czech Republic, Hungary, and Yugoslavia. He had no idea why he'd been awarded such an entrusted and sensitive position amidst the surreal and politically labyrinthine media realities of East Germany. He wasn't a party member, and he avoided the right people as best as he could.

Maier always suspected that his father had something to do with his meteoric trajectory. This father, who'd apparently passed nothing more to his son than his piercing green eyes and natural restlessness, had attended a few lectures at Universität Leipzig, bedded down with his mother for eleven months and simply vanished without a trace one day to leave her with nothing but a broken heart and a child. Scandalous behavior in the former East Germany. The neighbors never talked to Ruth again. But Maier knew she was secretly proud of her affair. She had hinted that the old man had had some role in anti-Nazi intelligence during World War II. His mother had told him that her mysterious lover had never let her take his photograph. Maier Sr. was an unknown entity that moved through his system like a ghost and stalked him in his dreams. Maier hoped and imagined that the old man was somewhere out there, keeping an eye on his son, following his path into adulthood and middle age.

He let go of the mirror and almost tumbled to the floor. Good times would do that to a man. It was easy to slide back into the drinking routine. He was so ready for work. In fact, Maier was already at work. His new mission demanded he let himself go immediately. He'd grow his hair, adopt mock slothdom, and return to the Far East. He'd look like one of those old hippies who wouldn't hurt a fly, had made a fortune in stocks and greenhouses, and had come back to Asia to relive the dream, man. He'd reinvent himself as a boutique bohemian.

We have a chance to save the world.

Or at least have a drink and let the old times roll before the mornings got so familiar that they'd enter his bones and make him feel his years.

There was an unearthly quiet in the suite of the Atlantic, which Julia Rendel had occupied for at least three days. That's how long Maier had had his mobile phone switched off, had not been at home nor in the street.

The job had been cleared with his boss. And he could hear his client's gentle breathing, intermittently punctuated by vodka-filled snorts.

He looked down at his flaccid cock and grinned to himself. How much better could life get? The Atlantic was one of the city's swankiest watering holes. The chandeliers, the gallons of vodka diluted with freshly squeezed orange juice, the drunken sex and his client's story of a lifetime, which, told from one inebriated person to another, had quickly taken on epic proportions in his addled mind. They'd even filmed a Bond movie in the Atlantic. High times.

It had been some journey getting here for Maier. When the satellite states of the great Soviet experiment started to crumble, Maier absconded to West Germany. He integrated into the capitalist media apparatus and his new employers in Hamburg sent him on the road, just as his old employers in East Berlin had. For some years, he covered German interests around the world, until he maneuvered himself into the most extreme corner of his profession, graduating from roving German reporter to international conflict journalist.

Maier covered many of the dirty little wars at the close of the twentieth century. But he found himself to be too restless even for this most intense and reactive employment.

After eight years on the front lines, Maier quit his career as a high-testosterone reporter and slunk back to Hamburg. At age forty, tired but not finished, he retrained and joined Sundermann, the city's most renowned detective agency. Four years later, he was the agency's Asia expert and one of its top operatives.

And now he was on his way to Laos. A beautiful woman had hired a jaded detective to find her father's killer in one of the world's least-understood nations. With a treasure of American war loot thrown into the mix.

Gold!

The quickest way to Laos was via Bangkok. He would be on a plane to Thailand in a couple of days. A Hmong hill tribe man, a member of one of the communist nation's countless ethnic minorities, had appeared with new information as to her father's demise. That's all she'd told him. About the job.

Maier had visited Laos several times as a journalist. Following the collapse of the Soviet Union, the country's main source of cash, he'd covered the slow opening of this sleepy backwater in a handful of feature articles. He'd traveled widely around this ancient, landlocked empire, which was covered in dense, primordial forests stretching across uncountable mountain ridges. The forests were interspersed with reassuringly insignificant villages, and dotted with otherworldly temples, their curved roofs shining like medieval receivers attracting distant starships.

He sucked in his stomach, then let himself go slack again. The Atlantic wasn't the place to start a weight-loss program. It was also a long way from Laos, a country many Germans would be hard-pushed to find on a map.

"Come to bed, Mr. Detective," Julia whispered from the four-poster. He staggered back to her and sat heavily on the edge of the bed. She looked at him with eyes full of pleasure.

"When you get to Vientiane, go to the Red Bar or the Insomniacs Club and ask for Léon. The young Hmong. That's our man. Kanitha is his girl. Meet them. I'll join you there once you have made some headway with him."

Maier smiled down at her. He liked the way she weaved the mission and the night together into a heady mix of mystery and, well, more mystery. He was sure Julia had so much more to tell.

In the suite's living room, a doorbell rang with the urgency of a wind chime.

"That must be room service," he said, and stumbled into a pair of shorts. Julia passed out again. Maier thought about ignoring the door. They hadn't called for anything. The bell tinkled a second time.

He couldn't find his shirt. Well, if they were happy to put up with rock stars, they'd be able to cope with his opening the door in nothing much at all.

He left the bedroom and crossed the immaculately lit teak-floored hallway to the living room. The Chet Baker CD Julia had put on at his request had finished.

He pulled the security chain off the hook and opened the door.

The fist came at him at an unlikely velocity. Maier swayed out of the way and instinctively threw a right hook at his assailant. He could hear a man's nose crack. His satisfaction lasted less than a second. The hand of a second attacker came wrapped in a knuckleduster. Professionals never arrived alone. A flash of brass, and Maier blacked out faster than Chet.

And it had all started so well.

3

ENTER THE DRAGON

THAILAND/LAO PEOPLE'S DEMOCRATIC REPUBLIC, NOVEMBER 2001

MAIER HAD ALWAYS LIKED the shallow easiness of Bangkok. The Thai capital was a mind-your-own-business-unless-you-would-like-us-to-mind-it-for-you kind of place. A city where the unchangeable was not tampered with and everything else mutated as quickly as possible. Sometimes even quicker. A metropolis of ten million people who never talked to each other but smiled and smiled and smiled. Every now and then, the Thais' reluctance to communicate erupted in wild cataclysms of political violence and military coups, sponsored by aspiring demagogues. The streets would run red with blood, and the violence triggered by deep-rooted dissatisfaction was almost always manipulated or paid for and eventually petered out. The very same people who'd been killing each other a few days earlier would now clean up the mess they'd made, so that both rich and poor could get back to their assigned places in this world and smile until the next cataclysm. Buddhism, a rigid social hierarchy and a widely held belief amongst the country's venal elite that knowledge of almost any kind was dangerous, kept people in their places.

But this time, Maier worried and the famous Thai smile, multifaceted and ambiguous, failed to touch him. His client had been kidnapped, had been virtually pulled from his arms. His eye hurt. Maier knew he'd never catch up with the two men who had knocked him out. They'd been anonymous, faceless messengers of doom

Shortly after he'd returned home from the Atlantic, following a long interview with the police and Kreuzwieser, the hotel detective, he'd received an email from a 1000 Elephant Trading Company. He quickly established that no such entity existed.

He could have Ms. Rendel back in exchange for a spot of professional consultancy, the message assured him. Further instructions were to follow by email once he'd reached the Laotian capital Vientiane. The IP address pinpointed an internet café in the city.

His case was going Fu Manchu before it had started. His client had touched him. He had the weird and completely inexplicable feeling that she was a soulmate. As if they'd shared more than a few nights together, as if she'd given him more than his mission. Irrationally, he also sensed that she'd come out of it just as fine and dandy as when he'd last seen her lying in her four-poster bed in the Atlantic, drunk and full of sex. But he couldn't rely on an emotional hunch. Men of violence connected to the pursuit of the gold had taken her. After conferring with Sundermann, his boss, he'd jumped the first plane east.

He took a small room in Chinatown and lost himself in the city's back streets for a day until he was sure that no one had noticed his arrival. He visited Wat Traimit and queued with camera-toting tourists to catch a glimpse of the temple's enormous solid-gold Buddha, the world's largest. It seemed like an auspicious thing to do, given that he was on a gold hunt. He talked to no one but the roadside noodle sellers.

Reasonably sure his anonymity was intact, he took the overnight train to the Thai-Laotian border. He entered Laos quietly, cloaked in the tribal conformity of an ageing hippie – he wore gleaming leather chapals, khaki cotton pants, a white shirt with too many buttons undone and one of those sleeveless vests with countless pockets favoured by photojournalists and would-be adventurers. Sunglasses covered his black eye, which remained dark as night. He looked fit enough not to be mistaken for a sex tourist. He didn't sleep and kept an eye on who was coming and going in his second-class carriage.

At the crack of a pale, cool dawn, he disembarked at the Nong Khai railhead and grabbed a taxi for the Thai-Lao Friendship Bridge that spanned the Mekong and connected one vaguely cruel world to another. The Thai immigration officers wore brown uniforms so tight they looked like they'd been sewn into them. They were surly and disinterested. Their Laotian counterparts wore ill-fitting bright green outfits and caps that were too large. They smiled with faux embarrassment as they demanded additional fees for their dedicated work. The bribes were modest, mere fractions of a dollar.

"Welcome to Laos."

They turned up their smiles to genuine happiness once he'd paid up. Maier cleared immigration and emerged onto a dusty road.

Arriving in Laos was a bit like being released from prison. Freedom and loss rolled in equal waves. A feeling of what now? welcomed visitors.

The road into Vientiane was barely paved, and lined with fenced-in fallow plots, interspersed with minor ministries, shops selling farming equipment and national pharmaceutical factories that looked like they'd not produced a pill in years. International NGO offices with fat cars parked outside looked more with it than the destitute government buildings. Advertising billboards and consumer goods were noticeably absent. Laos was one of the poorest countries in the world.

Hunter-gatherers had been living in the region as far back as forty thousand years ago. In the fifteenth century, the Lan Xang Empire, ambitiously named the Land of a Million Elephants and the White Parasol, established itself as a nation-state of sorts. A couple of hundred years later, the fledgling affair was virtually crushed between larger neighbors and almost went out of business. The French showed up in the nineteenth century and saved Laos for its Indochina experiment, though this protectorate never made the colonizers a great deal of cash.

During World War II, the Japanese briefly ran the show, allowed the Laotians to declare independence, which was quickly denied by a resurgent France, smarting from its collaboration with the Nazis. Only in 1953, following France's defeat at the hands of the Vietnamese in Dien Bien Phu, did Laos achieve independence. A monarchy, a right-wing dictatorship, a dysfunctional democracy, almost three decades of US-sponsored war, and four years of secret carpet-bombing paved the way into the current and slowly declining socialist paradise.

Essentially Laos remained what it always had been, a sparsely populated land of mountain ridges, few roads and an atrophied political system dependent on foreign donors and neighboring states. Even now, a significant number of the six million Laotians had little or no contact with their government. There was no economy to speak of. People did the same now as they had then; they grew rice and took it easy. Hammocks were more important than cars, rice wine more ubiquitous than beer.

An hour of avoiding sleeping dogs, pedestrian monks, and cycling Jehovah's Witnesses later, a rickety Toyota Camry dropped Maier off by the Mekong in the heart of the Laotian capital, Vientiane. Population one hundred sixty thousand. He paid the modest cab fare and decided to walk around town to catch his bearings before checking into a hotel.

Lao national flags fluttered next to hammers and sickles along the riverfront, tattered cloth flapping above modest outdoor restaurants overlooking the uncertain embankment. As on previous visits, Maier felt like he had re-entered a dream world, a land where everything had slowed down to the bare necessities, the opposite of exuberant, decadent and hedonistic Bangkok. Laotians had modest aspirations – one had to live with a stagnant economy and a government that ruled, just barely, as if it had experienced a bad spell of taxidermy. It was quiet. No one was watching, because there was nothing to do. This was a brand of communism so very different from the former East Germany's heavy-handed realities he had experienced as a young man.

For a while he crisscrossed streets aimlessly and passed temples, carrying his modest, stylishly tattered backpack, making sure that no one followed him. The attack at the Atlantic had made him übercautious. The men who'd knocked him out in Julia Rendel's suite had been Asian. Someone had sent two able messengers to Hamburg. They'd managed to enter one of the city's most salubrious hotels and stolen away with one of its guests.

The dream of a luxury holiday with his Poirot-style deductions on the side had evaporated. Laos wasn't going to be as easy or glamorous as he'd first assumed. He worried about Julia Rendel. Others were on the same trail as him, and they were somewhere ahead.

Maier checked into a modest hotel off Samsenthai, took a shower and fell asleep.

As night fell, the detective headed for the river. Open-air food stalls offered salted fish baked over open coals, accompanied by papaya salad laced with chili and crabs. On a small square, the decidedly uncommunist sounds of the Village People pumped out of a portable stereo with maximum distortion, loud enough to banish any thoughts of revolution.

The buildings that lined Fa Ngum Quai Road, the long avenue that ran through the capital along the Mekong, made up an eclectic mixture of traditional wooden homes, Chinese shop houses, colonial piles, modern US-financed structures and cheerless Soviet-built concrete boxes, offering visitors a quick run-down of the country's recent history by way of its architecture. He passed cheap restaurants geared towards young backpackers and stalls selling pirate video CDs of the newest Hollywood blockbusters – one of the world's last Stalinist regimes wasn't immune to the tepid cultural temptations of the decadent West.

No further messages waited in his email account. No news on Julia Rendel. No lead on his client.

Maier had to double back a couple of times before he found the rather innocuous entrance to the Red Bar, a three-story affair trapped in a hundred-year-old shop house, and the only happening night spot on the riverfront. Even so, the receptionist in his hotel had assured him that the Red Bar, along with every other watering hole, would close at midnight. Vientiane had never been a dynamic metropolis.

In the Sixties, the Americans had pumped more money into Laos than into any other country in the world, with predictable results – widespread corruption, a burgeoning sex industry and heavily manipulated elections undertaken by a populace accustomed to centuries of feudal rule. As a result, the city had come to life as something of a modest party place, though it had never been a refuge of debauchery and ruin comparable to Bangkok or Saigon. But this was history. The revolution in 1975 had put an end to the good times. Socialism had stamped out the evils of decadence, whether of Western or Eastern origin. And while Laotians knew where to go and have a moderately good time behind closed doors, foreign visitors were herded to the Red Bar.

Maier headed upstairs. The first floor gave way to a large, barely lit room with several pool tables, occupied by a smattering of bored bar girls who, in the absence of cash-flashing Western visitors, played desultory games amongst themselves. A Britney Spears song leaked from invisible speakers, putting a further downer on the scene. As he passed, a collective cry of professionally enthusiastic delight emanated from the tables, but Maier didn't stop.

The second floor was more amenable to his tastes. A round bar of heavy teak stood in the center of a large, well-lit room. Floor to ceiling windows opened onto the river with views across to Thailand and the free world. Punters sat at low wooden tables, roughly hewn from illegally logged teak, knocking back the country's most coveted product, Beerlao. Bar girls toyed with the umbrellas in their cocktails, appraising each new arrival with the seasoned eye of a quality checker on an assembly line. The Who threatened to escape from the speakers. Old music for old people. Not quite Babylon, but better than Britney Spears.

The barkeep was a squat, careful-looking guy. He was decidedly not Laotian and combed his white hair like a Fifties newspaperman, strands of silver brushed across his slowly balding head. He wore thick, horn-rimmed glasses. Around fifty years old. There was something in his eyes that gave him the appearance of a man toying with going downhill, but he still teetered at the top of the crest, and any uncertainties in his movements might have been for show. He was clean-shaven and plucked the hair from his nostrils. He looked more like a history teacher than a bar manager in his plain white shirt tucked carefully into his neatly pressed blue jeans. A man who probably cared too much about what others thought of him.

Maier broke all the local rules and ordered a vodka orange, his preferred poison.

"Hey, I'm looking for the Insomniacs Club."

The little man pushed the glass across the gleaming teak counter and eyed him without great interest.

"Who's asking?"

"My name is Maier. I'm a friend of Julia Rendel. Of TreeLine."

"She's not here."

"I know she's not in town. But she asked me to drop by the Red Bar and find her friend Léon. Or ask for the Insomniacs Club. But you're not Léon?"

The barman registered Maier properly. The joint might have been red but its manager was decidedly North American.

"Can't place your fucking accent, dude. You German as well?"

The detective nodded, keeping his eyes to himself.

"Maier, from Hamburg. Professional traveler. Mostly harmless."

"Vincent Laughton. Pleased to fucking meet you, Maier. You don't look harmless. But you do look German. You had a fight with a water buffalo?"

Maier shrugged, trying to place the man's accent.

"I ran into a beauty on a moonless night, Vincent."

The bar man smiled with as little sympathy as he could muster.

"Must've been some gal. Not Julia, I presume."

"No, it was her cousin Arthur."

Something prickled between the two men. Maier wondered whether Vincent knew Julia was missing. The barman snorted and pushed another vodka orange across the counter.

"I haven't seen Julia in a while. I'd like to think she's out in the sticks somewhere. As a matter of fact, Léon was looking for her, too. So, I'll give you the benefit of the doubt, being the generous kind of guy that I am."

"Where does one acquire an accent like yours, Vincent?" Maier asked carefully.

"Small town, Ontario. Canada. Nothing like Laos. We got fucking roads there. Fuck, I never walked more than three hundred yards in my life until I arrived in Laos, unless it was into absolute wilderness. Some irony ending up in this dump, ha?"

Maier laughed politely. He'd rarely heard a man swear so much. Vincent had a slow and deliberate way of expressing himself, and a lazy melodic drawl in his voice that Maier associated more with the southern United States than with Canada. He also had an air of noisy resignation about him, a need to let the world know that he hadn't been treated fairly. Perhaps that had something to do with his diminutive size and unattractive shape. Some men were like that.

"Back home, we drive cars, ride horses and shoot bears from pickups. No need for fancy footwork. Arriving here was a bit of a shock – there are few rides in the Lao PDR. It's a pedestrian kind of place."

"You own a great bar."

The Canadian shrugged, marginally more friendly, "Just filling in for a friend. I'm a freelance journalist based out of Bangkok. I got stuck here somehow. There just isn't enough writing work around anymore. Fucking Internet is killing the profession."

Vincent scanned the bar to see if anyone was listening into the conversation. Maier assumed that the level of privacy they enjoyed would determine the amount of bragging his new friend would come up with.

"But you came to the right place. I'm the founder of the Insomniacs Club. And I keep a tight check on who gets to join and who doesn't. We're the only exclusive after-hours speakeasy in town. In the country. The only cool fucking place to go to in the Lao PDR."

The Canadian, surely the most laconic man east of the Mekong, wasn't finished. He leaned across the bar with all the authority his short frame could supply him with and grinned at Maier with a conspiring air of self-importance.

"We're totally under the radar. Even the government pretends we don't exist, because it enjoys a drink here. And we like to keep it that way. Otherwise, we get closed down. Like all good things in Laos."

"What does the Insomniacs Club offer that the Red Bar cannot provide?"

Vincent shrugged, lit a cigarette and stepped out from behind the bar.

"Man, you can't compare the two. It's like day and night. Anyone and his fucking uncle can sit in the Red Bar. The club is a different proposition. It has an eclectic members list. The backpackers aren't allowed in. And as I said, the government snoops come to drink, not to give us trouble. Fuck the closing time. Fuck the drug laws. An escape from the tawdry communist bullshit. Unheard of in the region, man. You really a friend of Julia's?"

Maier nodded as earnestly as he could. The Canadian looked appeased.

"Follow me. You'll be the second German to be admitted. And you're a bit early. The Insomniacs Club doesn't get started properly until everyone in the Red Bar starts going the fuck home."

The Canadian exuded all the charm of an overfed spider. He didn't reach to Maier's shoulder but he probably weighed as much as the detective. He led Maier to the exit and back down the stairs. They crossed the pool hall on the first floor, meriting barely a glance from the bored young women around the tables. Three doors loomed at the back of the room: Ladies, Gents and a third which sported a metal plaque that read Tired, bored and lonely? Go back upstairs!

Vincent pulled a pass key from his pocket; the kind usually used on trains, and turned to Maier. "In case she failed to mention it, Julia's my girlfriend. And she's your pass into our exclusive little circle. She told me to look out for you. Otherwise, you'd never be here. You look like a slippery fucker to me. That's why I was testing you. Old journo trick, you know."

Maier was sure the Canadian lied, at least about Julia warning Vincent about his arrival, but he didn't press the point. Perhaps she'd emailed him after their first meeting.

The cowboy from small town Ontario flicked his cigarette into a dark corner, opened the door and grinned back at the detective. The relative warmth in his expression surprised Maier almost as much as the fact that he was Julia Rendel's partner. He just couldn't imagine the two in the sack together.

"Welcome to Vientiane's best-kept secret, Maier. Don't be too fucking bad."

4

THE INSOMNIACS CLUB

Long couches and low tables spread around the lounge. Black curtains covered walls and ceiling. The Insomniacs Club had no windows. A large fridge with a glass door packed with Beerlao bottles was the main light source, throwing long shadows. The smell of marijuana wafted through the air-conditioned room. Small groups of people mooched around talking in hushed tones. Jazz, not quite insipid, but certainly not free, poured from invisible speakers.

A feisty-looking girl sat on the green felt of the only pool table, nursing a beer, looking distractedly in his direction. The dim glow of the table's overhead lights lent her a wonderfully remote aura.

The fridge was guarded by a dwarf who perched on a low stool like a retired albatross. A small person. A very small person sucking on a joint almost as long as his arm.

"This is No-No. My little fucker. Keeps tabs on what you drink. He's a picture of integrity. Don't fuck with him or you'll be removed from this place, never to return."

Having completed his precise instructions, Vincent turned and made for the door to resume his duties upstairs.

"See you later, Maier. Don't do anything I wouldn't do."

With his wizened sad face and his tiny body strapped into a white shirt and black tie, a waistcoat and black pants, No-No looked like the gatekeeper to undesirable realities. He opened the fridge and, without a word, handed Maier a Beerlao.

"Vodka?" Maier asked gently.

No-No shook his head.

"Beerlao. You want?"

Against his better judgment, Maier took the bottle.

"Who is Léon?"

No-No pointed towards the pool table and resumed his love affair with the joint. Maier passed a group of older white men sitting in a tight circle. They glanced up as he made his way past them, several sets of hard eyes following his steps. Considering the dreamy ambience, there seemed to be an inordinate amount of unhappy types in the Insomniacs Club. These guys would have been more at home in one of Bangkok's nightlife ghettos. He heard American accents and kept moving.

"Hi, you Léon?"

The girl on the table smiled and nodded, just a little. Her short black hair was a carefully crafted mess, and she wore her black eyeliner thicker than her purple lipstick.

"Who wants to know?"

"Maier, friend of Julia's."

"Ah yes, she mailed me a few days back, told me you're coming. Didn't tell me you were one-eyed. Nice to meet you, Mr. Maier. I'm Kanitha."

"Just Maier, please. The dwarf seems to think you are Léon."

The girl jumped off the table. She wasn't quite a midget herself, but she didn't reach past his chest either. Still, she was too tall for No-No. She threw Maier an impish firecracker smile.

"We know so much about you. The famous PI from Hamburg."

Maier was stumped. She had the cutie sheen of a Japanese manga character, with perfect features, light immaculate skin and a figure that suggested she either did yoga all day long or was familiar with tantric sex practices inappropriate for her age group. She wore a critically short skirt and her perfect legs reached down into high black leather boots that wouldn't have looked out of place on a dominatrix. Maier started to warm to the Insomniacs Club.

"What else do you know about me?"

"Julia told me you used to be a journalist. Like a top guy. A great writer. Like me."

Maier felt uneasy. What else had Julia mailed her friends?

"Don't worry; only me and Léon know who you are. Léon knows where the gold is. He also knows where Julia's father died."

"How is that?"

"The man who killed Julia's father also killed Léon's sister. Tried to kill Léon too. Bad guy, definitely. That's what Léon says."

She had a strong American accent with a soft Asian lilt. Maier pushed dark thoughts away. She was young.

"Where are you from?"

"Bangkok. But my mom's Laotian."

"And how old are you?"

She pulled a face and strained to look like a grown-up.

"That's a loaded question, coming from you, Maier. Old enough to make all the same mistakes you made. In a girl's way, of course."

Maier smiled at her and refrained from commenting.

Her eyes narrowed.

"Twenty-three and counting, if you must know."

He nodded and left her remark standing in the room. He could sense that any comeback would only rile her.

"Is Léon here tonight?"

The girl shook her head, "No, he's out of town. But I can take you to see him. And then he can take you to the gold. I mean us. It's still there, he thinks. So, get it into your head right away: You need me."

"You're a friend of Julia's?"

"I've known her for about six months, Maier. And I plan to be a real journalist, just like you. I graduated from Thammasat with a first in media studies. You know, the best, like, university in Bangkok. I also spent a year in Texas and did an internship at a local paper there. I've lived in New York. I've been places. I know people."

Maier was intrigued. She knew people.

"I am not a journalist."

"But you used to be, I looked you up on the Internet. You're legend, dude."

"Writers are only as good as their last story, and I stopped writing a long time ago."

She shrugged in a dismissive way that befitted her permanent air of youthful discontent and quietly grinned into her beer. Maier had the feeling that his protestations were meaningless.

"It must be journo night tonight. Your smooth-talking friend Vincent is a writer, too."

She shook her head. "No, Vincent is a hack. And he'd sell his mother for a story. He's desperate. I'm eager. There's a difference. And he's not my fucking friend."

Maier grinned, "Maybe the twenty years separating you have something to do with it? But you swear almost as much as him."

Kanitha shrugged, "The way he charms people with his linguistic fireworks is way beyond my abilities, Maier. And I reckon he was always like this. Probably not a bad writer at the beginning, but no pride and too much envy. As you said, we're only as good as our last story. I'll remember that one."

Maier looked at her more closely. This girl was sharp. Asian hardware, Western software. He'd noticed that he was patronizing her and changed the subject.

"And how does No-No fit into all this?"

Kanitha laughed, her teeth shining like a priceless pearl necklace.

"I'm just telling you because we'll see more of Vincent. He sometimes looks like he can't think his way from here to the toilet, but he has his ear close to the ground. Everything that happens in this country washes through this club sooner or later. And past No-No. He's just the beer clown. A good soul. And Vincent's spider."

"I thought Vincent was just filling in for someone?"

"Is that what he said? Playing the great writer?"

Maier wasn't sure whether the local rivalries had any bearing on his case. He'd cross that bridge when he got to it.

"So, Julia told you I was coming, but omitted to tell her boyfriend?"

"Ah, Maier, you're beginning to get up to speed. Brilliant. Julia and I know each other from TreeLine. I did a short internship with them in Bangkok. And I read your stuff. You're tops."

Maier frowned into his bottle.

"The Beerlao's not bad, but I usually drink vodka orange."

"Don't go off subject like that, dude Maier. I read your stories from Palestine, Yugoslavia, Nepal and Cambodia. They were all translated into English, ran in the Tribune. All over. You've seen a lot of war,

Maier. You've been around. You were at the top of your game. Why'd you pack it in?"

"My best friend in Cambodia was killed during an attempt on my life, dude Kanitha. After that, it was time for a change. I had enough."

Seeing her take a step back, he added, "Slow down a bit. Otherwise, there won't be any mysteries left in the world by the morning."

"Are you making a pass at me, Maier?"

"No, you're too young."

The girl threw him an ungrateful look. His last quip had slowed her down. But she hardly missed a beat.

"In 1971, the then government created an artificial lake north of Vientiane. Following the revolution, the Pathet Lao, our victorious armed forces, banished all the capital's undesirables to two islands located on this lake. One island for all the female sex workers, another for the pimps and the drug dealers. Most of them have either died or gone, of course. The lake is called Ang Nam Ngum."

"Great story, Kanitha, but it is not going to force me out of retirement."

She laughed. "Ah, you're so German. Léon is on the island that once held the female exiles. He has a small house there."

"Hm, that sounds like paradise. How far is it?"

"You'll see tomorrow. I've rented a car. It'll be a bumpy ride; the road up there is no good. Meet me outside the Red Bar at 8. And don't get your hopes up too high. The female subversives that are left are of retirement age. Even older than you, Maier. So old."

The tiny dance floor at the back was almost deserted, and it was so dark Maier could barely make out the other customers. Just as well. A middle-aged foreigner with a tired bar girl attempted a Lao-style dance. It looked sad.

"As old as Mr. Mookie," she added.

The man she pointed at discreetly looked around sixty. He had short white hair and was decked out unfashionably in gray pants and a blue anorak. He sat next to the dance floor, surrounded by younger men in leather jackets. Perhaps he was a government official. He looked like a war criminal. He had the best table and the youngest girl. As he rose slowly from his couch, the chicken song blasted from the speakers. Mr. Mookie was in a dancing mood.

Maier assumed that the Insomniacs Club had seen this before and that the chicken song was the old man's favorite tune. Why else would one want to make the rest of the punters in Vientiane's only speakeasy squirm? Wealthy and influential men in Southeast Asia appreciated small, torrid gestures that appeared to reaffirm their usually undeserved status and helped them, for a few blissful moments, to forget about who they were going to screw next.

Mr. Mookie grabbed the girl and hit the center of the dance floor. Some of his companions drifted around the edges, but the old man had the limelight all to himself. The girl, dressed in tight jeans, equipped with WTC-sized platforms and a mobile tied to her belt, a rarity in Laos, pirouetted around the old man and giggled as if scared to death. Mr. Mookie broke into a sweat. The song mutated into another 'Agadoo' style party number, and the old swinger changed his step into a backwards-forwards penguin shuffle, accentuated by the anorak's shimmer under the mirror ball. It was all too much. The music finished and the girl led the blue anorak back to his table. Minutes later he got up, slowly, ever so slowly, and with the help of his lady friend and his bodyguards, headed for the exit.

"Laotian Intelligence, that guy," the young siren to Maier's right laughed, "Mookie's his nickname. Welcome to Laos."

A handful of Beerlao down the line, Maier began to appreciate the people's utopia brew, but he'd had enough for the day and arranged to meet the young reporter the next morning. The evening had been more productive than he'd expected. Léon knew who'd killed Manfred Rendel. Perhaps the twenty-five-year-old murder would be resolved after all. He touched her shoulder as he waved her farewell. That did make him feel old, older than Mr. Mookie.

As he crossed the dark room for the exit, a huge, broad shadow, a bear of a man, moved into his path.

"Well, evening. Don't think we've had the pleasure. And I usually make everybody who drops by the Insomniacs Club. You new in town?"

Maier took a step back to gauge the unwanted human obstacle. The man was nearly as tall as the detective but twice as wide. American. His pockmarked face was pale and leery. A moustache fit for a walrus divided it neatly into up – mottled cheeks, red veined nose and tiny, curious eyes – and down – numerous chins, covered in dirty stubble. Since Maier had lost his own moustache to his slowly improving taste, he looked with pity upon others who wore them. He'd come to think of moustaches as an affliction, like a terrible skin rash.

While the man had no shortage of facial hair, his head was polished like a slippery bowling ball. His breath wasn't good. Maier guessed him in his early sixties. Once upon a time, he'd been in very good shape. Perhaps even handsome. That time had passed and it had left few traces. Life could be cruel.

"Maier, professional traveler. Who are you?"

The American with the oversized whiskers shot him a searching look. Maier sensed that his name had preceded him to this unfortunate encounter. This guy knew who he was, what he was. But the older man caught himself instantly and smiled without passion.

"A devil in his own right, Maier, a devil in his own right. Name's Charlie Bryson. I'm an American, and a veteran. Back in the Seventies, I worked in Laos as a pilot for Air America. Now I'm running some MIA ops north of here. We're looking for our buddies who gave their lives for the agency. Some of them were lost up around Long Cheng. Heard of it?"

Maier shrugged a fake smile onto his face and shook his head. This guy was more dangerous than the faded military tattoos on his hairy arms suggested. He was a smooth liar.

"Well, I saw you talking to young Kanitha there; I assumed you were a journo like her, looking for that mega-scoop, snooping around. I keep telling her it ain't gonna happen. Not in Laos. And now that I look at you, you don't really look like a hack. So, what's your game, Maier: just looking for girls?"

Bryson was trying to provoke the detective. Did the old American refer to his client or was he making an innocuous comment about Kanitha? Maier was right at the heart of things. Perhaps Bryson knew of the gold. Perhaps he had Julia. Maier abandoned his strategy of verbal non-aggression to see if he could make the old guy blow his top.

"Ah, you don't think me very classy, Charlie. Try shooting closer to the mark. In time you might hit something. We all have our dark sides. Yours is bad attitude, friend."

The old American gripped Maier's wrist, hard. For a split second, the detective thought of freeing himself and decking the insolent, drunken soldier. But he checked himself. A bar room brawl was the last thing he wanted. Bryson had friends no more than two metres away.

Bryson knew things. And Maier didn't want to be barred from the city's most exclusive drinking hole on his first night in town. He wasn't going to get his client back by getting into a punch-up with this hard man. He relaxed and waited for the American to calm down.

"Hear this, Maier. I saw you walking down the street earlier. It didn't look right. You're a know-it-all. Be careful with our circus; otherwise, the tigers might get nervous."

He let go of Maier's wrist.

The detective, sorely tempted to tell Bryson he'd already seen the clown act, smiled with as much naivety as he could muster, "Charlie, so great to meet you. You look nervous already and I have no desire to see your tigers miss one of the hoops you undoubtedly make them jump through."

The American grinned, his expression sour.

"Well, Maier, nice talking in analogies. Now we both know we're clever. One day soon we'll have a real conversation. But for the time being, fuck you and the fuckin' horse you rode in on."

"That's what Mr. Mookie just said about you, Charlie," Maier replied flippantly, not really sure why. The older American recoiled and stared hard at the detective. But he didn't say anything else. Strange for a man who looked like he always had to have the last word.

5

THE ISLAND OF LOST DEALS

KANITHA PROVED to be an efficient guide. The jeep's silent driver raced, slid and pushed through eighty hellish kilometers of muddy roads in four hours and deposited Maier and the girl on the shores of Ang Nam Ngum just after midday. In the shadow of a rickety sala, its grass roof torn away by the rains, Kanitha negotiated the hire of an equally unsteady-looking long-tail boat. The boat man took his time filling his plastic fuel tank, and Maier could feel the girl getting restless. But she didn't complain and sat silently in the prow as they pushed off towards Léon's home.

The small island rose from the water like a magical place in a fairy tale. Fields graced the tree-lined hillsides, and small canoes lay on the grassy shore. Old people pottered around between water and sky. There were no roads or towns. Nothing had happened here for years. The island looked like the world's last idyllic hideaway.

Smoke rose from the next cove. They rounded a headland and paradise was gone to hell in an instant.

The boatman switched off his engine and they drifted towards the shore in near silence. Flames rose from a small property close to a jetty. One look at Kanitha, and Maier knew they were too late.

As soon as the boat touched the jetty, Maier jumped off and ran to the burning building. Kanitha followed him with uncertain steps, crying. Her sobs, the crackling of dying flames and the small waves lapping against the shore made for a dismal soundtrack. The modest inferno had the atmosphere of a heavy scene in a Peckinpah movie. But there was no movie, only real life, bleeding slowly into the placid water.

An old woman sidled up to Maier as he picked through the charred remains of what had been a modest beach hut. Flames still licked around the blackened stumps that once held the structure upright. The woman wore a tattered, bright red Chinese polyester dress, the kind that was popular all-over Southeast Asia during Chinese New Year, and too much make-up. Her mouth, smothered in cheap lipstick, looked like a wound. In the harsh November sunlight, she had all the charm of a starving vampire.

The ground was charred; fences had melted away. Half-burnt garbage lay everywhere. The carcass of a dog had been impaled and roasted on a wooden pole in the center of the inferno. Its head, stuck on a second pole, greeted Maier from the space that must have once been the hut's front porch.

Whoever had taken Léon had made sure he had nothing to return to. The scorched earth reached all the way down to the lake shore. This hadn't just been a kidnapping. The scene smelled of erasure.

Maier smiled at the woman and took her hand. She was happy to be led. He took her to the water's edge and found a dry piece of wood for her to sit on. He asked her name but she only smiled vaguely and gave the standard Laotian answer to uncomfortable questions.

"Bo pen yang."

Never mind.

He turned to Kanitha, who'd slowly followed Maier onto solid ground.

"What's her name?"

"I only know her stage name, which she got when the Americans were here. During the war. She was called May Lik then. Fucking sad."

"Ask May Lik what happened."

The woman started talking, more to herself than to the two arrivals. Kanitha was still struggling to come to grips with the signs of recent violence.

"I met her when I stayed here with Léon. Vincent and others from the Insomniacs Club have also been here, and she always comes down when we sit on the shore, drinking, having a good time. She's been here since the Seventies. She's mad as a box of frogs."

Maier stifled a laugh, listening to the girl's appraisal while observing the carnage. Sometimes, he couldn't stand his own cynicism.

"We will not have a more reliable witness."

Kanitha nodded and swallowed her tears.

"The dog's name was Poe."

"As in the American writer?"

"No, Maier, as in Tony Poe, CIA case officer in Laos in the Sixties."

Maier looked at her blankly.

"Tony Poe, Maier. Where have you been? The wildest, craziest of the Secret War warriors who lived in Long Cheng. Remember Brando in Apocalypse Now? That character was based on Poe. I thought you were the Southeast Asia expert."

"Where is Poe now? Still around?"

The girl shrugged.

"No idea. But Léon met him when he was a kid and named his dog after him. The guy must have left an impression. Léon told me that Poe used to walk around with a necklace made from human ears. His flower bed in Long Cheng was framed by communist skulls. He was the business."

Maier shook his head. The rules of commonly accepted conduct disappeared as soon as the first shot was fired. The war pig came out. And stayed out. It squealed and ravaged, pillaged and raped, while generals, politicians and the media told the world the beast was extinct and that an honorable creature sat in its place, spreading justice and punishing those who deserved it. Simple stuff. One look at May Lik told a different story.

"So, what happened here today?"

"She said that a boat arrived very early in the morning. She can't sleep at night because it's so quiet here. She sits in her cabin, up on the hill. She saw a motorboat. Five or six men got off. They knew exactly which house to go to. They took Léon and burnt his hut and killed his dog. They had a machine that spat fire."

"They were Asians or white men?"

"She says they were Laotian and Vietnamese. With a white man. Very tall and fat and wearing a colorful shirt."

"The white man had a bald head and a moustache?"

May Lik shook her head and stared hopefully at Maier.

Despite the pale sun, high above them now, Maier felt a chill.

Everything had been said.

The story of the old woman had set new wheels in his head in motion, but he couldn't place the man in the colorful shirt. Not unpleasant Charlie Bryson from the Insomniacs Club. But there were other objectionable characters around. And if the Vietnamese were crowding in on his case, there would be more complications. If the kidnappers were government people, they could do anything they wanted in Laos. If they were a private outfit, they would do anything they wanted in Laos. The difference was merely in the language. Vietnam was a powerful neighbor. Still, those were a lot of ifs.

With the air of a funeral procession, a smattering of old women slowly walked down the hill, gathered in a wide circle and stared at what was left of the cabin. No one spoke to the visitors. Everyone kept their eyes on the burnt-out shell of the hut. No one made eye contact. One bunch of strangers in a day was quite enough.

May Lik spoke into the long silence.

"She says they beat Léon until the white man made them stop. They were very angry. That's why they chopped and burned Poe."

Kanitha picked herself up. She was pale but composed. She put her arm around May Lik and asked her to continue.

Maier shook his head. What was a white man doing with a bunch of Vietnamese enforcers?

May Lik brushed the girl off and walked to the lake shore, where she continued to mumble at no one. The old woman in her tattered dress implored unseen friends and enemies, begging for a better deck of cards than the one she'd been dealt. Then she lapsed into a loud silence that stretched as far as the water around them. Maier was moved by her desperation. No winners today.

"She says that Léon was a good man. They should not have taken him."

"Why did Léon choose to stay on the island of the old ladies, rather than the one with the pimps and hustlers?"

Kanitha shrugged, "Where would you've stayed, Maier? He wasn't well. He'd been shot in the war. He thinks the bullet grazed his lung, but with medical facilities in Laos being almost nonexistent and he being a Hmong whose parents had clearly been on the US side..."

"You and Léon are pretty tight, right?"

The young woman gestured helplessly, as only a near-teenager could. She wouldn't meet his eye.

"With me and Léon, it's one day at a time, Maier. But that has nothing to do with how I feel about what happened here. We have to find him. We gotta find my buddy, my soulmate. And I want to know which bastard killed and burned Poe."

Maier got up and kicked the pole that supported the dog's head into the dying flames of Léon's inferno. It was time to go.

"I don't suppose May Lik has any idea where they took Léon?"

"She does. She told me immediately. They took him to Muang Khua. Little more than an obscure river outpost, it's in the north, near the Vietnamese border and very close to Dien Bien Phu. You know, the last stand of the French in Indochina. They told May Lik to tell anyone who was coming to look for him. They said they'd be waiting."

Maier mulled the kidnappers' message and made a snap decision.

"Julia already told you that she hired me to find out about her father. Do you know she was kidnapped in Hamburg last week?"

He watched the younger woman pale, stagger to her feet and throw up into the shallow water.

"Maier," she shouted between heaving saliva and air, "why didn't you tell me this when we met?"

He didn't answer. The case was slipping through his hands. Both his client and his only local source of information had been kidnapped by at least one opposition he hadn't known existed. His trail to the gold was quickly wearing thin.

Maier caught a flash of light across the water. The sun was behind them. It was probably the reflection from a piece of glass lying on the distant shore.

"I think we need to go to Muang Khua. Have you been there?"

Kanitha shot him a weary look and nodded, "I went there for a travel magazine. A wild, beautiful stretch of the Nam Ou River. There's some talk of re-education camps in the area, built for enemies of the state after the revolution. My story was on trekking, though. And I didn't see any camps."

Maier smiled, "You are a writer after all. Maybe you can show an old dog a few new tricks."

Kanitha smiled into her shirt and said nothing. Maier gave May Lik a fistful of kip, Laotian bank notes, and started towards the boat.

"Great, you'll be my guide, then."

"And we'll find Julia."

Whatever lurked on the far side of the water flashed again. A signal? Maier's hair stood on end. Not a signal. He threw himself onto Kanitha and they both tumbled into the shallow water. The shot rang out a second later, the sound delayed by the distance.

A sniper.

"You OK?"

Kanitha tried to get up but Maier pushed her behind the boat and crawled through the shallow water next to her. She nodded; her eyes wide with fear.

"It's OK; they missed."

He turned to scan the shore behind them. They, whoever they were, hadn't missed. May Lik had collapsed, a hole in her thin chest, her smudged mouth a silent scream. Everyone else had disappeared.

Maier waited thirty seconds and then crawled over to the old woman.

She was dead. He slowly crawled back to the boat.

6

BAD ELEMENTS

They stayed in the water until they couldn't stand the cold any longer. They pushed the boat – a petrified boatman lying motionless in the water-filled bottom of his vessel – around the island until Maier felt it safe enough to get out of the water. Once it got dark, the boatman agreed to return to the shore. There was no sign of the shooter.

Shaking, wet and cold, they rested in an abandoned farm hut before hitching a ride with a tourist group in the morning. The vacationers were somewhat excited at seeing an older Western man and a young Asian woman, both of them caked in mud, emerge on the side of the road and flag down their four-wheel drive. Maier spun them a story about being a journalist on the trail of illegal loggers with his fixer, having run into trouble in the forest.

Certain that his hotel was being watched, Maier didn't bother returning to his room. He stayed with Kanitha in her cramped two-room apartment above a Chinese goods store set a couple of blocks back from the river. He slept on a tattered sofa that was covered in cigarette burns and held together by duct tape. The perfumed sheets of the Atlantic in Hamburg were a distant memory. The actual life of the private eye had caught up with him.

No matter how many times the detective turned the events at the lake over in his mind, he couldn't understand why the Vietnamese had shot the old woman. And if May Lik hadn't been the intended target, then why would anyone have taken a shot at him? The kidnappers' message had been loud and clear: Try to come after us and we'll kill you. It also meant that Léon was of no value to them dead.

There was of course another, more troubling possibility. Maier and Kanitha could have been followed from the capital to the lake. While the detective and his companion had been in pursuit of Léon's kidnappers, others had been in pursuit of them. And where was Julia?

Maier was in the deep end.

He knew next to nothing about the kidnappers, even less about the killers who might have been on their trail. Unpleasant thoughts formed in his mind like heavily laden monsoon clouds. One could imagine enemies everywhere.

"Maier, I'm scared. And we need to talk."

The detective, showered but not shaved, sat on the small terrace of Kanitha's apartment and studied a map of northern Laos. Children played on the unpaved road below. A woman passed, pushing a cart with steaming corn on the cob under a tree, calling for hungry customers. From their vantage point, the world looked non-threatening and idyllic.

"You have information for me that you previously withheld?"

"Of course, Maier. I'm a journalist, remember, not a public information service that spills all its secrets because a tall, handsome German correspondent turned private eye steps into the picture. And you didn't tell me Julia was kidnapped. You don't trust me."

Maier shrugged, "Get over the celebrity thing, Kanitha. I am just another Joe making a buck. And my journalist days are long gone. I am no longer interested in investigating truths and then finding out that my employer has an agenda that contradicts my story."

"You think the truth shouldn't be told at all?" she asked defiantly.

He looked at her in what he thought might be a disarming way, "When you are young, you know that you can change the world. When you are my age, you know it's impossible. Both insights are close to the truth. Does that make sense?"

She thought about it and shook her head.

"Why won't you sleep with me, Maier?"

He looked up from the map and focused on the girl.

"I am not looking for attachments."

Kanitha rolled her eyes and pushed wayward hair from her face.

"I'm not asking you to marry me, dick."

"You're a beautiful girl, Kanitha…"

She cut him off.

"Blah blah blah…"

"Your boyfriend's been kidnapped."

Her face was a mixture of shame and fury.

"Like I said, Maier, with me and Léon, it's one day at a time."

Maier cut her off with a curt gesture.

"You are my understudy. Perhaps I can help you get a scoop, an important exclusive, if you help me get to the bottom of this gold saga. This case just smells of things larger than the sum of the parts we have seen so far. We have a deal?"

He held his hand out and tried for his most genuine smile.

After a moment's hesitation, she took it and tried for a tight, manly grip.

"Old men are such pussies. You're probably right. I'll take a shower and get myself together, don't disturb. And know what you're missing."

With that she got up, turned theatrically, pulled off her T-shirt, and walked inside. Her perfectly smooth, pale back swayed away from him, out of reach, and he hoped half-heartedly, out of mind. He wasn't sure how the conversation might have ameliorated any of her fears. He'd avoided all her questions. And she was avoiding most of his while toying with him.

Maier left the apartment and found an Internet café. This time he had a message waiting. From the 1000 Elephant Trading Company.

We offer Julia Rendel in exchange for Léon Sangster. When you find him, get in touch. Refrain from all other investigations or you will be stopped with maximum force.

An hour later, Kanitha was back at his side, wearing a black blouse and a long skirt over her boots. She looked like an Asian rockabilly cat.

"Ready for the wilderness, Maier? Are you?"

Maier held up the maps. "Sure, but how do we get there?"

"Let's go to the Insomniacs Club. Vincent knows a good boatman."

Maier shook his head, "Kanitha, I've been doing some thinking. We met at the Insomniacs Club, and Vincent knows I came looking for

Léon. When I left, I was stopped by this MIA guy, Charlie, who wanted to know whether I was interested in Long Cheng. The old US airport? Ring a bell?"

Kanitha thought about it.

"I know Charlie. He and his crew work all over the country, especially in the north. Retired Air America, CIA. Long Cheng isn't far as the crow flies but hard to get to. Bad roads, Hmong rebels, Lao military. Off limits to tourists and snoops like us. Even Charlie and his guys can't go there unless they have prior clearance from the right ministry. But his lot have lobby groups in the US who pressure congressmen who in turn might be talking to the Laotians. There's big money involved in digging up American soldiers. I've tried to go to Long Cheng. But I got stopped at the first army roadblock and was sent back. Definitely a story."

As an afterthought, she added, "And Léon has been there, too. He was there as a kid. He told me that his parents died there. But he was pretty sketchy about it. I mean, he was definitely holding out on me."

"Is there anything else I need to know about before we head north?"

Maier didn't try to keep the hard tone out of his voice. If he was to travel with this unpredictable young woman, he needed to know everything she did.

"He told me that he got shot there. That his sister was killed there. In the Seventies. By a double agent. I dunno, that just sounds mad. But as I said, he was a kid then."

Maier said nothing and looked at her expectantly. There was more.

"Léon's second name is Sangster. His father was American. His mother was Hmong. He told me she was a princess. The whole family lived in Long Cheng."

Maier thought about the information she was spoon-feeding him.

"The gold is in Long Cheng, I think. It must be."

He scanned the maps again. Long Cheng was a long way from where Léon had been taken. "But I don't think his kidnappers know that. And I am sure they are Vietnamese, as May Lik said. They are playing safe, keeping him near the border so they can whisk him away quickly if necessary. And they are not just careful because I am nosing around. There are other players out there. This 1000 Elephant Trading Company and the Vietnamese are hunting for the same prize. One lot have Julia, the other lot have Léon. One lot burned down Léon's house, the other lot shot May Lik. And both parties think I have the key to the gold. That's my theory at present. It comes with a fifty percent margin of error."

"What do we do?" Kanitha asked impatiently.

"We take a trip to Muang Khua. Quietly and carefully."

Maier, marooned on Kanitha's tatty sofa for a second night, was alone in his dream. *His world was on fire. Way ahead in the distance, partly obscured by flames, wavering like a mirage, he could see the silhouette of a man, standing on a wide-open plain dotted with villages. Broad shoulders, short-cropped hair, a fierce gait, his arms apparently embracing the world. Every time the figure vibrated slightly, a huge roar sounded across the plain. Maier knew that the ground shook, though he couldn't feel it. The man started walking through the fire towards Maier.*

The closer he came, the more familiar Maier felt about the lean features and the purposeful, economic movements. Soon he'd be able to make out his identity. Just a few more meters. As the man got closer, Maier noticed something else. Wherever this black shadow walked, his outline defined against the inferno around him, villages went up in flames, forests burnt like matchsticks, rivers dried up in seconds and people died and died. Maier moved towards a village that the black shadow, the broad-shouldered man with the short-cropped hair had just passed. The second the detective's mind touched the village, he recoiled and woke up, breathing much too quickly. But he was immediately sucked down into the dream again. All the houses were burning. People ran from their homes, their backs and hair in flames. Children watched their skin peel away from their arms as clouds of chemical warfare washed across their community. Mothers and fathers, uncles and aunts, grandparents and neighbors, builders and tailors, idiots and wise men wilted away in an instant. While one village burned, a great silence descended on the next, as another shock wave hit buildings and tore them to pieces, seconds before the noise of the explosion deafened every living being within a mile radius. He looked up into the sky but saw nothing but silence.

"Gods," an old man shouted. "These are gods that spit fire from the sky. We cannot fight them. We must go underground."

The next moment, the old man had gone, had been atomized by the harbinger of sorrows. The black shadow continued walking through a land it emptied with its passing. Every time Maier could almost make out the ogre's face, another huge explosion would light up behind him, leaving his identity obscured.

Dawn came and Maier woke up, grappling with the fading visions, trying to fall back down into it a third time to find out where it might take him.

7

NEVER GET OFF THE BOAT

The Lao Airlines jet banked dangerously and wobbled towards the Luang Prabang runway. The flight had been short and frightening. The plane was as ancient as the hills it had crossed and in much worse condition. The tourists on board applauded when the pilot touched down and got his machine under control as they rattled towards the ramshackle airport building.

Maier had been to Luang Prabang on an assignment covering German restoration efforts of the historic city center just after Laos had opened its doors to foreign visitors, a cover for his investigative work on the Hmong rebels who continued to fight the Laotian government in the mountain ranges to the south of the city, decades after the CIA, their erstwhile paymaster, had abandoned them.

The city itself had escaped the war unscathed – the Americans and Vietnamese had decided early on that Luang Prabang was too beautiful to be destroyed. Perhaps it had been the town's spectacular collection of sixteenth century temples, each one a striking physical poem to form and faith, that had saved the city. More likely, both factions had decided to use the former royal capital as a holiday spot while the rest of the country was being vaporized. Twenty-five years later, Luang Prabang was the Laotians' most magnanimous tourist cash cow, a UNESCO world heritage site with a rapidly expanding infrastructure of hotels, restaurants, bakeries, shops and cybercafés.

Maier and Kanitha carried only hand luggage and caught a taxi straight to the town's ferry pier. They were too late. Their destination, Muang Khua, lay on the banks of the Nam Ou River, a day's journey north on a long-tail. The regular boat had left.

"Bo pen yang," the ticket seller smiled, "Never mind. Another boat tomorrow."

They ambled down to the waterline, where a group of boat captains sat under a tree and played cards. Half an hour of intermittent bargaining later, they sat in the back of a long-tail boat.

The captain, a cheroot-smoking old man with arms as thin as matchsticks, grinned at Maier and asked, "Honeymoon?"

Maier first assumed the boatman to be sarcastic, but when he turned to fix him with a stare, the poor soul, intimidated and embarrassed, simply wilted and squeezed out another *bo pen yang*.

The Laotians were keen to avoid confrontation.

"Why rock the boat, Maier? Leave him his assumptions," Kanitha said and hooked her arms around his. Maier didn't resist.

A few minutes later, they'd left Luang Prabang behind, headed up the Mekong and entered one of its countless tributaries, the Nam Ou. Small villages lined the river banks. Gardens stretched all the way down to the water's edge. Buffalo stood and stared at them as they passed. Children waved and jumped into the floods while their mothers showered or beat their washing on flat stones, clothed in sarongs that clung tightly to their skins and shimmered in the afternoon sun. From the passing boat, the scenes were bucolic, framed by the natural poetry of the world's honest and hard-working people, the salt of the Earth. Maier relaxed, knowing he was lucky to enjoy these glimpses of partial truths and to be able to separate them from other realities the country's rural population faced.

Four hours upriver, they approached Nong Khiaw, the halfway point between Luang Prabang and their destination. The boat slowed to a crawl as the captain made ready to pull in and stop. Like other villages they'd passed, Nong Khiaw, a modest collection of homes and shops, a few guest houses and a jetty cum bus terminal, clung to a steep embankment. A concrete bridge crossed the river high above the village. Karst stone cliffs topped by clusters of bamboo framed the idyllic view. The pandas couldn't be far. For a second, Maier had that tourist feeling that he almost never got. Innocence had its benefits.

"Shit," Kanitha suddenly exclaimed and pointed to the jetty.

Charlie Bryson, his shining bald plate poking out behind a jeep, was directing a group of workers to transfer tarpaulin bags to a longtail boat. As they neared, he abandoned his mission and scanned the river.

With a mad hug, Kanitha fell on top of Maier. They tumbled into the bottom of the boat. He smelled her faintly delicious perfume mixed with sweat.

"Mai yud, baw yud, don't stop," she shouted to the boatman in both Thai and Laotian. The driver looked at her, confused. Naturally, he'd made no connection between her sudden affection for her partner, the commotion on the river bank and her desire to continue at top speed. Embarrassed, he decelerated to a crawl. Kanitha continued imploring him. They drifted by the jetty in slow motion just as one of the workers dropped a large bundle he was carrying. The American turned and shouted at the man. The boat passed. Maier glanced back. Kanitha continued to berate the boatman. A few seconds later, they'd cleared the spot and Kanitha let go of Maier, sat up and returned to her seat. She grinned at him victoriously. They'd been lucky.

Almost.

As they crossed under the bridge, Vincent, Ontario's greatest journalist, appeared on the balcony of a restaurant shack overlooking the river. The Canadian stared straight at Maier. He gave no sign of acknowledgement. But as the boat passed the bridge, Maier saw him get up and hurry away. Then they were gone.

Maier had regained his composure and laughed.

"Quick thinking, Kanitha. But we have been spotted. How close is that Canadian guy to the MIA program?"

The young Thai shook her head, somewhat dejectedly.

"I didn't even think they had anything to say to each other. Never seen Vincent sit down with Charlie. In fact, Vincent always talks about how he'll one day expose the MIA activity in northern Laos having as much to do with recovering loot from the war as with finding the remains of American soldiers."

"He changed sides, perhaps?"

"Anything's possible. He thinks the world owes him. He'd naturally see you as a challenge just because you're a new face in town and you appear to be doing something. You're a man of action, Maier. That can make expats stranded in small-town Asia homicidal. And Charlie is a regular at the Insomniacs Club."

Anything was possible with anyone in this game, Maier thought as he listened to his companion. How the hell did these guys get on the river here? Did Kanitha have another agenda other than springing her one-day-at-a-time boyfriend and getting her scoop? How innocent was innocent? And why did she have to smell so damn good?

The boat man started shouting above the noise of the engine. Maier understood a smattering of Laotian, but this man was almost completely unintelligible. The detective experienced a momentary lack of confidence in his beautiful travel companion. But he needed to trust her.

"We need petrol. We don't have enough juice to get all the way to Muang Khua. And it's getting late. Our man doesn't want to travel in the dark. He says there might be bandits. The closer we get to the Vietnamese and Chinese border, the higher the risk of an ambush at night."

Maier pulled a map from his vest and scanned the river villages. Muang Ngoi, a tourist outpost on a peninsula in the Nam Ou, was close. The boat man confirmed the availability of gasoline at the village. They'd be able to melt into the tourist population without attracting attention. It was time to get off the boat.

8

THE GOOD AMERICANS

She lay deep in his arms as if she belonged there. Music drifted from a campfire through the small gaggle of riverside huts occupied by young Western travelers. Someone was strumming a guitar, not too competently, but it hardly mattered. Maier could see fireflies bouncing around in front of the window.

Muang Ngoi was the last frontier for the Lonely Planet set – a laid-back Lao village that had made the necessary concessions to the twenty-first century nomads that scoured the Earth in search of cheap foreign thrills packed with the necessities to keep the comfort zone intact – beer, marijuana, pancakes and fried rice. The Internet wasn't long off. Travelers needed little more to continue their consumption-driven lifestyles in front of a more exotic background than the suburbs they came from. Luckily, the young people traveling the Asian pancake trench weren't particularly observant. For the most part, they were busy positioning their own narrative in a strange land, posturing with disc players, singing songs that had originated, like themselves, thousands of miles away, falling in love with the Other but sleeping with others like themselves, people they met on the road. They talked about the price of this and that across Asia – where to scuba-dive cheaply, how to beat the entrance fee to a temple, which beer had the best flavor at the lowest price with the smallest headache factor. They were experts in scrimping and saving but learned little about the land they passed through or the people that lived in it. A generation entranced by the conformity of individualism. No one had looked at Maier and Kanitha as they'd checked into one of the huts. In the travelers' world, old age made men and women invisible.

Maier loved being unseen, though he knew the locals would remember him.

Kanitha, her eyes closed, her breath hot against his chest, didn't appear to remember anything. The worm had turned and no one was more surprised than the detective. He'd been so determined not to fly. She was part of the case. She was the second woman connected to the case he'd ended up in bed with. She was too young. Perhaps he'd entangled himself in more than he could keep track of. He didn't know whether to feel happy, stupid or a tad too predatory.

He could tell she wasn't sleeping.

"So, tomorrow we try to spring your boyfriend from captivity, and tonight we are having a ball? I mean, I like you. A great deal. You are a wonderful woman, Kanitha. I have the feeling you have been digging away at me ever since we met in the Insomniacs Club. But I can't figure out why. I am sorry, but I don't quite buy the cub-reporter story. I did a little checking on you myself. You are widely published in the region in the past six months. You have a pretty good reputation amongst the NGO set and expat readers in Thailand. You don't need me."

He gently placed her head on the moldy pillow they shared and pushed himself up on the worn-out mattress. She didn't react. Maier slunk out from underneath the mosquito net and reached for his clothes. The girl grumbled, but she made no move to follow him.

"There must be more to this than what you have told me."

Kanitha opened her eyes and looked at him as he pulled on his faded khaki pants.

"Where you going?"

"Beer run. And when I get back, you better have a story. Otherwise, I may be gone when you wake up tomorrow. We detectives move in silent and mysterious ways, you know."

As he opened the door, she spat angrily after him, "Come back to bed, Maier. We're so drunk, we'll never notice if someone comes and tries to kill us in our sleep. What do you need more alcohol for? And the boatman won't go without me."

Maier laughed. "Oh yes, he will. Money talks, bullshit squawks."

"Marry me, Maier."

He turned back to see her sitting up under the net, laughing, flashing her breasts.

"Get that shock off your face, old man. Relax. You're so old-fashioned. We're on the river of dreams. It's a trip. Get some beer and when you get back, if I can figure out which side you're on, I will tell you the rest. And then we make love properly."

Outside, the party had almost finished. Village children cleared away beer bottles and other debris. A campfire behind the huts was burning down. The flames, the only light source other than the moon, threw long shadows. Maier found the bungalow colony's owner sitting on a plastic stool by the river. When the woman saw him coming, she pulled a nylon net filled with Beerlao bottles from the water. He handed her a bundle of kip. The Nam Ou flowed all the way down from southern China into Laos, but its temperature was lukewarm. Maier disliked warm beer more than cold beer. But he understood that the day the first fridge arrived here would be the end of an era.

The woman smiled at Maier in the dim light and said in broken English, "You very old man, monsieur. Tourist in Muang Ngoi always young. Why you come? You not look like tourist. Which country?"

Maier looked her straight in the eye.

"I am German. From Germany."

She didn't flinch.

"Ah, Deutschland," she said, and fell silent.

He guessed her about sixty, though she might have been ten years younger.

"Many visitor from Deutschland, but not look like you."

"What is your name?"

"Bua Kham," she said, smiling.

"You have lived here for a long time?"

"All my life."

"You have family?"

She looked at him with eyes long inhabited by sorrow.

"My husband dead. My son dead. My daughter, she cannot walk. Stay in Luang Prabang with auntie, sister. Only me, alone. Make money for family."

She thought about her words and a vague smile passed her lips.

"Every year, more and more tourist coming. More and more money coming."

Maier already knew she had something to tell him. But one didn't press the point with older people in Southeast Asia. She'd get around to it in her own time.

"I sell beer, rent room. Good job. I too old to work in the field."

She nodded to herself.

"In the war, American planes fly across Muang Ngoi. So much bombing. We live in the cave. Everybody live in the cave. Only at night we come outside and do the farming. I grow rice with my husband. But not enough to eat like this, so sometime we plant in the day. One day the plane come. You hear the sound of the bomb falling, you know in few seconds you maybe die. So much explosion and everything dark. The tree falling, the river like boiling water. My husband die that day. Many people die that day. I never see American people at that time. Only see the plane. I don't know how far away is America and why they come halfway round the world to kill Lao farmer. I not understand."

She lapsed into silence, her face a mask of suffering.

"After the bomb, so many body. We put all dead together and put petrol and burn. No time to take to pagoda. Maybe more planes coming. Sometime we leave the body in the field because too much danger. And then very bad smell. We go back to the cave and hide."

She nodded, to herself more than to Maier.

"After the war finish, my children they go out to play, they find American bomb. Small bomb, like toy. Boom. My son die. My daughter lose one leg."

"Do you hate America?"

She shook her head, got up and walked to her nearby home. Maier sat alone and stared into the silent, dark river. He wondered how often the woman had told her story to visitors. A few minutes later, Bua Kham was back and pressed a tennis ball sized object into his hand.

"Bombi," was all she said.

Maier felt the cold metal of the explosive. During the Secret War, American planes had pummeled Laos for almost a decade, dropping off gigantic payloads round the clock, day in, day out. B52s filled the skies and carpet-bombed village after village into oblivion to cut the Ho Chi

Minh Trail, the Vietcong's supply line that ran from North Vietnam through Laos and Cambodia into South Vietnam. Pilots who failed to use up their payloads were ordered to return to their Thai bases empty and dropped their remaining munitions indiscriminately over Laos. The country became the Vietnam War's dumping ground. By the time the US exited Southeast Asia, Laos and neighboring Cambodia had earned the sad monikers of being the most heavily bombed countries on Earth.

The bomb Maier was holding had originated from a large cluster bomb case dropped by a plane. The case was designed to open in mid-air releasing thousands of these bombis, packed with nuts, nails and bolts, and operated with a spring. The ball-shaped bombs needed to turn several times before exploding. Some malfunctioned and hit the ground in one piece. Children, mistaking them for toys, played with the bombis and completed the final turn necessary to detonate the device.

Bua Kham continued in a more upbeat manner, "Now young American come back. Bring money, buy beer, rent room, eat fry rice. No problem. Different American. Very nice."

Maier opened one of the beers and took a swig.

"But Vietnamese very bad. No buy beer, no friend. No smile. Just make problem."

"But the Vietnamese left a long time ago, didn't they?"

The woman looked at Maier, as if trying to fathom his reasons for appearing on her doorstep.

"Yes, they go. But they never go. Sometime come back. Lao government build prison upriver. Near Muang Khua. But prison not Lao, prison Vietnam."

Maier assumed she meant one of the re-education camps the communists had established across the country following the departure of the Americans. In these tropical jails, bureaucrats and soldiers loyal to the old regime were indoctrinated and sometimes killed, or simply kept out of circulation for a decade or more. The camps were self-defeating, the resultant brain drain on the country catastrophic. But the communists, like their imperialist nemesis further west, had long understood one thing: keeping people stupid, either by depriving them of stimulation or forcing them to be constantly stimulated, made them malleable. It kept the number of rebels to a minimum, made accountability unnecessary, and when the war pig made its return, no one was likely to question its appearance.

"Aren't these places all closed?"

The woman shook her head violently. "Not closed. Only few days ago, Vietnamese stop here for petrol. Very bad men. They have one prisoner in the boat. I can see he is prisoner."

"A white man?"

Bua Kham thought about her answer for a while. "I not sure. He have bag over head. But I think maybe Asian, maybe local. They not pay for petrol. Just take and go. But they talk Lao with prisoner. Tell him they wait for his friend, then shoot him dead. You his friend?"

Maier felt sorry for the woman and admired her shrewdness. But he wasn't sure whether he could trust her. He remained silent and concentrated on the river again.

"And some young tourist go upriver. Never come back."

Her expression swung from compassion to indifference and back.

"What do you mean? Never come back? They might go up to Phongsali. And then leave by road. Into China. Or back down to Udomxai. They don't have to come back this way."

She shook her head and brushed a strand of thin hair from her narrow face.

"They never go Phongsali."

"How do you know?"

Bua Kham rose slowly.

"Enough beer? I go sleep."

Maier wasn't going to get an answer to his last question and nodded in silent agreement to end the conversation.

She broke into her vague smile again, "I think you good man, monsieur Deutschland. I think you here because of Vietnamese. You careful in Muang Khua. These men make me very much scare. Very danger. And they travel with big white man, very nice shirt. Very loud man. Your friend?"

Maier shook his head.

May Lik, the woman who'd died because of his visit to the island, had told them the same thing. The Vietnamese were traveling with a Westerner. Not a prisoner. An operator. At least Maier now knew that Léon was alive.

Bua Kham faded into the night. By the time the detective returned to their hut, Kanitha was asleep. He sat on the small porch, drinking, watching the fireflies, too lazy to fend off the mosquitoes that devoured him, in too much turmoil to lie next to the young woman whose dreams and stories were waiting for him.

The case was beginning to eat at Maier. The same questions rolled around his head like empty Beerlao bottles, making a vague, undefined sound he didn't care for. Was he being played? Was Kanitha a spy? Or was he just such a smooth, handsome and beautiful guy that twenty-three-year-olds latched on to, the way flies were drawn to honey? And what the hell had happened to his client? Where was Julia? Just ahead, the river rushed on, not offering a single answer.

9

ONE VELVET MORNING

THE FRIED EGGS Bua Kham served with strong Lao coffee were only mildly appetizing. Kanitha had dark rings under her eyes that kept pace with Maier's slowly healing injury. Despite her wasted countenance, she looked ravishing, and the detective watched her for a small eternity as she put on and laced up her boots and made sure her spiky black hair rose to disorderly attention. As she stood up and walked down to the shore, she looked like a pygmy warrior queen about to rouse her troops. She didn't have any troops, of course. She just had Maier. Or perhaps it was the other way around.

Mist hung over the Nam Ou. The sun still hid behind the craggy mountains to the west. The first light of dawn caressed the ridges; shadows rippled across tree lines. The movement gave the forested ravines the appearance of a slowly moving reptile. The air was cool, and a thin film of dew covered the world like a glass blanket. A couple of egrets rose from the far shore, drifted across the brown water to find a perch on a nearby hut and proceeded to clean their white plumage. If only it was as easy as that.

Despite the night's excesses, Maier and Kanitha were the first guests to greet the new day. The backpackers were still asleep in their hovels. The silence was waiting to be shattered by the noise of boat engines and transistor radios.

"I'm so hungover," she groaned, obviously enjoying her destitute state as much as the changed energy between them. Maier felt awful, but he had no urge to report on his physical state.

"I'm so hungover," she announced once more, more forcefully this time.

Maier wasn't forthcoming with prattle this morning. "Go tell the boatman," he said.

The detective drank his second coffee and watched a small, almost transparent paddy field crab move through the dust by his feet. The crab moved sideways, stopped and started, scuttled a short distance before coming to a complete halt once more. Maier likened the crustacean's journey to his work. He moved about a little, usually sideways rather than straight ahead, talked to some people and then stopped and took stock, assembling the available information, hypothesizing various realities. He did it instinctively, like the crab which had now pushed off towards the river.

And what a great moment to take stock it was. He was stuck with a keen child in the middle of the Laotian jungle, about to confront a dangerous mob of Vietnamese assassins accompanied by a fat white man in a loud shirt. He'd set off to spring the child's boyfriend from the clutches of men whose agenda was unknown to him. He remembered that Kanitha had confessed during the night, not in so many words, but in essence, that her stories had been half-truths, selected facts, perhaps even red herrings. Having lured each other into rolling around in the hot night made things more difficult, not easier.

But Maier enjoyed the feisty woman's company.

"Never underestimate your charisma, Maier. These eyes of yours know how to melt a girl's heart. Even when one of them is black. That's why I wanted to sleep with you. But it's not a hanging matter. It's not a capital crime."

He didn't have it in him to remind her that they were together so she would get her big break and they would both get their man. A second later, he realized she was toying with his ego. The girl from Bangkok was still one step ahead.

"Don't be so serious, Mr. Detective," she laughed, "You're an amazing guy, Maier. Don't be too humble. I would love to spend more time with you when this is finished."

"And what is this exactly?" he countered.

"Good question, Maier. Since you turned up, it's all been tightening somehow, racing towards a darker place."

"Come on, journalist, don't give me poetry. We need facts."

A somber voice shattered the peace. Prehistoric tannoys suspended from a pole near Bua Kham's collection of huts coughed to life. As in every village in Laos, the morning propaganda was pumped into the day whether people wanted it or not. The Laotian government's reminder of its existence. Speech was followed by marching music, followed by more sonorous speech. A sleep-deprived tourist complained loudly from his hut, to no avail. The Laotians were reminded daily that their government had saved them from a fate worse than death – capitalism – and that it would always be there for them, even if it did absolutely nothing to support them. Totalitarian political systems demanded total attention, as Maier knew from his own childhood in Leipzig. Democracies, on the other hand, didn't want you to give any attention to its caretakers at all.

Laos still had some way to go before it would reach an unhappy medium.

The detective turned to the girl, "Tell me what else you know, and tell me all of it. If I get the impression you are holding more stuff back, I will continue the journey upriver by myself."

He realized immediately that this wasn't the way to get the best answers out of his companion. Threats didn't work with all-or-nothing rebels.

"And if you tell me more, I will help you get your scoop."

Kanitha, barely suppressing her anger at his condescending strategy, managed to smile with remarkable sweetness, "As long as you don't take me seriously, you're not getting anything out of me."

Maier stared across the water.

She added, with a modicum of youthful menace in her voice, "But I'll be nice to you. Again. And you can be nice to me. Again."

One of the travelers nearby cranked up his stereo. Bad resort funk drowned out the communist sermon. The egrets rose from their perches. The village had turned into a noisy bus stop. It was time to go.

Kanitha looked around, perhaps to see if anyone else might be listening. It was a rather theatrical effort. When she turned back to Maier, her face was deadly serious.

"I'll tell you the rest. What I know. You promise you'll look after me up there. You won't leave me behind?"

Maier tried to assure her with a stern look.

"Have you ever heard of the U48?"

He shook his head.

"This has to be our secret. This is my story. This is the story. No one gives a damn about gold or drugs. The Vietnamese upriver, the Americans behind us, perhaps even Julia, they are all after the U48."

"What is it?"

She chewed her lower lip, "I'm not sure. But Léon does know. And he told me that the U48 would reunite him with the man who tried to kill him. Soon."

Maier had no idea what she was talking about. More subterfuge, perhaps. Without a word, he got up and went to find Bua Kham. He paid the bill and said goodbye to the old woman. This morning, her face was closed. He was just another transient. Maier was disappointed to see her so cautious, but he said nothing and waved goodbye.

When he returned to the hut, Kanitha had already moved their belongings into the boat. He followed and jumped in. The boatman cranked up the engine and they pushed out into the Nam Ou River. The sun rose quickly and would soon touch the water. A beautiful day was on its way. A day with answers.

Muang Ngoi receded behind them as they pushed north. They rounded a bend in the river and the village disappeared. They had the world to themselves. The trees grew taller. The brush by the river's banks was impenetrable. The Nam Ou narrowed and the jungle closed in from both sides. All signs of human habitation vanished. The river snaked deeper and deeper into the evergreen forest. Maier leaned back and relaxed. Everything would work out OK. He didn't have anything to offer to the Vietnamese when they got to Muang Khua, but he knew from past experience that a deal of some kind was always possible with them. The Vietnamese were extra-rational and wanted to get things done. He drifted into daydreams and watched the elemental scenery slide past. Strange birdcalls he'd never heard before could be made out over the din of the engine. A clan of monkeys lounged in the trees by the water's edge, only vaguely upset by the passing vessel. Kanitha, who sat in front of him, turned and smiled. They rounded another bend. He watched his young companion scan the forest to their right. He saw her smile fade.

A shot rang out, clearly audible over the engine noise. It was Maier's turn to grab the girl and pull her to the bottom of the boat, with somewhat less affection than she'd shown him the day before in Nong Kiaw. This was turning into a killer honeymoon.

He turned, but the boatman had gone. The long-tail's screw ripped out of the water and the boat immediately turned sideways in the swift current. It started to take water. They would capsize in seconds. Maier jumped up and grabbed the tiller. The engine howled. Kanitha lay frozen, a look of terror on her face. He pushed the screw back into the water and tried to turn the boat back into the on-coming current. The girl screamed and pointed to the shore. Maier saw a man rest his rifle on a rock less than a hundred meters away, its sights pointed straight at the boat. He couldn't make out the shooter's features in the few seconds it took to move past.

"Down! Sniper!" Maier screamed. He turned the boat. Just. He pulled hard on the wire that served as the throttle. They shot away from the riverbank. The narrow vessel shook wildly as Maier fought to control the engine. The river curved again and Maier pushed ahead at full speed. They would make it. Maier lowered himself into the boat as much as he could without abandoning the tiller. He pushed the screw deep into the water and banked hard. The engine roared. The long-tail shot forward.

They were out of the gunman's line of sight. Maier could feel sweat dripping off his brow as he straightened up and looked back. Nothing but forest. The boat was taking water. The detective thought he'd gone deaf; then he became aware of the noise of the engine.

Kanitha sat up and scanned the jungle on both sides of the river. Pale and troubled, but on the rebound, her spiky hair wet and screaming in all directions, she looked striking.

"The boatman?" she shouted, her voice breaking up with the adrenaline she was pumping.

He shook his head.

"Do you think there are more?"

Maier had no idea what lay in store for them. He didn't answer but pushed ahead at maximum speed and kept his eye on the water, in shock. He tried to keep the boat in the center of the river, as far as possible from either bank. Every tree, every bush, every blade of grass looked hostile.

The boatman had been the second innocent Laotian who'd been killed because of his investigation. Someone was toying with him. Someone with a sensitive trigger finger and perfect aim. Maier shuddered as he banked another curve in the river. Right then, he didn't want the girl to see his face.

10

THE FREE STATE OF MIND

MAIER DIDN'T DARE STOP the boat to check how badly damaged it was. He wanted get as much distance between themselves and the boatman's killing as possible. If the boat leaked critically, they would still have time to swim ashore and hide from whoever followed them on the opposite bank of the river. This time he was pretty sure the shot had been meant for him rather than the boat's captain. Pretty sure. But not completely sure. Perhaps he was being warned or tested. This was the second time a sniper with considerable experience had killed the person closest to himself and Kanitha. Maier had seen snipers at work in Sarajevo, gunning for moving targets. At a hundred meters, the shot had been a routine target for a professional. But the sniper had only pulled the trigger once. The detective knew that a man who didn't go for the double tap would be someone with extreme confidence in his abilities.

The river narrowed further. Ancient evergreen trees, some more than thirty meters tall, leaned out over the water like old drunken men whispering to one another, their canopies almost touching, suggesting a tunnel. Maier thought he could spot a swing hanging from a thick branch above the waterline. The nearest road or village was miles away, but they weren't as alone on this stretch of water as he'd expected. He slowed the boat, wary of another attack.

"Watch out," Kanitha shouted, and dropped back on all fours.

Several ropes dropped out of nowhere and tightened across the water. Maier cut the engine, but it was too late. As the boat zipped underneath the taut lines he leant back. He was too slow. The detective was ripped overboard.

The shock of the cool, fast-moving water took his breath away. As he surfaced, tree branches rushed towards him, suspended by more ropes. Before he had time to dive, a piece of heavy wood connected with his skull, a rough net closed around him, and Maier went under.

"You have a jungle visa?"

Maier slowly returned to the here and now but he kept his eyes closed and remained motionless. It was best to play dead detective until he could sense in how much trouble they'd landed. He could hear the river rushing near-by. His clothes were wet. The day smelled of morning. He hadn't been out long.

"What the fuck is a jungle visa? You guys can't be serious. You sank our fucking boat."

Kanitha was alive.

"No pass without a jungle visa, lady. That's the law in the Free State of Mind."

Kanitha sounded more angry than scared. Maier pretended to come around slowly and blinked into their newfound situation with what he hoped looked like the innocence of a newborn.

"He's coming around. He's coming around," a chorus of voices whispered in unison.

Maier raised his head to confront an incredible sight.

Kanitha sat on the forest floor, a few meters to his right, stripped to her underwear. A gaggle of young men – at least that's what Maier thought they were – stood gathered in a tight knot around her, staring. They wore torn shorts and little else. They were all barefoot. Their expressions were pretty vacant. Perhaps they'd all smoked strong marijuana. Perhaps they were opium addicts. A few carried outdated guns. War antiques from the Seventies. The rest carried more traditional weaponry – spears, knives, axes, and machetes – and puffed on cheroots. But the eclectic armory wasn't nearly as strange as what had been done to their bodies – every man's torso was covered in strange swirly patterns. As Maier took a closer look, he realized the men were tattooed, all over their chests and arms, all in a similar way. Some had their foreheads and necks inked. Intricate diagrams and geometric patterns, and a script – familiar, clearly Asian, though he couldn't decipher it – covered almost every inch of bare skin. Tigers, buffaloes, elephants, snakes, crocodiles, dragons and other obscure creatures, hermits, monks, martial arts fighters, and Hindu deities complemented the abstract designs. The writing looked like Khmer but the letters were unfamiliar. Maier had rarely seen a bunch of white boys more flipped out. These kids had been in the jungle a long time.

The young men were mesmerized by Kanitha's state of undress, but there was little sexual tension in the air. Maier wasn't sure what to make of it. He sat up. They shrunk back as one and shifted their focus to the detective.

"Without a jungle visa, you can't pass," they crowed in unison.

Kanitha shouted back at them. "Fuck you and your jungle visa. Boats travel up this river every day and you can't possibly be attacking all of them. Why us? Why? And give me back my clothes, motherfucker!"

The young man who'd first spoken to Kanitha moved away from the rest of his gang and turned to Maier. He couldn't be more than twenty years old. A circular diagram had been etched onto his shaved skull. Blue lines described a shape somewhere between a bull's-eye and a Ouija board. He didn't look threatening, just ever so slightly mad.

"You! Where's your jungle visa?"

British, judging by his accent.

Maier turned to Kanitha.

"You OK?"

"I'm courageous when I have to be, Maier. But they took my clothes, these clowns. They're trying to figure out whether we have sak yant."

"What's sak yant?"

She pointed at the men behind her.

"These tattoos they are covered with. They call them jungle visas. They're sacred tattoos. Sak yant in Thai. Lots of people in Thailand and Cambodia wear them. Maybe in Laos, too. The wearers believe they have magic powers."

"These guys do not look like they have magic powers," Maier

muttered under his breath, but she'd heard him and he could see that she took courage from his quip. He didn't get the feeling that these forest hippies were out for blood. Still, they'd sunk the boat. He turned to their captors.

The young man with the head tattoo waved impatiently and two of his minions pulled Maier to his feet. He felt dizzy and wanted to sit back down. They stripped off his shirt and, despite vague efforts to resist, untied and pulled down his pants and looked him over. They had no interest in the bundle of documents and money he wore taped to his right thigh. Disappointed, they let him drop back to the forest floor.

"No jungle visa," their young leader muttered.

"You entered the Free State of Mind without valid permission. You infringed on our territorial sovereignty. You will have to come and see the Teacher."

"We didn't enter anything. We were just passing on the river," Maier answered with as much authority as he could gather with his pants around his ankles.

The boy didn't answer. His companions pulled Kanitha off the ground, grabbed Maier and marched them off into the forest.

11

THE TEACHER OF AVERAGES

THE NOISE of the river was swallowed up by the dense vegetation, and they walked in a soundscape of insects and birds, of things moving in the bush, of the jungle inhaling and letting its breath go slowly in a subsonic hum of growth and decay. Maier hadn't been this far from a city in a while.

A narrow trail, almost invisible, led east and upwards. There were no views from which the detective might have been able to orient himself, though he guessed they were walking roughly in the right direction, towards Muang Khua and the Vietnamese. The group's leader was ahead and made no attempt to communicate again. The rest of his gang also remained silent.

The sun stood high in the sky and tried to find its way through the canopy into the jungle twilight below.

The Teacher of the Free State of Mind started to speak, "You have to give it to them straight, you see. But when we do that the usual way, when we talk in the straight and hard way and tell them what their problem is, they become defensive. They don't think about what we say, they just think that we aren't nice. And all this being straight will do nothing for us. It won't have any effect. The message is lost. We're better off telling it straight but with a smile. We're open. We make eye contact. The same way we're making eye contact with you now. And you'll take it and not be able to reject it or hate us for giving it to you – straight. And this is the secret of our success. And you, Maier, have beautiful eyes, but not much success. Except with the ladies, perhaps."

The small community's leader flashed a semi-pleasant grin at Kanitha and swayed on the edge of drooling. His eyes shone out of his withered face. His receding hairline gave way to a blue ribbon of the same strange alphabet Maier had observed on their captors, snaking across his wrinkled forehead. He was dressed in the white cotton pajamas of a Buddhist layman. He'd dyed his long hair black and wore his beard like a nineteenth century Chinese warlord, but he was obviously a white man in his early sixties.

"My troops took legitimate action. You were attacked downriver. Your driver was shot. The opposition's boat was faster than yours. Somewhere on the shore, they had a crack shot who can tickle a flea from two hundred yards. We had to intercept. Another half mile upriver and they would have sunk your vessel. The Viets don't play around. They'd have cut off your cock and tits and stuffed them down your throats. It's a war out there."

The Teacher offered no apologies for his imaginative descriptions but paused for dramatic effect before relaunching into his speech.

"My men pulled the mission off with utmost precision. No injuries besides wounded prides. They take their jungle visas very seriously. But they're well disciplined. No funny stuff, na?"

He looked at Kanitha for confirmation. She looked right back, her dark eyes on fire. His faint, unhealthy smile suggested he didn't care either way.

"Our listening posts downriver heard shooting. You were deemed a security risk. Your boat wasn't steered by a local. That's unusual. All boats must be steered by local people."

The Teacher sat on a throne of sorts, which appeared to have grown from the roots of an enormous strangler fig. Animal skins, perhaps once worn by unlucky leopards, served as cushioning. His seating pad was raised above the forest floor, so that he looked down at them.

He was American, though he had the uncertain air of a man who'd spent considerable effort to deconstruct the very essence of who and what he'd been in his last life. Every square centimeter on his ageing but very fit body was covered in blue squiggles, shapes, figures, numbers and diagrams. As he leaned forward, Maier detected older, less traditional tattoos on both his arms. This guy had been in the US military once. The Teacher noticed Maier's interest.

"Ah, you're an observant type. You smell a bit like a spook. In some ways you look almost familiar. As if I'd met you before. But…Welcome to spook heaven. Who'd you work for? What do you want? What are you doing on my stretch of the river? Are you a threat my country, to the Free State of Mind?"

Maier knew it was pointless to play the tourist. But what to tell this man? He needed more information before he'd be able to voice credible excuses for their presence. He shrugged and tried to turn the tables.

"We did not know that you control this part of the river. We are on our way to Muang Khua. What is the Free State of Mind? What are all these young people doing here?"

The Teacher shifted on his throne but made no attempt to get down.

"Questions and counter-questions. Hm. In the old days, I would have started cutting bits off the lady to get answers. No one likes subterfuge. No one knows you're here. Hardly anyone knows we're here. And I want to keep it that way. Understand?"

"You're MIA?" Kanitha blurted out. "You're one of those guys who disappeared in '75? Huge and wealthy organizations are looking for guys like you. You'd be a massive story if you walked out of the forest."

The Teacher laughed, flashing a row of black teeth. Years of chewing betel did that to a man. He leaned towards Kanitha and pulled his lower lip down. The word SILENCE had been crudely hand-poked into the inside of his mouth.

"OK, so you're a journalist. Good to see your breed hasn't become extinct yet. During the war, our military realized that it was of utmost importance to keep you guys out of the real business and in the show business, on our side of the story. And most of you cooperated and wrote the pap we wanted to you to write. Are you one of those agreeable kinds of writers? Or are you the rare, contrary kind, obsessed with the truth, one of those who contributed to our defeat? Cause you know, the truth is just another story."

He looked her straight in the eye and leaned back, roaring with laughter. The boys around them joined in, guffawing as if it was the law. It probably was. The assembly smelled like a weird cult.

"I don't suppose there's too much about you that's agreeable. You're young and probably stubborn."

He leaned back and began pulling on his fingers. His followers immediately fell quiet. Every now and then one of the joints in his knuckles cracked. In the near silence of the forest clearing, the grinding bones sounded like small explosions.

"Come on, guys, it's good to be here. It's good to be anywhere. We're all survivors. Let's make a deal. I'm a reasonable guy. Otherwise, you would be at the bottom of the Nam Ou by now. I tell you a little and you tell me a little. OK? That way, we won't have to kill you. Maybe."

Maier had no choice but to agree. They needed to get moving again soon. They had a mission. He had a case as impenetrable as the jungle around them.

"We were on our way to Muang Khua."

The Teacher smiled benevolently.

"You already told us."

"Our boat man was shot downriver by persons unknown. That wouldn't have been any one of your guys?"

The Teacher snapped upright and craned down towards the detective, "What do you take us for? Savages? The Free State of Mind is a civilized country. The world's smallest and least known nation. An independent entity since 1975. An open society. We have no police and no judges. No foreign embassies and shopping malls. And no assassins and sharpshooters. There's no executive except me and I'm not one for executing. Unless you threaten us directly, I don't mind what you do. I didn't put snipers on the river to engage in a pre-emptive strike. We made that kind of mistake when we came to Indochina in the Sixties. Phoenix Program and all that. And so many of us died. And we killed so many of them. Millions in fact. Millions."

With the disengaged mannerisms of a compulsive obsessive, the old king of the jungle pulled his beard straight.

"But I was lucky. I was reborn. I got a second chance. And I built myself a world where I give the orders, not some incompetent, careerist general looking to pay for his kitchen extension or his wife's new set of tits. I give the orders. To live and let live. To die. My way."

"My way," his disciples bellowed.

"You were with Special Forces in Laos?"

The Teacher laughed, "There were no Special Forces to speak of here after Kennedy and Khrushchev made their neutrality deal for Laos in '62. Only a few hundred guys from the agency. Low-key. We trained local militias. We used Thai border police to do the donkey work. Showing these montagnards, as the French called them, mostly Hmong and Yao hill tribes, how to hold a gun, fly planes and kill commies. Stone age to space age in six weeks for those guys. But we were discreet. We hardly left a footprint."

The Teacher paused and cracked knuckles again. The man was quite mad. But he got his wind back and returned to his story with the enthusiasm of a lonely pensioner who'd found an audience for the tales of his glorious youth.

"US aid pumped in money, rice and infrastructure. They built hundreds of airstrips across the country, called them Lima Sites. Those were the key to the Secret War. There were no roads in Laos, like none. All supplies, rice drops for refugees, ammo and troop drops, the constant movement of money, all that could only be achieved with small planes and a network of hardly noticeable landing strips. It worked for a while. But we got what we deserved supporting two parties on opposing sides. Corruption and chaos. The very best weapons to fight communism. It was a childish game, really. If you guys won't let go, we'll destroy everything. That was the way we did things."

Maier looked at the citizens of the Free State of Mind. He couldn't read anything but admiration in the young faces around him. He was touched by their need to belong, to follow. These kids would kill in an instant if this man so much as lifted a finger against his captives. The Teacher had clearly gone rogue.

"You were CIA?"

The Teacher nodded.

"Twelve years in the field. Worked with all the greats in Laos. Bill Lair, Tony Poe, Vint Lawrence. We were on the side of the angels in the early Sixties. We were fighting the good fight. We needed to stop the Reds. We trained these mountain peoples to fight with us. We paid them. It was an honorable relationship."

A film of sorrow settled over his eyes and he paused, lost in time and space. Maier remained silent. The boys expected more and leaned into their leader. They'd heard the story before, in the same way a congregation had been comforted by their religious leader on countless Sundays past.

"But then, in the late Sixties, we lost our way. The Vietnamese started helping the Pathet Lao and killed many of our local troops. The US military wanted a look-in on the action and we started to bomb the hell out of this place. That's when I began to have my doubts. Throwing napalm and CBUs on farming communities wasn't my idea of fighting the good fight."

"So you quit?"

The Teacher laughed and looked at Maier with a paternalistic expression. "I left. I had to. There was an incident in Long Cheng in '73. One day, I caught a transport back to Vientiane. When I returned, several case officers with whom I'd shared bunks had been killed. Shot at close range. One had disappeared altogether. No body. It all got blamed on communist infiltrators, but I never bought that idea. I think it was an inside job. They'd have done me too if I'd been there. That was the moment when I thought, ah, I better get out if I want to survive the war. I got cold feet."

The Teacher had checked out of the program.

"What's with the jungle visa?"

The Teacher laughed and ran his tattooed fingers down his equally tattooed left arm.

"So many questions. You're not British, are you?"

"German."

"Never been there, buddy. I gather Germany is doing quite well these days. But why are they sending people into the jungle? You BND or something? German secret service? Ex-Stasi?"

Maier shook his head and threw a quick glance at Kanitha. She'd regained her composure.

"How about some clothes, at least for my companion?"

The young Thai woman looked to the ground and smiled.

The Teacher shrugged and snapped his fingers. The boy who'd led them through the jungle ran off. The rest of the group, perhaps thirty in all, sat in a wide circle on the forest floor. Maier felt ridiculous standing in front of these crazies in his underpants like some lost Tarzan. He felt even more ridiculous telling them who he was.

"I am a private eye. I work for a detective agency in Hamburg. I have no government affiliations. I have been sent by a client to find out about her father's murder which took place in Laos in 1976. My client's father was the cultural attaché to the East German Embassy at the time. He probably was Stasi. He was killed by forces unknown."

"So you're not here for the U48?"

Maier looked at the Teacher in surprise.

"What is it?"

The Teacher watched him closely, then shrugged. "I guess you don't know, judging by your expression. But you have heard about it?"

"It's been mentioned. But I don't know what it is."

"Can't help you there, Mr. Detective. Your job to find out. But what are you doing here? The German attaché was killed around here? And what was his name?"

Maier tried to weigh up how much he would have to tell this man. They no longer had a boat. Muang Khua was at least three hours away via the river. Walking up there would take a long time.

"His name was Manfred Rendel. I don't think he was killed here. Does the name mean anything to you?"

The Teacher shook his head, his expression unreadable.

"But what, Mr. Detective, are you doing here, on my doorstep?"

"My client gave me the name of an informant in Vientiane. A Hmong whose father was an American agent here during the war. One of your colleagues."

This time the Teacher raised both tattooed eyebrows.

"That wouldn't be one young Léon Sangster, son of Jimmy Sangster and his Hmong princess, by any chance?"

Kanitha jumped up. "Wow, you know Léon? You know where they've taken him?"

The apparent leader of the Free State of Mind looked at her with intense concentration.

"This gets more interesting all the time. Let's say that I did know his father."

His eyes flicked back and forth between his captives.

"Perhaps there are higher reasons why you washed up on our jungle doorstep."

"Higher reasons," the young citizens of the Teacher's jungle empire echoed in reverential unison.

The Teacher sat back, letting the sycophantic mutterings of his disciples run their course. He pulled at his long beard and took his time processing the information.

The young man who'd been sent off to fetch their clothes returned.

"Get dressed. You're my interesting guests tonight. Make yourselves at home in the Free State of Mind. But don't try to run; we've mined and laid traps in the forest. You'd lose a limb if you walked five hundred meters by yourselves. Trust me on this. Have dinner with us tonight and we will talk."

The Teacher's disciples rose as one and spoke as one.

"What about the jungle visa?"

The Teacher got off his throne and descended to the forest floor. Only now did Maier notice that the man had a false leg. Not a modern plastic prosthetic but a rather crude wooden stump that had all the charm of an unvarnished chair leg. Even standing amongst his devotees on a single limb, he was a towering figure, a man who'd found his vocation in life. He noticed the detective looking at his defect and grinned at Maier.

"I know all about landmines, Mr. Detective. I laid hundreds if not thousands of them in the war. I taught the Hmong how to lay them. And then one day, I stepped on one and in an instant, I became an office slave. Served me right, I suppose. Life-changing experience, trust me. Losing my leg and seeing my best friends killed by one of our own caused a seismic shift. I mean, my mind was gone. Once I'd left Long Cheng, I decided never to follow an order again. A few are bound to lead. The rest are meant to bleed."

He laughed madly at his inept rhyme, grabbed a crutch one of the young men was holding and moved surprisingly swiftly away from them. His disciples flowed around him like a tide of amoebas, repeating his slogan, "A few are bound to lead. The rest are meant to bleed."

"In time, children, in time. We all know the rules. No one can pass through the Free State of Mind without the jungle visa."

12

THE JUNGLE VISA

SECONDS after the Teacher had finished speaking, the clearing around the throne lay deserted. The show had simply melted away. Only Kanitha, Maier, and the boy who had returned with their clothes remained. Their captor waved them to follow, away from the river, deeper into the jungle.

"What do you think?" Kanitha whispered. Maier detected no fear in her question, only curiosity. What a girl.

He wasn't quite sure why, but he smiled at her reassuringly and answered, "I think we will be able to make a deal. I suspect it might cost a bit, but we will get out of here alive. If they wanted to kill us, they would have done so already. And anyway, this guy is just a stooge."

"He is?" she asked with obvious doubt in her voice.

The detective slowed to create some distance between them and the boy ahead.

"Well, who tattooed the tattooed? He must have learned about these magic diagrams somewhere. We are yet to meet the Teacher's teacher."

They hit a narrow path hemmed in by giant ferns and clusters of bamboo, and marched in single file. When Maier tapped their young guide on the shoulder to get his attention, the boy snapped around with a solemn expression and shook his head. The kids were either highly disciplined or brainwashed. How had the Teacher gathered them in the forest, tattooed them from top to bottom and kept them here? Didn't these young men miss their creature comforts, girls, technological gadgets, the football scores and the latest episode of their favorite TV series, or were there still romantics left in the world?

Hundreds of thousands of travelers stepped off flights from the developed world into Asia every year. Most came to carry on their lives in the sun with a little soft adventure thrown in – full-moon parties and hill tribe treks, the ubiquitous visit to a sex show, a toke on an opium pipe or a scuba-dive course. Some came because they knew their parents wouldn't follow them into the jungle. A few came looking for more, though they hardly knew what they were so desperate to find out here, other than the loss of the certainties of home. The sacrifices the Free State of Mind demanded from its citizens were considerable.

Maier stopped himself judging his younger compatriots. Everyone had to work out their own stuff. He'd never had the opportunity to become part of a tribe. In East Germany, subcultures had been viewed as a direct threat to socialist cohesion.

The trail led into dense forest. Even from a helicopter hovering right over the canopy, all signs of life beneath the trees would likely remain undetected. The boy led them around camouflaged pits peppered with sharpened wooden spikes or alerted them to almost-invisible ropes crossing the path that would presumably trigger a swift demise if pulled or stepped on unwittingly. Maier shook his head at the set-up. This could be going on in the twenty-first century?

A couple of hours into nowhere, the path snaked steeply upwards around a scattered group of boulders the color of ash and the size of small houses. They crossed a low pass, little more than a hump between two stone cliffs, and the trees gave way to sheer rock and open skies. From the crest of the pass, they caught the sun dropping towards the Nam Ou behind them. From their vantage point, he couldn't make out any traffic on the short stretch of river visible below. As he turned to Kanitha, he could see the entire scene reflected in her eyes. The river, the looming silhouette of the jungle, the quickly sinking red fireball made for an immense, otherworldly view. The panorama danced on her glistening eyeballs. She was clearly moved by the scene. He was touched, watching her while she was watching it. He caught himself thinking about her the way he'd promised himself not to. As they started moving again, he considered trying to ask her outright what was really driving her to accompany him into this quagmire. But he had a hunch that this would lead to some kind of schism in their communion and he remained silent.

Their guide signaled them to push on, and the trio dropped away from the sky back down into the forest without time to catch its collective breath. Maier's thoughts returned to the immediate prospect of facing the Teacher's teacher, the man who ruled this fleck of jungle.

Maier and Kanitha sat with the Teacher and his disciples on straw mats that had been spread in the ragged-toothed mouth of an enormous cave. It was quite a refuge for a group of children who'd thrown it all away, who'd moved farther from the center of things than most of their compatriots back home could imagine.

Floodlights had been installed along one of the cave walls and on steel poles rammed into the solid stone floor around them, lending the austere space a festive ambience. An orchestra playing Mahler symphonies wouldn't have looked or sounded out of place.

The monk made an impressive entrance. The community fell silent. Two boys led the old man to a low wooden bench that had been positioned a little deeper into the cave. The bench was flanked by several low stools and a free-standing shelf that served as a rack for the monk's steel needles and other accessories. Wooden masks of hermits and deities lined the top of the shelf. The master had arrived.

The monk sat heavily and crossed his legs while facing his visitors. Every inch of skin that protruded from his robes was covered in sacred diagrams and prayers. Only his lean, deeply lined face was unmarked. Maier guessed the monk to be in his eighties. Kanitha approached the old, wizened man, got down on her knees and bowed three times. The monk showed no reaction and stared into space.

"Luong Pho Mai is very happy to have you and your journalist friend here, Maier. We hope to get some answers about what's going on north of here in Muang Khua, and your arrival has thrown a new light on the affair," the Teacher explained, deeply touched by the appearance of the monk. His young followers were in awe. Maier relaxed.

"Everything I've learned about sak yant, I know from this man.

Everything I know about compassion, I have understood because of his teaching. And the teaching of his needle. The teaching of his tattoos. What the disciples call jungle visa. Sacred designs that the Hindus brought to Southeast Asia from India millennia ago and that we apply to the human skin."

"Why are you in the jungle?"

The Teacher smiled broadly.

"I didn't have it in my heart to go back to Minnesota after the war. I needed saving. Jesus was no longer my ticket after what I'd seen in the jungle. But the war saved me. And Luong Pho Mai saved me. And in a way, I saved him. Couldn't save the war, though. And now the venerable Luong Pho Mai will save you too."

Maier looked at the blind man. There would be no shortfall of salvation today.

The Teacher got up remarkably quickly and waved Maier to follow him towards the back of the cave.

"You see, the communists weren't keen on the old animist worlds the Laotians lived in. And still live in. Buddhism was ok; it could be coerced, controlled, organized along revolutionary lines. It was inherently socially conservative, so that fitted in well with the new program. The monasteries had to agree to teach communist propaganda to the novices. I guess whether you learn to read and write with the help of Pali scriptures or Das Kapital is academic. Anyway, once the deal with the sangha– the Buddhist council – had been made, animist rituals were suppressed. And sak yant, a tradition the sangha never liked anyway, was banned, and its masters, those who didn't escape to Thailand, were sent to re-education camps. Luong Pho Mai was incarcerated in Muang Khua. He was tortured and blinded. And I got him out. You can imagine how much he hates the Vietnamese."

Maier said nothing. The old American was on a roll; it was best to let him pour out his story.

"Since the revolution, the tradition has died. Serious adherents go to Thailand to get tattooed. Luong Pho Mai is the last of the great Laotian masters left."

"You saved all these kids by branding them so badly that they are permanently excluded from the rest of the human race, only in order to spite the local government?"

"I saved them. I did. Don't be so... old, Maier."

Kanitha chuckled next to him. Maier remained calm as the old American continued with his far-out realizations.

"The world isn't a level playing field. It doesn't care to include everyone. One has to make one's own way. Even in Vietnam, the blacks had a much harder time than the white grunts. The war taught me ground realities. In extreme moments of life and death, you can really see what we're made of, what we are. None of these kids would have come to this point of self-realization by themselves. They'd have all gone back home, and the more ambitious of them would work in offices, while the lazier ones would either end up slaving in the local fast food joint, join the military or sell drugs and go to jail. Don't judge our little jungle state too harshly. Which brings me to the point. It's not like our modest empire here isn't profitable."

He hobbled a little further into a natural alcove. Maier and Kanitha followed. The smell inside the narrow space was intense.

Maier recognized it immediately. Plastic crates were stacked several meters high. A long table stood covered with plants. A group of young women, probably from one of the minorities living in the area, stood separating the buds into different piles of varying quality. They barely acknowledged the Teacher and his guests. The old American waved his arms in a wide sweep across the scene. There was no need to explain just how special a life he and the young disciples led. For most young men, a free state built on dope and sex was about as good as it got. Maier looked at the Teacher, who grinned at the girls.

"Now you understand why the boys are here. You see, no one gets anything for nothing. And that includes you two. I'll let you in on something else."

Maier wasn't sure he wanted in on any more of this man's secrets. Knowing about the little cottage industry would cost them.

The Teacher brushed a long strand of hair from his leathery face.

"Right now, we have a potential conflict of interest with our neighbors to the north. A situation. The Vietnamese and some old Pathet Laos retirees recently revived the old re-education camp in Muang Khua, the very place where Luong Pho Mai was held. Apparently, they're building some kind of debriefing center there. A place where they can hold someone in complete isolation. I don't think it's Léon Sangster they are after. But they have him there."

The Teacher pulled a packet of cigarette papers out of his trouser pocket and handed it to Maier. "Do us a favor, Mr. Detective, and roll us a number. It's a pain with my bad leg, doing the balancing act with the crutch."

The girls were almost done. Maier noticed that they too were tattooed, though they hadn't gone for total alienation. The table was covered with the remnants of a long plant-trimming session. The boxes were packed tight with marijuana, destined, Maier assumed, for Thailand. The dope would be loaded onto boats and shipped downriver, all the way to the Thai border at Huay Xay. This place was making cold, hard cash.

"Why the dope?"

Maier pulled a dry bud from the table, stripped the tiny leaves off their stalks and rolled them into the paper. He passed the sorry-looking joint to the Teacher, who pulled a lighter from his pocket and lit up.

"In an earlier incarnation, Luong Pho Mai used to be an officer in the Royal Laotian Army. We used to haul packages of opium from the Air America flights that rolled into Long Cheng. We ran a narcotics industry in those days. The stuff was packed so tight and there was so much of it that it would leak from the canvas sacks like syrup. We pulled them off the planes and into the lab, right by the runway. And every day, planes would fly junk out of there, number-one-quality heroin. It became too successful. By the late Sixties, we had a third of our buddies in Vietnam hooked on the stuff. And we never saw any of that cash. The agency used it to finance our damn war. A war we were going to lose anyway, one day. But that made me think, Maier. Losing the leg just made things clearer in my head. Loyalty to the agency didn't pay. I went rogue just before Long Cheng fell."

He took a long drag and offered the joint to the detective.

Maier shook his head.

"Does the monk know his following is in the drug business?"

The Teacher laughed gently, "Does the monk know? What a question. I told you we used to haul junk together in Long Cheng. The monk knows everything, Maier. He can see with the needle. The moment he cuts you, he can see."

The Teacher turned to go but stopped in his tracks and grabbed Maier by the shoulder.

"We're showing you our darkest secrets for good reason, Maier. We're not doing it lightly, and if we thought you had impure motivations in this work of yours, we'd kill you without hesitation. But you'll understand our dilemma. I'll show you tomorrow. And then we'll go and get Léon in Muang Khua and encourage his captors to vacate the area. You see, we have similar interests. We should accept this opportunity by reaching together for a common goal."

"Which is?"

"Anyone who knows anything about tattoos will know who put the yant on you and the girl. You'll be branded with his needle. That's the price of knowledge, Maier."

The Teacher laughed and limped away, back into the main part of the cave, towards his master, trailing marijuana smoke behind.

"You see, the re-establishment of the Muang Khua camp is threatening our country. The Laotians know that we exist and leave us to it. We pay them every time we transit with our product. A routine has been established. The Vietnamese hopefully don't know yet. But they're bound to find out if we leave things as they are. They're inquisitive people. If they send troops up here, we're done for. The Laotians who take our money will lose a little face and will no longer deal with us. But Luong Pho Mai suggested we intimidate his erstwhile captors a bit. Do a raid. In fact, he insists."

He sighed and appeared to look inside himself as if he'd misplaced his heart.

"Nothing lasts forever, of course."

13

NINE PILLARS

IN THE MORNING, Luong Pho Mai sat on his bench as if he'd never slept, staring straight ahead. The Teacher sat next to his master on the cave floor. The kids, both girls and boys, gathered in a wide circle as Maier rubbed the sleep from his eyes.

"Jungle visa, jungle visa," they chorused quietly as the old monk got his needles ready.

Maier was skeptical.

"Tattoos last forever, I am told. Do I really need to have one?"

The old monk gave no indication he understood Maier's protest, and waved for his guests to come closer. The Teacher laughed softly. He turned towards Maier and explained, in a near-whisper, "I wouldn't be happy to watch one of my boys shoot you in front of our modest abode. It's not up to me or Luong Pho Mai. The kids won't let you go without one. Our authority is limited when it comes to laws of faith. They respect us because we live by the same rules as they do."

Maier shook his head at the collective lunacy. The kids were crowding in, prayers on their lips, caught up in a sway of tribal currents it was impossible to fight.

The Teacher rose and addressed the small congregation. "Brothers and sisters, the time has come for each and every one of you to choose. You have ten heartbeats to choose."

The congregation gasped at their leader's poetic eloquence and turned to Maier and Kanitha to repeat their leader's wisdom.

"Ten heartbeats."

The Teacher continued, "Our guests have chosen. They will accompany us north to fight the enemies of the Free State of Mind. They'll travel with their jungle visas."

The old monk dipped a long steel needle into a tiny pot of black ink, and intoned a mantra to bless his tool. The Teacher walked across the smooth floor of the cave to Kanitha. She looked up at him with a jaded, unsympathetic expression.

"You think you can make me, you boneless old cripple?"

The congregation took a collective breath and the old blind monk stopped his prayers. The Teacher smiled and limped through the crowd like a royal emissary, soothing ruffled egos with simple hand movements. The boy who'd just collected them from their hammocks walked up behind Maier and pointed a gun at the detective's head.

"Jungle visa, jungle visa," his companions chorused.

Kanitha shrugged, got up and approached the old monk. This time, she did not offer the traditional bows of respect. Two boys peeled away from the crowd and made her sit with her back facing the old tattooist.

"Put the bloody gun down," Maier told the boy behind him, who stared at the detective with glazed eyes.

The two kids flanking Kanitha made her take her shirt off. No one appeared to be interested in the young woman's nakedness. For the devotees, she was a canvas.

Luong Pho Mai started into another mantra as the two boys next to Kanitha pushed her forward and stretched the skin on her left shoulder. The blind monk didn't need guidance. The needle went in. The young men and women gasped and strained to catch the master at work. Kanitha faced Maier head-on, her face without expression, looking straight into his eyes. There was nothing he could do. The boy behind him still had the gun in his hand.

The monk worked quickly. His hand was steady; he knew where to put his needle. Every now and then, one of the boys wiped the blood from Kanitha's back. They'd done this many times before; their communication was silent. The devotees drifted into reverence. The needle played across her skin. The monk mumbled another prayer. It was done.

Kanitha got up slowly and faced the crowd. Her perfect breasts pointed beyond the young men towards the forest and freedom. The two boys who'd been assisting the old monk turned her around and a wave of adulation went through the congregation. Five strips of archaic calligraphy stretched down the girl's left shoulder blade, a trickle of blood running from the design down her back.

It was Maier's turn, and the boy pushed the detective to get up.

He walked through the crowd towards the monk. He sensed that the cave's inhabitants were getting excited at the prospect of a fellow white man getting inked. He passed Kanitha, who offered him a crooked grin.

"It's meant to help me make a fortune and protect me from harm, Maier. Let's see if it works."

Maier sat and the two boys to his left and right stretched his skin. He could hear the monk pray behind him. Luong Pho Mai shifted on his bench.

The needle went in just below the neck. Laos was taking more from him than he had bargained for. He watched Kanitha float away, her lithe silhouette in sharp focus against the morning light, giving her the aura of a sacred waif, a picture of great beauty, wholly lost on the congregation. As she moved out of his field of vision, he closed his eyes and concentrated on the needle that traced shapes he couldn't guess at across the center of his upper back. There was nothing spiritual about this procedure, he told himself. Maier exhaled and let himself fall into the rhythm of the steel point piercing his skin. Soon, there was only the needle playing around his breath.

He had left the cave in the jungle. He stood on a runway surrounded by high karst mountains.

A man walked towards him. Maier couldn't make out his face. He needed to make eye contact with this man if he was going to solve his case. The gold, his client, the U48, the men who were hunting him... everything led to the man on the runway. But Maier couldn't move. He stood rooted to the ground, a huge weight tied to his back, pressing him down. The man walked past him, the sun behind him. Maier couldn't see anything but his squat, well-trained physique, his quiet, sure step, his long breath. The man didn't turn his head as he passed.

He was back. Luong Pho Mai mumbled a last prayer. The tattooed children in front of him stared. Some cried. Others shook their heads in beatific mindlessness. He could see Kanitha at the mouth of the cave, her back turned to the Free State of Mind, watching the forest. Maier lingered in his trance, watching the world from within, quite unable to speak.

"It's time to go," the Teacher said.

His disciples crowed agreement, "Time to go."

14

WALK THAT WALK

The Teacher proved to be surprisingly spry for a one-legged man. For almost two days, he'd managed to make good speed on his crutches, all the while pontificating across his shoulder. He truly spoke to the jungle. The kids, still dressed in little more than rags, were now heavily armed. The entire group of tattooed warriors marched silently, in single file. They looked fearsome and they'd had some military training. Their weapons were ancient but in good condition. Perhaps they had stumbled upon a cache from the war. What these tooled-up hippies would do when they reached the prison camp was another matter.

The detective hadn't seen his own tattoo. There were no mirrors in the cave.

"Don't worry; the image is not important. It's the rules you need to follow if the jungle visa is to work," the Teacher said, "But you should be pleased, you're wearing a gao yod, the nine pillars yant. The top pillar, the one right in the center of your neck, represents nirvana, Maier. Remember that. It'll protect you from harm."

Maier looked at the Teacher, trying not to appear opinionated.

Far out, man.

His mind wandered back to the hallucinatory journey the tattooing had taken him on. The vision of standing on the runway had shaken him. Who was the man walking towards him every time he closed his eyes? As the intensity of the imagined near-encounter faded, he shrugged into his shirt and tried to push the memory aside. He had more immediate problems.

Both he and Kanitha knew too much.

Many of the plants stood two meters tall and were heavy with buds. The forest was pungent with dope for miles in all directions. During the war, napalm dropped from US planes had gutted patches of jungle. The citizens of the Free State of Mind had cut down the brush. They'd left the larger trees that had grown back stand and planted marijuana around them. Lots of it. Maier guessed at an area as large as a football field.

They stopped by the Nam Ou for lunch, hidden from river travelers by dense foliage, but close enough to hear passing boats. Several boys climbed up into surrounding trees to keep a lookout for unwanted guests.

The Teacher bristled with self-confidence. A man with a plan, Maier thought, watching warily.

"My kids will bring a couple of boats upriver that we'll sink once we have sprung Léon and scared the Viets. They'll think we have gone down with the boats. It'll look like a massacre. It's all about surprise."

Maier couldn't imagine any kind of surprise would faze members of the TS2, the Vietnamese secret service. Those guys were hard.

The Teacher called the boy who'd captured them.

"Give our new friend your revolver."

Maier could see that the inclusion of two strangers in this expedition flustered the young man with the tattooed skull, but he obeyed without hesitation.

"Tomorrow is our day, Maier. Are you ready?"

Maier didn't like carrying a weapon, but he kept his mouth shut.

He wasn't ready.

Getting Léon out without attacking his captors was unrealistic. With this gang of outlaws, they stood a chance. But what could they do, kill all the Vietnamese secret service men? No one would get away with that. It would mean the end of the Free State of Mind.

Perhaps the Teacher knew this. That he'd made a deal with the devil, the old monk, a long time ago and had now been asked to deliver his side of the bargain.

Maier worried while flashing his best smile. The death of his best friend and fixer in Cambodia four years earlier had made him extremely averse to violent confrontations. He knew there was nothing anyone could do to stop people killing each other. They did it for the most trivial reasons. But death was never trivial. It was waiting ahead of them, somewhere along the trail.

The young citizens of the Free State of Mind were tense and spoke little while they ate. Eventually, the Teacher got up and took Maier and Kanitha aside. He wore his long hair piled up like Audrey Hepburn and a bullet belt stretched across his bare, tattooed chest. He looked as mad as Colonel Kurtz. Maier doubted the American really knew just how far he'd drifted from the program. In some ways, the detective admired the former CIA man for taking his chances away from the crowd. The Teacher was the most extroverted drug peddler the detective had ever met. But now, away from his group, he seemed a little worried, paranoid even.

"We go in as a tight group. We will have the advantage of surprise and altitude – the camp is ringed by low hills. We will hit them just as it gets dark. You get your man Léon. We make it look like a bandit shoot-out. Just between you and me, I think it's madness, but Luong Pho Mai insisted. He has bad memories of that place. His anger is considerable, even though he's meditated on his incarceration since he got out. Now, to increase our chances of total success, I have a suggestion."

15

DEATH COMES IN SURPRISES

MAIER ALMOST SAW the trap before it sprang. Everything just happened a little too quickly. He'd been ground down by the Teacher's incessant talking.

As the long day slowly faded into night, Kanitha, wearing a torn pair of trekking pants, a lycra sports top and a faded baseball cap, was the first to go in. Shouting for help in Laotian, she slowly descended from the ridge above the camp. The prettiest Trojan horse Maier could imagine was on its way.

The compound looked like the stage set for an action B-movie, a square space dotted with simple huts and ringed by a bamboo palisade three meters high, topped by barbed wire. A couple of makeshift watchtowers, little more than wooden platforms with grass roofs looming above the bamboo walls, stood unguarded. Jungle LEGO.

As soon as the girl reached the camp, the guards switched on a couple of flood lights. The bamboo gate remained closed.

Maier could see several armed soldiers in the harsh glare of their lamps.

It didn't look like they'd have to fight the entire Vietnamese army. With a little negotiation, a bloodbath might be avoided. The kids far outnumbered the camp guards.

One of the soldiers climbed onto the watchtower closest to the front gate and shone his light at the girl. Maier couldn't hear the words the man and Kanitha exchanged. But she had her story down pat. She was from Vientiane on a trekking tour. Her boyfriend had broken his leg upriver and she was desperately looking for help. Any fear she betrayed would only be natural under the circumstances, the Teacher had suggested.

The soldier in the tower signaled back to his companions and the gate opened. Sometimes, the simplest plans worked.

The boy next to Maier pulled the trigger on his rifle.

The soldier in the tower fell.

The citizens of the Free State of Mind broke into a mad run, howling like banshees all the way down the hill. It hadn't been much of a feint, but it worked. They rolled towards the camp like a primitive wave of doom. Seconds later, they broke through the gate, Maier swept along in their midst. The solar lights died. Shots rang out. Men screamed into the darkness. Maier found Kanitha and they scrambled for the protection of one of the compound's huts. In the strobe lights of a few weak torches, the kids let themselves go and butchered two more soldiers. By the time the Teacher limped into the camp, an older man in military fatigues was the only opposition alive. The Teacher stood facing the prisoner, looking unhappy. Maier understood that this was not a victory. One could win a battle against the Vietnamese, but never a war.

"You have a prisoner here?"

The older man knelt on the ground, blinded by two portable floodlights that the kids held just inches from his face. He didn't answer. Maier doubted he spoke English. The man looked up at the Teacher with undisguised hostility and spat on the ground. This guy wasn't going to talk.

The Teacher waved to his kids and they swarmed out into the night. Then he called Maier and Kanitha into the circle of light and addressed everyone, breathing heavily like an overworked devil.

"You see, Mr. Detective, it's hard to guess how much you are with me on this. I'm assuming you are a shrewd fella and know that you will be dead in a few minutes. As soon as we find that Hmong rat Sangster, we can pack up and go home. And you and your teenage monster here will be blamed for the deed."

He laughed and added, "The Free State of Mind has prevailed, Maier. You get Léon. We get peace."

The boy who had sunk their boat days earlier came up behind Maier and took his gun.

The detective turned to Kanitha who looked at him expectantly and whispered, "You better have an ace up your sleeve, Sherlock; otherwise we're screwed."

Maier had been called Sherlock before, under less strenuous circumstances. He couldn't think of a flippant reply. But he didn't show her his fear either. He'd been tricked by a cripple who hadn't seen a road in twenty-five years. And he'd find a way out.

Maier stepped into the light to look at the Vietnamese. The old man raised his head and stared. The boy handed the Teacher the gun Maier had been carrying.

Time took a deep breath and the night, what was left of it, crowded in. He thought of looking at Kanitha. He tried to think of ways of how they could still be of some use to the Teacher. The intense stare of the intelligence officer kneeling in front of him pulled him back into the vortex of the mess they were in. The man was looking at Maier like someone who was struggling to accept the existence of ghosts. There was nothing desperate or hopeful about his intense gaze. All his men were dead and he knew he was next. Yet the Vietnamese soldier pointed calmly at the detective and started talking, quietly, succinctly. The kids, their weapons now slung casually across their shoulders, drunk on blood and victory, gathered around the small group.

"Who speaks Vietnamese?" the Teacher demanded, but Maier knew his heart wasn't in it. There was nothing to be gained here for the one-legged soldier, no matter what the Vietnamese had to offer. The Teacher had written the script for this scene long before the attack. He needed everyone dead, and he needed Maier's corpse to get away with his ruse.

"Weltmeister," the Vietnamese said.

Maier clearly heard the man speak German. The soldier pointed at the detective and repeated the word.

"What's he saying?" the Teacher demanded.

Maier answered quickly, "No idea; he's speaking Vietnamese. I don't understand a word."

"Can't be that important," the Teacher said, and shot the old soldier in the head.

"Can't be that important," the kids huffed as one, and shrank away from the executioner.

A commotion behind them prevented Maier from going into shock. He turned just as two of the kids led a middle-aged man into the light.

"You must be Léon Sangster?"

The Teacher smiled at the new arrival. He had the killing fever in his eyes; everything about him was dangerous.

Léon looked tired but unharmed. His hair came down to his shoulders. His handsome face, darkened to an attractive copper hue by years spent in the sun, was on the verge of going to seed. The white, flowing beard he tried to grow made him look a little more imposing than he might have been otherwise. He wore a thin cotton shirt and a ripped pair of jeans. He looked from Kanitha to Maier, expressionless and silent. As Léon made eye contact with the detective for the second time, he jerked back, an expression of deep bewilderment on his face. For an instant, nothing and nobody existed except the two men and an undefined space between them. Léon, Maier thought, looked at him as if he'd recognized a long-lost cousin or someone he'd met before and never expected to meet again. The dead Vietnamese officer on the ground in front of them had looked at Maier the same way. Maier had never met either of them. Not in this life.

"Impossible," the prisoner muttered under his breath.

The Teacher hadn't noticed. His script was still playing. And Maier was about to be written out of it.

The Teacher beckoned his disciples closer to Maier, Kanitha and Léon. Thirty guns pointed at three heads.

"We've been waiting for this opportunity for months. I remember you, Léon, when you were a kid. I liked your dad. He was a good agent. Shame he perished when the shit came down. But he was always stubborn. He valued his wife and children more than the duty to his country. Admirable, really."

The Teacher laughed a laugh that looked like the mouth of his cave, and brought his warriors into the conversation.

"We've been trying to figure out how to get rid of this camp before it ate our business. We even thought we could arrange a shoot-out between you, Léon, and the guards which would have left everyone dead. But five against one wasn't going to stick. Then these guys actually come to free you. With a little help from us, you'll create the perfect finale and allow the Free State of Mind to remain a rumor, a dumb tale that tourists tell around camp fires."

Maier doubted the Vietnamese were as dense as the Teacher hoped them to be. The one-legged dope dealer had fought for more than a decade in the jungle and seemed none the wiser for it.

Léon continued to stare at Maier. Kanitha, who hadn't said a word to either her new or her old boyfriend, was crying quietly and blew snot into the night.

"Weltmeister?" Léon asked, a mixture of utter disbelief and barely suppressed hate in his voice, and leaned closer to Maier.

The Teacher grabbed hold of Léon's hair and pulled his head up. "What's that? You know this guy? What did you call him? I thought that was Vietnamese. Tell me."

Léon looked at his captor and grinned. "I've got nothing to tell you and nothing to lose. You're gonna kill me anyway."

The younger man turned his head so hard that the Teacher was left standing with a fistful of hair. Léon dropped to the ground. Furious, the old American soldier raised his gun.

Léon ignored his captor and continued to stare at Maier, a cruel smile on his lined face. Maier could smell an end between them. Dust particles swirled in slow motion around the two men as death settled on whatever it was that connected them. The detective thought them beautiful, like the snowflakes that had dropped onto his childhood in Leipzig.

The Teacher turned to Maier, a sudden understanding in his eyes as he looked at the detective again.

"You are…"

The sound of the shot rang out as if from miles away. Léon continued to stare, his eyes glazed with deep guttural anger.

The Teacher fell into the circle of light with a heavy thud. His chest exploded the very same instant.

Kanitha screamed silently.

The next two shots took out the solar lights. Everything went black.

For the third time, a sniper had found his mark right next to Maier.

Then something louder, much louder and much closer, blew him up and away.

16

REUNION HALL

"Young man, the first time I met you, you'd been beaten by ghosts. And now I find you bleeding to death in paradise and not a soul but you to tell the tale. Maier, I decided to save your life. Again. Because of our great friendship. You owe me. What is it the Americans always say? Big time."

Maier opened his eyes. Too bright. The world flashed as if armed with swords of light. He closed his eyes. He knew this voice. He could tell this voice from a thousand others. Sounded like a Hollywood bad guy. So much to think about. He'd been shot. He wriggled his toes. Both legs still there. What the hell had happened? Tattoos, ambush, Léon, Weltmeister. He was dead. He was definitely dead.

The likelihood of being resurrected by a gay Russian hit man was infinitesimally small. But there it was, that voice.

He sank away into unconsciousness.

"How long have I been here?"

The man wore a white coat and a face mask. He looked at Maier gravely but didn't answer. This time Maier was sure. He was alive. He was in a hospital, in Asia, and the man was a doctor. The white coat left the room and closed the door. A key turned in the lock.

A couple of drips were running into a catheter in his left hand.

There were no electronic monitoring systems in the room, no blood pressure gauge, no heart rate monitor. He was probably still in Laos. The hand was heavily bandaged.

He looked down the bed. His feet, all toes included, stuck out from the bottom of a sheet that was too short and had been washed too many times. He pulled his legs up and pushed them back down and put his right hand between his legs. Everything was still there. He tried to wriggle his toes. They responded. He lifted his left arm. The tubes from the drip were short. His left hand looked too small.

Mikhail wore a loud shirt and a sweaty grin. The last time Maier had seen him had been months ago in the Cambodian jungle, in what seemed another lifetime. Mikhail was a dangerous man, but he had saved Maier's life once. Twice? The huge Russian drank from a glass. That looked strange. Vodka. Neat. Maier could smell it. His sense of smell remained highly sensitive. The drink in the other man's hand had woken him up. He felt euphoric.

"Am I dead?"

Mikhail laughed and winked at the detective.

"You better hope that the relevant people out there believe you are, my dear. Otherwise, I suspect they'll be in here very soon to finish the job. Maier, you're in a shitload of trouble. Just like last time we met. Welcome back. You're still handsome and you're wasted on those ladies."

Maier said nothing. He could feel a tear running from his left eye. He felt the tear intensely, like hot wax, as it made its way down his cheek. He wasn't sure why he was crying. It felt good. Every emotion that washed through him was magnified to enormous, obscene proportions. But why was the Russian in his room?

"Did you get me out of there?"

The Russian nodded, "It's ok, young man; the important bits are still there. I got you the best medical attention this part of the world has to offer."

"What's wrong with me?"

The Russian put his glass down, brushed his long, greasy gray hair from his puffed, red face and pulled a bottle from behind his chair. He refilled the glass and got up. He was as enormous and fat as Maier remembered him. A jolly giant, a specialist in murder and discretion. A rare breed. He handed the drink to the detective.

"No orange juice in here. That'll have to wait. But you will need this, my friend."

Maier took a modest swig. His throat burnt. It was great.

"You want it straight?"

Maier felt dizzy. He nodded, worried his head would slip off his shoulders, and took another swig.

"Someone shot you. Close up. Not a very good shot and it came from the ground. He blew off the two smallest digits on your left hand and the bullet tore through your shoulder. No serious veins or bones hit. Shoulder is good, fingers are gone."

Maier raised his left hand again and stared at it.

"I arrived seconds after the attack by your tattooed holiday club. Daniels is dead."

"Who is Daniels?"

The Russian snorted in disbelief. "Come on, Maier, don't start playing with me. I have your life in my hands. Daniels, that one-legged macho CIA freak gone native. The leader of the tattoo gang. The guy who set you up. No great loss anyhow; he had too much body hair. Really not my type."

Maier nodded. The Teacher had set them up.

"How long have I been here?"

"The attack happened a week ago. We kept you under, to make sure everyone thinks you're dead. We also needed to wait and see if you would develop any serious infections from the surgery. I know you're capable of great mischief, Maier."

Maier laughed without wanting to.

"My hand?"

Mikhail shrugged.

"We did what we could. I couldn't medevac you. The job's not finished. It wouldn't have done much good, anyway. The fingers were gone, shredded. I had you sewn up, and you're getting a morphine shot twice a day. Tell me if the dope wears off. The doc says I can take you out of here in a couple of days. Minus your digits. You're coming back into the jungle with me."

Maier chuckled. The chance of meeting an assassin of Mikhail's caliber twice and living to tell the tale was slim. Happy as a clam, he took another sip and asked, "So, to what do I owe the honor this time?"

Mikhail raised the glass and grinned.

"You said you wanted it straight and I admire that. This story is big. You know nothing yet. This is your biggest case, Maier. Your pivotal moment."

"Did you shoot the Teacher? Daniels?"

"No, Maier, this is the thing. This is why I came out, so to speak. To save you, my good friend. Otherwise, you'd never have seen me. You know I'm the man in the shadows, bulky but invisible."

He threw his head back, roared with laughter and drained the glass.

"The only way to drink vodka."

Maier wasn't sure whether mixing vodka and morphine was a good idea. He doubted there was a name for it. But it was textbook treatment for a private eye who'd lost two fingers in a case he didn't understand. Then his mind, quite of its own accord, took the next step and he felt the hair on his arms stand up.

"Who shot the Teacher?"

"The same person that shot the old woman on the island and your boatman up in Muang Ngoi. That's three down. The same person who lured you to Laos. And who keeps shooting across your bow."

"You call killing innocents shooting across the bow? He shot May Lik in cold blood. She was the intended target. The murder of the boatman was another killing without reason, without motive."

The Russian grinned and winked at Maier. "The first killing was a kind of greeting. The second one saved you from your pursuers. The third saved your life. Someone is coming closer, Maier. Someone is coming for you."

"What, I have the devil on my trail?"

Mikhail snorted, "Ah, young man, your detecting faculties are obviously still intact."

His comment was laced with sarcasm, but Maier was too burnt out to counter the Russian's wit. He'd just lost two fingers. He didn't have a clue what was going on, and his girl had vanished. The morphine made him happy.

"What happened to Kanitha? Is she ok?"

Mikhail made an uncertain hand gesture.

"We're not sure, Maier, not sure. By the time I had secured the area, she and Léon were gone. Whether he took her or whether she went, we don't know."

"He was her boyfriend."

The Russian laughed. "So were you, Maier. What does it mean, I wonder? So many players in this show, it's hard to see who belongs to which side. Or what each side actually signifies. Very hard to tell."

"What happened to the tattooed kids? The Free State of Mind?"

"Gone."

"What do you mean, gone? And how did you secure the area? How did you even come to be there?"

"In time, detective. We have more pressing things to discuss."

Maier sighed and lifted his left arm. The shoulder felt stiff, but it was functioning. He had problems looking at his hand. It was his, but it had changed. He could feel all five fingers but he could only see three of them. The case had gone to hell. He would call Sundermann and discuss his next move. His boss didn't like his employees getting maimed.

"Where am I, Mikhail?"

The older man got up and pulled the curtain from the only window in the room. With his right arm, Maier pushed himself up. The view was familiar. Temple roofs flashed in the distance the north. He was in Luang Prabang.

"We flew a doctor in from Vietnam. The older intelligence agent you saw at the camp was my friend and boss. He died from a shot to the head that was sloppily executed. It took him the whole night to go. The doctor came for him but he only managed to fix you."

"Can I make a phone call?"

The Russian laughed. "This isn't an American cop movie, Maier. You're not down at the precinct. You're in deep shit. Your life isn't worth your weight in borscht. Well, actually, your life is worth a lot to all the wrong people. We all love you for the connection you don't even know you have."

Maier was back at the prison camp and remembered the look in the eye of the Vietnamese agent just before the Teacher had executed him. It wasn't Maier he'd recognized when he'd looked at the detective. Léon too had stared at him in a similarly intense way, out of it, shocked to the bone.

"Let's start at the beginning. Weltmeister? Who is he and why do people mention his name when they see me?"

The Russian seemed to read his mind.

"This man is an enigma. A spy, an assassin. He's worked for everyone on all sides. No one knows who he is. Until now."

Maier felt uncomfortable in his own skin, like an old snake ready to shed.

"So, who is Weltmeister?"

"Don't be slow on me, Maier. And you know what the wise men say. We all choose our parents. Your father's in town. And he's in a killing mood."

Maier passed out.

17

STICKY FINGERS

MAIER WOKE IN A DIFFERENT ROOM. He was no longer in hospital. The euphoria had gone. His shoulder felt stiff and his body hurt as if he'd been beaten with clubs. The catheter had been removed and his hand had been re-bandaged. It still looked too small. Maier shivered when he looked at it. He'd have adjustment problems for some time to come.

The world had carried on in his absence. The sky was blue, the winter sun pale, the air dry and full of life that he wanted to capture, consume, inhale. A dog barked in the distance, unseen. Another answered, even further removed from his current frame of operations. People were still loving and killing each other, also unseen.

The Buddha recommended that one ought not to worry about things one couldn't change. Maier worried anyhow. When one lost two digits, even the Buddha's advice found its limits. Perhaps he'd be reborn with two good hands.

He got up. He stood. He felt a little dizzy, but no more so than in an average state of inebriation. The steel door was locked and probably tank-resistant. Definitely detective-resistant. The only thing he could hang himself with was the rough toilet paper. The only window was barred. The smaller window in the tiny bathroom was just large enough to fit a monkey. If they starved him long enough, he would be able to make a run for it. Maier wasn't in a monkey mood.

The walls were painted government green and had started to flake. The view of the Mekong had been replaced by a view of paddy fields. A concrete wall topped by shards of glass, ugly as concrete walls can be, ringed the property he was locked up in.

One day, he'd be able to turn the loss of his fingers into something positive. It would make him look more lived-in. It would impress the girls, or give him a villainous sheen when needed. He studied the bandage. He moved his hand. He felt a little pain that burned to his very core. He could feel the missing fingers, as if the crippled hand were just a hallucination.

Life was ugly.

Except for a plastic bottle of water and the bed, the room was empty. No more vodka. After doing three desultory rounds and promising himself never to go to a zoo again, Maier lay back down and considered his non-existent options. A few moments of vapid meditation pulled him under, back to sleep.

"And how is our patient today?"

Mikhail entered the room with all the panache of an overweight torero, followed by a small man in a red Ferrari polo shirt. Collar up. Hair shaved back and sides. The Russian's companion, in his early sixties, looked familiar. The loud shirt which stretched across his stomach did nothing to dispel his military background. He wore a gun in a shoulder holster on top of his shirt. No anorak in sight today. A flashy entrance for Mr. Mookie, the dancing fool from the Insomniacs Club.

Behind the Laotian, a young woman in uniform tried to remain unseen. A bona fide member of the Lao PDR's heroic military. She was slim, dark-skinned and devastatingly beautiful.

"We're going to love you back to life, Maier," the Russian laughed.

The Laotian didn't laugh, but held out his hand and introduced himself in fluent German.

"I'm your local case officer, Detective Maier. You can call me Mr. Mookie. The man who was shot by Daniels, or the Teacher, as you knew him, was my brother-in-law. I'm Laotian Intelligence. We work with the Vietnamese on resolving this issue, and I'll bring you up to date with your investigation. Then you will help us. Failure to follow our instructions will result in your disposal. Our mutual friend Mikhail has been tasked with this mission in case you forfeit the trust we invest in you in the coming days. He'll not show mercy, nor will he take your previous association into account. He won't torture you. We're revolutionaries, not barbarians. But if you deceive us, keep us from our goal or lead us down blind alleys, you will lose a lot more than two fingers."

Maier shook the man's hand. His "case officer" still had his ten fingers, he noticed. The detective was very sensitive about other people's limbs, even the most insignificant and smallest.

Mr. Mookie watched Maier attentively.

Mikhail looked out of the window, presumably at unseen dogs, leaving the playing field to his employer.

"Where am I?"

Mr. Mookie ignored the question. The Laotian's finesse probably lay in interrogation. The Russian turned and brushed his gray hair from his face to throw the detective an unhealthy grin.

"You are in the Lao PDR, Maier. On a tourist visa, in case you want reminding. Jungle visa doesn't count in the real world. And you're up to your neck in shit. I mean real shit. Asian shit. Laotian shit. European shit. American shit. Shit that stretches from one side of the planet to the other. But mostly you're in Vietnamese shit."

Mikhail laughed so hard that Maier felt exhausted.

"What were you thinking? You took part in an assault on a Vietnamese intelligence unit. And you got caught. My clients don't take lightly to the murder of their operatives. Remember this when you consider your options in the coming days."

Maier didn't like being berated or lectured.

"These kids kidnapped me and Kanitha. Took us right off our boat. I didn't know this tattoo cult was going to burn down the valley and kill everyone."

Mr. Mookie smiled mildly, as if he'd just stepped off the dance floor.

"You did, Maier. And as I said, we're not savages. We reacted with utmost pragmatism. We dragged Daniels back to the plantation and hung him right in the middle of his ganja plants. A deterrent."

"And what happened to Luong Pho Mai?"

"My assistant here – you may call her Miss Darany – shot the old monk. He was an unrepentant reactionary we should have finished off after the revolution. We were too soft. But not this time. The Free State of Mind no longer exists."

"What happened to those kids?"

Mikhail laughed, "Oh, Maier, always compassionate. You're the classic private eye, on the side of the downtrodden and the helpless, fighting the forces of darkness. Like in American movies. But this time you picked the wrong darkness, my dear."

The Russian slapped his huge hands on his thighs and looked like he was about to dance like a bear. This was turning into quite a party.

"The tattooed kids ran back south through the jungle and emerged in Muang Ngoi where the Lao police picked them up and charged them with overstaying their visas. They have been deported and blacklisted. Growing marijuana on an industrial scale is illegal in the Lao PDR. But the Laotians don't bear grudges. The government will take the plantation over for research purposes."

Mikhail left his words hanging in the ugly room.

Mr. Mookie coughed and pulled a battered pack of cheap Laotian cigarettes from his pocket. He offered Maier a smoke.

"I have given up. Ask Mikhail. He will vouch for that."

"And for very little else, Maier."

"This is the good cop, bad cop routine?"

The door was open. The walls of the corridor outside were painted the same color as those of the room they were in. Maier had a longing to get up and walk out. As if Mikhail could read his mind, he stepped up to the bed.

"Tell my friend Mr. Mookie why you're here. Please choose your words carefully. I do like you, you know. I mean, not in that way, of course, but still… we could have a future…"

Maier repeated his story, starting with his encounter with Julia Rendel in Hamburg. When he had finished, the room lapsed into silence.

Mr. Mookie lit another cigarette. The room stank of cheap smoke.

Maier sensed that Mikhail and the Laotian were a tight team. They barely needed to make eye contact to exchange information.

Mikhail broke the silence first.

"You see Maier, this is way bigger than you think. We believe your story. Julia Rendel did hire you to find out about how her father was killed, but this is just a smokescreen. And behind the smokescreen is another smokescreen, and behind that smokescreen lie a number of truths. We're not here to get at the truth. We are merely interested in making it all stop. You understand?"

Maier shook his head.

"Your father was an intelligence agent, one of the best in business. He worked for TS2 towards the end of the American War. And now he's cropped up in Laos with something everyone wants. And believe me, a lot of people would like to get hold of him. The Laotians, our Vietnamese brothers, the Americans, all his old paymasters..."

His voice trailed off.

"My father? In Laos?"

Maier sat stunned on his bed and stared into the middle distance, assembling his new reality. He remembered that this was the second time the Russian had shocked him with the news of his father's alleged appearance. Even as he struggled to cope with the news, he knew the Russian wasn't telling him everything. He looked at Mikhail, but the hit man's eyes were neutral. Was this a message of some kind that was only meant for him?

Maier couldn't keep the bitterness from his voice. Whom were they kidding?

"You are playing games. This is all about a haul of gold from the Secret War, right? American drug money?"

The Russian laughed maniacally.

"Gold, Maier? Gold? Drugs? You don't think the Vietnamese government would send a top intelligence agent into the Laotian jungle because of gold and a few kilos of heroin that the Americans forgot to take with them? No, Maier, you weren't recruited for a treasure hunt. Get that out of your head! You were hired to help your father take revenge. He's calling the shots."

Mr. Mookie flicked his burning cigarette butt into a corner of the room and leaned into the conversation.

"You didn't tell us you slept with Rendel at the Atlantic prior to her abduction."

"I'm not asking you who you're sleeping with. Or how old they are," Maier shot back.

The old Laotian smiled faintly. It didn't look good on him.

"We had a look at your email account. You received an email from the 1000 Elephant Trading Company a few days ago. If you want to see your Thai friend Kanitha again, you'll have to meet up with them."

"She is Laotian."

Mr. Mookie smiled sourly, "It remains to be seen exactly what she is. In the meantime, get moving."

"I don't know who is behind the 1000 Elephant Trading Company." Mikhail laughed.

"You had a run-in with Charlie Bryson in Vientiane, didn't you?"

"The MIA guy at the Insomniacs Club? Sure, he is a creep."

"He's an American agent. A very good one. Don't be fooled by his brash character or his unhealthy complexion. He's looking for the same man we are looking for. Your father. He must not find him first. This is why you are now working for us."

Maier felt distraught but tried not to show it. It was all fine except the "father" bit. Why here, why now? Hadn't he long ago learned to live with his sense of mystery and loss?

"Who is my father? This Weltmeister everyone is scared of? And why is he in Laos at the same time as me? The chances of that are non-existent, given that I have never met him."

"Maier, he set you up. You're here because he is here. He wants to make some kind of deal. But we don't know with whom. Or perhaps he simply wants to make trouble, show off to his son. He always was a romantic."

Mr. Mookie looked irritated. Maier must have looked doubtful.

"When did you first hear about Weltmeister?"

"I told you, I first heard this name at the camp the other day. From the man you say was your brother-in-law, moments before Daniels shot him. He stared at me as if he recognized me. So did Léon Sangster. And Daniels also got that weird look, right before he died. I had never met any of them before."

Mr. Mookie answered, "We think he gave that name to himself. He has a high opinion of his abilities."

Maier shook his head.

"Can you prove any of this?"

The Laotian shrugged and looked the detective straight in the eye, "Do we have to? The look my brother-in-law gave you prior to his murder should be evidence enough."

374

The Russian tried to defuse the tension in the room and continued, "Weltmeister was last seen in Long Cheng, the secret US airbase, in 1976. We're sure he'd changed his name and worked for Stasi at the time. We lost track of him after that. Decades of silence. Until now."

Mr. Mookie calmed down and put on an almost paternalistic smile, "You know it's him, right?"

Maier nodded. Sections of this secret mandala were coming together, though he couldn't see any decodable patterns yet. An awful picture was emerging in his mind, its center blurred, its frayed edges coming into focus.

"So where is Julia? They wanted Léon Sangster in exchange for Julia."

Mikhail shrugged. "We aren't sure. We don't think that the 1000 Elephant Trading Company is holding her. I mean, they were holding her and then lost her. We have reports of a house being hit by some kind of a death squad, origin unknown, in Luang Prabang. Unheard of in Laos. Signature Weltmeister, if you ask me. The second email Bryson sent you didn't mention her. That only reaffirms our suspicions as to who freed her."

Maier looked sourly at the Russian, "If it didn't tell me that they killed her and threw her down a mine shaft, what did the email say?"

Mikhail laughed, "Oh, Maier, young man. Don't get angry over everything or I'll hug you to death. It said that you must meet them if you want to see Kanitha again. We assume they have Léon as well. But he might not be a strong enough bait to draw Weltmeister out. You are. You'll meet them and find out what they want. And you meet your father."

Two women, connected to this case in entirely different ways, had been used to haul Maier in. Perhaps the kidnappings were mere distractions, tools to guide the detective towards the elusive Weltmeister.

Maier played his only trump card.

"So, what about the U48?"

The room fell silent. Mr. Mookie turned to Mikhail, then back to Maier. He didn't speak for a long time, but simply watched the German detective, a look of intense concentration on his wizened face.

Maier left the question standing and continued. "What will I have to bargain with? I want to try and get Kanitha back. And we need to find Julia."

Mr. Mookie laughed, softly clapping his small hands, turned to Mikhail and said, in German. "You were right. He really is the sentimental type."

He snorted derisively at the detective. "You will offer them your father. And yourself, of course. It's the only deal in town, Maier."

"They will kill me."

Mr. Mookie countered gently, "Maier, you're getting there. The moment your father truly believes his son will die, he will show his hand. It's our only chance to get the U48. And Weltmeister. You wouldn't believe how much our Vietnamese friends want to get their hands on this man. And the Americans are no different. Trust us, this goes all the way up to the White House. And right now, the White House is concerned. Not just about planes flying into buildings. We spoke to the US ambassador in Vientiane a couple of days ago. I had a feeling he was waiting for my call. For the US, the Weltmeister affair is a diplomatic tsunami in the making, an ugly aftertaste of their Vietnam War. For us, it's merely a coming to terms with the past. If we apprehend Weltmeister, perhaps even honor him if necessary, Laos will be able to draw a line under the conflict, our American War. Trust me, Maier. If Weltmeister falls into American hands, he' stead. And Vietnam loses prestige. If we get to him first, anything is possible. Like it or not, you're embroiled in the biggest spy scandal since World War II."

Maier emphatically didn't trust anyone. He wouldn't have believed Mr. Mookie if the agent had told him that he was missing two fingers on his left hand. Maier wasn't in a trusting mood.

Mr. Mookie waved for Miss Darany to step up to the bed.

"This is my cousin's wife. She is a mid-level intelligence agent. Someone who does dirty work. But she's not very bright. She helped facilitate the passage of the drugs from the cave to the Thai border to line her own pockets. She got too close to these tattooed kids. She cheated my cousin and she cheated her country. She doesn't speak German. She thinks her killing the monk has redeemed her somehow. She expects us to order her to sleep with you. Or to kill you. What do you think?"

"You will sacrifice your cousin's moral standing or mental health to keep an eye on me? There must be less-compromising options at your disposal."

The intelligence agent picked at his collar as if looking for dandruff. He became, quite suddenly, as remote as a cloud.

"I need to impress just one thing on you one more time. This is not a game. Your father is the most sought-after intelligence asset of the twentieth century. And we will have him. You will be the bait to draw him out. That's the only reason you're alive. And I will demonstrate the difference between life and death to you in the best way I can."

Maier nodded, trying his best to look agreeable.

"You're from Leipzig, Maier, aren't you?"

Looking agreeable wasn't enough.

Mr. Mookie smiled faintly as if listening to a sad piece of music far, far away in his head.

"I studied there. Then I went back home and helped beat the Americans. You see, Maier, there was only one way to beat these white devils, to win the war. We had to be ruthless. We had to be cruel. We had to sacrifice that which we cherished most. We had to lose everything to win the war. We lost hundreds of thousands of our own people. Fathers, mothers, brothers, sisters, sons and daughters. And the Vietnamese, whom we have much to thank for, threw millions into a furnace to save their great nation."

Mr. Mookie stepped back behind the young woman, who looked at Maier without expression. Her uncle said something in Laotian and she looked at the detective uncertainly, unable to grasp the situation.

Maier nodded gratefully, though he knew enough of people to feel sick. Sick of the world, sick of his job, sick of this room he couldn't escape from.

"We will use Miss Darany to impress our utmost seriousness on you. She's a spent force, anyway."

Mr. Mookie pulled his gun. Before Maier had time to move out of the way, the Laotian agent shot his cousin's beautiful wife in the back of the head. The girl jerked violently forward and splattered on top of Maier, the spray of disintegrating facial tissue showering the detective. The bullet had whizzed past Maier into the bed's mattress. Mr. Mookie threw the gun onto the bed next to Maier's good hand and pulled a small camera from his trouser pocket. He pressed the shutter to capture Maier amidst his bloodbath and grinned.

"You can't run, Maier; you belong to me. We'll meet again."

The old man laughed severely and left the room. Maier fought to wipe the girl's skin and bones off his face with his one good hand while trying to direct the projectile vomit that shot up his throat in the direction of the killer with the other.

18

PLAY ME A SONG OF DEATH

The Plain of Jars, a high, windswept plateau that stretched across the central region of northern Laos, looked like a giant's golf course. The scars of the American war were clearly visible. Almost perfectly circular bomb craters dotted the land in all directions. Tall grasses grew around the craters. There wasn't a single tree in sight. A cold wind blew across the rolling hills of northeastern Laos.

There were few towns and villages in the area. The old provincial capital of Xieng Khouang had been blasted to rubble.

The region had taken its name from several collections of huge, roughly hewn megalithic stone jars, obscure remnants of a culture long lost from memory. The Americans had airlifted one of the jars back to the US, which now stood at CIA headquarters in Langley, Virginia. Scholars claimed the jars had been used as funeral containers. Others suggested they'd been used to brew alcohol.

The jars reminded Maier of the stone virgin of Dölau, a menhir he'd visited with his mother when he'd been ten years old. As he scanned the hills around him, he clearly remembered a story of the stone his mother had told him: A woman had been shopping. When she'd been on her way home, it had started to rain. Her trail was full of muddy puddles, so she threw a loaf of bread on the ground and used it as a stepping stone to avoid getting her feet dirty. The gods were incensed about her squandering of fresh bread and turned her to stone the very same instant.

Maier assumed the Laotians had been more sensible and had really used the jars to brew local beer, not minding how dirty their feet got during the wet season.

The new capital, Phonsavan, was a dusty collection of shacks. The tumbledown township was interspersed with garish houses fronted by Roman-style pillars, painted in dirty pink or fluorescent green – the homes of officials, connected entrepreneurs or drug and gem barons. The fences that ran through town were constructed of CBU cases and other war scrap that had rained down on the plateau in the Sixties.

Maier and Mikhail checked into a couple of rooms in the dusty center. The hotel looked like a Swiss chalet and was decorated with war junk. Guided tours to crash sites of US jets and the final resting places of gutted Laotian tanks provided the only source of income on the Plain of Jars besides subsistence farming.

Maier spent a long time looking at himself in his room's mirror. His black eye had faded. He kept his moustache at bay. His bandages were off. He raised his ruined hand to the mirror, touching the cold glass with his index finger. The short stumps tingled. He'd never be a guitar player. Nor a typist. He didn't think women would give him any credit for having lived dangerously.

Other than that, his situation was precarious and unsettling. He suddenly had a father. The last two women he'd slept with had been kidnapped. Or not. He was watched around the clock by a fat Russian hit man, half friend, half foe, all monster. He missed Kanitha, her feisty attitude, her curiosity and her company. He had little to bargain with and no idea which side of the fence she was on. He'd never gone into a situation with a worse deck of cards. He felt old, used, unwanted, and he was crippled.

In Europe, they called this midlife crisis. In Asia, most people were happy to live to his age and had no time for periodic self-doubt. That in itself was a depressing thought.

At first light, Maier left the hotel and walked due east, unarmed, not a single ace up his sleeve. The most recent email from the 1000 Elephant Trading Company had stipulated he come alone. No tricks, no weapons.

He walked carefully and stuck to well-trodden paths. Sweat was trickling down the back of his cotton shirt. The hills around looked safe enough, tranquil, but this was an illusion. Unexploded ordnance lurked everywhere under the shifting soils of the highlands. One false step could spell the end. At the close of every monsoon, locals got their feet blown off by bombs that had shifted during the rains. The weather was everything out here. It made and broke adversaries.

Maier knew the story well. From 1960, the US had secretly set out to dominate the Plain of Jars to create a buffer between the North Vietnamese and Thailand. A US secret army of montagnards – thirty thousand hill tribe soldiers trained by the CIA – had fought the communists each dry season, supported by bombers flown by Hmong pilots out of Long Cheng. But each year, they quickly lost their gains in the rains when the Pathet Lao pushed back with heavy artillery. The war washed back and forth like a sick, deadly tide. As the Sixties wound down and the summer of love went to hell in Southeast Asia, the US military wrested the war from the secret service. The ground war abandoned, the US now bombed the country back into the stone age it had barely emerged from. The Plain of Jars, or PDJ, as the locals called it, became one of the most heavily bombed places on the planet.

The grass was knee-deep, and every time Maier lost track of the path, he retraced his steps. The going was slow. The dirty, leaking sky pushed down on the grassland, threatening to squash the hills and all that moved amongst them. Large raindrops splashed on his head.

When he reached the road, a black SUV sat waiting for him. A couple of white men armed with large-caliber scowls served as his welcoming committee. There was no need for introductions.

Middle-aged suburban guys, tooled up and professional, most likely comfortably semi-retired with Asian wives and war loot in Florida, out for a short stretch of nostalgic hurrah and shit-kicking. One wore an MIA patch on his polo shirt. The other one wore a toupée that looked like it would blow off in a heavy gust of wind or turn into a mushroom if the skies opened.

They asked him politely to sit in the back of the four-wheel drive. One of the men sat next to him, bound his hands with double cuffs and put a bag over his head. The other got in the front and started driving as if his life depended on it. That made Maier feel marginally better. They were being theatrical and he was being taken to a show. He wasn't sure whether he'd be the main act or merely part of a supporting cast. Trapped in darkness and breathing stale cotton, he felt like he had all the time in the world.

Ten minutes later, the hood came off in the middle of nowhere. As Maier slowly opened his eyes to adjust to the dull daylight, he saw Charlie Bryson standing outside a typical thatch-roofed family home raised on stilts on the edge of a village. The American looked grim. Out of sorts, even. There'd be no hugs this time.

The house stood surrounded by a low, broken fence. A high wooden gate yawned in front of the building like gallows. The village spread across a low knoll, a great vantage point with a 360-degree panorama of rolling, almost featureless hills. The highlands of Saxony-Anhalt in autumn couldn't have looked more desolate.

Mikhail would have to keep his distance. There was no rock or tree cover and no way for anyone to creep up on their meeting. Not even a sniper, Maier feared.

"Well, Merry Christmas, Maier. I thought we'd meet again. I made you right then in the Insomniacs Club. You're Julia Rendel's sniffer."

The American wore the uniform of his MIA outfit. He'd recently shaved his head, which gleamed like a lopsided bowling ball. He'd kept the walrus moustache. Neither the haircut nor the furry lip extension made him any more welcoming or agreeable than on their first encounter.

Maier stood with his hands bound and slowly stopped squinting into the pale light. He could see for miles. Besides the village, a collection of fragile looking huts teetering on the edge of insignificance, there was no other sign of habitation. No shopping centers, theme parks, airports or other distractions. Except for the men around the house, the world was empty. A cool wind blew around them and kicked up dust beneath the hut. A family of chicken picked its way through life underneath the modest building. A bow-legged, slack-backed sow roamed the trail that led to the rest of the village, followed by a brood of mud-splattered piglets. Two more black SUVs stood parked near the hut. It was the perfect place for a hostage trade-off.

Maier had nothing to trade.

The old American walked around his de facto prisoner. The driver and guard leaned against the car he'd arrived in and smoked.

"I see you lost a couple of fingers on your left hand there, Maier.

Laos getting to ya? Better be careful or there won't be anything left of you by the time the little cooperation I have in mind for us is through."

"Where is Kanitha?"

Bryson coughed and spat onto the ground next to Maier.

"Still into young girls, then? Well, she's around. Though she's traded you in for a slightly younger model. But you might get to see her alive before you expire. That depends on how we progress from here."

Bryson emphasized the first syllable of progress.

As Maier considered the hammy aspect of his predicament, the hair on his arms stood up again. He scanned the hills around the village. There was nothing to see but shifting monochrome grasses and pastel horizons. But the electricity was changing. He knew what was likely to happen shortly. He knew that Bryson and his gang wouldn't get what they wanted. He knew he had nothing to worry about. He knew. For the first time in his life, he felt loved by a father, no matter how crazy this father might be, loved unconditionally, the way he'd always wanted to love somebody. He also knew that this longing was deeply rooted in him and that reality never played out the way one imagined it.

Never.

19

A BULLET FOR WELTMEISTER

BRYSON MUST HAVE PICKED up the change in the atmosphere. He barked at his enforcers. Three more armed men, younger and meaner, their eyes hidden behind wrap-around shades, emerged from the hut. They clung to automatic rifles and binoculars. They wore little earpieces and looked like B-movie actors on steroids. One of the men carried a guitar instead of a gun. Vince Laughton, the owner of the Insomniacs Club, dressed all in black, wearing a bulletproof vest and looking decidedly uncomfortable in this get-up, followed them. Maier doubted the rotund Canadian had any idea how ridiculous he looked.

Vince grinned at the detective with a sour expression filled with violence and sloth, "My grandfather was a pilot in World War II, Maier. He spent the war killing fucking Germans. Then he got shot down. Imagine how I fucking feel about that."

This guy could spoil all the fun with the f-word, Maier thought.

"Your girlfriend is German, in case you hadn't noticed."

Vincent stepped up to Maier and hit him in the stomach. Maier dropped to the ground retching and watched the chicken, surprised the Canadian had it in him to resort to violence.

"My ex-girlfriend since you fucked her in Hamburg. I don't take kindly to that kind of thing."

He moved in to hurt the detective, but Bryson restrained him, "Hey,

hey, hey. Take it easy. We need this guy. He's the only asset worth anything in this godforsaken place."

Maier groaned and cursed his captors. Whatever they hoped was out there amongst the jars, now was the time.

Bryson bent down and laughed, "Well, you know, in the end I couldn't help myself. I mean you broke my man's nose in Hamburg. It cost money to fix that. I told my friend Vince about Julia Rendel's unique recruitment drive. Vince, by the way, is an excellent help. He spotted you on the Nam Ou the other day. Eyes like a buzzard. Foul mouth. A real journalist. Good man to have around. Always thought Canadians were just pale Mexicans wearing anoraks. Anyway, I told Vincent what it had taken to extract Julia. If you hadn't slept with your client, he would never have come over to us."

"So where is she?"

"I lost three good men over that bitch. At first, I thought you'd sent these devils to free her, but now that I look at you, lying in the dust with fingers missing, that notion's clearly off the mark. We put her in a nice room in Luang Prabang, and then one morning last week, boom. Someone came in, killed my buddies, burned down half the building, freed the maiden and disappeared without a trace. A real pro operation. Reminded me of the old days. Audacious, brutal, efficient. Nice. Couldn't have done it better myself. Which makes me think… it wasn't you. You smell a bit like a loser. So you tell me. Where's Julia Rendel?"

Maier couldn't help smiling.

"I hope it wasn't on the national register, Bryson. They take that kind of thing serious in Luang Prabang."

The American threw him a sick look but remained calm.

"The Vietnamese getting to you, Bryson?"

"This wasn't a Vietnamese operation. They could've just walked in with the local cops and taken her out. No, there's another operator out there, silent as a grave, heavy as a Dallas hit. I mean heavy."

Maier said nothing. He liked the Amercan's comic turn of phrase. Bryson was growing on him.

"Well, I've a pretty good idea who it is. And you do too, I reckon."

Maier said nothing. Vince made moves towards Maier again, then thought better of it and angrily turned to the old American.

"Shut your fucking hole, Charlie. Let's get on with it. Let's string this creep up and see what happens. I wanna see some American justice done here."

Bryson straightened up and laughed.

"You really do have one filthy mouth on you, Vince. This isn't about justice. This is all about advantage. That's all. Let's not get all lofty here."

He waved to one of his goons, who disappeared promptly into the house. How many heavily armed Americans could one fit into a Laotian farmhouse?

"Fan out; keep your eyes peeled. I think we're close."

The old soldier didn't look worried. He took his time. He was dangerous. He nodded to the guitar player, who started playing a mournful country & western song.

Charlie Bryson liked his killing spiced up with a spot of entertainment, "We try to make our executions unforgettable experiences for everyone involved. It's all about projection, you know. Everyone loves a spectacle. It's all Triumph of the Will, really. In that respect, the Nazis got it just right."

Maier concentrated, not just on what this man had to say, but on how he said it. His southern drawl stretched slowly towards the hills before it was whipped away by the breeze.

Bryson got into one of the SUVs and backed it up until it faced the hut's front gate. He jumped out and opened the back doors. The last row of seats had been replaced by a mounted machine gun. It looked ready to assault.

Maier sat up and looked at Bryson, "I know where the gold is, Charlie."

The American laughed. "We do too, Maier. Léon's on our side. Remember? You've managed to alienate just about everyone who counts in this little saga. No one likes you, Maier. Or rather, no one likes your old man."

The CIA man clapped his hands, and seconds later Léon and Kanitha emerged from the hut. It was hard to tell who was prisoner and who wasn't. Things were confused. The guitar player switched to a slow, torturous flamenco. The execution threatened to slide into the absurd before it got started. Triumph of the swill.

"You see, Maier, without a bit of theatrics, we aren't going to get anywhere. If my hunch is right, Weltmeister's already in the building, so to speak. I mean, I got respect for the guy. Léon told me you're his son. That's why we're gonna test the father-son bond, right here and now. We're in the anger business. The music might just bring him along to where we want him."

Kanitha looked at Maier wide-eyed. Léon kept her close by his side. There was no way to communicate, no way to connect. Vince came up behind Maier and pulled him back to his feet. Despite his small size, the Canadian was strong and propelled by furies. His round, clean-shaven face was twisted with enough anger to turn water into turpentine. His thin, unsmiling lips moved silently, perhaps reciting a mantra that spelled revenge. He had a rope in his hand and looked like a man who'd dressed up for a futuristic round of cowboys and Indians. With some people, it was hard to imagine they'd ever had mothers. They seemed to have emerged into the world not from a woman, but from a hole in hell, birthplace of assholes.

"We gonna have ourselves a bit of old-fucking-fashioned Wild West fun here in the Wild East," he intoned with a football field's worth of glee surrounded by rusty barbed wire in his laconic manner.

He threw the noose around Maier's neck, tightened it and pulled the detective underneath the gate to the hut before throwing the rope across the gate's main beam and pulling it tight. It seemed unlikely, but he moved like a man who'd hanged people before and had taken a fancy to the process.

One of Bryson's soldiers pushed Kanitha forward. She pushed right back, but the agent slapped her just hard enough to make her fall. He dragged her underneath the gate. Léon looked on, his withered face impassive. So much for love. Maier wondered what kind of reunion they'd had since they'd escaped from the Vietnamese camp in Muang Khua.

"Well, Maier, in this game, you got to have some patience. We have been trying to find Weltmeister for a quarter century. And now we're getting close. And a little sacrifice here and there to draw him out of the tall grass is entirely reasonable."

Bryson scanned the scene around the village again.

"The hills have eyes," he murmured, more to himself than anyone else.

"We'll play a little game. A game of losers."

Two of Bryson's soldiers of fortune forced Kanitha to kneel down and motioned Maier to stand on her back. He didn't budge. They raised their guns. He took his shoes off. As gingerly as possible, he stepped on his partner in crime. She groaned. The noose tightened around his neck a second time. If he slid off her back he was done for. Cold sweat soaked his shirt in seconds. The guitar went into crescendo. The player began to stomp one foot on the dusty ground. He wasn't a bad player.

Bryson looked satisfied and smiled down at Kanitha, "I know, I know, he's a big man. Far too big for such a delicate waif as yourself, little lady. Next time, choose your bedfellows more carefully."

He pulled a length of cotton string from his pocket, threw one end to the girl and ordered her to wrap it around her fist until it was taut.

"I'm telling you this because you're a Buddhist, and you'll get a next time."

He walked to the car, trailing string, and tied the other end to the machine gun's trigger. After some maneuvering, the gun's muzzle pointed at Maier's stomach and the string was taut. Bryson snapped the gun's safety off. Vincent positioned himself in front of Maier and stared up at the detective.

"If you fall, you hang. If she moves, you hang. If she pulls the thread, you get shot. If she lets it go slack, I will shoot her. It's failsafe. In a few minutes, the pain on her back will be unbearable, or you will lose your balance or she'll let go of the string. So many possibilities. You better pray that Daddy is coming to bail you out."

Maier stared straight ahead across the hills into a bleak gunmetal sky. If he didn't move his head, he couldn't see a soul. The view was clear, all the way to heaven. He used the tension on the rope around his neck to lighten his weight on the girl's back, but it made little difference. He remembered Mikhail and Mr. Mookie, assuring him that a deal could be struck with the Americans. Some deal. Outnumbered and outgunned. The rope cut into his throat, but there was nothing to say anyway.

Kanitha cried, "You're very heavy, Maier. Not sure how long..."

The men fanned out in a semicircle around the makeshift gallows. Maier swayed. His eyes blurred. His shoulder stung. The girl groaned. The guitar player started a new song. The wind picked up and Maier could make out tall grasses sway back and forth as if led by the somber chord progressions. The gunman with the six-string started to sing.

Well, I'm tired and so weary but I must go alone, Till the Lord comes and calls, calls me away, oh, yes.

His voice carried well. Maier, sorely tempted to give in to unreason, grasped the beauty in everything, even as Vincent leant in and feinted a kick to the detective's legs. Maier no longer cared about his torturer. All was forgiven. The game was up. Time rushed on. He met Bryson's eye. The American didn't look happy. Perhaps he didn't enjoy executions. But that was all irrelevant now. The sky went time-lapse. The clouds opened and the sun broke through and lit the moment in an unearthly light. And everything was good and blue. The abyss was near, and this time there'd be no return. Maier remembered the kind of things one was said to remember in these last lucid seconds – the sea, his mother, a long-lost love, her breasts, his crippled hand.

There'll be no sadness, no sorrow, no trouble, trouble I see, There will be peace in the valley for me.

The wind picked up. Bryson's men moved in closer. These guys didn't want to miss a little death on the range. They were keen to see Maier hang. He swallowed hard. The guitar player strummed his last chord.

20

THE COMEDOWN

THE FIRST SHOT cut the rope. Maier dropped to the ground. He fell so quick, he didn't see the shooter emerge from the sliding door of one of the cars parked next to the house. As he fell, Kanitha pulled hard at the cotton string wrapped around her fist. The machine gun in the back of the SUV jerked hard to the left and started spitting bullets.

"Fuck," Vincent coughed as he took a hit in the throat and slammed into the dust next to Maier, leaking life and fear for all they were worth.

Bryson's men scattered, but the shooter from the car was fast and took out the two soldiers closest to Maier. Maier and Kanitha crawled away and hid behind the vehicle that held the automatic weapon. Maier slunk to the SUV's door. The Americans had their hands full and paid them no attention. The front seats were empty and the key stuck in the ignition. Maier jumped in and started the engine. The steering wheel was slippery in his sweat-soaked hands. As the girl jumped in next to him, he put his foot down and the heavy four-wheel drive jerked forward. He slammed the gear stick into second and hit the bumpy road on which he'd arrived, bound and blindfolded, an hour earlier. The mayhem receded quickly in the rear-view.

Léon popped up in front of the windshield. Maier almost pushed his foot through the floor of the car as he hit the brakes.

He stalled the engine. A shot shattered the window and passed between him and the girl. The Hmong, a desperate grin on his face, was gone as quickly as he'd appeared, jumping into the tall grass to the side of the road.

Maier hesitated. The man they all claimed to be his father was somewhere behind them, killing people. He was very close. Maier had never met his father, a father who'd just saved his life. A man who could shock the world with his secrets, they'd said. A man wanted by intelligence agencies across the planet. A father, everyone had been telling him, who'd brought him into this case in the first place.

His father.

Father.

Dad.

Son.

"Let's go," Kanitha screamed, and shook him out of his stupor.

Maier restarted the engine and gunned the accelerator. The car howled and they raced forward, into the hills. After ten minutes of dust and potholes, they hit a larger road. Maier stopped the car and got out. He told Kanitha to wait and ran up a small outcrop the shape of an upturned soup bowl, a hundred meters off the road. At the top, he stood breathing heavily, trying to get a sense of himself, trying to get a grip. He was alive. Kanitha was alive. They'd escaped.

He could see most of the trail they'd come along. Smoke rose in the distance and he hoped his father hadn't burned down the entire village. No one had followed them.

Weltmeister had saved the day.

Kanitha shuffled up the hill, took his arm and leant into his side.

"You came for me. You saved my life."

Maier remained silent.

"I killed Vince," she added solemnly, her voice brittle with stress. He pressed her close, but he couldn't feel a thing. He had no words for her or anyone. He just stood for a while, catching his breath, listening to his heart trying to escape from his chest, scratching his neck where the rope had cut him. Kanitha pulled at his shirt and started descending the hill towards the car.

"Come on, Maier, I'm wasted; we need to get out of here. Miles to go before we sleep."

When they got back to the vehicle, Charlie Bryson stood waiting for them.

21

FRIENDSHIP

LAOS, SEPTEMBER 1973

Beginnings were easy. Dressed in black fatigues, his face darkened by paint, a black cotton skullcap on his head, Weltmeister slipped out of his hooch and made his way down to the runway. For a few hours each night, Long Cheng was silent, before supply planes and bombers started landing and taking off at the crack of dawn. For almost eight years, the secret US base had been the nerve center of the war in Laos. He was at the heart of things, a heart no one knew existed.

He'd picked a moonless night. His friends, Cronin, Taylor, Herr, Flitman and Daniels, would have passed out by now. He'd worked and drunk, killed and laughed with these guys for close to a decade. They'd shared good times and bad, both stateside and in Indochina's darkest jungles.

Nothing brought men closer together than the atrocities they committed in the name of God or country. They were tight. They were fighting the good fight. If they didn't look too closely at what they were doing, the professional justifications they were served by their handlers were sufficient to allow them to take pride in their work and to absolve them of the demons that arrived on the scene in the wake of rape and murder.

Weltmeister wasn't a drinker and he did look closely.

An owl sounded into the night, and Valentina's eyes, dark, almond-shaped, full of love and sorrow, washed over him briefly, piercing his heart deeper and more painfully than any bullet could. Bullets were easy; love was a killer. His mind played with the fringe of her short black hair, put his arms around her waist and remembered her sitting on top of him, moving gently like a tide, while he gripped her wide mother-hips and cried, eclipsed by the closest thing he knew to that feeling that bled across all the others. No one else had ever seen Weltmeister cry and no one ever would. It was near impossible to be a romantic and a pragmatist at the same time, but these were the cards he'd dealt himself. And he was about to play his last trump.

He was certain he'd never see Valentina again. No one came back from the secret American prison in Cuba. They had him by the throat.

In war, everything and everyone eventually became expendable. Everyone became a lever in the pursuit of Realpolitik. And that included the love of America's most sophisticated assassin. He had a feeling for catastrophe. He'd juggled it often enough, but now the different elements of control, loyalty, action and reaction had slipped from his hands. Weltmeister was on the way out. The darkest recesses of the US government had decided that its most prized asset was disposable.

The phone call from the Secretary had been personal and succinct. The secret bombing of Laotian villages would need more justification. One day soon, the querulous American public would want answers.

Weltmeister, a man rarely surprised, was taken aback by the loathing the Secretary expressed towards his countrymen's intelligence. The agency man had been in the game long enough to get a feel for when he was getting fucked. A word he didn't use often or lightly and only to himself.

Weltmeister was a private man.

He rechecked his gun, a German Luger, a 1969 reissue produced by Mauser in Oberndorf. He'd been given the old Nazi favorite by a black GI called Leroy in Danang a couple of years earlier. He liked the irony of Leroy's gesture as well as the weapon itself. He'd killed with it before. The Luger was precisely that marriage of romanticism and pragmatism he so often missed in life. He screwed the silencer on.

During the night, he'd disassembled the weapon several times, fastidiously cleaned and oiled each part, put it back together, loaded, unloaded, reloaded. He'd tied a snub-nosed .38 Special to his left ankle, no silencer, noisy bang-bang death in its short barrel.

He didn't expect any challenges. He'd killed many times before. But even in his world of far-out values, this was different. This job would propel him into a state of beyond he had glimpsed in the eyes of others, men and women he'd dispatched himself. For the first time in his long and illustrious career as spy and "cleaner," he'd run out of choices. He was about to do a great wrong. He'd step up to the edge of the abyss and tip forward into the darkness from which one could only return with fever dreams, with reports on loathing and defeat. He was about to cross the threshold that separated the men from the monsters and the good folks from the motherfuckers. He'd become an oblivion seeker, an outsider's outsider. Love could make a man lose everything, give up anything, do everything and anything. Love had a long breath and a short fuse.

He wiped the tears with the cloth his gun was wrapped in and started for the living quarters of the field agents. His mind turned to granite. Valentina's scent, her eyes, her shape, her essence slipped away. She became unreal, her perfume faded; her eyes retreated into the shadows, her words turned from song into memory. Today, he hated the metamorphosis. He hated getting into the killing state. But the sorrow of change turned quickly into a sense of liberation. Everything became easy in an instant. He was qualified. He knew how to do his job.

He was Weltmeister.

In complete silence, he made his way to the living quarters of the top CIA men who operated Long Cheng.

An owl's hoot followed him through the narrow alleys of wooden huts that housed the Hmong rebels and their dependents. He passed the house of their leader, General Vang Pao, unseen by his guards and carefully approached the shacks used by the Americans.

The free-standing house of the Sangsters loomed ahead, the only building one might have called a home in Laos' second largest city. Why Jimmy kept his wife and children in one of the most dangerous places on Earth was beyond Weltmeister. He'd never liked the man, a staunch ideologist who hated communists to a point where they no longer counted as human. For a while, Sangster had paid a fistful of dollars to the Hmong soldiers for every set of enemy ears they brought back from the front. Then one day, he'd flown up to a remote Lima Site in the far north of the country and noticed that all the

Hmong children who lived near the runway had had their ears cut off by their parents. Some get-rich-quick scheme. After that, he'd asked for heads. Weltmeister sighed into the silence. Everyone had their own reasons, obsessions and justifications for being in the spook business.

The low shack where the rest of the Americans slept was just ahead. He approached slowly, mindful of the shadows around him. He stopped in his tracks and crouched down into the soil as he caught a noise to his right, ever so obscure. A dog?

He sat, controlling his breath like a yogi, letting his eyes roam where there was nothing to be seen. A false alarm. He gripped the gun harder and checked the silencer one more time. He slid the safety off and waited. Nothing. And waited. He felt someone else breathing nearby, almost inaudibly. He could not exactly put his finger on the direction the faint sound came from. He tried to smell others in the darkness, but there was nothing. Perhaps he was overcautious.

It was time to go.

Weltmeister rose and moved quickly to the shack he had slept in countless times. The door stood ajar, as he'd hoped. Security was not an issue inside the dark heart of America's most secret base. These guys felt safe. He crossed the threshold unseen.

The bunks were occupied by the right men in the right state of inebriation. The room smelled of sweat and alcohol. He knew them so well; he could tell them apart by the way they inhaled and exhaled. They were his friends. He stepped into the center of the shack and thought of Valentina and how they'd taken her and how he'd run out of choices. It was the only way to go through with the unspeakable.

He moved between the two middle bunks and raised his gun. Weltmeister shot Cronin, the man closest to him, first and covered the weapon with a scarf to silence the slide action, then quickly put Flitman out and repeated the precautionary move. The third shot went into Herr's brain, just as Taylor, woken by the muffled gunfire and smell of cordite, raised his head and took a bullet in the throat. The medulla oblongata kill. Death came immediately.

Silence.

He was one man short of completing his assignment. Daniels was not in his bunk. He checked the bathroom. It was empty. The fifth man must have flown down to Vientiane for a debriefing or a spot of R&R.

There was nothing to be done. His handlers had screwed up. Or they'd simply screwed him.

He had one more chore to fulfill. He would shoot himself in the shoulder and bury the gun in a hollow under the floor he had prepared the previous day. Weltmeister didn't worry about shooting himself. He knew how to inflict a horrific-looking but ultimately harmless wound which would divert attention from his involvement in an incident that was bound to rock the war establishment. No one would suspect an injured survivor. For a second, he grinned at his own audacity. The Secretary knew that Weltmeister was still the only man for the most difficult jobs. That's why he was being sacrificed.

He turned around and caught the eye of young Léon Sangster in the shack's window. The boy recoiled in fright and ran into the night.

Weltmeister had been seen. He wasn't sure whether the boy had managed to get a good look at him. Change of plan.

Ten minutes later, America's most secretive assassin, frequent visitor to the White House and treasurer of American dreams, crossed Skyline Ridge. He killed a young Hmong guard who, half asleep, stepped in his way, probably wondering what the commotion in the valley below was about the instant he died. Long Cheng had woken up. Léon must have alerted his parents. Troops fanned out beyond the runway. In the cold dawn of war, Weltmeister threw one more glance at America's secret city. Then he started walking east, towards Vietnam. He'd lost his love and his country. It was time to lose himself. He'd need to find another employer to stay alive. One day, perhaps, he would reclaim it all.

PART II

WELTMEISTER

22

THE WHITE HOUSE

HAMBURG, DECEMBER 2001

The Weiße Haus an der Alster, Hamburg's White House, a handsome late nineteenth-century building located in the Rotherbaum quarter of Germany's wealthiest city, had seen several illustrious owners. During the war, the sprawling property had served as the Nazis' city headquarters. Following Germany's defeat, the British squatted the grounds until the US purchased the Hamburg White House in 1950 and opened a consulate a year later.

Sundermann liked the striking edifice, though he hadn't come to admire the architecture. He'd never been inside the consulate, but there'd been no question of refusing a personal invitation. The consul's PA had informed the owner of Hamburg's most prestigious detective agency that the casual meeting would touch on one of his most troubled cases, Maier's gold saga in Laos.

Now he stood in front of the building, collecting his thoughts, arranging his very expensive tie and wiping his delicate rimless glasses on a fine cotton kerchief. Sundermann never rushed into things. He had his detectives to do that, on the ground. In the lofty social stratospheres, the agency boss operated in, reticence, detachment and discretion were the most useful tools for survival. Of course, he was being watched, and if he stood in front of the building long enough, security would come out and question him, no matter how much his Armani suit cost.

America had just been attacked and the world was nervous. But he was ready. And on time.

As he approached the main gate, he could see that his visit was of some importance. A woman and a man dressed in business suits just slightly less snappy than his own were waiting.

It was time to get out of the miserable November rain.

"You see, we have a very delicate situation on hand here," the consul intoned while playing with her coffee cup. She was a rather large woman, a career diplomat from the Midwest who'd made it to a prestigious coastal school and done well. Sundermann guessed Pennsylvania, Boston, foreign shores. Hamburg was a good posting.

The man was a different customer, a hard face attached to a fighter's body gone to seed, a player who'd seen America's interests around the world rise and wane for decades. He'd most likely put his boot in a few times to improve the country's prospects. He was completely bald and, like Sundermann, in his late fifties, perhaps a little older. The over-the-top walrus moustache should have made him look like a kind uncle. It didn't.

The consul's name was Lieb, which she pronounced Liab, perhaps a subconscious move to distance herself from her German ancestry. First name Margaret. A bit nervous, compulsively flicking her shortish hair – dyed red – from her wide forehead with voluminous fingers.

She introduced the man as Bryson. No position, no job description.

Sundermann opened his file on the Laos case and scanned Maier's reports. He had all the pertinent information in his head, but he wanted to settle into the mood of the somber room and its occupants. No point rushing into anything with Ms. Velvet Glove and Mr. Rottweiler across the table, both laden with expectations. He took in a rather heavy painting of settlers with high collars, offering baubles to naked Native Americans, before turning his attention back to his two disparate hosts.

"Detective Maier's off the case. He lost two fingers in a shoot-out. He also reported that you guys almost executed him in order to draw out a German double agent from the Cold War days who some people claim to be his father. A rather outlandish scenario. Should I get in touch with the authorities to inform them that the CIA kidnaps and tortures German citizens in third countries?"

The consul hid behind her files and said nothing. Bryson took control of the conversation, cutting right to the issue.

"You ever heard of an agent called Weltmeister, a German guy, a veteran with decades of experience in the field? A double agent, as it turned out."

Sundermann shrugged. "I've already heard all this from my own man, Maier. This story about a mythical US operative and an obscure file that you and the Vietnamese would like to get their fingers on is a little fantastical. Good for you if it turns out to be something of substance. The fact that this man might be of German origin is neither here nor there. And I don't see why you almost hung Maier from a village gate. And if indeed this man who you say is his father freed him and killed several of your men, then why would it be my business to influence my detective one way or another in relation to this situation? If your scenario's true, this is a rather personal affair."

Lieb raised her hands in a conciliatory manner, "This is all a misunderstanding. We've been on edge since the attacks on New York and the Pentagon. Our foreign policy is evolving faster than the Internet, and the executive branch is rewriting the way we deal with the rest of the world. America is at war, Mr. Sundermann. And this meeting should serve in part as an explanation to your detective as well as to you. We'd rather you didn't involve German authorities. Trust me, apart from hunting down the terrorists who killed so many people on 9/11, the 'Weltmeister' case is the top foreign affairs priority at the White House this week."

She chuckled modestly into her double chin and continued. "And I don't mean our cozy little Weiße Haus an der Alster, I mean the real deal in DC. The President himself is looking at how we screwed up in Laos. Then and now, by the way. And we need to get things right before…"

Lieb didn't finish her sentence. Sundermann turned to Bryson.

"Maier told me it was you who personally set up his hanging. He reported that you used a female Thai journalist as his footstool for your makeshift gallows. Are you people out of your minds?"

Bryson grinned at the German without a hint of contrition. "Well, let's not ride our moral bicycles through the parking lot here. Your man's in Laos to find his father. I'm in Laos to find his father. The Vietnamese have lost one of their top intelligence operators in the pursuit of his father. They lost soldiers. I've lost soldiers. I admit, it's all a bit Alice in Wonderland out there, and we did abuse privileges between friends. But if Weltmeister isn't caught soon, we'll have an international spy scandal on our hands that'll put the Guillaume affair to shame. This man whom we thought dead for decades sits on information so compromising, it might lead to a very unfavorable rewriting of our recent history. It could lead to nasty political purges both in the US and in Vietnam at a sensitive time. A bilateral trade agreement between the US and Vietnam is about to come into force. I mean, this German used to be a guest in the White House, a trusted man, a good friend to our then Secretary of State. He turned and sold us out to the commies in 1973. And now he's back, and we think he wants to go public with our old laundry. We can't have that."

Sundermann laughed politely and made sure not to keep a hint of condescension from his voice, "You mean he fed Kissinger false intelligence? Are you serious?"

The Americans said nothing.

"Oh, well. Now you're breaking my heart. I am almost tempted to bring Maier back on the case just to expose a few old war crimes. But I guess that would be testing the great friendship between our nations?"

Sundermann caught himself and continued in a more conciliatory tone. "Consul, Mr. Bryson, please, understand my irritation. There's a need to look at this affair with utmost sobriety. I run a respectable and well-connected business, not a fly-by-night outfit of divorce investigators and sleaze peddlers. My agency isn't interested in decades-old political crimes unless they become pertinent in current cases we've been asked to investigate. I answered your request for a meeting on a voluntary basis. And we have something called a Rechtsstaat in Germany at present. It means rule of law. I'm sure you've heard of it."

Bryson was staring at the agency boss with barely suppressed anger, when Lieb interjected softly, "Let's not get all twisted up here. We're all friends in this room. What Mr. Bryson would like to move towards here today is cooperation."

Sundermann countered, "Detective Maier is one of my best men. He gets outstanding results. And he's seriously injured at this point. He's off the case and no longer in Laos…"

Bryson interjected angrily, "Put him back on the case or we'll make some calls and close your agency. And you can go on food stamps or whatever they call it here and kiss your nice suits goodbye."

The consul, wearing a pained expression, waved Bryson's threats away and added, "That would be a last resort."

Bryson snorted at the diplomat, "Last resort, my ass, Margaret Lieb. And listen, Sundermann, if we don't catch this Weltmeister guy, and if he publishes the contents of the U48, then some of our finest citizens will go to court and to jail, and our rapprochement with Vietnam will go down the toilet. Our influence in Southeast Asia will take a serious hit, and the man you describe as mythical will kill every single person who may be able to identify him. And that could include his son and, by association, yourself. If this particular scenario comes to pass, I swear to you, I'll personally chop you up after he is finished with you."

Sundermann took off his glasses, pulled his kerchief from his breast pocket and started meticulously cleaning the lenses.

"This U48? What exactly is it?"

The consul exchanged glances with Bryson. Sundermann doubted that she knew anything of any real value about this affair. No more than she absolutely needed to. Intelligence was very compartmentalized in the US, and even cooperating outfits often operated without any inkling of what their colleagues were up to in the same theater.

But Margaret Lieb answered, hesitantly, "A secret file containing information about some obscure but pertinent details of our involvement in Vietnam."

Sundermann looked at her impassively, "Surely there are countless files like that floating around. And this is all history."

Bryson cut in, "As we explained, the contents of this one are explosive. We believe Weltmeister is planning to sell to the highest bidder."

"Can you furnish me with evidence? Or is this a kind of Tonkin Bay maneuver to get my detective into a fray he doesn't belong in?" Sundermann quipped.

The two officials in front of him glanced at each other and remained silent.

Sundermann laughed politely, "You must have done something stupid if this Weltmeister was one of your top agents and went into business for himself. A little respect goes a long way, gentlemen."

Bryson countered, "Well, the only mistake we made was that we didn't kill this guy when we realized he was turning into a monster.

But there's no point crying over spilled milk that has since turned to cheese. We're pragmatic people, Sundermann. We live very much in the here and now. We want Weltmeister and his file, and we'll get both. We can't have our country's secrets on the open market."

The German smiled sardonically.

"Then you better pray that no one ever hacks into all these computers of yours. Imagine all the dirty laundry that would spill into the street. It would be on the wrong side of depressing."

Bryson nodded, "Well, it ain't our computers I am tasked with keeping secure. That'll be some other guy you should talk to."

Sundermann got up.

"Ms. Lieb, Mr. Bryson, it's been an interesting meeting. But these problems you have with your Weltmeister have little connection with the Sundermann Detective Agency. And they may not affect my case. Though I do see that they might. I'll talk to Maier. Another file, as damaging as your U48, which outlines the threats uttered as part of this conversation as well as the details of your mock execution, is being created and will shortly make its way to representatives of the German government. And believe me, I'm trusted in the corridors of power. You can flout international law in a small, developing country like Laos. You've done it before; you'll do it again. 9/11 will encourage guys like you, Bryson, to murder people you have no evidence against. Before you know it, you'll get carte blanche from your president to kill with impunity. America will be disliked around the world and Germany may well be coerced into covering your asses. But today, the buck stops here."

He stopped to observe the CIA man stare into space defiantly. Mr. Rottweiler was probably one of those public servants that couldn't be corrupted by money or by the enemy, but he was dangerous. He'd always follow orders. He'd never question his handlers.

"In the meantime, don't get so emotional. If you want cooperation, make a deal. Offer me something other than threats. If you want me to consider putting Maier on site, do me two favors."

Lieb opened her arms in a conciliatory gesture and looked at Sundermann questioningly. He was certain she had no idea about espionage, though she apparently felt safe as long as proceedings were wrapped in the language of diplomacy.

"I'm looking for an operator, a freelancer, currently active in Laos.

His name is Mikhail. Second name unknown. A Russian. Homosexual and extrovert. Extremely skilled. He's involved."

The consul looked dumbstruck, but Bryson betrayed no reaction at all.

"If you have a file on him, I want his file. I want more than his file. I want to meet Mikhail. If you help me get to the Russian, I'll get Maier back on the case."

Bryson asked, his voice dripping with menace, "And what was the second favor?"

"Keep your fingers off my detective. Stop threatening me, my agency or my operatives. I'm not a government official and I can't be strong-armed by a CIA assassin with a nice mug of coffee in his hand. In the event of another incident like the one on the Plain of Jars, this meeting along with the case file accumulated by my operative will be made available not just to German authorities but to the global media. Trust me, the sympathy the US have garnered from the attacks on the World Trade Center will evaporate in no time at all. It'll crumble as soon as it becomes obvious that you're killing innocent people in poor countries. I thought you guys had packed that in after Vietnam."

The room fell silent. They sat facing each other, playing the roles they'd been assigned in life. Eventually, Bryson got up, walked across to the German and offered his hand.

"It's a deal. You get the Russian. He's not our man, but we have a line on him. We get Weltmeister. And we keep our hands off your sorry outfit. It's a price we're happy to pay. But we better be quick. And that includes Maier."

Sundermann knew instinctively that the agent's promises were almost worthless. He tried to meet the consul's eye, but Lieb preferred to stare at her carpet instead. These guys weren't happy. Someone else was out there, wanting a piece of the man they called Weltmeister. Someone more ruthless than Bryson and his Vietnamese counterparts put together.

He got up and shook hands.

It was still raining as Sundermann stepped outside. A cold winter drizzle, with ambitions to turn into sleet, molested the city. He walked away from the consulate to the Außenalster, an entirely artificial body of water which looked a great deal more genuine in the dying afternoon light than the farewell expressions worn by the two Americans.

These people always expected others to accept their sense of destiny. Everyone had a destiny.

Even Detective Maier did.

The agency boss pulled his phone from his coat and dialed his operative's number. It was time to put his best man back to work. Getting their hands on Weltmeister before the Americans and Vietnamese or other contenders did would be one hell of a scoop for Sundermann. Getting the lowdown on the Russian would be a nice bonus. It was a win-win situation, as the Americans liked to say. And he was looking forward to a bit of sunshine.

23

PARADISE

THAILAND, JANUARY 2002

MAIER LAY IN HIS HAMMOCK, counting the fingers on his left hand. He'd been counting for days. Christmas and New Year had come and gone, and he was still counting. He got to three fingers and two half fingers, then he started counting again.

The Thais had done a good job operating a second time, re-sculpting the stumps, into, well, stumps. Better stumps. Supreme stumps. The Thais were good at surgery. They'd also crafted him two state-of-the-art metal prosthetics.

He could still feel the end of his fingers. Touching the cold metal was reassuring. There was still something there. For now, the claws, as he called them, remained in the smart plastic box they'd come in.

He picked up a three-day-old copy of the Bangkok Post that was fluttering around the porch of his bungalow. Crooked politicians, unfeasibly large kickbacks, murderous generals, and a beauty pageant for fat women filled the front page. A short article in the bottom right corner caught his eye.

Former US Secretary of State on unprecedented visit to Laos to advise on investment. Bilateral trade agreement soon.

Maier lingered on the story. Was it a coincidence? American politicians always did trips to poor countries around the globe to level the way for US businesses into new markets. But Kissinger? Maier was surprised the grand old man of Realpolitik even got a visa from his old enemies. Obviously, the collective memory of the guys in the politburo was failing. The detective shrugged. This was all about wood, coffee and geopolitics. The Americans and Chinese were looking at expanding existing plantations on a massive scale. Local and international environmental organizations were protesting against the plans, which involved logging huge swathes of forest.

Kanitha had taken her skimpiest bikini for a walk down the beach and now ambled towards him from the waterline like a pocket-sized Ursula Andress. The Gulf of Thailand stretched like a lazy, luxurious blanket into the hazy distance of the tropical morning. To Maier, the girl was an expression of his limbo. He was off the case, his boss had seen to that, but Kanitha was part of the case. Every time he looked at her, the Laos quagmire came flooding back.

Sundermann had told him to write this one off. The client, Julia Rendel, had disappeared. Her fee had been spent. The gold hadn't been found. Everything pointed away from the loot, anyhow.

"Maier, there's a man coming down the beach, trying to take your attention away from me."

Maier raised himself out of the hammock quickly.

She grinned and threw a handful of sand in his direction. "Hey, relax, it isn't Weltmeister."

He shook his head. She was right. He wasn't himself. He was nervous.

Sundermann, wiping his glasses, stepped onto the porch, carrying nothing but a small overnight bag.

"Morning, Maier. How are the fingers?"

Maier raised his hand, "Gone."

Kanitha had disappeared inside the hut. With his good hand, Maier handed his boss a bottle of water and motioned him to sit on the only chair the porch had to offer. Sundermann dropped the bag next to Maier and sat.

"What are you doing here?"

"Come to check up on you. The Sundermann Detective Agency is worried. And, by the looks of it, with good reason."

"I'll be OK."

"You'll be dead."

Maier raised his eyebrows.

"You know things I don't."

It was not a question.

The older German laughed gently, "Of course I do. I'm your boss. And I've come to save your life. You're back on the case."

Maier was impressed. He'd envisaged time stretching into sunny infinity, a moderate retirement package and a beautiful woman to share his days, plenty of sunsets to mourn his fingers. Retirement, for the first time in his life, didn't sound like a dirty word.

Out in the bay, two men were racing a jet ski that sounded like a slowly approaching mechanical bee. Probably Russians, Maier thought.

"I answered an invitation to the White House on your behalf, Maier."

"I'm that important?"

Sundermann took a swig from the bottle and put it on the porch's banister.

"The Hamburg White House."

Maier grinned. "Still, I feel honored. Were they pleased I didn't try to kill their man Bryson in a fit of rage after he tried to execute me?"

"Bryson was present at the meeting. As was the rather ineffectual consul. A woman called Lieb. But they made their point. Unfortunately, the real White House is alarmed. We bit into a rather large fish this time, Maier, and it's make-or-break for me, too. Our reputation is on the line. Your life is on the line."

Kanitha stepped out onto the narrow porch, nodded at Sundermann and scanned the water.

"Those bloody Russians and their jet skis. Last week they killed a kid off the beach in Phuket. The cops tried to blame it on sharks."

The two men in the bay made their vehicle jump and spin, slowly washing closer to shore. Maier watched them distractedly. They looked like Russians, all right: skinheads, bodybuilder figures, Terminator shades, big tattoos, no smiles, despite the stupid twirls they managed to execute on their ride. Maier had a better tattoo.

Sundermann switched to English.

"Bryson's on our side, Maier."

The detective laughed sourly.

"Of course he is. That's why I didn't kill him after we escaped the mayhem on the PDJ. I do admit, he's a weird one. More sophisticated than he looks. He tried to kill me in true American showbiz fashion and then begged to hitch a ride with us when we managed to escape. How weird is that?"

"That's why I am here. To fill you in. And to check whether you're ready for work."

Sundermann glanced at Kanitha.

"You look ready to me."

The girl threw him a dark look.

"I apologize, Kanitha. I'd like to offer you temporary employment. With the agency. We need all the help we can get. You have good contacts in the region. And you're in danger as much as anyone."

The girl stood looking at the older German as if trying to make up her mind whether to pull his hair out. But she said nothing and retreated into the bungalow again.

"So, fill me in on our glorious new collaboration with the nice folks at the CIA."

Sundermann put his hand on Maier's shoulder. The detective shrank back involuntarily. He didn't know his boss was the paternal type. Maier couldn't remember Sundermann ever touching him.

"Open the bag."

Maier reached down from the hammock and unzipped the canvas holdall. A snub-nosed revolver lay on top of the agency boss' neatly folded shirts. A box of ammunition lay next to it.

"It's loaded. It's serious, Maier. Something could happen any time."

Maier sighed. "I don't like guns. And those shirts of yours probably cost more than your peashooter."

"Times change, Maier. We have to change with them or we go under. Weltmeister's coming and the world lives in fear of what will happen. He has plans. And he's your dad."

Maier felt sick as he listened to his boss' advice. Paradise was but a moment, and he could see it slipping though his remaining fingers like the fine sand on the beach in front of him. He wiped the sweat from his forehead.

"That remains to be seen. And the Viets and the Americans want to shut him down because he has a thirty-year-old file up his backside. So what? He's not coming for me."

He pushed the bag away and sank back into the hammock.

Sundermann touched his shoulder a second time, "Maier, don't lie to yourself. I'd love to give you a month off, to get over the trauma, come to terms with the loss of your fingers, forget the case, enjoy your very enjoyable company, but it's not going to happen. Your father will make the world explode. He has scores to settle. Old, old injustices are about to be revenged. And he called you out here, to his side. To bear witness. Your father's the first messiah of the twenty-first century."

Maier snorted. One of the jet ski riders fell in the water and the infernal buzzing stopped as the vehicle slowed fifty meters off the beach.

"I guess I should shoot these two thugs out there first," Maier laughed, "Then we can deal with the messiah."

Sundermann got up and stood facing the sea. The first shot hit him in the shoulder and he tumbled backwards. Maier spun out of the hammock onto the porch. The man who'd fallen off the jet ski stood waist-deep in the water and let off a second round from his semi-automatic, which ripped past Maier into the bungalow.

"Kanitha!"

The jet ski driver cranked up his engine and started accelerating towards the hut. A third shot ripped into the floor of the porch.

"Kanitha."

No answer.

Sundermann had slid into the sand in front of the hut, bleeding heavily. Maier grabbed the bag, pulled the revolver out and flicked off the safety.

He hated guns. But he took his time and aimed carefully.

He hit the man in the water square in the chest. The small gun almost jumped from his grip. Maier, shocked he'd found a target, rolled off the porch. Barely glancing at his boss, who was crawling behind the hut, the detective got up, brushed the sand off his chest and stepped into the light. He felt like lying in the sand and crying and never looking up into the sky again. But he was on his feet and started walking. The sun was behind him. Everything slowed down to the speed of sound and matter. Today, there would be no need for a sniper. Today, there was no longing for a father he had never known. Sundermann, he understood, was as close to family as he'd had in years. And Sundermann was down. Maier's will to live and fight back was very strong. His sacred tattoo burned into his back.

The jet ski ran out of water and slammed onto the beach, sliding towards the bungalow. The assassin jumped off in one fluid movement and sprinted towards Maier. The detective stood his ground and stared at what was coming with discontent. The world was on fire. He didn't need the CIA or the Laotians to tell him that. He didn't need to understand what was coming towards him right now. He raised his weapon with care and squeezed out a second shot. The jet ski pilot stumbled and fell. Maier felt tears running down his face. He didn't have the courage to turn. Had Kanitha been hit? Was Sundermann dead? He was too scared to check what was happening behind him. He marched forward, towards his attacker.

The man was alive and grappling for something in his pants. Maier stepped between the killer and the sun and shot him in the arm. The bullet from the peashooter almost severed his limb. His assailant stopped grappling; a slim throwing knife tumbled into the sand. Beyond the jet ski, which lay on its side pissing oil into the sand like a dying horse suffering from a last moment of incontinence, the water had turned red. The second man was drowning, slowly turning this way and that, his life seeping into the crystal-clear surf.

It was over. Almost. Maier stepped around the man on the beach. The assassin was still alive.

"What were you assholes thinking? And who are you working for?"

Maier reveled in his moment. He knew he was at his very worst. He didn't care for answers. He knew that he'd never wanted to arrive at this point. He could see himself walking past villages as they went up in flames. He pointed the gun at the killer's head. There was no fear in the man's eyes, just a whisper of disbelief and hate.

"Go to hell, you fucking kraut. We'll get you and your old man, dead or alive. This is just the beginning. And I'm not going to tell you anything."

Maier, in a daze, barely registered the man's American accent. Through his tears, he started laughing maniacally. He opened his eyes to let the man look inside.

"I don't want you to talk. I just want you to die. Don't fuck with the son of Weltmeister, my friend."

He pulled the trigger until the gun was empty. Times had changed. Oblivion-seekers ruled the land. Maier threw up into the sand next to the man he'd killed and passed out.

24

FATHER

Sitting in the Bangkok hospital's waiting room, Maier contemplated the benefits of technology. Helicopters were fine conveyances. The air ambulance that had plucked Sundermann from the beach had saved his boss' life after a passing boat of snorkelers had heard the shots and called the police.

The steel prosthetics the Thai doctors had given Maier were perfect tools to scratch his back with. Or someone else's back, for that matter.

But technology had its limits. Kanitha lay dead in the morgue a few floors below. Her parents, distraught, their lives smashed to pieces, their daughter lost to causes they couldn't comprehend nor cared for, had left. He hadn't even seen her after he'd collapsed next to his second victim. Bryson, gross Charlie Bryson, had broken the news, told him a headshot had disfigured her. Maier had no idea yet how Bryson had found out about the shooting and the medevac.

Maier was both empty and nervous. He was in a different place, a dark corner, full of anger and resentment at the cards he'd been dealt. His batteries were depleted, the joy for life punched out of him. Not since he'd lost his best friend to a bomb in Cambodia four years earlier had Maier felt so lost, so utterly alone, so ridden with guilt and regret. Sundermann, who'd instructed Maier to disappear, now lay sedated in ICU. Maier had ignored his order.

Bryson, who'd been at his side ever since the detective had gotten back to the Thai capital, forever wiping his bald plate and wittering on about security, only made it worse. Friend or foe, the man was a snake.

Sundermann would make it. The bullet had not hit any vital organs. Infection was unlikely. Thailand had good hospitals. Squadrons of nurses fussed around his boss, offering everything from new dressings to marriage proposals.

Kanitha had nothing to make. She would never smile again, never love again, never ridicule Maier for his hang-ups again. In time, her loss would turn into a wound. One day, the wound would close. Unless it got infected.

Maier almost wished for that infection. It would distract from his seething anger. It would slow the desire to murder a little more.

The gunmen had not been identified. The local papers talked of a Russian hit on German holidaymakers, with an unidentified Laotian woman the only casualty. The kingdom was so used to acts of violence and backroom monkey business perpetrated by foreign gangsters that the police, once briefed by the US and German embassies, were busy brushing the affair under the table. Thailand's reputation as a safe destination for millions of international holidaymakers was on the line. The tropical fantasy of the world's most easy-going playground, a clever marketing ploy the country had nurtured ever since seven million Americans had washed through during the Vietnam War, had been shaken and stirred. In the coming days, the apparent freak incident on a relatively remote beach would be explained away in a couple of lackluster newspaper paragraphs, and no one would ask pertinent questions. Thailand's Teflon image rested on this kind of crisis management. The local media was easily malleable, routinely threatened and paid by the government. Ethical reporting was dangerous and consequently almost unheard of.

Only now did Maier contemplate the softness of her skin, her sharp wit, the quiet encouragement and manic energy with which Kanitha had infused their brief moments together. He'd never let her close. He'd thought her too young. He hadn't really trusted her. But he hadn't stopped her from becoming more involved in his case either. Whatever suspicions he'd had about her motives, her death had neutralized them all. And now she was gone and his boss lay unconscious in intensive care, connected to countless tubes.

Distractedly, he ran his steel fingers along the metal arm of the chair he sat on, scraping off the hospital paint job. Bryson's phone rang. The American got up, nodded at the detective and walked off down the hall, barking into his device. Maier shuffled around in his seat. The corridor he sat in, in front of Sundermann's bed, lay deserted. All he could hear was the beeping of machines, of respirators keeping the seriously sick alive, and someone coughing desperately. It was around lunch and Maier assumed that most of the nurses were on their midday break. He was alone, for the first time since the attack on the beach.

"Maier, don't turn around."

The detective didn't recognize the voice. A German voice. Slight Saxony accent. Slightly overdone. He didn't know the voice, but he knew it for what it was. He started to turn but a heavy hand gripped his shoulder.

"You have to trust me on this one, Maier."

Maier relaxed back into his chair and stared straight ahead. The pressure on his shoulder diminished.

The man behind him chuckled, "Ruth didn't give you a first name? There must be one in your passport."

Maier had not spoken his first name in years. In his own world, in the construct he called life, he was just Maier.

"Ferdinand. But no one knows that."

A soft laugh rose from the other man. His voice had the subtle qualities of a good wine vintage, full-bodied, strong and aged.

"I'll keep your secret. Our secret. It might come in handy."

"Who are you?"

"Ah, Maier, you know who I am. I am Weltmeister. And I need your help. What's been started must be finished."

"Why don't you want me to turn around?"

The man behind Maier said nothing. Then he cleared his throat and said quietly, "I'm not ready."

Maier thought about it and replied, "There never is a good time."

"We have little time, good or bad, Ferdinand. Let's not waste it on essentials. We will have our moment. But first, we must... I must close down my legacy. Sometimes history throws a long shadow extending across a man's lifetime. Mine's coming to an end. I'm old. I'm not as strong and efficient as I used to be. But neither is the opposition, however formidable it thinks it is."

"Did you bring me to Laos?"

"I did."

"You used me in your damn schemes?"

"I did."

"And Julia was a set-up?"

"She was. She is."

Maier recoiled and the hand pressed down on his shoulder again. Someone nearby sighed and the detective stopped struggling.

"There's little time now for this, Ferdinand. Take it easy."

"Who's Julia Rendel?"

The voice behind him held its breath. The two men sat in near silence amongst the beeping machines.

"Julia's the daughter of Manfred Rendel, an old friend of mine whom I killed in Long Cheng in 1976. A useless man who was about to blow my cover."

Maier sat, waiting for more.

"And that's all you need to know about Julia right now."

Maier took note of the easy familiarity with which his father referred to his client. But he decided to stop pushing.

"Now there are others who want to expose me. I'll kill them all. Every last one of them."

Maier twisted uncomfortably in his chair.

"So, it's because of you I lost two fingers, my boss is lying over there with a bullet in his shoulder, and my girl is downstairs in the morgue."

"We're all responsible for our actions, Ferdinand. You know the risks. Kanitha knew what she was getting into when she hooked up with Léon Sangster. She wasn't innocent and she didn't do it for love. Your boss is a wily operator who'll come out of this as a winner. And so will you, your loss notwithstanding. But first…"

Maier brushed the hand off his shoulder. The touch electrified him, but he was unable to speak. Anger, sorrow and confusion raced through him.

The older man continued, "I have something that everyone wants. Information pertaining to the American War in Indochina, information as explosive today as it was then. Well, almost. Without it, I'm dead. I've kept it under wraps all these years. This information cost me dearly. I lost the woman I loved and I almost lost that which I now treasure most in this life, my anonymity. I thought it was all buried in the early Seventies, but people try digging it up again and again, for different reasons. The man who killed my wife, who betrayed me and the country I worked for, the man who made me change sides in the American War, is coming back. The two killers on the beach were his emissaries. They were like me, only younger and not as good. Otherwise, you'd also be dead."

Maier shook his head.

"But why did you abandon Ruth? You broke my mother."

He was suddenly overwhelmed by his father's presence. He no longer needed to turn around to see him. He just needed answers.

"All my life, anonymity has been my main weapon. And my passion. I loved your mother, but I was working as a US spy in Germany. She got pregnant, so as soon as you were born and I knew you were both healthy, I left her. I didn't even get to name you. My situation was too precarious. They'd have gotten to her. They get to everyone a guy like me loves. They'd have gotten to you, too. But over the years, the loneliness gets to everyone, even the best. I got married to a girl called Valentina, long after you were born. And I went off to work, and one day she was no longer there and I never found out how they killed her. I did the right thing with your mother. If I hadn't left her, she would've been killed. Instead, Valentina was murdered."

"You should've kept your hands off her, then," Maier retorted, but he realized in the same instant that he would have done the same. That his father was indeed his father.

"Sorry."

The man who called himself Weltmeister squeezed his shoulder once more, with less force. Maier reached out with his good hand and connected with old flesh. He tried to think of the gesture as comforting. He tried to feel something. For whom he wasn't sure.

"And now?"

"It started in Laos in 1973 and it will end in Laos. I'm not sure how it'll end, but I hope, I really, really hope that we'll be able to meet under better circumstances. It's my life's wish."

Maier tried for a long shot. "You're the sniper?"

"I am."

The detective inhaled deeply.

"Why did you shoot the old woman on the island? The boatman?"

The hand vanished from his shoulder. "I just wanted to see how persistent you are, whether you're up to it. Parents make mistakes, you know. And I'm sorry. So very sorry."

"Sorry you shot those people?"

Weltmeister coughed into the empty corridor.

"Not really."

Maier had no answer.

"I've been wanting to talk to my son for years, so many years. I was always watching from a distance, far away, seeing you grow up and do well. You're everything I hoped you might become. But I was never crazy enough to contact you. Too dangerous. Until now."

"And it has become less dangerous?"

"No, it just became more urgent."

The two men sat in silence.

Eventually, Maier snapped out of his thoughts. "So, now what?"

The older man laughed, not happily, "Now I'll set the world on fire. I'll close my life's story. I'll end the tyranny I've suffered under for the past thirty years, the tyranny of being a fugitive. I'll release my dark side into the world and challenge my old masters. And I want you to help me."

Maier shrugged defiantly, "How?"

The older man behind him sounded relieved, "You're reacting like a teenager angry with his old man, Ferdinand. I love it. Just trust me."

Maier didn't answer.

The hiss of an elevator door down the corridor made him turn his head. Bryson was running towards him, screaming, "Where is he?"

Maier turned but there was no one else. He was alone.

Weltmeister had left the building. And Maier hadn't even had a chance to ask what had happened to Julia.

He sighed. His father's words lingered.

25

PEACE IN THE VALLEY

LAO PDR, JANUARY 2002

"Of all places in Asia, why here? Why are we meeting here?"

Maier's mind loitered in an exotic semi-stupor. He was back at work. Early retirement hadn't worked out. It was hard to resist the Russian vodka and the freshly squeezed orange juice served by the painfully shy waitresses dressed in dark sarongs and shiny silk blouses who fussed around the group of middle-aged and jaded men. They sat on the shady balcony of the Phousi Hotel, one of the better addresses in town.

"The powers that be always meet in Luang Prabang. Historically, it's neutral ground. What's not to like?" Bryson replied lazily.

Sundermann, his arm in a sling, nursed a glass of expensive French wine. There'd been no shop talk. The conversation prattled on, tourism, bombs, economy, the impending visit of the former US Secretary of State. Maier kept his mouth shut. Nice stuff. No murder, no secret files, no explosive revelations. Like a couple of old friends. They all needed to work together, Sundermann said. His boss sounded like a politician. Bryson was polite, careful not to antagonize the detective.

Maier didn't like working with others. Not even with people who'd tried to kill him. He started digging his steel fingers into the white plaster of the balcony wall and watched as young backpacking tourists in the street below tried to discover the delights of Laos for as little money as possible, carrying hefty guidebooks in their hands. As his gaze drifted back to Bryson, he envied these kids. They didn't even know what bastards existed out here, on the fringes, just a few meters away from them.

The locals were setting up a street market to help the visitors spend their money. As the sun dipped into the hills to the west, they put up their stalls at a snail's speed, happy in the certainty that money would cash with very little effort. This was communist capitalism Laotian-style.

The two men he sat with exuded the charm of ancient reptiles about to devour the land beneath them. He wondered whether there was a sniper out there, training his sights on the balcony.

"Well, I know it's probably the last thing you expect from old Charlie Bryson, but I keep my promises, Sundermann. Of course, you guys know I'm not the sentimental type and I'm not looking for friends here, so just take it as good business practice."

The American got up and opened the door behind the small group.

"Surprise, surprise."

Mikhail, dressed in a loud shirt, Bermuda shorts and an unhinged grin partly obscured by strands of his long grayish-blond hair, stepped onto the balcony. A camera around his neck would have made him the archetypal package tourist. Instead, he carried a bottle in his hand.

"Ah, my friends, surrounded by lovely mamachtkas, guzzling high-quality vodka, waiting for the only real man with the only real game in town!"

Maier and Sundermann got up. The red-faced jolly giant opened his arms and embraced Maier. He was breathing heavily, as if he'd walked the four hundred kilometers up from Vientiane. He smelled, in equal parts, of expensive but carelessly chosen aftershave and pricey liqueur.

"Finally, we meet under a good sky, my handsome German friend."

His bear hug done, the Russian proceeded to vigorously shake Sundermann's good hand.

Maier's boss gave the huge man an appraising look and grinned, "A great opportunity to meet the elusive Mikhail. It might be the only one, so I won't waste my time. Are you for hire?"

The Russian roared with laughter loud enough to make heads turn in the street below and waved for one of the waitresses.

"I might be, once we have resolved our current conundrum. How is it that the Americans say? I keep you posted," he added with a wink towards Bryson

"We say, fuck off, you commie fag," the bald American retorted, but only Mikhail laughed.

"Ha, I've never worked for you guys and I never will. Americans are too uncertain. They always change direction when the going gets good. I blame the need for instant gratification. You're a young country. Immature. Not used enough to tragedy."

His next chuckle went straight into his glass, two thirds vodka, one third orange juice, with a few drops of mirth and anarchy to round off the flavor.

Bryson, Sundermann and Mikhail sat down. They were a little out of the ordinary, Maier thought, gazing at the odd team.

"You look like a bunch of heist vets."

This time, everyone laughed without smiling.

Bryson countered, "Well, I'm in, but this gotta be the worst place in the world to hit a bank. Biggest note is worth a couple of bucks. You'd have to bring a truck to move this monopoly money the commies trade in. But never mind; plenty of folks who start in the intelligence business go on to become gangsters."

"Ah, the Vietnamese would slap you, my American friend," the Russian interjected. "If there's any money in the banks here, it's probably theirs."

Sundermann struck his glass with a spoon and the lazy banter subsided. He turned to Mikhail.

"Are you still working for the Vietnamese?"

The huge man swallowed the last of his drink and waved for a refill.

He nodded severely, "You know how it is in this business. Never screw your client. I'm here representing Laotian and Vietnamese intelligence in my usual private capacity. My current employer, the very magnificent Mr. Mookie, sent me, and I have his trust. My old friend Maier had the rare honor to meet him and survive the encounter a couple weeks ago. Technically, Maier is working for us. But let's not snap spines here."

Mikhail laughed in Maier's direction. Everyone turned to the detective. Maier said nothing. He looked at his artificial fingers, then back at the men. What was happening to his life?

The Russian continued, "We're keen to make any deal to work with the CIA and your outfit on this, Sundermann, to find Weltmeister and talk him into coming in from the cold, so to speak, before the third party gets to him."

Maier shook his head. "And who might that third party be?"

Mikhail looked at the others.

No one answered.

Eventually, Bryson piped up, "We think the third party is American."

"The guys who attacked us on the beach in Thailand were Americans," Sundermann added.

Bryson looked to the street.

"These guys weren't government issue. At least not officially so. We might've trained them but they were working in a private capacity. Highly specialized machine operators. Very nasty. I mean very efficient."

He turned to Maier, "You did very well, detective, and I'm sorry you lost your little girl in the crossfire. These guys usually clean up. And you stopped them. Congratulations."

"That doesn't make me feel better, Charlie."

The American looked away and opened another beer.

Maier picked up the thread, "Basically, everyone and his dog is after a man called Weltmeister who may or may not be my dad–"

Bryson cut him off, "Stop playing games, Maier; I know he was at the hospital in Bangkok. You talked to him. He's your old man."

Maier nodded and grinned at Bryson, "He told me he's sick of being hunted and that he's turning the tables. He told me he's going to set the world on fire."

Bryson jerked back, then checked his composure.

"Sure looks like that," he agreed.

Mikhail laughed, "Then we should help him do it. I doubt we can stop him. He's back because someone forced him to show his cards. None of us, and that includes you, his son, would ever have heard from him otherwise. It's a second coming."

Maier had to agree with Mikhail. Love and altruism weren't part of his father's motivation for his reappearance, no matter what he'd told him at the hospital. And yet the old man's acknowledgement of his mother felt right to him. Maier hoped his father had always watched from a distance, had always been there as a shadow, had kept tabs on his son growing up over days, weeks, months, seasons, years and decades, had supported him from within the system he used and abused with so little effort.

Bryson nodded, "I have some classified intel that's for our ears only. This comes all the way from the top, right out of the Oval Office. Weltmeister was a US agent who crossed over to the Vietnamese in the final days of the Vietnam War. He'd been an extremely loyal and reliable man, a brilliant field agent, a ruthless killer, an all-around full-blooded American, even if he was a kraut. No Safety-First-Clive either. Took risks, did brilliant work. But in 1973, he turned. He murdered several CIA case officers in Long Cheng. Shortly after, we lost track of him. Along with the elusive file, the U48, which we're all after."

Mikhail raised his hand, "He did come over to the Vietnamese. But not because they turned him."

"So who did?" Maier interjected.

The Russian shrugged, "No idea what made him change sides. The killing of the American agents in Long Cheng was never made public, but under the table, the US used it as justification to intensify its bombing of a stretch of the Ho Chi Minh Trail that ran through Laos and Cambodia. I'm guessing it served as a secret trump card in case the Long Cheng story was blown at the wrong time and public protests back home got out of hand."

Sundermann leaned forward and played with his glass.

"It sounds to me as if his own people set him up. Made him kill those guys. Someone had leverage over him. And he got wind of it but did it anyway and escaped."

Bryson shook his head, "Well, we looked in our records, went through all the classified info within the agency. Nothing. It was an act of insanity. The men he killed were his buddies. He'd fought with them for years. That guy's a war monster."

Maier stayed silent. He didn't care to share his father's secrets and he felt no urge to convince Bryson of deeper truths. If the CIA man couldn't dig up what had happened, then there was a good chance his father's story of love and blackmail would be dismissed outright if anyone was ever taken to task for what had happened.

Mikhail continued, "He provided the Vietnamese with some excellent intel towards the end of the war. He was instrumental in the liberation, sorry, conquest of Long Cheng. He was as loyal and reliable as a Vietnamese agent. But they didn't trust the Vietnamese. They never understood why he'd done that killing and come over to them. They used him for two years – right until the end. A decision was made to dispose of him once the US had been driven out of Indochina. Somehow, he found out and had himself transferred to the Stasi. A year later, he was back in Long Cheng, killed his friend, the East German cultural attaché, and disappeared with a little gold and heroin, part of the stash the US had left behind. The stash that brought Maier to Laos. The Vietnamese never got that file."

"How do you know all this?"

The Russian smiled benevolently at Maier, "Mr. Mookie is very close to the Vietnamese. In those days, he also worked closely with the East Germans. We have good intel on your father until 1976."

No one spoke for a while. The sun had dropped behind the hills and the temperature fell quickly.

Mikhail got up and waved for a refill.

"I have some good news. We found Léon Sangster and we're watching him, from a distance. It seems he's gone over to the third party. Last week, he was spotted in Vang Vieng, a small tourist town a couple of hours north of Vientiane. He met several Americans there."

He glanced at Bryson, "They are yours?"

The American shook his head.

Maier shook his head, "It's pointless approaching them. They won't tell us a thing. The man I shot was laughing at me even as I pulled the trigger."

"Then we need to find Léon's weak point."

Maier said, "That's easy. He hates me almost as much as he hates my father. I'm the son of Weltmeister, who killed his sister. He'll do anything to have it out with me. He had murder in his eyes when he recognized me at the Vietnamese jungle prison."

The Russian clapped his hands, "Great. We get Léon. Then we know about the third party. Mr. Mookie has advised me to put a stop to any activities conducted by foreign mercenaries on Laotian soil."

Bryson waved the Russian's enthusiasm away, "Well, that doesn't tell us anything about Weltmeister's next steps."

Maier spoke quietly, "My father is angry, very, very angry. Someone forced him out of retirement, and he won't disappear until gets what he wants."

Maier felt exceedingly strange talking with so much certainty about family matters. Two fingers gone; one father gained. He wasn't sure what kind of deal that was.

26

FRONT PAGE NEWS

"I give you ten seconds to get lost."

Maier threw an empty glass at his boss, who quickly retreated from the detective's room. The editorial headline in the Bangkok Post, Thailand's most popular English-language newspaper, read *High-stakes spy game leaves trail of dead across Southeast Asia*.

Kanitha's parting shot was a good one and it hurt. The paper was three days old.

A high-stakes game of espionage stretching back forty years currently plays out across Laos and local authorities are suppressing a violent storm of cloak-and-dagger business raging right under their noses. In mid-November, a former sex worker was shot at Ang Nam Ngum Lake, an hour north of Vientiane. A week later, a boatman on the Nam Ou River was killed on his vessel by a sniper. Shortly after, an eminent monk was beaten to death in his jungle cave. A few days later, local police retrieved the body of an old white man, apparently brutally executed by persons unknown in a large marijuana plantation north of Nong Kiaw. Also in November, a former Laotian prison camp reopened and closed amidst rumors of a massacre. Shortly after, three Americans, employees of an MIA program, and a Canadian journalist were found dead, buried in a bomb crater on the Plain of Jars. Just days later, a female Laotian intelligence officer was executed in a farmhouse near Luang Prabang.

My investigation has led me to some of the country's most remote corners. I met Vietnamese intelligence officers, American spies, Hmong rebels, and private foreign contractors, all of them hunting an elusive prize from the Cold War, the U48, a file, perhaps mythical, perhaps real, that is said to list all the double agents of the Vietnam War era as well as other sensitive US policy details of the time.

Laotian police steadfastly rule out any connection between these murders and deny the very existence of the file. No mention of espionage has been made in local papers. Is the Laotian government killing bad-news stories fearing the murders might affect tourist arrivals? Is the much-touted increasing transparency of the reclusive communist state on a backslide just as Henry Kissinger, former US Secretary of State and Nobel Peace prize winner, is about to visit the country? US government representatives in Vientiane were not available for comment.

The comment was followed by an editor's note.

Up-and-coming travel writer and journalist Kanitha Amatakun sent us this incredible story on the condition that it be published only if she were found dead.

On Thursday, Amatakun was killed in a bizarre and unresolved shoot-out on the island of Ko Chang in Trat Province, where she had been holidaying. Local witnesses say her bungalow was attacked by two armed men who arrived on a jet ski. Police in Trat have since claimed the assailants were Russian and that the bodies had been returned to their country. The Russian Embassy was not available for comment. A foreigner who had been staying with Amatakun has not been found.

Maier grabbed the vodka bottle, raised it to his mouth and tilted it back until he'd emptied it. Gasoline, he thought, and passed out into a dirty dream.

27

JULIA

"Good morning, Maier. Your looks haven't improved since we last met. And what happened to your hand?"

Maier was slowly getting used to the metal prosthetics and vaguely waved them in Julia Rendel's direction as she stepped into the room. He was quite lost for words. The sun, the hangover and the vodka orange he was nursing for breakfast made it hard to focus on his visitor. But he was relieved to see her alive and in one spectacular piece.

Julia appeared to have survived the weeks in captivity well. One hell of a woman. Her hair was up in the unruly fashion he remembered. She wore practical but elegant clothes – a white, thin cotton blouse and low-slung, baggy beige pants, along with fashionable red leather slippers. Her high-maintenance hair extravaganza was accentuated by ethnically styled earrings and a tribal necklace of lapis lazuli big enough to serve as a generous dowry gift. There was not a hint of trauma in her eyes. She looked stunning, and Maier's thoughts briefly short-circuited back to the nights they'd spent together in Hamburg. He got up and embraced her.

"What are you doing here, Julia? Where have you been?"

"I was kidnapped, remember? By people you now work with. And then other guys kidnapped me again. People you know nothing about. You're not on top of things, Maier," she snapped, and pulled away.

"I certainly wasn't working with the people who took you then, and I am a reluctant colleague now," he shot back.

She sat down on the room's only chair and lit a cigarette. Maier hated cigarette smoke. He made a show of opening the windows.

"No need to rub it in, Maier. I understand you're not pleased to see me."

He fell back onto his bed, exhausted by his attempt to clear the air between them. The fact that she wasn't shattered by her kidnapping unsettled him. He was happy for her. But she reminded him of his father.

"Who busted you from Charlie's clutches? And what did they want?"

"That's top secret, Maier. Let your imagination lead you, detective. But count yourself out. We know it wasn't you who rescued me. You just kill people, by all accounts."

"So do the people who freed you, I heard."

"You don't have that kind of clearance."

"You hired me to find your father's murderer, and now you withhold information. You're just another wily operator. You string me along and you blow up cars. And I was so stupid as to worry about you. What kind of working relationship do we have?"

"A cold one, Maier, a cold one," she retorted.

Maier ignored her jibe.

"And what makes you hang around?"

"Other people's greed and crimes, of course, Maier."

"Making the world a better place for all of us, are we?"

"Just for some of us. A select few, in fact."

She pulled a face and blew smoke in his direction before stubbing her cigarette out on the barrel of the gun he'd smuggled across the border from Thailand and left lying on his night table. A poor way to make a point.

He looked straight at her, a sour expression on his face.

"Can't say I've found your gold just yet."

Julia grinned sheepishly and broke the eye contact, "It was never really about the gold. I would've thought you'd know that by now."

Maier said nothing and waved his metal claws at her again.

"Very handsome."

She smiled, but he saw no sweetness in her eyes.

"So you are back for some tree-hugging?"

She shot him a look that would have wilted a cat and growled, "No need to be mean, Maier. I did hire you to find out who killed my father. The gold was just an incentive. And I loved our time at the Atlantic until those thugs came and dragged me away."

He supposed he was looking for a hint of vulnerability, but he couldn't detect one.

"Do you know who killed your father? Do I have to tell you?"

She shook her head, and her hair did something Maier liked, despite his misgivings.

"I guess it was the same man who killed Vincent. You're not the only one who's learning painful lessons in Laos."

Maier left her answer standing in the room. He had no intention to offer his former client information about his father. In a manner of speaking, Weltmeister had indeed killed the Canadian, although Kanitha had pulled the machine gun's trigger. Maier thought back to how Bryson had described Julia's liberation. It had been efficient and bloody.

"No, Vincent died because he tried to have me killed. Bryson told him about us. What a coward that guy was."

"Vincent was a calculated mistake."

Julia stared furiously into space, unwilling to say more.

"So why did you come back?"

"Kissinger is coming."

Maier raised his eyebrows and refrained from telling Julia that he already knew.

Kissinger was coming. There was so much secret undertow in the way she'd said it. They looked at each other and Maier had the feeling that they both knew they knew. Something. Julia broke his gaze and walked to the window.

Kanitha had mentioned that the former US Secretary of State was about to drop in for an unofficial visit in her final news story. Had she left him a message? The man who'd ordered the carpet-bombing of Laos was returning to the scene of his misdeeds. Was there more to it than echoes of Realpolitik? What was the connection between the mayhem Maier had survived and the former US Secretary's visit? One look at Julia and he understood that the goalposts had shifted. The old diplomat's visit lay right at the heart of the schemes Julia was involved in.

"And?"

"Trees, Maier, are one of Laos' greatest assets. But they stand in the way of dam projects, road construction, mining and every other infrastructure project that the Chinese, the Americans, the World Bank, the Thais, the Vietnamese, the Asian Development Bank, and anyone else with cash and a profit motive have in mind. Don't get me wrong; we are not anti-development. But these projects benefit foreign powers and local gangsters. Laos is coming out of its communist isolation, sniffing cash, and we're hoping to slow the damage this entails. Tree-Line has a petition with three hundred thousand signatories, from Desmond Tutu to Paul the backpacker, calling for the enforcement of laws that already exist but are unfortunately never used. Laos has a good national park system, but logging and poaching go on anyhow."

The detective said nothing.

Julia continued. "Come on, Maier, don't be slow. Kissinger is coming to ink deals. To provide an unofficial counterweight to Chinese efforts in Laos. They can't send a US government delegation to a communist country. Not just yet. They send Henry. He has connections everywhere and the war is long past."

Maier scratched the stubble on his chin with his thumbnail.

"There lies some deeper secret in this?"

"Could be just a story. But I suspect not. Time will tell. And we aren't really friends today, Maier, are we? There's not much trust going around."

"Did you come here just to show off?"

She shook her head and pulled a long needle from her hair. It was a well-practiced gesture and an effective one. As she flashed him a winning smile, her hair cascaded down her back like a summer rain of precious jewels.

"No, Maier. I came to say sorry. I came to tell you how sad I was when I heard the journalist you traveled with was killed. I'm back to help you with your loss and depression, if you like. And you can help me with mine."

She looked around his messy room.

"And I came to tell you that I rented the suite. A more comfortable option than your current residence, Maier. Let's be friends."

He shook his head.

"I am quite happy here for the time being."

"No, you're not. You shot two men, executed one of them. You lost your girlfriend. And you know more about this case than anyone else, and yet you know almost nothing because you haven't put all the pieces together yet. I can help you do that. It will bring closure."

"Where did you hear I shot two men?"

"Oh, Maier, I'll let you figure that out. Come on, you're the detective. But in the meantime, scratch my back with those new fingers of yours. And I promise to scratch yours in ways you've never known."

She towered over him, offering him her hand. He saw a weird kind of love in her eyes, not a healthy one, to be sure. He saw she still had five fingers. And all the other bits were in place, too. She threw his clothes into his bag. She really had no clue who he was. As she brushed past him to reach for his jacket, he pulled her down towards him. He couldn't help it. He was Maier, private detective, survivor, veteran, killer. His father's son. In these moments, he hated it, all of it. All his monstrous selves.

"I was terribly worried about you, you know," she whispered under her breath. But Maier heard her remark clearly.

28

FLAME WAR

VANG VIENG MIGHT HAVE BEEN the world's most beautiful village. Surrounded by karst stone mountains that rose from paddy fields with primeval abandon, nestled along the banks of the swiftly moving Nam Song river, this modest collection of family homes, including a couple of banks and a dilapidated hospital, had an idyllic vibe. Farmers walked to and from their fields, local women fished khai phun, moss, from the fast-moving stream and threw it on the hot stones by the shore to dry, or set traps for freshwater prawns. Children caught lizards and rats in the rice paddy and carried them to the market. Stalls sold animals Maier didn't have names for. The surrounding villages were mostly Hmong, former anti-communists resettled by the government to discourage resistance.

Maier didn't care for the concessions that had been made to the dollar-strewing visitors. The backpackers were slowly overrunning Vang Vieng, attracted by the availability of opium, hallucinogenic mushrooms, marijuana and cheap alcohol. The entire community was about to turn into a university campus, without a university. Young Westerners floated in the river on inner tubes, beers and joints in hand, drowning frequently. The locals were friendly and a little overwhelmed. But the crowds of young travelers provided a modicum of cover for him. He checked into a cheap guesthouse by the main road and waited for dark.

. . .

"You shot off my damn fingers, Léon. I am very pissed off."

The Hmong jerked up from the low bench he sat on, but Maier waved him down with his snub-nosed revolver he pointed as discreetly as one could point a gun in a public place at the younger man.

"I'll kill you," Léon hissed through his teeth, and looked around as if expecting the cavalry to ride to the rescue.

"You've already tried to kill me a couple of times, Léon. It's my turn today."

Mikhail's info had been good. The young Hmong had been easy to find. The café Maier had spotted his nemesis in stood right on the edge of Lima Site 409, one of the old airfields from America's Secret War. The former landing strip was currently utilized for less ambitious purposes – as a bus terminal and playground for local children.

"Fuck you, Maier. You haven't got a clue what's going on. You're out of your depth."

Léon moved again but Maier let his smile fade quickly as he pointed the gun straight at the other man's chest.

"We have to talk, Léon."

Léon's black eyes tried to burn a hole through Maier's heart, but the weapon in the detective's hand kept him from trying to rip it out.

"We're long past talking, Maier. Your family has brought nothing but death and destruction into my life. I recognized you immediately in Muang Khua. Like father, like son. You got your old man hiding in the bushes somewhere? Is that why you've suddenly developed balls enough to shoot people? I took you for a more passive kind of guy when I first saw you on your knees, about to be blown away by that stoned creep, Daniels."

"Daniels spoke very highly of you."

Léon pulled at his wispy white beard absent-mindedly, perhaps glad to hear a compliment, any kind of compliment, but he quickly turned sour again. It was easy to hate.

"Well, he's dead. And so is Kanitha, thanks to you. And so are you. You just don't know it yet. You're up against people so terrible, you can't even imagine."

Maier expected Léon to start foaming at the mouth. Reason had nothing to do with it. Most likely, it was the people Léon was working with now who'd killed Kanitha. But he had to try and calm this man down. There was always something to be gained from people who did not have themselves under control – as long one stayed far enough away to avoid a physical confrontation and managed to push them in a useful direction. And in some ways, he liked Léon. Like himself, he was a child of subterfuge and secrets, quite unable to free himself from his past.

"You worked with Charlie Bryson until very recently, Léon. What happened?"

The younger man made an angry cutting gesture with the flat of his hand and grinned malevolently into the night.

"He went soft on me. He didn't even manage to kill you after getting you under the gallows. Just another sucker without a clear mission. They pass it from one generation to another. That's why the Americans lost the war. No clear mission, listening to the hippies back home while letting their soldiers get stoned in the jungle. Who's going to win a war like that?"

"That was a long time ago, Léon. History. All done. This is a new age. A former Secretary of State is coming to Laos next week."

He'd hit a nerve. Léon said nothing and stared at Maier, brooding. But he quickly found his sardonic wavelength again.

"The new age is going to eat you shortly, Maier."

He made motions to get up but Maier raised the gun again. Direct visual contact with the weapon was the only way to keep this guy in his seat.

Léon relaxed and grinned darkly, "You see Maier, in the end, we'll win the war. Laos won't choose communism. The Chinese will overrun my country. Every time they offer the government an infrastructure project, they bring their own workers. And when it's all done, the workers stay. It's the new colonial capitalism. The Vietnamese have pockets of their military all over the place, trying to hang on to what they see as their sphere of influence. But the government is no longer going to accept this. The Vietnamese are on their way out. Trade relations with the US are the first step in our emancipation. Absorbing the Chinese is the second. Communism is going down."

"None of this has anything to do with us, Léon."

The man across the table laughed bitterly.

"Yes, you're right, detective. I don't really care about any of this. Your father killed his best buddies. I saw him do it. He betrayed my parents. He betrayed everything we believed in then. I saw him shoot my sister. He almost killed me. I don't give a shit about anything else."

Maier understood the stateless, rootless man. His anger was genuine, lethal and in parts justified. The kind of history Léon wore like a suit of armor and a ball and chain would have turned anyone into a monster or a basket case.

But Maier was on his own learning curve when it came to loyalty, love and blood relations. He still had a father. A war criminal, a killer, a victim of circumstances, a prisoner to his vanity and love. A father he wanted to save.

Léon tied his long thinning hair into a pony tail and continued. "We all need closure, Maier. I was reasonably happy on my island with my dog. A year ago, I met Kanitha, and sometimes she would come and stay. It wasn't much of a life, but it was something. Then you turn up and take it all away. I've tried to kill you twice. Now I leave it to the pros to take you out. But not today. We still need you to lure your father out of the woodwork."

"Then why did you try and kill me on the Plain of Jars after I got away from the hanging?"

"You were escaping with my girl. I have many reasons to kill you, Maier. But as I said, it makes more sense to keep you alive. And close."

"Then why did your current associates try to kill me on the beach in Thailand?"

"They weren't trying to kill you; they were trying to kidnap you. They didn't expect armed resistance, I guess. They killed Kanitha and shot your boss because you resisted."

Maier could see that the boy was thinking in circles, desperately trying to attach guilt to anyone but himself for the mess he was part of.

A great silence settled between the two men. Maier relaxed and quietly released the hammer of his gun. He'd killed two men in self-defense. He was determined not to kill again. It wasn't part of his job description, nor his destiny. But he understood how one could get used to killing when it came to saving one's own life. One got used to it quickly.

As he faced Léon, he realized they were both trapped in this story. Their personal investment was so substantial that neither would be able to walk away from whatever was coming at them, no matter how cruel and repulsive it might turn out to be. They were both checkmated. They'd both lost their pawns and their queens. And the game had to be played to the end.

Léon laughed sadly, "It's funny, really. If you kill me, you won't be able to walk out of here tonight. If you let me go, I'll come back with everything I have when the time is right and take you out. Bad cards, Maier, very bad cards. We'll win the war and kill the last of the secret warriors. And his son."

A gaggle of drunken British girls entered the café and ordered beer. They were young and loud and had no eyes for the conversation at the next table. Maier noticed the two men who'd slipped in behind the girls too late. They sidled up behind the detective as Léon smiled triumphantly but without joy. The man to Maier's left wrested his gun from his hand and stuck it into the belt of his black jeans.

"You see, Maier. You're just never quite in the picture. The plans to catch your old man have been in motion ever since he first popped up again. Perhaps even longer. As soon as May Lik, my neighbor, was killed and I figured that it hadn't been the Viets who'd hit her, I knew something was afoot. When that idiot Daniels sprang me in Muang Khua, I made some phone calls. Charlie and his outfit became obsolete very quickly. They couldn't even hold on to the Rendel woman, Vincent's girl. Up in smoke, as they say. And now you're about to become obsolete. Your last mission in life is to serve as bait for your father."

Maier couldn't think of a way to reach out to this angry man, to contain his fury.

"I am not my father, Léon, and you should let go of your past," sounded lame even as he said it.

Léon grinned sourly, "Family runs deep in Hmong culture. It means so much more to us than it does for Westerners. It's our past and our future. My father died for his ideological beliefs, but my mother, she died because she loved her family, her children. And that's all that counts. We hit where it hurts most, detective. Your father's crimes are best avenged by taking you with us, Maier. At least it's a good start."

"I don't understand how you can hate someone you don't even know, Léon."

"You took my girl."

"She came voluntarily. And trust me, I wish she hadn't if it meant she was still alive."

"You killed her."

Maier shook his head and turned to the two men sitting next to him, "Your new friends, rogue killers, private mercenaries or whatever they say they are, killed her. Someone who isn't part of the unofficial official program of the Secret War killed her. Trust me, I was there."

The two men next to Maier shifted closer to him. They were neither upset nor nervous. For them it was just another job. The conversation didn't interest them. They were waiting on Léon's word to get on with it.

"Didn't make much difference, did it?"

He saw some doubt in Léon's eyes as they flicked from the detective to his two stone-faced guards. The man had been cheated of his life, had lost his family and his health to a war that had officially ended twenty-five years ago. A war that continued to rage through battle trenches in his mind, day after day. It was hard to get through.

"Look, Léon, we can resolve all this without further killings. At the end of the day, all parties involved in this affair want a peaceful outcome."

The Hmong brushed his hair from his face and grinned viciously, "Politician talk won't help, Maier."

Maier shook his head with irritation, "Which side are you on, Léon? Where is it going to go?"

"I'm on whichever side is out to squash you, Maier."

The detective held up his hand, "Listen to me. You loved Kanitha. I also liked her a great deal. She was a free spirit and she paid the ultimate price for following her hunches. She wanted the story. Your story, my story, whatever story was going in the wake of my father's reappearance. She understood the risks, and now she is gone and we should stop fighting. It is over. Let it go. Enjoy the time you have left; it isn't much even if you grow to a respectable age."

"Weltmeister shot my sister in the neck. He didn't hesitate. He shot her in the neck and she lies in a hole in Long Cheng to this day. Next to my mother and my father. My family hole, Maier. He promised me he would look after her, after he'd already killed her. He's an animal and he needs to be put down. And you're part of him."

Léon rose from the table and threw a punch at Maier, who jerked back fast enough to dodge the swipe.

"Not here," the man on Maier's left hissed.

The drunken girls at the next table piped down and stared as the two heavies pulled Maier to his feet. Léon snapped angrily at them and they instantly turned back to their holiday debaucheries. Seconds later, his captors marched Maier across the cracked tarmac of the runway towards a waiting SUV. Where were his friends when he needed them? Mikhail and Bryson had persuaded him walk into the lion's den. Did they really want him to disappear with these two murderers? He looked across the runway, but there was no one else in sight. Léon stayed behind in the café. His depressed laugh followed Maier into the night.

The two men beside him held him in an iron grip. As they approached the car, the man to his right pulled the keys from his pocket. The vehicle, a black SUV with tinted windows, good enough for anyone's final journey, beeped as the electronic locks sprang open.

Then it exploded.

Maier was thrown onto his back by the blast. A part of the windscreen flew past him and smashed into the man to his right, severing his right arm. The second abductor, peppered with glass and bleeding heavily, rose uncertainly, looked at his fallen colleague and stumbled into the night. The British girls at the café yelled in panic and spilled outside, clutching their drinks. One of them vomited in the light of a single solitary bulb above the café's front door. Another lifted her point-and-shoot camera at the carnage. The ground shook as bits of sport utility vehicle bounced off the tarmac. Maier lay still, too stunned to move, watching the fireworks.

A motorbike pulled up next to the detective. Julia, hair in disarray and eyes shining brightly, bent down towards him and smiled innocently, waving a mobile phone in the detective's direction.

"I just love technology. Saved the night, Maier. Saved your hide. Let's go."

He slowly got up and looked around. The tourists stood frozen and sober. A few Laotians peeled out of the night and carefully stepped onto the runway. No one moved towards the burning vehicle or the dying foreigner next to it. Léon, master of the great disappearing act, was gone. The injured operative stared madly and silently at Maier, gripping his gun in his left, too far gone to pull the trigger. He wasn't going to answer any questions. Maier waited until he'd lost consciousness and took his gun back.

"Find out anything interesting, detective?" she asked, her voice ripe with tense sarcasm.

"Family runs deep in Hmong culture, apparently."

She threw him an opaque look and answered, "That's a universal thing. Your aversion to the natural order of things proves you're dysfunctional."

"So is Léon, a bitter crisis of a man."

She shrugged, gunning the engine, "Léon Sangster is a victim, Maier. Dangerous when he has a gun pointed at you. We have to see that we don't become victims as well."

Maier sensed a dark undertone in her voice, so dark he quickly began to get over the flames rising from the shattered vehicle and the dead man on the ground in front of him. She'd put an emphasis on the *we* that he couldn't put his finger on, nor was he sure whether he cared for her certitude. The vehicle coughed and exploded again.

He walked away from the heat.

"You just made their hit list, I think."

She laughed bitterly and gunned the engine, "I was already on their hit list. These guys kidnapped me from Charlie and they weren't nice."

When he looked into her eyes, he knew she wasn't lying. He knew war was like this, messy, dirty, terrible, full of irredeemable moments that punched holes into people. He also knew that he'd never seen this woman like this before and that he had no idea who she really was. Something about her was so familiar, it frightened him. The detective, stunned but happy to be anywhere, jumped onto the bike.

As the old Lima Site burned, Vang Vieng receded behind them.

29

THE BIG MAN

MAIER WOKE UP AT MIDDAY, pushed an empty vodka bottle off his bed and stared down into the street. Vientiane was hardly its sleepy, good-natured self today. Troops, armed and not nearly as bored as one might have expected, stood on street corners and in temple forecourts behind low piles of sandbags. Ancient diesel-spewing trucks packed with soldiers drove around town in a show of disheveled force. The government paper alluded to nothing, but Maier didn't expect revelations from the secretive communist leadership or its tightly controlled media. Hangover bearable. Brain intact. Breakfast first.

He had decided to be conspicuous upon his return to the Laotian capital. Carelessness had taken over. The game was almost up, anyhow.

He'd taken a room at the Lane Xang Hotel, with a view of the riverfront. From his window, he could see a long stretch of the main road along the Mekong. An agricultural trade fair was being set up, nothing to get excited about unless you were a farmer in search of an imported tractor.

Julia had stayed the night and they'd drunk together without trust or tenderness. She had told him nothing about herself or her plans or, for that matter, his father's designs. He was sure trees had little to do with whatever they were up to. She'd said nothing more about who her captors were nor how she had escaped or how she'd known he was meeting Léon in Vang Vieng.

When he'd regained consciousness, his former client had gone.

Bleary-eyed, he watched a helicopter sweep low over the riverfront, reminding Laotians that the politburo had nothing but their welfare in mind. Still, people raised their heads at this unusual spectacle. Airborne helicopters were a rarity in the impoverished nation by the Mekong.

Across the river, a balloon, bright yellow, the slogan of a fertilizer company emblazoned on its bulging skin, had risen into the sky, representing Thailand's free market contribution to the upcoming fair. The basket underneath the balloon was crammed with tourists.

Her perfume lingered like a curse. But it wasn't just Julia Rendel that Maier was worried about. An invisible hand, all five fingers intact, had settled over the Lao affair, picking at its innards like a starving vulture. Alliances around him were shifting quicker than the clouds that raced across the communist sky.

The knock on the door shook him out of his morning daze. He grabbed his gun and took a peek through the door viewer.

His father stared straight at him.

Maier dropped the security chain and pulled the door open.

"Ferdinand."

The old man quickly looked up and down the corridor and slipped past Maier into the room. Maier shut the door and dropped the gun to his side. They stood looking at each other. The two-dimensional silhouette that had followed the detective through his dreams had morphed into a real person.

"Vater."

Maier couldn't help but use the most formal title as he addressed his father properly for the first time.

"Call me Weltmeister. It's the only name I have left," the older man replied.

They embraced, awkwardly. Maier took a step back and continued to stare at the man he'd been dreaming of meeting all his life.

The man stared right back.

Maier Sr. was a head smaller than his son. They shared the same broad shoulders, the same large hands and the same intensely curious green eyes. He must have been a handsome devil, all right. His face was deeply lined with life and sorrow, with victories and defeats. His hair might have been blond once; now it was gunmetal gray. He wore a white, short-sleeved shirt and gray slacks. As he came further into the room, he kicked off his simple black leather shoes the way any man who'd spent years in Asia would. Maier guessed him to be in his mid-seventies, though his body was that of a healthy man twenty years younger. Apart from the subtle charisma he exuded, he looked unremarkable, but Maier could tell straight away that his father's ordinariness was studied and refined to the point where he might pass through a crowd of people without anyone noticing him. Except for the eyes, of course.

"It's been a long time. I've only ever held you as a baby…"

The older man's voice faded with emotion.

Maier didn't know what to say. So many questions. So little time. As if his father could read his thoughts, he walked over to the unmade bed, pulled a gun from under his shirt, gently deposited it on the night table and sat down. As Maier deposited his own gun next to his father's, he realized that the distance between them was narrowing. Maier too had killed.

"What are you doing here?"

Weltmeister turned his head and beckoned his son.

"I'm not sure. Trying to set a few things straight, I guess. I know it's late. Very late."

"Why did you never contact me?"

"I told you at the hospital. If I'd stayed with Ruth, she would have been killed. If I'd been too close to you while you were growing up, you might have been killed. Anonymity's the only way in this game."

"So, why do it? Why did you become a spy?"

Maier was acutely aware that his own choice of careers – that of journalist, war correspondent and private investigator – looked like a progression into eccentricity. Being an international spook was another ball game altogether.

Weltmeister sighed, "Fighting the Nazis, working for the resistance in Germany, it was the ultimate adventure for a young man, a near teenager, full of half-baked ideas of justice and values. When the war finished, espionage was all I knew. I was good at it; I loved the subterfuge, the honesty in the dishonesty, that quiet perversity in the subversive element. I came to love the privilege that spooks enjoy, the access to information, the being apart from the rest of humanity. I fell into it, completely. It absorbed me, like a fever."

He looked around the room and back at his son, his eyes shining with the memories of past conquests.

"I've been to all the front lines of all the wars of our time, Ferdinand. I've seen things most people can't even imagine. I've walked through firefights in Vietnam and cowered in caves in Laos while napalm peeled the skin off life itself a few meters away. I have seen B-52 bombers split mountains in half and pulverize entire civilizations. I have fallen into the abyss and climbed back out so many times, I can't remember. I only learned one lesson, son. The same one you're learning now. If you're going to do something, do it with gusto, or stay home, watch TV, and leave it to the professionals. If you let yourself fall down into the abyss, by your own volition, then be damned sure you come back with a story."

Maier tried hard to keep his resentment in check. He forced himself to take a step back from his anger, to absorb his father's words without reacting from the pit of his stomach. He forced himself to look.

The old man, the spook of spooks, looked his age. His years showed in the stoop of his back, the wrinkles in his huge hands, the slight sag of the skin on his lower arms. The most hunted man in Southeast Asia looked tired.

"It was a great life. For a long time, I was with the good guys. But after they took Valentina, after I killed those men in Long Cheng, I began to hate the world. And I no longer cared who I was working for. I became a gun for hire. You know, like in the Wild West."

Maier sat on the room's only chair, transfixed. Weltmeister lapsed into silence. Maier waited. But his father just sat there, trapped by memories.

The older man's heavy breathing filled Maier's world. The detective had no idea whether he should comfort his father or question him about his sanity. Neither of them knew how to deal with the moment. They both knew it was all they had; all they would ever have.

Weltmeister raised his wounded eyes to his son and tapped the side of his head.

"I am the U48. If I die, it's all gone. All that knowledge about the war. Including my orders to kill my best friends. Including the White House plans to nuke Laos."

Maier stared at his father in astonishment.

"Nukes?"

Weltmeister nodded, "The US contemplated dropping a nuclear bomb on the country as early as the Fifties. By the early Seventies, they were almost ready. They would have done it if the war in Vietnam hadn't turned against them. I have the file names and file numbers, all the right references to reams of classified material in my head. I know the names of all the officials involved, from the Secretary of State down."

"The same Secretary of State who is about to visit Laos?"

"The very same. We used to be close. I'd be the only person in the room who'd call him Heinz. It was Henry or Mr. Secretary for everyone else. We had a special relationship."

Maier understood his father, understood his reappearance, understood how the old man imagined the near future. As the detective was about to speak, his father raised his hand.

"Julia is your step-sister, Ferdinand. I adopted her. And I trained her in the arts of killing so that she'll always be able to look after herself. You see, after losing Valentina to the CIA, I couldn't risk having another relationship. I changed sides too many times; someone else would have gotten to me. But then, in the late Eighties, when I got out of the game, I was lonely. I still felt bad for killing Rendel. He was a sleazy bastard but we went way back. I' been to university with him. His daughter needed help. Life's never the way you plan it. And she has grown into a formidable woman, as you know. I worked as a painter in London through the Eighties and Nineties. I no longer had anything do with the intelligence community, I thought. Julia's adoption was my atonement…"

He let the sentence drift away.

Maier was speechless. Almost.

"Does she know that I am your son?"

The older man shook his head.

"She knows on one level, of course. But she's in denial. I've tried, quite successfully, to keep some of the more fantastical events of my life from her. But not for much longer. I'll tell her soon that the family is bigger than she thought."

"Everyone else in the world has made the connection. She deserves to know. Now."

Weltmeister was silent.

"Why didn't you tell me at the hospital?"

The old man looked at his son, his eyes glazed and far away. "You'd just lost your girlfriend. Your boss was in ICU. We had to talk. But there wasn't time. It wasn't the right moment."

"You told me there never is a right moment."

Weltmeister made a conciliatory gesture.

"I'm here now."

"You are here to kill the Secretary."

His father let the remark float between them before answering. "I'm here to close the Weltmeister file. I want to see the man who killed Valentina. I want to look into his eyes. Time is short and we're getting old. We're almost the same age, the Secretary and I."

Maier shook his head and walked to the window.

"Where does that leave us?"

Weltmeister pulled a CD from his pocket. "The U48. The only copy. Everyone wants it. The US, the Vietnamese, the Secretary. It's yours. After I leave, you can do what you want with it. Sell it to the highest bidder and retire if you like. Make a deal with Mikhail. The Vietnamese probably deserve it the most."

"What do I deserve?"

"The money."

Maier felt himself getting angry.

"I make a living, Father. I don't need your money. Your shenanigans have cost me two fingers and a friend."

He stopped himself from giving in to the rising frustration and calmed down.

His father rose slowly and bent over to put his arms around his son, "I know, I know. So many mistakes. War and love don't lie together well. Family always pays the price."

Maier didn't resist, though he felt uncomfortable at his father's emotional touch. Julia his stepsister? Far out. Disquieting thoughts chased one another as he tried to pull all the different strands of his case together. Case as life, life as case, it was hard to keep it apart. Maier felt being subsumed by his job.

"You already told me you sent Julia to recruit me."

The old man stepped away.

"I put the idea into her head. She was desperate to reconnect with her past, ever since her mother died a couple of years ago. She wanted to know more about her real father. At the same time, I found out that my anonymity was no longer watertight. Léon was telling stories, after being so quiet I didn't even know he'd survived our encounter in Long Cheng in '76. With him back in the picture, I needed to act before they'd come after me again. I told her it would be best if she made efforts to find out what had happened to her father."

"Thereby condemning yourself? She'll find out who killed her father sooner or later."

"Not unless you or Léon tell her."

"Or you," Maier snapped back.

The old man sank back onto the bed.

"It's incredible that anyone would care about all this Secret War business today."

Weltmeister shrugged, "Secret wars have a habit of continuing in secret. The Americans are desperate to come back into this part of the world. It's the same old game. The Great Game. It wasn't about ideology then and it isn't now. It's money. Power. Greed. Resources. Laos sits at the crossroads between China and Southeast Asia. Remember the domino theory? Kennedy said if Laos fell, the commies would overrun the world. That's how it all started. He lied about Lao neutrality in the early Sixties, claiming no Americans worked in Laos, while building up a secret US presence at the same time. All they really wanted was the oil in the South China Sea. That kind of thinking hasn't evolved. If the U48 becomes public, the US will struggle to get a foot in the door. Trade agreements will be that much harder to sign, and Coca-Cola will face obstacles. America making a fast buck may take second place to China making two fast bucks."

Maier shook his head, "But the CIA is no longer after you. Charlie Bryson is on our side."

The old man laughed gently, "It's not that simple. Bryson and the agency are no longer in the loop. They've been instructed to hunt me down, so that the third force can quietly make diplomatic inroads against the Chinese and get rid of me quietly at the same time. The CIA screwed up in Laos in the Seventies. So, now it's done via secret diplomatic channels that the former Secretary of State has cultivated. He's the puppet master, and Bryson, the Vietnamese and Léon and his

Hmong, they're all tools, distractions in a much larger game plan. The secret agents aren't in on the secret this time around."

Maier stared into space, trying to distill the information his father threw at him piecemeal into a coherent narrative.

"Family, money, politics, ideology, old war stories, new capitalist realities all thrown together. Isn't it all a bit much for you?"

"The time machine is ruthless; even when bored, it throws you ahead and there's nothing to hold onto."

"All the more reason to retire, right?"

His father smiled sadly, "I tried to wash my hands of it when I moved to the UK. I thought it was all over and that I was safe. I thought I'd killed everyone who knew who I was and who might have had an interest in exposing me. I had a good life there, despite the food. The British like true eccentrics. I painted. I was quite good at it. I made money. I watched Julia grow up and came to feel that she was my daughter. Someone I could trust. Someone who made me miss my son a little less. When my cover was about to be blown again, I sent her to you, in the hope that you'd be able to throw a spanner in the works."

He shuddered and continued, "And you have, of course."

"I threw two fingers in the works."

"I'm very proud of you, Ferdinand."

"I'll never get used to you calling me by my first name. No one calls me Ferdinand."

Weltmeister looked up at Maier. "You might miss it when I'm gone."

Maier let the thought go. His father had only just arrived. And nothing really added up.

"What happens next?"

The old man pointed at the CD, "We should go and talk to the Vietnamese. They have more to lose than anyone if the Chinese or the Americans come into Laos in a big way. They might help."

"Help with what? Do you really think you can change the course of history?

"I've done it before, Ferdinand," Weltmeister snapped, and got up.

Maier looked at his old man looming up above him, his squat shape an overbearing, impermanent silhouette against the bright hotel windows. Hello and goodbye lay close together in this family.

Maier suddenly felt tired. So many people had died. The matrix his father had weaved for decades continued to expand, on and on. He reminded himself that Weltmeister's sway had reached all the way to the White House. The entire affair was epic. His father. His father was truly crazy.

"I have a line to Mikhail, the rep for the Vietnamese. It's a good idea to end this before more people get killed over lives and loves long gone. I can set up a meeting."

His father stepped out of the light, smiling. "I was sure you could do that, son."

30

ENLIGHTENMENT

Weltmeister and Maier left the car behind a shack by the side of the main road and walked through a dry rice paddy. The morning mist hung above the sluggish Mekong like a gray blanket. The water level was low. The monsoon floods had gone. The fields on the riverbanks were covered in dew. It was cold despite the first rays of milky sunlight that washed over the untainted landscape. Mornings in Asia had an ethereal quality. The crimes and defeats of the previous day had been forgotten. The hope for the coming day remained intact. Village girls wrapped in sarongs carried steel pots and bags of washing along the riverbank, giggling and shouting quietly as only girls in Laos would, their long raven-black hair trailing behind them, giving them the solidity of feys. A couple of buffaloes ambled across the fields on the opposite side, dark and solid shapes heading for the water's edge. No traffic noise, no loudspeakers, nothing but bird calls and the laughter of the girls penetrated through the mist and lent the scenery a dignity that was unlikely to survive the day. Laos could be that way, timeless, unhurried, busy with a quiet sensuality that was all its own.

A huge bird-like creature loomed out of the mist. A fierce stone garuda, some fifteen meters high, its wings spread wide, stared at them with an expression of overbearing authority. Maier had never seen a statue so impatient.

Mikhail had suggested meeting away from the capital, at Xieng

Khouang, an otherworldly collection of gigantic religious sculptures, constructed in the late Fifties and located in an overgrown park. The eccentric founder of this sacred medway, a self-proclaimed yogi, had combined elements of Buddhism and Hinduism to forge his own popular cult. When the communists took over, the yogi escaped across the Mekong to build another Buddha park in Thailand. His sculptures, some of them twenty meters high, lingered as ghostly reminders of more magical times.

Even at the very first light of day, several old women had lined up along the broken fence around the property, selling freshly steamed khao tom – sticky rice mixed with black beans and banana, wrapped in banana leaf. With toothless smiles and hopeful eyes, they told Maier that the two men were the first visitors this morning. They showed no surprise or interest in the heavy black canvas bag that the older man carried.

Maier pointed an imaginary camera at them and clicked off a couple of shots. The snack sellers laughed at his antics and settled back behind their produce.

The two men drifted into the park. They passed a giant reclining Buddha, a fierce Shiva, and a garish Rahu which sat amidst countless human and animal shapes that rose out of the knee-high grass. Skeletons danced and frogs cowered, warriors mauled mythical creatures, and ladies bowed their heads in prayer. It was easy to become disoriented amongst the sculptures; many were virtually identical. As the sun rose, the lingering fog sustained the labyrinthine ambience. They reached a bulging pumpkin-shaped edifice that rose from dry grass in the center of the park. Weltmeister and Maier entered through a circular doorway and ascended three levels of narrow, damp stairs to the top of the construct. From here they had a perfect view over most of the area.

As they emerged onto the building's roof, Mikhail sat waiting for them.

"Good morning, my dear friends," he declared with his usual bonhomie, and stood to embrace Maier. He wore his lank gray hair in a ponytail. With the wraparound shades covering half his bright red face and his garish short-sleeved polyester shirt, he looked every bit the Russian hit man. He didn't seem to feel the cold. A revolver poked out of his khaki shorts.

He bowed politely to Weltmeister. "It's a great honor to meet you. We did our best to hunt you down. We even had a nice jungle hotel ready for you. And now here you are, free as a bird and on your own terms. My employers send utmost felicitations and are appreciative that you have agreed to this meeting. And I would like to add that your son is a handsome devil and the best detective active in the region today. You should be proud."

Weltmeister smiled politely and carefully scanned the park below them.

The Russian's smile vanished instantly, "There is a problem?"

Maier grinned. "This is the first time I've seen you surprised, Mikhail. What's up?"

Weltmeister sat on the curved roof and pulled his bag open. He waved Maier closer. The black canvas rucksack contained a sniper rifle.

He looked up at the Russian, "For once I trust the Vietnamese. More than they ever trusted me. The U48's in my head. It's the only copy there is. I destroyed the file I took from Long Cheng in '76."

Mikhail waved the old man's comments away, "I will protect your life to the best of my abilities."

He observed Weltmeister with respect, his eyes alight with real curiosity. Maier didn't buy it. To him the Russian looked like a man asking the deranged inmate of a closed institution for the weather forecast. Everyone was lying.

"But why you have come back to Laos? You've been sitting on the file for twenty-five years. You might have taken it to your grave with you. Why did you come out, so to speak?"

Mikhail's comment was infused with high camp but turned into a whisper as he looked around the deserted park below.

Weltmeister shrugged, "Léon was making noises. The Americans are coming back into Laos. The former Secretary of State's on his way."

The Russian nodded, "He's the man who ordered you to assassinate your friends in Long Cheng? He caused you to cross over?"

Weltmeister didn't contradict Mikhail.

The Russian grinned, "So romantic. Maier's boss, Sundermann, guessed as much. Bryson wouldn't have it. He said he couldn't find any evidence."

"Secretaries of State don't leave evidence. They killed my woman."

"So macho. I like it. You're the last real man on the planet. Apart from your handsome son."

Weltmeister started to pull rifle parts from his bag.

Mikhail looked on with wide eyes, "I don't believe it; you use a Dragunov."

The German grinned, "I'm old-school. The gun is great. Only the sight is terrible, mounted to the left of the barrel's centerline and inaccurate. I took it off and put a Zeiss on the top. I can hit a leaf from a kilometer away."

He assembled the weapon with a few assured movements. The Russian was clearly impressed.

"You expect company?"

He brushed Mikhail's remarks away.

"Did you know they followed you?"

Mikhail shook his head and showed his teeth.

"Maier checked into one of Vientiane's largest hotels last night. The whole country knows you're in town. Do we have a deal?"

Weltmeister slotted the sight onto his gun and rested its bipod on the structure's stone roof. He offered the Russian his hand. "Integrity and anonymity are everything in this job. If we walk away from this, the Laotians and Vietnamese can have the file. I'm definitely not giving it to these guys."

He pointed down to the ground. Some of the life-size statues moored in the park were shifting in the fog. Weltmeister waved Maier and the Russian to retreat back into the structure they sat on. With the assured agility of an old leopard, he climbed to the very top of the building and pointed his weapon at the advancing shapes below.

A howl of electronic feedback, the sound of a speaker cranking up, shattered the morning's quiet and instantly transported them into the here and now.

"Weltmeister and associates, you have five seconds to come down here. Otherwise, we will blast you into the seventh Buddhist hell and no one will ever hear of any one of you again."

Weltmeister called down to the Russian, "Did you bring backup?"

Mikhail shook his head, "I always work alone. Ask your son."

The man with the megaphone emerged from the dissipating fog and slowly approached the structure they sat in. It was Charlie Bryson.

Maier shouted to the American, "Hey, Charlie, you're on the wrong side of the road."

The CIA man laughed, "Maier, it don't matter which side of the road I'm going down or you're going down. It's our road, you see. Americans like to keep it simple."

"In that case, you're still on the wrong side," Weltmeister mumbled, and shook his left hand as if trying to readjust the position of his wristwatch. Bryson almost fell the same instant, the sonic whiplash of the shot bouncing around the concrete guardians a second later.

Before the American had hit the ground, the old man lifted his rifle and started picking off the men below one by one. Several of the attackers shrank back. A second sniper shot them down. Automatic weapons fire echoed between the concrete structures. A couple of minutes later, it was all over. Julia Rendel emerged from the back of the reclining Buddha, carrying a rifle. She waved silently and disappeared.

They found five dead men below. Bryson had suffered a shot to his upper chest that had grazed his bulletproof vest, close to his armpit. He sat in the grass, pressing his fist into the wound to slow the bleeding.

"Julia left you alive so we might get some answers."

"Help me. Call backup; they will send a helicopter. Please."

Maier could see Bryson's eyelids flutter; the American would lose consciousness any second. Rivulets of sweat ran down his bald plate as his face turned green. Maier looked across to his father, who knelt down next to the CIA man.

"I can save your life, Bryson. Give me one good reason."

"These are not my men. They made me come here. My unit has been ordered to cooperate with a new outfit… the agency co-opted from within."

Weltmeister shook his head, "I don't care about you changing sides whenever the wind changes. That's not news. Give me news. Now. Or I will take your fist away and your life will slide into this field. It's a beautiful day to die, Bryson."

The American shook with increasing shock.

"What about Vientiane? The agricultural show? You guys are paying for that, no?"

Bryson managed a feeble nod, "A trap. Too many troops, Laotian police, Vietnamese intelligence, Léon and his guys, everything.

Everyone waiting for Weltmeister. But they're all proxies for the Secretary. Get used to the new age of borderless diplomacy."

"Weltmeister's just a story, Bryson; he doesn't really exist. You know that, don't you?"

"Always keep my word… this just business."

The old man opened his bag and pulled out a tourniquet. Maier sat the American up and they removed his jacket, wrapped the bandage around his chest and pulled it tight. Weltmeister fished a phone from Bryson's pocket.

"How long?"

The American whose complexion changed from green to gray to white and back every few seconds, smiled in the weird dislocated way badly injured men pumping adrenaline usually do.

"I have a son too, Weltmeister. I give you my word… please make the call. You'll have two minutes to get away. There's a boat moored at the bottom of the park."

Weltmeister passed the phone to Bryson and pulled a small first aid kit from his trouser pocket as the American auto-dialed. The old man popped the cap on a vial of morphine and filled a syringe. As the American's call connected, Weltmeister found a vein and pushed the needle in and rammed the plunger home.

"You're lucky that I once loved your country and that I've killed enough Americans in this life. You'll make it. And if you do survive, they will punish you for letting me slip away. No winners in this game, Bryson," he said, got up and walked towards the river.

Maier and the Russian followed quickly. The boat lay ready. For once, Bryson had told the truth. Julia started the engine as they reached the riverbank. They jumped in and raced southeast.

Maier watched his father, who sat in the front of the boat, his eyes on the river. The old man's ability to show ruthlessness and compassion in the same instant was a thing of unsettling beauty. Maier, former conflict journalist, detective, a man with three fingers on his left hand and a magic tattoo on his back, was in shock and in awe of his father. Yesterday he'd thought him almost demented. Now he seemed more lucid than anyone else around. He turned back to look at Julia. She wouldn't make eye contact but held the rudder with the determination of a warrior Amazon as she raced their vessel at full throttle away from the morning's killing fields.

Mikhail signaled for Julia to slow the boat. She cut the engine. Silence descended on the river. The Russian waved her to the eastern shore. The last of the long-tail boat's momentum propelled them against the low embankment. The welcoming party stood waiting, guns cocked. So was Weltmeister, his rifle pointing straight at Mr. Mookie.

"Hey, take it easy; we're all friends here. No need for anyone to die now," the Russian hissed behind Maier.

The old Laotian soldier who wore a tight-fitting polo shirt embroidered with a Lamborghini logo underneath his anorak, laughed down at the travelers with false bonhomie, "Good morning, Maier and family. I see you have already livened up this wonderful day with a little murder. No need to remind you that killing isn't allowed while visiting the Lao PDR on a tourist visa."

Mr. Mookie smiled at the travelers with barely disguised disdain, though he didn't dare make eye contact with Weltmeister. Maier got off the boat first, walked quickly up to his so-called case officer, pushed him hard with his right hand and unfurled the metal prosthetics on his left towards the Laotian's neck. Mr. Mookie stumbled backwards into the wet grass. His men raised their weapons to Maier's head. The detective ignored them and put his boot on their superior's chest. His heart racing, he was barely able to contain the anger he felt towards his erstwhile captor. He bent down and scraped his steel prosthetics along the man's chin. His thoughts tumbled from his mouth, "This is the new Maier. I no longer work for you. Neither does my father. We're not here to make deals and we're not scared."

The safeties of several rifles clicked off.

Weltmeister, standing in the boat, raised his voice towards the Laotian. "So much macho bullshit. You're completely outgunned and we will have you floating in the Mekong in thirty seconds if you don't drop your guns. My son will cut your throat from ear to ear before any of your boys pull the trigger. Half the American cavalry is right behind us. Visa or no visa, they'll shoot it out with you lot just to have a conversation with me."

Julia, who'd kept the Russian covered, jumped off the boat like a cat, her rifle now pointing at the handful of soldiers, who looked to their fallen boss for orders. Mr. Mookie nodded almost imperceptibly. Julia collected their weapons.

"Now," Weltmeister continued as he grabbed his bag, jumped onto solid ground and offered the prostrate Laotian his hand, "Let's make a deal."

Mr. Mookie smiled thinly as the older man pulled him to his feet. The Laotian brushed the dust off his anorak and nodded softly. Weltmeister laughed along with him.

"Let's make a deal," the Laotian smiled. "Hand over the U48."

"Three million dollars."

The Laotian nodded without hesitation.

31

FAMILY AFFAIR

Just after dark, Mikhail and his Laotian paymasters dropped the Maier family off at the Lane Xang Hotel and drove away into the Vientiane night.

The hotel bar offered no foreign liqueur, but Julia had gone out into the night and procured several cans of too-sweet orange juice and a litre of Smirnoff. She'd rented the hotel's honeymoon suite, a tired affair with a huge bed covered in the most garish polyester spread south of the Chinese Wall. They sat and drank, their rifles propped up by the door, ready to go. There could be no more surprises.

Maier, halfway through his second glass, was the first to get back to the case.

"Why did you save Bryson's life?"

Weltmeister sighed.

"I don't like killing Americans."

Maier's look must have appeared doubtful at best.

His father continued, "It's a generational thing. I fought the Nazis. At the end of the war, the Americans were the good guys. They helped liberate Germany. My generation owes the US. The first banana I ever ate, the first orange I ever tasted, all thanks to these foreigners who occupied Germany after the war. And then in the Fifties and Sixties, I worked with Americans. That's how I met Ruth. I went to university in Leipzig and spied on people. Easy stuff after working for the resistance in World War II. I mean, think about it. Kissinger, a German, made it all the way to the top of the government. I, another German, made it all the way to the top of their secret service. I was judged by my abilities and my loyalty, not by where I'd come from. It's a psychological debt I could never quite repay, even after I killed my friends in Long Cheng. Seeing Bryson bleed to death in Xieng Khouang, my reaction was automatic."

He laughed dryly, "Don't get me wrong; it wasn't informed by compassion for the man, only by my sympathy, however misplaced and nostalgic, for what he represents. At heart, I always wanted to work for the Americans. I wasn't going to let this son of a bitch die, unless it put us in danger."

"He tried to kill us."

Weltmeister discarded Maier's remark with a curt hand movement and stood up.

"You do make me think, son."

The room was suddenly dead silent. Julia stared at the two men, her eyes drifting from one to another in disbelief.

Coasting effortlessly around the bombshell he'd just dropped, Weltmeister looked at Maier appreciatively and continued, "Your mother did a good job, you know. Your heart's in the right place. You have standards. That's nice. But understand this, Ferdinand: this century is not one for the underdog. The rich flex their muscles, muscles like me, only younger and less inclined to question their motives, to get what they want. Right now, they want market shares. And Laos is a market untapped. The Vietnamese have been logging here for decades and have barely made a dent. There's so much more to steal. Hydro power, minerals, monoculture plantations, you name it. Southeast Asia, Africa, South America, all new frontiers in a new economic war. They call this globalization in the West, but we're wolves in sheep's clothing, thieves in the night."

Maier cut in while keeping an eye on Julia, who was still struggling with the revelation that she had a stepbrother. "We can't stop it; we can't even slow it."

She was a hard cookie. She was already losing that hard-drive-is-full look in her eyes. She was busy adjusting to her new reality.

His father nodded and continued, "You're right. But for personal reasons, I feel obliged to leave a mark, to send a signal, perhaps to build a monument to commemorate the losses that underdogs suffer as a consequence of the endless pursuit of money. I was part of it for so long. I've killed so many people in the name of democracy, progress, liberation and wishful thinking. Always for others. To fuel the dreams of the wealthy. It comes easy to me; you saw that this morning. It comes easy to my daughter, too. I'm as proud of her as I am of you. In fact, I'm gloating in the presence of my wonderful children. A rare moment I've been longing for."

Julia, sitting bolt upright on the far side of the bed, nervously lit a cigarette and said nothing. She couldn't bring herself to look at the two men.

"Now, at the end of my life, if I have to kill more, I'll kill more. Killing isn't everything it's cracked up to be, son. It's actually quite easy if you have sufficient motivation. I've never lost any sleep over it. And I'm so happy that you, Ferdinand, don't share the curse of feeling at ease with taking another man's life."

"You'll kill the Secretary?"

"This is the second time you've asked me. I don't know what I'll do. But whatever we do, we'll have fun doing it, right?"

Maier and Julia looked at each other. Maier felt an immediate poignancy. Life could be heartbreaking. His father was a cold bastard alright, dropping the truth on Julia like this.

Weltmeister grinned, "I won't share the marital suite with my kids, so I'll leave you to it. The first international agriculture trade show starts tomorrow. I think we should all attend, don't you? Liven things up a bit. See if Mr. Mookie sticks to his side of the bargain and brings three million dollars with him. I have no doubts he won't."

As the old man slid out of the door, Maier waved him to stop.

"Dad."

The master spy stepped back into the room.

"That's the first time you've called me that."

"What's your real name, your first name? I would really like to know."

The old man grinned and made moves to leave again.

"When this is all over, Ferdinand. I'll tell you everything you want to know. Everything. We'll have time. As long as I'm a wanted man, the less you know, the higher your chances of survival. And mine."

32

FARMER'S LAMENT

JULIA HAD GONE when Maier woke up on the couch. He drank a liter of water and stood under a cold shower until he couldn't take it any longer. She'd taken her bags, including her rifle, and disappeared, the same way she'd done in Luang Prabang. Only, this time she'd left as a sister, not a lover. The inner world of Weltmeister was quite unhinged. His father was nuts, a crazy puppeteer, guiding people on invisible threads to furnish him with a narrative twisted to suit his jaded emotional palate.

Maier was the sole occupant of the honeymoon suite at the Lane Xang Hotel. A phone call to the lobby told him that his father had checked out. There was no plan he was in on. He had no idea where they'd gone. He opened the window and leaned on the sill. Turning back into the room, he noticed the cigarette packet Julia had left lying on the small Formica table by the bed. The only thing she'd left. He leaned back and picked it up. His little stepsister wasn't trying to get him to start smoking again. The packet contained a scrap of paper and a key.

Maier,

Go to the main branch of the Laotian State Bank and retrieve a suitcase with a million dollars from security box 6235. Check the cash and make sure it's packed in waterproof plastic. The agricultural fair will have a few stalls of NGOs. Today, our father will give a short talk about the threat of unchecked development and the importance of the remaining forests in Southeast Asia. At 2.30pm sharp. Stall 1009. TreeLine. After the speech, we will all travel to Thailand together.

Transport has been arranged. Be sure to be at the stall, with your gun, at 2.30pm sharp. Wear your passport, the U48, the money and other documents in watertight packaging underneath your clothes. We love you. I'm in shock. And I'm giddy.

Julia

Maier found a lighter, burned the paper and flushed the ashes down the toilet. He packed his bag and wrapped his passport and the CD his father had given him in plastic. He was annoyed with his father's parting shot. What a control freak, dropping the bomb about Maier on Julia while lecturing on global politics. He taped his package to his chest, put on a shirt, stuck the gun into his belt, slipped the metal prosthetics over his stumps and left the hotel.

The river road was packed with Laotians in from the countryside. The agricultural fair had been well advertised on local television. Countless farmers arrived on huge flatbed trailers pulled by motorbikes and stayed in cheap flophouses. Some slept in or underneath the trailers. It looked like half the country of six million had turned up in the capital. Most of the exhibits at the fair were beyond the budget of the average Laotian village, but that didn't stop people's curiosity. The lure of a capitalist dream and the better life associated with it was strong.

The former US Secretary of State and the Laotian Trade Minister were billed to take a brief walk around the stalls at 3pm.

Maier was early. The pale winter sun was high up in the sky, providing the warmth of a late spring day in central Europe. A bit too cold to go swimming, a bit too warm to die.

He walked along the river road until he'd hit the bank. He asked a girl behind the foreign exchange counter for the safety deposit boxes and she led him to the back of the room.

Box 6235 was empty.

Maier left the key in the lock and walked out of the bank and into the city, away from the river. The Laotians hadn't kept to their side of the bargain. What would Mikhail, who had brokered the deal, make of that?

Maier had thought it unlikely he'd be able to enter a bank, open a safe and walk away with a million US dollars in cash. He was sure his father expected the double-cross. The family reunion was stressing him out. Whatever happened today, Maier would do his best to look after his own skin. He no longer had a client; he no longer had a case and he had lost control of his destiny. It was all making him nervous. Everything had always gone so well for him. He'd never be sure whether that was thanks to his father. The possibility that his life and career had been manipulated by outside forces, no matter how benign, now haunted him with the same persistence his father's silhouette had stalked him with in his dreams before their encounter.

He drank a coffee, black, no sugar, in a café by That Dam, a large moss-covered stupa, a mound containing Buddhist relics, a stone's throw from the US Embassy. There seemed to be no change in the security detail as Maier walked past the American compound on his way back to the river. The former US Secretary must have been keeping a very low profile.

Clouds moved across the sun and Vientiane went a little monochrome, befitting its socialist decrepitude. Maier walked in a roundabout way, past police and troops. The closer he got to the Mekong, the more the streets filled up. The sedate traffic had been blocked off around the city center.

Once he hit the river road, he turned north and made his way down to the embankment. One day, the municipal authorities would concrete over the land between the road and the river, but for now this strip of brush, ravines, sandbanks and unruly lawns was where the locals set up small restaurants and bars, parked their long-tail boats, flew kites, promenaded or simply sat and watched the mighty Mekong flow by. As the water level declined, the land expanded and some enterprising urban farmers grew a quick round of cabbages on the nutrient-rich soil, before the next monsoon would submerge their temporary real estate.

The agricultural fair had been set up on a piece of uneven ground at street level. A metal fence appeared to run around the land on three sides. The fair was open towards the river. The fairground rose high above the water, a steep ravine tumbled down to the water's edge. No long-tail would be able to stop here. No sand banks. Deep, muddy brown water stretched towards Thailand. A Ferris wheel stood near the ravine, its baskets dangling over the river. It was ancient, operated manually by young men who climbed the contraption like spiders and made the wheel turn by adding enough weight at the top. On the way back down, they had to jump. It looked like a tough life.

Maier entered the fair through one of three gates and made his way to the river's edge. Security was tight. The entrance was guarded by what must have been Laos' crack troops, tough-looking men in fitting uniforms, wearing boots, earpieces and brand-new weapons. There were only a few, but the artillery they had strapped on put the cops, some of whom carried Kalashnikovs, to shame. With this many people around, firing any of their large-caliber guns would create a bloodbath of epic proportions. The detective was swept along in the crowd. The gun bit into his stomach. At least he wouldn't forget it was there.

He watched a trio of teenagers wriggle out of their T-shirts as they stood on the edge of the ravine. A couple of camera-toting tourists, aliens from another world as far as the kids were concerned, had spotted them and were egging them on to jump. Maier watched the kids leap off with a loud whoop of joy. One of the tourists cursed in a language Maier didn't know because she'd missed the shot. As soon as the boys hit the water, they were washed downstream, arms flailing, living the dream.

He walked carefully around the entire fair and watched bug-eyed country people suck up farm porn – harvesters, tractors, trailers, silos, GM seeds, and toxically pink candy floss. Many of the punters carried plastic bags filled with *lao lao*, rice wine potent enough to drown a Mekong catfish. The roaming snack vendors sold sweet sticky rice with beans and boiled peanuts.

At 2pm, he noticed a change in the atmosphere. Police reinforcements arrived and the efficient-looking troopers who'd guarded the entrances now swarmed across the grounds, moving in pairs, mumbling into their mikes and headsets. It was all going James Bond. Maier hadn't spotted the other two members of his illustrious family yet, though he'd twice slunk past the TreeLine stall near the river. He returned to the main entrance, pulling a pair of cheap shades into his face. In a worn batik T-shirt and his vest, which helped hide the gun, he looked like any middle-aged hippie doing the Lonely Planet.

A couple of limos had somehow managed to get through the pedestrian chaos on the river road. A police escort was clearing the entrance, pushing the crowd in front of Maier. He could no longer see the cars. Why would a rich, influential seventy-eight-year-old veteran of international politics come here, to this field by the Mekong, to be squashed by incompetent cops and farmers who had no idea who he was?

It was 2.25pm. They were more than half an hour early. Maier fell into the slipstream of the VIP commotion which flowed slowly through the fair, towards the river, but he couldn't get any closer to where he assumed the special guests were walking. He could see neither the US Secretary nor the Laotian minister.

He suddenly had the feeling that he was in danger and discreetly pulled his gun from his waistband, holding it with both hands stretched out and pointed to the ground. He stopped and shuddered, realizing that all the cops he'd seen were locals. No US government security, no huge, beefy foreign bodyguards. No advance troop of discreet spooks. It was all a con. There'd be no foreign guest of honor.

He abandoned the throng and turned towards the river. Straining his head above the crowd, he saw several soldiers bearing down on the area where the TreeLine stall stood.

"Maier."

Léon had a flick knife at the detective's midriff. He'd appeared like a flash out of the heaving crowd. Maier let the Hmong feel the steel of the gun.

"Léon."

"Maier."

They were both pulled along slowly in an unhealthy near-embrace. Léon wasn't drunk. He was cold and rational and no less angry than the last time the two men had met.

"I have the U48, Léon. Let's make a deal."

He retracted the blade of the knife.

"Now we're talking, Maier."

Maier lowered the gun to where he'd held it before. They were still moving towards the river.

Léon was slowing him down, trying to pull him out of the current of people they were being swept along in. Maier was sure he was floating towards a trap. A trap set for Weltmeister. And Léon was making things more complicated.

"I have the file, Léon. What do you think?"

The Hmong looked at Maier intensely as they walked on at a snail's speed.

"Your father shot my sister."

"I didn't even know I had a father until last week, Léon. Stop blaming the wrong people. Get on with your life."

"This file is worth a lot of money? A lot?"

Maier nodded and tried to sound convincing.

"The Vietnamese will pay top dollar for it, Léon. Take it and let it go. Money is better than revenge."

The son of another secret agent who'd grown up without his parents and without a country looked at Maier severely. The irony of the desperate expression in Léon Sangster's eyes wasn't lost on the detective. They were both refugees from madness.

They reached the TreeLine stall. Two pairs of soldiers were moving in from the sides. Music blasted from the nearby Ferris wheel that was just starting to move. His father stood inside the booth, watching the approaching police, his hands in the pockets of a thin cotton jacket. He wore shorts and looked comical. From his left, Maier saw Mr. Mookie, a gun in his hand, pushing towards him. The old Laotian spotted the detective and Léon and started barking orders into a walkie-talkie. They reached the stall. Weltmeister looked faintly rushed, but he squeezed off a quick smile for Maier. The detective caught his father's next expression – a mixture of joy, concentration, love and murder that bubbled like lava – with pride and dismay.

Everything sped up. Mr. Mookie now shouted out orders. Two uniformed soldiers pushed Léon to the ground and lunged for Maier. Mr. Mookie raised his gun. He stood stock-still and took aim. Maier was hemmed in by farmers and soldiers. The Laotian agent was too close. Maier raised his hands and fell back.

Mr. Mookie's face disappeared. It simply disappeared. Maier couldn't hear the shot above the din of the fair. The killer must have used a silencer. The old intelligence man had dropped his gun and tumbled to the ground. The monster had just lost one of its heads. Another monster, more familiar and emotionally involving, had pulled the trigger. The family had spoken again.

Léon shouted, "Long Cheng, this time next week, we make a deal," and was gone, pulled away by uniforms. A couple of police were kneeling down next to Mr. Mookie to stop him being trampled on. Few of the revelers had noticed what had happened.

The sun broke through the milky clouds. As Maier looked up, he saw Julia next to him drop her gun, silencer still attached, into a neoprene bag she wore across her shoulder. The cops missed it altogether. His father had trained her well. He had created another killer.

Maier pushed towards the TreeLine booth, his stepsister right behind him. He almost tripped over the prostrate Mr. Mookie, guarded haphazardly by his men. He had no choice but to step over the dead man and squeezed between the two cops, who had no idea who he was. The stall was empty. Maier jumped across the table at the front of the cubicle, scattering brochures and documents. A blanket hung from the stall's ceiling. He pushed behind it.

Weltmeister handed him a diving mask.

"We have to be quick. This ruse will only work for so long. The money?"

Maier shook his head.

"Did you really think Mookie would pay up?" the detective asked, looking down at three sets of scuba jackets and tanks. A helicopter passed overhead. Julia pulled one of the scuba jackets up and heaved it onto her shoulder, silently watching the two men argue.

"Yin and yang. I wanted to switch Mookie off once and for all. Of course, they set a trap for us. Of course, there would be no money. The only reason they let us go on the river yesterday was because they believed my bluff of overwhelming American firepower coming up right behind us."

Weltmeister grinned from ear to ear. He lived for these moments. The close shave, the narrow escape, the ultimate gamble. He'd been at the edge of this cliff so many times before. Had trusted his luck and jumped. He pointed at the helicopter.

"And we have yet to get away. It's going to be tight. But here is Plan B. Spread your arms and hold your breath and off we go."

Maier could suddenly see the essence of his father, the thing that made him tick.

He got angry, "We are diving across to Thailand? That's the plan? You are seventy-five years old and you are diving to Thailand? You are crazy, Father."

The moment he said it, he realized that stating obvious truths wasn't going to get them anywhere.

His father shrugged, "Relax. It's been done before, son. A journalist kidnapped his Laotian girlfriend with scuba gear, from near here, back in 1978, after the Laotians didn't let her leave. There's even a Hollywood film about it."

"I can't believe you thought you could confront Kissinger in a mud field by the Mekong," Maier countered.

"I had my hopes. He was in Bangkok last night. Probably still is."

A shot rang out behind them. This time, the crowd panicked. More shots. The cops were firing in the air to stop people from stepping on their boss.

Maier was tempted to stay but he knew he'd be arrested. It was time to get out of Vientiane.

He put the mask on his head, stashed the gun in the pocket of his BCD, and lifted the heavy tank onto his back. He knew the drill. Though he'd never dived anywhere as murky as the Mekong.

Weltmeister had already strapped on the second tank. He showed Maier the two ends of a thin orange rope.

"As soon as we hit the water, we dive, connected by the rope. We all have a compass and swim due west. It doesn't matter how far downstream we drift before we hit the other side. We just need to get across."

Without another word, his father stepped to the edge of the ravine and jumped. Julia followed. She never looked back. Maier stood sweating with the tank on his back. He pulled the mask over his face and pushed the regulator in his mouth, tasting stale rubber. The blanket behind him was ripped down. He turned and faced several police with guns drawn, looking at him in astonishment.

Maier, seriously crowded by the authorities, bewildered by the antics of his family and without an idea in his head, did the sensible thing and jumped into the brown floods of the Mekong.

33

UNDERTOW

VIENTIANE TO BANGKOK, JANUARY 2002

WELTMEISTER AND JULIA SUBMERGED. Maier took a quick look back at the fair and heard more shots. He released the air from his jacket and sank.

The water was a shock. Sight was usually the only useful sense below the surface. Not in the Mekong.

Nothing. He couldn't see a thing. He'd gone blind. He started equalizing as soon as he fell away from the water's surface. He picked up the depth and air gauge that was dangling from his jacket and held it right in front of his face. Visibility twenty centimeters. Depth, four meters, five meters. Bottle full, facing west. They moved in a dark brown shit storm.

He couldn't see anything of his father and Julia until she bumped into him. A second later, she was sucked back into the great brown nothing. He kept the compass right in front of his eyes and swam as hard as he could, tugging at the cord that connected him to his stepsister. He wasn't sure whether they would reach the shore before their tanks were empty. The current got stronger the farther they got away from the Laotian capital. It was getting harder to move forward and he found himself breathing faster. Soon he would be hyperventilating, pushing used-up air back and forth in the tube between the tank and the regulator.

A boat passed overhead; its engine noise reduced to the whine of a dentist's drill.

The cord between Maier and Julia tightened and stretched downwards. Maier followed while trying to hold the depth gauge right in front of his left eye. It got darker. The water temperature dropped. Twelve meters. The light faded.

With barely a warning, he hit the bottom and moved forward in a murky twilight that flickered on and off like a faraway strobe. Far out, he thought. The boat came back, now barely audible, passing slowly overhead.

Maier hauled himself along the rope to Julia. The moment he bumped into her he saw that she was crawling along the river floor, holding on to rocks and plants to pull herself forward, kicking up silt that was swept away into the river current with slow-motion hurricane force. Maier almost choked into his regulator. Here he was with his new family on their first-ever holiday together. Scuba diving, no less. In the tropics. But this was the Maier reality, a far cry from the brochures. They were crawling along the muddy bottom of one of Asia's mightiest river like failing crabs, with half the Laotian capital's police in pursuit.

He pulled his air gauge close to his eye. He had about a third of his tank left. Somewhere ahead, it was getting brighter. They were now clawing their way along a barely noticeable incline. Maier clawed best with his metal fingers. He was sure of it. He took solace in it. The visibility improved slightly. The current slowed and garbage started to cover the river bottom – glass bottles, batteries, oil drums. Welcome to the free world. It was getting too dangerous to dig their way through the mud. They had to go up. He could see Julia, a meter away, crawling. His father, the mighty Weltmeister, the originator of their brilliant escape plan, was lost in the dust. Maier pulled the cord, hard. As Julia drifted into focus, he jerked his thumb upwards. She nodded.

It became easier to swim west as they slowly rose. The current seemed to pull them in the right direction. Maier surfaced. They were in a bend, about to be washed onto a sandbank. Forest reached from the waterline into the sky. Maier pulled Julia to the surface. They were in Thailand.

"Where's the old man?" he coughed. She held up her cord. It had been sheared off clean. Maier spat into the river. He wasn't surprised. Weltmeister had made alternative arrangements for his escape. There was some larger, overarching plan at play to which the kids weren't privy. Or perhaps it was just him who was left floating in the dark.

They drifted slowly to the nearest reach of sand and crawled onto solid ground. Maier felt like he'd done all the crawling he could ever have wished for. For a while, they lay side by side on the baking sand, drying, breathing, looking at the sky.

"Quite a creative way to leave a country."

She looked at him, her eyes both proud and troubled, "He's a great man in his own way."

"He shot two innocent people right next to me to 'warn' me. He is… He's a lot to take in."

She sat up with a quizzical look in her eyes, scanning the forest. For what?

"Would you give him up?"

Maier turned and pulled the gun from the scuba jacket. It was dry. He stuck it into the front of his pants and lay back down.

"No, I wouldn't give him up. But I am not sure how healthy it is to be around him for any length of time."

"I've lived with him for years," she shot back, and lunged for the gun.

Maier didn't try to stop her. She pulled the slide back and clicked off the safety.

"And how difficult do you think it would be to be around you? You're his son," she spat.

She turned her head. Three men had slipped out of the jungle and walked towards them. Two of them were armed with assault rifles. The third man was Bryson, his arm in a sling. He walked slowly, dragging his feet.

"Well, this was supposed to be Plan B. Mr. Mookie had the best crack team of cops in the country on the ground. And gets himself killed. By Ms. Rendel here. We thought, just in case you do escape from Laos, we'll have our people along the river. And now you're minus Papa. I mean, kids, we're just going in a circle here. One round after another. I'd love to just kill you and be done with it, but then I got that damn Weltmeister on my back. I love you guys."

Standing directly between Maier and the sun, Bryson droned down at the detective, a disembodied voice without much consequence. He wasn't making any decisions here. He was merely a messenger of bad tidings. He sounded weak. He had to be. Weltmeister had saved this guy from certain death just a week ago and now he was back in the game, without imagination or initiative.

Julia sneered at him, "I thought you'd died in that field, Bryson. All on your own, slipping away with the thought of young girls but not getting any."

The two men behind Bryson were young Americans with finely chiseled cold faces. Professional killers. Secret murderers. The shadow front line. Every country had them.

Now Maier had them.

One of the men wrenched the neoprene bag off Julia's back. As he stepped into Maier's line of vision blocking the sun, the detective could see Bryson clearly. The American vet looked almost dead. His face gray, his moustache droopy like a dying bird, his eyes full of pain. Gray stubble on his head. He wasn't here by choice.

"Never a dull moment with you and Weltmeister," Maier said lamely to Julia.

She wouldn't look at him. They were both living through their father's narrative now. The feeling of having lost control of his destiny overcame Maier again.

One of the two heavies picked up the two bottles and masks and motioned Maier and Julia towards the jungle with his gun.

The detective suddenly knew that he'd arrived at that point again. The point of departure. It was his life and his death that were on the line here. Not his father's, but his own.

"In the end, we've all been had, friends," Bryson coughed, wheezing.

Maier turned and watched the soft afternoon rays of the sun break in broad golden strips through the trees onto the sandbank, lighting up the speck of earth like a stage. The second man had stayed behind with the old American. Maier saw Bryson go down on his knees facing the river. He didn't fall. He wasn't pushed. He just kind of crumpled slowly and with somber finality. They were just a few meters apart. The veteran didn't turn his head to Maier.

"How I wish my guitar player was with me," Bryson mumbled.

Maier remembered standing on Kanitha's shoulders under gallows. But he couldn't feel anger right now.

Bryson was humming to himself. He consumed his last Asian sunset. His body heaved with sorrow. It looked so bloody dignified. The young American shadow soldier pulled the trigger. Bryson, American hero, expendable liability, fell face first into the sand. A couple of birds rose from the forest. That was all. But it was enough to take the men's attention off Julia.

She shot the man in front of her and turned quick enough to catch the executioner in the arm. The bullet propelled him into the sand next to his victim. Before he could sit up, she stood over him and pulled the trigger of Maier's gun again.

The silence that followed the shots was eerie, as if they were standing inside an empty cathedral, seconds after the echoes of a child's handclap had faded. The three fallen bodies had kicked up fine dust that must have rained down from the canopies. The light strips that fell across the sandbank became almost solid, a fine haze of gold and amber tones, a ladder to the heavens, or the bars of a jail; Maier wasn't sure what they reminded him of. He pulled his pants down and dug a spare clip out of the plastic pouch he had strapped around his leg and threw it to his sister.

She caught the clip and smiled sardonically, "You're becoming just like him, Maier. That's your destiny. To be like your father. It's something that happens to many men. You can't change it. All you can do is be aware of it. Especially when you live the more extreme aspects of his personality."

He shook his head. He had no urge to tell her or his father anything more. Maier was different. His father had always worked for a master, even killed for a master. He'd always been a part in grander schemes. Maier on the other hand, was a lone wolf, a man in charge of his own destiny. He wasn't a killer.

"Let's head for Bangkok."

34

ABSOLUTE POWER

THAILAND, JANUARY 2002

"Heinz."

"Sebastian."

So that was his father's name, Sebastian.

The sound was a little muffled, but with the help of a small cordless microphone Maier had fitted to the frame of a painting in the main corridor on the ground floor of Bangkok's Mandarin Oriental Hotel, he could hear what the men were saying.

The former US Secretary had emerged from a conference room, flanked by two bodyguards, and accompanied by a diminutive PA with pale skin and slicked-back hair. Maier understood immediately that all the stories his father had told him were true. These two men had once been close, he could see it in their body language. And Heinz, better known as Henry Kissinger, was a formidable presence; he filled the corridor with the easy aura of a Roman emperor.

Maier couldn't make out the young Asian woman's face from his discreet vantage point at a garden table, just outside the corridor his father had disappeared down two minutes earlier. She wore a short black skirt and had the poise of an angel. The kind of woman that looked right on the arm of an infinitely rich and influential man.

Hotel guests were coming and going around Maier, and the other tables in the hotel garden were all busy. He felt safe. Everything had been prepared.

Maier hadn't seen his father since emerging from the Mekong, watching Bryson perish and his stepsister kill two American agents. After arriving back in the Thai capital, he'd made all the arrangements Julia had asked him for. He'd been tasked with creating an escape route from the Oriental Hotel following his father's meeting with the former Secretary of State. Beyond that, he'd been left in the dark. But Julia had given him the feeling that he was almost part of the family and that they might all ride off into the sunset together. Deep down, he was certain it was all a sham. Maier knew little about family, and the situation reminded him of a spoilt love affair in which one party had lost the passion and the other was in denial. He'd always be stressed with these two around. His loyalty would never be rewarded. And yet, the security, even affection of sorts, which the family appeared to offer was seductive. The temptation to throw his present life away and run off into the sunset with his father was strong. And he didn't even know whether his father would take him along. No one had asked him. For the first time in his life, Maier wished for simpler, irrevocably lost times.

Weltmeister wore a sharp, dark suit that looked like it had been tailored for him. An expensive pair of mirrored sunglasses hid his eyes, but as the two old men started sizing each other up he took them off and beamed at his nemesis. He had that same look on his face as at the fair in Laos. He was ready to jump off the cliff again. Everything had moved towards this moment. He'd planned it all, starting with Maier's recruitment.

"It's been years," Weltmeister said in German.

"Twenty-seven to be exact. And it's not a reunion I relish particularly, I can tell you that."

The former Secretary's voice, usually laden with diplomatic rhyme, carried a barely audible, dark, menacing tone. One devil challenging another.

"What did you want to see me about? All this wahoo about the U48? Who cares about this today? The only pertinent fact that's not public knowledge is that we considered nuking Laos. We might have changed the situation in Vietnam that way. But that's history. This is 2002. The twenty-first century. The new dawn. Didn't you see the planes flying into the Twin Towers? Our brief encounter boils down to just one thing: What does an old relic like you want from an old relic like me?"

A couple of hotel guests walked past wrapped in beach towels. Recognizing the former US Secretary, they blushed and hurried on. The statesman's PA shifted her narrow back. Maier couldn't see her face through the glass, though there was something familiar about her.

Layers within layers within layers. Every reality in this game had alibis. The entire case was like an onion. You pulled one skin off to find another. And each one made you cry a little more.

Weltmeister said nothing and grinned. Lesser men might have been distracted by his intensely disturbing expression, but Heinz didn't seem to mind. He droned on, like an archaic oracle, "It was the war, you know. Wars need to be won. Go ask the Vietnamese if you don't believe me. They sacrificed millions to get us out of Indochina. And look at them now, poor, corrupt, hardly worth a thing. But their pride is intact. It means a lot to people. More than truth, more than reality. You knew the risks when you joined the outfit. You were our best man. We courted you. We trained you. You were the only sniper working for the agency that didn't have a military background. That's how special you were. But you got weak, fell in love, thought you could live like a normal person half the time. The moment that happened, you became a liability and an asset that could be exploited. Long Cheng was your downfall. Ours, too. We lost so much there."

"Is that why you didn't cross the border?"

Heinz did something to his face; perhaps it was his idea of a smile. Maier couldn't tell.

"I was never going to go to Laos. That was just a story put out by our embassy. It was part of my plan to bring Weltmeister out of the woodwork. It was me who found Léon and put it into his head that he could get his revenge. And it worked."

"A lot of people died in the process."

The former US Secretary shrugged.

"What was that old story about the omelet? If only you'd stayed in London painting your avant-garde crap, everything would have been fine, and I would not be standing here doing the secretarial shit with some guy I should have fired decades ago. But I guess you never managed to let go of that girl you loved. Germans are such bloody romantics."

The old diplomat's voice never wavered. He was becoming almost jovial and moved closer to the young Asian woman by his side. The two bodyguards were rattling in their frames, pumping adrenalin, studying the threat in front of them. Weltmeister, the best-dressed man in Bangkok's most exclusive hotel, stood his ground and smiled that golden smile.

To Maier, old men either looked like war criminals or hippies. He supposed that the growing depository of the decisions one made during a long life slowly assembled into facial expressions, body language, wardrobe and sometimes aura.

"What's on your mind, Sebastian? You'll strangle me in a hotel corridor in Bangkok? You couldn't have picked a more salubrious address for my passing? New York, perhaps, on the grounds of the UN? Or Angkor Wat? I'll be there on Monday. Life goes on. You know the game."

"I won't kill you, Heinz," Weltmeister said, switching to English. "I came unarmed. I just wanted to see you one more time before you die. And to take the only thing you really care about."

The old American said nothing and the two men lapsed into an odd silence. At the far end of the corridor, a young woman in a tight, long dress came clicking along on high heels, wrestling with a large shopping bag, cursing under her breath.

"Why did you have Valentina killed?"

"What, the girl we had taken to Cuba? When we realized that you'd disappeared, we handed her over to the Cubans."

He paused, either for dramatic effect or in shock at the way he'd just said what he'd just said.

"When you popped up again this year, I took another look at the file. She's alive, as far as we know. She lives in Santiago de Cuba. I suppose she must be in her fifties now. We have a phone number."

Maier could see his father's expression change. An unsound look came into his eyes. This look was the cliff about to be stepped off and left behind, with only the flimsiest of safety backups, the slightest of trumps up the proverbial sleeve. Weltmeister was ready to parachute with a cocktail umbrella.

The old diplomat sighed. His entire huge body seemed to heave. Then his posture was back to what passed for normal, full of self-confidence and bounce as he seamlessly transitioned into a different scenario.

"OK. I don't want to lie to you, Sebastian. You won't leave this hotel the way you came in. It's over for Weltmeister. We'll take you and you will never be seen again. But you knew that before you came here, didn't you? And you have some incredible ace up your sleeve and will try and make a daring and honorable escape? Isn't this all about honor, Sebastian? Right?"

The former US Secretary's young PA stepped away from her boss and unzipped her handbag. As Maier rose, he could see her pull out a small gun. He spotted the tattoo on her back in the same instant. The five sacred strips on her skin, the narrow, lithe shoulders.

The jungle visa.

He tore the door to the corridor open.

"Kanitha."

She was alive. She hadn't died on the beach. Maier's mind was reeling. Everything came down like a monsoon shower, heavy, immediately and without mercy. He'd been played.

Played by his father. Played by Kanitha. Played by everyone who counted in this case.

Kanitha looked at him as if at a stranger, raised the gun and fired. The shot was deafening in the narrow corridor. Maier hit the ground unscathed. Now he understood where this girl was coming from. His thoughts raced back to their first night together in Muang Ngoi and to all the lies that she'd furnished him with ever since their very first meeting. Life could be so twisted. He had to admit to himself, very much against his will, that Kanitha had truly fooled him. And she'd missed.

"Stop," Kissinger shouted. "Stop. Don't shoot. Not here."

His bodyguards lunged between the former US Secretary and the girl.

"We can't afford to have an incident here, of any kind, Mr. Kissinger," one of his minders warned his employer, only to earn a withering look from the former statesman.

Kanitha turned towards Weltmeister.

The former Secretary of State, loser of several wars, winner of countless prizes and author of books recounting his triumphs, tried to stop her, but he was too old and it was too late. As he pushed past his minders and pulled at Kanitha's sleeve, the young woman in the long ballgown closed in on the group, dropped her shopping bag and pulled a wooden hairpin from a pile of unruly hair that now gave way to gravity and tumbled across her naked shoulders. In one swift movement, she plunged her beauty utensil into Kanitha's throat. The gun dropped to the ground. One of the minders kicked it away but made no attempt to grab the assailant. Julia was back and she was in a killing mood.

Kanitha collapsed, her eyes wide, retching for air. Without gracing anyone with so much as a look, Julia carried on walking, the click of her high heels fading like a weakening pulse as she moved away. Maier stayed close to the glass outside, looking in, in complete shock. Julia had told him there'd be no more killing unless absolutely necessary.

Weltmeister stood motionless, relaxed, offering his empty hands to the bodyguards. They stuck close to their boss.

The former Secretary knelt heavily next to Kanitha. His face was white, his savoir-vivre had given way to something he seemed unfamiliar with. He patted her hand like a dog, but she had already lost consciousness.

"Mr. Kissinger," one of the security men said quietly. "It's time to go. We can't have a diplomatic incident involving a killing here. We'll have this cleaned up for you in no time. But we must leave now."

He nodded, dazed, and got to his feet without their assistance.

"I want that woman dead."

His minders looked nonplussed, "We will leave now, Mr. Kissinger, without delay. You'll have to leave Miss Kanitha here. And we can't run around the hotel after the assailant. Another time, another place."

The former Secretary of State looked like he wanted his men dead too, but he pulled himself together and turned to Weltmeister.

"Yoga, you see," he said, squeezing out a savage smile for Weltmeister, "prepares you for anything."

With that he strode off in the direction of the lobby, his steps uncertain, flanked closely by his men, leaving Kanitha behind, lying on the cold, smudged marble floor. Maier pulled the door to the garden open and motioned his father outside. Julia was right behind him, her high heels in her hands, her long skirt hitched up to her knees. Maier pulled the door shut and locked it. For a second, he stood transfixed, looking through the glass at the dead young woman. What was this job all about? What was life about? Finding truths and watching people die? Getting to like people who never let empathy get in the way of their agendas? Falling for girls who bedded him one day and tried to kill him the next? Who died and came back to life and died again? Kanitha had been a great woman, so much energy, so much determination, so much subterfuge. Even now he found it hard to match her with the fading statesman he'd just seen. And he found it much harder to accept, a second time, that she was gone.

"To the pier?" Julia asked urgently, pulling at his sleeve.

Weltmeister seemed to be in a world all his own. A beatific smile lingered on his face. He'd stepped off the cliff but he hadn't hit the bottom yet. Perhaps he never would.

"No, to the lobby," Maier said.

Julia looked at him with skepticism, the way one doubted a child that claimed to be able to levitate.

"Half the US security forces in this city are going to be there in about two minutes."

"Exactly, and the other half will be on the river. And I am not going diving again. If we are lucky, they will be so busy looking for us that they will not see us. Trust me."

Julia looked at Weltmeister, expecting her stepfather to assert his authority, but he just shrugged like a happy drunk, "I'm on holiday. I deserve it. I saw it in his eyes. Whoever said that revenge can't be sweet is a fool. I tell you it is, even when one revenges the unimaginable. Let's follow my son's game plan."

Maier ignored his father's ambiguous proclamations and moved them along a garden path towards the hotel's main building. Someone shouted behind them, but he motioned them to keep walking.

As they passed the pool, the doors to the lobby flew open. Guests and staff rushed out into the sun, shrieking in panic. A young, heavy woman fell into the pool as they walked into the oncoming crowd. A child stood lost, wailing for her parents. It was pandemonium.

"Now is the right moment."

Maier took Julia's hand and pulled her along. They entered the lobby and plunged into chaos. Right in the center of the sumptuous first port of call of Bangkok's finest lodgings, two skinhead thugs, dressed in shorts, sleeveless shirts and expensive garish trainers, their arms bulging with crude tattoos, stood slugging each other on the now blood-spattered reception carpet. Twenty more men, all of them Russian and armed with cans of beer and angry, red faces that invited no appeals to reason, screamed at each other, supporting one fighter or the other, occasionally lashing out at guests or staff who hadn't fled. The few people who remained in the lobby stood close to the walls or scrambled behind the reception counter, petrified. The atmosphere was electric. The simple, physical danger the men exuded was palpable. Any wrong move and someone could die. As Maier pulled his family gingerly through this tableau, the bedlam slowed down to a pinhole moment, and he had a feeling that the entire hotel lobby hovered on a precipice of a larger, more brutal unleashing of violence. Maier knew things unseen were happening.

He pushed Julia and his father past the fighters and towards the main hotel entrance. One of the thugs guarded the door. As Maier moved towards him, he stepped to the side and joined his friends closer to the action.

A bus had pulled up outside. A huge fat man wearing shorts and a Hawaiian shirt, sweating profusely, wiping his bright red face continuously, beckoned to them.

"All aboard; time for a round of sightseeing. I'm your tour guide."

Julia pulled a second pin from her hair.

Weltmeister shook his head and looked at Maier.

"Ferdinand."

"Sebastian."

"I did, of course, think of killing you too. If I wanted to be my usual one hundred percent, I would have taken you and Mikhail here out of the game. You know too much. But, as the former US Secretary said, it's all history, and who really cares. I got what I came for. I'm gone."

"Cuba is nice."

"Heinz was telling fibs. He was scared. He had his story ready. Even if they'd given Valentina to the Cubans, she would've been a white female non-person amongst male police with no accountability. I don't go for this kind of hope. I'm romantic but not stupid."

Two motorbike taxis pulled up next to the bus. The riders were dressed in black and wore helmets, dark visors down, gloves, black leather shoes. The bikes had no plates.

"You think of everything."

His father clearly took Maier's remark as a compliment and grinned. "I'll have to give the submarine I have waiting at the Oriental's pier the all-clear."

Maier stood lost for words. He was acutely aware of the seconds slipping away. He stared intensely at his father. Julia smirked at him, and he didn't like it much. The old man stepped forward as if to hug Maier but then just grabbed his arm to lean closer.

"Kill the Russian now and come with us. Prove yourself to me, son. Show some loyalty to the old man and we'll take you along."

Maier gently pushed his father away and looked into his eyes. The man known as Weltmeister wore the same mocking expression on his face as Julia.

Maier didn't move. His father shrugged, "You're not made for the secret life, Maier. I did my best to get you up to Weltmeister level. But you'll never have that freedom of self that's called for in a true child of mine. Always remember, without me, you wouldn't be who you are; you wouldn't be anywhere."

Maier thought the old man's speech grandiose, absurd and, for want of a better word, depressing. He'd just pulled his family out of the frying pan, and they were threatening to kill him and called him soft. He looked across at the Russian. Mikhail stood sweating. He knew. His eyes flicked from the motorcycle drivers to Weltmeister and Julia and back. Maier could hear his heart beat away the seconds.

Julia pulled his father away, "Time to go; the cops are almost here."

A smile crossed Weltmeister's face as he looked at his son for the last time. Maier knew that it was not meant for him, but for his stepsister. She had internalized the same kind of freedom his father had gone for. Maier took a step back. It was all he could do. Julia and Weltmeister got on the bikes and shot off. His father never looked back.

Maier, dazed, boarded the Russian's bus. Mikhail handed him a vodka orange, the juice fresh, the ice clinking in the glass.

He filled his own glass and looked at the detective thoughtfully, "It was very dicey out there. Your old man is dangerous. He's like a loaded gun. He was really thinking of getting rid of us there and then. You played it just right. Thank you, Maier," he lifted his glass, "When this is over, we will have to have a drink together."

Seconds later, the police poured into Bangkok's finest hotel from all sides and herded all but the two lobby fighters back onto the bus.

35

THE BEGINNING

LAO PDR, JANUARY 2002

MAIER LAY IN TALL, dry grass just above the runway, pointing his binoculars at a cluster of wooden huts that spread like mushrooms along both sides of the tarmac. His heart was racing. Long Cheng, the legendary CIA airport, the nerve center of the agency's largest operation, lay just below. Despite the city's dilapidated state, the view and everything it implied was mind-blowing. An obscure but crucial moment in twentieth-century history had played itself out in this valley. And if one cared to look right into the dark heart of men and their games in this remote, subtropical and stunningly beautiful fleck on the planet, one might be able to spot the silhouette of a man walking straight ahead, while the world burned to either side of him. His father had been betrayed here, had killed his best friends and colleagues here, had thrown his humanity to the winds here. A man could only start his journey once he'd arrived somewhere. Maier had arrived at the family shrine. He couldn't think of a better description for the place.

Sundermann's last call still bounced around his head.

"Your father planned brilliantly. He recruits his detective son to help him clean up his old ghosts and to find closure. I suppose one might say this is a plan twenty-five years in the making. Most people aren't able to think past the end of next week. A few, like your father, have very long memory. You should be proud that he entrusted you this mission. And he paid well. We can't complain. Except for the bullet."

His boss moaned in mock pain, "I won't come out to do field work again anytime soon. It's too dangerous. I'll stick to politics. That kills you a lot slower. I have the utmost respect for operatives who live through these painful, difficult projects, come out virtually unscathed and go straight into another one. Laos has been a humbling lesson."

That was one way of looking at it. But Maier felt anything but unscathed. He felt used. He'd lost fingers and bits of mind out there. He'd killed two men. He'd been played by a wonderful girl who'd died. He had a tattoo on his back. He'd gained a father who had barely a passing interest in his son and an assassin stepsister he'd slept with.

His boss' respect for his father's creative faculties outweighed the lack of any moral judgment on Sundermann's part on the deeds of Weltmeister.

"He has a brilliant mind. If he was a chess player, he'd be able to play ten masters at the same time and think five moves ahead in each game. He writes his own destiny, that man. Very few of us manage to do that. You're his son, and you're so much like him."

They'd both laughed at the cunning distraction Mikhail had pulled off at the Oriental Hotel.

"Look at it as time well spent with your family."

But Maier had his doubts about his life's new realities. And while Sundermann's optimism was infectious, the detective was in two minds whether to honor his agreement with Léon. He knew his father would be there. He knew there'd be more killing.

His boss would have none of it.

"Finish the job, Maier. Go to Long Cheng, find out what happened to Julia Rendel's father. See if the gold is still around. Face off your father. Find some closure. I'm sure he'll find you there. Then we write our report and it's another case for the archives and you can go back to less emotionally searing work. Oh, and train the new guy. Bring him up to speed. Show him the ropes. And teach him some German; he'll need it."

Maier had a habit of not contradicting his boss, but sometimes Sundermann was too much of a hard nut. Maier had silently nodded into the phone and, without saying another word, hung up, coming to a decision about the outstanding deal with Léon. He knew he couldn't save the Hmong but he had to try. Maier would have to outwit Weltmeister to stop the killing.

Long Cheng looked deserted. The landing strip was cracked and dotted with sprouting weeds. Crows circled ominously in front of the rocky cliffs at the end of the runway. The infamous CIA lair had collapsed in on itself. The wooden buildings were falling into the fertile soil. Papaya and banana sprouted everywhere. There was no electricity. A few more rainy seasons and only the runway would be left.

The road on which he'd traveled, on a dirt bike and mostly by night, had been atrocious. His back was killing him. Long Cheng wasn't about to be rediscovered by the world. National Geographic wanted nothing to do with it. But that didn't matter. For Maier, this was a pilgrimage. He needed to discover something essential about his father and perhaps himself. He hoped to learn something from visiting Weltmeister's moment of crisis. Just enough to make peace.

Maier was still wondering why the old man had come back, killed so many people, only to disappear again. Nothing was quite a secret anymore. The Internet had seen to that. Time had seen to that. Mobile phones, digital cameras, personal computers; the number of technological conveyances for our dreams and nightmares grew every day. Soon everyone would be a photographer, cameraman and storyteller. Everyone would be a spy. Everyone would be in the detection business. The increasing information overload made uncomfortable truths more available but less relevant, hardly evident in the tsunami of digital garbage that rolled across the world's virtual highways. Nothing was taboo and nothing quite mattered anymore. Everyone and his cat could be a superstar in the digital universe. A message was always just one amongst many. In a world like this, a man could barely be a man anymore. Hunters, their spears abandoned, their backs bent over computer terminals, their teeth blunted from eating processed garbage, were turning into geeks and nerds playing war games on their consoles, killing thousands while never experiencing the proximity of death. Soon, machines would rule the skies and take out undesirables and 'enemies of the state'.

Hard times for true outlaws.

Perhaps Weltmeister had simply followed his ego for one last blast out in the open. Men with secrets had no audience unless they hung those secrets out to dry and basked in the attendant sunshine. But the coming-out corrupted them, their experiences became cheapened once shared, their mystery turned into the banality of the everyday exceptional. It had occurred to Maier that this might hardly mattered to a seventy-five-year-old man who enjoyed killing people.

Maier suppressed the anger he could feel rising in his chest. He relaxed and sucked up the view once more. Then he slowly got to his feet, stashed his binoculars and descended towards the base. He was unarmed. They knew he was coming. He was just a delivery boy. And one way or another, he would meet his father down there for the last time. It was all in Maier's script. He was taking charge of his destiny.

Maier stuck to the well-trodden trails on his way down to the airbase. Unexploded ordnance was likely to be buried around the covert war's nerve center. He walked carefully. He'd brought the CD his father had given him. The U48. The very last copy of America's most secret military file from a war long gone.

"Guten Abend."

Just as Maier reached the first huts, Léon and a small band of Hmong soldiers appeared from a muddy alley. They looked like they'd been living out in the open for some time, unkempt and dressed in rags, all with the same unhealthy sheen that men who rarely slept and ate poorly acquired. They stared at Maier in silence, the silence of people who never get good news. He wasn't sure whether he appeared as potential threat or savior to them.

Léon, a baseball cap hiding his long hair, a gun in his belt and his hand on it, looked at him sourly, "I can't believe you're dumb enough to come here. But then, I also knew you'd come. You want to make the world a better place. You want to die with honor. You want to undo what your father did. You're so German, Maier."

"I don't want to die at all. No one does. And I can't do anything about my father's crimes. What do you know about honor?"

"I saw a man without honor kill his friends when I was a teenager. I'll never forget it."

He nodded to his men. They searched Maier quickly and got moving, dropping right into the warren of small abandoned homes that stretched down to the runway.

"I met your father right here, twenty-five years ago. Just a year or so after the war had ended. He'd come with his friend, Rendel. And my sister Mona. We were walking down this same alley together. I'd like you to show me where he killed them," Léon turned as he walked and grinned savagely, "Don't worry, Mr. Detective; I'll show you where Weltmeister murdered them."

"Aren't there any Laotian troops here?"

The leader of the rebel group spat onto the ground and muttered, "Nothing ever happens up here anymore. No plane has landed here for decades. The soldiers are scared of ghosts. By afternoon they all disappear to their compound and leave the town to fall apart by itself."

A feral, skinny dog lurked underneath the stairs of a stilted hut that leaned towards the earth at a sick angle. The mutt barked at them with cholera breath. Léon snarled back at the animal.

It took no notice and continued barking. The other men walked in silence. Maier could smell the desperation on them. They'd been abandoned by their erstwhile American paymasters. They were being manipulated by Hmong who had emigrated to the US and made a living by keeping the dream of a return to Laos alive in their communities. These rebels were too stubborn to give up their desperate fight against the Laotian government. They followed Léon in the hope that he would lead them to freedom. Maier had no hope for them.

They reached the runway. Léon motioned Maier to keep out of sight and off the tarmac, and they made their way to one of the concrete buildings along the airstrip. Apart from birdsong and the hound behind them, it was quiet. They entered through a shattered and boarded-up doorway. As soon as they stepped inside, Maier could smell dried blood. His hair stood on end and he knew that Léon had brought him to the right place. The wrong place. And he knew his father was here, too.

"My sister was lying there. She died almost instantly. I was hit in the chest. I didn't want to leave. I wanted to die, Maier. My soldiers took me out of here and saved my life."

The Hmong fighters stayed outside. Léon stood in the door of what must have been a master bedroom. Two metal bed frames stood in the center of the room, over a gaping hole in the floor.

Maier looked around.

"I have a feeling my father is here in the area somewhere. And that he wants to kill you."

The Hmong American grinned, "I know. That's why I asked you to come. What goes around comes around. Give me the U48."

Maier opened the pocket of his jacket and handed Léon the plastic case. Without a word, the rebel leader took his backpack off and pulled out a laptop.

"Léon, you're the last link to his past in Laos. He will kill you."

The Hmong shook his head, "He has to get me first."

"Kanitha is dead."

Léon snapped around and looked at Maier with contempt.

"What do you mean, Kanitha is dead? Of course she's dead. Are you deluded, man? She was killed by those two CIA guys in Thailand."

"That's what I thought. But she wasn't hit during the beach attack. That's only what Bryson told me. The official story they put out and hoodwinked us with. I never saw the body. He made her disappear. She was a plant all along. When you started talking about CIA gold in Vientiane, Kissinger got wind of it. Suddenly Kanitha showed up, established herself as a travel journalist with a handful of stories under her belt and latched on to you. When she thought I'd be more effective at shaking Weltmeister out of the trees, she latched on to me. She was waiting for Weltmeister. They were waiting for him. You brought them both out into the open."

The Hmong-American looked at Maier in disbelief.

"Yes, I remember now. She asked me about the gold. Several times. And I told her about Weltmeister killing my family."

Maier nodded, glad his face was hidden in the dark. Everything became clear, and he liked the version of the truth that was about to establish itself in his head. He was smiling.

"You were the bait they used to reel my father in. The US want a closer working relationship in Indochina and the U48 had to be tracked down, its originator silenced."

"When did she die?"

"Four days ago, in Bangkok. In a corridor of the Oriental Hotel. She pulled a gun when Weltmeister intercepted the former US Secretary on his way to his suite."

Deep lines formed on Léon's forehead, threatening to tear him apart.

"Who killed her?"

"Julia Rendel."

Léon rolled his eyes. The expression in his face softened. They both knew that a speck of trust had been established between them.

"Why?"

"She's Weltmeister's adopted daughter."

"He was trying to make amends after killing his friend, that sleazy East German cultural attaché, here all those years ago?"

The Hmong-American didn't expect an answer.

Maier continued carefully, "Kanitha pulled a gun on my father. Julia walked past in a ball dress and stabbed her with a hairpin. I think my father played through every possibility in this scenario a thousand times. It was his last assignment. In its own cruel way, it was beautiful, elegant, sophisticated. It all looked so effortless. They're really good at killing people."

"Who was Kanitha working for?"

"She was the former US Secretary's PA. And perhaps girlfriend. Kissinger looked beside himself when she died."

In the pale light of the laptop screen, Léon looked like a convalescing ghost. He was almost convinced.

"She lived with me, on and off, for almost a year."

Maier looked at this child of the war, this man trapped by his violent history, his voice full of sorrow and doubt.

Léon understood Maier's look and faltered. Maier could tell when a man had been beaten. The detective relaxed slightly. The truth could bring almost anyone down to the wire.

"I know. She told me. One day at a time. It sounds different now to the way she said it then."

Léon sat down heavily on the edge of one of the metal bed frames.

"She played us?"

Maier nodded.

"And your old man, he played us, too. The CD is a blank."

Maier carefully moved around the Hmong and looked at the laptop screen. Léon was right. Maier could not bring himself to feel surprised. He'd not bothered to check the CD himself. When it came to his father, he had very little faith, tempered by a faint longing that receded with every breath he took. Still, he knew that his sense of loss, loss of something he'd never experienced in the first place, would never completely go away.

"Another ruse, then. Weltmeister is here, Léon, and he wants to kill you. He will kill you. He told me in Bangkok that he was tempted to kill me too, just to bring the story to a neat conclusion."

The Hmong-American shut down his computer and replaced it in his backpack.

"I don't really care about the CD. That file. I don't need it. Look at this."

He pulled a powerful torch from his bag, switched it on and pointed it into the hole underneath the bed frames.

"In '76, after your father shot me, my men pulled me out. They also pulled out my sister and the German diplomat. Both were dead. We left them lying right here on the beds, and the troops that were chasing us never bothered to move them. Nor did they ever find out what was underneath."

Maier looked around the room. The bodies had gone.

"The gold is still down there?"

Léon nodded. "I buried them later, years later. Just out the back. Couldn't carry them very far. They share the same grave."

He flashed the beam around and got down on his knees.

"The gold is still here. My parents are still down there, too. Over the years, I managed to come back twice. To pay my respects and get some gold for my soldiers. And only I know about it. No one else does. Except Weltmeister, of course."

He clambered down into the hole. Maier looked at him impatiently.

"Léon, you're in serious trouble. You cannot take the gold with you to where you're going if my father catches you here."

The Hmong looked up at Maier.

"How many people have you killed since coming to Laos, Maier?"

"I killed two men in Thailand. In self-defense."

"Of course, Maier. I forgot. Thanks for reminding me. You have a life to live yet."

Léon laughed bitterly.

"You could go and live in the States–"

Léon cut him off, "In a fucking trailer, with eight other Hmong families, with the men drunk and unemployed, and I gotta sit and listen to them beating their wives and kids every night because they can't assimilate into the American Dream. Come on, Maier, I'm not stupid. There's no place in the sun for the undereducated bastard children of America. Not even the gold would make us part of the American Dream."

He disappeared out of sight and the room plunged into almost complete darkness. Maier walked to one of windows. The sun had already sunk behind the mountain ridges to the west. It would be dark soon. It could get very dark in Long Cheng. Time was short. Always short.

"You know, Maier, I'm not a hundred percent sure about you. You turn up and warn me about your old man coming to take me out. And I can't fathom whether you're part of his scheme. Or maybe the bait. Like I was bait. I mean, these guys don't care. Your father doesn't care. The former US Secretary doesn't care. I believe your story about Kanitha. It makes sense. Why else would she hang around with two old sacks like us?"

Maier didn't feel as humble about himself as the Hmong did. Kissinger was considerably more advanced in age than either of them. But he also had more money, charm, a good tailor and a better sense of humor.

The detective kept his mouth shut and let Léon talk.

"The fact that she's dead tells me that the former Secretary, the man who ultimately caused all this shit, is in pain right now. The man who pulled the strings on everyone including Weltmeister got what was coming to him. And one day, he'll deal with true Hmong justice in the court of the afterlife. Weltmeister, too."

Maier wasn't sure. If there was one person in the world who could escape such a Hmong court of the afterlife, it was his father.

As Léon dropped down into the hole beneath the floor again, Maier opened his bag and pulled out two small packages that Mikhail had given him. He quickly laid them in the darkest corner of the room. There was no furniture or rubbish to hide them under.

Maier returned to the hole in the center of the room just as Léon heaved a gold bar onto the floor. It made a dull thud and kicked up a small dust of cloud.

"There's quite a bit of heroin down here too, but lots of the bags have split open. A real mess. How long does that stuff keep?"

"Forget about the gold and the drugs, Léon. You can come back for it another time. Think of a way to get yourself out of here alive."

The Hmong laughed, "Oh, that's easy. I just go with whatever arrangement you've made for your getaway."

"There's no room."

Léon slapped a second bar of gold onto the floor in front of Maier.

"Oh yes, there is. I just hoped you'd be clever enough to save a space for yourself."

36

FLYING WITHOUT A LICENSE

Maier stepped out of the building. He carried two gold bars in his backpack. They were so heavy; he could barely stand. He wore Léon's clothes.

"Well, Maier. My men are gone. And I will leave presently on a conveyance of your choice. And I bet you anything, somewhere out there in the hills, a sniper is getting his scope in focus, even as we speak. You're not so bad, Maier. Once your father has shot you, I consider us even. Weltmeister will have his moment of loss just as the Secretary did. Just like I did."

The Hmong-American looked ridiculous in Maier's far-too large hippie shirt and vest. Maier wasn't sure the ruse would work. Léon pulled his gun and motioned the detective onto the runway. He scanned the hills, but he couldn't see anything but monochrome forest. His heart was heavy. He wanted the killing to stop and his father to crawl back under the stone he'd emerged from. He didn't want to die, nor did he particularly want Léon, another victim of the Secret War, to die. They had a lot in common. Old wars couldn't be won in the minds of old men who'd fought decades earlier.

Maier, wearing Léon's army boots, kicked some gravel across the runway. The light was fading quickly. Soon, he'd no longer be a realistic target, even for the best sharpshooter in the world. Léon disappeared back inside the building. Maier thought of dumping the gold and running for it, but he didn't rate his chances of escape too high. Best to stick to the original, haphazard scenario he'd cooked up with the Russian.

A white bird rose from a tree on a slope to his right and drifted down towards the detective. Everything was about to come to an end.

Léon emerged from the building once again, carrying a gold bar, dropping it by the side of the runway. He barely looked at the detective and went back inside for more.

Maier truly hated the kind of decisions he'd have to make in the next few minutes. No matter what he did, it would make him feel worse afterwards. He couldn't see the Russian yet, but he could feel the sniper's rifle on him, caressing his form, settling for the weakest point. He felt the hair on his arms stand up.

"Still alive, Maier?"

Léon laughed as he emerged, sweating profusely, with another gold bar. Maier looked at him, feeling sorry for himself. The Hmong-American pulled his gun, a quite unnecessary gesture.

"Come on, Maier; give the old man a chance before it gets dark. He's only got a few more minutes to get a clean shot."

Maier smiled beatifically, holding his breath.

"Otherwise, I might be tempted to do it when your pickup gets here," Léon added, and left to pull more gold from his family grave.

For a second, total silence hung over the valley. Maier looked up to see the white bird circle cautiously in the darkening sky, high above his head.

Everything was so broken.

The shot went straight into his back and propelled him forward. He hit the ground and lay on his side, helpless. Pain shot through him from all sides. Part of him had exploded. Maybe it had. Maybe he'd gone into shock. Maybe everything was totally irrelevant. The rifle's echo made the bird soar away across the nearest ridge. In the same instant, he could hear a faint but quickly approaching buzzing sound. The cavalry was on its way. A tear dropped from his left eye onto the warm tarmac.

Weltmeister had shot his son.

The buzzing of the microlight quickly grew louder. Maier couldn't move. He was looking straight at the entrance to the building that contained half the bad dreams of the CIA's Secret War. He could see

Léon emerge from the hole in the ground and, with some difficulty, lift a gold bar. For a second, the two men looked at each other. Like soul brothers, Maier thought. Léon smiled. He stood up and carried the gold bar onto the tarmac. The bullet hit him the very second the building exploded. The explosives Maier had left in the room had done the trick.

Maier turned his head away from the billowing smoke that quickly spread towards him and down the runway. The buzzing sound turned into a mechanical scream. Flames licked around him as the microlight touched down and rolled past. His ride had arrived. Mikhail climbed out of the tiny aircraft and ran across to Maier.

"All OK?"

Maier nodded weakly, "The good times are killing me."

"That's because your father shot you in the back."

"He thought I was someone else."

"No, he didn't."

The Russian pulled the heavy backpack off the detective's back and ripped it open. The sniper's bullet had buried itself deep into one of the gold bars that Maier had been wearing in lieu of a Kevlar jacket.

"Don't go soft on me now. You want to live, right?"

Maier managed to sit up. He shook his head. There was nothing left of the final resting place of Léon Sangster, his parents, and the bad dreams of Indochina. The building had disappeared. The explosive Mikhail had given to Maier had buried the U48, the file that probably no longer existed. Léon lay where he'd fallen, his legs crossed at an odd angle. The bullet had caught him in the back of the head and made a mess of things. The small pile of gold bars that lay by the runway looked pathetic, but Mikhail scooped the first one up and loaded it onto the small plane.

"How many of these can we take if we want to take off?"

"Just one or two. It doesn't matter. We need to leave. Weltmeister may think you're dead, but he's a cautious guy, and seeing the building explode, he might hang around to see what happens next. I don't think he saw me coming in with the microlight, but you never know."

The Russian came back to help Maier up.

"You're in shock. You know what we'll have to do?"

The detective nodded. With Mikhail's help, he limped to the small plane and climbed into the passenger seat. The Russian dumped one of the bars of gold on Maier's lap and handed him a headset. After Maier had put his seat belt on, Mikhail pressed a piece of steel wire into his hands that led out of the cockpit down the side of the aircraft.

"When I say now, you yank that wire hard. Then we go home."

"What is it?"

"You'll see; it's the proverbial string that pulls it all together and tears it all apart, Maier."

37

SILENCE IS MY HOBBY

"So how was that, sleeping with my son?"

"You're jealous?"

"There's no one to be jealous about."

"He was actually pretty decent, as lonely and proud men can be."

The man called Weltmeister grinned into the coming cool evening. He felt tired. He looked back across Skyline Ridge one more time. The fireball was gone, but a huge plume of smoke and dust still billowed across the valley. It was getting too dark to see whether there was any movement on the runway.

He looked at Julia. He was late. Twenty-five years late. He took her hand and pulled her up. A last look into the valley. There couldn't be any survivors. Even if Maier or Léon had not been killed by his shots or the explosion, the Laotian troops would finish them off.

They started walking towards their jeep. He sped up. He knew she didn't mind the spring in his step. She started jogging beside him, full of the years he no longer had.

"What about Maier? Was that really necessary?" she asked when they reached the bottom of the hill.

Weltmeister snorted, "He was my son. That was always a thorn in my side. Kind of a loose end."

"Aren't you overdoing it a bit?"

He snapped around to her then, a white flame in his eyes. Julia shrank back and kept her distance.

"Hundred percent. It's the only way. I have little time left and I want it for us. With Bryson, my Vietnamese handler, Mr. Mookie, and Daniels dead, Léon and Maier were the only guys still alive who could identify me. I couldn't let them live. It's against my principles."

She laughed drily and hooked her arm under his.

"Anybody ever tell you that you think too much, Sebastian?"

He smiled, not a care in the world, "Just call me Weltmeister."

In their green fatigues, they soon melted into the surrounding brush, barely visible for another few seconds, then they were gone.

38

OPERATION MENU

MAIER COULD HEAR Mikhail singing as they picked up speed and bumped along the runway like a demented rabbit on wheels. An old song from Mother Russia. It sounded mad. He was mad. The world was mad.

A bullet zipped past the glass cockpit. The microlight raced towards the karst stone formations at the end of the runway. Maier thought he could see shadows by the side of the tarmac. Laotian troops. The aircraft wobbled and left the ground, and Maier heard the Russian yank the stick with a sickening crunch to get the plane to rise and turn quickly into the coming night.

They were away. As they rose from the valley, the sun's last rays caressed the ridges in golden light. The former airbase below had already sunk into obscure darkness. Maier felt volatile in the tiny bouncing capsule, but it was a definite improvement to lying on the tarmac below.

"The shots that got you and Léon came from the east, so we'll buzz over there and take a look. They wouldn't have walked very far. We have about twenty minutes' worth of fuel, then we need to turn and make our way to Thailand."

"You don't think we'll get scrambled by the Laotian air force?"

Mikhail laughed loud enough to almost shatter Maier's eardrums.

"Air force? There's a good reason why not a single plane has taken off from Long Cheng for twenty-five years. Their planes are all wrecked. We'll have more to worry about when we come into Thai airspace."

Maier, glad to be putting some distance between himself and his family, wondered about the Russian's motivation to save him.

"What would you have done if things had not worked out and Mr. Mookie had ordered you to kill me?"

The Russian chuckled into Maier's headset.

"I always finish the job and I never cheat the client, Maier. It's nothing personal, trust me. You're my favorite heterosexual friend. We're both from the East. I love you like my brother. In future, I'll refuse any job that involves the assassination of Detective Maier. I promise. Anyhow, my client's dead and gone, and I don't care for Cold War secrets. I have my career to take care of."

They left the valley and flew over dense forest. The Russian brought the plane down low over the trees. Quite suddenly, Maier could make out a road beneath them.

It was almost too dark to see anything moving down there, but Mikhail swooped lower and Maier spotted the headlights of the jeep before the Russian did. He held his breath. It was his father's getaway car. As they passed low, really low, he could see Julia open the door, lean out and fire her revolver at them. She looked beautiful, proud, and unhinged. She was his father's true child. He felt no jealousy.

"We will turn and come up behind them once more," Mikhail cackled into the headphones. He made a wide swoop upwards above the trees and turned the plane around. Five minutes later, they were back chasing the tail lights of Weltmeister's jeep.

"When I shout 'Go', you yank the cord, OK? It's not much, but it's also everything."

Maier nodded half-heartedly, to himself. The philosophical Russian dropped the plane, its engine buzzing like a sick hornet.

"Go."

They passed the jeep. Maier didn't touch the cord. He tried to turn, but all he could see was the bright flash of the exploding vehicle.

They flew on in near silence.

Mikhail shouted, "That was your chance to get even, to make peace with yourself. And you made me pull the damn cord. You left it to the professional."

The Russian roared with laughter.

Maier looked down at his two metal fingers. As his eyes drifted to the landscape below, the small aircraft banked, and the earth fell away from them in a flamboyant swoop. He inhaled deeply, suddenly thinking of the job done, of new beginnings, and of freshly squeezed orange juice and quality vodka. He was free.

"This family holiday really took it out of me. I am tempted to celebrate. And to retire."

The Russian shouted, "No problem, my German friend; I'll take your job."

THE MONSOON GHOST IMAGE

DETECTIVE MAIER MYSTERIES BOOK 3

To Scott,

Thanks for the good times on the road, the sage advice on the first two Maier books, & the friendship... I wish you could read what happens next.

"A good photograph is knowing where to stand."

— ANSEL ADAMS

1

ANDAMAN SEA, THAI TERRITORIAL WATERS, OCTOBER 2002

THE CARABAO

MARTIN RITTER WAS READY, as ready as he'd ever be. Ritter was ready to die.

He'd collected and paid his debts. He'd made peace and hard choices. In a few moments, the ocean would take him away, into its impenetrable depths, or into a new life. The thirty-eight-year-old combat photographer was calm and focused. He'd played the life lottery many times, had stared into the abyss over and over, and had reemerged, loaded with tales of horror, triumph, and despair. Congo, Cambodia, Afghanistan, he'd seen it all. This was just another trip to the bottom of everything.

There was no land in sight, no matter which way he turned. The sun was about to come up and the slight breeze, fresh and salty, would presently give way to merciless tropical heat reflecting off the water from here to the edge of the world. He'd prepared everything and now stood at the stern of the *Carabao*, the luxury fishing yacht that had got him here, amongst neatly coiled ropes, buckets for the burley, and the seat which his best friend and assistant Fat Fred had broken a couple of days earlier while trying to pull a huge marlin from the great wet.

Deep sea fishing could be so much fun.

But Fat Fred had caught his last fish. Ritter's life was compromised. He'd made the deal at the crossroads and all who'd traveled with him had to go. It was time for a purge. The common term describing the likely fallout from Ritter's next move was collateral damage.

A few years earlier, in the wake of civilian killings in Kosovo, a bunch of German linguists had named collateral damage the un-word of the year. *Too right*, Ritter thought. Yet everyone was living in an un-world, talking to each other in un-words. Most people just didn't know. Anything. He knew. He was about to kill seven people, including his corpulent friend.

He knew.

He inhaled deeply and tried to listen to his inner voices. There were none. He was calm enough, all things considered. He'd never killed anyone. In fact, he'd saved quite a few lives in his time. Perhaps now, things would even out.

The point of arrival and the moment of departure were close. Martin Ritter was ready to let go – of his career, his friends, his routines and aspirations, his half-baked ideas about life and love and justice and the loss thereof, all the big questions. He was ready to let go of Emilie.

Even of Emilie.

This was radical stuff. In some ways, he'd be killing her too. And he was ready to let go of everything he'd seen through his view finder.

He smiled vaguely into the dawn and took stock the way his father, a reliable accountant from Düsseldorf, would have done.

Martin Ritter had been one of the good guys, one of the heroes of his time, a familiar face on television, a man who encapsulated the Zeitgeist, a winner. He'd taken great risks and had done great things. He'd witnessed history in all its beauty and terror and then some. He'd rolled with more punches than the great Ali and he'd enjoyed his victories.

At the height of his career as one of the world's most committed conflict photographers he'd loved and married a great woman. And yet, despite all the tales of heroism and the ensuing success, financial and otherwise, he had, as only a post-war German could, fastidiously held on to the fact that he was but one tiny cog in a giant matrix, a player with an exaggerated sense of self, stumbling through an age that had begun to frown upon the cult of individuality.

Had he been American, he might have believed that his work, discovering and documenting ugly truths, would be a modest but important contribution to the greater good, part of a valiant effort towards stopping all wars. But he was German, blighted and liberated by his particular history.

Martin had been photographing war and misery around the world for two decades. Stern, The Süddeutsche, TAZ and Bild, TIME, Newsweek, The New York Times, The Sunday Times, The Telegraph, he'd worked for everyone.

He'd been thrown out of countries by killers trying to hide their crimes. He'd been beaten by ordinary men on fire. He'd portrayed the down-trodden and poor as well as the cruel and the powerful. He'd dined with presidents and common garden variety torturers, with queens and with anti-queens. Sometimes it had been hard to tell them apart.

He'd traveled to the very heart of things that concerned people, all people, in all countries and cultures, that dark heart. He'd been down to the wire of common notions of success and decency, of fear, terror, and sublime elation. A life in images, assignments, war, corruption, nepotism, murder, and more awards than he cared to remember. Mansions made of mud had piled up inside him and around him, had filled with useless thoughts that had fragmented and washed away.

Ritter had been a reasonably honest man, a man of ideals and principles, but it hadn't been enough. His paradise was a featureless place, the absence of most things, much like the tranquil water of the Andaman Sea around him. Martin Ritter was tired of the high wire act. His hard drive was full, his emotional operating system dated and corrupted. He would crash or burn.

Despite his best efforts to help, to point, to cry, and to live, the world hadn't changed, only he'd gotten older, wiser, and less knowing. His long-held certainties had faded and every time he now pressed the shutter, it was as if casting a small stone into an expanse of water as immense as the one around him, watching the ripples the splash made extend a few metres towards infinity and then quickly fade into silent, blind insignificance.

He looked out across the calm water, half hoping for a storm, a typhoon, a huge wave, anything to carry him overboard and away from the traps he'd set for himself and jumped into, more or less consciously and always wholeheartedly.

That's what happened in life.

But not this time. He'd walked into traps before, eyes wide open, convinced of his righteousness. This time, the last time, he'd bent it as far as he could without breaking it. Perhaps his certainty was a tad overplayed. But the thought passed as quickly as the bird that fluttered above the placid, dark ocean, not quite decided on a resting place, even as the *Carabao* was the only solid opportunity visible.

As he leaned over the side of the boat, he spotted his reflection, distorted by the languid movement of the water and by his recent actions, his last assignment. His face flickered back at him, part handsome hero, part ugly other.

Martin Ritter looked at the GPS data on his watch again. The water was deep, almost a mile deep. He'd mapped out the currents and discreetly packed water and food for a couple of days. The next fishing boat wouldn't be far. He had a flare gun. It was a risk, a risk worth taking.

The crew was still sleeping in hammocks towards the bow of the *Carabao*, snoring in semi-unison, oblivious to his plans. With a last look around, he strapped on a weight belt, pulled the fins over his rubber shoes, took a deep breath, and then let himself slide over the railing in silence, making sure he held his cell phone above the waterline. As he drifted away from the boat, he zipped up both his wetsuits, pulled the mask onto his face, and pressed the call button. Then he dropped the phone into the ocean and dived straight down, as far into the dark void as he could.

The ocean shook briefly.

The *Carabao* combusted in a roaring fireball, shooting fiberglass panels, fishing rods, and scuba bottles into the faint morning sky as if loosening a celebratory firework display upon the world that found no audience.

By the time Martin Ritter resurfaced, the waves and ripples caused by the explosion were dissolving into the vast, featureless mass of water around him.

He was alone.
He was alive.

2

HAMBURG, GERMANY, NOVEMBER 2002

MAIER

MAIER FELT LIKE SHIT. He stared up at the pale, German afternoon sun pouring through his bedroom window, a sickly disc filtering through the haze of Altona and too many Camparis barely diluted by the night before. And the night before that. And...

Maier recalled that Campari Orange, to which he'd been introduced by a worn transvestite from Magdeburg who'd lost an ear and a half to a gang of Neo-Nazis, was his new favorite drink. A drink made from crushed insects, sweet at first and then bitter, and finally sweet again, just like that series of moments he called his life. Forty-eight years of life.

He'd also discovered that he had a soft spot for transvestites.

Oh, fucking dear.

Maier was down.

Detective Maier hadn't worked in six months, not since he'd slept with his stepsister. Not since his father had tried to kill him. Not since he'd lost a couple of fingers in an ambush on a Vietnamese prison camp in the jungles of northern Laos.

He'd been trying, halfheartedly, to get out of the desperate corner he found himself in, but the deck was stacked. Every morning he woke up surprised to have lived through the drink and sweat sodden night and a familiar process of deconstruction started anew.

He read the papers and hated the world. Why solve a crime when everything he read about was criminal?

Maier had been trained to be a political animal. While he'd never been enthusiastic about the communist propaganda he'd grown up with, he'd absorbed it and it had shaped him. His political sensibilities had their origins in his Cold War Eastern German youth and young adulthood, but those old certainties had long gone.

He'd worked as a foreign correspondent for the state-owned GDR media until the Wall had come down. Then he'd worked for West German media, on the road, out of hotel rooms both shabby and sumptuous. Assignments from Cameroon to Mallorca. A couple of years of that and he'd started to get bored.

He'd joined the Deutsche Presse-Agentur, better known as DPA, and by the mid-90s, Maier had begun to drift through most of the dirty little wars of the late 20th century – from the Israeli occupation of the Palestinian Territories to the civil wars in the former Yugoslavia and the high-altitude conflict in Nepal. But he'd left it all behind when he'd lost a Cambodian friend to a Khmer Rouge bomb five years earlier. He'd wanted nothing more to do with war.

And now it was all around him.

The twin towers had tumbled. A clear demarcation line had been drawn in the collective narrative of the brotherhood of man. People weren't arguing about issues anymore. People were arguing about what had happened and what was happening. People were arguing about the course history had taken and was taking, about who was writing it and how it was being broadcast and consumed, and they no longer agreed on the broad strokes. The truth was becoming just another story. For better or for worse, certainty was fragmenting. A hard bread for a German whose world had already fragmented.

Maier could hear the war drums without getting out of bed. He could feel the ripples of the attacks in New York expanding on and on, to the four corners of the world, to the rim of infinity. He could feel them because he had no other life to speak of, no partner, no family, and few friends who weren't connected to his demi-monde. He was disillusioned with the media he had once been a part of because it so rarely questioned its own questionable narratives.

By the time he'd had his first drink, vague thoughts of self-help he sometimes nourished had gone out the window. Maier felt impotent. Perhaps he should quit his job, retire from the detective business and work in a bar. He spent almost all his time in bars anyway. Perhaps he should blow the rest of his savings on a couple of months of Cocaine Carolina on the Kiez, drifting through the after-hours clubs with other happy souls like himself. He felt like he'd worked enough. Loved enough. Seen enough, done enough.

When he looked in the mirror, his inner life was on full display, spotty skin, shoulder-length, greasy hair from another age, deepening lines in his almost gaunt cheeks, his green eyes dulled by booze, self-inflicted monotony, and isolation. Wasn't this exactly the place private detectives were meant to occupy?

His cell phone rang. Maier retrieved his battered Nokia from a two-week-old pile of tired underwear that lay scattered around his fetid bed.

"Maier," he said as a way of answering.

"Morning, Maier. There's a job. Time to rejoin the family," his boss Sundermann said.

Maier grunted at Sundermann, tempted to throw the phone through the closed window at the sun.

"I don't have a family."

"Yes you do."

"What, some cousin I have never heard about wants to suck away the last shreds of kindness I have in me?"

"No Maier, we're your family. The family of noseys. There's a job, and you and Mikhail are on it."

Maier grunted again and coughed up the phlegm of a heavy smoker twice his age. God, he hoped he wouldn't be around at 96, drooling like a fool, unable to remember the good times. He could barely recall them now. He was tempted to laugh but remembered that Germans usually went to the basement to do that.

"Time to take a trip down memory lane, Maier."

"I have just been there. It wasn't good."

"Stay morose, Maier, it doesn't suit you."

"Nothing suits me right now, *Herr* Sundermann."

His boss paused. Perhaps the owner of Hamburg's most prestigious detective agency was hung-over too. It was possible, though it would hardly be the result of a three-day Campari Orange binge. Sundermann had the sensibilities, connections, and wherewithal to live it up in the more salubrious social circles of Germany's second city. He wouldn't be sipping crushed insects.

"That's why I put Mikhail on the job with you. You know, you train him and he covers your back."

"You are telling me I am losing it?"

This time his boss did not hesitate.

"You've lost it, Maier. And no one regrets that more than the family. And no one's blaming you, the last case was…difficult."

Maier sat on the edge of his bed and looked at the holes in his dirty socks, not sure whether to feel rage or sorrow. Sundermann was a man of few words, so this should have meant a lot.

"Emilie Ritter just called us. Her husband is missing, presumed dead."

Maier sat up and coughed past his phone. The mention of Emilie Ritter had jerked him back to half-life.

Fuck memory lane.

"I know that. It was in the papers. It had to happen one day. Combat journos have a high mortality rate. That is why I became a detective, remember?"

"Then you also know he wasn't shot by a sniper. Funeral's on Tuesday in Berlin. At the dome. Ritter really was something. A good German."

"I know that too, I read the papers. National hero killed in boating accident. Nation in mourning for our greatest post-war photo journalist. I am with it, *Herr* Sundermann."

"Good to hear that, because Ritter was seen alive and well in Bangkok a couple of days ago. And that's not in the papers. It's what his wife says."

Maier felt sick. His bedroom started to turn.

"I'll be there in an hour."

"Good man." Sundermann chuckled and then hung up.

"I doubt it," Maier answered to no one but himself.

3

BERLIN, GERMANY, NOVEMBER 2002

DEATH AND GLORY

MAIER STOOD by the front pews in the Berlin Cathedral, the Berliner Dom as the Germans called it, wearing his only suit, fresh from the dry cleaners and a little frayed around the edges. He tried to take in the whole damn travesty, sure that Martin Ritter would never have wanted this. It reeked of state funeral.

The world was desperate for heroes.

Ritter had grown up in Berlin and he'd be buried here. Maier doubted a journalist had ever been awarded a service in this Kaiserzeit edifice. Everyone from Nina Hagen to Oliver Kahn was milling round under the church's huge domed and frescoed ceiling amidst the quiet cacophony of several hundred subdued voices. Maier felt quite alone amongst the hushed chunks of glitterati gossip. Of course, he felt alone. He was alone. He was a lonely drunk, feeling sorry for himself.

His new partner and one-time assassin for hire Mikhail had disappeared into the VIP funeral crowd. The Russian was surprisingly agile in his black tuxedo, which added a touch of sophistication to his camp-thuggishness. He wore his shoulder-length, gray-blonde hair with the clout of an aging sports star. He had the airs of an eastern Mike Tyson who read Bulgakow on Quaaludes. He was the heaviest, most dangerous man on the premises. Probably. On the periphery of the occasion, Maier had spotted other men used to wet work – muscles straining in a couple of conservative suits, right by the doors, the only spot it was almost acceptable to be wearing wrap-around shades. The two looked too fashionably dangerous to be German.

Americans perhaps.

Maier remembered Ritter, the celebrated conflict photographer from several conflict zones, a rather intense young man with plenty of brooding charisma, a quick dry wit, and an uncanny ability to make good career moves. The two men had never worked together, but they had bumped into each other in Kashmir, East Timor, and Cambodia— Asian hells Maier had covered as a war reporter for DPA.

They'd known each other casually in Hamburg, with Martin and Emilie dropping by Maier's apartment a few times to drink copious amounts of vodka and exchange war stories. They'd never gotten close. Probably because Maier had liked the German photographer's French wife more than the man himself, and she too had seemed rather positively inclined towards the older writer. But those sentiments had never been articulated and their association lay ten years back.

As he looked at Ritter's coffin, the detective was acutely aware of time passing. Every day the finite became more certain.

The black casket stood a little to the right of the altar. Everyone kept their distance, perhaps because it was empty. Following the mysterious destruction of the deep-sea fishing yacht they'd been traveling on, neither Ritter's body, nor that of his long-time side-kick, cameraman Frederick, had been recovered.

Maier pushed a few graying strands of hair from his face and smiled to himself, ever so slightly, so as not to upset the solemn atmosphere. He was glad to have left the war business. Happy to be a living loser. Nowadays, he merely joined little wars, involving just a few people and a limited number of dirty secrets and atrocities that could be examined, dissected, analyzed, and occasionally resolved without the immediate risk of severe injury or death. Well, not altogether without risk. Maier had no death wish. He thought of himself as just moderately self-destructive. Despite his depressions and misgivings, he had miles of crushed insects ahead of him.

He drifted off into daydreaming about the good years he'd spent on the front lines, amongst men of violence and infinite sorrow. Those were times past, and he was alive. And for some reason, Martin Ritter, who'd never stopped pursuing just one more shot and one more story in the cold hearts of men, was not.

Officially at least.

"Hallo, Maier, it's been a long time."

"Hi, Emilie."

For once, Maier's usually decent social skills evaporated as soon as he'd gotten past the formal greetings. Emilie Ritter was sadly radiant, dressed in an elegant black pinstripe suit, a pillbox hat with a black veil partly obscuring her tanned and drawn face, a simple gold chain on her right wrist, and a conservative timepiece on her left. The shoes, all pointy black leather, needed spurs and served as the *piece de resistance* of her outfit.

In her younger years, Ritter's wife had been a bit of a rock-n-roller, a countercultural type who'd liked to flaunt protocol. In the 90s, she'd worked for an organization helping Palestinian refugees. She'd been a cool, honest, and fierce activist, though not quite as risk dependent as her younger and brasher husband.

Despite the somber light and the occasion, Maier could see that Emilie looked well. She was almost as tall as him, lithe and straight shouldered. She carried herself like someone who swam a mile a day. Every day. Her grey eyes had lost a little of their wicked sheen as she gazed through the short veil at the detective. Their meeting, the first in a decade, sent a small shock wave down his spine and he wasn't sure why. He hadn't felt interested in women in a while. He'd been too drunk.

He smiled politely, trying to remember what his face might look like to assemble it appropriately.

She held out her hand and grinned without happiness.

"You're looking...good."

The detective shivered into his shirt. She knew he'd blown it, that he was past his sell-by date. Everyone knew.

Maier forced a smile and scanned past Emilie, trying to get a sense of who was watching him. Too many people. Clearly, he was paranoid. He tried to calm his breathing and focused on his client.

"Thanks for coming. I appreciate it. I take it you are working for me," Ritter's wife offered.

"Yes," was all Maier said.

"I appreciate that too. I didn't know where else to turn. You were my first and only choice," Emilie added.

Maier suppressed the urge to cough alcohol-laced bile into Berlin's most hallowed venue. *Trap*, was all that went through his mind, though he couldn't put his finger on the how and why just yet.

"Yes," the detective mumbled once again.

"Let's talk later when this travesty is over and you've sobered up. I'll pop over to Hamburg," Emilie said, dry ice in her voice. She raised an inquisitive eyebrow beneath her netted veil, "You're still up to this kind of thing, aren't you, Maier? You look a bit… lived in. What happened to you?"

Maier managed his second smile of the day.

"Yes. I am still the best. I just don't go to war anymore. Leave that to the kids. They are better with prosthetics and funerals."

He hoped she would catch the irony. But Emilie just looked bitter. Maier had lost his tact too.

"You don't look your best, Maier. But your *Herr* Sundermann assured me that you and your partner can deal with extreme investigations. I suspect the fact that Martin is not in that coffin over there and that he might still be walking around without feeling the need to get in touch with the woman who loves and adores him, is just such an occasion."

Before he could think of something witty, severe, or at least appropriate to say, she'd turned and elegantly floated across the marble floor to chit-chat with the surgically enhanced mistress of a former German president who greeted her with the professional smile that belonged exclusively to wealthy vampires. Not Maier's world. Not anyone's world.

Maier hoped his own deeply lined and worn face had communicated some degree of the genuine warmth he still felt towards the French woman. But he couldn't be sure. Of anything.

At least she hadn't noticed his missing fingers or their replacements. Maier was still shy about his loss of digits. The prosthetics, however useful, were making him more freakish than he cared to be.

It was almost time for a drink, he thought, sweating, aware of his own faint odor that appeared to become more pervasive with each clusterfuck catastrophe he lived through. Maier nodded to himself like one of those plastic dashboard dogs so popular with a certain class of Germans and retreated to the back of the church.

Being a little further from godliness would make him feel more comfortable.

One hundred and fifty kilos of Russian super-power sidled up next to the detective. "Some strange people here."

Maier turned towards Mikhail. "You mean the celebs? Ritter is a national hero. He went where no man has gone before. Over and over again. I didn't like him too much, but he was the real deal."

"I saw you talking to his *babushka* just then," Mikhail said. "Watch your body language, Maier. Obvious that you're still fond of her."

His new colleague was also sweating, despite the cool temperature inside the Dom.

Maier grinned defensively.

"Hey, that's the first time you've smiled since you failed to kill that pig, your father," Mikhail added.

"So, what of strange people?"

"Oh, I don't mean the beautifully loving, famous people. It's the cold-hearted males by the doors that caught my interest. Definitely not German security. Americans, no sense of humor. Hardly friends of war reporters," Mikhail said. "Asked one of them for a light. Told him I was from Kazakhstan and had spent years on the world's battlefields. He didn't ask what battlefields. He didn't care. Had the feeling he was trading in darkness. But restrained. A guy used to do wet work under strict orders. These are interesting times, Maier. Those doorstoppers are messengers of the new game, the one of the nine-eleven world. They made me feel old school."

"You are a romantic, Mikhail."

"Yes, I'm a proud and gay Russian. But I'm a pragmatist too and we're working, not mourning. As are the fashionable doormen."

"You have your camera?" Maier asked.

"All done," the Russian grinned.

4

BANGKOK, THAILAND, NOVEMBER 2002

WET WORK

THE ROOM WAS small and windowless with cameras stuck in the high corners. The concrete floor was smooth. It smelled of old and new wars. Ritter had set up his tripod opposite the bench that the HVD, what they called the high-value detainee, was tied to. The space between them felt airless, but that was an illusion. Everything was an illusion. That's why he was there. He'd be the first to capture the illusion, the fallacy.

Welcome to the end of the world. Another end. There were so many. But this was different, dark matter of a new school. Ritter was in a whole new world here, a political space that was being carved out as he pulled his lens into focus, a space that would never go away again. Not in his lifetime anyway. He felt detached, kind of at ease, but also wired to the max, a constant quiet shiver passing through him, licking at his core. This was the next level. A Western nation letting go of so much— dignity, pride, aspiration, perhaps even hope.

The two Americans, Dobbs and Williams, were in shirtsleeves, not nearly as detached as Ritter.

A farmer's kid from Ohio fighting the good fight, Dobbs was handsome in the way men in fashion catalogues were handsome— smooth as a polished rock face and instantly forgotten. Ritter knew Dobbs from

Afghanistan. The photographer was working hard on becoming his current jaded self then and Dobbs had long been connected to the dark side of heroin, girls, and undocumented renditions.

A versatile guy. Dobbs had been chosen for his zeal and commitment as well as for his impunity. They'd called him Mr. Innocence out there.

Williams, a much smaller man with office posture and thinning hair, was a psychologist. He had some medical skills, if not ethics, but he was clearly being led. Dobbs called the shots and Williams looked like the kind of guy who would chew through his own arm for his master. He was here to make sure that the prisoner didn't die or go insane as a result of the enhanced interrogation techniques they employed. Williams was also the intellectual back-up of the project. It was his organization, the American Psychological Association, that provided the intellectual rationale for turning men into meat.

The two Thais were something else. General Thongsap had been drafted in from some secretive military unit that stretched back to the Vietnam War. The man was used to wet work. In his early fifties, a square head and a bronzed broad face, his strong arms covered in faded magic tattoos promising protection from bullets, knives, and, presumably, unknown devils. His eyes told the story. Whatever was coming was routine work, in the service of the nation. Thongsap gave himself the air of a dependable lapdog.

The other man, Suraporn, came from a different world.

A plastic surgeon by day, and a well-known Bangkok socialite by night, the doctor— and from an ethical perspective this term had to be applied with great caution or insane abandon— had done skin grafts for several politicians' mistresses who'd been victims of acid attacks.

One day, the police had caught him disposing of a mutilated corpse. He'd killed a prostitute and sown a dog's face onto her peeled skull. Suraporn knew the right people to call for help, the case had disappeared, and he'd been sent to Thailand's restless south to torture alleged Muslim rebels using the same guidelines for institutionalized brutality that the Americans had unleashed a year earlier. Suraporn was one of those men who considered themselves artists in their fields.

The agency had gotten wind of his skills and recruited him. They didn't trust him, but they'd been told that he was the best cleaner in the region and that he produced results quickly. Suraporn had confided most of this, with a little understated glee in his voice, to Ritter on their first meeting, establishing his credentials while gently instructing the photographer about the need for commitment, discretion, and humility. A crippled fist in a silk glove.

Suraporn was respectable through and through. Family man, three children, houses, BMWs, the whole brood regularly in the society pages of Thai Rath, the country's largest newspaper. Suraporn's American wife, his most highly prized possession, had fake boobs and Botox lips that put Angelina Jolie's to shame.

Just as importantly, Mrs. Chantal Suraporn dutifully accepted the traditional Thai code of conduct a high society woman was meant to adhere to and waited for her busy husband in their Sathorn villa or down south in their apartment in Hua Hin, where she would get distracted by the pool boy or the foreign photographer her husband had once brought for dinner, the one who liked taking kinky pictures. That had been after Suraporn had transformed Ritter's face, had smashed his features, and reconstructed them. No dogs' faces that time around.

Bad cop and worse cop.

Past and present. Concrete and abstract. Painful and painful. Fucking dangerous. Very.

Some kind of life.

Ritter grinned and adjusted his tripod.

Some kind of life insurance.

The room was geographically on Thai soil. Legally, if that term could be applied to the situation, they were on American soil. But really, Ritter felt, it was located in a kind of no man's land, an ocean of darkness far below somewhere, populated by the truly cursed. It was an exclusive club, for sure. Membership demanded culpability. He could barely perceive the surface of what was going on. They were operating so far beneath ideas of soundness that even the devil squealed in discomfort at the thought of this submersion. Right now, the squeal was about to turn into the high-pitched whine of a million furies.

For the fifth day in a row, the four men, tense and aroused by their power, went to work on the HVD.

Ritter pressed the shutter.

Again, and again.

5

HAMBURG, GERMANY, DECEMBER 2002

THE FAMILY

"My husband is alive."

Emilie Ritter looked as drawn and resolute as she had at her husband's funeral a couple of weeks earlier. She'd cut her hair short and she had the air of a beautiful lost soul doing penance for someone else's misdeeds.

Sundermann, dressed immaculately in a black suit and tie, delicately pushed a glass of port across the table towards his client.

Maier hid behind laptop screens and the file on the Ritters, concentrating on his coffee that was long cold.

Mikhail, dressed in one of his ubiquitous Hawaiian shirts and jeans, had propped his considerable frame against the edge of the office's bay window that looked into Venusberg below. He was bare foot and when he stepped outside, he did so in luminescent green Crocs, a new kind of plastic shoe he loved. Sundermann thought them so ugly that he encouraged his new employee to leave them in the hall outside. This, Maier supposed, was what family was all about.

. . .

Emilie Ritter raised the glass and then knocked her drink back in one movement.

Her statement, delivered with the authoritative certainty Maier remembered her for, hung in the room, waiting to be shot down or accepted. The pale sun got a break in the usually doom-laden, dirty, grey winter sky and tried to push across the Nordelbe into the plush offices of Hamburg's most prestigious detective agency.

Sundermann's bunker, as its owner liked to call it, resided in a nondescript office block a little north of the Baumwall U-Bahn station. Maier usually walked to work from his apartment in Altona, on the rare occasion he bothered to go in. He had to admit it. He loved the walk. He loved the Altstadt's troubled street life, the tourist traps on Reeperbahn. He loved meandering along Hafenstraße through rain, sleet, and occasional sunshine.

Walking was good. It emptied the mind.

Right now though, his mind was in gear, more than it had been in months.

The job was on and he wanted to help. He also wanted to work. He needed to work. He needed to feel himself again.

Miles of crushed insects felt like hollow victories.

"Do you have any concrete proof, Mrs. Ritter?" Sundermann inquired, not a hint of judgment or predisposition in his voice, while gently pushing contractual paperwork into her hands. Maier never stopped admiring his boss's diplomatic skills. That man could charm a snail onto a razorblade.

Emilie looked at Maier and shrugged.

"There were two men in dark suits at the funeral," Emilie said. "Right at the back of the Dom. Not on any guest list, but they got in despite security. The same men showed up at our house three days ago. Rang the doorbell and then more or less forced their way in. They then sat down like professionals and told me they were working with the US government, following up on leads they wouldn't divulge, and that Martin was part of their investigation. No ID forthcoming. Asked me where my husband was. I think they were trying to figure out whether I told them the truth about not having heard from Martin since he disappeared. That convinced me he's alive. I'd really like you to tell me otherwise, so I can have some peace. It's driving me crazy."

Maier looked at Mikhail and pushed the photographs of the two goons from the Berliner Dom across at Emilie.

"These two?"

She nodded silently, half impressed that the detectives had already done some homework.

"Did you call the police?" Maier asked.

Emilie looked directly at Maier, her expression sour. "You know I wouldn't do that. The cops are useless. Period. Don't trust them. ACAB, remember?"

Maier refrained from commenting on her ideology. Everyone had to find their dignity somewhere.

"When did you first hear about Martin possibly having survived the sinking of the yacht?"

It was Emilie's turn to push an A4 sheet of paper across to Maier.

"I received this email in July. I couldn't bring myself to do anything about it. I thought it was a hoax, a mean-spirited attack by someone who didn't like Martin's work. Or someone from my past. I did make some people uncomfortable in my younger days. You know, we used to get a lot of hate mail when he was… still active."

Maier took the note and read it.

Your husband is alive. He lives in Bangkok and is involved in the crime of the century. Thought you should know.
  The Wicked Witch of the East

"The Wicked Witch has been in touch again since sending this email?" he asked.

Emilie shook her head.

"Black Audi with smudged Berlin plates passed the third time below our window."

Mikhail was out the door before he'd finished the sentence. Sundermann raised an eyebrow at Maier and turned to their client, who was visibly shaken.

"You're quite safe here, Mrs. Ritter. Another port?"

. . .

It snowed lightly as Maier stepped out of the building. Mikhail stood a few metres to the right, his arms raised. His plastic shoes were filling with snow.

The black Audi had a long steel pole stuck through its windscreen.

Two men, one with blood on his face, stood behind the open doors of the car, guns pointing at the Russian. The guns were identical small and deadly Glock 19s, typical equipment for American government agents. They were the men who'd gate-crashed Ritter's funeral.

Maier moved forward. The guns followed him.

"Do we kill them?" the bleeding man asked.

The question was casual and remote, made even more so by the snowflakes that swirled around the four men. A few pedestrians rushed past, shocked at what they saw. Someone would call the police. This was Germany in 2002, not the OK Corral. Germans always called the cops.

Maier stepped forward calmly, but he could hear his heart beating like the wings of a stressed starling.

"Hands up, Detective Maier."

One of the men moved away from the car towards Mikhail. Maier pulled himself together, half-hoping the man was stupid enough to get close to his colleague.

"Guys, stop harassing my client or we will call the police," Maier said.

The closer man, with a ginger buzz cut, big chin, good East Coast school accent, and cold and clever eyes, laughed gently.

"We're the police, Maier. Call whoever you want if you get the chance."

Ginger held the 9mm steadily on Mikhail. His companion, a larger and darker specimen with shorter black hair gelled to his broad semi-handsome head, stood bleeding, exhaling clouds of pain-filled breath. He looked like movie tough guy Charles Bronson, like a man who'd been left out in the sun too long. The blood threatened to blind him, but he was calm. Fake Bronson stepped from behind the car door and pulled the steel pole out of the Audi's windshield. He looked a little less in the mood for diplomacy than his ginger-haired colleague.

"I should put this down your throat, you fucking Ivan. You're as good as dead," Fake Bronson said.

The loud clank of the pole hitting the tarmac was enough distraction for the Russian to make his move. Mikhail stepped forward in a way that seemed entirely impossible given his bulk, and kicked the Glock out of Ginger's hand. His plastic shoe cut through the cold air fast enough to make the snow in its path melt. A split second later he'd closed in. Headbutt. Broken nose. Blood bubbling. Ginger was about to go down, but Mikhail caught him as the second American opened fire. Maier dived to the hard ground.

Fake Bronson had shot Ginger.

"Drop the gun or I break your friend's neck and use him to make an even bigger hole in your fucking car window, darling," Mikhail said.

Maier could hear the glee in his partner's voice. *Don't fuck with the Russian bear. Mad.*

The gun in the hands of the injured American who'd just shot his colleague never wavered. These guys were on course.

"OK. Let him go," Fake Bronson said as if ordering a cup of tea.

Mikhail's answer was equally calm and measured. "Drop the gun on the ground. No guns. I'll snap his head off now. I'll make you eat it."

Fake Bronson dropped the gun. Maier got up, sidled past his friend, and then retrieved the weapon. The bleeder smelt of studied anger.

"Get back in the car. Put your fingers on the steering wheel. If you move, he's gone."

Mikhail slowly moved around the car and lifted the unconscious Ginger into the Audi's passenger seat, gave him a gentle pat on the head, and then shut the door. He kept the American's gun.

"I see you again, the Ivan in me will devour you guys. Ass first."

He stepped away from the car and pulled the magazine from the gun, nodding to Maier to do the same. The Audi moved past them at a snail's pace, the blazing eyes of the bleeder, Fake Bronson, at the wheel, burning through the two detectives. As the car pulled away, Mikhail threw both guns, one after another, through the back window. He threw hard and he had good aim. Perhaps he'd been a gun thrower in a past life. As the window exploded, the Audi rolled on, unhurried, in a world of its own.

"You sure you want to be a detective?" Maier asked, jokingly.

Mikhail laughed. "You really want to go up against men like that without having a guy like me around?"

. . .

"The US Embassy just called."

Emilie lay on the office couch, a third sherry half gone, the coffee in her hand steaming warmth into the room.

Sundermann eyed Mikhail with newfound curiosity.

"Really, against two armed special whatever guys? Unprovoked attack? This is Germany, you know, not Chechnya. We have rule of law here. And America is our closest ally and all that."

"Not today."

"That's what I told the embassy. The police will be here shortly. We have most of it on our security camera."

Maier turned to Emilie and said, "Presuming there's something in this, and it certainly looks that way now, what is the crime of the century the email refers to? And why is it unsettling you rather than making you angry?"

She shrugged. She was troubled, not outraged by the message.

"My husband's relationship with reality became more and more tenuous," Emilie said. "That had been going on for a while. All those years in the field looking through his viewfinder at one atrocity after another. Even with the camera between himself and all that killing, it started to get to him. A couple of years ago, I saw him edit images that were terrible. I mean totally unusable. Out of order. Nothing any paper in the world would ever print. When he noticed my shock, he hid those images from me. I was losing him to darker forces before he blew up on that boat. And now it turns out that this might be a story, some kind of weird elaborate cover-up, I'm shocked but not totally surprised. We were no longer on the same journey."

Emilie finished her coffee, got up, and then put on her jacket.

"But I really need to know what's going on, what happened to Martin. He is or was my husband. I loved him. Make haste, detectives. I leave you to the snow and the thugs."

6

BANGKOK, THAILAND, JANUARY 2003

THE CITY GLOWS

People came to Bangkok to roll around in it, to wallow in its neon-lit troughs, to commune with its countless ghosts on crumbling street corners, to fall into its cheaply perfumed sheets, to experience vulgarity at its least refined and most institutionalized. The Thai capital was something else. Eleven million souls and then some, crammed onto a skyscraper-strewn flood plain on the banks of the tarry Chao Praya River that snaked like a python stuffed with garbage and miscreants towards the Gulf of Thailand.

There was nothing to look at in downtown Bangkok, but there was plenty to see.

From morning to morning, a haze of mediocrity hung above the area, an insipid film of average, best reflected in the prevalence of Hitler T-Shirts in the tourist markets, the alleys populated by hustlers, the overpriced restaurants selling Thai food no Thai would eat, the awful cover bands that churned out uninspired, hollow rock standards to drunken degenerates, the mean, beady eyes of white men and Arabs that poked out of decrepit sports bars and followed passers-by like persistent venereal diseases, the incredible cacophony of terrible tattoos displayed on wilting flesh, and the thousands of burnt out and beaten women who were waiting to open their legs, mouths, and asses for less than fifty bucks.

Warlords, perverts, sex fiends, bank robbers, murderers, white-collar criminals, illustrious devotees of both the short and the long con, fugitives from all five continents, and a whole lot of people who didn't quite fit into any category but veered from suspect to unsound dropped by. The Thais welcomed them the way Europeans welcomed Santa Claus, like an old, rather distant friend who came to play and left presents.

Fellinis, that's what Maier called the holiday psychos who arrived in their thousands every day. These men roamed the nightlife strips of Nana, Patpong, and Soi Cowboy, hungry expressions on their taut, love-starved faces as they scanned thousands of women, men, and transgenders, looking for the one. The one. The one who'd agree to be abused in exchange for cash, in whatever way the client dreamed up.

The Thais smiled into this ongoing tropical apocalypse of crass impunity tempered by an unhealthy dose of gonorrhea, superstition, and chili sauce, with exceptional detachment. One had to go with it, float in its odd current, soak up its magic. Politicians relied on fortune tellers. Sacred tattoos that stopped bullets and attracted partners of the opposite sex and, of course, money, were highly sought after. Bangkok was really all about the money in the right pockets, to keep the locals either driving fancy foreign SUVs, or living impoverished in the shadows of concrete fly-overs.

Bangkok had a sick charm, despite itself. A charm that foreigners found difficult to capture. Photographers produced sleazy images. Writers wrote nasty stories about nastier men and women gambling away their dignity. Painters, poets, and posers all contributed to the haze, some as participants, and others as mere observers lacking the wit and substance to find inspiration on the edge of yesterday's broken dreams.

It had been like that since Maier had first visited in the 80s. Bangkok was static in a dynamic way, a unique metropolis of vibrant activity in a constant flux of regeneration that led nowhere. Between shrines and shopping centers, massage parlors, and private zoos, the locals weren't encouraged to think about it. In the far eastern City of Angels, it was both unfashionable and dangerous to think about the bigger picture.

Perhaps that's why Maier wasn't any closer to the answer either. He'd passed through Bangkok many times and he'd never quite made up his mind whether he liked the place or whether it merely frightened him into acceptance. One had to be reckless or extremely disciplined, perhaps both, to subsist here.

This time he'd been in town almost a month. There was no sign of Ritter.

He'd trawled through hi-so rooftop bars in five-star hotels and curbside hellholes, karaoke gulags and massage dream stations, neon-lit diners, fine dining eateries, underground punk clubs, and tourist go-go bars. He'd been high and low and in between.

Not a trace.

No one had raised so much as a manicured eyebrow at Ritter's mugshot.

Perhaps, Maier considered, the photographer had changed his appearance. When they'd met in conflict zones, Ritter had always adopted local colors, grown beards, and worn caps and anything else that he felt would make him blend in more. His battlefront penchant for going native had been legendary.

It was 2 am. The Dolly House, which had all the warmth of a recently abandoned abattoir, was more than half dead. The night and possibly the entire world were winding down. Most of the tables stood unoccupied. The place smelt of ashtray, toilet, and dreams that had never quite had the opportunity to flourish between the two.

An impossibly fat woman was fleecing an Arab wearing shorts, trainers, a T-shirt, and a baseball cap, all in matching colors, over a last game of pool. Maier had been watching them intermittently while Mikhail had used his considerable charm at the far end of the bar to interest a gaggle of ladyboys in their quest. The fat woman had been losing several games in a row and the Arab had increased his stake accordingly. If she won this one, she'd be able to take a month's holiday from this neon-colored death row.

Maier, half-felled by Campari orange, sat engrossed at the bar, watching the woman's gambit when someone started pulling his arm.

"Hey you, handsome man. You want to take me outside? Go somewhere. I show you good time."

The detective turned to face the skinny, pockmarked face of an upcountry girl who'd seen too much down country. She spoke decent English and tried her best professional smile on Maier.

The detective shook his head and grinned, indifferent to yet another inane conversation about sex and money.

"I'm not going anywhere. It's hot out there. It's like a swimming pool changing room."

"Or like in my pussy," the upcountry girl said.

"You mean as if I were in your pussy?"

"Yes."

"So, everyone else from the swimming pool changing room would be in there as well?" Maier quipped.

"No, just you!" the girl said in sing-song way.

She pulled a face that made her somehow prettier and then slunk away.

The Arab lost his money and started shouting. The fat woman stuffed bills down her cleavage and headed for the toilets. Or the back door. Maier had the urge to return to his hotel room and nail the door shut.

"Hey, handsome man, we won the lottery."

The stunning blonde that Mikhail was pushing towards Maier was the same height as the detective but in much better shape. The blonde hair was a wig and her breasts were considerable and almost looked real in the bad light, thrusting as they were, out of her pink, V-neck, Playboy T-shirt. She wore tight, ripped jeans, also pink, and high heels, not too extravagant. Not pink. Black, with some glitter, and, well, a little extravagant.

A pink sex giant, he thought.

Maier joined them at an empty table away from the bar.

"This is Ruby. Ruby is Martin Ritter's girlfriend. Ruby, this is my partner, Maier."

The *kathoey* or ladyboy as the Thais called transgender, giggled and flicked her blonde mane back. She'd invested thousands of dollars to look like a million.

"Your partner?" The ladyboy spoke with a soft lilt, a little exaggerated, a little too woman.

Every move she made closer to Maier was elegant, studied, calculating, and sublime. *Who said there wasn't any class in hell?*

"What wrong with your fingers, baby? You feed the street dogs, or you forget to pay the rent?" She arched two tattooed eyebrows at the detective. "We all have to pay the rent, you know, darling. How you gonna pay me?"

Maier raised his left hand and wriggled the metal prosthetics that had replaced two of his digits in front of the lady boy's face and gave her his best heterosexual stare.

"I stuck them in someone's bottom, and they broke off. That's who I am, Maier."

Ruby pulled a face and ladled out substantial portions of mock disgust.

Mikhail shook his head. "Maier here is lost to the ladies. You know, ladies that are born ladies."

"So sad."

The ladyboy's expression had the air of a starlet's scream in a silent comedy— garish, exaggerated, and sweet. Maier was touched.

"You are trying to expand my sexual horizons, Mikhail?"

"Always." His partner laughed and waved for a round of drinks.

Ruby moved her shoulders to give Maier a better look at her breasts and switched to a new smile, so radiant it looked like it had been designed in space, close to the sun. Mikhail slapped a photo of Ritter onto the bar.

"He not look like this in the picture anymore. He changed, but same man, really. He's my boyfriend. He takes photos. He makes movie also."

A cloud passed the ladyboy's finely sculpted face. When Ruby caught the detective watching her, it vanished as quickly as it had appeared, replaced by more blinding plastic sunshine.

"He's a good man. But so much change on face and hair and everything. He is handsome man like you, but young. Germany like you."

Mikhail pushed a tablet of tequila slammers between them and winked at Maier. "Let's have a good time.

The Russian smiled at the detective. "Courtesy of the Wicked Witch, my dear. She mailed Emilie about Ruby. I think we have an ally."

"Yeah," Ruby squealed in the most girlish register she could muster and drank her shot down like a man.

Then she put his arm around the detective and hissed, "Who is Emilie?"

Maier drank and stared off into the teary distance.

"My girlfriend."

Ruby pulled a face that had nothing to do with the liqueur.

"You know, he give me one photo. I don't understand. But he tell me that the photo is insurance. Very important. Not to show anyone. But now I am so worried. And I meet you. Make me more worry"

Maier and Mikhail stood guard in the unlit alley off Nana Plaza as Ruby cowered next to a couple of bins and yanked down her pink jeans. The pavement sloped downwards as pavements in Bangkok were prone to and a river of piss made the two men jump. A couple of busy rats scuttled past them towards the drains on the main road behind them.

"What are we doing here?" Maier, reeling a little from the shock of the sudden rise in temperature after their drinking binge in sub-arctic air-con, absentmindedly noticed Ruby was pre-op.

"Getting lucky, Maier."

Ruby zipped up and Mikhail gave her a bear hug, "We just want to help. Maier is a detective and an old friend of Martin's. They go back years. They were in the war together. And now he's looking for his friend. Just like you."

"Very dangerous. I feel it," Ruby said.

"Yes," the Russian admitted. "Martin is involved in some bad stuff. He is running from serious problems."

Ruby smiled. "He show me the newspaper. His funeral. In Berlin. Many VIP people coming. He's a very clever man. Famous man."

"But he's in trouble."

Ruby shrugged like an obstinate child. "I want to help him. I don't care danger. I can defend myself."

Mikhail led the *kathoey* towards Sukhumvit Road.

"Ruby, you have to trust us. It's the only way to find Martin."

Maier could see Ruby trying to wriggle out of his partner's soft but firm embrace.

"Ruby, there were people at Ritter's funeral in Berlin, people who came to visit us in Hamburg at our office. Bad people. People who will stop at nothing to find Martin and silence him. That's why he faked his own death. To escape those people. But it didn't work. They know he's alive just as we do. Just as you do. And they'll come after him and kill anyone in their path, anyone connected to Martin. If we find out why they're coming, we can stop them. We need that picture. With the picture, we can find Martin," Mikhail said.

That wasn't entirely true, but it was clear that Ruby feared for Ritter's life.

Mikhail turned up the heat.

"Ruby, they'll kill you too. They'll find out you are Martin's friend."

Ruby looked torn, with little choice but to trust Maier and Mikhail and betray the man she loved.

They'd reached the main road.

Maier scanned the four-lane traffic artery, clogged with taxies, vendors pushing their stalls home, a lost elephant done begging for the day, and a gaggle of middle-aged Americans in matching batik Buddha shirts led astray by three girls and a dwarf.

Everything looked as one would expect downtown Bangkok to look like in the small weekend hours.

A gang of cops was stopping traffic a little up the road, flagging taxis, robbing tourists too drunk to stash their drugs. One of the policemen turned towards the trio and shot them a bored, hungry glance.

"OK, we go my place."

7

THE GOOD DOCTOR

The reception area was dressed in hushed beige. A glass fridge bulged with small cartons of cold mineral water and vitamin juices, complimentary for waiting patients. TIME Magazine and the local English language papers sat neatly stacked alongside interior design magazines on the glass table in the center of the room. Ambient music hummed from invisible speakers.

It was cool, rather than arctic. A framed photograph of the Thai king holding a camera graced a wall.

A photo of the doctor taken in front of the Statue of Liberty, accompanied by his wife, shirt unbuttoned and vivacious, and three kids, faced Maier. It looked like an ad for American family values. Except that the doctor was Thai.

The remaining walls were bare.

Dr. Suraporn, one of the country's leading plastic surgeons, would have time for Maier in a few minutes, the lady at reception had told the detective in lilting but flawless English. Maier judged, by the professional attention she was bestowing on him, that dropping Ritter's name carried weight.

Ruby had furnished Maier and Mikhail with the doctor's identity in the early hours of the previous night, dead drunk and psychologically strong-armed by the detectives to help find the photographer. A wad of cash, Vitamin M as the Thais sometimes called it, had smoothed the passage.

Despite the crushing hangover, Maier felt optimistic. He was closing in on Martin Ritter. This was bigger than a man's disappearance. This stank of the serious stuff— life, death, dignity, history. Maier also knew he was back, doing what he did best. He wasn't sure whether he wanted to be back, but at least it was more agreeable than waking up in his apartment in Altona, surprised to be alive. Maier had risen from a dark slumber. Bangkok had a rejuvenating effect, it seemed. For a split second the detective wondered whether he was deluding himself in the same manner as the Fellinis on the street.

"Good morning. Let's get right to the point as I have a consultation in fifteen minutes. What can I do for you? You're not a prospective patient, I understand. You are here to inquire about someone else's surgery?"

Dr. Suraporn was reasonably handsome, 40ish, almost tall, sharp grey suit and hair cut out of a 90s John Woo movie, an expensive but rather small and effeminate watch on his left wrist, and a pair of almost square rimless and impossibly delicate glasses on his nose. His face looked like it enjoyed the world's best moisturizers and spa treatments.

"Thanks for taking a moment to see me, doctor."

Shaking hands, Maier detected something unsettling in the doctor's radiant expression, the same undercurrent he'd felt when he'd studied the family picture outside. Suraporn welcomed the detective with a curious, apparently open smile that was grounded in utter fakery before turning into seasoned and earnest professionalism in a matter of nanoseconds. A small shock passed through the detective. This man was very dangerous. He'd shown his true face, on purpose.

Maier tried to look detached and at ease.

"You're here about the famous war photographer who blew up in Thailand. Incredible story, Detective…Mr. Maier. I read all about it."

"When was the last time you saw Martin Ritter?"

Suraporn waved Maier onto a leather couch so white, the detective was sure he'd leave part of his shadow behind when he got up again.

"Even if Mr. Ritter had been my patient, I'm sure you understand, I'm not in a position to divulge information about any procedure he might have had here. It would clearly be unethical. Even, I should say, if you come to me in the name of this man's widow."

Maier chose conversational, though he felt increasingly uneasy in the too-cold office.

"You have a great reputation for skin grafts and cosmetic surgery, Dr. Suraporn."

The doctor let the question drop to the dead ground as if it had never been uttered.

"By the way, who told you that your Mr. Ritter has been to see me?"

Maier didn't answer. This was as far as he was going to get here.

Nothing happened. Smiles on both sides of the table started to wane. The doctor leaned forward. His presence moved the glacial air which had gone stale around the office.

"Mr. Maier, in a few seconds, you will get up and leave my office. You will never return. We will never meet again. I don't know what you want but I understand very well what you are. You are trouble. And trouble invites more trouble. But you have a choice. A little bit of a choice. Because we take these haters who trouble us to the afterlife where they will be dealt true justice in the afterlife court."

The doctor didn't blink.

"And sometimes, very rarely, we get them into the afterlife court before they have died."

Maier waited for more, short of breath, on the spotless white couch.

The doctor grew across his desk towards the detective.

"Where is it?"

Maier managed a faint stammer, "Where is what?"

"The image. Where is the image? The Monsoon Ghost image? Where is it?"

Suraporn leaned back and began to bark, like a small dog. Maier was suffocating. Whatever air hadn't been used up by the barking was toxic. As the doctor grew hoarse, his vocal efforts grew in intensity.

Maier rose to leave. He swayed, his eyes on Suraporn. The man's face looked twisted. Sweet, but wrong. As the detective turned with effort, he noticed that a part, a small grey sliver of his soul remained imprinted on the surface of the couch. Perhaps he'd been drugged, he couldn't be sure. He had to get out. He never wanted to meet this man again.

Back on the street, he vomited his breakfast into a rubbish bin.

8

THE BIGGER PICTURE

"It was so bad it made me want to cry shit," Maier said.

"You're still in your sentimental phase, Maier," Mikhail said. "That's OK."

Mikhail looked at the detective intently. Maier felt better. He sat propped up on his bed at their hotel in Ari, a few kilometres north of downtown Bangkok. Quiet, discreet, out of the way. CNN flickered silently on the hotel TV. George Bush and Saddam Hussein gesticulated without poise between ten-second bursts of archive footage of American troops running around the Hindu Kush. It was a cheap show, but it was enough.

"You look like you've seen a ghost."

"I could not breathe. Like he cut off the airflow in the room with his mind. I thought maybe he had drugged me, but I did not consume anything while I was on the premises. And of course, he knew Ritter. I'm sure we will be followed and watched from now on. We're not the only ones wanting to get their hands on Ritter. My appearance at the doctor's, whatever he is, set wheels in motion and we have to be very careful, we don't get ground up underneath them."

"You think that Suraporn is connected to the two Americans we met in Germany?" Mikhail asked.

Maier had been kicking that thought around since he'd left the doctor's practice.

"I am not sure I want to do this," Maier answered.

"I understand."

"I want to go back to Altona and drink crushed insects. This is very fucked up stuff. Beyond our competence."

Mikhail knew Maier well enough to know when he was serious. Maier opened a bottle of ice-cold water and drank half of it down in one gulp. It did nothing to make him feel better. Only that morning, he'd been riding the wave. Now he was out of sorts, scared.

"Let's call Sundermann," Maier suggested

"Let's go up on the roof," the Russian answered.

The sun set over an unruly collection of multi-story buildings. The hotel's rooftop was level with several other properties, but the two detectives were the only people outside.

Maier, not wanting to panic their boss, recounted his meeting with the doctor as slowly and deliberately as he could manage.

Sundermann didn't sound happy.

"No doubt connected. A psychic shock, you said? I can hear it in your voice. The man used hypnosis perhaps."

The detective nodded into the hot gun-metal sky. He waited a few seconds before he answered.

"The man barked, in his office. Like a little dog. And it was the most serious thing I have ever seen. I mean, it was like being back in the war. Worse. We are both, let's say, worried, for just about everyone we know. Ritter is the key to something…unsound."

Mikhail's mobile beeped with a message.

"It's Ruby. An attachment. I'll call him."

There was no answer.

Sundermann, 6.000 miles away in Hamburg, had a fine nose for trouble. "Forward the mail to me and delete it immediately."

The Russian transferred the phone's SIM to his laptop. Seconds later, the computer's photo viewer came to life.

The two detectives stared at the image in silence.

Sundermann, a man not prone to swearing was shouting at them, "You two should listen when your boss tells you something. Now you're fucked, royally fucked. And so is Agency Sundermann."

Mikhail put the SIM back in his phone, sent the mail to Sundermann, and deleted it. Their boss didn't miss a beat.

"As I said. The case is closed. Come back to Hamburg."

Maier felt relieved.

"Are you sure?"

Mikhail's phone beeped again.

"An address. From Ruby. In Chinatown. I will call him," Mikhail said.

Ruby still didn't answer her phone.

Maier relayed the message to his boss.

"It's a trap," Sundermann warned. Don't—"

The line went dead. Maier stared at his phone, then at the Russian.

"Something just happened. Sundermann hung up."

Maier called their boss back, but there was no answer. Mikhail grinned at his partner, looking unhappy, fatalistic as only a Russian would.

"This is no longer a case, Maier, it's a hunt. And I'm not sure who the hunter is now."

The sun dipped behind disorderly columns of skyscrapers, its diminishing power leaving behind a purple bruise in the orange sky that looked like it belonged on someone who'd been beaten for a long time. The two detectives were slipping into something worse than men turning into barking dogs. Something that could blow them away in an instant. They were on their own.

Mikhail copied the image onto a CD. He handed the disc to Maier. "Life insurance, maybe."

Maier almost felt the disc burning into his hand. He thought about ditching it in the nearest drain.

The Russian closed his laptop, pulled a Sig 9 from his shirt, attached his silencer, and then, after one more look round the neighborhood, shot the computer several times.

"Give me your SIM."

Mikhail took their two SIM cards, snapped them in half, and crushed them between two bricks.

"Let's go."

"To the airport?" Maier asked.

"I think it's too late for that. We get new cards for the phones on the way. Take your battery out. Let's stay off the grid for a few hours.

I think we need to go a bit Russian on this one. Let's go to Chinatown."

The photo had seared itself into Maier's memory. A little grainy shot under tungsten in what looked like a prison cell. Maier suspected the grain was there for aesthetic reasons, not because of bad light. Suraporn was clearly visible, so were two white men, one a thug, the other a pencil pusher. The two white men looked excited, perhaps aroused. Definitely in their element, digging into salvation. Another Thai man, older than the rest and holding an Alsatian on a very short chain, stood to the side, his face only partially visible. He looked bored. Suraporn wore a vague smile and was staring at a point somewhere above and beyond the photographer. The dog also smiled, much like the doctor.

In the centre of the photograph, the fifth man lay barely conscious and grey-faced, bruised almost beyond recognition, naked and smeared in excrement at the feet of the others, staring wildly into nothingness. He had dark skin and a beard.

It looked like a post-hunt calm down. The beast had been slain and it was time for the beers.

"I think we're looking at the front line of the War on Terror."

Mikhail sighed.

"Where might this be?"

The detective shrugged. "I doubt it is in Bangkok. This is …sensitive, to say the least. Maybe in one of the old Vietnam War-era facilities the Americans built here in the 60s. Somewhere where they have some control or pseudo-jurisdiction. This is…radical. In all the wrong senses of the word."

The Monsoon Ghost image was a masterpiece. Perhaps, today, it was the world's most wanted photograph, the 21st century's Zapruder document. It was Ritter's *coup de grace*. If photography was mostly about access, then this one was the world's best reportage photos. If it was about capturing inhumanity, it did the job as well as American images of the liberation of Belsen and Auschwitz. But there was an essential difference and neither Maier nor Mikhail had any trouble spotting it. In this case, the shooter was part of the picture and part of the action. The photographer was an accessory to the crime.

Maier tossed the image from one corner of his panicked brain to another. These guys would not stop until everyone who knew anything about this was dead.

And Ritter was a pig.

"Let's publish it," Mikhail muttered as they hit the street, light travel bags slung across their shoulders, looking like a couple of expats heading for the nearest gym.

Maier looked at his friend, weighing up his suggestion. "No. We need to find out what happened to Sundermann first. And check on Emilie."

His partner nodded, scanning the broken litter-strewn pavement ahead. Maier knew that look. Everyone was an enemy now. Everyone except Maier. Stall vendors, evening shoppers, office workers, couriers, lottery vendors, and street musicians, old men coughing phlegm into the rat-infested gutter, young backpackers clutching guidebooks, and middle-aged tourists holding on to their young butterflies, clogged both sides of the road. Bangkok life. All of them enemies. Sometimes Mikhail's mistrust of everyone made Maier feel safe. Tonight, it didn't.

Half an hour later they reached Victory Monument, an obelisk surrounded by quasi-fascist 1940s bronze heroes commemorating the brief Sino-French war which had gained Siam a little territory it was going to lose again a few years later.

This ugly reminder of past glories also served as a vast two-story circular intersection. The early evening traffic made the place look like a metal ant hill. Exhaust fumes belched from buses, taxis, and motorcycles. Above street level, sky trains rushed past every couple of minutes, disgorging thousands of commuters. Cops flagged down motorists and robbed them for water money, to be pissed against the wall in bars around the city at the weekend.

The traffic circle looked like the outflow of a diseased urban sphincter, forever spasming fumes into the world.

Mikhail made a path through the crowd to the south side of the monument and flagged down a couple of motorcycle taxis.

"*Yaowarat*," was all he said to the two young punks in orange jackets.

There were tens of thousands of these men in the city, wearing face masks and sacred tattoos with the same laissez-faire attitude they utilized as they weaved through the city's clogged streets.

"Two-hundred Baht, mister, kap," the more sober of the two

suggested with cheerful weariness. He pointed at each of the foreigners in turn.

Mikhail nodded. They weren't here to save money. One of the boys — neither could be much older than 18— collected two battered helmets that hung off the side of a phone box. They slipped into dense traffic along Phayathai Road. Maier, on the back of the lead bike, relaxed a little. He felt almost invisible.

9

BURN BABY BURN

THE MOTORCYCLES DROPPED them off next to Wat Traimit, its courtyard deserted. The temple was home to the world's largest solid gold Buddha. But even the net worth of this edifice wouldn't be enough to get them out of trouble. The two men turned onto Yaowarat and walked towards Chinatown as briskly as the crowded pavements would allow. The buildings sprouted countless neon signs in Chinese that looked to have survived from the 50s.

Mikhail led the way. After a few minutes of ducking and weaving, they turned left and found Kampeng Lane, a wholesale market selling plastic trash, fake jewelry, and textiles.

Chinatown hardly slept and as business in the narrow lane wound down, young toughs in shorts and broken trainers carried huge sacks of new product into the cramped, tiny stores.

A couple of hundred metres into this warren and Mikhail took a sharp left down an alley barely wide enough for a motorbike. They reached a filthy *khlong*, a rubbish-sodden canal alive with giant monitor lizards. Two old men played chess on a narrow bridge, barely glancing up from their evening game as the foreigners passed. The bustle of the market and the city traffic faded to a dirty low hum. Maier felt like he'd gone deaf.

On the far side of the bridge, they passed between rows of restaurants and flop-houses and emerged on a deserted street. The smell of curry and pan lingered in grimy, rat-infested alleys. They were in Pahurat, Bangkok's Indian quarter.

"This is it." Mikhail pointed across the street.

They were looking at an old shophouse on a quiet back alley, the ground floor built from concrete, the second floor from wood. The roof was made from corrugated iron. Flames licked the wooden frame of a first-floor window.

"We're late." Mikhail looked up and down the street.

"Maybe not," Maier said. "The cops aren't here yet. Our American friends or the doctor aren't here either, there isn't an SUV in sight."

"But they will be here soon."

"So we best go and take a look quickly, don't you think? Before the fire really gets going."

Without another word, they crossed the road. In the distance, a lone motorcycle was approaching. The driver would surely see the building was catching fire and call emergency services.

The house was slightly set back from the street, surrounded by an iron fence. One could only see the fire on the upper floor if one stood directly in front of it. Maier could smell the flames devouring the wood.

The gate was unlocked, and Mikhail pushed through to the front door, his revolver in hand. Maier followed. He had no weapon other than his disillusionment.

"Help!" a woman's voice called. "*Shuai, shuai- leuâ!*"

The front door, flimsy to the touch, old and rotten, painted an age ago in pastel blue which was now coming off like peeling skin, was locked. Mikhail kicked hard against it and put his foot through the wood. They were inside in seconds.

It was always too late for someone. Ruby hung from a hook in the ceiling, her long bare and perfectly waxed legs almost touching the ground. A puddle of piss and blood had spread beneath the slowly turning, naked corpse. Her killer, or killers had, cut her penis off and stuffed it down her mouth.

Maier stood in the centre of the room taking it in. They'd spent hours talking Ruby into betraying his partner. Acrid, chemical smoke was billowing down the staircase. The temperature was going up quickly. The ceiling above their heads was made from teak and would catch fire soon.

The back wall was lined with metal desks covered in camera gear.

"Help."

Maier made for the nearest door into the kitchen. Gas hissed from the cheap cooking plates that rested on a stone shelf. He crossed the room, closed the bottle, and then dialed the plates to zero.

A woman lay trussed up behind the door, staring at him with wide, black eyes.

"Cut me loose, man. Quick, this place will go in a second. Ritter's long gone," She pleaded.

"There is a back door?" Maier asked as he untied her.

Mikhail was in the room.

"They're here. We can no longer go out the way we came in," the Russian shouted.

"There's a backdoor upstairs at the back of Ritter's studio," the woman explained. "We can get onto next door's roof from there. Not sure I can walk, though."

Mikhail pulled a knife from his pocket and began to cut through the computer cables that had been used to tie the woman up.

She looked Asian but she spoke with an American accent. Her wide, round face was dark and her eyes were darker still. She didn't look scared, but she was clearly worried. Not a citizen. She had herself under control in a very tight spot. She was a pro. Maier guessed her in her mid-forties.

He stepped back into the living room turned execution chamber. The smoke wafting down the stairs had gotten thicker. He could see blue and red lights flashing outside. Mikhail emerged behind him, the woman leaning heavily into his arms.

He handed Maier his gun and bag.

"You have a copy of the picture, you dumb idiots?" she asked, exasperated.

Maier took a deep breath.

"If you have a copy of the picture, you must give it to me now. Otherwise, you're definitely and absolutely dead. I'm the only one who can help you. The people who are after this picture will kill everyone they find it on," she shouted.

Mikhail coughed and shook his head. "We have to get out of here."

Maier looked at the woman, unsure what to do.

"They will kill you too then," Maier suggested.

548

"Don't get smart with me, Maier. I'm one of them. I'm your only hope," she shouted.

Mikhail, in no mood for great decisions either, pointed towards the stairs. The woman nodded vigorously.

Mikhail said, "Maier, you first. Up the stairs, straight ahead. There's a door. If it's locked, shoot the lock until it opens. It's our road to freedom. Don't inhale, those burning photo chemicals are toxic."

The Russian lifted the woman off the ground as if she were a toy. She didn't protest. Maier took a deep breath and sprinted up the concrete steps into the inferno.

10

HEALTH SCARE

"Where are we at?" Maier wondered.

Maier and Mikhail sat in the accident and emergency waiting area of Bumrungrad Hospital, the city's most exclusive medical facility. The woman had insisted to be taken there. Since they'd been waiting to hear how badly injured their new 'friend' was— this was how Maier had described their relationship to the nurses— the detective was becoming more and more restless.

A hospital, and a private one mostly frequented by foreigners, was not as safe a place as he'd wished to be in right now. It wasn't nearly crowded or anonymous enough. Every now and then a doctor or a nurse passed them, barely acknowledging the two men in the corner, minds focused on the typical Friday evening injuries— a man with a bullet in his throat who'd driven himself right to the doors in a Lexus, a heavily pregnant teenager and her boyfriend freaking out. But mostly it was quiet but for the electronic hum the place generated.

"The cops knew. Otherwise, the fire engines would have been there first. I don't think we have all that long 'round here. They will come for us, one way or another," Maier said.

Mikhail nodded. "I'll go and check the entrance for trouble."

Maier shook his head. "This place has several entrances. There's so many people, it's impossible."

"Has it occurred to you that she might be a honey trap, or just a trap, with the honey being incidental?"

"You're so elegant with your choice of words," Maier remarked.

"Do you think she is?"

"No, but we can't trust anyone."

"I agree."

A door opened with a low sucking noise, suggesting a more hygienic, screened, and controlled world beyond, and a young, pale, and harassed-looking doctor approached them. Judging by his sallow expression, the Friday nightshift with the wealthier casualties of the city's downtown area wasn't much fun.

Mikhail nodded at him as he approached and left the room. The doctor turned to Maier.

"You are the two gentlemen who brought in Khun Puttama?"

Maier introduced himself as Miller and pretended to be American.

"My name is Dr. Karawan. Khun Puttama is in stable condition. She suffered two broken ribs and a twisted ankle, a little head trauma, some minor respiratory issues. She needs to rest up a few days and she will be fine. We have alerted the embassy."

Maier tried to look non-committal and flashed an open, reassuring smile.

"Yes, the US embassy," the doctor went on. "There's an alert out for Miss Puttama. Apparently, she disappeared several days ago from her office. There's been something of a manhunt going on."

The doctor broke into a wry smile at his own joke, then, perhaps finding the detective's reaction wanting, looked at Maier suspiciously. "You do know she is a diplomat based here? You are colleagues perhaps?"

Maier shrugged and answered easily, "Yes, of course."

The doctor continued to stare at him.

"Is there a problem, Dr. Karawan?"

"Is there, mister…?"

"Miller, my name is Miller. And I'm not at liberty to say more."

The doctor nodded, unsure of what to say. "Hm. I understand you saved her life. She said so. She is lucid and rational. In fact, she is extremely robust. And that's confusing me."

Maier waited for more. Sundermann had said this was a trap and that had been a couple of traps ago. But the doctor stared into the middle distance and said nothing else. A question was as good as anything right now.

"Why are you confused, Dr. Karawan?"

"You work closely with Khun Puttama, Mr. Miller?"

Maier looked at the doctor again and realized that the man was scared. The doctor could sense the blowback of the catastrophe that was enveloping the three people who'd entered his world tonight. His sense of self-preservation had kicked in and was starting to conflict with the oath he'd taken.

"I...we saved her from a fire. In Chinatown. To be honest Dr. Karawan, I have no idea what's going on. I brought her here because she was injured and because many of our colleagues are treated at Bumrungrad. And now I'm just waiting to liaise with those very colleagues." That was as much as he would say.

The doctor looked torn between professionalism and something else. He knew that the detective was making it all up. He glanced nervously around the deserted waiting area.

"My colleague is sewing up some lesions on Khun Puttama's legs. She asked me to tell you that the police will be here soon and that you should leave."

The doctor looked at the floor searching for words.

"I don't usually tell strangers in the waiting area something like this … but she seems very sincere and very worried. And she is very strange."

Maier got up. It was time to go.

"Why strange?" he asked.

"Because Khun Puttama was tortured, quite severely and she is not showing the usual mental trauma we associate with victims of torture." As an afterthought, he mumbled, "Not that I'm an expert."

Maier fell back into his seat.

"What?"

"You should leave. Now. That was her advice. Odd, if you're attached to the embassy."

Mikhail stormed through the doors. "Bad news, they're on their way."

The doctor, now clearly frightened, scuttled off towards the emergency rooms. The double doors made the same sucking swish as before, but now it sounded futile, like a tired fart escaping the failing bowels of a geriatric patient.

"This hospital wing must have backdoors. Let's split and meet downstairs," Maier said.

Without another word, Maier followed the doctor. He still had Mikhail's gun; he'd get out.

He burst through the double doors. There was more silence, just a few machine beeps here and there. A nurse wearing a face mask came out of a treatment room, looked at the detective, and then rushed on, several vials of blood in her gloved hands. Maier stuck his head around the corner but the room she'd emerged from was empty. He continued down a narrow corridor. More empty rooms. He got lucky on the third door.

Puttama, if that was her name, lay on a bed, her right wrist connected to a drip, her legs bare and covered in bandages. She recoiled ever so slightly as he came in.

"Maier, you mustn't be here," she said. "You'll be arrested. Go now. You don't know what you're getting into." She looked angry.

"Are you OK?" Maier ventured.

"Of course I'm not fucking OK. But I will be a lot worse if they see us together. Give me the disc."

Maier didn't move. He could hear a commotion in the corridor.

The woman on the bed hissed at him, "I am the Wicked Witch and I will curse you if you don't give me that image, Maier."

The coin had dropped. He wasn't sure which coin, but he clearly heard it hitting the ground.

Maier pulled the CD from his pants and passed it to her.

"Only copy we have. Deleted the mail it came in."

She gave him an almost bemused smile.

"Now you have a fighting chance. Get out."

Maier looked around the room. Someone had left a white nurse's coat draped on a chair. He grabbed it and put it on. There was a box of face masks and disposable gloves on a sideboard. He slid a mask over his face, buttoned-up, and then pulled the gloves on. She nodded approvingly.

"Now we're talking. I'll be in touch."

Maier stepped into the corridor. Uniforms at the far end. He turned the other way and walked slowly ahead.

There'd better be another exit.

The back doors opened onto a hot, putrid yard, and several huge containers containing medical waste. The bright yellow labels on the containers screamed warnings.

The gate at the far end of the yard was locked and there was a uniform in the little guardhouse to the side. Maier could also see several security cameras pointing at the gate. If he crossed the yard he'd be seen.

No way out, he thought.

Maier ran. As he heard the sucking noise of the doors behind him, he noticed a small door on the nearest container that stood open. He got down on his knees and crawled inside, pulling the door shut behind him.

It didn't smell good in there. He leaned back and heard shouting outside. First in Thai, then in English. American English.

"Fucker's gotta be round here somewhere," a voice sounded close to him.

He'd heard that voice before.

"We got the doctor. He said one guy was called Miller. Probably a fake name. Probably the detective I met in Hamburg. I want CCTV footage of these men. I have a bad feeling about this."

A Thai man answered in fluent, heavily accented English. "She is your asset. She can tell you what happened."

"General, she was tortured. She's in shock."

The other man retorted with some bite in his voice, "She is Asian. Don't trust her. You don't know shit."

"You got something on my colleague? You have proof Puttama is bent? Spit it out."

The Thai man didn't answer. He was very close, perhaps just millimetres away on the other side of the plastic box Maier crouched in. He could hear more talking in Thai.

Then the man right by his head spoke again. "These containers are full of garbage from the operation theatres— organs, needles, blood. They are going to the ovens tomorrow. We will keep a guard on them for the night just in case your man was crazy enough to climb inside. I would keep an eye on your colleague."

"Calm down, General. This is the twenty-first century. Some of our best agents are women. Even Asian women."

Maier could picture him now. It was Ginger from Hamburg, trying to be smart. The woman they'd saved *was* from the agency.

He needed to get moving. He was liable to catch Hepatitis or worse if he stayed much longer in his hiding place.

The general droned on, his voice devoid of passion, emotion, and guile.

"Perhaps she is as you say. But perhaps she is a traitor who wants to harm our mission. Your mission. We have to find that photograph and those who took it before anyone else does. The damage to my reputation would be terminal if it ended up in the papers."

The Thai coughed old age. Maier was pretty sure that this was the bored-looking man with the Alsatian in the Monsoon Ghost Image.

He was close to the center of things.

The American laughed. "That's impossible. We have insurance. Even if this cowboy detective has the image, he can't release it. We have renditioned his boss. He's in-country, on his way to Cat's Eye now. We already disposed of the client, Ritter's wife."

Maier swallowed hard. The other man said nothing. After a theatrical pause, the American's tone changed. "And your reputation will be the least we'll be worried about if the image does get out. I'd go as far as to say no one in the world will give a flying fuck about your reputation, General, if we're fingered. It's the reputation of my country that'll be on the line."

"And mine," the other man retorted, suppressed anger in his silken voice.

Ginger wasn't having it. "No one gives a fuck about your shitty little country. Get yourself a dose of reality, friend. Foreigners just holiday here to tan and fuck. You guys live in the middle ages. That's why we come here. To get medieval in a place where we can blend in. We pay you and you shut up and kill whom we tell you to kill. Our special friendship has been like this for half a century, and it won't change now. And I'd like to tell you something else, General. If necessary, we will get rid of Dobbs and Williams, so don't doubt me for a second when I tell you that in the greater scheme of things, you're as disposable as the trash in these containers. You introduced us to Ritter and got us exposed. When we find him, we'll grind this indiscreet, dishonest, scheming piece of shit into the dust. People think they can fuck us, they got another thing coming. Give that reality a thought,

General. And remember, I'm not scared of your Far Eastern hocus-pocus, your barking assistant, you sick fucking clowns. We wrote the book on hypnosis and thought manipulation and your boy is nothing but a gifted amateur."

Ginger sounded like he was foaming from the mouth. The man was a failed stage actor. But the final curtain had now dropped on the scene.

Maier could hear them walking away. The other man barked some instructions in Thai. Then they were gone. Maier was alone and all he could smell through his mask was blood.

What now? Emilie was dead. The Wicked Witch had the photo. The Americans had Sundermann. Here in Thailand. A straight exchange wouldn't work. And in any case, he no longer had the image.

After waiting for an hour, he switched on the torch on his phone. He was inside a garbage container, up to his ankles in bloodied bandages, medical equipment, and thousands of syringes that glinted in the beam of his phone like needles from a Christmas tree grown in hell.

He dug a pocketknife from his bag and cut a hole into the plastic wall of his prison. It was a slow and arduous task. He finally cut a slit big enough to see through. The hospital back door was closed. There was no one around. He watched and waited another twenty minutes.

He needed to contact Mikhail or Puttama. She'd said she'd be in touch. Email was the only means of communication. He needed to cross the yard. He needed to cross the cameras.

He pulled the revolver from his bag and stared at it for too long. He was glad for the coat, the mask, and the gloves but he had no illusions that he was in a highly toxic environment. Hospitals were death traps and hospital garbage bins were coffins. He wouldn't survive the night. He had to get out.

He flicked off his torch, threw the bag over his shoulder, and then slowly eased the container's small door open. The hot, tropical night air outside smelt almost alpine as he emerged into the yard. He crouched to the side of the container and took a deep breath.

He was alone.

· · ·

Maier turned towards the gate, leaving the iron smell of dried blood behind. The guard was in his box. Maier waited. The man might eventually fall asleep. After a few minutes, the guard's phone rang. This was his best chance. The detective quickly made his way to the back of the guardhouse. Four CCTV screens flickered empty panoramas of the yard in front of the guard's empty bored face. Maier could see himself clearly, but the guard wasn't looking. He slunk past. The main gate was locked but a smaller side door opened onto a back road.

Maier ran.

11

NORTH-EAST OF HEAVEN

MAIER LOOPED AROUND THE HOSPITAL, gradually ditching the gloves, mask, and coat in separate rubbish bins, and disappeared into Little Arabia, a string of restaurants, hotels, shops, and travel agents catering to Bangkok's floating Middle Eastern population.

A day on the run now felt like an eternity. Maier was spent, stumbling into another vortex he didn't care for.

The back alleys branching off from Sukhumvit Soi 3 were incredibly crowded at night. This part of the city was aglow with malevolent spirits. Sex, drugs, and crime dripped out of short-time hotels and back street beer bars where young Africans sold meta-amphetamines, the drug of choice in this urban labyrinth of decrepitude.

He ducked into the coffee shop of the Grace Hotel, once a salubrious Vietnam War era edifice, now a degrading hang-out for men from anywhere between Turkey and Pakistan and an army of corpulent, aging sex workers used to years of heavy combat.

The coffee shop was thick with smoke rising from countless shisha bowls, shared by the male customers and their temporary friends. Some women sat dressed in burqas, adding some much-needed mystery to the open wound atmosphere. Everyone looked like they'd won the lottery of life.

Maier passed through the back of the shop and took the stairs two at a time to emerge into the hotel's crowded lobby a few seconds later. He quickly made for the men's room.

His face looked drawn in the mirror. His hands shook. He checked his legs and the soles of his shoes for needles or anything else that might have attached itself to him during his stint in the container. He washed the grime off his skin with cheap hotel soap, feeling no cleaner, and inhaled deeply.

What a day. What a nightmare. He'd never felt hunted like this.

This kind of stress took him back to the days when he'd worked as a conflict journalist when days of boredom had been intermittently punctured by cruel insanity. He was too old for this. He silently cursed Emilie. He didn't feel proud that he had half the US Secret Service after him.

He hoped Mikhail was still on the run. He needed access to the Internet. Maier felt like he was burnt out from being burnt out.

He made his way down the back of the hotel ramp into the car park and via a small alley into Soi 3 ½ where he was swept away by a crowd of evening strollers— a cacophonic assortment of covered-up women pushing trams, their husbands in shorts and T-shirts, of hawkers selling plastic trash from China like fake sunglasses, watches and cheap dreams printed onto glossy flyers that promised instant girl experience right around the corner. Some Thais called the road Soi Bin Laden.

Maier escaped the throng onto the patio of an open-air restaurant and tried to relax. Middle Eastern TV and European football flickered across two opposing screens hanging above late-night diners. Colin Powell looked authoritative on the Arab channel, pointing at maps of Iraq. Waiters flew past, carrying trays loaded with hummus, kebab, and nan.

He ordered a glass of limonana and watched the street. Ladyboys from central Asia, a blind man led by a child belting out a song no one wanted to hear, a family of central European travelers with father fascinated, mother disgusted, teenage daughter bored, and teenage son frustrated, plenty of Fellinis— perverts, gamblers, killers, shady men wearing ill-fitting toupees, drug addicts....no one who looked nearly together enough to be tailing the detective. But pros would never show their hand until it was too late.

Leaving the container in the hospital had been too easy. Maier had been on camera. They had to be close.

He sat for a while, lonely, sweating, his head swimming with too much stuff and too few ideas. He wasn't sure whether giving the image to Puttama had been a wise move.

Why had she been at Ritter's studio, trussed up and about to burn alive, if she was an American asset? She must have gone to see Ritter under her own steam and he'd overpowered her. Perhaps with Ruby's help. Tits of steel but a very soft heart. It had cost the ladyboy dearly. Ritter must have killed her.

Maier found it hard to accept that Sundermann had been abducted in Germany, from the agency's office in broad daylight. He thought the man untouchable. His boss schmoozed with Hamburg's elite day in, day out. Sundermann was connected.

This was some job. The whole world was lurching into unknown territory with this kind of pioneering shit going on. An extreme investigation, Emilie Ritter had asked for in Hamburg. There no longer was an investigation. There no longer was a detective agency. There no longer was an Emilie Ritter. Just men on the run, hiding in cheap restaurants.

It was a bloody massacre.

Half an hour down this road of despair and another limonana later, Maier got up and crossed Sukhumvit Road. A hundred metres past the Vegas lights of Nana Plaza, he found an Internet café, filled with teenagers playing search and destroy video games. Maier logged in.

Mikhail was still out there.

I talked to some people in Hamburg. Sundermann's kidnapping was in the news briefly. German police have been informed by the Americans that Sundermann is being held as part of a terrorist investigation. Media is playing along. Amazing, KGB tactics from our American friends. Behind the scenes, some of his well-positioned friends have been exerting pressure, but so far, no results. This could turn into an embarrassing incident, good for us perhaps, but how?

Emilie is dead. Suicide. Found in her apartment with a bottle of pills by her bedside. They did a good job. Coroner didn't find any signs of foul play.

IF YOU READ THIS, AMERICANS, DON'T COME NEAR ME. I

WILL NOT GO GENTLY INTO THAT GOOD NIGHT AND I WILL TAKE AS MANY OF YOU WITH ME AS I CAN.

I am laying low. Mail me at the place where we first met @yahoo.com. I am closing this account.

Maier had no idea whether the Americans had hacked into their email accounts yet. He imagined so. He got his answer when he opened the next mail, signed by the Wicked Witch.

They have access to your accounts. Delete all pertaining correspondence. Disappear until things get sorted. Expect casualties.

Maier deleted the correspondence, changed his password, and closed his account. He opened a new email account under a false name and mailed Mikhail.

He sat quietly in front of a screen saver that was zapping tropical fish past his eyeballs. The answer to everything lay in the Monsoon Ghost Image. Publishing the image wouldn't work. Sundermann would be killed. In fact, most media wouldn't want to touch it without some context.

Who exactly were those people in the image?

He needed to find out the who, the where, the when. Only then would the picture be complete. Only then would it be truly dangerous for the Americans. Maier needed information, the only weapon out there that was of any use.

"You're still paying for your online time, friend, you know that, don't you?" American southern states accent, mid-sixties, skinny, dressed well enough, like any moderately wealthy old white guy in the tropics — green Lacoste polo shirt, beige slacks, shoes, watch, phone, a little bug-eyed.

Maier's smile froze as he turned his head. Was the man sitting in the cubicle next to him one of them? Was this it? Were they toying with him? Was he about to have a hood slipped over his head?

"What do you mean?"

"Well, I noticed you sitting there, zoning out, and staring at the fish. Got your heart broken by a lady?"

"Maybe. Yes."

Something like sympathy flashed across the American's haggard face.

"Thought so. You're in the best place in the world to have your heart broken, your mind melted, and your cash stolen. Welcome to Thailand, Land of Smiles. A land where you can buy happiness by the kilo. I'm a forty-kilo guy."

Maier leaned back, trying to get a little distance between himself and his talky neighbor.

"I mean, I don't want to interfere, you can stay as unhappy as you like. It's a free country." He laughed at his joke, but he didn't look funny. "Something we say back home. Not sure the Thais use the expression much."

Maier felt reckless.

"You are attached to the embassy?"

"Ha, if I was, I wouldn't be advertising it. But no, I'm not. My name's Mason. Mason the Poet. Everybody knows me in Nana, in Bangkok even. Well, the white guys do, you know. I don't suppose you live here? Business or pleasure? For most business travelers, the two kind of overlap in this town. Or maybe you're a German spook? Asking me a question like that, sounding like that." Mason took a breath and stared at Maier. This man could talk. "What did you say your name was? I got a gig around the corner tonight in a little bar. I mean literally around the corner. Great place to stare into the void and contemplate the injustice of your existence with a beer in your hand and some intellectual stimulation on stage. I promise you, a real rarity in these parts. Poets' night. Not a broken woman shooting darts from her nether regions in sight. Some great people meeting up for a drink. Fantastic band in between the spoken bits, so it doesn't get too boring."

The man was a compulsive talker with an unhealthy level of ADHD, but he was sharp and observant too. Maier had to make up his mind. He was dead tired, but he needed time to work out what to do. He had nowhere else to go. The streets were dangerous. His life expectancy could be measured in seconds. And he was hungry.

"Really?" was all he could manage.

His newfound friend looked at him expectantly.

"I see you're in an exceptionally good mood tonight, with a total sense of well-being, optimism, and faith in humanity…channeling Diogenes is always good for the inner soul…"

Maier laughed, for the first time in quite some time. He missed living. He remembered, for just an instant, that he quite liked it. He'd wasted months on his couch in Altona escaping the very thought. Now that he was thoroughly screwed, alone, and hunted by US Secret Service men, he would have given anything to piss the night away with Mason the Poet, get uproariously drunk and live towards another day.

"You have a gig at midnight?" Maier asked.

"Sure, all the best shows happen in the small hours of the night. You know, in the seventies in San Francisco, when I was hanging out with Fleetwood Mac, we'd never even start before one in the morning when everyone would be really far out wasted. That was back then back home. Bangkok can be like that today. Tonight even."

Mason the Poet got up and handed a few bills to the woman running the Internet café. Maier noticed that the man's clothes were shabby and worn, his polo shirt washed too many times. Clearly, poetry didn't pay.

"Come, buy me a beer. You won't regret it."

Maier gave in to the gentle entrapment and followed the gangly man into the night, his bag across his shoulder, Mikhail's gun inside, weighing it down, pushing him closer to the earth than he cared to be.

They crossed Sukhumvit Road with thousands of other revelers in various stages of inebriation. Tired stall owners were pushing their creaky metal carts towards Asoke, their last fried insects and watered-down orange juice sold for the night. Taxis looking for rides but refusing to use their metres clogged up the road hoping to scoop up drunken foreigners.

Progress was slow on the pavement. Maier got stuck behind a couple of overweight Indian businessmen deliberating with a less than handsome ladyboy.

"You said one thousand baht for a blowjob and a fuck. I get the blowjob and he gets to fuck? OK?"

"Not OK," the *kathoey* drooled back. "Two guys, two thousand. Cheap price. I show you good time."

Maier squeezed past. Mason the Poet disappeared into a narrow doorway guarded by a dwarf in a purple silk suit, smoking a cheap cigar. Maier had no energy to contemplate the city's cruel eccentricities.

They passed along a short hallway. A few steps led down into a cavernous club with sticky floor tiles and emergency storm lighting. Women in short black skirts and tight white blouses, most in their fifties, served a dozen low tables. A stage loomed at the back of the room, guarded by plastic unicorns. Mason hadn't lied, it was poetry night at the Sunshine Bar. There was no sunshine on the menu though.

An elderly white man with a beer paunch and a scar across his bald skull, his expression suggesting whatever had once been inside his head had long been sold to the highest bidder, sat on a stool to the front of the stage. He was reading a story, presumably of one of his exploits, about screwing a sex worker while she talked on her mobile to her German husband 5000 miles away, begging him to send more money.

He did the accents quite well. Every paragraph got a couple of tired laughs from the audience. Old white men sipped beers while their bored and discontented Thai partners sucked on Coca-Colas. There was something endearing about a bar that sold a vibe that no longer existed, to people who were no longer quite there. And there was the dwarf at the door. Maier was coming around a little.

He ordered two beers and a burger and picked an empty table in the worst lit part of the bar. Mason followed.

"I tell you, we got some real talent here," Mason said. "That man up there's a legend. He's been here since the sixties. He had a newspaper column for years, recommending the hottest new girls in town. That's not politically correct these days. I tell you, man, the sixties. Everyone was free. There was fucking in the streets. I first came to Thailand was sixty-nine, it was crazy, man. They had an underground blow job room. We used to take the girls in there four at a time and bet money on who could hold on the longest. Want to take a look?"

"You're offering me oral sex, Mason? We only just met. Your hospitality is incredible."

The woman who dropped the burger and the beer on his table looked at neither man.

"Ah, German sense of humor perhaps..." he drifted off. "Enjoy yourself, live a little, relax. No wonder you guys lost two wars."

With that, he grabbed his beer and joined a table of disheveled, balding veterans closer to the lights. Well, Mason was on the winning team tonight. Relaxing wasn't on the agenda.

Maier consumed the burger and beer in record time and stood up to head for the toilets. He saw Mason the Poet turn and look back at him while typing into his mobile phone. It was time to leave. He walked past the restroom to the bar, dropped 500 baht on the counter, gently eased the wallet from the back pocket of a distracted drunkard next to him, and left without waiting for change. Too weird. Perhaps he was being paranoid, but his inner voice told him to hit the streets again.

Maier stepped out onto Sukhumvit and quickly crossed four lanes of traffic. He rushed into the nearest 7/11, ice-cold air-con making his shirt cling to his chest, and pretended to read a newspaper on its rack by the door.

His inner voice was intact. A cop car pulled up outside the Sunshine Bar. Two policemen got out of the front. A tall white man with a mane of long blonde hair, dressed in a decent suit, stepped out of the back. The man had his jacket draped across his shoulders; his forearms were heavily tattooed. He wasn't carrying, as far as Maier could see, but that didn't make the detective feel any better.

The two cops disappeared into the Sunshine Bar. The man didn't follow the two officers immediately. Instead, he stood by the curb and took the scene around him in slowly, systematically. Maier walked to the back of the shop, collected a bottle of water from the fridge, and moved to the cashier. He paid and took another interested look at the newspaper.

The two policemen re-emerged from the club, Mason the Poet between them, cuffed and protesting. Maier guessed his hunters weren't taking risks. They were collecting anyone who'd spoken to him.

Mason had a less than lyrical night ahead. As the poet ducked into the back of the cop car he glanced fearfully across the road. For a split second, his eyes locked into Maier's. Then he was gone. The large blonde man followed Mason into the vehicle without another look, and the car, lights flashing, moved into the traffic that pushed towards Asoke.

Maier had been lucky, frighteningly lucky. He'd have to be less trusting if he was going to survive the night. And if Mason was spilling his beans across the backseat of the car, the cops would be back shortly. Mason would never return. The stakes were too high.

The detective flicked through the wallet he'd lifted. A few thousand baht and a couple of hundred dollars came in handy. The man had plenty of ID, credit, and debit cards. Winston Powers, a lift maintenance man for the sky train, trained by Siemens. Powers was the same age as Maier, but he looked a decade ahead in the race to the bottom.

Maier stepped out onto the hot pavement and flagged down the first vehicle that went past— a tuk-tuk, a moving tourist trap.

He'd be Winston Powers for a while.

"Chinatown."

12

THIRD-PARTY COLLATERAL

Maier woke with a start. Daylight filtered through the wooden blinds shuttering the only window in his shabby, non-descript hotel room. He cursed the mosquitoes that had been buzzing around his head all night, despite the hurricane-power fan spinning at fluctuating velocities above him. He stumbled into the bathroom and stood under a lukewarm and modest water cascade for a short eternity.

An hour later he sat in a dim sum hole-in-the-wall restaurant off Yaowarat Road, his back to the wall and his eyes on the street.

He'd bought a pair of cheap sunglasses, a new SIM, and the day's edition of The Bangkok Post. The SIM stayed in his pocket for the time being.

Mason the Poet, real name Springdale, had made page three. The long-term Bangkok resident and minor light on the city's minor literary ex-pat scene had fallen off the first-floor balcony of his condo in Ekkamai. The police were treating the death as a suicide. The paper hadn't done any digging. Someone must have called the newsroom. Balcony deaths, usually a euphemism for a little push and shove, were common in Bangkok and usually elicited no more than a mention in the back pages.

Springdale, from North Carolina, 64, had suffered from depression and alcoholism. A service would be held at a temple in Thong Lo the coming Sunday. Maier didn't know what day it was. But he wouldn't be at the poet's send-off. He felt sorry for Mason, even if he'd tried to shop him. No one deserved to die for the Monsoon Ghost Image.

His thoughts returned to the tall man who'd arrived at The Sunshine Bar with the cops. The way he'd dressed and carried himself was particular, flamboyant even. Ginger and his friend weren't cut from that guy's freaky cloth.

Is there a third force out there, chasing the Monsoon Ghost Image? And if so, how do they know the picture existed?

The only way to stop the killing was to get the photo published. He had to find out who was in the picture, what they'd been doing to whom, and whether Sundermann could be saved.

Maier had no clear idea who was in possession of the picture, Sundermann, Mikhail, Puttama. But he did understand there was a manhunt on to make him disappear.

He headed off to another Internet café, opened his new email account, and mailed Mikhail again.

His message was simple.

Are you still in the country? Any plans for the holidays?

He had thought of printing out the picture, cutting it up, and sniffing around to see who the three remaining torturers were. But it was too dangerous to ask Mikhail for his copy. Maier found himself zoning out in front of the screen again and scanned through the news. US Foreign Secretary Colin Powell proved to the world that Iraq had weapons of mass destruction. British Prime Minister Blair announced that the United Kingdom was under imminent threat from Saddam Hussein's missiles. UN weapons inspector Hans Blix gently denied Blair's evidence.

The articles and op-eds he scrolled through all shouted for war, selling fear and earning traction. The Americans were getting ready to invade. Maier was a tiny fraction of this war, and not of his own choosing. Despite the fact that the detective had experienced conflict first-hand, he struggled to align the doomsday news pouring from the media with his personal stake in the Monsoon Ghost Image.

As he got himself together to return to his hotel Mikhail sent a reply.

"Holidays are splendid. The beach is wonderful, the men are gorgeous and it's party time in a couple of days."

Maier typed Party, Thailand, and the date into the browser's search engine. Koh Phangan's Full Moon Party, a monthly event that attracted thousands of kids from the Western world's suburbs and tempted them into cultural insensitivity, was due to kick-off two days hence.

He signed out, bought two bowls of noodles and enough water for 24 hours, and picked up a strip of valium at a pharmacy. As he passed a 7/11, he contemplated buying a bottle of Sangsom, an efficient poison that passed for rum in Thailand, but he walked on. But for the beer in the Sunshine Bar, he hadn't drunk since they'd received the photo. There'd been no time. If having the world's best-trained spies after you wasn't enough to sober up, nothing ever would be. For the first time in his adult life, he neither drank nor smoked. He almost felt better about himself.

Maier returned to his room and closed the shades. The world would continue to turn without his input for a few hours.

13

SOUTHERN THAILAND, JANUARY 2003

ANIMALS

THE CAR FERRY was packed with backpacking tourists— a few disheveled hippie types, the rest credit card-carrying hedonists, all of them looking forward to a few days of beach-side debauchery.

The ferry, traveling from the coastal town of Surat Thani, was an old steel vessel that had seen too many voyages. The passenger cabin smelled of old socks and most of the travelers sat on deck in the bright, tropical sun.

Small forested islands dotted the horizon, rising from the perfectly placid Gulf of Thailand like the spine of a sleeping dragon. Except for the smoke belching from the ferry's rusty chimneys, it was postcard paradise.

On deck, shirts had come off, bikinis were taken for a walk and bodies glistened in self-satisfied, oiled-up repose. Maier had nothing better to do than watch the kids. They didn't look as excited about travel in exotic lands as he'd had been when he'd first started working abroad and hadn't been able to get enough of The Other.

This lot was more comfortable with itself, admiring each other's tattoos, reveling in a shared tribal experience that encompassed doubtful fashions and earnest discussions on wellness and how to save money on the road.

Maier lasted just a few minutes in the sun and retreated inside where the Thais sat eating snacks made from sea creatures, watching a badly flickering CD copy of a Hong Kong action movie, waiting to get it over with. For the locals, there was nothing romantic about the scenery or the sea. None of them had to bear all the sophisticated constructs with which the Europeans on deck had to wrestle. They were on their way home or on their way to work, many couldn't swim and were scared of the water.

Maier entered the ship's small convenience store and ordered a coffee. The sour-faced *kathoey* behind the counter pointed him to a large steel container on a table to the back. A middle-aged woman, a hippie type with a huge pile of dreadlocks rising from her head like a coiled cobra, held a young girl in her arms and tried to pour herself a coffee, but most of the brew spilled onto the tabletop.

She laughed nervously as Maier stood next to her. He took her cup, refilled it with a second pouch of instant, and then poured hot water to the brim. The woman smiled, took the cup, and left, the child staring at Maier with large vacant eyes.

"Where you go, mister?"

The woman waved at Maier from a table a few metres away. Her dark arms were tattooed and she wore studs in her ears that looked like they'd been made from animal bone. Maier feared her. *She could be a trap.* If she wasn't and anyone saw them together, she might become a victim.

"I visit friends." He realized that other than ordering food, these were the first words he'd spoken in a couple of days.

The woman nodded as if she could see right through his head.

"Where you stay, mister?"

"Chalok Lam," Maier answered wearily, the name of a village he'd remembered from a tourist map in the minibus.

"Oh, I live in Chalok Lam, I have a pick-up downstairs. I give you a lift, mister. You look like a nice man, OK."

Maier thanked her as the cranky, tannoy system came to life and informed passengers that Koh Phangan was just minutes away. He felt too paranoid to consider the woman's offer and went outside.

. . .

The ferry pulled into Thong Sala, the island's port town, at mid-day. Maier half expected the cops to be waiting for him. He hoped to see Mikhail at the pier. As the ship tied to the single concrete jetty, Maier scanned the waiting crowd from the sundeck.

No cops. No Mikhail. No professionals.

Hotel touts in pick-ups or on motorbikes, holding up signs promising paradise and more, jostled for space with business owners picking up supplies, and sun-seared, hung-over tourists, their holidays and libido spent, looking significantly more disheveled than the new arrivals on the ferry, waiting to leave paradise.

But something was wrong. He had a hunch that trouble was waiting down there. A brand-new black pick-up sat empty fifty metres back in the sun, windows down. A metal awning stretched back to the ferry company's office, erected so that passengers who walked onto or off the ferry didn't fry in the sun. Maier moved to the far side of the deck to be able to see who was under the awning. He cursed. The tall blonde guy who'd arrived with the cops at the Sunshine Club in Bangkok, now dressed in beige shorts and a gleaming white shirt open almost to his navel, stood smoking a cigarette, watching the boat pull in. He looked like a sailor in a whaler's novel. Only the harpoon was missing. He probably had one in his pick-up.

Maier crossed the deck and rushed back into the passenger cabin. The room was deserted, the Thais, keen to get off the ship had left. The woman who'd offered him a lift was gone. Maier crossed the cabin to the far side of the ferry which wasn't visible from the jetty and found the stairs that led down to the cars. He descended and emerged into a tangle of smoke-belching vehicles just as the ferry's loading door started to descend. If the big man had moved closer to the ship, Maier would be exposed in a few seconds. He stood on the lowest step scanning the sea of vehicles.

The door came down and the first cars and trucks at the front started revving their engines.

"Where you go, mister?"

The woman had wound down the window of her truck, parked a couple of the vehicles to his right, and smiled brightly at him. Maier did his best to hide his distress and walked over to her.

"You might give me a lift after all?"

"Sure, mister. you come to Chalok Lam with me, no problem."

She laughed at Maier with such warmth that it jolted the detective into a world quite alien to the one he currently traveled through, a world of people who cared for one another. *Who could resist such first-degree charm?* He squeezed between vehicles to get to the passenger door and jumped in.

"You sit in the back, mister. If you are scared that someone is looking for you. I understand, no problem."

Maier turned around and saw the young girl, sitting in the back, staring at him with intense curiosity. With some difficulty, he squeezed between the front seats and crunched himself up next to the girl.

"My name is Hom, *sawadee kaa*, please to meet you, mister. This is my daughter, Mae." The woman laughed as she pulled out of the belly of the ship.

Maier shrunk deeper into the back of the pick-up, though he needn't have, the windows were tinted, and they were coming up as the air-con blew ice-cold into the car.

"My name... Maier."

They pulled up onto the jetty in a long line of vehicles. The tall man was right ahead at the end of the ramp leading up to the jetty, scanning the crowd and vehicles as they passed him. He stood like a giant rock in a sea of mechanized movement, clearly intent on checking every single vehicle.

Hom wound the window on the passenger side down and the man looked inside. There was no way he could see Maier who cowered behind the woman. The man recognized Hom and recoiled. Maier thought the woman looked angrily at his pursuer. A second later they were approaching Thong Sala's only traffic circle and the detective sat back and relaxed.

"You in trouble, Mr. Maier? You don't look like a tourist."

He shook his head in silence.

"Come sit in front with me, Mr. Maier."

Maier squeezed past Mae and slumped in the passenger seat, staring glumly out of the window. He felt drained. Another close shave. Whom or what had he just escaped? Was this guy connected to the two Americans in Berlin, Hamburg, and Bangkok? He was most likely involved in the death of Mason the Poet. And had Maier escaped? Hom had worked out quickly that he was in trouble.

Within a few minutes, they'd left the town behind. Coconut plantations, patches of giant bamboo, and a few remnants of the rainforest that had once covered most of the island zoomed past. A Chinese cemetery, its broad white gravestones and mausoleums gleaming in the sun with the intensity of burning magnesium, rose from the forest amidst a thousand shades of green.

Koh Phangan, population less than 10.000, half a million visitors a year, lay in the shallow Gulf like a precious jewel, ringed by palm-fringed beaches. The island's name was derived from the Siamese word *ngan* which translated as sandbank. But Phangan was a sandbank no more. Money had arrived and taken over like a new predator species and was more desperate to multiply than the local flora.

The island's first dalliance with outsiders had been both more glamorous and humbler. During the 19th century, a Thai king visited the island eighteen times and put it firmly on the map, or at least into the Siamese subconscious. The British noticed Phangan in the dying throes of World War II when they sunk a Japanese supply ship off its coast. In the 70s, the hippies discovered the Phangan, and the three hundred or so local farming and fishing families catered to their increasingly sophisticated demands ever since.

In those early days, the ferry took eight hours to cross from the mainland, so most visitors stayed for months, smoked bongs, and made out in the shallows. The Full Moon Party arrived in the late 80s and opened Phangan to mass tourism. Land disputes, unregulated development, and real estate-related murders followed.

Growing pains, Maier thought.

The Full Moon Party remained the major draw. The local authorities liked earning the cash the kids brought but showed their disdain for their young unkempt guests by busting them for small amounts of drugs. Harmless stuff, really. The usual cultural disconnect with both sides too lazy to think about it. The kids and the money kept coming. Everyone called it progress and development.

The road curved gently uphill as they headed north, deeper into dense jungle, further from his pursuer.

Hom asked no more questions but smiled at him with a mixture of nervousness and hope that Maier couldn't fathom.

After fifteen minutes of silence, she cleared her throat. "My house is one kilometre from Chalok Lam. Where you go, mister?"

"I don't know. Anywhere. Please drop me at the beach."

She slowed down and turned to him.

"Why did you come to my island?"

"If I tell you that, you might get in trouble."

She contemplated this.

"You're a good man, Mr. Maier. I feel and I trust you, no problem, you can come to my house. Maybe I can help you, and you can help me."

That sounded ominous, not least because she knew the blonde man at the port, but he was pretty sure that his benefactor knew nothing about him or his situation. She liked him. That was enough. And he already owed this woman for getting him off the boat in one piece.

"And no sexy stuff," she added.

He nodded.

She smiled.

They rode on in silence.

14

THE HOUSE

For the first time since he'd stood on the hotel roof in Ari, watching his Russian friend and colleague destroy their communication devices, Maier felt safe. Reasonably safe. The impulse to constantly look across his shoulder had subsided. In fact, he was quite pleased with himself. He'd pulled his head out of a lot of slings between Bangkok and the beach.

Lying back in a hammock on the verandah of Hom's stilt house, surrounded by flowering epiphytes, watching her child play in the front yard, he thought about the mad last days.

Oh, Maier.

He remembered the German title of an obscure Grimm's Fairy Tale— *Von einem der auszog um das Fürchten zu lernen* — which roughly translated as 'Of someone who left home to learn to fear'. That's where Maier was at. He was busy learning and failing his lessons.

He needed to find Mikhail and they needed to save Sundermann.

Watching Mae in the golden afternoon light, kicking up dust as cicadas started their shrill evening concert in the forest behind the house, Maier remembered his boss' phone call that had snapped him out of his self-pitying revelry in Altona a few weeks ago.

"I don't have a family," he'd said then.

Yes, he did.

"The family of noseys," Sundermann had countered and pulled him back to work and a semblance of a life.

Sundermann, Mikhail, they were more than colleagues. They had to be because Maier had no other friends or family and there was nothing else worth fighting for.

Hom emerged from the house, a joint in her hand, and sat down next to Maier.

"You smoke?"

He took the joint. The hit was immediate and his head started to swirl. The woman laughed and climbed down the stairs. Mother and daughter chased each other around the yard. Their shouts cut across the insect chorus in the trees and the gentle splashing of waves lapping the shore less than a hundred metres away. Maier drifted off into exhaustion.

Much later, they sat on rattan mats on the verandah, a single candle, a mosquito coil, and the remnants of a fiery fish curry between them. Mae had fallen asleep in the hammock, only her feet visible above the netting that cocooned her.

"I want to tell you a story, Maier. Before, when you sit here and get stoned, I went in the room and look in your bag. You have a gun. You're not police, I think. But you're not *nakleng*, not criminal either, I think. That's why I want to tell you my story. After you can stay or go. Up to you. You can leave or help me, up to you. But you have to listen to my story first. And I need your help, *ka*."

Maier nodded, from another world altogether.

"I am forty-five years old. I come from Krung Thep, Bangkok. I was a student in Bangkok in the late seventies. We had many problems with the military government at that time. I came down here for time out and I met a man, Boy. His nickname was Boy, because he look like a boy. He was a young man from the island. I fell in love with this boy, and I stayed on the island and we married and we build bungalows for tourists, we made a restaurant, we sold ganja, we made parties for many years. And then one day, about ten years ago, a man came to the island, a *farang*, a very rich *farang* who had a big company in US. And this man, with some partner in the military, decide to build an airport on Koh Phangan. On my husband's family's land, the land of many other people, and on national park land. He offered some money, some compensation. But my husband and I organized with other farmers here, like we did in the seventies. We wanted to keep Koh Phangan beautiful. We made demonstrations on our land against the airport." She paused.

Maier could guess what was coming. The night contracted around them and the darkness made the candle between them flicker and almost faint.

"This man, he paid everyone, the major, the police. And my husband, one day, five years ago, he drowned."

Maier saw only sadness in Hom's face. She laughed with bitterness.

"My husband was a very good swimmer."

After a long silence, Maier asked her, "Why are you telling me this? I'm not a killer."

She looked at him directly and without pity. "The big man at the boat. He killed my husband. He works for the rich *farang*. His name is Wuttke-something. I think he is looking for you. I'm sure."

Maier said nothing for a long time. He looked out into the night, uncertain whether to leave this madness or stay. As soon as he escaped one trap, another one opened. How could this man have a long connection to an island Maier was visiting to escape from this very same man? It didn't make sense. He'd spoken to no one in Bangkok, to no one on the bus, and only to Hom on the ferry. For Wuttke to appear at the jetty couldn't be a coincidence, but Maier could see no logic in what had happened. At least one of the parties looking for him was looking for him in places he'd never been to.

"This *farang* who wants to build the airport. What nationality is he?"

"He is German. Wuttke is German, same. Same as you, Maier. The big man with the money is called Krieger. He is a famous German *poo yai*, like a strong man, big man. He is in the news here sometimes. He owns many telephone companies, he has so much money. Same like our Thailand prime minister. Rich man and very corrupt. Krieger owns one island not so far from here. It's in a national park. People say there are wild animals, a very dangerous island, has tigers, has big snakes. He has a big house, with place for helicopter, jetty, speed boat, everything there. You go there, you don't come back. That's what the *chao ley*, sea gypsies, say who travel through the park sometimes. These rich people killed my husband. For money."

"What is it you expect me to do, Hom?"

She shrugged at him, a dark look on her face. "Why did you meet me on the boat and why did I help you, Mr. Maier? And why is the man who killed my husband looking for you? Maybe it's magic. Maybe karma. Maybe it's lucky, no lucky. But you are here now and you…I don't know how to explain, my English is not so good…you are part of the story. I know. I feel it."

Maier nodded. "Me too, and I don't like it."

"So, I think you don't come to help me, but you come for another reason and maybe now something will change for me, because I miss my husband very much and I have so much pain and I have to hide it from my daughter all the time. And she will never see her father. She was too young. It is very hard. I don't like this rich *farang* and these local people who only like the money and let the foreigners do what they want in my country, even kill our own people. I want to stop this man building the airport where my husband died. Stop destroying the island. I want to kill Wuttke. That is my wish."

Maier drifted off under a mosquito net in the back room of the house while mother and daughter slept outside. The cicadas stopped singing around midnight and only the gentle rhythm of the waves remained, interrupted every now and then by the call of a gecko in the distance, sounding like a quickly tiring windup toy.

"Kick me, kick me, kick me, urgh."

Then he was gone, both eyes closed.

15

THE BUCKET PEOPLE

THE POLICE HAD SET up several roadblocks between the island's capital and Haad Rin, the crescent-shaped beach that served as the venue for the monthly Full Moon Party.

Motorbikes and *songthaews*, open carriages carrying up to thirty young, mostly drunk tourists, were stopped and checked for drugs. There wouldn't be much of a catch. These youngsters purchased their drugs on the beach, from local toughs who worked with the cops. Or they were already off their heads, leisure chemicals laughing at the police through glazed eyes. The cops waved Hom through with curt nods and never looked at Maier.

The road traversed several steep hills, ascending and descending at crazy inclines that killed a handful of drunken scooter riding foreigners every season, a small sacrifice the island exacted for the debauchery that washed across its beaches, year in, year out.

A few minutes later they pulled into the town that fronted Haad Rin beach, a traffic-clogged, unruly collection of shops, resorts, and restaurants that stretched from the road down to the seashore.

Hom parked the car behind a friend's clothes shop, tied Mae to her back with a checkered cotton scarf, and led Maier towards the party.

It was 11 pm. The vibe by the water's edge was both wonderful and nauseating, like a huge, fatty meal in progress.

Several thousand kids between sixteen and thirty spread across the wide curve of Haad Rin Nok beach, consuming lethal mixes of liqueur, energy drinks, and sodas from plastic buckets that were for sale everywhere. Even the pharmacies behind the beach sold buckets for a fistful of baht.

A dozen sound systems pumped house beats across the sand as they walked away from the crowds along the shore, which was lined with young men relieving themselves into the shallow water that was barely visible under a carpet of beer cans and party debris. Other, less able revelers lie drunk in the surf between land and sea, their happy, leering faces raised upwards towards the perfect cold disc of the moon.

Up on the beach, it was dark. The bars had light systems that flashed across the sand but there were enough shadows for an endless chain of drug deals and drug busts, for casual and damaged moments of intimacy or for the solitary drift into a narcotic coma.

Most males wore no shirts and most bodies were covered in luminous paint. Silly hats and buckets were ubiquitous. Maier stood out in this crowd, but he didn't feel like going native.

It wasn't all bad. The air was balmy, the headland that rose to the north end of the beach, occupied by a giant luminous neon mushroom, was part Walt Disney, part King Kong and many of the kids looked unearthly and wraithlike in their mindless abandon. There was no message here, no struggle, no fight, and no War on Terror. The world was normal. Everything was under control.

"There is ladyboy bar near Tommy Resort. Maybe your friend is there. We try?" Hom said.

Maier nodded and they pushed on through the crowd. Mae was wide awake, watching the lights with unfiltered curiosity.

They passed a man with a giant lizard on his shoulder. A group of upper-class English boys wearing bikini tops and wigs danced next to a party of street-wise French kids, all dressed in Muay Thai boxing shorts, Paris scrawled in luminous letters across their puffed-up, shaved chests. It was all one happy family.

Scores of feeders moved amongst the revelers— drug sellers and undercover cops, working in groups to bust as many foreigners with the same pack of pills as possible, each time extracting an excessive bribe. Ladyboys offered semi-public blowjobs, a maneuver designed to lift the punters' wallets. Good time girls looking for holiday boyfriends and all sorts of vendors sold stuff half-naked drunken people needed in the middle of the night. There was something about the absurdity that was endearing.

Don't they know there's a war on out there? Don't they care?

Hom led Maier north hugging the waterline, dodging party people both upright and horizontal. A few hundred metres before they reached the neon mushroom, Hom took off up the beach, into the swirling masses. Maier followed her dreadlocks, piled high on her head, as Mae looked back at him, her eyes widening every time they were about to lose eye contact.

"My long-lost brother."

Mikhail towered in front of them, in shorts, his Hawaiian shirt barely buttoned. He looked drunk, but his eyes were sharp. Maier was very pleased to see his colleague.

"We can talk?" Maier asked him.

"Can. Must."

"This is Hom. She helped me get here. She is connected to all this."

Mikhail offered his giant right paw to the woman. "*Sawadee kap*, young lady. Pleased to meet you."

He waved at Mae and pulled an inebriated clown face. The girl smiled back at the giant, surprising both Maier and her mother.

"We're human after all," he grinned.

Maier hugged his friend, realizing it was a first.

"Maier, you're finally warming up to my hidden charms?" His partner laughed at his own joke as he led them along a sandy path between two resorts.

"What's going on? Why are we here?" Hom asked. "Why is a huge man named Wuttke, a German with blonde hair, looking a bit like you, but uglier, chasing me through Bangkok and then stands at the jetty here on the island when I arrive?"

Mikhail turned back to Hom. "He told you that we are in a tight spot. You being with us is dangerous. He told you that?"

She nodded. "This man Wuttke killed my husband."

Mikhail raised his eyebrows and walked on. Maier recounted his last couple of days. The light of a small hole-in-the-wall bar loomed ahead. The sound of Celine Dion dripped onto the sand. A hand-drawn sign welcomed them to the Dream Boy Bar. Next to the entrance, the toilet door was marked with another hand-drawn sign that read 'Customer free, Outsider 20 baht. No poo-poo.'

The Dream Boy Bar was skid row.

The Russian stopped.

"Ritter's in there. With Ruby's friends from Bangkok," Mikhail said. "He owns a house here where he used to take Ruby. It was my only lead, so when I found him, his friends joined me. They aren't happy with what he did to Ruby. So tonight, they'll punish him."

"Punish him?" Maier asked.

"Yes, they'll cut his nuts off."

Maier cringed. Hom looked at Mikhail in disbelief.

"What did he do, this man?" Hom asked.

"He killed his partner, a *kathoey*, and castrated him. Now he has the same coming to him. But he'll live. His partner Ruby didn't."

Maier felt sick.

"You are going to stop them?" Hom asked.

Mikhail shrugged.

"They're determined. And they're friends of convenience. It's not a true love affair, Maier. But we want to talk to Ritter beforehand. Now. I don't know who the man is you think is looking for you, but I have a hunch he's looking for Ritter, not you. Sorry to dent your ego there, Maier. There must be a third party involved. He's not with the Americans, I'm sure of that."

Maier agreed, the Monsoon Ghost Image was sought by someone else.

The Russian grabbed Maier's arm and pulled him a few feet away from the bar's entrance.

"And there's a caveat to all this. A doctor will attend Ritter's possible demise…it's your Suraporn, the barking quack."

Maier stopped in his tracks.

"You have met him?"

"No, they're still waiting for him. Apparently, Ritter negotiated his presence. How mad is that?"

"Confusing," was all Maier could think to say.

"And dangerous."

Mikhail nodded. "Your account of your meeting with him is still with me, friend."

"If Suraporn turns up here, the Americans won't be far behind."

"I fear that too. But is it reason enough to kill the doctor?"

"We are not killers, Mikhail."

His partner laughed. "Maybe not, but we do like to live another day and these people are out to get us. Hitting them first is what I've been taught to do."

"You don't work for the FSB now, Mikhail."

"I don't work for anyone, other than myself."

"You work for Sundermann," Maier pointed out.

"He's disappeared."

"Yes, so let us kidnap the spooky doctor and see if we can trade him for our boss." Mikhail looked at his partner with sad pride. "Maier, you have strange ideas. I'm proud to be working with you. And you're right. We both grew up under communism. We understand each other. We're friends. I have been thinking about this for some days and I came to the same conclusion as you. We must spring the boss. Everything else is failure."

"Plan?" Maier asked.

"Can. Must. Now. We get offensive. They get offended."

Ritter sat tied to a barber chair to the back of the small bar. Maier barely recognized him. The plastic surgery by Suraporn had been extensive and it had healed well. The man who sat defiantly in front of the ladyboys was clearly a different creature than the war photographer Maier had met years earlier. But he was the same person.

No one served beer behind the counter. The music had stopped. The cacophony of sound on the beach was a low, mangled hum that drifted through the door. The fairy lights strung along the bar's low ceiling blinked on unconsciously, blind to the misery below.

Ruby's four transgender friends sat in a semi-circle around their prisoner, passing around a long piece of aluminum foil, chasing the dragon. Maier recognized the acrid smell, these ladies were smoking what the Thais called *yaba*, mad medicine, cheap meta-amphetamine, mass-produced in the jungles of Burma.

Ritter addressed him in German.

"Ah, Maier, still fighting the good fight, are we?"

Maier was taken aback by Ritter's tone. The man knew what was coming. He was fighting for his life, but he sounded defiant.

Maier pulled up a stool and faced him. Tired men looking at each other across vast distances. No one was having any fun.

The detective replied in English. Mikhail, who stood outside with Hom, just out of sight, needed to understand. The *kathoeys* needed to understand.

"Emilie hired me to find you. She paid with her life to get you back."

The photographer snorted in disgust.

"Emilie. Maier. You should've fucked her when you had the chance all those years ago. Maybe I would've been able to get rid of her then and she'd still be alive today. Anyway, I know you're a former commie turned humanist, hard shell but kind heart and all that, so you'll stop these crazies here from going ahead with their revenge plans. Believe me, Maier, you need me alive. You got the devil on your tail. I know what I'm talking about. I worked with him."

Maier coughed, a late reaction to the weed he'd smoked the night before, or perhaps it was revulsion.

"What did you think you were doing, taking that picture?" Maier asked.

Ritter laughed. "That picture, what they call the Monsoon Ghost Image, has everyone in a twist. But you see, it's just the tip of the iceberg. The Americans have been disappearing Muslims since nine-eleven. They pick these people off the street anywhere in the world, dope them and fly them to poor, lawless countries, where they employ a combination of homegrown skills and local traditions to extract information. It's radical stuff, Maier, deeply disturbing and deeply honest, when you think of what we really need to do when we face evil. We have to embrace evil. We have to become evil. You should know this. You've been down to the wire. The Americans are reaching for higher truths here."

"By torture?"

Ritter grinned. "Yes."

"And what does it have to do with you?"

Ritter laughed so hard that the *kathoeys* who sat on the bar's white floor tiles, passing a huge blade and a sharpening stone between them, took a unified breath and shrunk away. Even Macbeth's three witches would have been scared away from their cauldron by this man.

"Maier, I photographed everything there is to photograph in this world. My career is coming to an end. The Internet is producing so many images now that guys like me will become irrelevant soon. Just as well you got out of the journo business when you did. Newspapers will no longer pay money for images from the world's front lines. It's over. I asked myself, what didn't I shoot in all these years of covering misery and violence? And the only thing I could think of, the only thing I could come up with, was a change in perspective. I always shot from the perspective of the underdog, the victim, the good guys. I wanted to see it another way, show it another way. And it turns out, I'm right with the times, didn't even have to change sides. You know, us Germans, we understand better than anyone how fragile morality is, how we strain towards the light for decades and then tumble into darkness in an instant, how we construct cathedrals of lofty thoughts only to negate them entirely with realities of barbed wire and small cells where terrible things happen. I was making an ambiguous contribution. I took up the CIA's offer to witness and record their most covert efforts to contain Muslim aggression. In return, they promised me a new start. So far so good."

"It doesn't look good for you, Ritter."

The photographer looked down at the ladyboys and laughed. "You'll stop them, Maier. You won't let these savages kill me. The rest is all a question of negotiation."

"Martin, your wife was murdered."

The photographer said nothing and looked away. For a second, Maier recognized the ambitious young man of the battlefields. He put his arm out to touch Ritter's shoulder.

"And they won't kill you."

Ritter jerked back, almost toppling his chair.

"I know what they said. You can stop them. If you do, I'll tell you where that stupid two-faced bitch Puttama is held and maybe you can free her with your queer Russian Rambo friend."

Maier thought it over. Ritter might have been bluffing or he might have been telling the truth. *Hard to judge a deranged man under duress.* People were prone to say anything under torture.

"You asked Suraporn to come here. You know what'll happen to you."

"I asked the doctor because he's the scariest man imaginable and he will put some reason into you lot. And then he'll walk out with me and kill me round the next corner. And if you're still alive, it'll be your job to see that doesn't happen, because if it does, the CIA lady and your boss are dead as doornails. You get the doctor, you have some bargaining power. The Americans won't stop. They want to kill me as much as anyone who's seen the picture. They don't want this to go public."

Maier smiled sadly at his old acquaintance.

"You think we are doing your wet work for you?" Maier asked.

Ritter laughed.

"I'm your only chance. Puttama is a whistleblower, an honest Joe who wants to make the world a better place. She'd give the picture away if she could. If you hadn't pulled her from my place in Chinatown, I'd have one problem less. I should have killed her with Ruby."

At the mention of their friend, the ladyboys perked up. The tallest, a thirty-something with a pockmarked face and a perm from hell, stopped sliding the knife across his stone and stared at Ritter with bestial aggression.

"Ruby blabbed to you guys. She gave you the disc, right? That was a no-no. And I must admit, I misjudged her. I thought she liked my money enough to not give my business a second thought. I was wrong. She paid for his thirst for knowledge. And so will Puttama if you don't get me out of here."

Maier shook his head. "Ruby compromised you because she wanted to save you."

Ritter shot back, "Ruby betrayed me because you two got her drunk and pressured her into giving you the photo. And with that, you have brought nothing but shit upon yourselves and the rest of the world."

Maier pulled the conversation back to the here and now.

"So, Suraporn will turn up with his American minders and we will have a late 19th century American West style shoot-out on the beach, and you will ride off into the sunset?"

Ritter laughed more and spat on the tiles in front of him.

"You think the Thais are slaves to the CIA? You really think a man like Suraporn can be bought, that his loyalty can be assured? You think these guys, Suraporn, and that crazy walking dead general will let the Americans humiliate them on their own turf and then stick with them when the going gets bumpy? Thais are your best and most loyal friends when it suits them, no matter how bad you treat them, and then, when you're weak, they turn on you and take you for everything you have. In the case of the doctor, that probably includes your liver."

The photographer stopped in his tracks. His anger had gotten the better of him. He'd said too much.

Maier weighed the other man's silence and took his time.

"Martin, who is Wuttke and why is he after you?"

Ritter jerked back in his chair and stared at the detective, eyes bulging with fear.

"You've been talking to Wuttke?"

Maier shrugged and got up.

"Maier, Wuttke is a mad dog. Ex-Stasi man, works for Krieger, the richest German in Thailand. The locals fear him. And with good reason. He's really taken to local standards of impunity. You don't want to go down that road. That guy is psychotic."

"And Suraporn isn't? Seems there is no short supply of psychos in the War on Terror."

Ritter was starting to relax again.

"Don't be so naïve. This isn't about the War on Terror. Maybe for the CIA and for Puttama it is. For everyone else, it's about money."

"What money?" Maier asked.

"Can you imagine how much people will pay for that picture? I can sell it in five seconds for two million US dollars. Give you half. Give them half, kill Suraporn and let me go." He laughed, pointing his chin towards the transgender by his feet.

"I think you're dreaming. The New York Times will not give you two million dollars for a photo, no matter how explosive, unless the purchase turns out to be a way to suppress the image. But with digital files that is virtually impossible. The moment is gone. The image is already everywhere even if it is nowhere at all."

"I'm not talking about the media, Maier. They probably need clearance from the US government to publish that kind of shit. Get real. No, I'm talking about the mavericks out there, the wealthy fringe."

Maier put it all together.

"Wuttke represents the wealthy fringe. You made a deal with this Krieger guy. You did not honor the deal. That is why he is coming after you."

Ritter remained silent.

"Every minute you remain tied to that chair and fail to put distance between your betrayals and your future, you die a little more, Martin. I don't pity you, but the place you are going, one way or another, is pitiful."

Ritter shifted uneasily, as much as he could, straining the masking tape across his chest that kept him immobile.

"Ah, my German connection will save me, you have to. Otherwise, your boss will die."

Maier rose.

"Perhaps there is another way. I will let your friends get on with it. If the doctor comes on time, he may save you, or sow a dog's head to your scrotum, who knows? After that, we can renegotiate."

16

WUTTKE

Maier left the building and waved Mikhail and Hom around the corner.

"Ritter is a stubborn bastard. I don't want him to get cut up, but nothing seems to scare him."

Mikhail shrugged. "It's always like that. You start a war and the rules of conduct are the first casualty. We need Sundermann back."

"You mean we should let those people in there cut his cock off?"

"Stop it by all means. But don't expect anything from that man. He's crossed over and he's not looking for a way in from the cold."

Maier had to stop the ladyboys savaging the photographer. But Emilie's drawn face, half-hidden under her funeral veil and his boss' last words kept crowding into his thoughts.

"There are too many players in force now. It is no longer about us running after an image and the Americans running after us."

Mikhail grinned sourly and looked skywards at the blinking lights of a helicopter that was about to descend into Haad Rin, no more than a couple of blocks away.

"Welcome to the twenty-first century. All the old certainties gone."

Hom stood behind the two men watching the entrance to the bar.

"You really let the *kathoey* cut this man? Maybe he dies. And how does he know Wuttke?"

Mikhail turned to her.

"I think he tried to sell Wuttke's boss Krieger something that Krieger wants." He looked at Maier. "Maybe we should meet this man."

Hom's eyes lit up, then she checked herself.

"He will kill you like he killed my husband."

"No doubt. Unless we have something that he wants."

Maier considered the cast of characters involved in the Monsoon Ghost Image affair the way he might have considered a streak of tigers facing him. You had to keep eye contact with all of them all the time if you didn't want to get mauled.

"What if the Americans found out Krieger had the image and Suraporn gave it to him? We'd be out of the loop then, no? Suraporn obviously betrayed their cause."

Maier wasn't sure, "They want to plug all holes. The more people are associated with the image, the more people they will send after them. Our best hope is still Puttama. If they haven't found out she is on our side, then we have a chance to get away with this."

Mikhail looked at Maier questioningly. "On our side?"

"Let us hope so," the detective answered.

"Ritter said she'd been found out."

Maier shook his head. "I think he is lying. I don't think he has had any contact with the Americans since the fire in Chinatown."

Hom, who'd been watching the bar, pushed Maier and the Russian further behind the building.

A minute later, they heard Ritter scream.

Maier felt sick.

"Suraporn must have arrived," the detective said.

Mikhail grinned towards the moon and said to no one in particular, "For a mad dog, seven versets is not a long detour."

Ritter continued to scream.

Maier cowered against the wall of the building retching up the dinner he'd never had.

Mikhail turned to Maier. "Where is my gun?"

"I don't have it with me," Maier grunted.

"I'll stop them."

The Russian turned to go. Wuttke came around the corner, a revolver in his hand. Mikhail wasn't close enough to make a move.

"*Guten Abend*. Seems like half of Germany is at the Full Moon Party tonight."

Maier looked at his friend and shrugged.

Hom stepped between the two men and opened her bag.

Maier saw the glint of the Russian's Sig. Wuttke was staring at Hom. His gun wavered away from Mikhail towards the woman. She dropped the bag into the sand and backed off.

"You. Again. The airport slut. I definitely don't need you in this story."

Maier bent down and pulled the gun from Hom's bag. He flipped the safety off, pushed Mikhail out of the way, and pulled the trigger.

The huge German took the bullet in his upper chest and went down into the sand, a look of disbelief fading from his broad face.

"Looks like an ugly version of me. Big, blond, but not handsome," Mikhail commented. Unfazed, the Russian stretched his hand out to Maier. "You saved my life, Maier. You definitely saved her life. You're a good friend. Now give me the gun. You killed enough today."

Maier handed him the weapon.

Mikhail disappeared into the alley, towards the Boy Dream Bar which, by now, was unlikely to harbor dreams of any kind. Maier got up and followed. What else was he going to do? He'd just killed a complete stranger.

Suraporn had been too late. The *kateoys* were dead, he'd shot all four of them with a steel crossbow that now lay abandoned on the tiles amidst the detritus of drug paraphernalia, in imminent danger of being submerged by a quickly spreading pool of blood leaking from Ritter's groin.

The photographer was unconscious and apparently post-op, and Suraporn was working feverishly on his wound, wearing rubber gloves, a small powerful torch on his head, and a magnifying glass in front of his eyes. The man had an uncanny speed. He'd stitched Ritter's crotch and was now staying the bleeding with a cotton press while plunging a syringe into the photographer's right arm.

He turned his head and both Maier and Mikhail sucked in their breath.

The doctor focused on Maier and smiled vaguely. "I warned you, Mr. Maier. I suggested we never meet again, and you did not follow my advice. And now you are dead."

He turned back to Ritter, pulled the syringe from his vein, dropped it to the floor, and pulled a tiny scalpel from his breast pocket with which he proceeded to cut the tape that kept Ritter upright. When he had the photographer cut loose, he wrapped his groin with a new cotton press weighed down with a tablet of lead.

"He's ready for transport. You'll help me get him to my helicopter."

Mikhail took one more step into the bar, raised the gun with a shaking hand, and shot the doctor in the leg. Suraporn slumped back onto the tiles and into the other man's blood and hissed at the two men standing over him.

Mikhail turned to Maier. "You're right, this man is strange, he can suck the air out of a room. Maybe we should put him down?"

Maier stood speechless, staring at the savage tableau in front of him. Four dead transgenders, a butchered man, and a savage serial killer with a bullet in his leg in a pool of blood in a back alley on Thailand's party island. No police. Unless the cops walked right past, they'd never notice.

"*Guten Abend, meine Herren.*"

The detective turned to see a little man in an open-necked white shirt and white cotton pants, his tanned feet bare in the sand, stand outside the door of the bar. The man wore his perfectly even grey hair brushed back across his head like a thirties movie star. Behind him, a dozen young Thai men dressed in identical black shirts and pants, armed with short-barreled automatic rifles, had blocked off the escape routes.

Mikhail kept his eyes on the doctor who was sliding through the blood towards the crossbow.

"If you move any further, I'll shoot you in the head, Dr. Suraporn. I doubt you'd survive that."

The little man continued, unfazed.

"Gentlemen, gentlemen. Enough killing. This is all ghastly. Here, Wuttke, my most loyal servant lies in the sand having breathed his last. I'm beside myself with sorrow and anger. But I can see that the situation is confusing and that men have their mad minutes. I'll forgive all of you if you are so kind and follow me onto my boat, so we can leave this dreadful, vulgar place and negotiate in more amenable circumstances. *Was meint ihr? Gebt meinen Leuten hier eure Waffen."*

Mikhail threw his gun towards one of the young men and pointed at the doctor.

"I think you need to tie this one up, Mr. Krieger. He's dangerous."

The little German man laughed through perfect pearl-white teeth. The fine tanned lines on his face barely moved, but in this moment of false joviality, his true age was shining through the money and surgery.

"So kind of you to point this out, Russian comrade. Actually, all four of you are lethal. Though Herr Ritter is largely a danger to himself at present. In any case, don't be concerned about your travel companions; we will make sure you don't scratch each other on the way to my modest home."

A couple of the henchmen moved past Maier and Mikhail and tied the doctor's hands and feet with zip ties One of the men opened a first aid pack. He picked out a syringe and stuck it unceremoniously into the doctor's arm. When Suraporn turned and muttered something barely audible, the man shrunk back before pushing the plunger all the way down. The doctor growled and spat a big gob of phlegm at his captor. Then he was out. The two men who guarded Suraporn looked shaken.

"I agree with you, comrade, this man is…problematic. His cruelty is immense. And there is something else, he has these powers…very worrying. We'll have to put him down when we're done with him."

Krieger clapped his hands.

"But join me now on my modest vessel. Follow my men through the crowd to the water. Don't try to run, they will catch you and hurt you."

The old German sighed and added, "I wish you hadn't shot Wuttke. I shouldn't be standing here explaining all this. I worked hard, in my professional and in my private life, never ever to be around assholes. And today I find myself breaking my own rules. All for this fucking picture."

With that, he was off.

His men drove Maier and Mikhail along behind the little man. Wuttke's corpse had already been moved. The spot where Maier had killed him had been cleaned. Ritter and Suraporn had been wrapped in dark oversize beach towels and tied onto stretchers Krieger's men had brought along. Four of the men now donned white jackets embroidered with Red Cross insignia. They picked up their injured prisoners and set off behind their boss.

The party was over.

As they crossed the beach, bombarded from all sides by drunks and bass beats, Maier noticed that Hom had gone. She'd gotten what she had come for. She'd held up her part of the deal and once her husband had been avenged, she'd faded into the shadows.

Maier was happy she'd extracted herself from the affair. He had no way to do so. Killing Wuttke only dragged him closer to the Monsoon Ghost Image.

17

THE BAD GERMAN

The white hull of the speed boat slid out of the Haad Rin shallows in almost complete silence.

No one spoke.

The moon hung trapped behind thick swirls of cloud. The sound of the party faded away. The captain opened up the twin-turbo engines and they sped across the placid water towards the bright lights of neighboring Koh Samui.

Krieger sat up front while his crew kept a wary eye on their two conscious prisoners. Ritter lay bleeding through his beach towel. Suraporn was out cold on the floor of the open deck. A few minutes into their journey the vessel veered westwards towards what Maier assumed to be nearby Ang Thong Marine National Park. But they didn't steer for the two large islands, Koh Phaluai and Koh Phi, and headed north instead. As the clouds let go of the moon and drifted eastwards, a small chain of islands became visible, stretching further north.

They raced towards the last outcrop, an island a couple of kilometres long, covered in dense jungle rising high from the sea and ringed by limestone rock formations. Other than a few squid boats, their huge light bulbs shining like alien heads across the water, there were no other vessels moving out here. No coast guard was going to intercept them. No one knew they'd been kidnapped.

The boat slowed well off-shore. One of the crew members balanced on the boat's starboard side to shine a powerful searchlight into the water. The seabed erupted in a thousand colors. Coral formations became visible just below the surface, jutting up from the seafloor, a natural guard against intruders.

They proceeded at a snail's pace, guided by the crewman's shouts. Maier got up but one of the crew motioned him to sit back down. Then they were through the island's coral defense and picked up speed again, towards a wide bay which appeared to offer a 300-degree jungle panorama, now but a black wall of foliage intersected by occasional white shards of moonlight dropping through the trees to the forest floor.

Götterdämmerung. Maier thought the scene Wagnerian. Nature being ominously bombastic.

The captain reduced the throttle and they slid towards a small wooden jetty. The only other vessel visible in the water was a 70-foot yacht, shrouded in darkness with not a soul visible on board. The only other life in the water were several respectable-looking shark fins that cut through the deep blue in lazy circles on the edge of the jetty's single light.

As the boat cut its engines and moved underneath the canopy, the neon power of the full moon was almost completely extinguished. Silence and darkness descended on Krieger's vessel.

Maier could smell the jungle. He could sense more than see the huge trees that stood back from the bay. He'd seen a lot of forest around the tropics, and this didn't feel like a private adjunct to a national park. This was a different world altogether.

A flock of giant fruit bats crossed the bay and sailed low across the boat, their leathery wings making a swooshing sound as they passed. In the distance, they could hear an animal roar.

Maier looked at Mikhail across the boat.

"What was it?" Maier wondered.

"Whatever it was, it's about as native as we are. There's something weird about this place. Everything's too big. Jurassic Park maybe?" the Russian answered.

The light on the jetty threw long, gloomy shadows devoid of color, rendering the scene like a 1940s Noir movie. The passengers were meant to be impressed, intimidated even.

Krieger was the first man off the speed boat, jumping onto the jetty with the agility of a teenager, where he was welcomed by several young women who carried towels, an icebox, and a gun, a Python .357 by the looks of it, a rather showy killing machine.

The women were all white and wore almost transparent silk *ao dais*, the Vietnamese national costumes. Krieger didn't appear particularly enthused by their presence. They were part of the furniture.

One of the women opened the icebox, elegantly extracted a glass of deep red liquid, and then handed it to the old, ageless man. He drank it down in one gulp and took the gun from another young woman. This man dripped vanity in the way others drip sweat. Every time he moved, he needed to reconfirm his own brilliance.

"Gentlemen, I get few visitors here on Koh Krieger. You'll soon see why. Even more extraordinary is the fact that I'm standing here with a gun in my hand. I haven't held a weapon for decades. I've never shot anyone. But you took my adjutant Wuttke from me prematurely, so I must react. And this by the way—" he held the glass into the light— "is not the blood of a virgin or some very rare animal, or anything else cruel and barbaric. It's beetroot, a good detox cleanser. It's just for effect. I rarely get the chance to put on a show like this."

Krieger relished the moment. Maier feared a lengthy tirade at the end of a hard day more than the rest of his frightening future. The last thing the detective wanted now was the philosophy of a rich island-Castro with a flashy gun in his hand.

"I'm the law, the only law on Koh Krieger. Killing all of you at that ghastly event would have been possible, but such a mess. Bad enough our friend, though that's a very loose term, Dr. Suraporn had already skinned the ladyboys. On Koh Krieger, it's another story. No one knows you're here and no one will find you. No cavalry, no hope. Just me."

The two injured men had been transferred onto the jetty and now lie on camping cots. Suraporn looked relaxed and stared at the moon as if in a trance. Ritter remained out cold. He looked close to death. Two of the women were examining the photographer. One pushed a catheter into his right arm and connected him to a drip. Another girl monitored his blood pressure. They were efficient. Possibly life-saving.

Maier and Mikhail were the last guests to disembark. The young men who'd forced them onto the boat now stood in a tight semi-circle behind the prisoners.

Maier could see few lights beyond the jetty. He didn't like the brooding impenetrable silence of the jungle. Not here. The forest was watching them, with distrust.

The German tycoon cast a long shadow on the jetty. The entire scene was choreographed. He was flamboyant, this small white-haired man.

"As you have probably surmised by now, I want what some of you call the Monsoon Ghost Image. Mr. Ritter here first brought the image to my attention. I offered him money for the image and paid him a substantial amount. But he hasn't delivered and by all accounts he's no longer in possession of the image."

Ritter began to stir and opened his eyes. Looking up from his cot, he stared straight at Maier.

Maier stared back but saw nothing he liked. Just Ritter post-surgery, post-op, post-everything. It wasn't death Maier feared. It was the step into the unsound, into the black surf of the bad sea that threatened to envelop everyone all of the time. Not the mad minute but the black hour. A place one reached more or less consciously, voluntarily. A place of no return.

Krieger stepped up to the two men, demanding attention.

He lowered the gun past Maier and put it to the photographer's head.

"This man owes me a million dollars. Or he owes me an image. Either way, he owes me more than he can possibly pay right now. And don't get me wrong, gentlemen, this isn't about money." He laughed. "Well, in the larger scheme of things it is, of course. But it's not about the million I advanced Mr. Ritter for the picture. It's about the damn principle. Imagine word got around that old Krieger down there in southern Thailand could be cheated out of a million bucks."

He took a deep breath and turned to Mikhail. "I've studied your background. You're wasted at the Sundermann detective agency. I will triple your income if you join me. I need a replacement for Wuttke and you have all the right qualifications. You even look like him. All you have to do is prove your loyalty."

"Cannot," the Russian answered calmly.

"Oh sweetie, don't discount the deal before it's out of the bag," Krieger countered, a camp tone in his voice.

Mikhail didn't look pleased.

"I renew my offer. Think past your current associations. They're all done anyhow. I'm in charge of your destiny. But you can be in charge of yours again if you join me."

Krieger offered the Colt to the Russian.

"Shoot Mr. Ritter here, and then shoot Maier and we're in business."

Mikhail looked at the gun, then looked down at the injured photographer who continued to stare blankly at the moon.

Maier was so lucid he felt the sharks passing underneath the jetty. *Sharks everywhere.*

"Sure, Krieger." Mikhail chuckled carefully, took the gun, turned it on their captor, and pulled the trigger.

Click.

The German tycoon laughed, first a little nervously, but then he put his heart and soul into it.

"You know I made most of my money selling telecommunications to the former communists in Eastern Europe. I get government grants from the Germans to help you backward lot get connected so you all buy into my service. It works in all emerging markets."

Krieger enjoyed being an orator; he reveled in his performance. Maier thought his little audience, one man in a coma with his testicles missing, a barely human mad dog, and two dirty, sweaty and burnt-out private dicks from Hamburg, didn't really amount to much. The same thought seemed to enter Krieger's mind and he wound down his show. He threw a sick glance at Mikhail and laughed sourly.

"I know so well how some of you Russians are far too loyal."

Krieger sighed. One of the men behind Maier and the Russian grabbed the gun.

Perhaps the beetroot high was wearing off, Maier thought. The man's shoulders seemed to be sagging. But the tycoon wasn't done. He pulled himself together and beamed his best smile into the round.

"Today was better than yesterday and tomorrow will be better than today, gentlemen. I am tired. Too much drama, too close to the street for my taste. My staff will escort you to your lodgings. You're free to roam the island and free to try and escape. But a word of warning—

Koh Krieger is a game reserve. It was populated with African and Asian mammals by an eccentric general some twenty years back. Every millionaire dingbat round here has his own zoo. Now, this one's mine, and in line with local tradition, I have kept the beasties around. Whatever's out there has little fear of humans since I rarely go hunting. A very special game reserve, as you could easily end up being the game, gentlemen. Let's talk in a few days when Ritter is with us again. Then we will see who will live and who will die and how I get my picture."

He shot Mikhail a testy look and added, "No one's tried to take me out in a long time. You have significantly reduced your chances of survival. That goes for your friend Maier too. In fact, you're all doomed."

With that he turned and marched off the jetty, followed by his female assistants. The men from the boat picked up Ritter and Suraporn, before herding Maier and Mikhail through a metal gate into darkness. The jungle roared again.

18

THE PRISONERS

MAIER WOKE WITH A START. It was cool and the first light was spreading through the forest and into the bungalow they'd been put in the previous night. He raised his head to look outside, to remind himself that they were trapped on a tropical island teeming with wild animals.

The detective had his wildest thoughts confirmed. A monkey, an adult langur, sat on the banister of the veranda, looking in his direction. As it saw Maier, it bared its teeth and rocked back and forth in threatening silence. Maier shook his head and shouted, but the monkey didn't budge.

"What's happened?" Mikhail groaned.

"A monkey. On the veranda. It is showing me its dental work. It's not scared."

"You want me to kill it?"

Maier looked across the room and smiled. "I don't think so. I want to get out of here."

"Can't be more than ten miles to the national park headquarters, no more than a couple of kilometres to the next island south. A leisurely swim. Lots of sharks in the water, though. Krieger or the previous owner must have trapped them inside the reef. I don't think a raft or anything like that will do. We might have to talk our way out."

"We have nothing to bargain with."

"But we do, Maier, we do. We have the image. Sundermann has the image. Krieger wants the image. The Americans have Sundermann. It's almost too neat. There has to be a deal in there somewhere to get our heads out of the sling."

"There is no reason to escape then?" Maier asked.

The Russian coughed.

"Well, darling, sometimes I think you're madder than me. We're trapped on an island safari park with a psychopathic surgeon and a man so rich he can bury us in the swamp of his back garden and never worry about it again. I say those are solid reasons to leave if possible."

"Ritter will tell Krieger that we have the image."

"Perhaps. I can barely keep up with the fringes of this affair. No one strikes me as particularly ideological when it comes to the image. It's all about money."

"Not for the Americans."

"Yes, the Americans, out there, fighting a long and losing battle against ghosts of their own making. This War on Terror will go on and on until half the world lies in ashes…again. But it's the other half, the far away half, and the *devotschkas* in Florida or Ohio won't even notice it because they'll be too busy getting their minds raped by Reality TV."

Maier laughed. "Hm, you are angry. Ideologically angry."

Mikhail sunk back onto his cot and grumbled. "Yes, even thugs enjoy occasional wandering thoughts. Especially Russian thugs, Maier. We have a long tradition of violent thinkers."

The bungalow was part of a small collection of buildings in a wide valley that led upwards between two mountain ridges that straddled the island like humps on a camel. A strong, two-metre fence cordoned off the jungle on all sides. Low watchtowers lined the steel wall on the inside every hundred metres or so.

Coconut and banana trees dotted the compound. A dirt track, also fenced, continued up to the top of the valley. They could see the sea from their porch and a simple double gate, which opened to the unprotected trail they'd walked up from the jetty the night before. The two karst stone mountains were densely covered in jungle and brush. Maier couldn't see any trails or other traces of human presence further up the valley, but he did spot two panthers, their fur black and shiny, slip out of the forest and meander along the barrier, their heads close to the ground. Very much a game reserve. Now in the daytime, he had the same feeling as the night before. There was something too much about this place, something wrong. He couldn't see it, but he knew it was there. *What kind of a man lives in a fortress, protected by a small army and surrounded by wild animals?*

The kitchen in the bungalow was well equipped. Krieger's private death row resort offered fresh eggs, coffee, and bread. The two men ate in silence, concerned their conversation might be recorded.

By mid-morning, they'd packed some fruit, eggs, and water into a pillowcase and began to check out the valley. An infirmary housed the two other prisoners. Ritter had dropped off into a coma and floated on the edge of this world and the next one, watched over by a Chinese doctor and two local nurses in what looked like a well-equipped, air-conditioned emergency room.

Suraporn was better. He sat on a cot, his left hand and leg chained to the wall. Krieger wasn't taking any chances. Mikhail's bullet had left a deep flesh wound above his right ankle, but it had missed bone and arteries. Maier half-wished Mikhail had finished him off. Two guards, armed with AKs, sat facing the doctor, watching him from a safe distance, looking unhappy.

The rest of the buildings housed Krieger's staff, from his troop of bodyguards to a regiment of cleaners, mechanics, cooks, and farmers. The girls, Mikhail noted, stayed somewhere else.

As they tried to head further up the valley towards the road, they were stopped by a couple of armed guards. The two men said nothing, merely pointed Maier and the Russian back down the hill.

They passed the buildings a second time and headed for the gate. Once again, two men stopped them, to hand each of them a spear, a proper spear with a long wooden shaft and sharp steel point.

"You go too far, you're dead man," one of them explained, pointing at the jungle.

They sat on the jetty. The sea bottom inside the lagoon was no more than fifteen metres below and they could see straight down into a dense coral garden broken up by patches of fine, luminescent white sand. The sharks they'd spotted the night before now cruised restlessly below them. Most looked like bull sharks, fat, gray bodies and broad, flat snouts. Bull sharks were dangerous. En masse they were an effective deterrent against marine escape. There were so many, they looked hungry, but here, on the edge of Thailand's most prestigious national marine park, there were plenty of fish in the sea. Breakfast, lunch, and dinner for the bull sharks, with an occasional undesirable thrown in for dessert.

The speed boat they'd arrived on was manned by four sailors, all of them armed and alert. The yacht out in the bay looked deserted. Maier could just make out the name on its hull, *Störtebeker*, the name of a notorious 14th-century German pirate who'd been beheaded in front of his crew in Hamburg. The presiding judge had promised the condemned outlaw that all those of his sailors he'd manage to walk past after his beheading would be spared. The headless pirate allegedly stumbled past eleven of his men before the executioner tripped him up. The judge then had his entire crew executed anyway.

How very apt. Just the kind of thing Krieger might do himself.

The detective felt as restless as the bull sharks. It was too hot to bake in the sun all day.

"There is no easy way out of here," Maier said.

"The forces of nature are against us, and Krieger's men are merciless pros. There are too many, they're too well trained and we don't speak their language properly. Not a good start if we wanted to manipulate them. We can't fight them head-on either. The only way off this island is by our wits, Maier."

They walked back along the jetty, away from the men, and turned left along the fence. The guards inside didn't seem particularly concerned, so the two men, spears in hand, continued uphill, close to the wire mesh. To their left, thick brush, giant ferns, and wild clusters of bamboo loomed amongst giant tree trunks.

After fifteen minutes' walk, they stopped and turned. The village lay beneath them. With the fence and the watchtowers around it, it formed a tropical gulag. The jungle made a dent here, courtesy of a wide, smooth rock that jutted twenty metres high from the ground.

Maier glanced upwards and glimpsed another large monkey, high up on the rock, silhouetted against streams of light that pushed through the canopy to the forest floor. He blinked and the figure had gone. The figure. Not a monkey. A man. Or woman.

He turned to Mikhail who looked at him expectantly.

"We are being watched."

"From all sides, Maier. Perhaps we should try and climb that rock to get a better view of the valley. We might even get a better idea as to what we can do to get out of here."

They struggled through a few metres of brush, using their spears to push the dense foliage out of the way until they emerged at the foot of the rock. A metre-wide gap of moist grass surrounded the boulder. The stone, dull grey in the sun, was incredibly smooth. A couple of monitor lizards, looking well-fed and surely, scuttled away as the men passed.

At the back of the rock, deeper in the forest, they glimpsed their way up. A teak trunk, perhaps a half century old, had been hit by lightning, and now lay dying, split in half. The weaker side had collapsed onto the rock and provided a pretty usable bridge, almost from ground level halfway up the flat backside of the boulder.

"Leave the spears down here," Maier warned and began to climb onto the trunk.

Mikhail followed and a couple of minutes later, they'd scaled the boulder. Maier guessed it to be thirty metres across. Several narrow and deep crevices and natural walls dotted the rock's surface. They looked at each other and took their shoes off to get some traction on the smooth stone.

Maier couldn't see anyone but he could smell sweat, human sweat. He could smell fear.

"We're not alone."

The man had once been fat. His skin was sallow and hung in small folds from his skinny, hairy body. His long beard had seen better days. He wore a ripped pair of Muay Thai boxing shorts that had been colored by the jungle long enough to blend in with the scenery. He was balding, in his mid-40s, and not in good shape. He'd been shot, a graze on his arm had become infected, the wound black and festering. It would not heal by itself under the tropical sun.

The man was waiting for them in the center of the platform, out of sight of the valley, a machete blade attached to a thick tree branch his only weapon. He waved his primitive tool at the two men.

"*Salam alaikum*," he offered with a hoarse voice. He seemed surprised at his ability to speak.

"*Wa-alaikum salam*," Mikhail answered and continued in Russian, "Who are you? We're prisoners here."

Maier had also spotted the accent. The man looked and sounded eastern European.

Their new acquaintance sat on the warm stone and stared at the pillowcase filled with food that Maier carried across his shoulder. Then he threw a glance back at the Russian, filled with fear and disgust.

"This guy is starving," Maier said before handing the man a couple of boiled eggs, some bread, and a pineapple.

The man nodded nervously and took no more notice of the detectives. He swallowed the eggs and the bread whole before ripping the pineapple open with his hands, spilling its juice all over himself. It was a desperate sight.

Mikhail fired a couple of questions at the skid-row Tarzan.

Only when the man had devoured everything, did he begin to talk. Maier understood his story in broad strokes, but the Russian he'd learned in school was too rusty to catch the details.

"His name is Shamil. He's a Muslim from Chechnya," Mikhail explained. "Fought the Russians there. He's a bit confused. His story doesn't make too much sense yet. And I'm the enemy for him. He knows we're prisoners. He saw us arrive. But he's finding it hard to talk to me. He thinks I might be a trap, a set-up to lure him into the open and get him killed. I don't blame him."

Mikhail switched back to Russian and put on his most soothing voice. He talked for a while, almost conversational, occasionally gesticulating down to the valley and mentioning Krieger and Suraporn. When Mikhail recounted their meeting with Wuttke, pointing at Maier, the man threw a glance at Maier for confirmation the detective was real, and relaxed a little. He began to talk in a more succinct and even tone.

"He's from Grozny. He was in Milan to meet Arab donors to raise funds for his war when his comrades occupied a cinema in Moscow and the Russian cops pumped a toxin in there that killed almost everyone. The next day, he was picked up by American Secret Service, bag over the head, doped, put on a plane, and flown to Bangkok. Krieger told him that the Russians had shopped him to the Americans because they know that since nine-eleven, the US pick up any Muslim who smells of radical Islam, even if the guy is just a cousin of a guy who once attended a madrasa in Pakistan. Well anyway, Shamil is the real deal, he's a bona fide Muslim extremist. Essentially, he's a Chechen nationalist who uses religion to gain autonomy for his people. The Russians are cruel in Chechnya. For men like Shamil, extremism is the answer. In another time and place, it would be called resistance. But the planes flying into the towers changed all that. So, occasionally, the FSB get the CIA to get rid of their trash, Shamil here included. The Americans are so hot for terror right now that they don't care if Shamil has never even thought about the USA. One day he might, and current policy is coming down on the pre-emptive side of the wire."

The Chechen nodded, half there, half not, along to Mikhail's translation.

"From Milan, he was flown to an old airbase here in Thailand, where he was kept in an underground cell," Mikhail went on. "He says that the ground moved every time he moved and they kept him in complete darkness for days. Then they put on the light, also for days, and played music at ear-splitting levels. They took away his clothes and dropped the temperature, for days. He was then exposed to series of procedures by two Americans and a few Thais, including the good doctor down there in the village. One of the Americans was a civilian, some kind of psychologist. He was called Williams. The other man was called Dobbs, a CIA vet. They called him Mr. Innocence. He doesn't know the name of the Thais he saw there. They locked him into tiny boxes, hung him from hooks, kept his head under a hood for days on end, mock executed him, stuck tubes in his arse, and told him his mother and sisters had been raped. They realized quickly that he had no useful information on threats against America. They understood they'd been had and that the Russians wanted him buried. The Americans continued to torture him to see what their methods would do to a man. Then they brought Shamil here to have him killed."

"The Americans are kidnapping, torturing, and killing suspected Muslim terrorists around the world? With the Russians helping them along?" Maier asked.

"Strange bedfellows but in this case, they have a common enemy. We guessed as much when we saw Ritter's photo," Mikhail replied.

"Krieger is CIA?"

The Russian shook his head. He asked the Chechen. The words were now pouring out of the man.

"Not really. Krieger and the agency are in an unhealthy partnership. Shamil tells me that Krieger is a former Stasi guy. In the nineties he became a powerful man in the telecom business in countries where America didn't want to appear publicly but was active behind the scenes. Nasty regimes, some burdened with UN or even US sanctions, so any investment had to be hush-hush. Nations where he had connections from the old days. Venezuela, Cuba, Iran. Krieger was their frontman. The fact that he wasn't American made it all the more desirable for them."

"How does he know all this?" Maier asked.

"He had dinner with Krieger when he was brought here. Shamil was not a fighter, he was a money man. Krieger liked him so he wined and dined him and then told him to get lost in the jungle. He wouldn't betray his American friends and let him go."

The German tycoon took an even more nefarious shape in Maier's mind.

"He told him all this and let him go to be killed by a panther?"

The Russian shook his head and looked at the Chechen with a somber expression. "Not quite. This is where it gets different. Every time the Americans drop off a secret prisoner, Krieger organizes a hunt. Prisoners are chased across the island until they are trapped and shot. Shamil is the one they never found, never tracked down because he says, he lives right under their noses. He says he can get in and out of the camp without being seen. He's more scared of Suraporn than of Krieger. All he wants is to get off the island and back to his war, but he hasn't found a way."

The pieces of an outlandish jigsaw started to assemble in Maier's head, not necessarily in a desired or discernible order.

"Have other prisoners been dropped here and killed since he has arrived?" Maier asked.

Mikhail asked the Chechen. The man nodded.

"Two others. Both Arabs. One of them managed to kill one of his pursuers. And they weren't held here in Thailand. They came from other black sites. This island is a dumping ground for the disappeared in the War on Terror."

"Who are the pursuers?"

The Russian shook his head, brushing his ash blonde hair from his face. "Men who pay a million bucks to go hunting humans. Men who're tired of shooting rhinos and lions. Mostly Asians. Mostly Chinese. Though he saw a couple of white guys with big guns out there too. Krieger told him that he had European aristocracy and a rock star signing up for the ultimate game."

"This does bring us closer to the reason why Krieger will pay Ritter two million bucks to get that image of one of these guys getting tortured. But I still don't quite see it. Why would he need the photograph when he just kills them here for fun and saves the Americans the mess to clean up?"

Mikhail asked the Chechen.

"He says he's not sure. Perhaps as insurance. They never talked about the picture. He says this is the first time he's heard of it. But he said that Krieger seemed frustrated by his arrangement. That he wanted to get into the telecom markets in Dagestan, another Russian republic, together with some Russian tycoon the Americans didn't like."

"Why would Krieger tell Shamil about this?"

Mikhail shrugged. "He must have figured that Shamil was as good as dead. And Dagestan is right next to Chechnya. Four years ago, Chechen Islamists invaded Dagestan only to be beaten back by the Russians. Maybe Shamil was involved in this attack and Krieger tried to squeeze him about the situation there."

The Chechen couldn't possibly understand what Mikhail was saying but he picked up enough from the name dropping to smile savagely at his companions.

"Yes, he was," Mikhail explained. "And he thinks Krieger is a nut. A rich nut, but a nut. His house is full of weapons. Hidden in weird places. Trap doors everywhere. And a guillotine in the shape of an old rotary dial telephone in the hall. Krieger told him he'd only used it once. The head of the prisoner goes in the microphone bit. The blade's in the receiver. The headset kind of stands next to the body of the phone with the dial. It's made from shellac, the whole thing, except for the blade of course. Far-fucking-out, as the Americans used to say. More flamboyant than a tin pot dictator from the Russian *taiga*."

"This guy is reliable you think? Maier asked. "He could be a plant."

Mikhail shook his head. "That thought crossed my mind. But his injury is horrific. The infection might kill him if he doesn't get some medicine. And he really does believe in a caliphate and will go to great lengths to make it happen. In a calm and rational way. He's frightening but he's not a honey trap, no matter how much you stretch that term."

Maier looked the man over again. The Chechen was on his last legs, there was no doubt about it.

"Shamil also told me he shared the slain pursuer with a couple of tigers. Other than jungle fruit, some of which make him sick, he has eaten nothing for a month except for a Chinese. He's useless at hunting anything faster than a frog and has no way to make a fire."

The Russian continued, "I told him that we may well become the next hunt. He said there are places on the island where it's possible to hide, but there's no way to get away except by boat, plane, or helicopter. There's a helipad up at Krieger's house and another jetty with a second speed boat on the other side of the island, also manned and armed and in sight of Krieger's residence. And Krieger has a water plane somewhere. Not sure what we can do. Best way is still to talk our way out of here. Make a deal."

Maier agreed. "We'll have to wait until Ritter has either died or recovered and his Excellency takes some of his very precious time out to deal with his current batch of trouble makers."

"Shamil says we should kill the doctor. He thinks Suraporn uses hypnotic techniques or drugs to get people to react to him physically. He almost suffocated Shamil with his stare when he was prisoner of the CIA."

Maier laughed. "So the CIA is looking for us under every rock in this country and we're guests of their best friend."

"Which means it's only a question of time until he tells them that we're here."

Maier shook his head. "Depends. He wants the picture. We can get him the picture only if he keeps *stumm* with the Americans. We just have to get him to believe we can deliver."

The Chechen was starting to get restless and started ranting at Mikhail.

"This guy is fucked up. And a bit too excited speaking to us after three months on the run. He wants to know what we can do for him if he helps us."

"Tell him we can get him food, fix his arm, and if we find a way off this rock, we will take him with us."

Mikhail translated and the Chechen grabbed his shoulder, imploring the Russian.

Maier interjected, "I don't think Suraporn should be killed now. He is another independent unpredictable player, and we may be able to use him."

"You're playing with fire, Maier."

"I am not in this business to kill people, Mikhail and you changed jobs, remember? You used to be an assassin. Now you are a detective."

"Maybe I should get my notebook and magnifying glass out, Maier?" his partner shot back.

"I don't think that will be enough to contain Suraporn or anyone else involved with the image, but murder is not the answer," Maier replied calmly.

The Russian flicked a strand of grey hair from his sunburnt face and grinned. "I know we understand each other, Maier."

Maier went through his pillowcase and handed Shamil a couple of chocolate bars and a kitchen knife, the only items they carried that were of use to the man.

"Let's go back before they send out a search party. Tell him we'll return tomorrow with food and medicine. Same time, same place if no one follows us."

Maier got up and walked to the far side of the rock to take a look at the valley. As he scanned the perimeter fence, he was momentarily blinded by the sun reflected in a mirror. Not a mirror. Binoculars.

Company Krieger was keeping an eye on them. He called Mikhail to show himself and they stood admiring the view for a few minutes, gesticulating at the valley, with the Chechen shuffling back and forth behind them, out of sight and muttering to himself, perhaps praying.

19

RITTER'S RETURN

Maier and Mikhail established a routine. Every day they'd leave the compound and walk along its perimeter fence. They explored the opposite side of the valley, but the jungle was leaning on the metal barrier there and walking out of sight of their captors was impossible. Instead, they settled on trips to the rock where they met Shamil with antibiotics Mikhail had lifted from the infirmary.

Once the Chechen began to recover, he took them around one of the karst stone humps, along deserted beaches, clusters of mangroves teeming with young sharks, and patches of dense forest clustered around the foot of the rock formation. The island was crowded, its ecosystem running at full speed. They came upon herds of deer, large populations of monkeys, all sorts of lizards, and snakes. Every now and then they sensed something big moving in the forest nearby.

After they'd circumvented the mountain, Shamil showed them a cave entrance, well hidden by clumps of giant fern. With nothing more to help guide them than three disposable lighters, they descended several hundred metres into an interlocking system of underground chambers.

Shamil had come down here with a burning branch he'd saved after lightning had set a tree on fire. He had left small markers at the entrances to the passages between the chambers to remind himself how to find the way out. Maier didn't share his faith or dedication to his cause, to any cause, but he had respect for the man. For an office terrorist, he was pretty resourceful. He was a survivor.

There were no signs of human activity in the cave system. Each new cavern they entered loomed empty but for remains of deer and monkeys that predators must have dragged in. A few bats hung among clusters of stalactites.

They placed more markers and left.

Outside, a tiger passed them in the forest, huge, sleek, and fast, not interested in three men armed with spears. They spotted birds of paradise and giant hornbills in the trees, eagles, and vultures in the sky. In the small patches of grasslands around the humps, they saw a few zebras and hundreds more deer. The beaches served as nesting places for sea turtles. While Shamil collected a handful of eggs, they noticed a couple of saltwater crocodiles in the surf.

They never met another soul.

Days turned to weeks, and weeks turned to a month. They rarely talked to anyone. The men who worked in the camp were either disciplined or frightened and didn't make friends easily. Suraporn recovered and had his other arm chained to the wall. The nurses released him only to eat and to use the toilet, where he was accompanied by two men with their fingers on their triggers. The entire compound was spooked by the man.

Ritter remained in a coma.

Mikhail and Maier lost weight and got fitter as they shared their food and days with the Chechen. They were sun-burnt and started to look like men who had lived in the wilderness for a long time. Maier had stopped shaving and was racing his beard with the Chechen's. The guards still watched them, but no one ever followed them into the forest. They never saw Krieger or the girls.

Once he'd gotten used to the two detectives, Shamil talked about the Quran, about his wish for a caliphate in the Caucasus, about how only the Muslims could resist and fight the Russians. They discussed the War on Terror, the war in Afghanistan, the coming war in Iraq.

The longer Maier listened to the Chechen, the more he feared the future. This was going to get bigger and bigger. This war would give birth to thousands of men like Shamil in dozens of countries and then sweep them all away to hell. And there would be thousands of Gingers to chase Maier and Mikhail to the ends of the earth. He didn't want to spend the rest of his life marooned in a tropical paradise over-populated by sometimes articulate predator animals.

Maier thought of Sundermann and hoped he wasn't held in the same kind of place Shamil had described to them. They had to get their boss out. They had to make a deal.

They prepared for the eventual flight. With great patience, Maier befriended one of the nurses at the infirmary and quietly pilfered a small supply of antibiotics, bandages, dressings, and other items. Mikhail managed to steal a couple of torches from one of the guardhouses. They didn't dare take any weapons. They buried their supplies behind the large rock where they'd met Shamil.

They heard the helicopter come and go. Krieger was a busy man.

In the small hours of another monotonous day in late January, Ritter returned to the living with a scream that woke every single creature on the island.

The next day, Krieger appeared on the detectives' veranda, dressed as before in immaculate white, his millionaire rictus smile firmly fixed in place.

"Ah, gentlemen, good morning. *доброе утро.*"

"*Спасибо,*" Mikhail grunted from his cot. "*ебать себя.*"

Krieger sat down outside and laughed lightly.

"Your Russian isn't getting rusty, Mikhail. Can't imagine you get a lot of practice round here."

"Can't imagine you do either, Krieger."

The answer came back in a glacial tone. "Indeed, my Russian is rusty. And you call me Mr. Krieger. And meet me at the infirmary, both of you, now."

Ritter was back. He didn't look happy about it. When Maier and Mikhail entered the room, he threw a string of expletives at the detectives until he sunk back onto his bed, exhausted.

Krieger, back in his good-natured incarnation of the gregarious entertainer, accompanied by a couple of young women in clothes as showy as his own, welcomed them. One of the girls carried the tycoon's revolver, on a silver tablet, for maximum effect.

"Gentlemen, for the first time since your arrival in my home, you're all *corpus mentis*, as far as it goes. You're all adults and all responsible for yourselves and I'm asking you today to make educated decisions that will go some way towards increasing the chances of your continued presence amongst us. It's time to reach out and find agreement or part in failure. And none of you, I promise, will want to go down the road of failure."

Ritter looked surprisingly strong, defiant, and half-mad. The anger that had seethed through him when he'd been tied to the chair at the ladyboy bar a month earlier was clawing its way back into his abrasive personality.

Suraporn had grown a thin, wispy beard and looked more feral than ever. His vague, distant smile hadn't changed, the man remained unbowed by weeks of captivity, chained to a wall.

No one spoke. Only the electric whirr of the ceiling fan separated the men from the jungle outside.

"Why do you want the picture?" Suraporn offered into the silence, looking at his captor blandly. Krieger was the first man Maier had come across who didn't struggle under the doctor's stare. His answer though was curt as he turned towards the chained man. He didn't make eye contact.

"I ask the questions. Then I decide whether to throw you away or not."

The doctor smiled his vague smile.

Today, things would change. Despite his bonhomie, Krieger was short on patience.

"Let's do this just the way we did way back in school. Whoever's got the image or can get the image without too much hooh-hah, raise their hands."

All four men raised their hands, with Suraporn gently rattling his chains. Maier felt stupid.

"Ah, you guys, you should've started a photo agency between your good selves when you had the chance. You'd be rolling in it. But I can tell you, the Monsoon Ghost Image, as it's been called, is still not in the public domain. Only a couple handfuls of people know of its existence. The US's dirty secret remains just that. And in so many ways, it's best to keep it that way. Here's the deal. Whoever gets me the picture before it's published, stays alive."

Suraporn began to speak, "These two clowns from Germany have nothing. The agency has renditioned their boss and they're wanted men. As soon as they're off the island they will be arrested. Perhaps, one day, when they're no longer what they're now when they've been through the American machine, they'll be brought back here to enjoy your fun and games, Krieger. You might as well kill them now. I'll do it for you. Free of charge."

The doctor's voice was soft now, barely audible above the noise of the fan.

"I need to take Ritter back to the Americans, a gesture of good faith, let's say. I know who has copies of the image stashed away. I can get the files if I give Ritter up and ingratiate myself again. I have… certain techniques… to achieve that."

The morning heat in the low-ceilinged building stood still. Maier could barely breathe. If Krieger was a flamboyant performer, Suraporn was a deviant one, divulging his methods while applying them to his captor.

One look at Krieger and Maier knew they were in trouble. Whatever Suraporn was doing now was affecting the old German. He wasn't immune after all. The tycoon's facial muscles slackened. He stared at the doctor in unpleasant surprise. His steely determination began to fade. He swayed and mellowed, surely against his very nature, and stared off into the half distance. One of the young women behind the tycoon swooned and collapsed against the wall.

The doctor continued.

"Let me go and I will retrieve Ritter's million and get you the image. I will take Ritter's payment as reward for my services. You can trust me. You can't trust them. The Russian already pulled the trigger on you."

Krieger laughed uneasily. "You don't really expect me to let you kill them in my home?"

"Send them into the jungle. Nature will run its course."

The doctor had won. Krieger stood in the center of the room, lost in thought. His staff, clearly confused by his altered state, were shifting away from the doctor uneasily.

Maier could see that some of the men were trying to point their weapons at Suraporn, but none quite managed. It was all over and it was all weird. Krieger had temporarily been hypnotized into another dimension. Suraporn was in control.

Without another word, Krieger led Maier and Mikhail outside. They stood in front of the infirmary in the high morning sun for several silent moments. The tycoon tried to make the most of it, putting as much severity into his words as he could muster. He was trying to look frightening. But the role of the monster had been taken.

"You have twenty-four hours. Tomorrow morning, I will send a hunting party into the forest. You and that Chechen will be gone in a couple of days, barely remembered as anything but a headache. Take whatever you want from the bungalow and leave."

Mikhail grinned at the German. "You're making a mistake, Krieger. The doctor is lying. You let those guys go and kill us and you'll never get anything. And we'll not go down easily."

The tycoon laughed. "That's what I'm banking on. I'm charging each hunter a cool half million. And as you know Suraporn is into his money. He asked me if he could participate. Bear that in mind when you dig your own grave tomorrow. Because that's the only sensible thing you can do."

With that he marched off towards his villa, Mikhail's laughter following him up the hill. Seconds later Suraporn emerged into the sun behind them, free of his chains, surrounded by Krieger's men. Maier could feel that Mikhail would have taken him out right here, but the guards formed a tight cordon around the doctor as he walked away towards the fence. This man was making the world a worse place than it was. Maier was annoyed, mostly with himself. He clearly lacked the killer instinct when it was needed.

Maier and Mikhail trotted back to their bungalow, packed what they could— mosquito nets, a few kitchen utensils, the rest of their food rations, and then made their way down to the gate. Ritter was waiting for them in a wheelchair, smiling, dreaming perhaps.

"Well, Maier, this is the last good-bye," Ritter said. "Tomorrow Suraporn will skin you alive. He told me that was his plan."

Maier laughed uneasily. There was just so much jolliness he could take before he had to get funny himself.

"He saved your life because he thinks you have the picture, Martin. When he hands you over to the CIA, he'll find out that you don't. Your life will be less than worthless. Enjoy the time and give Emilie a thought or two."

Ritter looked nervous but he caught himself quickly for a man who'd lost his marbles.

"They'll send me back to the real world, guys. Don't you have a message for anyone, last note for a loved one?"

"You're the only one we love, Ritter," Mikhail said, interrupting the photographer. "And when we get off this island, we'll come and we'll find you and return all your affection in kind."

Ritter flinched and spat on the ground, "I was going to give you a gun, so you can defend yourselves. I don't think I will now. You're a brute, Mikhail."

The Russian laughed. "Thanks, Ritter. You are a buffoon. And remember, you started this entire chain of events when you agreed to become the devil's photographer. And then you fucked up when you stole evidence of the devil's work and were too stupid to hang on to it. And it's cost you your nuts. And you sit here lecturing me, you impotent, sad cripple."

, "Hey, let's stop calling each other names here," Maier interjected. "We have to get into survival mode. All of us. Even you, Ritter."

With that, he stepped around the photographer's wheelchair and wrested a cotton bag off its backrest.

"Presume this is where you keep your arsenal, Martin. See you when we see you."

20

THE HUNT

They carried a few days' worth of food, several knives, a couple of machetes and the gun Maier had wrested off Ritter, a Ruger SR22, a pea shooter with half a box of bullets, hardly a match for the AKs that would be coming after them.

Maier couldn't quite fathom where Ritter had gotten the gun, having been in a coma for so long. The detective assumed that the weapon had been meant for himself all along, a sporting initiative by Krieger, something that suggested the tycoon was keen to manipulate the scales in his twisted gladiator game. Perhaps he saw it as German fair play.

Shamil explained that the hunters were rich amateurs, barely able to discharge their weapons, though each one would be armed to the teeth and accompanied by one of Krieger's men who kept in the background. The tycoon's enforcers had been told not to steal the shine off the clients, but they stepped in if things got out of hand for the guests or if real competence was needed.

Mikhail looked grim, in the mood for a bit of real competence, as they made their way to the boulder as quickly as possible.

Shamil was waiting for them, his primitive weapon in hand, his eyes fearful, searching the foliage beyond the two friends. He'd dug up the supplies that the three men had buried.

"It's time," Mikhail told the Chechen, as they set off laden with food and weapons.

They fought their way to the base of the hump closest to the camp. As they emerged from the trees at the foot of the karst stone formation, the forest fell silent.

Shamil looked around wild-eyed. "There must be a tiger nearby or something."

Mikhail didn't bother to translate for Maier and pointed at the mountain in front of them. Shamil knew the way. The men got off the forest floor and worked hard, using small trees that grew from the incline as leverage to ascend. They were barely ten metres up when they saw a rhino, a fully-grown beast, with two adolescent cubs, breaking cover from the brush, moving back and forth on the spot the three men had just left.

The adult animal was huge and agitated. It could smell them, but it couldn't see them.

Maier was glad rhinos couldn't fly. Not even here.

There was no real trail. But Shamil had been to the top before and had marked the route he'd taken the previous time. He was an assiduous man. Maier thought perhaps that's what had kept him alive.

Halfway up the hump, they stopped on a narrow ledge and looked back to the valley. Even without binoculars, they could see that all the watchtowers were occupied today and that all eyes were on their efforts to get away. Whether they'd been spotted in the rock wall was anyone's guess.

Mikhail laughed.

"Our friend tells us that we'll get a good night's sleep. There's water up there, a small source in the rock, and the top is easy to defend by three men. And there's a natural chimney that leads down into the cave system."

"So, what do we do? Fight machine gun-wielding, Asian playboys with rocks, like Vikings?"

Mikhail nodded grimly. "We kill them one by one until Krieger comes around and talks to us. I can't think of another way."

"Only one of us is trained for that kind of thing."

The Russian pushed his grey-blonde hair out of his face and started climbing again.

"Can, Maier. Will. Leave it to me. They have no chance. We just have to watch out for the good doctor."

They reached the top an hour later. They could see the entire island and, across the second hump a mile away, a string of other islands that stretched south, the marine national park. To the east, Koh Samui rose from the Gulf, its clusters of tourist resorts along the beaches clearly visible. Down by the second jetty, next to the tycoon's alternate speed boat, a water plane bounced in the shallow surf.

"I can fly that thing," Mikhail mentioned drily.

The Chechen couldn't have understood him, but he followed the Russian's gaze and got excited. A giraffe passed in the grassland below.

The men strung up a piece of tarpaulin to protect their supplies and began to fortify the mountain top.

Mikhail had cut several bamboo trunks from the brush on top of the hump and was busy sawing them into what looked like machine parts.

The Russian looked up from his work and pointed to a green fruit from a small nearby tree.

"Only God knows how guava come to grow up here. But collect all the ones you can find that are hard."

They gathered a sizeable pile of fruit. Mikhail pulled a sack of nails he had pilfered from his bag. He began to push the nails into the green pieces of fruit, a couple of dozen a piece.

"Watch me fire an opening salvo at our pursuers."

He grabbed one of the armed fruits and dropped it into a sling made from vine that sat in the centre of the small but robust bamboo contraption he'd built. He pulled the sling back to breaking point and secured it with a short thick stick against the frame of his machine. He then picked up his weapon and carried it to the edge of the plateau.

As the sun set, they took turns keeping an eye on the valley below. A warm breeze played around the cliff edge. Krieger's helicopter had been making two trips to the mainland, presumably picking up the hunters. Down in the compound, the tycoon's staff was busy amassing supplies for the clients. They had set up long tables and were lighting wax torches that had been rammed into the sand. The tables were covered in weapons, tracking devices and ammunition boxes.

The watchtowers were lit up. In the last flickering of the day, they saw Krieger with two other men arrive in what looked like an electric cart, a kind of refurbished gold buggy that had been made to look like an all-terrain vehicle.

"What do you think, Maier, three-hundred metres as the crow flies?"

The Chechen answered.

"Shamil thinks it's more like four-hundred metres to the buggy. Let's see how accurate my little machine is."

He moved his contraption slightly to the left and flicked its wooden leaver. The leaver snapped. The bamboo cannon jumped. The guava was gone. A second later, the screen of the buggy exploded, showering Krieger and his guests with glass, fruit, and nails. The driver slid from his seat onto the ground.

"One down, three hundred to go," Mikhail laughed grimly. "The hunt is on."

The Chechen looked at Mikhail with respect.

Maier whistled. "Where did you learn this?"

"Burma."

"You worked in Burma for whom? FSB?"

Mikhail answered, "Classified, Maier. Will tell you another time."

Staff and clients had bolted as soon as the fruit missile had hit the vehicle. A few shots rang out, but no one could tell where the projectile had come from. They didn't know the three men were on the hump. Not yet anyway. The small victory was important for Maier. It was the first time they'd fought back. The crush of attrition he'd felt since leaving Hamburg had left little space to do anything but react. This time, they were on the offensive, if only for a moment. It was a beautiful moment.

Mikhail re-armed his weapon and slid another prepared guava into its slot.

"It'll take them a while to work out that we are like Hanuman, the monkey god, throwing fruit at them. And it's too dark for them to see where we're shooting from."

The Russian fired a dozen more pieces of fruit into the compound, trying to hit Krieger where it hurt. Two of his projectiles smashed through the windows of the shack where the generator was housed, but the force of the guava was not enough to damage the machines inside.

Darkness came quickly in the tropics. They'd been watching fruit flying through a bruised purple sky until the world had been swallowed by the night. All but the watchtowers with their searchlights in the valley below.

Mikhail hoisted his machine off the ground and carried it across the plateau. The other two men followed. When he reached the opposite edge, he laughed. "They didn't think of turning the lights off down there. Which one do we take out? The boat or the plane?"

"You can really fly that thing?"

"You know I can, Maier."

"Trash the boat."

Mikhail adjusted his contraption, placed a fruit crammed with nails inside, pulled the leaver and let it fly. They couldn't see the projectile until it hit the boat, or rather one of its two outboard motors, which snapped off instantly and dropped into the sea. The crew jumped off the deck onto the jetty, pointing their rifles into the night. He reloaded and smashed the second engine.

"Always was the best shot in the army," Mikhail bragged.

"Which army?" Maier asked.

The Russian shot him an exasperated look.

"Maier, darling, really, don't ask me such personal questions. We've only just met."

The Chechen stared in horror at the giant's obscene body language.

The helicopter woke Maier. He barely had time to roll from under the blue tarpaulin into the brush that covered part of the hump's plateau. The machine came in below the plateau and appeared only as it crossed its crest.

Everything happened in a second or two. One of Krieger's men hung in the open door, an automatic rifle pointing at their camp. Shots slammed into the ground and their supplies.

"He's not going to hit a thing with his automatic at that speed," Mikhail shouted over the roar of the rotors. "This isn't Hollywood."

As the aircraft rushed past over their heads, Mikhail emptied the SR22 on the shooter. He missed, but one of the bullets hit the tail rotor.

The helicopter's engines screamed. And screamed. The three fugitives ran to the far edge of the plateau to see the metal bird spin and tumble from the sky into the jungle below, taking a swathe of trees with it before smashing into the forest floor. The world shook. The jungle buckled.

Mikhail looked sheepish. "Hey, me, I'm not Bond. I'm just your Russian friend. Hey, this is Mikhail, your jilted lover. I can assure you I haven't done anything like this in a long time. That was sheer luck. That did have a touch of Hollywood. One in a million."

Maier shook his head. He had his own private one-man army with him on the mountain. *What could go wrong?*

"Bond was not a huge, fat, gay man with greasy blonde hair and a red face that serves as testament to having drunk industrial quantities of vodka. Hats off to you, Mikhail," Maier joked.

Maier's partner walked back to their shot-up camp only to return seconds later, triumphantly.

"I have one bottle here, of Gilbey's. That's what the guards drink. So that's what we have. One bottle."

The Chechen didn't look impressed.

Mikhail snorted. "The world will never stop fighting and drinking."

Maier looked at his friend uncomfortably. What was happening to them? They were detectives, not mercenaries. This case was war. He hated it. He could no longer imagine normality. He took the bottle and felt like an impostor.

"Do you think the fireworks will discourage Krieger?"

Mikhail nodded. "Yes. He'd be totally out of touch if it didn't. We just punched a hole through his fleet. Killed at least two of his men. Cost him a couple million dollars. Tomorrow he'll send the clowns for us, no doubt. He'll send Suraporn. He scares me more than a helicopter. I should have shot him at the Full Moon Party, when I had the chance."

21

THE CHASE

They came the next morning.

Maier sat on the edge of the plateau from sunrise, watching the camp. Suraporn snuck out of the camp at first light, alone, armed only with a backpack, and headed straight towards the boulder. The detective soon lost sight of him in the vegetation. Four, two-man teams, each one a client armed with an exotic array of weapons along with one of Krieger's men, soon followed.

Krieger had moved the plane further out to sea, right to the reef's drop off. At very low tide, one might consider walking there with the right shoes. It looked like it might be too shallow for the sharks. Maier dropped the thought.

The speedboat at the second jetty had sunk overnight.

The doctor would be here soon.

A drunken Mikhail and a sober Shamil had talked late into the night, but his partner had translated little, and Maier had drifted off into his own thoughts. Whatever plan there was today was all news to him. He felt disjointed, out of his element, mentally breathless.

"We go down."

Maier looked up at the huge bulk of the Russian by his side.

"We have to kill all these people?"

Even after a month in captivity on an island populated by beasts, the detective couldn't quite get his head around the realities of his day.

A few miles away, tranced-out teenagers danced themselves into hedonistic corners, drank, smoked, laughed, fucked, cried, and spent money like sand, without a worry in the world. A couple of islands north of this never-ending party, a savage struggle for survival, for a single photograph, for money, for a war within a war that unspooled like a snapped film reel, spilling scenes packed with casualties across the tropical postcard paradise, unfolded unseen.

But their little heart of darkness was no more than a detail of the larger forces at work out there. Beyond Thailand there was likely to be a web of black sites in amenable and weak nations that played host to gulags similar to the place where Shamil and the prisoner in the Monsoon Ghost Image had been incarcerated in.

Maier knew a thing or two about torture. He'd been in the hands of mercilessly transfixed Khmer Rouge children with sadistic streaks and a routine with steel needles in Cambodia, a dark moment he'd barely survived. He sensed the same extremist cruelty in Suraporn as he'd seen in those brainwashed teenagers. Nothing scared Maier more than ending up in the hands of the Americans in some hole that was never mentioned on CNN, with the good doctor as his guard. But as he struggled with his thoughts, he only felt the web tightening, the ripples spreading.

Mikhail was more pragmatic.

"We're out of bullets. I go down and I kill one of the teams, we get their weapons. We talk to Suraporn. Then we talk to Krieger. Without sending another signal, he won't talk to us. The helicopter alone didn't do it. And he knows we were lucky. He knows how good Suraporn is."

"We talk to Suraporn?" Maier pondered.

"Yes, Shamil has an idea. I have a feeling Suraporn is worth more alive and dangerous than dead. As much as that pains my Russian soul."

They found the first two bodies as soon as they reached the forest floor. Krieger's man had his throat cut from behind. The man's head was almost severed, a scalpel had probably caused the butchery. The client, a middle-aged, formerly sporty Asian with a hard face and soft hands, had been shot in the head. The doctor had dismembered the man and placed his liver on a near-by rock. Animist stuff. Maier stood retching.

"I don't think we'll need to do any killing today," Mikhail quietly intoned, picking up the guard's Beretta 9M, and throwing a couple of ostentatious revolvers and an Uzi to Maier and Shamil. The giant looked a little worried,

"Why?" Maier asked the forest as much as his companions.

"He's taking them all out because the survivors might talk about us. That's why the Americans hired him in the first place. This man frightens, tortures, and kills for …fun, but he's still in the program. He gets the job done."

Shamil led the way, away from the hump, away from the valley, towards the sea. There were no trails, and the going was slow. A half hour later, they reached a clearing with a water hole at the edge of the jungle. Beyond, tall grasses stretched to the ocean.

Maier could smell him before they could see him.

There were no animals around, unless one considered Dr. Suraporn to be part of the impossible menagerie. Every now and then, the breeze washed the sound of the sea into the deceptively peaceful scene, rendering the Hieronymus Bosch tableau vivant that unfolded in front of them almost bucolic. Otherwise, it was perfectly quiet. The jungle had retreated in disgust, its moveable parts as far away as possible from the scene unfurling around the water hole.

Suraporn was down by the water's edge, his back turned to the three men. He was naked, but for his rubber gloves. Another team of hunters sat disemboweled on the edge of the clearing a few metres away. The doctor had made a fire near the bodies which was now merely smoldering. The carcass of a bird of paradise lay in the bushes a few feet away. A wallet of medical instruments lay open near his victims, bloodied blades strewn across its oilskin fabric. Suraporn's clothes lay neatly folded, far enough away not to get splattered with the bits of humanity he'd cut off his victims.

Maier looked closer at the two dead men. Both their faces were awash with blood.

Mikhail pushed him gently. "Don't look at that for too long. It's not right."

It took Maier another few seconds to realize that neither man had a face. Suraporn had pulled the skin off their skulls, all the way down to their jaws. Krieger's man had had his nose removed. The doctor had skillfully replaced it with the head of a bird. The client was worse. His eye sockets had become the home of tiny snakes, which writhed behind a black web of thread Suraporn had sewn onto the man's face.

Maier was particularly disturbed by the fact that the web was shaped into a beautiful geometric pattern, a mandala.

When the detective looked up, the doctor stared straight at him.

"You're the first admirers of my work today. And I must say, your longevity is remarkable."

Suraporn had a small knife in his gloved right hand. He was twisting the blade around so it would catch the sun. He seemed relaxed, even as he stood bleeding from a wound in his shoulder that he had roughly stitched himself. The man was bionic, almost super human. Maier never saw him blink.

They were about thirty feet from the water's edge

"Are they all dead?" Maier asked.

Suraporn surveyed the clearing.

"All except for you. Is this a trap? Are you bringing the cavalry?" he answered calmly.

Mikhail nodded carefully and looked directly at the doctor. Maier sensed that Mikhail was trying to stare him down, cut off his mind control stuff, if that's what it was. The detective also noticed that none of them were pointing their guns at the doctor. As the thought was about to send him into a panic, Suraporn began to speak again.

"The jungle doesn't worry me. I don't register with animals much. It's humans who fear me."

"You just sowed a bird's head onto a man's face." Maier said.

The doctor grinned. "Yes, and in record time too. Still, despite my skills, the man expired before my work was completed. The bird didn't mind. Nature is forgiving to creatures like me." He laughed softly.

"What are you?" Maier asked.

"I'm the secret weapon in your War on Terror. I go where ordinary men don't go. To his credit, Ritter tried to cross the threshold too, but he's not strong enough. You *farang* are too close to your egos. Your sense of destiny…it's overdeveloped. We're all part of something bigger. Even me."

It was obvious that the doctor relished the situation, relished the tussle with Mikhail, and relished their powerlessness. Maier's head was screaming, but he looked on, unable to move, in sick fascination.

The doctor was touching his penis with his left hand while keeping an eye on his captives. Maier had no doubt that that's what they were — prisoners.

"I could stand here playing with myself until Krieger turns up and has you killed. Probably in a theatrical kind of way. He might bring his toy guillotine down the mountain. You never know with him. As I said, egos."

Absentmindedly, he slid his blade along his penis. It was enough to bring Mikhail out of his trance.

"Small cock, not worth cutting," he grunted with difficulty. He raised his Beretta and continued. "You don't have enough respect for us, my dear. Especially not for impatient Russians. I'm trained to resist your bag of tricks."

Beads of sweat ran down his red face and his grey mane clung to his head like a dish mop. He started firing. The bullets zipped past the doctor into the water.

Suraporn didn't move.

The three men stood in complete silence again. Mikhail had missed.

"You know, I love Agatha Christie," Suraporn said. "When I studied medicine in Ohio, I had little money, so I went to thrift shops to buy secondhand books. Christie's were always the cheapest. I learned about *farang* from her books. Ten Little Niggers was my favorite."

Suraporn stood in reverie, alone in his world, inhaling darkness, exhaling something worse. "Four little Indian Boys going out to sea. A red herring swallowed one and then there were three."

His blade zipped past Maier's head. Shamil collapsed behind the detectives, the small piece of metal in his throat. He looked surprised. As his gaze drifted away to the canopy, he whispered, "*Allahu Akbar.*"

Then he was gone.

"*Allahu Akbar.*" Mikhail repeated as he quickly pulled the scalpel from the wound and tied it off to stop the bleeding.

Maier stared at the injured man. "Will he make it?"

His partner looked uncertain. "He's a hard bastard. But we can't take him with us. All we can do is leave him our medical supplies. If the wound closes, he might have a chance."

The doctor had moved away from the water hole towards his bag.

"What do we do?" Maier whispered.

"We can't kill the doctor. He's too strong. He knows every mind trick in the book. Hypnosis with memory techniques, PWA, and ideomotor suggestion, a whole arsenal of weapons. On top of his... other skills. I've never met anyone who can use this stuff so well."

Mikhail shot Maier a tired look.

"We should leave if we can."

"Can we?" Maier asked himself as much as his partner, looking down at the wounded Chechen.

"Three little Indian Boys walking in the zoo," the doctor said. "A big bear hugged one and then there were two."

The doctor had reached his clothes and murder utensils. At great leisure, he picked up his boxers while he continued to sing under his breath.

"Two little Indian Boys sitting in the sun. One got frizzled up and then there was one."

Mikhail turned, with difficulty, and grabbed Maier by the shoulder.

"When we get back to the city," he said, "we will have to check what happens in the last verse."

The only path open to them was around the water hole into the grasslands and towards the sea. Maier didn't have the strength to run past the doctor back into the forest, the safer option.

"Agatha Christie was widely read in the Soviet days," Mikhail said. "Personally, I was never a great fan. Some good plotting, but a terrible writer."

The detective nodded at his partner's sudden bout of literary criticism, wondering who'd gone mad.

"You know how we always do it, Maier. Never run. Face it head-on."

The doctor started whistling. The two detectives couldn't move.

Suraporn picked up his spotless, green T-shirt when a snake jumped. Bright green and no more than a metre in length, it shot like a ripcord at the doctor's leg and sank its fangs into his calf. He screamed and sunk to the ground.

Mikhail moved in and kicked the doctor in the head and walked on. Maier hesitated. He couldn't believe their luck, but he remained frozen to the spot. Suraporn, snake attached to his leg, looked up at the detective and grinned.

"Three little Indian Boys walking in the zoo. A big bear hugged one and then there were two."

The snake was not letting go and chewed its way deeper into the doctor's flesh. Suraporn bent down, grabbed it in the middle, pulled it up to his mouth and bit down hard. His focus on the animal and a shout from Mikhail snapped Maier back into real time.

The detective started walking. He stumbled. He ran. He slowed as he reached the doctor. The man had almost chewed his way through the snake, brilliant green and dark red writhing savagely, but it hadn't let go. The reptile's flat skull was locked tight into Suraporn's calf. Perhaps only a cold-blooded animal could take him out. The jungle was resourceful.

Maier stepped right over the man.

Suraporn loosened his bite on the animal and raised his head. "Help me," he said.

His voice was so calm, so devoid of fear or panic that Maier stopped. He couldn't breathe, he couldn't turn. He stared at the doctor who had his teeth in the snake again.

Then the utter absurdity of his situation hit him. He had nothing to lose here other than his life. And the man who wanted to kill him was chewing on a snake.

Maier got moving.

As soon as they were out of sight of the doctor, they ran. Ran through the bush, the same way they'd come, furiously beating away at the vegetation that snapped into their path with every step. Ran, ran, ran, until they reached the foot of the hump.

The first Krieger team they'd come upon still lay where they'd last seen them, covered in flies.

Mikhail lifted a couple more guns and a backpack off the client and they began to climb to the top once again. They summited half an hour later and found a third team, also dead and partially dismembered, in their shot-up camp.

Neither man had spoken since they'd run. Now they looked at each other in disbelief. How had the doctor gotten up here, killed these men after they'd found the other team at the bottom of the mountain and the man himself half an hour later with another slain team by the waterhole?

"Fucking scary," Mikhail muttered.

Maier stepped away from the corpses. "If that snake doesn't kill him, he will be here soon."

The Russian shook his head. "It won't kill him. That was a pit viper, poisonous, painful, but not deadly. A normal man wouldn't be able to do anything for a while after having been bitten by one of these. But Suraporn…"

"So, eventually he will crawl up here with his voodoo hypnosis powers and make us both jump off the mountain."

"I think he's more into killing us off following the Agatha Christie poem. The bear should've been next. Instead, it was the snake. Nature trumping art? I don't know. We just got lucky. But you're right, Maier, we can't stay up here. He may just come up in the middle of the night and make tartar of our innards. It's not worth hanging around for."

They scavenged what they could off the two dead men and descended into the chimney that led to the cave system, laden with backpacks full of water, food, and ammunition. They used their torches, but the descent was slow.

There were plenty of foot and handholds in the narrow vertical passage, but the stone was soft and crumbled easily and Mikhail, the heavier of the two and the first to descend, had to test each step while trying to hang on to vines that grew from the rock.

Maier took comfort in the fact that Shamil had been down this way. The detective was euphoric as he followed his friend. His elation sprang from the fact that his mind was not controlled by someone else and that they'd gotten away from a proper monster. Again. The doctor's touch had left him violated and dirty inside. He tried to feel no more than a child would, totally absorbed in the movement, the action, for fear of reliving Suraporn's aura.

The daylight receded as they continued to move downwards, accompanied by the rich ecosystem that lived inside the chimney. Snakes and lizards, small rodents and a cornucopia of insect life passed them from all directions along the rock wall.

Then they hit bottom. Both men dropped to the cave floor and sat staring at the small circles of light their torches threw around the cavern.

"I'm exhausted," Mikhail managed.

Maier nodded into the darkness.

"Let's move a bit closer to the cave exit and get some rest."

They could smell the sea.

22

NOMADS

MAIER WAS AWOKEN BY VOICES. He flicked his torch on and held his palm in front of the light. He turned to Mikhail. His partner was already sitting up.

"Krieger's men?"

"I don't think so," Mikhail answered. "They're not speaking Thai and they sound happy. And I can hear female voices."

They pulled their bags onto their backs. Shamil's marker lay by a tunnel entrance that led towards the voices.

"What do we do?" Maier asked.

Mikhail took his time answering. "I'm trying to figure out what language they're speaking. Can't think who they might be. It isn't Burmese or Khmer either."

Maier remembered his conversation with Hom at her house.

"Sea gypsies. They could be sea gypsies. Hom mentioned that they travel through the park on their boats. You know, stateless people who live on the water."

Mikhail slapped his partner's back. "Ah, Maier, the Asia expert. You're right of course. I recognize the language now, it's a type of Malay. Didn't know they came into the Gulf. They're fine people and they don't like the authorities. Maybe they can help us."

Maier entered the tunnel first. After a few metres, the ceiling closed in on them and the walls shifted together.

"Hope I don't get stuck in here," his partner grumbled behind him, "I might come to regret all that fine food and excellent drink I've consumed in my life."

Fifty metres in, the tunnel widened and opened onto a large cavern, its ceiling heavy with stalactites.

A man and a woman were about to couple in the center of the cave. A pair of torn shorts and a sarong lay next to them. A crude torch dropped wax onto the cave floor at another entrance a few metres to their right. The scene looked moderately romantic.

Maier stumbled into the cave, gun in hand. The man grabbed a spear and jumped up, barely slowed by his arousal. The woman stood up and stared at them in surprise, unafraid. She turned towards the detective and slowly stuck her middle finger in her mouth, raising her eyebrows. Her smile was cold and suggestive. Then she picked up her sarong and walked from the cavern the way an actress left the stage.

Maier lowered his gun.

"Oh," was all Mikhail said, as he emerged behind the detective.

The man stared at them with menace, but Maier also detected confusion and bemusement in his face. No fear. He was in his forties, stocky, and dark-skinned. His thick hair, as far as Maier could make out in the flickering light, was a dark shade of red.

Mikhail started laughing and laid his weapon on the cave floor. The man looked surprised, his face alert, but his body started to relax, and he lowered his spear.

"*Chao Ley*?" the Russian asked, "*Chao Ley*?"

"*Moken*," the man answered as he looked at them with mild curiosity. He pointed at both of them and asked, "*Farang*?"

They nodded.

"I can't speak their language, but he understood the Thai word for sea gypsies, and he told me the name of his group."

The man grabbed his pants and pulled them on, picked up the torch and motioned them to follow him. They entered another tunnel, emerged in another cave and headed into yet another tunnel. Maier noticed after a couple of caverns that Shamil's markers had disappeared. If their new friend left them now, they'd be lost in the bowels of the mountain.

But their guide didn't abandon them. A few minutes later, they emerged into the open, a different way out than the one Shamil had found, beneath a rocky headland close to the beach. Several long-roofed boats bounced up and down in the shallow surf. A few women sat on the edge of the forest. A group of kids played hide and seek in the water, yelling and chasing each other.

"They live on these boats?"

Maier nodded. "Part of the year, yes. During the monsoon season, they live on the beach. But these days, most of them live in slums along the west coast. There is nowhere left for them to go. All the islands are colonized by tourists. And they are stateless, so they get abused by the cops, local authorities, and the military. But they are never seen in the Gulf. And they rarely travel on these boats; they call them *kabang*. They use ordinary long tails. This encounter is very odd. Like something out of a fairy tale."

The man had gone to the water and pulled a teenager out of the group of kids.

He led the boy to the two detectives. The boy looked sixteen going on thirty, the skin on his arms and legs hard and scarred. He avoided eye contact with the strangers.

"English," he said.

"What's your name?" Maier tried.

The boy smiled uncertainly and shot the detective a quick, surreptitious glance.

"Toe."

"And the man's name?" Maier asked.

"His name Dunung."

Maier introduced himself and his partner.

"Where do you live?"

Toe pointed to the boats.

"Do you know the owner of this island?"

Toe shook his head and looked back to his friends by the water.

"Owner," he answered to no one in particular.

"I don't think he understood that question," Mikhail interjected.

The women who'd sat at the edge of the jungle, joined the four men, pulling their thinning sarongs over their breasts, and stared at the foreigners with undisguised fascination.

Dunung started a discussion with the teenager. The women threw in the odd comment. Most of it sounded frivolous. The woman they'd met in the cave cracked a joke and everyone burst out laughing.

Toe turned back to the two *farang*.

"Where you go?"

"Bangkok," Maier answered. The entire group exploded in laughter again.

The boy shook his head.

"Oh no, very far."

"Where you go?" Maier countered.

"Another island," the boy answered.

Another woman muscled her way into the group and was now examining Maier and Mikhail at close quarters. She pulled at Mikhail's graying hair. Her comments elicited yet more laughter.

"We have to go to the mainland," Maier said. "Chumphon, Surat Thani."

The boy shrugged, translated, and they were almost rolling in the sand again.

"Oh no, very far," the boy repeated, clearly amused at the detective's ignorance.

"You can take us?"

Toe translated. More laughter. Then he turned, and rejoined his friends by the water. The women strolled to the edge of the forest, collected a pile of roots they had dug up and carried them to the boats, while continuing their banter. The two *farang* were the main attraction today.

Dunung pointed them to one of the vessels. They waded through the surf and climbed aboard.

The Moken boats served as mobile homes. About ten metres long and three metres wide, the *kabang* wore rattan roofs and carried a small outboard diesel engine with an unfeasibly long pole, a screw mounted on its end. The engine block was mounted on a rotating steel plinth so that the screw could be lifted clear of the water, giving the vessel the best possible turning circle. Inside the boat, underneath the flimsy roof, an open fireplace served as the kitchen. Pots and pans were stashed in the boat's side walls. Clothes and food supplies hung in plastic bags from the roof.

Maier and Mikhail sat to the back, out of sight.

Dunung manned the engine. One of the women and a couple of

kids pushed the boat out into the surf. They were off, moving across the reef. Dunung slowed the boat as they reached the circle of coral that enclosed the island. The kids were out on the bow, shouting directions, helping to navigate the *kabang* through the shallows. The Moken boats were slow conveyances, not suitable to outrun anything faster than a jellyfish, but they could be steered with great precision.

As soon as they cleared the reef, Maier spotted Krieger's surviving speedboat rounding the headland they'd just left behind. They'd been spotted. Krieger's boat quickly approached the five Moken vessels. Maier and Mikhail crawled further under the roof and lay down flat on the *kabang*'s floor.

Dunung, standing behind them besides the engine, grinned and nodded reassuringly. Seconds later, the speedboat pulled up next to them.

Maier recognized a couple of the men on the vessel. The tycoon wasn't on board. The men shouted at the Moken in Thai. Dunung shouted back, not making eye contact with anyone, gently recalcitrant in the face of overwhelming firepower. Krieger's men stood to the back of the speedboat, flashing their guns, berating the nomads about entering private property.

They steered the boat right into the centre of the small flotilla, the crew craning its collective neck to see inside the *kabang*. They drifted by and immediately turned, approaching Dunung's boat once more. As they passed again, the woman on board, perhaps Dunung's wife, stood up in the stern and absentmindedly readjusted her sarong. It was enough to distract the men. They shouted another warning before heading back towards the island.

Dunung stared straight out to sea, steering with one hand while rolling a cigarette with the other. The sea gypsies were used to this kind of harassment.

Across the border in Burma, they were beaten, robbed, raped, and forced into bonded labor. In Thailand, they were trafficked to work as slaves on fishing boats or became alcoholics in depressed coastal communities. Being free, truly free, living the life of a nomad, without government and consequently without rights, had its price.

The Moken had never dropped out. They'd simply chosen not to join the larger picture. He appreciated their rescue, and the woman's gesture all the more. The Moken had courage. And their own obscure reasons for their incredible empathy.

The *kabang* put some distance between themselves and Krieger's island. The two humps receded and soon their prison was just one more outcrop in a chain of jungle covered sand banks stretching south. Koh Tao, the turtle island, another tourist trap, lay straight ahead. Maier looked back at Dunung who pointed at the much larger island, then at the two passengers. This was as far as the Moken were prepared to go.

They pulled into Mae Haad, the island's only town, which rested in a wide bay backed up against jungle covered hillsides in the early evening. Dunung piloted his *kabang* close to the seafront, but he didn't head for the island's jetty. The other four Moken boats stayed offshore. To the left of the small town, a narrow beach meandered south. The Moken steered his boat to the point that was furthest from bungalows, restaurants, and shops. Fifty metres from the sand, he cut the engine and moved the screw around to stop the boat from getting any closer to the island.

He stood silently in the stern, his eyes searching towards the lights and techno music that drifted across the water. He wore no impression that Maier could interpret. After a while the Moken turned towards the setting sun.

No one spoke.

Mikhail wrapped the guns in a couple of plastic bags. He took his clothes off and stuffed them into his bag.

"We swim."

Maier followed suit. A few seconds later, they quietly dropped over the side of the *kabang*. The detective felt guilty. These people had saved their lives. He wanted to return the favor but other than his farewells, he had nothing they wanted.

They swam quickly. The beach was deserted. Maier turned to wave at Dunung but the *kabang* was nowhere to be seen. The entire flotilla had disappeared.

Mikhail seemed to read his thoughts.

"These sea gypsies haven't been seen in these waters for a half century. They don't really exist in this stretch of ocean. But they weren't lost. They live here. I don't understand how that can be possible. And now they're gone, simply gone as if we've dreamed them, the meeting, the rescue, Krieger's patrol, everything. It never happened unless you and I continue to convince each other that we were with them, and that it did happen."

Maier felt himself sliding off into metaphysical contemplation.

"You're saying we were rescued by ghosts?"

His partner grinned. "I like you, Maier, you understand me."

Koh Tao was Thailand's scuba diving mecca, right at the top of the bucket list for young Westerners who were wealthy, mobile and in search of soft adventure. Hilly and covered in jungle and coconut trees, it took its name from the turtles that lived in the coral reefs around the island. Sightings of whale sharks and bull sharks were frequent, and the tourist dollars flowed in with considerably more force and effect than the barely noticeable tide.

This small spec of land was a cash machine.

A half century earlier, Koh Tao had served as a prison for political opponents of the military. Maier had heard that the island was a lawless place, run by a handful of families who did what they could to bring the money in. Suspicious accidental deaths and assassinations of over-ambitious entrepreneurs were not uncommon. Koh Tao was the Wild East.

The Russian counted the money in his wallet.

"Tonight, we drink, Maier. We need it. We need to look at life askance, to get our bearings. That world in which we find ourselves is without love or pity."

Maier remembered the Thai baht he had borrowed from the liftman and pulled a roll of soggy bills from his pocket.

Mikhail laughed. "I hope you swiped that cash somewhere, Maier. I don't assume you used your plastic or washed dishes during our separation."

His voice sounded a touch morose. Maier felt it too. They'd come to some kind of end of the road. They couldn't check into a hotel on Maier's stolen ID alone. They couldn't get off this island without being seen. They were alive and that was about it. The elation the detective had felt during their escape evaporated in the face of their pathetic reality.

His partner took the money and disappeared towards Mae Haad.

Maier sat in the sand, guarding their bags and arsenal, hoping nosey cops looking to bust tourists for drugs wouldn't pass.

He needn't have worried, the beach remained deserted.

Night fell quickly and Maier's thoughts drifted away with the memories of the past weeks. He'd survived a month on a desert island inhabited by wild animals and a feral rich man. He'd seen more death than he cared for. He'd witnessed the work of a proper madman. He felt wired and tired at the same time.

Sudden passing voices made him turn too quick. He was nervous all the time. *Is this what trauma feels like?*

He tried to process the essential truths he'd picked up like contagious diseases in the past weeks— the sickness of men like Suraporn, the greed of Krieger and the generosity and calm love of nature and all things the Moken and Hom had shown them. But despite all the far-out stuff they'd seen and lived, nothing had really changed. They were still on the run with literally nowhere to go. Their boss was still the involuntary guest of the world's greatest superpower. The superpower was still going through a dark phase. There was nothing Maier could do about it. He couldn't change the ugliness around him. He couldn't tell all these killers, whether state sponsored or entrepreneurial, to go home and grow tomatoes. He'd long lost the optimism of the young hoping for a better world. But he wasn't a down and out cynic either. He would try and spring his boss and save part of his world. They needed a new plan.

23

MAYBELLE

THE TWO MEN sat in stoic silence, a metre or so apart. They were both splattered, an empty bottle of rum and a half empty bottle of vodka lying in the sand between them, surrounded by a dozen cans of soda, a depleted bag of ice and oily sheets of wrapping paper that had harbored generous portions of fried chicken and sticky rice.

Maier noticed the girl the first time she walked past them, down by the waterline. A few minutes later she was back, looking lost, though Maier thought her uncertain steps a little studied. She stared. Maier stared back briefly, then looked away. She appeared surrounded by an orange haze. It made her look ethereal and saintly. The alcohol he'd consumed most likely helped to detect her aura and he cursed himself for getting drunk, but then his head swam and he focused back on the lone beach comber. Just another bored, young backpacker.

She was in her late twenties, heavily tattooed and willowy. Pretty and a little worn around the edges, and she looked like she lived the life that corresponded to her offbeat vibe. She wore her hair in an unruly bob. The left side of her head was shaved and sported a tattoo, a geometric diagram, a mandala perhaps.

Maier didn't care much for tattoos. Everyone and their dog were inked these days. His own tattoo, a *sak yant*, a sacred mark received under duress from a blind anti-communist monk in Laos, was on his back. He never saw it and he'd had almost forgotten about it. He remembered it when he saw other people's tattoos.

Twenty minutes later, she was back. This time she appeared to have made up her mind and headed towards the two men.

"Here comes trouble," Mikhail grunted.

"Well, how y'all tonight?" the woman asked.

She wore a torn T-shirt that read 'Real Chicks Dig Scars' and a Rajasthani style skirt, bright colors, covered in tiny mirrors that reflected the lights along the beach in moving sparkles. She stood between the men and the sea, and she knew it disturbed Maier and Mikhail. She had an accent as American as it could get, deep South, cousin of Elvis land.

"We're the beach drunks," Mikhail laughed at her, but Maier could hear a subtle reticence in his friend's voice.

"I like drunks. If they're not men of violence. I've met too many of those. Fuckers."

Neither man said anything. She smiled benevolently, as if she felt sorry for them or perhaps for herself, and continued. "You guys don't look violent. You look like some weird art installation, sitting in there, your own detritus. Cool. Are you violent?"

"Never to women," Mikhail joked.

Maier noticed her flinch. But she didn't leave. She simply stood over the two men, seemed to reach into herself and extract an extra ounce of courage and nonchalance. That's what the haze was telling the detective. Despite finding her vaguely attractive, he longed for a bed all for himself and a hundred hours without harassment.

She sat down, a couple of metres away from them and gathered her wits about her. "The wanted posters say that yours truly is armed and dangerous."

Maier sucked in his breath. "Wanted posters?"

"Yes," the woman responded. "They're all over the island, in every bar, hotel and restaurant. Saw them on Koh Phangan as well. You guys are hot."

Mikhail filled his plastic cup with vodka and offered it to the young woman. "What's your name?"

"Hey, I'm Maybelle." She took the cup and bumped fists with the giant and got up again, to tower over the two men.

"You must be Mikhail Kozakov. It's you they call armed and dangerous. Fred Maier here seems to be a little less gun-crazy."

Maier worried as he shook the cocky woman's pale hand. She took a step back and remained between the detectives and the sea. She was making a statement. She knew who they were. She wanted more than a shot of liqueur. She was dangerous.

The sounds of a Bob Marley song drifted over from the tourist ghetto of Sai Ri, and Maybelle retreated a little, dancing across the sand, her drink raised, her cruel youth in flawless motion.

"It's a testament to the hard work of Thailand's police force that they're looking everywhere and you're sitting on a beach getting tanked."

Mikhail grunted. "Maybe it's a testament to our resourcefulness."

She danced back towards the Russian, small brass bells around her ankles ringing in bad news.

"I was hoping you'd say that."

Maier raised an eyebrow when she stole a glance in his direction.

"I can help you if you help me," Maybelle said. "We could benefit each other..." She drifted off across the sand again, swinging her hips, tinkling, throwing back coy glances.

Her beauty was brutal. It had a price, but it was not for sale. And the tattoos on her head told disturbing stories. Maybelle had let go of a thing or two. Maier had enough of edgy people.

She came to rest in the sand a few metres away, pulled a crumpled cigarette, papers, and a little weed from her bra and started rolling a joint.

"I don't want to sit too close to you guys, in case an assault team turns up and the bullets start flying." She laughed hoarsely to herself.

"What do you want, Maybelle?" Maier asked quietly.

She shot the detective a testy glance.

"Come on Frederick Maier, don't spoil a beautiful evening. Play the game. Don't be so crude. So German. I'm a lady. An American lady. My momma called me Maybelle. I'm like a flower. I need lots and lots of fresh air and water and minerals and sunshine to sustain myself. I want everything in the world you can possibly imagine..."

She broke into a sweet, seductive grin and continued.

"So, I'm minding my own business tonight, taking a walk on the beach, thinking about this and that and I see you guys sitting there and

I go back to Mae Haad and look at the artwork they have on the wall and get real sure that it's your mugs they put up every few metres. And the weirdest thing is, it don't say why the authorities are after you. That tells me you're not the usual criminal shysters innocent and gullible girls like yours truly meet in Thailand. You're not rapists or murderers. You guys go deep. I get my courage together and I'm thinking to myself, Maybelle, you're in a damn tight spot and you need help. And these here two individuals sitting in the sand, are Thailand's most wanted. And I look at the date on the poster and it's a month old and I got me thinking some more. These guys must be pretty resourceful or pretty cocky if they sit in full view on the beach, drinking their heads silly, without a place to go and half the world looking for them after a month of being hunted up and down the land. A full month on the run."

She finished rolling her joint, stashed her accessories, and then lit up. Reefer in hand, sparks flying, she jumped up and started dancing to more or less imagined music.

The two detectives said nothing. Maybelle was beautiful trouble, a boatload of trouble when all they needed was a boat.

"Anyway, hanging out with you two on this tropical isle sure beats spending evenings in parking lots back home." She laughed with bitter innocence. "I could write a book about all the things that happened to me in parking lots. Maybe one day. Maybe Maybelle. That's what they called me at the liquor store. Fuckers."

Maybelle drifted to the water's edge.

"She's got us by the balls. Shit," Mikhail muttered.

"Maybe she wants us to kill some guy she has a turf war with."

The Russian shrugged, his entire frame making a huge subtle movement.

"What she wants only partly worries me. What she is capable of…is very uncertain. I have a bad feeling. But let's see. Maybe we can frighten her away."

Maier shook his head. "Piss this woman off and she will report us."

Mikhail nodded as Maybelle flicked her spent joint into the surf and walked back up the sand towards them.

"The most amazing thing about the wanted posters is the fact that there's a price on your heads. Anyone who sends information to the police hotline that leads to your arrest will get ten-thousand dollars.

Lucky for you, I'm not short of cash, though I can always do with more."

"You know they never pay the reward money to anyone but themselves," Mikhail tried.

She threw back her hair to draw attention to the mandala on the side of her head, a much-practiced movement that screamed, 'Look at me, this is how beautiful I am'.

"No matter. I'm no snitch. So…I'd like you gents to consider a business proposition I have in mind. I think it'll have something for everyone. A win-win as we say. I help you and you help me."

"We're all ears, Maybelle," Maier answered and then added, "How can we resist a proposition from someone as selfless and beautiful as yourself?"

She pulled a face. "Ah, Freddy, you're *so* cold."

"Call him Maier," Mikhail interjected softly. "Like everyone else. If not, get your nasty personality off this beach and leave us alone."

Maybelle stopped her dancing and focused on the Russian. "Ah, mean, are we? Scary we want to look? Try again, buster. My daddy taught me how to shoot when I was seven. I sucked my first cock when I was twelve and smoked my first crystal the same day. I ain't scared of two punks on the run, no matter who you are. I've broken into stuff. I've been around. One little phone call from me to the authorities and you guys are toast and I get a little richer."

She smiled sweetly and Maier wouldn't have been surprised if she'd shown them her tail and cloven hoof. The detective smiled right back.

Mikhail looked up and down the beach, opened the bag which rested by his side, pulled out his automatic, got up and pointed it at the woman.

"You're quite right. We're just two punks on the run. We have nothing to lose. And I was lying when I said I never hurt women. I'm open to change and opportunities. I adapt as the situation demands and I'll shoot you right here and bury you in a shallow grave quicker than you can roll a joint. And maybe we'd be caught disposing of you, but chances are, in Thailand no one ever sees a thing and we'll just get back to drinking in half an hour. Tell us what the fuck you want or get lost."

She lost her cockiness, looking down the barrel of the giant's weapon. But she caught herself a few beats later and danced around Mikhail like a woman instinctively certain of her charm. Mikhail pulled the trigger and sent a bullet into the sand by her feet. Maybelle stopped dancing.

"Are you crazy, you fuckin' Russki? You guys are going to hell in a handbasket if you're not a bit more careful. Calm down guys. Maybelle didn't mean it. She was just kidding," she laughed.

Neither Maier nor Mikhail moved. The two detectives looked at each other. They shared the same sentiment. They had to shut her down.

"Maybe we should just shoot her. Save us some trouble, I think," Mikhail suggested.

Maier wasn't sure whether the Russian was kidding or not. Right now, perhaps that wasn't important. There didn't seem to be a middle path with Maybelle. Or with Mikhail.

His partner's words had some effect. She quieted down and tried to read the two men's faces before she responded with a more diplomatic back volley.

"You two guys are a godsend. Yes, I think the good Lord sent you. And I'm just kidding. I'd never rat on you. It's against my principles."

Mikhail raised his brows, an ironic smile on his face. She didn't like it.

"Fuck you, Russki, and take me serious. We're not in the Taiga now, where men are men and sheep are nervous. This is civilization." She gestured and started to laugh, hiding her fear well.

But it was there, and Maier was almost glad for his partner's utter lack of sentimentality and compassion on days that took them down to the wire.

"What do you want, Maybelle?" he asked her again.

She did a pretty good imitation of the Russian's shrug that made Maier laugh. The haze was receding, and he just couldn't believe that their months of bad luck simply continued. Out of one shit shower into the next.

"You want to get off this island, right? Y'all will be caught here, and your weapons aren't going to save you. The cops will kill you and collect the reward. If they posted a ten-K price on your head, someone's paying them a lot more than that. It's got to be a hassle for them to do a nationwide poster campaign. You guys are special. And special desperate. Why else would you shoot in the sand next to an unarmed, vulnerable, and peace-loving woman?"

She shrunk away from Mikhail as if a few metres difference made his automatic any less deadly. Perhaps she thought she could dodge his bullets.

"What do you want from us?" Maier prodded her again.

"I have a boat. I need to go up to Petchaburi and land on a beach near town, discreetly. In fact, I have done the trip several times. It's easy as pissing your pants, gents. Just need a couple of able-bodied, clear-thinking, and opportunity-seeking gentlemen like yourselves to remove several obstacles en route."

Maier knew where Petchaburi was. It was a small, unremarkable coastal town within a stone's throw of the capital. Not a bad destination. From there they'd be able to hitch a ride into Bangkok. It was a step in the right direction. Staying on Koh Tao was dangerous, and daylight was likely to bring more trouble. Maybelle wouldn't be the only person who'd recognize them once the sun came up.

"If you have done the trip several times, why do you need us?" Maier asked.

Maybelle pointed theatrically at the boats that anchored off Mae Haad. "The kids need to be entertained. They must be offered the right amenities and services if they're to come back again and again. Personally, I think weed is enough, but most of those boats out there, any that don't look like dive-boats, are bringing in drugs. They use Koh Tao as a transit point. A pretty lawless place, all things considered. By my conservative estimate, there are at least fifty keys of weed on these ships at any given time. More around Christmas and New Year. The other boats are stacked with cocaine, ecstasy, yaba, ketamine, you name it, they got it. It's a floating infirmary, a water borne drugs supermarket for the jaded palates of the party dogs on the islands and probably for the rest of the country. You with me?"

The detectives sat waiting for more. Maybelle took her time to get to the point.

"There are two armed men on board my boat, holding my captain hostage."

"A dive boat?" Maier asked.

The American grinned. "No, Maier, not a dive boat."

"The men on board? Navy, Army, police, private?" Maier asked.

Maybelle laughed her pearl-white best. "I'm not sure. It doesn't matter much. One's as dangerous and corrupt as the next. They're private, but they may well be connected to a state agency."

"And?" Maier asked.

She looked at the two detectives hopefully.

"We need to get on board tonight, disarm these guys and head off into the dawn, cargo intact."

"And the cargo is?" Mikhail asked.

She pushed the sand around with her feet and looked a little sheepish. "Thirty-nine kilos of fine hashish from Nepal. They're mine, all mine. I got them this far. My babies. I paid off all the right people. I have folks waiting in Petchaburi offering a way better price than the island. I just need to get the fuck away from here. It's your ticket out, gents. I really don't see another way for you."

"These men on the boat, how professional are they?" Mikhail asked.

Maybelle shrugged. "They're armed. My captain is shitting it, said they're serious about taking the boat. They know that I'm *farang* and that I don't have the kind of connections that might hurt them. Well," she said with a mischievous grin. "They think I don't."

"And what makes you think we can help you? That we would risk our lives for a cargo of dope?" Maier asked.

She laughed gaily. "I'm not deluded, y'all. I might be from the South but I ain't simple. It's not Deliverance, no banjo player, no ass rape, just little ole' Maybelle and her sack of goodies. And Maybelle would never assume you gents would help me for altruistic, selfless reasons. Nor would I allow myself to think that you might be tempted into this endeavor by my stunning beauty, though it is considerable and has twisted many a guy's noodle. No, I think you guys are in a tight spot. And that got me thinking."

"And where did your thinking take you, Maybelle?" Mikhail asked, all darkness and threat.

The American took a couple of steps away. "Now don't you try and scare me, you damn Russki. I don't scare easy, ya know."

Maier motioned Mikhail to lower his Beretta and said, "In the unlikely case that we are a couple Rambos who can swim to a fishing boat and take out two armed men Ninja-style in the middle of the night, what would there be to stop us, once on the way, from killing you and throwing you overboard and putting a gun to the captain's head while suggesting a change of course? You are too optimistic."

She hissed at the detective.

Maier continued, "Wouldn't it be much better to do this on a friendly basis, without greed and coercion?"

Maybelle rolled her dark eyes. "You guys stupid or what? You're basically telling me to call the cops right now."

Mikhail smiled as he stashed his weapon. "You do that, you're dead."

"I'll do it in ten minutes, buster, when I'm back in my room."

"I'll be sitting next to you," the Russian countered. "You know who we are. We can't let you go anywhere by yourself. Consider yourself kidnapped, Maybelle."

She looked at the giant with disbelief. But Maier could see the wheels turning in her head as a bright smile spread across her broad face.

Maybelle was a match for the two detectives.

"We got a deal then, gents? Wanna come to my bungalow, take a shower, oil your guns and do whatever it is you do before we spring into action just before dawn?"

Mikhail nodded sagely.

"Can you get us three wetsuits, masks, fins and snorkels, a couple of dive knives and a good dive torch with fresh batteries? We'll take care of the rest," Mikhail said.

"Now you're talking, boys." The girl laughed, full of life and cunning.

24

THE BOAT

THE NIGHT WAS WINDING DOWN. Maier and Mikhail had had a shower, several cups of coffee, and a bite to eat in Maybelle's bungalow. Mikhail had spread their arsenal, an AK47 and two handguns, a Beretta and a Glock, along with a single full magazine for the AK and a handful of bullets, and a hunting knife, all taken from the clients and their helpers on Koh Krieger, on the girl's bed.

"What will we do with her? She will fuck this up or shop us," Maier wondered aloud.

Mikhail looked grim as he nodded. "Yes, the entire maneuver is dangerous. We're paying a high price to get off this island. But the opportunity did drop into our laps. Never stop drinking! Never look a gift horse in the mouth. Especially not when she's as twisted and pretty as Maybelle."

"Twisted?"

"If we get away in the boat, we'll be killed as soon as we hit the mainland. There's a lot riding on that boat. I suspect there's more than a few keys of weed on board. Maybelle is in at the deep end but she's so cocky, she doesn't see it. That's our opportunity."

The girl entered the small beach hut with a wide grin.

"*Muchachos*, I got all you wanted and more." She dropped a sack of dive gear on the floor. "Easy to break into these dive shops. Got in and out in a few minutes. And I got this!"

She proudly held up a harpoon. Mikhail raised his eyebrows, looking impressed.

"Good, we need to have our thinking heads on, all of us."

All three got into their wetsuits.

Mikhail laid out the plan. "We go to the beach. You two stay there for fifteen minutes. Then you start swimming to the boat as fast as you can. By the time you get there, we'll be ready to go."

Maybelle looked happy.

"Just be sure you untie the boat captain as soon as you eliminate the other two guys, so he can get the ship running." She threw a humorous look at the Mikhail. "I don't expect you to kill these guys. Just putting them out of action and tipping them overboard is enough. Otherwise, we'll all end up wanted as serial killers. Not that you guys got much to lose. But Maybelle does, so keep that in mind."

They left the bungalow and made their way to the beach. A group of young backpackers had made a small fire and were playing songs from another time on beat-up guitars. The smell of marijuana wafted across the sand. They were flying without a license and barely noticed the three snorkelers.

The two friends and the girl hid in the shadows of a rocky headland. Maybelle pointed the boat out to Mikhail. The small fishing vessel lay in complete darkness a hundred metres offshore. There was no movement on board.

The sky was cloudy, the moon hidden. The fire was the only bright light around. Mikhail looked satisfied. He sat watching the beach for a while. Then he rose into the night and gathered a small pile of garbage which he threw into the shallow water— torn ropes, polystyrene boards, water bottles.

As the Russian tied the flotsam together as best as he could, Maybelle stepped from behind the rock into the light, half out of the wetsuit, showing off her white bikini top.

"Hey, they're going to see us," Mikhail hissed at her angrily. "If they know I'm coming, we have no chance."

The American giggled. "Can't make things that easy for a Russki. You're gonna earn your life tonight, buster. Nothing is free, ya know. You gotta earn your ticket."

Mikhail turned and grabbed Maybelle by her hair and jerked her down into the water.

"You said you didn't kill women," she hissed, her eyes wide.

"You're trying to screw us. And I lied," he said and plunged his knife into her throat. He pulled her into the shallows and held her under as she struggled feebly. The small waves her splashes made soon faded.

Maier looked away.

A few seconds later, Mikhail called him.

"Let's go."

"You didn't have to kill her," Maier said.

"Yes, I did. Them or us. She was going to shop us."

Maier stared at his friend in disbelief.

"Maier, now's not the time. We have to get off the island. That's all."

The detective's eyes followed the woman's corpse as it began to drift away. Mikhail grabbed hold of her, pulled rocks from the seabed and stuffed them into her wetsuit as he zipped her up. A few seconds later and she was gone.

"I'll wait here," Maier said.

The Russian shook his head. "We're not sure what's going on. They might already know we're coming. Maybelle prancing around might have been a signal. I might need you there. There could be a trap on the beach. I take out the two guys on the boat, you might get caught here at the same time. Better we stay together."

Mikhail strapped the Beretta to his chest and handed the Glock to Maier. He motioned the detective into the water, and they pulled on their fins and masks. Maier zipped up the few belongings Krieger had returned to him after their arrival on his island— a phone, his fake ID, the last of their money— in a plastic bag inside his suit.

The Russian whispered by his side, "There's only one way to approach that boat— with stealth. Which means you don't do anything. You lie in the water looking down, but you don't move. Stay absolutely still. Not one move. You breathe slowly and silently. I will pull you to the boat. When we get there, you grab hold of the stern, with both hands. Don't try and climb in, just kind of hang there. Don't let go under any circumstances. I'll do the rest."

He handed Maier the Glock.

"If they start shooting at us before we get to the boat, you pull your gun above the surface, open the breach, and expel the water inside. Then you shoot at whatever is moving."

"If I am looking down into nothingness, how will I know when we reach the boat?"

Mikhail chuckled. "You'll know. I'll let go of you, you put your head up, the stern will be right ahead."

Mikhail pushed the small float of garbage out to sea, strapped the AK to his shoulder and slid into the dark water. Maier followed suit. He submerged looking down onto the sand. He lay completely motionless and tried to breathe in near silence. He relaxed. He felt a push and shove and moved into deeper water, garbage floating around him. It got darker and he strained to see the seafloor. Then Mikhail was past him, grabbed his arm and pulled him along. He hoped they looked like floating trash to anyone watching from the boats moored offshore.

As Maier focused on the encroaching darkness, mindful not to panic, Maybelle stared up from the depths below, her eyes wide and dead and white. Her corpse hung suspended in the calm water weaving with the soft currents, a black shape receding into its night. Maier shook a little. Maybelle had touched him with her crude pragmatism. It was all or nothing, semi-elegantly packaged as a southern belle, and in the end, it was nothing. He'd never forget his partner cutting her throat with the same absence of mind he'd cut a piece of meat at the dinner table. In a way, he'd plunged in the blade himself. He too had murdered the woman.

The corpse drifted off into the shadows, continuing to leak a little blood. Then she was gone, on her last and silent journey. Maier felt himself being pulled further out to sea, slowly, very slowly, further than he'd ever been and further than he cared to know about. He realized, staring into the gloom, that he was entirely dependent on his friend and colleague, a former hit man.

They barely seemed to move. Maier floated and his mind drifted. The water was now entirely impenetrable, a sea of black ink, a sea of death and dreams. The girl's eyes came back at him out of the wet darkness, again and again. If there were sharks, attracted by the leaking corpse, they'd never see them coming. He was drifting on and on, losing orientation, losing the connection between body and mind, losing his mind. Perhaps this was how Ritter had felt when he'd blown up his boat, his best friend, and his life. But Maier had better friends than most.

After a small eternity, his partner let go of him. A second later Maier gently bumped into the boat.

It was time.

He raised his head above the surface. His eyes used to the darkness, he saw the stern of the boat loom above him. He kicked upwards with his fins and grabbed hold of the boat. The small ship moved.

Using the detective as a ladder, Mikhail climbed across Maier's back a second later. For an instant the giant rested on his shoulders, pushing him down into the soup. His fingers began to slip. Maier heard a thud and a surprised yell. Mikhail was on board the vessel. A single shot rang out, then silence, only the waves lapping against the boat.

He didn't dare move, simply hung on for life, staring at the wooden hull in front of him.

"Maier," the Russian hissed from above. "On board now."

The detective pulled himself up and fell onto the deck. A man lay next to him, the steel arrow of the harpoon sticking from his chest. The man was breathing rapidly, bleeding across the deck. He was Thai and he was dying. Maier moved away and got up. A second man lay dead towards the bow of the small ship, a small crater in his smashed forehead.

Mikhail had moved forward to the small pilot's cabin, his 9mm in his hand. Maier stayed a couple of metres behind his friend.

As Maybelle had told them, the boat's captain lay trussed up and gagged on a small bench inside the cabin. The man now struggled against the ropes. Mikhail tucked his gun into his wetsuit and pulled his knife. The captain relaxed. The Russian slit his throat and pulled him out of the cabin. In one swift movement he heaved the dying man over the side of the boat and tipped him into the water. The body landed with a soft splash and drifted away.

Maier had the feeling he was standing knee deep in blood as he watched the butchery in near darkness. Mikhail returned to the two guards. His movements were economic. His huge bulk weaved with the elegance of a ballet dancer from one kill to the next. He grabbed the still breathing man with the harpoon injury and pulled him to the stern where he heaved him overboard. The third man followed seconds later.

Mikhail stopped and looked at Maier with a grim expression on his face. "If that doesn't bring the sharks, nothing will."

Maier had nothing to say. The abyss was staring back at him, and it was leaving him lost for words.

Mikhail shrugged his bear shrug, as much to himself as to his partner.

"One does what one has to do."

Maier smiled without enthusiasm. "Start the engine. I find the cargo. As soon as we have cleared the island, I start ditching it into the sea. We need this boat to be clean if we are to stand any chance of getting to the mainland."

As the vessel rumbled to life, Maier didn't take long to track down Maybelle's stash. Tightly wrapped in oilskin and plastic, twenty or so bundles sat next to the engine block. Way more than thirty-nine kilos. He heaved the parcels on deck and lined them up on the starboard side of their vessel.

Mikhail cranked up the engine and they moved away from the island. The fire on the beach receded. Neither man spoke as they watched surrounding boats and the island for pursuers.

"Now," the Russian shouted above the engine noise from the cabin.

Maier began to heave the bundles overboard, one by one. He watched them drift away in the vessel's wake, a chain of white dots quickly disappearing into the night. Most of the bundles would wash up on Koh Tao's beaches in the coming days. Maier almost laughed to himself. The island would go out of its mind with so much free drugs. But he didn't really feel much like laughing. Maybelle's eyes followed him from the murky depths across the Gulf of Thailand towards the mainland.

25

BANGKOK, THAILAND, FEBRUARY 2003

LONELINESS IS A HOT GUN

Maier walked down Sukhumvit Road in the early evening hours, enthusiastically inhaling traffic fumes. It was good to be free. He wore shorts, a T-shirt and flip-flops. Deep, deep undercover.

He'd lost a lot of weight, was tanned, and had cut his hair short. His haggard face sported a thin beard he'd had trimmed at an Arab hairdressers'. He felt pretty anonymous despite his size and he was still using the ID of Powers, the lift operator. He had half the money they'd found on the boat, several hundred dollars, in his pocket. Everything was going according to plan.

Except that Sundermann was still imprisoned somewhere.

Except that the Americans were still looking for him.

Except that there was no longer a case, a job, a family, and barely a plan.

Maier wanted it all to go back to the depressing time before this even more depressing time. But nothing and nobody cared what Maier wanted.

He'd read about protests against the coming war... Tokyo, Moscow, Paris, London, Montreal, Ottawa, Toronto, Cologne, Bonn, Goteborg, Istanbul, and Cairo. Half the world was out on the streets, but it wouldn't make any difference.

The momentum was with the war, not with protesters or the voters. Voters, like typewriters, telephone landlines, hand-written letters, and cash were becoming obsolete.

He'd watched the UN crawling around Iraq looking for weapons of mass destruction. Information about the country's military capabilities and arsenals changed depending to whom one listened to, perhaps because the men who'd confessed to the officially paraded truths had done so while being tortured somewhere in Thailand.

Maier found it difficult to align the processes that shaped the world on the TV screens he had passed since his reinsertion into society with his own story, with his hunters, with all the parties who wanted to get their hands on the Monsoon Ghost Image. There was the narrative and here was life. Every collision between the two he'd been privy to had been deadly.

He turned off into On Nut, a suburb to the east of Bangkok's busy downtown area.

He'd spent three days alone in the city, staying mostly in his hotel room, talking to no one. Mikhail had gone to ground to find out how hot they were. He'd gladly taken a break from his partner. Mikhail had saved their lives by killing everyone connected to the drug ferry they'd ditched on a deserted beach a few miles north of Chumphon. But he couldn't get himself to feel happy about their escape and eventual return to Bangkok.

The price they'd paid was high. People continued to die in the wake of the Monsoon Ghost Image. People who'd never heard of the photograph, who had no stake in or knowledge of the frontline of the War on Terror, were being swept away by its pernicious, angry force that rushed over them like a tsunami leaving a vast swathe of the world broken in its wake.

The detective couldn't quite remember how many people Mikhail had killed since they'd arrived in Southeast Asia. His own shooting of the German tycoon's henchman, Wuttke, was a burden. The second man he'd killed. But the crazy blood-soaked Full Moon Party was a lifetime or two ago. Maier was no closer to finding his boss or getting his hands on the image. And he had murder on his hands.

. . .

The city embraced Maier like an old friend. After ditching the boat, the two detectives had hitched a ride to Bangkok in a truck and split up on its outskirts to catch separate taxis into town. Maier had headed east to the end of the sky train line and taken a room in an anonymous hotel off Sukhumvit Road, favored by Chinese salesmen and British furniture dealers who worked a nearby fair. The stolen company ID he carried was good enough to check into the hotel.

Mikhail had told him that he was checking sources. The detective felt that his partner was tired of his own company and perhaps his too. The Koh Tao massacre hung between them like a rotting carcass.

What next? Maier sent an email from his new account to Puttama and waited.

As he stepped from the lift the following morning, he spotted a familiar face behind the potted palm trees in the lobby. Ginger, the American he'd last seen when he'd been hiding in the hospital bins, sat reading the paper, a cup of coffee steaming on a low table in front of him.

The agent hadn't seen the detective yet. Maier turned to get back into the lift but the doors had closed. He set off to the café at the back of the lobby. As he passed the toilet doors, the men's room door snapped open and the incredibly pale Fake Bronson stepped out, his head to the ground, his hands concentrating on doing up his fly.

Maier slipped past.

A glass door led out onto the terrace. He climbed over a low fence into the hotel garden and made his way around the building to the street. Without a look back he flagged down a taxi and headed downtown.

In Asoke he got out, ditched his alter ego Powers-the-lift-operator ID in a pile of pavement rubbish, and walked east.

It was hopeless. They were always behind him, snapping at his heels, getting ready to make a grab. There was nowhere to run. They occupied his entire universe. Even if they hadn't caught up with him yet, they'd already taken him over. He was a free prisoner, not quite here anymore but not quite over the threshold into another place yet either.

Maier walked east along Sukhumvit Road. The heat pushed down onto him; a hot wind breathed along the concrete canyon he followed.

He scanned the crowd around him for familiar faces, strained his neck to spot pursuers.

As he passed Soi 23, he was done for. Puttama was moving through the throng towards him. Their eyes met. Hers were full of something that touched Maier to the core. He noticed a black Lexus with tinted windows keeping pace with him on the road. She smiled. His heart rate increased. He started to sweat profusely and his shirt clung to his chest.

A few more metres between them. Maybe everything was OK. Maybe she'd come to warn him. But Maier had gut feelings about the likelihoods of rescue when he found himself in a tight spot. And today his guts told him that he was about to be disappeared.

"Hello, Maier," she said. "Everything will be OK. It's all been resolved. We know you're innocent."

He barely felt the needle prick. As he turned and began to lose consciousness, he wondered why Ginger was doing his own wet work, in public, exposed. Then he saw Suraporn. But it was Ginger who caught him from tumbling to the ground.

"You'll be traveling first class, Maier. We have a nice room at Cat's Eye for you, where you can relax. Maybe."

As Maier passed from one world to another, he could've sworn that the doctor was drooling through canine fangs.

Heavy shit, this.

Then he was gone.

26

THAILAND, FEBRUARY 2003

CAT'S EYE

MAIER NEEDED TO PISS.

It was pitch black around him. He couldn't see a thing. He tried to stand up, but the floor underneath him moved and he fell backwards into a wall. His eyes adjusted to the darkness. He thought he could detect a faint neon glimmer between wall and ceiling. The room was small, just large enough to stretch out in. There was no furniture or other features of any kind. The walls were smooth concrete, the floor was covered in a linoleum-type material.

Maier moved and so did the floor, and he tumbled back into the wall. He tried to get up and stretch towards the light but the floor was too treacherous. Panic rose in his throat. No one knew he was here. The last man he'd seen on the street in Bangkok had been the crazy doctor.

He checked his body; his vital organs were still where they should have been. Maier didn't know where or what here was. He was cold. He didn't want to be tortured. He really didn't. He wanted to be free. He started hyperventilating, as he bathed in the stress his captivity induced. Nothing happened. He could have a heart attack in the box he was caged in and the world would never know. There'd probably be a headline on page three in the Bangkok Post, 'German detective falls from condominium balcony'. The same route Mason the Poet had taken.

Maier moved a few more times. Each time the room moved with him. He figured out that the false floor must have been resting on ball bearings, keeping prisoners permanently off-balance. *Who thinks of stuff like that?* He maneuvered himself into the best position possible and peed on the floor.

Eventually, he nodded off, lying flat on the ground at a slight angle against a cold wall, his mind spinning through an infinite sea of darkness, unable to fully grasp how wonderfully glorious life had been before being locked up in this featureless nothing.

Sometime later he sat at a steel table in an empty room. They were all in front of him like a tableau from hell. A large mirror loomed behind them. Just like in the movies.

The Monsoon Ghost Image had come to life in front of him. From left to right, Dobbs, General Thongsap, Suraporn, the little man Williams. He was no HVD of course. Not in the traditional sense. Maier wasn't sure whether the term traditional applied to what the Americans were doing.

A camera attached to the wall behind his interrogators was watching him. He imagined another camera and a crack team of analysts hid behind the mirror. Five chairs, one table, four interrogators, one prisoner. He was right at the heart of it. He stomped his foot on the floor and pushed his prosthetic fingers into the palm of his hand. The tableau turned its attention to its subject and eyed him warily as if he were a deranged, possibly dangerous lunatic. If only. He half-hoped the entire scene would dissolve into a nightmare but it didn't. It remained far too tangible for his taste. The only object on the steel table was a CD in a clear plastic case, much like the one Ruby had passed to Maier and Mikhail.

Williams threw the opening gambit. "Detective Maier, for all intents and purposes, you're on US soil. This is a military facility. You have no rights here. We have all the rights. We decide over life and death, over punishment and pain. We're the forefront on the War on Terror, and we're going on the offensive against an enemy so cunning and immoral, asymmetric strategies in our fight are called for. This opens a window of opportunity for you, Maier. If you cooperate with us, if you bring our fight forward, we might let you live and you can crawl back under that rock in Hamburg you came from. If you tell us what we want to know, you might have a lifetime investigating bad guys ahead of you. If you don't satisfy our curiosity, you'll be in more trouble than you can imagine."

Williams leant back in his chair, smug and content with his speech. Maier said nothing. He tried to read the faces of his captors, all except the last one, the doctor.

Dobbs picked up where his skinny colleague had left off.

"We'll offer you the deal of the century, Maier. So please don't jump to rash decisions. They won't pay off. They'll cause pain."

Mr. Innocence shifted in his seat and smiled at the detective with what looked like genuine benevolence. Maier felt sick.

"Do you recognize the disc in front of you?"

The detective shrugged. "It looks like the one I got off Ruby, but an unlabeled CD in a plastic case is hardly something anyone would be able to identify with great certainty."

His voice was shaky. The time in the dark cell had softened him up for the next punch.

"But it could be the disc?"

Maier nodded.

What else could he do? It was all shot to several shades of mad. He felt like a defendant in the dock at the trials against the House of Un-American activities.

27

DAGESTAN

A DAY later he was back in the same room. This time the Thais weren't present. Instead, Puttama sat facing the detective along with the other two Americans.

Williams, the reedy psychologist, opened the conversation again.
"What can you tell us about Shamil Basayev?"
"The Chechen on Krieger's island? He's probably dead. We had to leave him in the jungle after Dr. Suraporn lodged a scalpel in his throat. We couldn't take him with us. He was…a good man."

Puttama looked off into the distance. Dobbs coughed.
"He's an Islamist, a terrorist. We think he was responsible for the theatre siege in Moscow last year."

Maier had no idea what he was supposed to say. He had no story to tell his captors other than what the Chechen had told him.

"You tortured that man. And then you gave him to Krieger to serve as bait for his hunting games. You fucking savages," Maier said. "Anyhow, he's almost certainly dead."

The Americans said nothing. Maier shifted uncomfortably on his chair.

"He's not dead? He got off the island?" Maier asked.
Puttama opened a plastic folder on the table in front of her and pulled out a photo. She showed it to Maier. The image was fuzzy, but

Shamil was recognizable, despite the beard. He wore a scarf around his neck and he looked healthier than Maier had ever seen him.

"This photograph is three weeks old. He's back in Chechnya, coordinating suicide attacks against the Russians."

Maier couldn't help but feel impressed. Shamil was harder and more capable than he'd shown himself in the jungle.

"How did he get off the island?"

Puttama answered, "He stole the water plane. Walked across the reef at low tide. In bare feet."

Maier inhaled deeply, trying to process the information, arrange it into his narrative. "He survived your treatment, survived Krieger's hunt, survived Suraporn's attack and he got away. One resourceful man."

"Quite, and partly thanks to you," Dobbs answered curtly.

"What did he tell you about Krieger?" Puttama asked.

"He told us he had dinner with him before he was chased into the jungle."

Maier's thoughts went into overdrive. The three Americans were fishing for something. Something that had nothing to do with the Muslim insurgency in Chechnya. This was all about the German telecom tycoon. And they were under pressure. Somewhere out there, Ginger and his killer friend, Fake Bronson, were waiting for news. Maier recalled the conversation Ginger had had with the general behind the hospital in Bangkok. All these people were expendable. They were almost in the same situation as him. They needed to produce results, otherwise, the next layer of assassins and torturers would eliminate them. That, he hoped, was his chance.

"Krieger wants the Monsoon Ghost Image. He almost had me killed in Bangkok. His right-hand man, a guy called Wuttke, ex-Stasi, nasty piece of work, was on my trail there. I saw him again on Koh Phangan a few days later."

Dobbs waved at the detective. "What happened to this man, Wuttke?"

"I killed him. At the Full Moon Party. Self-defense. Krieger wasn't happy."

Dobbs looked at Maier doubtfully. "You killed this man? How?"

"I had a gun. I shot him in the chest."

"Where did you get the gun?"

"It was Mikhail's. A woman called Hom, whose husband was killed by Wuttke because of a land dispute, handed it to me. I know that sounds a bit outlandish. And I am not a killer."

"You are now if your story checks out. What happened to the body?"

"Krieger took Wuttke with him back to his island when he extracted us from Koh Phangan."

Dobbs continued to look skeptical, but no one countered his claim. Puttama passed a piece of paper to the other men.

"What else did Shamil and Krieger discuss?" Puttama asked.

"Dagestan."

The air in the room contracted. Maier had hit the jackpot. Puttama looked at her colleagues. She said nothing, but it was obvious that some line of thought she had entertained had just been confirmed. She pushed on.

"What about Dagestan?"

"Shamil told us he'd fought there, that he'd been part of an Islamist invasion force a few years ago. And that Krieger tried to set up a telecom network there through a Russian proxy." The truth wouldn't be enough. The Americans wanted more. They wanted certainty where there was none. He was going to give it to them. His life depended on appeasing these people. He also understood that telling them a secret about themselves might forfeit his life. "Krieger told Shamil that you tried to stop him. That you did in fact shut him down in Dagestan. And he hated you for that."

"Pretty tall tales you're spinning there, Maier," Williams interjected, but Puttama cut him off with a curt hand movement to let Maier continue.

"Shamil told us that the CIA and Krieger have a long-standing business relationship that covers territories where the US cannot be seen to do business. And that Dagestan was one of those places and that you rescinded on this deal. Krieger wants the Monsoon Ghost Image so he can blackmail you into giving him a free hand anywhere he chooses to set up shop."

Maier now had the full attention of the three agents in front of him.

"Ironically, as Dagestan is Russian, letting Krieger have his way would kind of put you on the same side as the Islamists. Strange strategy."

Maier regretted his quip as soon as it had slipped from his mouth. Mr. Innocence got up, his face flushed with anger. Clearly, the truth hurt. The interrogation was over.

"Thank you, Maier, that's all for today. We'll talk more tomorrow."

Maier could not recall the last time anyone had thanked him for anything.

The detective was moved to a different cell. The ground was solid, there was a bunk with a blanket, a toilet and a sink, and a steel door with a small window that opened onto a bleak, barren corridor. A camera in a corner was the only other feature. He would refrain from masturbating or barking at the walls.

Occasionally he could hear guards passing outside. Sometimes he could hear other men scream, from a long way away. The screams were so faint he wasn't sure he was imagining them. Perhaps they were putting drugs in his food. He was grateful he was getting food. He hadn't seen daylight in more than a week and he was not altogether sure how long he'd been imprisoned. His life wasn't worth shit unless he convinced these people that he could be of use to them. The conversation he'd overheard between Ginger and General Thongsap at the hospital gave him some hope.

28

FUCK YOU

THE FOLLOWING day he sat facing the three Americans again. Not having a watch, he assumed it was the following day. He had slept, dreamt, shat, slept again. He was back in the same bare room with the table and the four chairs.

He had the impression there was some kind of struggle going on between the two men and Puttama, but perhaps they wanted him to think that. Every day he cared less what they wanted.

Williams started the conversation this time.

"Where's Mikhail Kozakov?"

"I have no idea. We separated in Bangkok after we fled Krieger's island."

"How quickly can you get hold of him?" "Where is my boss, Sundermann?" Maier countered.

Williams smiled without sympathy.

"He's safe, Maier. Whether he will remain so is to some extent up to you. We've been trying to build a relationship of trust here during the past few days. That's why we've not applied enhanced interrogation techniques."

For a second Maier felt grateful. No, they hadn't tortured him. Yet. But everything Williams and Dobbs said was entangled in threats.

They didn't need to be explicit. These men were obscene. They wanted him to be grateful because they'd been merciful. Because they'd not killed or maimed him. He hated them. All of them.

"Fuck you."

Puttama smiled at him sympathetically. Maier hated her too. He was half-tempted to tell her colleagues that she was a whistleblower. Only now he was no longer sure. Perhaps everyone was lying about everything. Perhaps the truth no longer mattered at all. Perhaps, in his absence from the world, during the months on the island and in captivity, the truth had been abolished altogether and everyone now told lies and half-truths to everyone else. Perhaps the Wicked Witch was exactly what she was supposed to be. Perhaps his sanity was slipping.

Emilie, Martin, Suraporn and Shamil, Wuttke and Hom, danced in his mind, night after night, yapping away in languages he couldn't understand. One moment he was on a Moken boat, the women laughing at him, the next he was trapped in a cave labyrinth, pursued by unknown, unseen forces. Over and other, the good doctor peeled away the faces of everyone Maier knew, certainly everyone he'd ever felt any kind of affection for. Maier could barely handle being a captive. He'd been here before, in the hands of brainwashed sadists, crooked authorities, psychotic assassins. The smell of everything was familiar and conjured up old traumas back that opened into his mind like bursting, puss-filled wounds. In fact, he was constantly in a state of near panic, kept under control only by a tiny glimmer of hope that the world would go back to how it had been. He knew that he was dreaming.

"Fuck you."

29

GINGER

Maier was back in the bare room, facing his interrogators across the table. Dobbs pushed a laptop across to the detective. The browser was open and they had hacked into his new, secret email account.

"Mail your Russian friend. Set up a meeting. It's your only way out of here."

Maier shook his head. "I want to see my boss."

Dobbs shrugged. "Or what?"

Maier gave him his best crooked, desperate smile.

"This is all about family. My family and your family. And it's time you guys respected that. Otherwise, you will perish as surely as I will."

Williams laughed under his breath. "Oh, and how is that?"

Maier leaned forward on his steel chair and tried to focus on Dobbs, Williams, and Puttama at the same time.

"Ginger told me that you guys are all expendable. You're all just another layer in this thing…this thing you belong to. Your organization, your family. I am scared of Ginger. Really, I am. Perhaps more than of Suraporn. I ran into him in Hamburg, in Berlin, in Bangkok. And every time I had the feeling that I was lucky to walk away alive. He is somewhere close by, but you guys can't see him. Ask your general what Ginger told him. You're all just so many digits with the shutters down and the curtains drawn, fucking up the lives of men who've been entrapped by a machine you barely understand. But that machine becomes a snake that eats its own tail. And you guys along with your local torture kings are about to become the tail."

Maier was ranting now, but he could see that his words were having an effect. He could sense more than see the beads of sweat that formed on the psychologist's forehead. He could see Dobbs' furrowed brow. Only Puttama was calm as set concrete. Perhaps he was wrong to doubt her.

There was complete silence.

Dobbs cleared his throat. "You can see your boss. And then you get in touch with the Russian. Otherwise, neither you, nor Sundermann, will ever see daylight again."

A day earlier, Maier would have recoiled in fear. Now he was only moderately agitated. He'd touched a nerve. There was a way out.

Dobbs pulled a phone from his trouser pocket and typed a message. He punched the keys a little too hard. Something had just ended. There was nothing more to say. The three Americans faced off their prisoner in silence. Puttama, her face unfathomable, stared at some point in space beyond Maier. Williams and Dobbs were watching him, impassively, spookily. They looked like they were on drugs.

The door behind them opened. Maier could see that it took the two Americans all their self-control not to turn their heads. Dobbs and Williams continued to stare down Maier, even as Ginger and Fake Bronson raised their tasers and pointed them to their colleagues' necks. Thin flexible wires shot into his two interrogators who slid to the floor screaming. A pool of piss quickly spread around Williams. Dobbs went bright red and howled furiously. But resistance was futile. The snake had made its move. And Maier had a VIP view.

He made eye contact with Puttama but the woman gave nothing away. Layers upon layers. Like an onion. Disinformation, lies, and subterfuge in the name of what? He felt an enormous amount of respect for the Wicked Witch. He hated her because she was clearly far ahead of him. He understood that she'd brought him into this mess to stir things up. Like an old-hand chess player, she was always a few moves ahead.

Fake Bronson cuffed Williams and Dobbs. His movements were economical, with not a pinch more cruelty than necessary.

Ginger dropped his weapon on the table and grinned at Maier.

"You're almost our best asset, detective. Good work for a washed-up German. But your job isn't done yet."

Puttama and Fake Bronson dragged the other two Americans from the room. *No more Mr. Innocence.*

Ginger motioned Maier to get up and follow him.

"We have a mission for you, detective. If you manage this last job, you'll never have to prove your courage again. And you'll live. Your family, such as it is, will live. And so will mine. You understand?"

The man didn't bother to turn his head to see Maier nod in agreement. They moved along the bare corridor past his cell into a reception room. This room too was grey and bare. Three body bags lay on the ground. General Thongsap, clearly dead, lay in one of the black bags, his pale face placid, his eyes as remote as they had been in life. A first aid kit lay opened next to the general. Puttama and Bronson pulled the two American torturers onto the remaining two bags.

Maier found his voice. "You figured out that their methods are unsound?"

Ginger shot him a pitying smile.

"No, Maier. We figured out that these guys were indiscreet. Bringing that old friend of yours, the crooked photographer, and the psycho doctor into the picture was a mistake. Too many generals know about this place, and they talk to their minor wives and weekend whores about it. We're here to rectify all that. There will be no photo, no scandal, no black ops, no torture, no human hunt in the media, nothing. We're going to shut down this perfect shit storm. And you'll help us achieve that. You've been perfect so far and you'll continue to be perfect. You and your Russian friend will bring us Krieger, Suraporn, and Ritter. If and when you do, your family, your agency, whatever you want to call it, your fantasy reality, can rejoin the living."

Maier swallowed hard as he watched Ginger pull two syringes from the first aid kit. The irony wasn't lost on the detective. The American calmly injected Williams first. Dobbs, still paralyzed, but more aware of what was coming, groaned desperately. Ginger plunged the second needle into the dedicated American. The two men faded fast, much faster than Shamil and all the others they'd tortured and maimed. Ginger would dispose of Maier as well once the detective had outlived his usefulness. The Monsoon Ghost Image had purge written all over it. There was a reason why he was in the room to witness the killing of Americans by Americans.

"By the way, I appreciate you calling me Ginger. I'm always stumped with code names and I can't very well tell anyone who I really am. Ginger works well for me. People remember that. What do you call my colleague?"

"You guys have drifted off somewhere few people are likely to follow you," Maier shot back

The American nodded, more to himself perhaps than anyone else.

"I wouldn't be too sure of that. Civilization's just a haircut. People are extreme. Always have been. You should know, with your experience as a front-line detective. If not, you're learning it now. Consider this an education, Maier. We're entering a new era of preemptive discussions. It's the Zeitgeist, as your countrymen would say."

Ginger turned his head. "And don't lambast me with your cheap sarcasm. It's not appropriate to jest with a man who just administered lethal injections to two of his subordinates. We're not joking around here. We're saving the world."

Maier nodded vaguely. "We call your friend Fake Bronson."

Ginger snapped around. "As I said, keep your jokes to yourself or I will cut your nose off." Then he laughed. "Ginger and Fake Bronson, come to think of it, not bad. As in Charles Bronson, I guess. Could be a TV series about a couple of American heroes. It might not save you, Maier, but your creative thinking sure entertains me."

The man was right of course, his jokes wouldn't save him. As a German, he understood this instinctively. And in a cosmic sense, Ginger was quite mad. Those who argued with him or disappointed him were dead because those who argued with him argued with his country. You were either with him or against him.

People were extreme.

Ginger.

30

BANGKOK, THAILAND, MARCH 2003

THE LOW COUNTRIES

THE ROOM SMELT of perfume and piss. Cheap perfume and cheaper piss. It wanted to look like a decadent opium den in 1920s China, with chintz and blood mixed into an unhealthy puddle of human misery.

Like almost everyone else on the planet, the two men in the room were racing towards happiness. The girls less so.

Dr. Suraporn lay sprawled on the fake leather couch, his exhausted, shriveled cock trailing a thread of tired cum onto the face of the girl that slumped motionless by his feet. This man, if that's what he could still be called, had sewn the heads of birds onto the faces of other men. He'd killed and barked and triumphed. He'd worked for the most secret of secret services. He'd altered Martin Ritter's face before the world got wise to the photographer's second coming. And now, it seemed, he was unemployed. Left to enjoy simple pleasures till his past caught up with him.

Ritter was immersed in capturing this final journey. He suspected that he himself was on the home stretch too. He'd lost his wife and his ability to procreate. He could pee, that was about it. It hurt every time.

A sharp shock shot through him every time his mind traveled back to the butchery on Koh Phangan. Anxiety didn't begin to describe how he felt. All he had left now were his photographer's eyes and his revenge. He grinned and adjusted his tripod. He was working on his last portfolio: Holidays in hell.

"You've captured every little detail?"

Suraporn's smooth chest glistened with sweat and blood. He smiled at Ritter with gentle savagery as the last girl reloaded his pipe with Special K. He was muscular despite his modest debauchery paunch that threatened to slide off his lower chest onto the floor next to the girl. As he gazed empty-eyed at Ritter, he had more than just ordinary murder in his eyes.

But Ritter didn't fear him. Suraporn had saved his life, had sewn his scrotum together. No one else would have been able to save him. And the German photographer knew too much about the doctor to feel cornered. In a way, he felt that he owed this man. And the doctor owed him as much. Mutually assured destruction was the only way out of this for the two men. But as a *farang*, a foreigner, he wasn't bound by notions of face. Ritter had other routes of escape.

The doctor briefly nodded off and defecated. The gagging sounds the girl made brought him back to life and he hit her across the side of the head. Ritter could see she almost passed out, but she didn't drop the pipe. She was desperate to live another minute, or two, just a few more crazy moments filled with nothing but terror. There was some dignity in the poor.

The ketamine was good. After a police tip-off, the doctor had killed two hapless dealers who'd gotten caught with a half key after their pick-up had broken down on the expressway. He'd shot them point blank and taken the whole load home while ordering the cops to clean up the mess. He'd bragged about it, and he felt good about it.

"These poor, they are not going anywhere. This is my country. My Land of Smiles. Everybody who has money is happy." He grinned at Ritter. "We really should get younger girls next time."

He pointed at the two bodies that already lay straightened out on clear plastic sheeting. Dead and cut up. Ready for postage. He half-laughed as he nodded off and lost his lunch over himself and his last victim.

Only the click of Ritter's camera and the falling tears of the girl broke the near silence in the soundproof, windowless room. The photographer paused in his work and took in the entire scene. A man and three broken girls in paraplegic disorder. The painting above the doctor's head of a half-naked, Asian damsel in the arms of a fierce gold dragon was so bad it was almost a crime.

Now he'd covered it all— the savagery of a democratic government abandoning the last shreds of its mythical narrative at Cat's Eye, and the private foibles of that government's most efficient henchman. National Geographic had nothing on him.

Ritter had no illusions on which side of the fence he was on. He'd crossed the line, given all to the need to see the human spirit for what he had always seen it— vengeful, cruel, and out of control. Somehow, he'd found himself there in the middle of this terrible vortex wielding his camera, pointing it at the black hole that produced all these men.

For Ritter, as much as for Dobbs, Williams, Thongsap, and Suraporn, and all the other creeps he'd worked with since joining the CIA renditions program, there was no way down from their privileged perch. They'd all tasted the Other. They'd all become aroused by their power, by their ability to inflict learned helplessness on other human beings. And they could feel safe in the knowledge that this had been authorized at the highest levels of the world's most open and egalitarian society. It wasn't pride exactly, that he felt. Something else.

The doctor forced himself out of his reverie and directed his ejaculation into the eyes of his victim. Her eyes were beautiful, and she was still twitching despite being almost completely paralyzed.

For a while, Ritter watched the doctor trying to get hard again, but he was too spaced out. He just sat there and started barking. Like a small dog. A yelp almost. The photographer was familiar with the doctor's sonic proclivities.

Suraporn stopped barking. The two men looked at each other. They were bonded by blood. In one fluent movement, the doctor rose from his chair, snapped off the head of his glass pipe, and pushed the crying girl to the side while slashing her throat with the pipe's stem.

"I'm partied out. It's a wrap."

. . .

Ritter could live for a year on the money he'd earned tonight. It wasn't the million he deserved, Krieger's million. Suraporn had gotten hold of that. In fact, Ritter had insisted the doctor take the money. He wasn't strong enough to keep it.

Ritter almost chuckled. It was a bit much. Snuff movies were really Grand Guignol, a little too medway. It was the rich losing it and things staying the same. The pocket money Suraporn had paid him would get him away from here. Away from Asia. Out of the CIA game. Away from the Monsoon Ghost Image.

Ritter was honest with himself. There was no denying that he'd had a good time tonight. After a few weeks of recuperation, he missed the vomitorium. He missed it more than his testicles. It was the new normal. He'd lost it when he'd stopped going to war. But he'd found it again. He had no idea where to go next, Colombia, Cuba perhaps.

As the doctor turned away from the photographer to wrap the girls, Ritter slipped one of the memory cards down the front of his trousers and reloaded the camera. He could handle his gear as well as any two-bit sadist who'd mastered the art of murder of helpless, drugged, and bound women. And he was pretty confident he'd get his money back eventually. All of it.

Much later, the doctor pulled himself together and got dressed. Ritter waited by the door.

As Suraporn passed, the photographer pressed the memory cards into his client's moist, soft hands. All but one. The doctor grinned.

"Good that we have common friends. I trust you. Otherwise...your soul might be next."

Ritter didn't flinch. It was just the drugs talking. He knew the drill. In a few days when everything had been cleaned up and whoever needed paying had been paid off, the doctor would invite the photographer to make merit at Wat Phra Dhammakaya and throw some money at the abbot. That always soothed his mind. Things were and things would be. The Buddha preached detachment and the doctor was a good student.

You had to be detached to rape and murder a bunch of nameless hill tribe girls every month.

For fun.

Ritter met Doctor Suraporn's animal stare with passive quietude, not a hint of fear nor arrogance in his foreign eyes. The apparently genuine expression of gratitude that flowed from Ritter's gaze had saved him many times.

In Africa, in Eastern Europe.

Now it would save him in hell. No need to make merit.

Glory days.

Outside, the balmy night air, heavy with petrol fumes and the burning oil of open roadside kitchens, took his breath away. He looked up and down the small road in Chinatown, there was no one around. And yet Ritter sensed he'd taken his last picture.

A taxi pulled up. Suraporn was busy locking his murder pad but the photographer didn't wait. He waved for the slowing cab and pulled the door open when the vehicle stopped.

"Ritter…" he heard the doctor's voice behind him.

He fell into the back seat and pulled the door shut. The cab moved off the curb. Ritter didn't want to turn his head. Intuition, clairvoyance, he wasn't sure. But then curiosity got the better of him and he turned to see Mikhail, the Russian, smash the doctor's face with a hammer. The taxi driver had seen it too and stared at his fare in the rearview mirror. But he didn't stop. Great men lived and fell in both darkness and light and the world never wavered. Ritter told the driver to take him to the airport.

3 1

DOCTOR'S ORDERS

MAIER and his captors found Mikhail on the steps to the house in Chinatown his Russian friend had asked to meet him in his last email. His breath was labored and smelled of alcohol. He sat pressing his hand onto the wound in his neck.

"He got me the same way he got Shamil. He was here with Ritter... probably up to no good. I can't believe he survived my hammer. I got drunk so as not to be too susceptible to his mind games. Didn't work."

Ginger dialed for an ambulance. Maier took his shirt off, tore the sleeve away, and then gently lifted the Russian's hand. The blood gushed. Maier tightened the short sleeve around his friend's neck. Mikhail looked at him passively, faint hope in his eyes.

"Krieger's island. Get the bastard."

Then he was gone.

Maier couldn't do anything but keep his hand pressed to the Russian's neck.

After an eternity, lights came flashing down the street.

With Mikhail on his way to hospital, Fake Bronson pushed Maier into the house. Crossing the threshold was enough to send any man into a state of permanent crisis. Maier threw up.

Fake Bronson inhaled deeply and remarked, "The locals will want to bring monks into the building to drive out the black magic."

"You employed this man," Maier spat.

Ginger shrugged as he surveyed the smashed, dead girls. "He was overqualified. Know where he went?"

"He's gone south."

The American nodded.

"In war, good does not always triumph. And evil sometimes has to fight on the side it most despises so that good can be victorious."

"You've been watching too many Rambo movies. You will do anything, no matter how debased, to come out on top. You are… unsound." Maier was playing for time. Whatever he said sounded pathetic as they stood amidst the sick massacre.

Ginger shrugged. "Keep it real, Maier."

"Ritter cashed out."

The two Americans looked to the detective.

"I think he repaid the million he took from Krieger for his photo to Suraporn who is on his way to return the money to its rightful owner," Maier said. "Or to kill him and keep the cash. Who knows? Ritter almost certainly took pictures in here tonight and if he did, he took some of them with him so he can blackmail Suraporn."

"Where's Ritter now?" Ginger asked.

"Gone before we got here. Mikhail saw him leave in a cab."

"We have nothing. Just three dead hookers and a half-dead Russian on his way into ICU. Sounds depressingly ordinary," Ginger shook his head in something akin to frustration and turned to his colleague. "Let's not you start to develop a sense of humor as well, Fake Bronson. One clown in the vicinity is enough when we're trying to save the world." Then he refocused on Maier. "You're starting to disappoint. Mikhail was your trump card. What have you got for me now, Maier?"

"I have you, Ginger. You will come south with me and we will finish this together." Maier found himself shaking, but he continued to press his point. "I would much rather travel by myself to somewhere you've never heard of. But my motivation to see the barking doctor out of action is strong. Mikhail hopes for nothing less as he fights for his life on an operating table. But I cannot do it by myself. No matter how much I might try, Ginger, I can never be like you guys."

Ginger nodded. "Don't get emotional, Maier. It's just a job."

The detective wanted to despair. Men, murder, torture, chaos. He looked at his companions. Ginger sensed his judgment.

"We're not fanatics you know. We're just…. keen. And thorough. Remember that, detective. Very thorough."

32

SOUTHERN THAILAND, MARCH 2003

DOCTORED

THE GRUMMAN MALLARD seaplane dropped quickly out of a clear afternoon sky towards Koh Krieger. From the cramped cabin, the island chain stretching south across the Gulf of Thailand looked picture postcard perfect.

That didn't make Maier feel any better. He had no desire to return to the tycoon's wildlife and killing safari. Duress and the War on Terror had brought him back.

Fake Bronson handled the small aircraft well and they soon spotted the jetty on the island's east side. The plane performed a low pass. Krieger's men were on the jetty, barking into walkie-talkies, but they didn't shoot. Fake Bronson turned and set them down gently. He cut the engines to leave them bouncing in the surf. Maier opened the cabin door and threw a rope to Krieger's men who pulled the aircraft close to the jetty. The detective jumped out with his arms raised. He couldn't be too careful with ten guns pointed at him. Fake Bronson stayed in the pilot's seat.

The water was turquoise and placid. The sharks were around, moving lazily on both sides of the jetty. The men formed a tight, silent circle around Maier and led him towards the island. He was surprised they didn't bother to search him. In a sense, he felt a little humiliated.

Krieger was so sure the detective wasn't capable of violence. Maier, the German pacifist. But Krieger should have known better. Drive any shark into a corner tight enough...

The German telecom tycoon stood waiting on the beach, sipping beetroot juice, surrounded by his gaggle of unsmiling girls.

Suraporn, the good doctor lingered further back where the jungle met the beach. His head was heavily bandaged and he wore a patch over his left eye. Hard to believe he'd survived Mikhail's hammer blow without brain damage.

There was no shaking hands and the only warmth provided came from the sun.

"Where is the Russian?" Krieger asked.

"Dead," Maier said.

"I don't believe it. Always thought that Russian was unkillable." Krieger turned to the doctor. "It's worth the hassle having to walk around with an eye patch and a headache for a while, killing that bastard. We almost got what we wanted."

The doctor's powers of engagement were down today. Maier couldn't feel his presence. Perhaps Mikhail had smashed more than just his eye socket.

But Maier didn't feel all that much respite either. The man was stressing him out, even if his voodoo was spent.

Krieger motioned his crew to search the plane. They were back soon, dragging Fake Bronson along, cuffed and silent as a grave.

Krieger turned around to Suraporn who slowly shook his head.

One of Krieger's men returned to the plane, pulled the pin on a grenade, and dropped it into the cockpit. Seconds later, the aircraft exploded, destroying half the jetty as it busts apart.

That would give the sharks a headache, Maier thought.

Despite the icy welcome, the tycoon, enjoying the pyrotechnic spectacle, had reconnected to his old flamboyant self. white flowing shirt, his grey sculpted hair a little shorter, the lines on his face a little deeper. A revolver hung from his waist in a velvet holster, and he had a bullet belt draped across his shoulder. It was a tad fancy dress. He looked like a boutique resort owner dressed up as a Zapatista for an office party.

And yet, in the face of so much infantile vulgarity, Maier had to take the crazy German as serious as cancer.

"So good to see you again, Maier. You know I have a flair for theatrics. When I heard you were coming down to visit, I thought to myself, how can I produce an appropriate welcome for the great detective, one of only a handful of men who left my little piece of paradise without my permission? How can I make a man who's given me so much trouble and caused me so much pain feel at home? You know, I miss Wuttke every day. Wuttke was reliable and loyal. He never let me down and he was always there for me. He was my friend. Perhaps my only friend. Not like this creepy gun for hire here, the dear doctor."

Suraporn stood a few metres to the side, in the shade.

"I thought long and hard about how I could ever repay you. I'll kill you and your new beefcake over there in due course. But before we get to that, I'd like to offer you a gift. I had to go to great lengths to make this happen, so I hope you appreciate the gesture. I know you will."

He waved to his girls. Two of his assistants stepped forward carrying a round serving tray covered by a shining metal lid.

"Welcome to Krieger Island, Maier, for the second and last time. Always good to be able to welcome a Landsmann with a local specialty."

With a showy flailing of arms, the little man turned and lifted the lid off the tray. Hom, or rather her severed head, stared up at Maier from a bed of crushed ice.

As the blood drained from his face, Maier felt as if he'd started bleeding internally. Disconcerted on a deep, silent level, the way a half-decent person would be when he or she was confronted with something unspeakably wrong. The beach, the sea, the sky, and the waves stopped existing. It was neither hot nor cold in Maier's world, neither bright nor dark. He didn't look away. He didn't want to look at Krieger. He didn't want to look at the severed head. But it wasn't a rational decision one way or another. He kept staring at the head of the woman who'd saved his life twice. They'd pulled her lips up ever so slightly to suggest a smile on her dead face.

"Where is Mae?" Maier asked.

"And who might Mae be, Maier?" Krieger chuckled with glee.

"Her daughter."

"Oh," was his simple answer as he waved towards the waves. "Did you notice that the bull sharks were a little slower and more relaxed today? Last thing we saw of her, she escaped into the waves."

Maier was almost blind with fury, partly at the world, partly at himself. He wasn't a killer. He wasn't an aggressive man. It wasn't his job to remove this unpleasant man from public life. From life. But someone would have to do it.

Krieger chuckled and pointed at Fake Bronson.

"Is that your new strongman? He doesn't look all that impressive."

"He has his strong sides, Krieger. He's immune to the doctor's charms. And he can be in two places at the same time."

The tycoon looked at the detective with a look of faint pity. "Are we getting metaphysical just as we're about to pass from one plain to another, Maier? You realize the world will keep turning without you and your little ideas of what's right and wrong. The big boys always get away with it. The boardrooms need filling. The money needs to keep changing hands. People need to keep talking. And I give them the tools to talk. And that's why the world needs me, why the Americans need me, and why I will always be safe and far away from assholes. I'm indispensable."

Maier pulled himself together. "This is exactly what we have come here to discuss, Krieger. *Und wenn ich das kurz auf Deutsch sagen kann. In zehn Minuten sind Sie tot, wenn Sie Ihren Männer nicht sofort befehlen, den guten Doktor auszuschalten und dann Ihrer Verhaftung zuzustimmen.*"

Krieger raised an eyebrow and answered in English. "To be arrested? To betray the doctor? You're going to kill me, Maier? You must have acquired new skills, detective. I feel a certain disconnect. Suraporn brought back my money, the money that Ritter stole. I let him keep it of course. Man like that needs to have some cash flow. He also brought me the biggest prize of all— the Monsoon Ghost Image."

Krieger needed to have the last word. His voice had gone from calm to slightly shrill.

Maier looked around to see what Fake Bronson was doing. The American agent shook his head.

"Oh, yes, yes. Your boss had the image on his smart phone, silly man. That's why the Americans picked him up. And Suraporn had access to Sundermann when he was held at Cat's Eye. Maier, see it for what it is. There's a good reason why I got to this place in life."

He waved effusively at the tropics. "I get things done. I pay people with a type of kindness they cannot refuse. I look after my own and I kill off the opposition. And with the help of the CIA, quite literally so. In fact, as you know, people pay me to come here and kill the people I need to have killed. Now, how smart is that? I mean, if that isn't the very definition of voodoo capitalism, then I don't know where you've been. In Cuba perhaps?"

Maier turned to Fake Bronson who nodded curtly behind his wrap-around glasses. This was going to hurt. Krieger hadn't noticed and carried on in his usual gregarious mode. He owned the world. And if not the world, then certainly the patch of fine powdery sand they stood on.

"Suraporn told me about the little poem he shared with you a while back. I am sure you'll recall. We're down to the last verse, Maier. 'One little Indian Boy left all alone. He went out and hanged himself and then there were none.' Will you do us the favor please?"

One of the girls stepped forward, holding a rope. Krieger took it from her and walked across the hot sand to an old palm tree that bent at a 45-degree angle towards the water. Perhaps sensing its owner's malevolence, it looked as if it were in the process of leaving the island.

Maier could hardly fault the tree.

Krieger threw the rope around the trunk and made a knot. The whole thing looked like he'd practiced the entire previous night. Longer than that perhaps. Satisfied, he waved for one of his girls. She was no older than fifteen, but she knew how to make a hangman's noose in a frighteningly short time.

"'One little Indian Boy left all alone. He went out and hanged himself and then there were none. One little Indian Boy left all alone. He went out and hanged himself and then there were none.'"

The more Krieger intoned his mantra, the more Maier thought him a spoiled old brat, a man to whom not enough people had said no to.

Krieger returned to the group of girls and Fake Bronson. This was the moment. Maier had banked on not being searched coming off the plane. He'd been correct. With Krieger absorbed in the preparations of the detective's imminent hanging and the doctor shaking his head nervously as if to check whether there was anything worth salvaging left inside it, the detective ceased to be a priority for a few seconds.

It was enough.

Maier pulled the stun grenade Ginger had given him from his

pants, pulled its steel chord, and rolled it into the small crowd. Fake Bronson had already stepped back and turned his head. The grenade went off. The beach flashed in impossible white light and shook for a split second.

Ginger, wearing wrap-around shades emerged from the sea like the devil he was. The garrote fastened around Krieger's neck before anyone had come to their senses.

When Maier could see again, the tycoon's head was lying in the sand next to Hom's which had tumbled off its tray. Krieger's men had joined their boss on his journey to another place, all of them shot by Ginger. The American walked around, barely looking at them, firing a single shot to each of their heads to be sure. Instant insurance cover. But the good doctor had disappeared. Having made sure that he'd killed everyone on his shit list, Ginger uncuffed Fake Bronson and both men began to zip tie the girls.

"We chase Suraporn?" Fake Bronson asked.

Ginger shrugged. "No point. That guy is too wily to be caught in the open. He'll have a plan B. You think Ritter is dead? Did Krieger tell the truth about the doctor getting hold of the photo off Sundermann?"

Ginger looked dangerous. The beach had gone back to normal but nothing was normal. The air was tense. Fake Bronson stood rubbing his wrists.

Maier realized that he was on the day's cleaning list.

"You can't kill me yet. You need me to get the image for you."

Ginger shrugged. "You got a copy? I doubt it. I think you're spent, Maier."

"You still need me."

Ginger laughed quietly into the surf and played with his blood-caked wire. "What in the world for? You're no good at killing and you won't catch us the doctor. You've seen the image and you know too much. If you have a copy, you're dead. If you don't, you're dangerous alive. God, you've seen me kill my own people. You're done, Maier. It's the way it works. Like in the old days, when they threw witches into rivers with stones on their feet. If they came back up, they were certainly witches. If they drowned, they were innocent. I know life's not fair and no one gets what they deserve, but hey. As long as you're walking around out there, men like me, men with the responsibility to protect national interests, will feel nervous. And you're so easy to kill,

Maier. I'm surprised it hasn't happened yet." Ginger took his glasses off and smiled an easy smile. He handed his companion the garrote.

"Do the honors, Fake Bronson. Then we can go home and start again. I hate this country. So damn vulgar. No one here is serious."

"The Wicked Witch will not forgive you," Maier said.

Ginger raised his hand. "What are you talking about, detective?"

"You're not with the program, Ginger. How do you think I got here?"

"You were hired by Ritter's wife. We checked through your agency files."

"Then you saw the emails from the Wicked Witch."

"We're losing time. That doctor will be fast on his feet," Fake Bronson interjected.

Maier laughed bitterly. This beach was too beautiful to die on. This sky was too beautiful to die under. This life hadn't been lived yet.

"You guys don't get it. You were had, right from the start. So was I. The doctor doesn't have the image. He never did. He never saw Sundermann. Apart from you two, only one other person saw Sundermann and interrogated him. That means only one other person could have harvested my boss's copy of the Monsoon Ghost Image. We had another copy, on the disc that Ruby, Ritter's ladyboy, gave us. I passed that disc to the Wicked Witch. She's in control of the image right now. Suraporn lied to Krieger to get his money. He has no loyalty to anyone or anything other than himself and his sickness. You fucked it all up, Ginger. You were too arrogant. You should have listened to the general you murdered. Remember what he told you at the hospital? But you were so proud, you had to put him in his place. You were busy humiliating the locals and you lost sight of where this whole affair had been going all along."

Ginger's smile faded. A little.

"You're full of shit, Maier. But I don't blame you for playing the game when you're about to walk the plank. Not one bit. It's a good show."

"I'm your only bargaining chip and you're going to throw me to the sharks? Think. I only just understood it myself. I'm the heart of this affair. Me, little Maier. I was brought in by the Wicked Witch to neutralize Ritter, to get the image. But we like to forget because we are old and we come from a time when the Internet did not exist. We forget that the image is already out there, whether it actually is or not. Once Ritter took the picture and it came off his memory card, that was it. This is Thailand, the Land of Smiles, the place where no one can keep a secret. What chance does a digital photograph with salacious content have of remaining a ghost image? What were you thinking to rendition high-value detainees to a place where no one takes anything seriously? A land where everyone is anyone's if the price is right. Can you imagine just how many people are gossiping about Cat's Eye right now? Next week your little joint will be on the nation's society pages. Even your ugly mugs might be featured. Thailand is a game-changer for almost anyone who gets stuck here. The country has a way of digging into you with its sunny disposition. Then, when you're flat out on your back, your cock burning from a thousand STDs, it's payday. And the only thing you have for sale is secrecy. In this place, you can buy secrecy in the market, for the same price as a couple of beers or a fuck. The Wicked Witch knew this from the start. The only thing that was not clear is where she stood on this. Would she fight the Zeitgeist as you called it, or go with the flow? Or did she have something else in mind altogether? Was she leading you right into the jungle? I suspect she had already made up her mind when she sent that first email to Emilie Ritter, the mail that brought me here. You get it?"

"They call this German gallows' humour, Maier?"

The waves gently brushed across the powdered sand. Maier was shaking a little. The adrenaline rush was intense, his fear palpable, at least to himself.

If these guys didn't have doubts right now, this beach would be the last thing he'd ever see. And he so wanted to live. He so wanted to talk himself out of his grave. To visit Mikhail in hospital. To tell Sundermann he was ready for work. To ask the Wicked Witch to give him his life back. After all, she'd been the one who'd taken it away from him, who'd manipulated and manoeuvred him from the start to bring him forward to this moment, where he was fighting for his life while declaring her victorious. He just didn't want to die for a cause that was so much bigger than himself. He was just some guy, formerly drunk, recently sober, who knew a thing or two about Asia.

The detective turned in time to see Fake Bronson's fist descend on his chin. He didn't quite have time to appreciate he wasn't feeling the wire that had just killed Krieger.

33

FUN HOUSE

Maier woke tied to the iron bars of a heavy four-poster bed as Ginger burst into the room, a hunting knife with a serrated blade in his hand. He had no idea where he was, he was sweating profusely and he couldn't move.

Ginger looked nuts, his eyes wide, a deep flesh wound on his right cheek. The American tore around the room, ripping the doors on a wall-length cupboard open and throwing them shut again with enough force to snap them off their hinges.

"Stop," the detective shouted.

Ginger stood in the centre of the room, catching his breath, staring at the detective as if he'd noticed him for the first time. Perhaps he had. He looked deranged.

"He is here?" Ginger asked.

"Who?"

"The monster?"

"No," was all Maier could muster. He knew exactly who Ginger was talking about.

"Where are we?"

"We must be in Krieger's villa," Maier answered.

Ginger stepped over to the detective and flashed his knife and a sad grin.

His eyes told the story. His self-confidence had moved on, probably never to return. Maier jerked back and remained where he was.

"I'm not going to kill you…now. I need all the help I can get."

He cut the plastic chords. Maier didn't move, but he did feel better.

"Where is Fake Bronson?" Maier asked.

"He's standing outside against a tree in the garden, minus a leg that a panther took earlier, with a pig's snout sewn to his face."

"Who else is here?"

"Krieger's men and most of the girls are dead. A few might have fled into the jungle. The gates to the compound have been opened and there are dangerous animals walking around outside. There's no one else. Only the doctor."

Maier laughed sourly.

"Your employee."

"We lost our way with that one."

Maier sensed how hard it was for the American to say this. He felt no sympathy for Ginger.

"It has become a monster competition for the Monsoon Ghost Image," Maier said. "What else?"

"The electricity is cut. There is no phone signal."

"Weapons?"

It was Ginger's turn to laugh. He liked his weapons and a hint of his belief in superior firepower returned to his expression.

"Plenty. The house is an arsenal."

"Food, water?"

"Maier, I've closed all the doors and windows I could find, we are inside a damn fortress here. He probably can't get in. But we can't get out."

Maier shrugged.

"You're a big boy. The cavalry will come."

Ginger sat down on the edge of the bed. "No, it won't. We didn't tell our handlers we were coming down here. Fake Bronson stole that water plane we boarded in Samui."

Maier looked at the American with disbelief.

"You disobeyed orders? You are just another money-grabbing gangster?"

Ginger shook his head.

"The next level up isn't happy with our performance in Thailand.

The Cat's Eye is out of the sack, the photo is out there, the interrogators are dead, two of the hired hands have gone rogue. We felt we needed to come down here and clean up before reporting back. Needed at least to get Krieger, you, and the fucking doctor out of the way."

"Mad."

"And now I'm trapped in this funhouse with the most dangerous, unhinged man in the world outside."

Maier shifted off the bed to the door and stared out into a broad, dark corridor.

"And me," Maier said.

Ginger threw a revolver onto the bed.

"Don't go anywhere without this. I know you're a peacenik, Maier, but we're in a tight spot here."

Maier pulled his phone from his trousers. Plenty of battery, no reception.

"There's reception on the roof. The last of the girls went up there yesterday. She is now hanging from a tree a little behind Fake Bronson. Never heard a thing."

Maier typed a message to Puttama, the Wicked Witch, and waved towards the door.

"It is pitch dark out there now. We just have to get to the patch where there is reception and the message will go out. You should have put your phone into the girl's pocket. Outside help is our best bet."

"You're crazy. You'll get killed."

"One of us might get killed, Ginger. The other one might get rescued."

Maier couldn't believe he was telling this man how to fight. CIA field agents were meant to be ruthless, heartless motherfuckers. He found it hard to believe he'd been so scared of Ginger.

The American sighed. "You're way too straight for this work, Maier."

The detective answered, "Right now, retirement does sound like an incredibly attractive deal. But it is not on the menu. We have a CIA torturer on our back for starters, mains, and desserts. And Mikhail is not here to lend a hand."

Ginger sagged against the wall. Neither man spoke for a while. Maier listened to the house breathe. The jungle sounded far away. He couldn't hear what had once been his life, not even when he concentrated on his breath.

"Fake Bronson was my partner."

Somehow Maier had known that this was the reason why Ginger had lost his drive. He didn't feel particularly reassured by the fact that the American displayed feelings so late in life.

"Three AM. It is time to go and send our smoke signal."

Ginger nodded.

"Maybe he won't be up there. He can't be everywhere at once." The words fell from his mouth straight onto the floor.

Ginger had little faith in his optimism.

"There are two trapdoors onto the roof," Ginger explained. "They open only from the inside. So, once we're done, close yours behind you, otherwise whatever's out there will follow you in."

Maier needed to urinate. He stepped over to one of the cupboards and relieved himself. The American carried on, talking through his master plan.

Desperate times.

"The best reception is in the middle between those doors. There are plenty of air-con units and other obstacles up there and tonight there's no moon. Easy to hide, hard to move quickly. My phone is dead, so yours is our only bet. Let's go. I don't want to wait till he finds a way in and sews your ugly face onto mine."

Maier said nothing. They were past horse-trading, past exchanging top-secret trivia. The Monsoon Ghost Image was running its course. In a sense, it was the perfect 21st-century weapon. Like a computer virus that had transmuted into a living organism, it had infected everyone who'd seen or owned it. It had rendered them utterly vulnerable. In time, some form of defragmentation or corruption would set in and destroy the carrier. Ruby, Wuttke, Emilie, Dobbs, Williams, Thongsap, Hom, Mae, Krieger, Fake Bronson… the number of casualties blown away by a mere digital photograph continued to grow.

34

IT'S A TRAP

MAIER HAD his finger on the send button as he followed Ginger into the corridor. He'd taped the screen of the mobile over to minimize the light coming off the device.

With every step they took, the house, a huge stone and wood bungalow, creaked like an old ship. The snarls and grins of wooden masks that lined the walls followed them as they made their way into the night. The detective had the American tape the phone to his left hand. He wore Ginger's pistol in his waistband. He needed his right hand to get on the roof. He wouldn't be able to jump out like a Jack in the Box, gun blazing. He hoped there wouldn't be any call for it.

They took their shoes off before they climbed a set of wooden stairs to the second floor. Another corridor yawned ahead. A narrow stairway led from where they'd emerged to a trap door on the roof. A second identical stairway loomed at the far end of the corridor.

Ginger stared at Maier with what the detective assumed was a look filled to the brim with meaning. This was their moment. Maier's mind was like a ghost ride, so taken in by the attractions, such as they were, that he didn't even have the idea to head for the exit. He was travelling on a set of rails without brakes, unable to deviate, unable to stop, batting off ogres and demons coming from all sides. He could no longer remember a world that was reasonably safe.

Ginger moved slowly along the corridor. They would climb up at the same time and then head for each other. Both of them were armed. As soon as the message was sent, they would retreat their separate ways back into the house. Or fight for their lives. Either way, it would all be over in minutes.

Ginger reached the foot of the stairs. Maier was too far away to make out his facial expression. Chances were one of them would be walking into death.

Taking the first step, Maier remembered climbing the ten-metre platform at the local swimming pool in Leipzig. He must've been eleven or twelve and he'd been under pressure from his more courageous classmates to make the leap. The teacher, a man called Stricker, probably an old Nazi turned ardent communist, had shown no sympathy for young Maier and shooed him up the stairs.

He remembered shaking all the way up. He also remembered reaching the top, standing against the banister of the dive platform, trying not to look down, watching a bunch of older boys show off their artificial fearlessness at the edge of the precipice. After a while, he'd gathered his wits, stopped shaking, let go of the banister, walked calmly amongst his peers to the edge, and let himself fall, head first. He survived. No one bullied him for a while. An older girl had kissed him behind the bike shed. If only he'd known then what he knew now.

He pushed the roof door slowly upwards, careful not to let it drop onto its back. It was pitch black up there.

Krieger's bungalow stood set back from a cliff facing the Gulf of Thailand. The jungle leant in from three sides, its canopies bending over the building's perimeter fence. The sound of the forest was incredible. Just before dawn, bird calls and the movements and growls of larger beasts flowed around Krieger's compound like the recordings of a pioneering ethnologist in deepest, darkest, tropical Asia.

Maier shook his head, climbed out onto the flat wooden roof, and then ducked behind an air-con unit. His phone showed no reception. He glanced across in the direction of the other door and saw a shadow rise against the black starless sky. The rains would be coming soon, the same way odd thoughts now flooded into Maier's mind. Extreme fear would do this.

He refrained from waving to Ginger and decided to crawl towards his unlikely companion, all the while looking at the small sliver of light emanating from his phone. Twice he had to crawl across pipes and wires, almost getting snagged. A minute or so passed. Maier stopped and started, raised his head occasionally to look across towards Ginger's door, but the American had disappeared.

Maier had a bad feeling.

He reached the centre of the roof. The reception bar on his phone rose weakly. The detective pressed send the same instant Ginger loomed above him. Maier had no time to see if his message had gone out. The American silently tumbled on top of him and the detective glimpsed the shadow of another man sail past. He pointed his taped-up phone at the fast-moving figure and caught but a sliver of Suraporn, naked, his head bandaged, rush past him towards the door he had emerged from.

Ginger fell by his side, spent. Maier checked for a pulse, but found only a small scalpel lodged in the American's throat.

There was no way he could catch up with the doctor. Maier shook himself. And why would he? Fighting this man was suicide. A second later he heard the door close.

The detective got up and rushed, as fast as he could, in the opposite direction. Ginger's door was open. But the doctor was down there. Or wasn't. Perhaps he'd merely closed the door to fool Maier and he was still up here.

The detective started sweating again, never a good sign. *Go down or don't go down?* Up here, he didn't have a chance. Down there he also had no hope unless the doctor was still outside, in which case, Maier could close the second hatch behind him and be safe. But if the doctor was in the house, Maier wouldn't even reach the bottom of the stairs.

He had no time to make a decision, not one with any informed certainty. This was Russian roulette and either choice could spell the end. He didn't want it to end. He hadn't jumped off that swimming pool tower for nothing.

But there was always a third way.

35

STUMBLE THROUGH THE JUNGLE

MAIER GOT UP, quietly closed the trapdoor, and ran as silently as he could to the back of the bungalow. A couple of coconut palms had grown across the roof at Maier's chest height. He pulled himself up on one of the trunks and began to crawl along the smooth, cool wood.

The voice came after him as he dropped into the jungle beyond Krieger's fence.

"Trying to fool me, Maier. I know you're out there. If the beasts don't get you, I will cut your throat at the crack of dawn."

Maier stood motionlessly on the forest floor. He couldn't see the doctor, but he could hear him bark like a dog. An incongruous, most frightening sound amidst the jungle orchestra.

Maier turned away from the house, downhill along the fence towards the jetty where he and Mikhail had arrived the first time. After a few minutes of stumbling barefoot through high grass, he pulled the tape off his phone and used its torch to make faster progress.

He soon reached the water. The gate to the compound had been ripped off its hinges. The sky had cleared, and Maier could see several large cats roaming around the buildings inside the fence. He only had five bullets and he didn't want the doctor to know where he was, though he wouldn't have been surprised if Suraporn had suddenly stood next to him and started barking again.

To the east, the detective could see the first hint of dawn. The doctor had told him that he'd cut his throat when the sun came up.

He thought of heading back to the hump to drop down into the cave system but Suraporn would catch up with him before he reached the top. He glanced along the pier. There was no speedboat, just a rubber dingy bobbing in the shallows. Maier looked out across the bay. The *Störtebeker*, Krieger's yacht, was still parked a couple of hundred metres away. A couple of hundred metres of shark-infested waters. Maier had no choice. He ran along the jetty and threw his gun into the small vessel before climbing down onto its thin wooden deck. There was no engine, which in any case would have given him away, but he found a couple of short oars.

He untied the dingy.

"Maier," a thin voice called out of the darkness below him.

Maier got down on the jetty's planks and peered beneath the wood. He could just make her out, Mae, Hom's daughter, clinging to one of the jetty's poles. He offered the girl his hand. She let go and he pulled her on board in one swift movement. She was light as a feather. Maier made sure she lay down in the dingy and pushed off.

The adrenaline he'd pumped on the rooftop and during his stumble through the jungle was beginning to wear off. Maier was weak, hungry, and exhausted, but he rowed like a champion, with silent even strokes towards temporary salvation.

Suraporn wouldn't easily be able to follow the detective. Swimming was not an option.

Every time he looked at the girl, who stared right back at him, he wanted to cry.

The first shark bumped into his boat some fifty metres out into the bay. It was very much a polite, friendly bump, but Maier jerked from half-sleep into hyper-alertness. He'd just escaped the CIA's most vicious killer and now he was being harassed by hungry man-eaters.

The detective put more force into his rowing efforts, keeping a wary eye on the eastern horizon. The next shark came at the dingy with greater force and Maier thought it ironic that he might fall overboard and thus cunningly evade the rendezvous with his hunter. But the sharks didn't appear to like the rubber feel of the boat and refrained from chomping down on it.

They reached the *Störtebeker*. He paddled around as fast as he could to get the dingy out of sight. He tied up at the back of the large, white vessel, to its dive deck and pulled the boat close so that it couldn't be seen from the jetty. He lifted Mae onto the larger vessel, grabbed his gun, and quickly crossed the dive deck, checked the pilot's cabin, and then descended back to where they'd climbed on board.

They entered the yacht's main upper cabin, a spacious and gaudy lounge befitting a German tycoon whose tastes had veered towards the classic, just as the upper rim of the sun rose from the sea like a burning, waking calamity. There was no one on board, but Maier didn't take this as a great promise of respite. Nor that he'd missed his date with Suraporn. Calamities were as certain as the sun rising if not quite so predictably regular. It made him manic.

The mini-bar carried champagne and water. Maier and Mae went for the latter, and bags of peanuts, which they chewed mindlessly. The girl didn't speak. After a while, she crawled onto a chair and fell asleep. Maier sunk into a couch on the cabin's starboard side. A second later he fell into a deep unsettled sleep. His body, mind, and soul went offline, all in the same instant.

36

SOUL CHARGE

THE FACE, dark and enormous, jerked back as Maier opened his eyes.

The boy hadn't expected Maier to return from wherever he'd been. Now standing at a safe distance, dressed in nothing but a torn, wet pair of shorts, he stared at Maier half-scared and half cocky. His body was covered in scars, he clearly lived a hard life. No more than thirteen, he stood very erect, not particularly contemplative. No, he looked like he expected entertainment from Maier, some foreign frivolity. Maier wasn't ready, but he was glad to be alive and smiled stupidly into the boat lounge he'd passed out in. The tinted windows distanced the world from the cabin. Maier had a strong urge to remain where he was.

The boy lost interest and headed for the door without further acknowledgement. The sound of the sea and the jungle invaded Maier's headspace, then he was alone.

It was only then he noticed that Krieger's bay was busier than he'd ever seen it. At least ten long boats bobbed in the gentle waves. The sea gypsies. *Kabang*. Maier drifted back to their first escape. He wished Mikhail was around. He had to find a way to overcome the doctor himself.

He remembered plucking the girl from the jetty. Mae had disappeared. Maier willed himself up, pulled another bottle of water from the fridge, and drank it in one go, before heading out on deck.

. . .

"Good afternoon, Maier," Sundermann said. "Glad to see you. Didn't want to wake you as you looked like death having a nap when we arrived this morning. Join us for lunch. The red snapper is excellent. And let me tell you. It's good to see you, but we're not clear yet."

Sundermann had risen from his seat with a tired smile. The table on the *Störtebeker's* lower deck was set for three. Puttama sat to the side, scanning the water between the yacht and the shore, quite obviously as relieved to see the detective as his boss.

"Mikhail sends his regards. They were having trouble finding the right blood for him in Bangkok. But he's out of the woods. Not quite strong enough to join us, which is a shame."

Maier was relieved.

"Where's Mae? The little girl? Hom's girl? I brought her back here last night."

Sundermann pointed vaguely out to sea. "When we came on board this morning, she was already up. We managed to trace an aunt in Bangkok, so we had her put on a speedboat. She's on the mainland by now, waiting for a flight."

Maier almost allowed himself to smile.

"Who's still alive up there?" Puttama interjected.

Maier stood rooted to the deck, unable to quite process the scene, the table, with cloth and dishes, wine glasses, the crystal, turquoise sea, the beautiful secret agent, his boss back from the dead. Either he was crazy, or these people were insane. Perhaps Suraporn had cut his throat after all and he was now in a surrealist waiting area before moving on to the next plain.

"You guys are eating?" Maier asked.

"Yes, Maier, it's two pm. No life signs since we got here. Just you utterly exhausted in deep sleep on Krieger's boat."

"Have you been to shore? Have any of these *kabang* tied to the jetty?"

Puttama shook her head. "No, they're being careful."

"Just the good doctor up there in the jungle, barking at us." Maier said.

"Krieger?"

"Ginger cut his head off."

"My colleagues?" she asked.

"They were killed by the doctor. Ginger died helping me get my message to you."

Puttama nodded grimly.

A Moken climbed on board with a fried fish, covered in chilli sauce, on a tablet. The young man handed the fish to Puttama and disappeared back onto his *kabang*, his home.

This was like lunch at the White House.

Sundermann seemed to read him well.

"You've become feral, Maier. Too long in the jungle. Sit down and eat. It'll get cold otherwise. We're not as mad as you think. Just tired."

"You have not met this man."

"Oh yes, I have."

Maier sat down.

"It's good to see you. It's good that all the staff of Detective Agency Sundermann connected with this case are alive. We might be able to swing this one yet."

"It hasn't been a case in a long while. It is one murder after another, one hunt after another, one inhuman moment after another. I don't need to be a detective to understand this."

Puttama gestured at the fish. "Eat."

Maier was starving. He shut up, grateful to be out in the sun without having to fear a scalpel flying towards his jugular.

"You have a plan." he said while he looked at his companions, pulling fish bones from his teeth with his prosthetics. He wasn't asking.

Puttama answered, "I brought you into this. I'll finish it. I've left the agency, but no one except you two knows that yet. I have the Monsoon Ghost Image. We'll publish it. But we need to get the doctor. We need to terminate this man. Mikhail really hurt him. He is weak. His abilities are spent. He's likely to have some brain damage. Your friend hit him with a hammer. The doctor sensed it coming. That's why he didn't die instantly."

"Your bosses…"

"Yes, of course. It won't last. Ritter sent the images he took of the doctor butchering those girls to the station chief in Bangkok. They're in damage control mode. I wouldn't survive it, even with the others connected to Cat's Eye all dead. It would be a lot to explain. But that's not my reason for quitting the program. I think people should know what America is doing. And trust me, as an Asian American, giving up my career, my mission, and crossing over to the other side, it's a hard path the Wicked Witch is on."

Maier looked at Puttama for a long time. She was tough and morally sound in a world gone insane. But none of this mattered.

"Irrespective of what I think of all this, this is not our war. We are detectives, not assassins. We fight for a better world or we don't, in ways in which we are qualified. I am not sure that one can be qualified for the kind of stuff you people are doing. When I look at you over the past month, I see a courageous woman, working under great pressure, presumably alone, to reveal her country's most intimate and unsavoury secrets. But the fact that you almost destroy three German detectives, chosen at random, by involving them in a war they cannot fight, gets me thinking that perhaps this is just another form of lunacy. Or that you have another agenda altogether," Maier said

Maier could read nothing in the woman's expression.

Puttama answered, "You weren't chosen at random. I looked into you. You knew the Ritters. You know how war works. You've seen enough of it. The jobs you recently did in Cambodia and Laos put you in harm's way. You're thorough. Mikhail is thorough. You were perfect. I couldn't have wished for a better backup. And I knew Emilie Ritter would come to you."

"The doctor told me yesterday that he would slit my throat this morning at the break of dawn," Maier said. "He failed, thanks to my creative thinking and a huge amount of sheer luck. What's stopping him doing it tomorrow?"

"That's why we came with the Moken. They won't kill him for us, but they will keep him from harming us or them. The doctor killed and disfigured a young Moken man on a previous visit to the island. They think he is a demon. But they can handle him if he isn't doing his mind tricks."

"But they won't kill him?" Maier asked.

"No."

"Why not?"

"Maier, you're being feral again," Sundermann interjected. "Like us, they're not killers. It's not their war."

Puttama added, "And they're scared of the authorities. They have no identification, they're stateless. They prefer to remain unseen in the

Gulf of Thailand. But they're great hunters. They know how to kill a shark with a spear. They know how to hunt an animal in the jungle."

Maier shook his head. He wanted to cry again.

"Krieger hosted hunts on humans on this island, using former CIA prisoners as fodder for high rollers. And now we are going back there to hunt down and kill another human being. I mean, I would like to see the doctor locked up somewhere for the rest of his life and exposed along with the program he served, or maybe killed by people like himself. I agree with your wanting to go public. But before this noble act, you plan to gather a hunting party of stone-age people and middle-aged Germans to track down and kill a cunning mass murderer on this island? I hope you see the irony here."

"They're not stone-age people and he's more than a mass murderer. And they won't kill him. We will," Puttama answered.

Maier, perplexed but wanting more, let the strange remark pass and merely nodded. "Bad choice of words. They saved my life getting off this island. They're special people. But in the context of what happened here... there seems to be no end. Everyone gets involved."

"The War on Terror, Maier, get used to it. It's only just starting."

"Then why fight it? Why the change of heart? Why become a traitor? Why pay so much to achieve so little?"

Puttama reached across the table and grabbed the detective's hand. He wanted to jerk back, but he steadied himself and relaxed.

"You know in the seventies, I was part of the student movement here in Thailand. On October sixth, 1976, I was at Thammasat University when the military, police, and militias attacked us. Dozens of students died. We were shot and beaten to death. Those who jumped into the Chao Praya River were shot in the water. Some of my classmates were raped and killed, others were killed first and then raped. I was saved that day by my father who was attached to the US Embassy. He walked me out through a phalanx of killers. He spoke Thai, otherwise, we would've died there. America saved me. And my father obliged me to pay the country back. The Asian way. That's why I joined the agency. And that's why I became the Wicked Witch. Everything that goes around, comes around, Maier. We've come full circle and America's exceptionalism means nothing."

Maier let that sink in. Of course, everyone had one's own motivations, sometimes obvious, often unfathomable even to oneself, for the actions that made up one's moral jacket. Life had a way of throwing people in opposite directions all at once. But this didn't make sense.

Finally, he asked, "You changed sides? Ideologically speaking?"

She withdrew her hands. "Yes, my father...he was a persuasive man, and he was cashing in emotionally on having saved my life. And in the wake of the Vietnam War, I believed what he told me— that the CIA would take on a new role, defend America's interests abroad, not those of venal politicians and the military industrial complex. And for a while, I did good work. In the early days, I worked in China and Southeast Asia. I was a good field agent. It was an amazing time. It was everything a young woman with a thirst for adventure could ask for. And I was glad to return stateside. What I'd seen in Bangkok in seventy-six and its aftermath...I was sure this country would never change. It was trapped in some ancient, archaic ritual that no modern inventions or ideas could temper. But I needed to remain connected...it was difficult. Don't judge me by what you know, Maier."

Maier sensed that there was more complexity at play in Puttama's account than he understood. He pushed a little.

"I noticed an odd sympathy for Suraporn in your earlier remark."

She sighed the way lovers sigh. "Suraporn was a student leader then. Medical faculty. A brilliant orator. Persuasive as you can imagine. We loved him. His nickname was Api. Everyone opposing military rule looked up to him. Everyone loved Api. That day at Thammasat, the military abducted him. It was a big deal. He was half-American, like me. When I later read his file, I found that it had been General Thongsap, then a young captain, who'd kidnapped him. In the early days, when I'd first joined the agency, I always hoped that I would find some trace of Api."

She stopped, caught up in her memories, looking at him with wide, empty eyes. Maier sensed that this was the first time she'd unburdened herself with this story. The story of her life. Perhaps Api had been her lover. *More onion layers.* What did any of this mean in the here and now?

"They didn't kill him. Anti-communist fever was high and they turned him and used him to interrogate leftists in the east. He was a pragmatist, not nearly as romantic as myself, and he had a knack for it and they taught him all this psychological stuff which he refined and refined... But he never shopped his old comrades in arms. That's how he stayed dead. No one knew. Last year, the CIA recruited him via General Thongsap. When I was drafted in to find the Monsoon Ghost Image, I didn't quite recognize him, but I had a look at his file. There were many more photos dating back to the seventies. I had no doubt. Even his turning made sense. As I said, everything was coming full circle."

Puttama stopped in her tracks. Maier understood her pain at this betrayal. But he was a long way from the truth. She gave it to him straight.

"Suraporn is my brother."

Maier and Sundermann inhaled sharply at the same time.

Oh, dear.

"I joined the agency to find him and to save myself and my father from heartbreak. It's been a long journey, but I finally found my little brother Api. The Monsoon Ghost Image led me to him. My father died seven years ago. He never knew his son was alive."

They sat into the sunset, the conversation suspended. Maier was relieved. The mad doctor had a sister who worked for the agency, who had searched for him for more than twenty years. She had the best chance to reign him in. Perhaps she also felt morally obliged to do so. Perhaps it was the mission she'd been waiting for all her life. A life devoted to tracking down her brother. And now she'd found him, all that was left to do was to not just face him, but to face the monster he'd become.

The circle of *kabang* around Krieger's floating palace tightened, as the last light faded from another bruised tropical evening sky. The Moken began to sing. A woman started up a chant, barely melodic, that sounded like a story, soon picked up by a man on a neighbouring boat. The song carried across the water, no doubt audible to the doctor who was somewhere out there, cowering in the jungle, sharpening his scalpels, waiting to kill.

37

CRAWLSPACE

THEY SET off before the break of dawn. The air smelt fresh and salty as they rowed the dingy across the bay to the headland furthest from Krieger's compound. The sharks followed them in silence, occasionally bumping into the sides of their vessel. Dunung and Toe looked grim and clutched machetes and spears. Spears.

Maier hadn't spoken with Puttama again. Whatever sympathy he'd felt for the woman and her mission to publish the Monsoon Ghost Image, it had suffered during the night. He had no idea what she had on her mind, heading towards the most dangerous man Maier had ever encountered, her brother.

Would she appeal to his better nature? Would he recognize his sister or attempt to graft the face of an animal onto her skull? Both perhaps.

Puttama had insisted they come along. She'd suggested they wouldn't be safe on the yacht without her. Maier couldn't think of a good reason why he'd agreed to return to the island with her.

Krieger's pirate vessel exploded as they hit the beach. Debris sprayed across the bay. A couple of *kabang* went down with Krieger's ship. They couldn't see whether Moken had been killed or injured.

Maier tried to read Puttama's expression. She looked as shocked as they did, but he had an uneasy feeling about the demise of the *Störtebeker*. This didn't carry Suraporn's signature.

"We have to get off the beach," Puttama said. "I've got the Monsoon

Ghost Image and much more on a hard drive in my backpack, so we're still good. The Moken know of a cave tunnel that leads to the house. I have the feeling my brother is waiting for me there. They've promised to take us to the cave entrance. Then, they told me, they'll leave."

They set off around the headland and followed the two Moken into dense brush. Maier had the safety off his Glock. He was becoming used to carrying a weapon. He was tempted to throw it into the forest, but it would be nothing more than an act of unadulterated stupidity. He also knew that carrying the gun wasn't going to save him.

They followed a shallow, fast-moving stream towards the hump where the helicopter had attacked Maier and Mikhail. The jungle orchestra was in full swing as they marched. Fifteen minutes into their journey, the two Moken stopped abruptly and pushed a couple of giant ferns out of their path. The stream had turned into a river and snaked into a low cave. Dunung and Toe disappeared into the jungle without another word.

"So much for the hunters. Now all you have is a couple of middle-aged Germans," Maier remarked sourly.

Puttama ignored his quip.

"The Moken told me that we'd be able to pick up a trail thirty or so metres inside."

Puttama waded into the current. Maier and Sundermann looked at each other. Both men smiled simultaneously. They both inhaled deeply and looked around.

"Nice place to die, Maier?" Sundermann said.

"Who said anything about dying?"

"I did. If we'd followed our instincts, perhaps we'd have stayed on the boat. But we got off the boat, the boat we thought was safe. Safer than following this mad woman into the mountain."

"Is she mad?"

Sundermann nodded. "She's certainly taken us for a ride. We'd all be living in a different world, if she hadn't emailed Emilie Ritter. The War on Terror would be something all of us would be seeing on the news, not blasted across a picture-perfect postcard bay in Southeast Asia."

"Maybe we should shoot her," Maier said.

Sundermann shook his head.

"Her brother will eat us if we do that."

Puttama turned, almost up to her chest in the water, and shouted, "Come on guys. He's onto us, he blew up the boat. We don't have a second to lose."

She didn't wait for an answer, but waded upriver into darkness.

They found the first girl as soon as they'd switched on their torches and stepped from the riverbed onto a narrow rock slab that led towards a low tunnel. She was one of Krieger's and the doctor had been creative on her. He'd left her the dignity of her face but instead of her own arms, she had a couple of what Maier feared to be monkey limbs implanted into her shoulder sockets. She sat open-eyed and very much dead in the entrance to the tunnel, blocking their passage.

Sundermann threw up into the river. Puttama shouted for Maier, but the detective didn't move when she grabbed the girl's corpse by one leg and pulled her towards the water. A second later, she pushed the grotesque body over the edge of the stone slab and she was gone. The sad shape of the woman's mangled remains lingered in Maier's mind as they pushed on.

The tunnel soon widened into another cave system. There was no way to get lost. Krieger's men had marked the trail with chalk arrows. Maier guessed the distance between the cave entrance and Krieger's villa to be more than a kilometre and they walked and sometimes crawled for an hour until they reached the second girl and one of Krieger's men. They sat, both dead and covered in flies, embracing each other like lovers in a suicide pact, at the entrance to another narrow passage. They had to be near an exit, there'd been no insects further down in the cave. The end of the tunnel couldn't be far off.

They stepped around the bodies as best as they could, trying not to inhale, and rushed on. The tunnel led upwards. Puttama's torch caught the door ahead of them and they slowed down.

"We must be at the villa," Puttama said. "Maier, you know the layout. Go ahead and lead us to the front door. And please take my backpack. When we have found my brother, you can go. Other than what's in my bag, all evidence at Cat's Eye has been deleted or shredded. You might be safe."

Maier had come to the limit of learned helplessness. He couldn't get himself to feel grateful to Puttama, but he took the bag from her.

He looked back at Sundermann who stood pale and grim. His boss was even less qualified to walk into Krieger's villa than Maier was.

The two men nodded to each other, and Maier felt relieved that the agency, his home, his family, was alive. Perhaps it even had a future. The contents of the bag on his shoulders, presuming Puttama had told the truth, would give them a sense of closure. He felt proud to be a detective. And he understood Puttama's life-long obsession with the disappearance of her brother. It would all work out.

The door had a handle. Maier squeezed past Puttama and pushed into the house.

The doctor was waiting for them.

"*Sawadee kap*, little sister."

Krieger's villa stank of death. There were corpses or parts of corpses everywhere. Dried heads stared from high shelves, one of Krieger's women, naked and partially dismembered hung from the front door. The door Maier would have to exit to get out.

Puttama had visibly aged, and her smile was kindly, almost infantile.

"*Hallo Pi* Api."

Her hands folded together in a respectful *wai*, she addressed her brother with the correct honorific title for someone older than her. Maier had a bad feeling. If she accepted the Thais' social hierarchy code, she wasn't going to fight this man.

Suraporn rose from a large chair in the centre of the villa's low-ceilinged living room, holding his hand out to his sister.

"You've been looking for me for a long time. I'm sorry. But we're together now. We can have fun. We don't need anyone else. We don't need the agency. We can disappear. We can be rich. You have the Monsoon Ghost Image?"

"Maier does."

"Will Maier give it to us, or will we have to take it?" the doctor asked.

She half-turned towards the detectives. Maier caught her eye for a split second and sensed a desperate struggle. But Suraporn's brotherly pull was too strong for her.

"We'll have to take it, I think," Puttama said.

The doctor laughed gently. It almost sounded like the man was crying. It was hard to tell, his head and part of his face remained heavily bandaged.

"*Pi* Api"

"*Nong Pui.*"

The siblings had reunited, existing only for one another.

Sundermann stepped past Maier, raised his gun, and shot Suraporn in the chest. The doctor jerked backwards and staggered in the centre of the hellish room, his eyes fixed on Puttama.

She turned, not waiting for her brother to fall, and shot Sundermann. Then she turned the gun on herself.

"We failed," she said to Maier.

Her face had turned into a death mask, infused with immeasurable anger and sorrow.

Maier nodded in shock.

"You have. But I won't," Maier told her.

Puttama pulled the trigger.

Sundermann was dead.

Maier checked on Puttama and the doctor. Dead too, without a doubt.

He looked around the room, expecting some audience perhaps, but very much hoping no one would see him do what he did next. He picked Puttama's gun from the floor and emptied it into the doctor's head. He had to be sure. But he still couldn't let it go. He dragged the doctor's smashed body across the room's floor to the giant telephone. He pulled Suraporn's corpse until his smashed head rested in the bottom of the handset. The lever was at chest height. Maier pulled the handle. Then he stepped out the front door and vomited onto the villa's patio.

Maier walked downhill towards the compound with tears in his eyes. He didn't think about the panthers and lions that might be looking for an easy lunch. He didn't think about the War on Terror. Maier didn't give a shit. His boss was dead. His life was smashed to pieces. History had converged on him and crushed him as if he were an insect on its way to becoming a tiny droplet of a cheap after-hours drink.

A few minutes later, he reached the jetty, confused and frightened. The sun reflected off the turquoise water, palm fronds flattered in a fresh breeze. The Moken woman he'd first met with Mikhail came walking down the beach towards Maier, a wide careless smile on her face. She stuck the middle finger of her right hand into her mouth and pushed it slowly in and out, her eyes never leaving the detective. Maier wished for nothing more than a pair of sunglasses. It was all he needed.

38

HAMBURG, GERMANY, APRIL 2003

THE MONSOON GHOST IMAGE

For an instant, a few days even, perhaps an entire week, the story of the Monsoon Ghost Image, the secret prison in Thailand, the CIA's alleged rendition program shook the world.

Mikhail had seen to that. The Russian had hacked into Puttama's email account and decrypted the hard drive in her backpack. Maier had assembled a persuasive file and sent it to several German and British newspapers. The flood of evidence was overwhelming and Maier, the ex-conflict journalist, knew how to tell a story.

Der Spiegel ran it first. The US media picked it up a few days later. The US government had punched a dark hole into the American Dream. Puttama was denounced as a spy and traitor. Sporadic revenge attacks on Asian Americans across the States made the news. Then the story faded. The war in Iraq had started and it had its own, complex momentum. The US was looking for imaginary weapons of mass destruction, cheap oil, a place to launder a lot of money, dictators who'd outlived their usefulness, and some kind of hackneyed need for simultaneous revenge and redemption when there was none to be had of either. It was quite a list, which thousands of young men and women carried onto the battlefield, destined to perish.

· · ·

For Maier, the War on Terror had almost become news again— abstract, at a safe distance, the usual ugly stuff that happened far away.

Sundermann's funeral had been an emotional affair. The agency had closed. Mae, Hom's daughter stayed with an aunt in Bangkok and went to school. She'd inherited her parents' land on the island. They'd talked a couple of times on the phone. The girl was grateful or had been told to be grateful. She was in safe hands. She was the only survivor who'd get another start in life. That made Maier smile every now and then.

Mikhail, fully recovered and his old joyful Russian self, and Maier were adrift, unemployed, perhaps retired. They sat in bars in Altona and made plans, discussed schemes, drank a lot, tread water.

The BND, the German secret service, followed them. They weren't too subtle about it. Perhaps the Americans had told their special partners to keep an eye on them, worried the Monsoon Ghost Image affair as it had been called in the media, would offer yet more salacious information on American misconduct on the world stage. They'd signed papers that obliged them never to speak of what had happened. The detectives shifted all the blame for the publication to Puttama. Apparently, it had worked.

They rarely discussed the affair directly, not because of the papers they'd signed, but because it was all too much. But in a way, they spoke of nothing else. Life, like the war, continued somehow. Even in a Kiez dive at 1 am.

"Nothing like drinking crushed insects, Mikhail," Maier said.

The Russian stared morosely at their glasses.

"We're waiting for something, Maier. What is it?"

The question shot through Maier like lightning. Of course, they were waiting for something. Everyone was. They were in a state of stasis. The entire planet seemed to be that way.

"You are right. I don't know what it is either. But I can feel it. Let's go back to my place."

The Russian laughed suggestively. "Better late than never Maier. It won't be a solution, but it will take the edge off things."

Maier waved his friend's joke away. He couldn't explain himself, but he felt vulnerable. Looking at his partner, he knew Mikhail had the same thoughts kicking around in his mind.

"It feels like Suraporn is still out there. But we know he's dead. You saw him unmistakably dead."

"I made him unmistakably dead."

It hadn't been a question. It wasn't an answer. They'd been through this many times. It had become a ritual. It wasn't funny. Too much had been lost. All, they had left, Maier felt, was each other. They'd become orphaned detectives.

They stepped out into the fresh Hamburg night. Maier sobered instantly. But the unease didn't leave him. He stuck his hands deep into the pockets of his jacket. He'd stopped carrying a gun. This was Hamburg. This was real life.

They walked down to the Elbe and crossed the Elbchaussee to get closer to the water.

Maier, watching nothing but his unsteady feet, heard a faint sound behind them. As he turned, Mikhail threw him towards a couple of recycling bins. A black Mercedes screeched to a halt in front of the two men. Maier tumbled backwards. He saw the back door of the car open.

A face emerged, a gun in its hand.

"Maier, I told you, you'd never be safe anywhere. Here's what you get for fucking up your old war buddy's life."

The face shot into focus the same instant the man behind the gun pulled the trigger. Maier saw Martin Ritter leer triumphantly. The detective smashed to the ground, this time with great force. As he fell backwards, he watched Mikhail step in. Like a pouncing cobra, his friend plunged an ice pick into Ritter's new face. But this didn't matter a great deal.

Maier's eyes let go and drifted to the featureless Hamburg sky, hoping for spring.

He heard music.

He saw a young girl he'd once saved, running down a beach, laughing.

Everything was fine.

ACKNOWLEDGMENTS

September 11th, 2001, a Tuesday, will always have a particular residence for anyone in my generation, no matter how much further the US has fallen since. I was in Camberwell, Southeast London, and saw the first plane crash into the World Trade Centre on a fuzzy black and white TV in a paint shop on Walworth Road.

I ran back to my friend Austin Cowdall's apartment, which was on the 20th floor of a 1960s council house tower block. When I got there, we stood next to each other in front of his TV, watching the planes go in over and over again. We looked at each other and both felt that the world, even our world, had changed ever so slightly, and that the future would be informed by the tremors that America felt that Tuesday.

The Monsoon Ghost Image is about those tremors. It's fiction, of course, but the book's look on US renditions of terror suspects is anchored in reality.

Thanks to my parents for their support and to my partner Laure Siegel for reading.

Thanks to Scott Nicholson, my quiet American in Detroit, for weighing in on the finer points of US politics and the War on Terror. You left early.

And hats off to James Newman for suggesting improvements.

Thanks also to my agent Philip Patterson at Marjacq in London.

ABOUT THE AUTHOR

Tom Vater is a writer and editor working predominantly in Asia.

He has published four novels, including The Devil's Road to Kathmandu, and the Detective Maier trilogy.

His articles on Asian politics, tourism, the environment, minorities, and pop culture have been published in many publications including The Wall Street Journal, The Daily Telegraph, The Guardian and Nikkei Asia.

∼

To learn more about Tom Vater and discover more Next Chapter authors, visit our website at www.nextchapter.pub.

Printed in Great Britain
by Amazon